THE SUNKEN CITY TRILOGY

UNDER ORDSHAW
BLUE ANGEL
THE VIOLENT FAE

PHIL WILLIAMS

MMXIX

ISBN-13: 978-1-913468-03-3

Cover design by P. Williams

Published by Rumian Publishing

Visit **www.phil-williams.co.uk** online for more information and regular news from Phil Williams. Join the newsletter to be the first to hear about new projects.

CONTENTS

Under Ordshaw

An Ordshaw Novel

Phil Williams

PART 1:
FRIDAY

1

Pax Kuranes peered over her whisky tumbler at a man in a turquoise vinyl trench coat. At 4am on what she still considered to be Thursday night, the bar was dead, and the only other occupant had approached her with a cheeky smile. A smile like Albie's, when he'd wanted a ride somewhere. This guy had olive skin and long, unwashed hair, but it was the same anxiously innocent smile. He couldn't be more than nineteen, and Pax doubted humouring him would threaten her life, challenge everything she knew or put the entire city in danger. Besides, she was already bored of reading poker news off her phone.

"Rufaizu." The young man held out a hand, the other raised defensively. "Not trying to hit on you, nothing like that. Just curious."

He pointed to his jacket, asking permission to put a hand in a pocket. Pax gave him a slight smile, but folded her arms to conceal her night's earnings in her coat.

"You're having a good time." Rufaizu nodded to the empty glasses on the bar, one hand still up.

"Yeah," she replied. The £3,237 in her pocket was two months' security and more. She'd taken the bulk of it from a pastel-vested finance prick who couldn't believe he'd lost *to a girl*. That arrogance put Pax on a path to join the World Poker Tour's first outing in Ordshaw, right when it had looked like she needed to choose between an entry ticket and paying rent. "It's been a productive night."

"May I?" Rufaizu indicated his pocket again.

Pax let him wait. Good manners were rare in Ordshaw, let alone in the Sticky Tap Sports Bar. Might as well savour the moment. Her eyes tracked to the muted TV crammed between vodka optics. The BBC World News was looping the same images of a bus crash that'd been rolling all night. Pax looked sideways at Rufaizu. He hadn't moved. "Go on then."

He took out a notepad, slowly, as though it might intimidate her. He took out a pen, just as slow.

"What's your problem?" Pax asked.

"No problem!" he replied brightly. "Lookit, I just gather answers." He thumbed through a few crumpled pages for her to see. "My father said you never meet a dull person after 3am. So I have three questions for people after 3am. First –"

"Let me," Pax said, reading a few of the answers upside down. She pulled his hand, and the pad, a little closer, to figure it out for herself.

Petey – payday – all-nighter, shots!

Tyler – been paving roads, beer's the most refreshing.

Luka – girlfriend left him – vodka is like home.

Pax looked from the pad to Rufaizu, then scanned the bar again. It was a weird hobby for a young man, lurking in places like this. Only the lowest people came here. The sort that didn't talk to one another, as Pax liked it. She pushed the pad back towards Rufaizu, concluding, "Name, reason they're out, what they're drinking. All guys, huh?"

Rufaizu whooped with delight, almost jumping. He slapped a hand into the pad and said, "*Damn* right! Damn right! You are *sharp*. I like you." He quickly backed off, face serious. "Not like that. Nothing creepy. I'll just ask the questions and go, okay? Not trying to sleep with you."

"You're making it creepy," Pax warned him. She found herself smiling, though. He was worse than Albie. Her little brother was a dork, but he tried to hide it with dignified quietness. This guy's dorkiness was bubbling out. "Why these questions?"

"Oh, these?" Rufaizu replied, as though surprised at the notepad himself. "I guess they're a start? To tell us if someone's . . . you know . . ."

Pax frowned, but he didn't elaborate.

"Okay. Shall we?" Rufaizu grinned. As quickly as the grin came, it disappeared, as something caught his eye. A suited man stood in the entrance doorway, watching them, coming no further into the bar. With a sharp intake of breath, Rufaizu said, "Lookit, I'll be on my way. Back to my booth, back to my booth."

"You're not gonna ask me my questions?" Pax said, eyeing the newcomer.

Rufaizu lowered his face to hide it. He clicked his pen and spoke rapidly, much quieter. "Um. Sure. Real quick. Can I have your name?"

"Why, you don't like yours?" Pax joked. He paused, not following. She used the momentary lull to sip her whisky.

"He bothering you?"

Pax jumped on her stool, the man in the suit suddenly at their shoulders.

"Son of a . . ." Pax uttered. He'd crossed the bar without a sound. The man's darkly handsome face was lit in the bar's archaic neon, skin like a Latino singer, not a hair out of place, suit freshly pressed. His white teeth shone like headlights in the dim bar and his smile killed Rufaizu's cheer.

"No trouble, friend," Rufaizu said. "Don't want none. Just shooting the breeze."

The suit's eyes stayed fixed on Rufaizu. "He's bothering me."

Pax searched for the barman, but he was nowhere to be seen. No one else in the room.

"The lady's not interested," the suit said.

"Hey," Pax said. "The *lady* can talk for herself."

The man gave her a wink. "Just trying to help."

"I don't need your help."

Rufaizu chipped in, then. "Yeah, man, she don't need –"

The suit pounced, pinning Rufaizu's arm behind his back and slamming his face into the bar. He yanked Rufaizu upright again, the younger man's nose bloody and his free arm snapping around. Pax stepped back, too late, as the two men collided with her and made her stumble, whisky spilling. Rufaizu made incoherent noises of protest as the suit hauled him across the floor. The suit flashed another smile back to Pax and said, "Enjoy your drink, miss."

"Leave it out," Pax replied hotly. "He didn't do anything."

Rufaizu tried to break free, but the man tightened his grip, forcing him still. As he marched Rufaizu to the exit, the suit said, "Trust me, he would've."

Rufaizu gave up struggling and started goading. "Tough guy, I'll set Barton on you, what're you gonna do? He's fought the *minotaur*!"

The door swung shut behind them. Pax stared into their absence.

4am lunacy. An irate office worker taking out his machismo on some mixed-up kid?

"What happened?" The barman's voice snapped Pax's attention back to the bar. He had a tray of clean glasses in his hands as he stared at an overturned stool. Rufaizu's notepad sat on the bar in front of him. Pax grabbed it.

"Fat use you are," she said. He gave her a bored look, said nothing and turned away.

Pax rolled the notepad in her hand. With the cash in her pocket, the Pax Kuranes Beer, Burger and Liveliness Fund was finally in good health. All she had to do was go home, pay the rent and enjoy the tournament starting Thursday. Revel in the memory of her ace-high flush holding up against an opponent's trips.

The notepad felt heavy, though. The handwriting was childish and the paper was warped from being repeatedly wet and dried. Painfully similar to Albie's books of ideas. He wouldn't visit places like this, would he? It might happen anywhere, though. Some suit pounding on some awkward kid for being different. The boy had raved about a minotaur, for crying out loud. Pax huffed. She'd already put one entitled prick in his place that evening. Why stop now?

She downed the whisky, pocketed the notepad and hurried outside.

The road was still, cracked tarmac dancing in the flicker of the Sticky Tap's light. An old air conditioning unit squeaked a few doors down. Pax scanned up and down, nothing moving anywhere nearby. She hadn't heard a car engine. Definitely no sounds of a struggle. They'd been bucking against each other on the way out; surely they couldn't have moved anywhere fast?

Pax frowned, reimagining the men's rapid departure. Rewinding to when the suit had struck. The men had bumped into her. Together. She shot a hand to her coat pocket.

Her fingers closed on empty space. The money was gone. £3,237. Gone.

No wait – there was the hard nugget of a £2 coin in there. Mocking her.
£3,235 gone.
The little bastard.
Pax held her breath. If she opened her mouth her whole venomous vocabulary might fly out. No. Keep calm. Be practical. She had lost more money quicker, in stupider ways, and recovered it – it was a bad beat. She could turn it around. Even if the Poker Tour started in six days. Even if the rent was due.
She took out her phone, bringing up a contact, fingers tapping on autopilot.
"Pax," Bees answered at once. "Heard you cleared up this evening."
"Yeah. The news might've spread faster than I'd have liked."
"Had some trouble?"
A chain-link fence rattled nearby. A black cat pounced to a higher vantage point to watch her. Pax met its green eyes as she answered. "Something like that. Guy called himself Rufaizu. Nineteen or twenty. Looked European, Roma maybe. Long green-blue coat."
"Not much to add to that."
"You know him?" Pax asked.
"Of him. Turned up a few weeks back, held his own in a game or two. Then made off with a chunk of money that wasn't his. The Row Street Rogues are after him. Out of St Alphege's."
She didn't need to be told where the Rogues came from. Some of the worst people from the worst part of town. They wouldn't have sent a suit out to collect. And Rufaizu wouldn't have made a grab for her cash in the middle of a serious confrontation, anyway. They were working together. She'd been robbed, simple as that.
Pax said, "Got a last known location?"

Rufaizu's apartment poked out the top of a red-brick terrace on the edge of the warehouse district, opposite the grimiest station of the K&S Underground. The windows were painted black, lessening the glare of the station's brightly lit sign. Pax drew an impression of the youth from the state of his home: the door locked by a piece of string looped over a nail; *STAY OUT* painted in sloppy red letters; smashed bottles on the floor testifying to the dual triumphs of drinking and hygiene problems. His dirt-encrusted blanket had been shredded, the mattress on the floor ripped apart. The stains and the scent of alcohol, partially masking what Pax feared was a more offensive odour underneath, suggested the place hadn't lost much charm when the guys from St Alphege's had turned it over.
Pax took in the peeling wallpaper, the uneven floorboards and the cracked single light bulb. The cafés in Ten Gardens spent a fortune trying to recreate this shabby look, and here this vagrant had stumbled across the real thing. He probably didn't know it, though; for someone who stole from affluent poker games, Rufaizu was light on luxuries. Pax trod lightly over the floorboards, listening for their creaks. She tugged at the ones that moved, and one came up. There was a crinkled

collection of men's magazines in the hollow underneath. A good, albeit disgusting, sign. Rufaizu had hidden stuff here, and the Row Street Rogues had failed to find it.

Pax ran a hand over the walls, checking the cracks and tears. Her finger bumped over a groove. Stopping to look closer, she found the crack ran up in a strangely straight line. She applied pressure, one side and then the other. Part of the wall flexed, a different material to the rest. She jammed a key in the crack and popped it open. The false front came off, a single panel wedged over a cavity in the lath and plaster, apparently containing Rufaizu's most prized possessions.

There were two items in the wall space: a thick leather-bound book and a glass tube trimmed with brass, a lever protruding from one side and a stack of interconnected cogs at one end. The contraption was dented and scratched; it looked like a nerd's desk ornament, but it had been tossed about. A lot. The book was also worn from rough handling. Pax skimmed through it, finding reams of handwritten symbols, with repeated combinations of circles, triangles and lines. The symbols surrounded maniacally etched illustrations and diagrams.

She hummed to herself, closing the tome and reading the title, carved into its cover as though by a knife: *Apothel's Miscellany*.

This would do.

It would work out, Pax told herself as she watched the city roll past the bus window. Whether the book's bizarre contents were the product of crazed mania or passionate creativity, the things hidden in the wall had to be important to Rufaizu. Albie protected this sort of creative crap with his life; she had to believe the vagrant kid was similar. If he wanted them back, they could do a deal. If not, they'd give a strong clue as to what he did want. Or at least where she could find him.

She rode the night bus with the items carefully stowed in her backpack, calm. Being calm was everything in a crisis. It was just theft. She was handling it. She had a few days yet, until the World Poker Tour. Eight days before rent was due. There was petty cash in the kitchen drawer. A stale loaf of bread on the counter that was probably still edible.

Everything would be fine.

When she came in sight of her apartment building, however, she gagged on the panic she was fighting to keep down. The man in the suit stood waiting, and everything she had assumed about Rufaizu's simple con, and what it would take to set it right, was shattered.

2

Unreliable people. Say to be somewhere and don't turn up. Unwanted, unreliable, bastard pigs. Give you an invite you want nothing to do with, then screw you. Dragging up the past for no good goddamned reason.

The angry thoughts shot through Darren Barton like a drill sergeant's shouts, encouraging one thick punch after another.

He typically coped with life in one of two ways. Strong enough liquor, drunk quick enough, could help him forget. The next best thing was to beat all hell out of something with his bare hands. He had run out of Johnnie Walker before it dulled the pain, so he was throwing punch after punch into the sack that hung in his garage. The bag swung like a pendulum as the supports shuddered. Half drunk and out of shape in a long-term way, Barton found his punches were glancing off the bag, inaccurate, but his full weight and loathing made each strike matter.

The noise of the impacts, the rattle of the chain and the creaking rafter were all blocked out by his heavy breathing and the sound of blood pumping in his ears. He might have woken up the wife, the kid, but it didn't matter. Their problem.

Another punch. Another animalistic noise to release some of the pressure.

That little scumbag, arranging meetings he couldn't keep.

At this damn hour.

His father's son, another stinking shadow you could trust for nothing more than trouble.

Barton took a step back and his foot caught a can of beer on the floor. Taking a sip from the can in his hand, he slowed down to focus. Catching his breath, he saw three empty cans, now. He blinked to check if it was his vision failing him. Definitely three of them. He must have been going for at least half an hour. His vest clung tight to his chest, skin slick with sweat, hot like a radiator.

Someone cleared their throat, up above.

He ignored it, passing the beer can to his right hand, then flung a stiff haymaker and took another swig.

"Oh for God's sake!" Holly finally erupted.

Barton turned from the bag with a frown, finding his defiant wife staring furiously from the top of the short flight of stairs that led into the house. Too weary from the booze and the boxing to conjure the energy for surprise, he spread his arms in a mock welcoming gesture. He heaved a few deep breaths, then said, "Did I wake you?"

"You think?"

Barton lumbered towards her, swaying on his tired legs. The severity of Holly's disapproving glare cranked up to maximum as he dropped forward to lean on the banister, looking up at her.

"You went out," Holly said.

"I got a message," Barton replied, unapologetic. "Asking me to meet him."

"Darren, it's almost *dawn*. We can't go back to this. I won't go through it again."

"You think I want to?" Barton snapped. Of course he was the one in the wrong. Having been forced to remember and getting stood up. It was his fault, like everything else. He pushed off from the stairs and walked unsteadily back through the garage. He took another swing at the bag as he passed, making it quake. He raised his voice, over his shoulder. "He didn't show. Wasn't there. So don't worry about it."

"Yet you're in this state, all the same."

Barton turned to hold his wife's gaze. She let her arms unfold.

"It's a lapse," Barton said. "I needed this" – he pointed at the punching bag, still swinging from his last blow – "from the moment his name showed on my phone. You think I'm happy?"

"What did he want?"

"Damned if I know." Barton took another swig of beer. "He didn't show."

"Darren." Holly descended a step towards him. That was all the conciliation she was willing to offer, placing a hand on the banister to show it. "For your sake, for our sake, for Grace's sake, it'd better just be a lapse. You told me this was behind us. I believed you."

"He didn't show." He said it one more time. "What else can I say?"

"If he contacts you again?"

Barton grumbled, "I owe it to his dad."

"After all he did for you?"

His face fell at the sarcasm, eyelids drooping. "You never understood."

"I understand" – Holly's voice took on a sharp edge – "that you wouldn't want your daughter to see you like this. Would you?"

Barton said nothing.

"You can sleep on the couch. Then we can talk about it in the morning, or you can let it go. Your call."

With that, she left, and Barton let her.

He put the beer can on the workbench and swayed on the spot. A door closed loudly as Holly made her way through the house. Barton leant on the punching bag, using it to hold himself up, then gave up. He slid down to the floor and sat in an unfocused daze.

His mind was almost blank, but not quite.

Somewhere in the haze, he could still see Apothel's face.

The hole in his head.

Rufaizu screaming.

3

Pax Kuranes lived in Ordshaw's student district, Hanton, the closest spot to the centre with even remotely affordable rent. It was lined with terraced houses, slightly more civilised than the tower-blocks that characterised the other impoverished areas. Pax's apartment was on the top floor of a converted church, and she was surrounded by people a few years younger than her. They rarely disturbed her, as their night-long parties seldom outlasted her night-long poker games. On her return that morning, a banner flapped from a window reading *Lisa's Home!*, but only a single lanky student held vigil on the stoop, hunched over a bottle of cider, red eyes vacant.

It was not the sort of location you found men in smart suits, especially not at the cusp of dawn, yet here one was. His hands in his pockets, he flashed his poster smile at Pax as she kept her distance, a dozen metres down the path to her building.

"I've got something for you," he said, lightly.

He reached into his jacket pocket and Pax took a quick step back. She held off from running, though. Granted, he had assaulted a young man and mysteriously vanished, but if it wasn't a con then maybe he had a genuine grievance with Rufaizu. Was it insane to hope he had her money? She was tired and desperate enough to believe it wasn't, and watched as he took out a piece of folded A4 paper. She caught a glimpse of something else under his lapel. A strap of leather. The unmistakable square of a gun handle.

It was too late to run, now.

He said, "It's a receipt, essentially, for the value of the money. A PO-42c. States that on completion of our investigation the private property that was confiscated will be returned. Assuming it was your money he took."

A dozen questions ran through Pax's mind. She asked the most burning one: "What do you need a gun for?"

"Shooting things," he replied candidly, as though it was obvious. He added, "But I haven't used it on a person in three years."

"Who'd you shoot?" Pax asked.

"An Armenian."

Pax hummed. The answer did not help, and demanded another question. Why had he specified *on a person*?

"There's nothing to worry about," the suit said. He moved a step closer and she took another step back, eyes on the gun bulge. "I'm sorry you had to see that, in the bar. I should've handled it better. He just – his sort irk me. But, please, take this."

He held out the paper. She stood rigidly as he closed the distance to her. She took the paper and unfolded it: a dense block of printed text dotted with legal jargon, headed with an important-looking crest and the title *Public Ordinance Issue 42c – Confiscation of Goods*. In the middle, the amount of money was written in bold: £3,235. At the bottom there was a printed valediction: *Yours Sincerely, Gertrude Gossinger, Acquisitions and Inventory Secretary*.

"What the hell is this?" Pax said. "What's this secretary got to do with my money?"

"It is your money, then?"

Pax gave him a challenging look. "How'd you know where I live?"

"The population of this city gets a lot smaller when you're filtering for nighthawks."

"*Why* are you filtering populations?"

"My name's Cano Casaria," he said, holding out a hand.

Without shaking, Pax rolled on, "Gertrude Gossinger and Cano Casaria? Your friends call you CC? Or KK?"

He let her agitation sit in the air, his hand waiting. His smile wavered slightly when she didn't shake. He said, "You're quick. But I'd imagine something we've got in common is our lack of friends."

"What's that supposed to mean?"

"We're both working unsociable hours when we needn't be. And neither of us, I sense, suffers fools lightly."

"I suffer tons of fools," Pax said. "You attack defenceless boys then stalk women outside their homes. Tell me again we've got something in common."

"I'm just here to do the right thing," Casaria said.

"And what's the right thing that got Cano Casaria out in a dive bar at 4am dressed like he's ready for a meeting, beating on a homeless boy? You want me to believe you're with some kind of government agency? Please – no civil servant has the gall to dye their hair and whiten their teeth. You wouldn't starch a shirt on Her Majesty's account, would you?"

His hand was still waiting to be shaken. The smile had barely faltered. She knew how to needle people, but he, in turn, clearly knew how to take it. Maybe he *was* a civil servant. He said, "I'm a field agent for the Ministry of Environmental Energy. The young man in the bar was a person of interest. And I genuinely thought he might've been bothering you."

Pax ran the unfamiliar Ministry's name through her head, not sure if it was obscure or made up, or if she was just ignorant of government affairs. She said, "And what the hell are you doing here?"

"Two things," Casaria said, finally lowering his unshaken hand. "First, following up on what happened. When I returned to the bar, you were gone. I wanted to ask if you knew that young man. I saw you talking, but –"

"Never seen him before," Pax said. "What's he supposed to have done?"

"You not knowing that will make both our lives a lot easier. Bringing us to the second thing . . ." He nodded to the paper in her hand. "I hoped that my gesture of goodwill might buy me a conversation."

"I don't know what your game is, but I read people for a living and I *know* you've got a game. I don't want your conversation. Just my money."

Casaria paused. "It could take two weeks, maybe more. There's a lot of red tape involved when property gets confiscated in the course of an investigation."

"Two *weeks*?" Pax exclaimed. "That's bullshit – I –"

"You'll get the money back, I can vouch for that. I'd like to know who you are, though."

"Who do you *think* I am?"

"If I'm honest," he said, eyes running from her bulky coat and dark hoodie down to her loose jeans and boots, "seeing a young lady out at that hour, with all that cash, dressed like this, raises some interesting questions."

Pax kept her face neutral, making an effort not to respond to the *young lady* comment, recalling his earlier use of *miss*. He couldn't have been five years older than her. She said, "What's this actually about? The guy you assaulted, the money, or me?"

"Let's talk about it over a coffee."

Pax looked up the road. The nearest café was at least forty minutes from opening, and she had no intention of inviting this stranger into her flat. She was tired, feeling the chill of dawn and wary that if he wasn't a government spook he had to be a psychopath. Either way, being the victim of a theft seemed like a blessing compared to this. "You say you're government. That you just apprehended that guy. Nothing to do with me? How do you explain him picking my pocket while being abducted?"

"He's compulsive," Casaria said. "Not rational. At all."

"Yeah," Pax replied. Shady guy in a suit kidnaps someone unstable because he's about to talk to a stranger. It screamed of a thousand possibilities she wanted nothing to do with. Yet she had to ask. "So why were you after him?"

Casaria held her gaze. There was no chance he was going to tell her, and that, it seemed, was the point. There was something she was not allowed to know. But he still wanted to talk to her.

"I've never heard of your Ministry of Environmental Energy," she said. "And unless you're gonna give me my money, right now, I'd like to go."

She paused, inviting him to respond. He let another smile fill the moment's silence, then said, "Of course, you're free to go. I've got one question, though. Where did you go after leaving the bar?"

"This stinks," Pax said, firmly.

"I get that you might not believe me." The smile escalated to a snigger, like this whole situation was a game to him. "But it *is* a matter of national security."

Pax stared, miffed at the contrast. His unprovoked attack on Rufaizu and his insincere smiles said one thing, while his suit, paperwork and gun said another. As if to punctuate it, he put his hands on his hips in a manner that pulled the jacket back, drawing attention to the pistol. National security was a perfect phrase, wasn't it. Throw national security into the mix and you can get away with murder, that's what he was telling her. Hesitating, Pax considered how best to answer him. She said, "People who work nights look out for each other. I asked my people and got a name, tried to follow it up."

For the first time, Casaria looked concerned. He shifted his weight from one leg to another and asked, "What did you find out?"

The truth, Pax knew, was always the best frame for a lie. "Rufaizu was new in town, knocked over a game in St Alphege's and no one's been able to find him since. I checked the Nothicker Slums, figuring he might have a shack there."

"The Nothicker Slums," Casaria said. Pax nodded. The homeless shanty town was close enough to Rufaizu's place, if he wanted to check her travel route. He said, "What do you mean by a game in St Alphege's?"

"A game," Pax repeated. "Poker."

"Ah." Casaria's face lit up, the penny dropping. "So you –"

"You said one question," Pax cut him off. "You going to leave me alone now?"

"There's more we could discuss."

"I'm going," she said, keeping her eyes on him as she took a cautious step forward. He didn't make a move. She took another step, then another, slow and deliberate. He rolled his eyes, giving up, and waved a hand, "Go on. I slid a card under your door. Call me, any time."

She hurried to her building and took the key from her pocket without looking back. As she let herself in, she sensed he was still watching her.

4

Pax threw off her coat and turned on the radio to try and restore some normalcy to her mood. The early morning presenters were discussing the bus crash. "Twelve dead – twelve – and three of them children. This guy should *not* have been driving, it's as simple as that."

"He wasn't drunk, Marty, he was doing his job same as ever –"

"He fell asleep at the wheel! Unfit – who's regulating these people – who's –"

Marty sounded like he was going to give himself a heart attack. Pax was happy to hear she wasn't the only one having a bad morning. She kicked off her boots and paused to study her thinning left sock. It'd survive a few more washes, but she couldn't wait until Christmas for new underwear. Whatever, socks were way down the list of things she needed that money for.

The radio host decided it was time to play some music, and Pax agreed. Better not to dwell on how shitty life was. Ignore her patchy socks, and the fact that a bad driver had cost a bunch of people their lives. Block out the thought that this apartment needed paying for. A pop song came on about love or dancing, or love of dancing, or some other banality. Much better.

Pax settled onto her sofa and spread *Apothel's Miscellany* out on the cushion. Its coded language had been scrawled with black ink in fits of emotion, surrounding pencil sketches of mechanical devices that combined pipes, tools, blades and arrows: creative ideas for modern medieval weapons. Then there were occasional floor plans of winding tunnels and mazes. There were strange, fantastic creatures. How did a creative kid with interests like this get into the spooks' crosshairs? What would it take for Albie to find himself on the same path? It didn't make sense. Then, this might be something completely different to his board-game miniatures. Maybe if she spoke to him more than once a year, she'd have a better idea.

Pax put that thought out of her mind, to study a creature drawn in different poses. Some sort of biped, the rough shape of a gorilla, with no head and an extra limb rising over one shoulder from its spine. Where the head should have been was a set of mandibles. Patches of alternating scaly and flat rocky textures covered its skin and lines ran between its panelled flesh like veins. The ends of its long arms, which hung just above its flat, elephant-like feet, had three angular claws.

This Apothel was a talented artist, Pax appreciated that. Someone of considerable imagination. It could have been concept artwork for a fantasy comic or a computer game. The annotations gave the same impression, written in that cryptic language. The symbols were a lexicon, repeated frequently and systematically. Occasional notes in the margins, scrawled in handwritten biro, in

English, hinted at a translation. Pax ran a finger from one or two of the comments to a few of the underlined symbols.

The monster's name, at the head of the page, appeared to be translated directly. *Glogockle.*

The title in symbols had the same number of letters. Another entry at the bottom had a comment, *What?! Seen one OUTRUN A MAN*, next to the number 13 and three symbols. Presumably those three symbols gave a speed: *mph* or *kph*. The word before 13 was five symbols. *Speed?*

Humming along to another irritating tune on the radio, Pax took a pad of paper and a pen from her side table and started to make notes. The cypher was simple, worthy of the man who had tried to lock his door with a piece of string. It substituted English letters with symbols. She made a list of the letters of the alphabet and started matching them to symbols. This was perfect. A mindless task to clear her head, to help her calm down before plotting her next move.

Deciphering the text, Pax ignored the sun rising. When only Q, Z and X eluded her, she started to translate sections of writing, starting at the back where a set of short paragraphs were surrounded by brainstormed words. She'd hoped there might be names or addresses, but the first lines suggested they were more likely to be nonsensical riddles. *The seeping sour flower rests before the needle of two days . . .* Pax flicked away from that nonsense. Back to the glogockle, might as well check something interesting. A series of short instructions annotated the pictures: *Always approach from behind. Soft spot in central abdomen. Feeds on small animals. Max seen speed 13mph.* There was the X.

The Miscellany was a colourful and creative project, no doubt about that. A labour of love and the result of painstaking hours of work. And it wasn't Rufaizu's work. His comments in the margin almost offered a conversation with the author. Going back to the beginning, Pax translated the title on the first page, finding the book's name repeated with an epitaph: *Apothel's Miscellany: Essential tips for mastering the Sunken City.* She sat back.

The radio presenter had started raving about something new. A problem with a construction site that people were worried might collapse. He claimed the people of Ordshaw were lazy and cutting corners. They needed a wake-up call. He yawned as he said it, though. Tired of his own vitriol.

Pax turned the radio off.

Checking back through the comments in the margins of the book, she imagined Rufaizu interpreting this nonsense with the same merry enthusiasm Albie had showed when he chattered at her about a race of greenskins when she'd walked him to a model store in London. That must've been over ten years ago. When she was a teenager. She'd ignored him to make mental plans for the £20 her mother had paid her to take him. It seemed Rufaizu had been even more neglected than that.

Pax looked at the odd book with a pang of guilt. When she got this thing turned around, she'd have Albie to stay for a few days. He'd love Ordshaw. Maybe after the tournament. If she could get hold of him without going through Mum or, worse, Dad. Pax shook herself out of it and fixed her eyes back on the book. Focus. There'd be nowhere to invite anyone to if she wasn't careful.

The book had brought her no closer to understanding what Rufaizu was about. What would a government Ministry of Energy want with him? Had he stolen from them, too? The card Casaria had slipped under Pax's door bore the same insignia as the PO-42c, a lion crest with grandiose laurels. Both matched the Ministry of Environmental Energy's website, which she'd checked on her phone. The website said nothing about what they did, though, it merely gave a list of nameless contact emails and stock images of models looking happy and important.

Casaria was troubling, even without this mystery ministry behind him. His wandering eyes, attempts at a charming smile and suggestions of wanting a casual chat all hinted at personal advances. Which was an immediate *no*. He'd dealt with Rufaizu barbarically, for one, and there were things she clearly wasn't supposed to know, for another. To say nothing of his edgy awkwardness, and the gun.

She decided to contact someone else from this Ministry. If they really did have her money, they could tell her when she'd get it back, and what had happened to Rufaizu. Or they could let her know Casaria was nothing to do with them. She pictured the gun again and considered another call to Bees, and as if on cue her phone chirped, making Pax jump.

She fumbled to answer, barely noticing the call came from a withheld number.

"All right bitch-sticks," a rough female voice shouted. "I know who you are and where you live – if I sniff a lie, I'll rain on you harder than a brick bull. You working with them?"

Pax held the phone a foot from her ear, too stunned to respond.

"You hearing me, cock burglar?" the voice snapped. "You working with them or what?"

"Who is this?" Pax replied.

"Are you fucking working with them?" the caller exploded.

"Working with who?" Pax answered almost as hotly, the hostility giving her a rise.

"The suit salesman, the slick prick – we *saw* you."

"The government?"

"Hallelujah, a ray of light in your simple skull."

"Who is this?"

"I'll come down this line and pull your tongue through your ear, you keep this up. Are you or are you not working with him?"

Pax paused. She'd dealt with plenty of angry people at the card table, and the best response was usually no response. But the night's events had her irate. To hell with the best response. She said, forcibly, "One, if you know who I am then you should already know if I'm working with them. Two, if you know where I live, then come say it to my face, instead of making threats through the phone."

Before the mad woman could respond, Pax hung up, as calmly as she could. Her hand was shaking, stung by the intensity of the caller's voice, but she kept her composure. The phone started ringing again, again showing a withheld number.

Pax waited three rings, then answered, holding the phone at a distance, expecting more shouting.

The caller was beyond incensed.

"Listen you tall sack of shit, if I tell you to talk you're –"

Pax hung up. Down this road, no rational conversation lay. She moved to the window. Her apartment gave a panoramic view of the sleeping street below. Curtains drawn in the windows, no one lingering in the street. Whoever was calling didn't appear to be in the immediate area.

She stared at the phone. There was someone else involved, apparently opposed to Casaria's lot, and hinting, rather strongly, that he genuinely was from the government. This angry woman had her phone number but had, for some reason, referred to Pax as *tall*. They couldn't actually know who she was, because 5'6" was hardly tall in anyone's books. She was safe, wasn't she? Besides, no one who wanted to hurt her would warn her with a crazed phone call.

Still, it was weird, getting weirder.

Pax returned to the sofa.

The book lay open on a sketch of an Underground train surrounded by what looked like lightning. There were people in the windows, with shaded doubles of themselves lifting from their bodies, as though something was pulling their souls out.

The evocative artwork made her frown. She read Rufaizu's marginal comment: *Minotaur's Grasp. Does this even need explaining?*

"Yes, it needs explaining, you dick," Pax grumbled, turning the page to see if there was any more. He'd said *minotaur* as he was dragged from the bar, clearly a focal point for him. The next few pages showed diagrams of tunnels with no text, though. Crazy people upon crazy people, and somewhere in the middle of all this Pax's livelihood was at risk, along with the life of an odd young man.

The phone vibrated again, once. A text message appeared on the screen.

WITHHELD: You are so fucked.

5

Barton took in Rufaizu's apartment grimly. There were boot-prints in the dust that said someone had visited recently, but they looked too small to have been the young man come home. Whoever it was, they'd raided his hiding places. That left only one option, and Barton hated it. Dr Mandy Rimes. Holly would be furious at him for even contemplating calling her.

It didn't matter.

He'd already breached Holly's trust by coming here. She hadn't cooled off when she woke him from his slumber on the couch, still dressed and smelling like a septic tank. She threw a towel at him and told him to go outside to hose himself down. Deadbeats don't get to use the shower, she'd said. He sat on the sofa for a while longer, rubbing his throbbing temples, while Grace watched him from the adjoining kitchen. Cautious whispers passed between his daughter and wife; he could guess what they were saying.

What's going on? Your father's an arsehole.

The usual sort of thing.

He could feel Grace staring, not venturing any closer. When Barton looked up, she ducked away, shaking her head, adopting the affected child routine. She wasn't a child any more, though, she was at that age where you took pride in hating your parents. It'd bring her kudos: *my dad is the worst.*

Holly got Grace's stuff together for school and huffed that she guessed it was her turn to drive, knowing full well it wasn't. Barton didn't respond. He let them go without any kind of explanation, just sat there staring at the carpet wishing he could stick a spike through his skull to release the pressure.

Holly slammed the door on her way out. Barton took it as a signal to finally get up.

Climbing the stairs to the shower felt like a monumental struggle. Twice he slid to his knees and groaned at the world for being too difficult to live in. Somehow he found it in himself to keep going, and the frosty water partly woke him. He threw on some clean clothes and dragged himself outside.

Struggling to keep his eyes open, swaying in his car seat, Barton suspected he still had more than the legal limit of alcohol in his blood.

It didn't matter.

Rufaizu's apartment was a forty-minute drive away, on the other side of the city, but he managed it in an hour twenty. It was the city's fault, not his; he'd taken the quickest route, using the ring road, but driving around Ordshaw during the day sucked at time like a leech. Damn Rufaizu for forcing him to travel. Barton had moved out to leafy Dalford to pretend he wasn't part of the heaving beast that was Ordshaw. Year by year the city was getting worse; more crowded, spreading into new, more colourfully wretched neighbourhoods that had once been villages in their own right. More like London every day, only less important. Two million people combining to create a monster you couldn't cross in under an hour.

He locked the car six times before he was satisfied that it was secure. If there was ever a place for your car to go missing, this was it. Even his twenty-year-old Scenic was fair game – it'd stopped being scenic a decade ago, but a thief around here could get it started better than he ever could.

Staring at the empty disappointment of Rufaizu's apartment, after the effort it had taken to get there, Barton considered sitting and waiting, but his hangover was getting worse and his ability to concentrate was fading. It wasn't worth it. Rufaizu was gone, not answering his phone, and it didn't look like he'd be here any time soon. It was either leave it all to rear its ugly head at a random point in the future, or call Rimes to try and figure this out.

Barton dialled and hoped, with each passing ring, that the doctor would not answer. It had been so long, maybe she had a new number. Maybe she was dead, who knew. Five rings. Six. Barton's finger hovered, preparing to hang up. The phone clicked.

"Citizen Barton?" Rimes' raspy voice answered, at once tired and surprised.

"Mandy," Barton said quietly. "How are you?"

"I've been expecting your call."

Barton could picture Holly's face. Her mouth and eyes screwing smaller like the narrowing points of intensely focusing lasers. She wouldn't say anything, just burn him with her gaze, letting him know how big a mistake he was making. Silently saying *you've ruined all our lives*. Sometimes she gave him that look when he folded his trousers the wrong way after doing the laundry, mind. It would make a change to receive it for something serious.

Rimes breathed patiently but loudly. Barton knew few people in the world who could so comfortably let a silence hang.

"Expecting me why?" he asked.

"Rufus got in touch. He said he had found something, but wouldn't tell me what."

"For God's sake," Barton groaned. "Did you meet with him?"

"Briefly. He told me to be ready. That your involvement would come first."

"I haven't spoken to him. He wanted to meet with me last night. He didn't show."

"That's not good. Not good at all."

Rimes' tone was completely neutral, but Barton knew well enough that her unemotional words could be taken at face value. He said, "What else did he tell you?"

"Just what I said. He thinks he's found the answer."

"To what?"

"To everything. To kill the beast."

Barton paused, holding back from saying something he might regret. Another question, another sentence, and he might be drawn back in without any way out. If there was a solution, it was not something he could walk away from. No matter what promises he had made to his family. He replied, "Rufaizu's been away so long. He was just a kid. What would he know?"

"I hoped you might tell me."

"Are you still working?"

"Mm."

He could picture Rimes in her laboratory, lights low and blinds down, examining some test-tube of luminous liquid through brass-rimmed goggles, even as they spoke. It was possible that the doctor had never left that unlikely hall of experiments. She might have been born there, for all he knew. It certainly felt like she would make it her grave.

The idea that he could ever have cheated on Holly with her was so far from reality that it wasn't even funny. It was borderline offensive. But Holly hadn't known who the doctor was. Rimes was a lady Barton had visited in the dead of the night. On numerous occasions. In Holly's eyes, those secret visits were a betrayal, no matter their purpose.

Guessing his thoughts, Rimes asked, "Did you tell your wife everything, in the end?"

"Enough to keep her from cutting my throat in my sleep," Barton said. "Not enough that she's any the wiser." Just enough to leave a permanent look of distrust on her face. He sighed. "She got the point that I wasn't having an affair, at least. Mandy, if you see Rufaizu again, let him know I tried to meet him. But it's best he not contact me again."

"Certainly. There's something else you might want to be aware of, though," Rimes said. "I believe he wasn't working alone. He said he had help. Friends."

"Well," Barton said, firming his decision. Apothel had found friends, too, and look where it got him. Rufaizu was his father's son. "Then I definitely want no part of it."

"Aren't you curious, Citizen Barton?" Rimes asked, before he could end the call.

"No," he told her. "I can't afford to be."

On the way home, Barton tried to convince himself that none of it mattered. There was no way to stop the minotaur, Apothel had been clear about that from the start. If he'd found a solution he would've told everyone, not disappeared up his own arse. And for Rufaizu to find something where his own father had failed was unthinkable. The boy was wayward, half mad.

There was no way.

And there were more important things to worry about. Holly's anger. Grace's trust. They needed him. Emotionally and financially. Even this impromptu day off would eat into their small buffer of disposable cash.

When the Scenic sputtered, pulling into the faster-moving traffic of the ring road, Barton pictured their faces on seeing the car he'd been saving for. It was small, the new Civic, but it meant cheaper journeys and fewer breakdowns. More money for holidays. A tour of Scotland. A seaside jaunt. A Christmas market. It was all possible. Holly would soften, at least for a moment. Grace, more importantly, would offer him her smile. She had the most charming smile of any young lady. A heartbreaker. That smile would say her dad was okay. There had been far too many disappointed smiles.

The imagined scenes of his happy family consoled him for the journey, his spirits lifting and the misery of his godforsaken hangover drifting into the background.

Life wasn't so bad.

Rufaizu's lunacy could not be allowed to ruin everything. Barton had the strength to ignore it. He decided he'd go in to work today, after all.

6

Pax had not slept. Years of enduring poker games that stretched into oblivion had taught her you could always find a second wind if you waited long enough. Or a third, or fourth. Rather than struggle to rest, she studied Rufaizu's book while she waited for the Ministry offices to open. After reading about glogockles and surveying tunnel layouts, she decoded notes on other unnatural creatures, taking satisfaction in solving the puzzles. She decoded the headings for *The Drummer Horse, Invisible Proclaimers,* and *Tuckles* before focusing on the entry for the *Sickle* in detail. Its image was a thing of nightmares, a humanoid torso atop four canine legs, with long, curved claws instead of hands. Its face had no eyes, just a jagged-toothed jawline that ran from top to bottom rather than left to right. The short misspelt paragraph curating it gave her the idea that Apothel was not exactly a scholar.

Sickles patrol on set lines. Strongest sense is touch; they look for vibrashans from movement. No eyes, no nose, no ears. Stay still and quiet, they mite not know your there. If cornered by a sickle, get the back legs, they lose balance easy. Sickles are very fast. Teef and claws rip flesh. Avoid – do not fite.

In the margin she found a clue to another person's involvement in this strange enterprise. A triumphant addendum read: *Tell that to Citizen Barton!*

Pax leafed through the book, looking for other names. She reached a long section with no images and a single solitary note in the margin: *Probably inaccurate.* She translated the title, *Layer Fae.* One to come back to. Following that was a list, with pictures of different containers: jars, cylinders and an elaborate flagon that gave Pax a yearning for a medieval banquet. Nothing like the object she'd taken from Rufaizu's place, though.

Continuing, she found a couple of pages stuck together and peeled them apart. She hadn't seen this one before, when she'd been looking for clues to the cypher. The image made Pax pause.

A full-page sketch depicted the insignia from Casaria's business card. There were symbols around it, passionately thick and underlined. It seemed Rufaizu, if the annotations were really his, wanted whoever found this book to know what this page had to say, because he'd already translated each block of text in small lettering:

Do not trust the Ministry of Environmental Energy. Investigations are baloney. Agents are dangerous. Spies everywhere. Protecting the labyrinth. In with the enemy.

"Jesus Christ," Pax said. She turned the page, but there was no more information. The book devolved into the half-dozen pages of short riddles, then, with their scattered words around them. Apparently Rufaizu had been trying to solve them.

And there ended the book.

Pax sat back and stared at the leather-bound tome. It was pure fantasy, except that it had thrown doubt on her plan of getting in touch with the Ministry. She wasn't sure what else she had hoped to find. More names, an address? There was nothing.

She bit her lip. Whether Rufaizu was half mad or the victim of an overactive imagination, nothing in what she'd seen suggested he deserved to be disappeared. In all likelihood he had no one looking out for him. He'd been squatting there alone, after all. Pestering night-time weirdos and squirrelling away bizarre books and devices.

Pax turned her attention back to the odd cylinder she had stolen.

Half glass, half brass, it looked like part of a Jules Verne machine, waiting to be filled with a magical fuel that could be used to travel through time. For example. Pax turned it over and found a fine set of markings on the underside: a symbol similar to a precious metal's hallmark. It was too small to make out clearly. The mechanisms at one end had cogs finer than a Swiss watch. She thumbed back through the book, searching the sketches for a page that might explain it, but none of the objects resembled this one.

Setting both items aside, she hummed to herself. Her eyes rested on her coat, hanging by the door, with Rufaizu's notepad poking out of a pocket.

That was another piece of the puzzle. Away from the distracting smells of the bar, she caught a whiff of stale sweat on its pages. Pax leafed through the unenlightening pages of notes. Hundreds of answers to three questions Rufaizu posed to night-dwelling strangers. Pax found herself answering the questions in her head as she read through others' answers.

What is your name? Pax Kuranes. Dad wasn't especially empathetic with that one.

What are you doing out? After-work drinks. I work later than most people.

Why did you choose that drink? To find luxury in at least one area of my life. Another legacy of my father's. Pound for pound, no other drink is as complex or rewarding as a whisky, he said. Always be a connoisseur, even in vice.

Was it any wonder she'd ended up here? Hustling and hiding, separate from the world, refusing to aspire. Was it any wonder that Albie took refuge in fantasy worlds? He'd learnt to escape from their bullshit quicker than her. Had Rufaizu done the same?

Pax grunted and abandoned the questions of life to grab a cubed bottle of cheap bourbon. To hell with being a connoisseur. She drank from the bottle, imagining herself a lowlife in a seedy American carpark. As far as she could get from her dad's House Rules and drink-specific glasses.

As she drank, she flipped through Rufaizu's notepad, reading about other nighthawks' habits. Most of their reasons for drinking were pathetic, either caused by minor tribulations or major personality defects: *My life sucks* or *Because I rock!*

Pax came to the name Darren, though, and saw it had been heavily circled in pencil, with a big tick next to it. Annotated in the same style as the book's margin notes. She realised, then, that the notepad, like the Miscellany, was not the work of one man. Many of the pages were written in slightly different handwriting. Similar, but with smaller letters, more angular. A more reserved, perhaps more mature writer than Rufaizu. Rufaizu had taken over this notebook from someone else, perhaps the Apothel who wrote the journal? With the Miscellany written in symbols, there was no way to be sure, but given how Rufaizu had revisited the original owner's notes here, too, it seemed a safe bet. And given the similar handwriting, were they related?

Rufaizu had celebrated this one name, in particular, with a scrawl alongside the entry: *Citizen Barton! YES!*

The excitement in Rufaizu's writing reminded Pax of his protests as he was being dragged out of the bar. He'd used the name then, too. Barton.

She read Darren's answers:

Darren – sleep wastes the night – strongest and cheapest shit possible.

Now we're getting –

Pax's phone buzzed. She froze for a second, took a breath and held it up. A withheld number again. She answered and said, "I don't find phone calls intimidating, okay?"

"Glad we're on the same page," the woman replied, calmer than before. "I want to be clear on how serious I am. Look behind you."

Pax stood perfectly still, her natural instinct being to not do as she was told, purely because she had been told to do it.

"It's not a trick," the caller assured. "I want to show you something."

Pax turned slowly, away from the kitchen area, back towards the open living room, where her ripped furniture, peeling walls and stacked bookshelves left a lot of untidy surfaces for hiding things. She looked through the window, too, the outside world still asleep.

"Good girl," the voice said.

Pax's skin tingled at the realisation that she was being watched. There was a terraced house across the street, the upper floor visible from here, the blinds in the window down. No sign of life there, but nowhere else for someone to hide.

"Eyes on your wall."

Fighting the urge to resist, Pax looked to the side. In the middle of the wall sat the red pinpoint of a laser. It traced a small circle. Pax looked back to the window, trying to see where it was coming from.

"You won't see us. No one *ever* sees us."

"Congratulations," Pax answered quietly, trying to muster more courage in her tone than she felt. "You've got a laser pen and found out where I live. What's the next step, knock-down ginger and a burning bag of crap on the doorstep?"

"The next step's a bullet through your ovaries, how about that?"

Pax cringed, but wasn't done. "I deal with a lot of talkers –"

There was a crack, and Pax jumped as the red dot exploded into a puff of wallpaper and mortar. She stared in shock for a moment, then slowly turned her gaze to the window. A line ran from the bottom of the pane up to halfway along the side, the glass split in two but still standing. In the middle of the line there was a web of smaller cracks. Pax couldn't so much as blink.

"You like your ovaries, right?" the voice on the phone asked, plainly.

Pax's lips moved for a few moments in silence before any words came out. "What do you want?"

"That's the easy bit," the woman said. "We want the boy you were with last night."

"Casaria?"

"The *boy*. Your boyfriend took him, right?"

Pax swallowed. "Who are you?"

"Just do what we fucking tell you, all right? Find out where he is and get him back."

"You've got the wrong person," Pax said, voice wavering. "I keep out of people's business, they keep out of mine. You want someone found –"

"You seem like a smart girl," the voice interrupted, "so I'll let you figure out what happens if you disappoint us. I'll be in touch."

The phone went dead and the red light disappeared. Pax kept the phone by her ear for a few moments, scarcely able to believe it. Then she ducked out of view of the window, skirted across the room and threw the curtains closed. Plunged into semi-darkness, she sat on the floor, back to the wall, and cursed herself for not going home after last night's game.

7

An hour since being fired at, Pax slumped on a park bench with her face buried in her hands. She had moved as quickly as possible, once she decided to get out of there, and after three Underground trains and a bus she was finally confident that she was not being followed. In the confusion, she'd left everything behind, bar what little cash she had, her keys and her phone.

When she'd calmed down from the chase, she tried to come up with a plan.

Pax liked to think she had friends. Acquaintances, at least. There were more than half a dozen contacts in her phone who could offer protection for a price. Linneman Forsyth, a weak five-card-stud player, could get her a gun in exchange for a commitment to join the working class when his revolution came. But that might get her on some kind of watch-list. And what would she do with a gun? Shoot an innocent bystander, probably. The host of a regular Chinese Poker game, Jack the Tee, could loan her a bodyguard. His thugs could dismember the woman caller. But the Tee was terrifyingly erratic. It was dangerous enough occasionally taking a pot from him in a game.

What else could she do? Contacting the Ministry seemed like a risk in itself, considering Rufaizu's notes and the fact that the lunatic with a gun apparently hated them. Doing as she'd been asked hardly seemed much better – there was no telling what the caller wanted Rufaizu for, let alone what she'd do to Pax if her usefulness ran out.

She had one lead to follow, and that was figuring out who this Barton character was.

In that, she thought of Bees again. Bees claimed to be in imports and exports, which everyone understood to mean drugs. You didn't ask, not unless you wanted to become involved. Bees himself was only a foot soldier, though, for a man of similar standing to Jack the Tee. Bees' apparently limited career aspirations led him to a hobby of collecting knowledge. At the card table, Bees candidly offered opinions on problems that ranged from the innocently simple, such as removing stains from kitchen towels, to the morbidly complex, such as hiding a corpse in plain sight. There was every possibility Bees would track down a person like this Darren Barton, AKA Citizen Barton, for the sheer curiosity of it. He'd probably revel in the mystery in Apothel's book, too, but Pax didn't want him that involved.

Pax texted Barton's name to Bees: *Only got the name and know he likes hard liquor.*

After another half hour, and a café croissant Pax could ill afford, the phone buzzed. Bees said, "Family man, works on IT servers for a blue chip, Raystaten. Wife Holly, kid Grace. If you're thinking he's a mark, you're misinformed. No expendable cash, not on his salary, with a wife and kid and a place in Dalford."

"How do you know it's him?" Pax replied, surprised.

"All hard drinkers end up down the Sticky Tap eventually," Bees explained. "And using a moniker like that, that's a way to get remembered."

"Ralph knows him?" The Sticky Tap's owner hadn't been in last night. Would he have known something about Rufaizu, and nipped all this in the bud, if he had?

"Barton was semi-regular a real long time ago. Ralph said it might've been as much as a decade."

"But he knew where he lived?"

"No. The guy never gave up much about himself in the bar. Just drank. A lot."

So Bees had used some other means to go from a physical description to knowing everything about him. Pax would grill him about it another time. Now, she had the lunatic sniper to consider.

"Send me his address, and his number if you've got it," she said. As an afterthought, she asked, "Do you know anything about the Ministry of Environmental Energy?"

Silence on the line for a moment, before Bees said, "Got involved in something, Pax?"

"Just someone I ran into. There's nothing about them online that I can find. Have you heard it used as part of a con?"

"Let's meet up. Best not to talk about it over the phone."

Pax hesitated. Another bad sign. "I need to find this guy first."

Mid-afternoon, Pax found herself on Darren Barton's doorstep, taking in Grace Barton as the slender teenager opened the door. She was fifteen at a push, and a natural beauty, perfect skin, a smile that could sell toothpaste. Her bright eyes regarded Pax with eager friendliness.

"They started you early, didn't they?" Pax commented, erasing that smile.

"Excuse me?" the girl answered.

"Nothing. I'm looking for your dad," Pax told her. "Is he home?"

"He's not back from work yet," Grace replied. "Can I help you with something?"

"Starting to doubt it," Pax said slowly, glancing over Grace's shoulder into the hallway. Clean carpet, wall hung with clinically simple picture frames. Photos of the family. Put it together with the closely trimmed front garden, the dull grey mini-van and the quiet suburban avenue, and nothing about this picture added up to a man involved in psychotic snipers, monster books or shady government ministries. The one positive about coming here was that the low-lying, leafy suburb left nowhere for a gunman to hide, and Pax felt more positive that she'd lost her tail, now. She said, "Can I ask you a strange question?"

"Sure," Grace said, her smile returning.

"Does your dad go out late much?"

"Not any more. Is that how you know him?"

Pax shook her head. "Friend of a friend. Thought he could help me with something."

"You should speak to my mum." Grace turned and called for her mum before Pax could warn her off. Pax suddenly felt very self-conscious. These areas rarely housed people with enough expendable cash to make a card game worthwhile, and the thought of happy families, boxed up in their detached houses with their detached lives, made Pax's skin crawl.

Holly Barton came down the hall asking, "Who is it, honey?"

She stopped and stared at Pax with unashamedly judging eyes as the two women got the measure of each other. Holly had a short bob of blonde hair and a shrewd face, petite but sharply unwelcoming. Objectively, she could be considered good-looking. Alongside her daughter, the bar was raised too high. Holly greeted Pax with raised eyebrows. "Oh, please tell me you're not a drug dealer."

Pax shifted uncomfortably. "I'm not. I was just looking for your husband. I can come back later."

She looked over her shoulder, towards the street. Her own appearance troubled her in the presence of these two. Her boots, her slightly-too-big trousers, and heavy coat all had a practical purpose – hiding her posture from scrutiny, or hiding wads of cash. Above all, they were comfortable. They were not, however, remotely feminine or fashionable. This suddenly seemed important, with a blossoming teenager and her eagle-eyed mum analysing this mess of an outfit, and she wanted to get out of there. Holly stepped aside, though, leaving the doorway wide open, and said, "Fancy coming inside, telling me what it's about?"

Pax stared at the entrance hall carpet, not a spot of dirt on it. She shook her head. "No. Oh no, I don't. Maybe I could leave my number, have him call me."

"Nonsense, you travelled all this way."

The implication was clear. Pax did not belong anywhere near here. Responding to the tone and not the words, Pax said, "You're right. I should just get going."

She spun and thrust her hands deep into her pockets, marching away. Holly called something after her, a half-hearted invitation to stay, but Pax ignored it, out of the driveway in moments. She turned onto the street and saw a boxy Renault approaching, a family vehicle with blotches of rust around the wheel-arches. She slowed down as the driver leant into his window, watching her. A heavyset man in his early 40s, with the slightly disfigured face of a fighter, head shaved. He'd seen her leaving the house.

It had to be Darren Barton.

8

Barton pulled over ten metres from his drive, five metres ahead of the stranger, eyes never leaving her. He had spent enough time in the ugliest hours of night to know a fellow transient when he saw one, and there was no mistaking the fact that she had come from his house. He felt Holly watching, waiting to see what he would do. The darkly clothed young woman had stopped to stare, too.

"Bollocks," Barton muttered, cutting the engine. He emerged from the car and called out, sure to be loud enough for Holly to hear, "Did he send you? What are you thinking, coming to my home?"

She raised her hands. "No idea what you're talking about, mate. I thought –"

"To my *home*?" He raised his voice.

Barton stormed towards her like a bull, for a moment unsure himself if he was going to stop. She didn't move, other than to raise her hands higher and cringe. When he got within striking distance, though, he caught himself, breathing into her face. She averted her eyes and he followed her gaze to the balled-up fist at his side. She took in the cracked skin on his knuckles.

"What the hell were you thinking?" Barton hissed, scanning his head around hers like a posturing animal. From her scruffy appearance there was no doubt she had something to do with Rufaizu.

"I thought you might be able to help me," she answered quietly.

"The others at least knew never to come anywhere near here," Barton snarled. He sensed Holly had wandered out to watch. Had to be convincing. "Who the hell are you?"

The woman squinted, recognition dancing across her eyes. If she knew Rufaizu, surely she knew his situation?

"I'm no one, definitely not who you think," she said, quickly, too softly for the others to hear. "This guy, last night, he took my money and disappeared. I found this book, and someone's put a bullet through my window. I don't know shit, only that your name came up and I need this to stop."

Barton kept glowering at her, but it was hard to maintain the anger looking into her eyes. Big, worried. He said, "You're not helping Rufaizu?"

The young woman shook her head. "Wish I'd never met him." She paused, like she was reconsidering, then added, "But he *does* need help."

Barton shot a quick look to his house. Holly hadn't come any closer; she wouldn't be able to hear them from that distance. "You know where he is?"

"Some guy in a suit got him. I mean, like, beat him out of a bar and took him away without making a sound, and I don't know what. Claimed to be from the government."

"Christ." Barton bit his lip. He ran a hand over his face. "I can't deal with this. I can't. For the sake of my mind," he tapped his temple, "and for the sake of my family. I can't go through it all again."

"I'm not asking you to. I don't even know what this is," the woman said. "But these people are out to get me – and this book said this Ministry is dangerous – and they took my money –"

"You going to introduce me to your friend, Darren?" Holly intervened. She crossed the road towards them as Barton waved at her with a forced smile. Through the side of his mouth, he said, "Forget your money. Don't go looking for Rufaizu. Talk to no one. Trust me."

"Someone *shot* at me!"

"Honey, I've never met her before, I was asking her to leave," Barton said, stepping aside and holding out an explanatory arm towards the girl. She gave him a questioning look as Holly joined them and folded her arms.

"Is that right," Holly said, hardly convinced.

"It's true," she said. "Rufaizu gave me your husband's name."

The name made Holly pause. "What for?"

"He wanted me" – the woman turned her eyes back to Barton – "to invite him back out. It's been too long. I heard your husband used to be the life of the party." Holly raised an eyebrow towards Barton, her suspicions confirmed. Hopefully the less dangerous suspicions, the ones that didn't entertain the thought of him being unfaithful. Before he could add anything to cement that, the girl continued, "We missed him last night. Rufaizu got the idea an invite from a stranger might work."

"I'll say," Holly said, keeping her eyes on Barton. "That family was no good for Darren and I'm sure they're no good for you. I'd appreciate it if you didn't come back here."

The woman nodded, backing off, "Sure. I get it. Sorry to bother you." She turned and went on down the street as Holly and Barton held each other's gaze. Her voice piped back again, though. "One thing. These people who've been calling me. Rufaizu's friends, I guess. Who are they?"

Holly watched Barton carefully, and he didn't dare take his eyes off her as he answered, frankly, "I don't know. But you oughta avoid everyone he knows. And everywhere he's been."

He listened without turning as she made a quiet, awkward sound, like a farewell from someone who wasn't used to it. As the girl's footsteps continued away, Barton put an awkward arm around Holly's shoulders to lead her back towards the house. They walked silently across the road. He slowed down, running the last question through his mind. He took a breath and turned to shout at the girl's retreating back. "This person who threatened you. You see their face?"

"No," the young woman called back. "We spoke over the phone. But they know where I live."

Barton cursed under his breath. Rufaizu might've made a thousand enemies in his life, wherever he'd been, but Barton's instincts pointed to one obvious one. He said, "Take their threats seriously. With the people he knew, if you never see them coming, chances are it's the Layer Fae."

The stranger offered him an empty smile, like it wasn't something she understood or wanted to hear. She waved again, and continued walking.

Holly stared at Barton to ask what he thought he was doing. He avoided her gaze and headed towards their home, leaving the car parked out on the road. She caught up to him and hissed, "Was that for my benefit?" Barton shook his head, aware that the more he said, the more she'd pick at. She said, "If you think I'm going to tell you to go help that girl, I'm not, you know that? It's her problem."

"It's her problem," Barton repeated, in agreement. "Nothing to do with me."

"What did she say to you, before I came over? What's happening?"

"Nothing. She got in with that crowd and wanted my take. I don't know why they're threatening her, probably because she knows Rufaizu." Barton's eyes wandered back down the road. The woman was gone. He said, "God's truth, Holly. I don't know who she is. She wouldn't be the first not to take this seriously, though, and I don't need another death on my conscience."

9

Cano Casaria woke for another night's work, glad to find the sun all but set. Relieved of the ugly innocence and ignorance exposed in the daylight. Only in the shadows did the truth of the world reveal itself. Only in the dark did people really come alive.

Thirteen storeys up, Casaria stood at his window for his daily ritual of watching the daylight ants scurrying back into their holes as the office-block lights blinked off. Making space for the real people to come out. The ones that railed against normalcy, ones who squeezed more from the world than their day jobs gave them. The drunkards, the insomniacs, the smugglers and the thieves. The sex pests and the night workers. Even the tourists who visited in passing; the victims of emergencies, the overnight journeyers, the desperate deadline-makers.

They were the people of his world. They enjoyed empty roads with abandoned shop fronts. With less distractions, they *noticed* one another, noticed every little thing.

From the panorama of his apartment, Casaria went to ground level to hover near the Underground station. He took his dinner in the window of the Indian restaurant opposite, watching the change take place up close. In the early evening, people blindly pushed past one another, pointedly ignoring the man offering free copies of the Ordshaw Evening Standard. As the population thinned, occasional enlightenment slipped in. With two people going for the same door, at night, one might let the other pass. People started to make eye contact with the newspaper vendor, just as he packed it in for the night.

This was the world that mattered to Casaria. Only in these hours could he find people with the two values most cherished by the Ministry, and himself: an acute awareness of, and openness to, the world around them, and the resilience necessary to live in the darkness. Many of these twilight wanderers were less than fully sane, and others could not cope with people, day or night. The ones who had chosen this life when another was possible, though, they were discoveries to be treasured. They were like him. Special.

Like the poker player.

Over dinner, Casaria cut back his people-watching time to think about Pax Kuranes. The Roma boy had seen her potential, no doubt. She was smart, bold and seemingly normal, yet she was drinking in a dive for pleasure. And it didn't hurt that she was easy enough on the eye. Sure, she was no ten, Casaria reflected, but she didn't need to be. A seven would do, combined with her other qualities. He could get tens, if that was all he wanted. It wasn't important, not necessarily.

The Kuranes girl's file had further convinced him of her potential. It had been opened when she crashed her father's car at the age of fourteen. The insurance company suspected her father hadn't been driving, as he claimed he had, because the timing didn't fit with his work schedule. Being an excellent lawyer, he had crushed the case, but the government had already started a file on Pax. Aged eighteen she went to university to study the Classics. Aged nineteen she dropped out. She created two hundred accounts for online casinos and poker rooms, but stopped using them within twelve months. She receded from society. Found work that left no record. Stopped using banks. The only evidence that she was still alive was that she continued to make National Insurance payments and submitted tax returns once a year. Always showing minimal earnings from what she described as consultancy work. For the most part, her gambling winnings went unreported.

As far as the government was concerned, Pax Kuranes became a vagrant who was thankfully keeping herself off the unemployment register.

It was easy to read between the lines. She had been raised by successful parents, was well-educated and had the capacity to do anything she set her mind to. She had run away, playing late-night card games, to avoid the trappings of conventional life. Most telling was that she had snubbed online gambling, too. It wasn't about making money; she was exposing herself to an underworld that held her interest. She played cards face-to-face at undesirable hours, with even less desirable people, for an interesting life. Maybe she enjoyed judging people face-to-face, too. Both concepts made her ideal.

The Rufaizu problem was under control, with no risk of him talking to anyone and no need to process him until Casaria bothered to file the paperwork, so there was plenty of time to concentrate on Pax instead. Get the measure of her. Casaria so rarely got the chance to introduce someone new to his world, and this time he was going to do it right. He wouldn't have a repeat of Sam Ward. Ward had never really belonged out at night; she'd tricked him. She was a day-dweller who'd strayed into his territory, and she'd been drawn right back into the bland conveyor belt of admin drudgery first chance she got. Damn Ward, now settled in a sixth-floor office with her five-man Inter-Species Relations Initiative team. Good riddance to her. With Pax Kuranes, Casaria had a fresh chance to draw in a kindred spirit, and he was sure she wouldn't be filing reports on Proper Conduct to wrangle a desk job. As long as he was careful, he could gently ease Pax in, without the attention of the bureaucracy. If it worked out, he'd simply tell the office he'd met her at a later date. He'd return the money in his glove compartment to her himself. Dispose of the forged PO-42c. It would be their little secret.

If it didn't work out, no one would ever need to know, and she certainly wasn't going to be offered promotions and a fast track to management.

But it would work out, wouldn't it?

Imagining a bright future, Casaria finished his curry with a smile.

All he needed to do was show her what he had to offer. Make the possibilities clear to her. And he had a good idea of where he'd find her.

10

"I want it fixed by Monday morning." Hank Cougan's broad Yorkshire accent droned through Pax's voicemail. "Or next Friday's rent doesn't even matter – you hear?"

The last thing Pax needed with a confirmed psycho watching her home was her landlord informing her he'd seen the broken window. That had to be another hundred quid or more down the drain, and if she didn't find *that* money, she wouldn't even be able to negotiate a late rent. If she could survive that long. As she raced to meet Bees, ruing the fact that she hadn't simply called Barton on the number Bees had found, she developed a short-sighted plan of action.

"I'm heading to Frankie's in about half an hour," Pax told Bees, without so much as a hello, slipping into the seat opposite him. She'd scraped together a little under £60 from her apartment that morning. Frankie would front her the rest of his game's £100 buy-in, knowing a female player would loosen up the action. She'd spend the evening making up the cost of the window and a little wriggle room for the rent. Forget the World Poker Tour, that dream was dead. Meanwhile she was counting on the psycho caller thinking she was out doing as she'd been asked. She'd avoid that problem by not going home, while she figured out what to do about Rufaizu's mess.

Bees had chosen a grimy pub to meet in, though his sunken posture, with an empty pint glass alongside his half-finished one, suggested he would have been here anyway.

"Enough time for a pint," he replied. He had a gravelly voice, the sort a man acquired after years of inhaling powdered stone down a mine. His darkly tinged skin and the uniform grey stubble which joined his shaved hair complemented this strange affinity with stone.

"No, I've got to keep my focus," Pax said, shuffling out of her coat. "It's payday at the club and I need the cash."

"Need a stake?" he offered. She didn't reply. Pax had refused a thousand stakes from the likes of Bees. She didn't begrudge criminals their trades at the table, within reason, as they tended to be honourable gamblers with high-stakes games, but she stayed well out of their debt. She wouldn't even take a marker for a hand she had pat. She'd lost sizable pots due to that caution, but she was happy to pay that price. In her silence, Bees nodded understanding. He wouldn't probe. Bankrolls came and went; if explanations weren't offered it was rude to ask. It was enough to know she needed to crash a small game like Frankie's.

"So?" Pax leant towards Bees. "What's so scary you can't talk about it on the phone?"

Bees rolled his eyes to check the pub, with the least amount of effort. He said, "What do you make of this bus crash on the news? One of the kids what died, he stood to inherit a lot from his dad. Divorced. Would've provided for his mum, but she's out on her ear, now. Think there's a connection?"

Pax waited for him to finish the thought, knowing better than to get drawn into it. He took a sip from his beer, foam collecting around his mouth like a second beard. Sure enough, he abandoned that pondering intro to get to the point.

"Ministry of Environmental Energy was created about fifteen years ago. Under the guise of tackling climate change and that sort of shit. But there's already the Department for Environment, see, and there was a Department of Energy and Climate Change until recently. Doing the jobs you'd assume Environmental Energy would."

"You think it's a cover," Pax concluded. Bees nodded.

"The MEE has never submitted any reports or shown any evidence of actually doing anything, see. You've seen their web portal? Nothing there. All records of them are so obscure you won't find anything else, neither. Except I happen to have seen a bit of their mandate. They have national jurisdiction to investigate – I kid you not, these are the words in their founding documents – *any and all circumstances relating to energy and environment*, with *practical powers to disband, restrain and otherwise enforce government policy regarding threats.* No one independently reviewing their work, though, just a few ministers paid a full-time wage to meet twice a year to go over the Ministry's budget."

"Okay," Pax said. "So they're siphoning money into what? Greedy politicians' pockets? Or something covert? Security?"

"They're not lining pockets," Bees said. He took his time to gulp down more beer, breathing deeply to savour the taste. Someone who didn't know him might have thought he had nothing left to say. His eyes were dull, resting on Pax without any particular interest. She waited. He said, "This Ministry, it was set up in 2001. There was a big shuffle in Environment departments, all this hoo-ha with foot and mouth disease. You ask me, it's got nothing to do with climate change, that was only a convenient umbrella to get it through parliament. But they're not doing nothing, the money's being used. I got a few ideas on it."

Pax waited again, sure he would tell her. He took his time, drinking again and staring into the glass as though his beer held the answers. It distracted him instead.

"You know these people have been doing whatever they've been doing longer than we've been allowed to keep pubs open all night? That was 2003. This Ministry had been going two years already, by then. Could be a connection."

"Why would there be a connection?" Pax asked, blunt enough to tell him his wandering thoughts weren't helpful.

"Not as crazy as you might think," Bees said, pointing a stubby finger upwards. "I've looked into the MEE a couple of times, and there's two things I've pegged them on. One's that they only seem to come out at night. Everyone that's met one of these guys has met them at the weirdest hours. I mean, any time after six is weird to meet a civil servant, ain't that right?"

"Tell me they're vampires and I walk," Pax said. Bees smiled. He had a thick, slightly sinister smile that suggested he might be considering punching your face off. His teeth were a little too big for his mouth.

"No, I don't believe they're of the supernatural," Bees replied, "But it's important. Because the other thing I know about them is that they make people disappear. Ronnie Sweet, you remember him?"

"Fat guy who plays at the Ocean Club. Sure."

"Seen him since last October?"

Pax pictured the ever-sweating sporting goods store manager, always late to a game and always eating. He was one of the many people she loved taking money from but hated being around. It was true, he hadn't been at a game for a long time. She shrugged. "Maybe he retired."

"Sweet asked Mr Monroe for some money, around a year ago. Wanted to open another shop. He'd found this nice property under the arches, near the West Quay. Disappeared before it got started. We got curious, found out he'd had a few meetings with someone from the MEE. Then, poof, vanished."

"Could've been discussing regulations," Pax said. "Could be anything. He was meeting with your boss too, you don't blame him for the disappearance."

"No," Bees grinned. "My boss didn't disappear him. Want to ask me how I know?"

Pax shook her head. His boss, Mr Monroe, was a gentleman at the card table, but had an ugly reputation. She had always taken care to distance Bees from the rumours she heard about Monroe, so she could hold conversations with him without a moral crisis.

"Anyway" – Bees' smile left his face – "it's not just him. I found three or four other people with similar stories. People who've had a meeting or two with someone from the MEE then vanished. Also found one or two who *hadn't* vanished, but met someone late at night claiming to be from the Ministry asking odd questions. Like if they'd seen anything strange on the train tracks."

"Right," Pax said. "What's your theory?"

"Clearly," Bees said, "they're hiding some nocturnal work. Seems to be something underground. Could be anything, though: illegal gas lines, sneaking war criminals across borders, who the fuck knows."

"Those are the two things that spring to your mind," Pax noted. "Not stockpiling chemical weapons or conducting experiments on aliens?"

"Could be anything. Nothing seemed to connect these people that disappeared. Maybe they're watering down alcohol on a national scale," Bees said, with an air of finality. "Who. The Fuck. Knows."

"Whatever the case," Pax said, "the point is they're shady and best avoided."

"Bingo. And being that they're government, that means don't talk about them on the phone and don't go searching on the internet. Now." Bees gulped down the last of his beer. "You gonna tell me how you came to meet one of them?"

"In the Sticky Tap. He made someone mysteriously disappear."

"Sounds juicy."

Pax took out her phone and checked the time. She had a moment of relief in seeing no one had tried to call her, but she needed to get to the game. All this was adding up to the simple conclusion that she wasn't likely to see Rufaizu or her money ever again, however much she wanted to end this, and whatever the lunatic caller threatened her with. "I'll tell you about it another time. One more quick question: you ever heard of a group called the Layer Fae?"

Bees shook his head. "Good name for a biker gang. Interesting word, fey. Could relate to magic, could relate to death and doom. Like, this fey guy, he's gonna die. No one says that any more, though."

"Yet you know it."

"Well . . ." Bees' smile returned. "I like to know things."

"Yeah, me too," Pax said. "And this ambiguous shit is starting to bug me."

Circling around thoughts of Rufaizu in a torture chamber and snipers ready to cripple her, Pax raced towards Frankie's game, hoping against hope to simply survive the night. If she could scrape her living costs together, maybe she could give the psycho caller the book and the weird device as a compromise. Barton had suggested the Layer Fae weren't likely to help Rufaizu, but maybe he was wrong – maybe they were his friends, after all. She could give them everything she knew and they could figure it out themselves, couldn't they? It was neater than the thought that no one was looking out for her brother.

No. Not her brother. Rufaizu. Some tramp.

She had to block the madness out, at least for the evening, to play her best and avoid eviction. It'd be easy. The lads at Frankie's club weren't the sort to ask about anything personal, they had their own shit to deal with and would sooner talk about that than worry about her. She could unwind. She could pick up on the hot streak she'd enjoyed the night before.

That was how it worked. You fall down, you recoup.

Her hopes of enjoying that relaxing evening disappeared before Frankie's door, though. She stopped in front of the club building behind its uneven parking area, the sign's wiry lettering and cocktail-glass silhouette flashing first green, then blue, then pink, then red.

"You've got to be kidding," Pax huffed under her breath.

Casaria pushed away from the wall he'd been leaning on to give her a small wave.

11

"Turning up like this," Pax told Casaria, "is stalking."

"Stops people from cancelling," he said.

"Removes the choice," Pax replied.

"Yes. There's something I want to show you. I guarantee you'll find it interesting. You *do* have a choice, though, I want to be clear. You can walk away. No harm done, no strings attached."

"I don't want to see your dick." The response simply jumped out. Casaria grinned, his straight-toothed smile a little too wide, like someone had once told him this is what charm looked like. Pax skirted to the side, trying to move closer to the club doorway without getting nearer to him. "I need to get to this game."

He put a hand into his jacket, making Pax freeze, fearing the gun. He ignored her reaction, taking out a fold of cash. Pax could judge money well enough by sight: a hundred in twenties.

"If that's all you've got, I still need to get to that game."

Casaria smirked again. He put his hand back in the pocket and drew out another, bigger wad of cash. "Let's be realistic. How well would you need to do to recover what you lost last night? How much luck is involved in that? Is that game" – he indicated Frankie's – "even big enough?"

Pax stared at the cash, unconsciously drifting closer like a moth drawn to light. That chunk of notes was definitely more than she could make at Frankie's table, even on the best of nights. And he knew it. Did he know how much she needed that money, too? A government agency might. But would they go around waving cash at people? Her eyes shifted back to Casaria's expectant face and she said, "Seriously. Is this a sex thing?"

Casaria put the money away. "Please. I'd be doing you a favour."

"Ouch," Pax said. He was smiling, of course. Thinking awfully highly of himself. A sex thing would've been simpler. "Rumour is it's best to avoid your Ministry like the plague."

"I'm sure you don't know anywhere near as much as you think."

"I know you beat on an innocent boy. And that you're waving your cash at me like it's . . ." Pax frowned. It was her own money, wasn't it? By rights, she could kick him in the nuts and take it back. "Where's the rest?"

"Safe," Casaria told her. "Like I said, you'll get it all back. I can speed things up, if you'll bear with me. A couple of nights, that should do it."

Pax looked at Frankie's sign, imagining the comfort of a night at the table with a sedate crowd. Going away with a little money and no additional complications beyond the promise of a bullet in the ovaries, and a guilty conscience if she didn't help Rufaizu. She looked back to Casaria's cash and imagined the other possibilities. Disappearing under the auspices of some violent government agency. Learning things she wouldn't be able to unlearn. The images from Apothel's Miscellany sprang to her mind. The fantastic creatures with strange names, capturing Rufaizu's excited attention. His connection to this ministry was a mystery. She said, "Tell me about Rufaizu."

"Huh?" The smile wasn't so permanent after all. Casaria's face was blank.

"What have you done with him? What are you going to do?"

"I thought you didn't know him."

"He took my money. I figured it out. Filtered for nighthawks, isn't that how you put it?"

Casaria's smile came back, apparently impressed that Pax had a memory.

"Where is he?" she pressed.

"Safe. It's our job to keep people safe, Pax."

"Why'd you take him, then?"

"A matter of national security." There was that expression again, telling her nothing. But Casaria elaborated this time. "He's not *innocent*, as you put it. At the very least, he knows something that would be dangerous to share. At the worst, he may have access to things he shouldn't have. He'll be interviewed and we'll take it from there. Is that enough? Will you come with me now?"

Pax kept her eyes on him, feeling something swelling in her chest. How was that supposed to be enough? "I need to see him. I need to see Rufaizu with my own eyes."

Casaria didn't speak for a moment. His blank expression broke, though, and he rolled his eyes away from her. "Fine. You can see the boy – but not until *after* you come with me. By then, though, I think your priorities will have shifted."

Whatever the hell that meant. By then she might be locked up along with Rufaizu, or worse? Disappeared like Ronnie Sweet?

Pax gave Frankie's another glance. She could go in and tell them all about this guy. She could call Bees and insist he come with her. She could run. But if she did any of those things, her money might disappear, and Rufaizu along with it. To say nothing of what these people, and the others, might do if she didn't play ball. Casaria was at least pretending this was an amicable deal, right now.

"You'll give my money back?" Pax asked. Casaria nodded. "All of it?"

"In time," he said. "But you need to give me some time. One evening is never enough."

"How's a statement like that ever lead anywhere good?" Even as she questioned it, though, Pax realised that shitty comment was good in itself. Whatever madness he had planned, Casaria wanted her consent to join him at a later date. He was watching her, waiting for her to reach a conclusion. She shook her head. "I've got bills to pay. I've got a tournament on Thursday."

"Give me until Monday, then."

"Why?" Pax narrowed her eyes. "What *for*?"

"It's something I have to show you, there's no point explaining it."

"Why?" she repeated, more firmly.

He nodded, realising it wasn't the process she was asking about. "Because there's not many people who can handle it, what I want to share with you, and there needs to be more of us. I'm playing a hunch here, but I think you'll be into it."

Pax didn't blink, taking in his squared-off posture, no hint from his body that he wasn't being honest. Unless he knew how to hide his emotions. Pax was good at reading eyes, though, and the way he broke her gaze, just for a second, confirmed her hunch that this was personal. "Three nights, that's what I'll agree to. But we see Rufaizu today. And you give me that cash now."

She held out her hand. Casaria stared at it, hesitating. He took out the hundred again, that was all. "This much. Only this, today." Pax started shaking her head, but he thrust the notes into her palm. "Believe me, seeing the boy is a *big* concession." He let go of the money in her hand, giving her a quick squeeze with his fingers to complete the handshake. The way fifteen-year-old boys give hugs. He immediately moved past her, pointing ahead. "This way. You'll enjoy this, seriously."

Watching him go, Pax told herself this was progress. He might've abducted someone and all but blackmailed her into coming with him, but he liked her. For the first time all day, she felt like she had some kind of leverage.

The icy silence of Letty's dinner was interrupted by her phone ringing. As she finished her mouthful and read Fresko's name off the Caller ID, she was aware that Mix and Gambay had frozen across the table, watching her like they thought she might shout at them for letting the phone ring. She tapped the green icon. "Speak."

"She's going with him," Fresko said. "Asked him about the kid, but nothing concrete. The mug agreed to take her to him after whatever they're up to."

"Finally," Letty said, closing her eyes with relief. "I'm coming to you." She hung up and returned Mix's rigid stare. He could've been a statue set in malice, his masonry block jaw set as squarely as his silver hair. Still pouting over the reams of insults she'd shouted at him earlier. She raised her eyebrows to prompt him to come out and say it.

"We're all going, right?" he said.

"Like shit. The Ministry's on her. I need subtle, not stupid."

Letty could predict Mix's follow-up before it left his lips. He was tough as cheap beef, and old enough to be a father-figure, but tough was all he knew. "We corner Casaria, we can make him talk."

"Spin on it." Letty pushed herself up from the table but kept her hands on it, looming over the others. "You're gonna start thinking now? It was yesterday I needed you. Now you'd just get in the damned way. Casaria's sweet on that girl, he's taking her where we want to go."

Gambay spread his arms across the table with the grace of a prowling lizard, leaning into her plan. "*Then* we ice that Ministry prick!"

"Stop being thick!" Letty commanded. She tossed her can at Gambay. He ducked, too slow, and it caught him on the temple. Toppling off his seat, Gambay turned on Letty with his teeth bared and fists clenched. Letty grabbed a curved knife, making Gambay freeze.

"Give me an excuse," Letty said. "It'd be less than you deserve."

Gambay glowered at her hatefully. He touched a hand to his reddening temple.

"*Please*," Letty said, savagely. He shook his head and sat back down. Letty continued, "Maybe it was good that you arseholes weren't on Rufaizu when you needed to be. The shit you might've done. We need the kid, we don't need a fucking war with the Ministry. Do I really have to spell that out?"

Gambay mumbled something that could have been a no.

"Here's what happens now," Letty said. "Me and Fresko keep on this broad and you two stay sober and wait for my call. Maybe – *maybe* – we put this behind us." She threw an arm to the ill-gotten gains that littered the room. Gold, cash and trinkets in abundance. "We put *all* this behind us. No more mugging pedestrians. Boosting cars. Knocking over card games."

Letty grabbed Mix's can from across the table and gulped down what was left of his drink. She wiped her mouth with her forearm, belched and turned to leave. Neither of the others moved or said anything, but she knew what they'd do in her absence. Gambay would grumble that he had no problem with mugging people and Mix would tell him to grow a pair and stand up to Letty. Then they'd down some vodka to make themselves feel like men. Not too much, though. They wouldn't risk getting blind drunk again after last night. Now that they'd screwed up and she'd chewed them out for it, they'd be ready to make good. They'd tracked down the girl from the bar's cameras in record time, after all, and Fresko had been a trooper trailing her all day. All she needed from the other two was their muscle, if it came to that. Hopefully it wouldn't.

Letty headed out feeling positive. Not great, exactly, but it was the first time in twenty-four hours that she didn't feel like punching her head through a wall with frustration. Rufaizu couldn't have been anywhere that secure. Casaria was promising to take the dumpy barfly to him, and no civilians got inside the fortress that was the Ministry offices. The prick must have put protocol on hold while he trotted after that piece of arse, and that was gonna save them all from an impossible situation.

12

Though visibly pleased with her choice, Casaria became quiet after Pax agreed to come. He led her away from Frankie's, towards an unlit street, and her worries mounted. Flanked by dumpsters and hidden from street lights, the road was a den of shadows. A billboard rose over the area beyond a building, the partly torn image advertising a Dyson vacuum cleaner. It said *The Future's Spotless*, but the image looked two or three decades old. A place that time had forgotten. He could rape her here, murder her. He had a gun, and even if he was unarmed she doubted she'd have the strength to fight him off. The exercise she paid lip-service to in bi-monthly twenty-minute bursts suddenly did not seem enough. She fought the fear, though: *I've handled worse situations.*

Onward they walked, out into the safety of the street lights.

Pax looked over her shoulder, to the passage they'd left behind, and told herself there was nothing to be afraid of. If he hadn't attacked her there, where would he?

As they continued, she decided talk would lighten her mood, and a comment came out unfiltered: "So definitely no rape, then?"

Casaria paused as he gave her an odd look. Common to so many people she'd met, he wasn't quite on board with her sense of humour. She tried an uneasy smile, which didn't help. He said, in a tone that begged to be believed, "Honestly, this isn't about sex."

"All right." Pax took a moment. "Are you gonna tell me where we're going?"

"Underground," he said, showing her his back as he continued.

"What's that mean? We need to get the Tube?"

"No," he answered. "Just its tunnels."

"What have you got to show me in the tunnels of the Tube?"

Casaria did not answer.

They continued to the end of the street and towards Wynbone Station. Its wide open stairs descended in the middle of the pavement, appearing incredibly foreboding. Wynbone was quiet at the best of times, far from the centre of the city, and at this time of night it was deserted.

Pax slowed as Casaria continued. Her earlier question was answered – an Underground tunnel might be a better place to attack her than that street. It could house the many things her father had always feared on her behalf. The nightmares of Ordshaw he brought up every Christmas. A sex dungeon? Human trafficking? *Keep working nights, with those people,* she could hear him say, *and you'll end up chained in a sex dungeon.*

She always growled at him that such things never happened.

Maybe they did, though.

Casaria stopped and turned back, realising she was not following. He said, "You'll be safe."

"Give me your gun and I'll believe you," she replied.

"That would make you *less* safe," he said. "I'll explain once you've seen it."

"Maybe you should explain now."

"I've done this before," Casaria told her calmly. "More than a few times. It's better to see it first. Otherwise, you'll just accuse me of making things up. More likely, you won't want to come."

"Now you really need to tell me what it is."

"No. I don't."

Pax watched him continue, towards the steps, and knew it was true. She had to go with him, to pay her rent and look out for that poor kid and to save her ovaries. More than all that, though, now she had a big fat dose of curiosity to satisfy. What could possibly be down there, and was it remotely close to Bees' idiotic ideas? As Casaria reached the station, never looking back, she rushed after him.

"At least tell me where it is," she said. "Give me *something*."

"You've got my word –"

"That's not enough."

"It's beyond the maintenance tunnels. I have a key that takes us to another set of tunnels. We'll go about three minutes into them, not far. Then you'll see it."

Pax kept walking, frowning. "Why are there extra tunnels that you have the keys to?"

"See what's there, then I'll explain. That's the deal."

They reached the bottom of the stairs, the station empty. It was one of the older stations, fading tile walls lined with cracks, steel-rimmed lights caked in so much grime that they gave only the vaguest yellow-green glow. The adverts here belonged in a collection with that Dyson billboard; there was a faded advert for Hooper's Hooch, a *Brand New!* alcoholic lemonade. Didn't that go out of fashion in the late 90s? As Pax tried to recall her alcopops history, Casaria stopped at a maintenance door a short way down the tunnel. He took out a key, opened the door and stepped aside. Pax stared into the darkness beyond.

"Okay." She took a breath. "Tell me one thing before we go another step. Where *exactly* is Rufaizu?"

Casaria shrugged. "I told you he's fine."

She folded her arms. He stared at her.

"All right. He's in St Alphege's. In a safe house. Waiting for me to process him. At that point he's going to the MEE building in central Ordshaw, which you would *not* be allowed into. Okay?"

Pax read his face, trying to judge how far to trust this. "Does anyone else know he's there?"

Casaria's silence gave her the answer.

"You're not on the level, are you?" Pax said. "You shouldn't be attacking suspects or imprisoning them in the sticks. Or bringing girls down here, for whatever this is . . ."

His smile came back crookedly. Pax was starting to notice the difference – straight and toothy was his show smile. This cock-eyed smirk betrayed genuine amusement. He said, "The Ministry has a great deal of rules and regulations. Forms to fill in. I like to keep things casual until it's absolutely necessary to go through the red tape. If I didn't, your money would be lost in the system. You should be thanking me, really."

He waited as though expecting her to say thanks.

"What'd he do?" Pax asked. "Exactly."

"It's connected to this." He indicated the doorway. "Again. The explanation will be so much easier after you see what's down there."

Pax shot him a fierce look, to say this was not cool. Acknowledging that didn't help, though. She walked on past him into whatever hell lay beyond.

"There's, what, three safe houses in St Alphege's?" Letty shouted at Fresko as they sped through the city. "Send the others to the east one, we'll cover the near two. We've got time to recover from this before he seals the deal with that vacant cow."

Fresko had his phone out, and quickly relayed her commands to Mix. He looked like a bloody banker, as always, in his shirt and suspenders, tie flapping over a shoulder. He hung up without waiting for a response and put the phone away, then shouted to Letty, "We could get more people, do this quicker. I don't like going to their places alone."

"Don't be a fucking pussy," Lett snapped. "We're fine on our own, even if you prats keep trying to prove otherwise. We'll find him in a half hour, tops."

"We gotta do more than find him."

Letty stopped suddenly, Fresko almost crashing into her. He was sharper than the others in every way, with his Wall Street wardrobe and selective vocabulary, but when she gave him an inch he was still an insubordinate arse. She told him, firmly, "We're doing this ourselves. *I'm* doing this. We haven't needed anyone in nine years, we don't need them now."

They continued in silence, side by side, before stopping at an intersection at the edge of St Alphege's. Fresko stared at Letty like he had something more to say, but her eyes warned him off. This was a time for everyone to do as they were told.

"Any problems, shout," she said.

"You too," Fresko replied.

"I'd rather shoot my own face off than admit to needing *your* help."

With that, she sped away from him, flipping a middle finger in his direction.

The idiots were cocky, never guessing that the Fae knew their safe house locations. Letty's target building stood three storeys high at the end of a terrace of derelict homes, with all the windows but the top one boarded up. That neglected one was Letty's way in. It was only open a crack, but that was enough for her.

Starting from the top floor, she searched her way down. Most of the rooms were empty, bar dust and the randomness of those occasional bricks that always appeared on the floors of abandoned properties. Complementing the beams of street light coming through the boarded windows, Letty scanned the walls and floors with a torch, looking for hidden rooms.

She made a quick circuit of the ground floor and discovered a single armchair with a magazine by it. Letty snorted at the cover, a half-naked man with his fists raised, every muscle on his torso tensed and bulging. *Martial Arts Illustrated*. She muttered to herself, "Christ, get out of the closet."

She continued to the kitchen, where the refrigerator hummed and emitted a dull blue light around its edges. A single washed glass sat by the sink. The place was in use, at least.

Letty spiralled around the bottom floor again. There was no other furniture and she doubted the whole building was dedicated to someone reading a magazine. Frustrated, she rested on the kitchen counter and took her phone out. A message from Fresko blinked up onto the screen: *Nothing but rats. Come to you?*

Letty replied: *Empty, too. Join the boys.*

As she put the phone away, she took another look at the fridge. It was a hulking ceramic model, like in a 1950s movie, and it looked like it would take three men to move it.

"Makes sense," she said, and dropped to the floor next to it, peering under. The glow wasn't coming from inside the fridge, but behind it. She rose and searched the wall around the fridge. Nothing there. Rushed back along the counter, searching the few empty cupboards, but still nothing. She headed back into the front room, where the armchair sat, and checked underneath it. Then under the magazine. Finally, she paused and saw another of those random bricks, on the floor, up against the wall.

"Why not," she said, and shifted it out of the way.

She stopped triumphantly. Behind the brick was what could have been a light switch, if it wasn't level with the floor and hidden. She flicked it and heard the fridge move, then raced back into the kitchen and found the blue glow expanding. A cellar door.

Fuck them *all*, she was about to save the day. Save everything and everyone.

She went through the opening and down a set of dimly illuminated stairs. At the bottom, there was a corridor that opened onto two closed doors. One of them had an electronic lock by its handle, lit with a red LED. She allowed herself a fist pump of success and approached it.

Something clicked.

She froze, eyes darting to all corners of the corridor. The walls were bare, besides the single fluorescent tube light.

Something hissed.

She spun and saw it. In the shadow above the stairs, a waft of almost invisible gas.

"Oh crap," Letty gasped and flung herself towards the stairs. She tried to keep low, to avoid the gas, but it was already too late. She smelt it and reeled away, back to the corridor. Gagging and coughing, she tore her phone from her pocket, but her vision blurred. She dropped the phone and it clattered across the floor. Unable to focus, she fell to the ground and bounced, once, before coming to a halt.

As she used her last strength to lift her head, her eyelids became too heavy to hold open.

She slumped onto the floor, into darkness.

13

Casaria stopped in the tight tunnel. He lowered his electric lantern to one side, its unnatural blue light stretching deep shadows across his face from below. "This'll do," he said.

Pax folded her arms again, hoping the lantern would give her expression the same campfire ghost-story effect. She had trained herself to hide or show emotions at the card table. She was determined to keep her posture rigid, defiant, to hide the anticipation she was starting to feel as they got closer to their goal. In this case, her scowl was to tell Casaria to cut the theatrics.

He smiled, another flash of perfect teeth. He leaned closer, lowering his voice, and said, "I need to insist that however you feel about what you are about to see, you must not react. That's something you're trained in, isn't it?"

"All right," she said. "Whatever you've hidden in this rape tunnel, I won't react."

"What is it with you and that word?" Casaria replied. "Besides, a rapist coming down here would be doing society a favour. Now stand as still as you can. See up ahead? Where the tunnels join? Something will be along any minute. Don't move, don't speak, don't freak out."

He lifted the lantern to light the tunnel. Ten metres ahead of them, the tunnel split into two, right and left. Pax narrowed her eyes, trying to pick out any details in the shadows that weren't just the lines of stacked brickwork. The place was empty, not a pipe or cable on the floor, walls or ceilings, only the occasional shells of old lights that might never have worked.

They waited in silence, Casaria's breath seemingly non-existent and Pax instinctively slowing and lowering hers. They waited long enough for her to start running his words back through her mind, as she wondered what indescribable thing could possibly be down here. She thought of the weird and wonderful creatures in Apothel's Miscellany. The creatures of nightmares with their bizarre rules. As she thought over some of them, Casaria whispered, almost inaudibly, "It's coming. What you're about to see senses things by touch. Vibrations. So if you don't move, and don't make a sound, it won't know we're here."

Pax screwed up her face. That sounded familiar.

"You're kidding," she replied, loudly enough for him to shoot her a warning look. She was surprised into quiet by his severity, and kept her eyes on the tunnel.

A scratching noise came from somewhere up ahead. Something was moving there. As the scrapes got louder, Pax picked out the distinct sound of two separate taps, almost at the same time. A creature on four legs. She stared hard, willing her first conclusion to be wrong.

It couldn't possibly be.

But it made sense. The book, the Roma boy being taken away before he could spread the secret. The government agency, covering something up.

The noise became louder, the creature getting closer.

It took all of Pax's willpower not to demand an answer from Casaria there and then, not to blurt out what she was afraid she was about to see.

Its shadow came across the tunnel intersection first, lancing over the floor as the creature jerked into the light. Then the claws. They looked like the curved blades of a farmyard tool; black, jagged shapes, stretching into the light. As they came further into view, it became clear they were attached to limbs. Arms that rose to a shoulder. A shoulder that sat below a head with no eyes. A bare head that bounced the light back towards them. A head that turned slightly to the side and revealed a set of teeth, running from the chin to the forehead like a zip.

Pax held her breath, digging her fingers into her palms to stop herself from moving. She couldn't take her eyes away, transfixed by how bizarre and fearsome it looked.

It stood over five foot tall and its legs were inhuman. The torso joined a lower body the size and shape of a large dog's, like a centaur. It wasn't furry, though; it was smooth, too smooth for human flesh. The creature had the same bare flesh all over, except for its terrifying claws, which had hardened into something like metal.

Its head turned in their direction, and for all the world Pax wanted to do nothing but run. She was rooted to the spot, though. All the panicked thoughts punching through her head had no command over her body. She stood staring, horrified, as it looked at her, as though about to pounce, and her heart pounded against her ribs, blood thumping in her ears.

It would hear her, she was sure.

It would charge.

It moved.

Out of the tunnel, through the intersection and into the next passage.

Its footfalls moved away, becoming quieter, as Pax quaked. She pulled her gaze away to find Casaria looking at her. He had been watching her the whole time, and as she caught his eye his lips spread into his overfamiliar smile.

"A sickle," she uttered, finally finding the presence of mind to say it. "It's real."

Casaria's smile was gone. "How'd you know that name?"

They drove in silence, Casaria shooting furtive glances at Pax as she stared out the window without focus. She hadn't been able to speak as they left the Underground, variously tackling the two conflicting thoughts that kept repeating in her mind: *It can't be real. It is real.* Casaria had asked if she was okay and she had said yes, he had asked if she wanted to leave and she had agreed. They had walked to the car and he had described where they were going next but it was all just noise. She was trying to process the creature, trying to figure out what it meant. If the sickle was real . . .

She didn't dare complete the thought.

"It wasn't a trick," Casaria said, after ten minutes on the road. "That thing could tear a person apart, if it knew you were there. That's where I come in."

Pax turned with the vague recollection that he existed.

"What was it?" she asked, quietly, and knew, as the words left her mouth, that this was her admission that it was true. It brought her back to reality with all the worried thoughts and confused images of the beast in the tunnel. She had seen something otherworldly. And this man could explain it.

"You knew its common name, apparently," Casaria replied, a touch irritated.

Pax stared at the side of his face, his indignation unbelievable at a time like this. She said, "Where did it come from?"

"How did you know its name?" Casaria shot her a look.

"What?" Pax gaped. "Who *cares*?"

"I saw him greet you," Casaria said. "You made a joke about him asking your name, remember? You didn't know each other. At what point did he tell you anything?"

"Who gives a shit?" she said. "After seeing that thing –"

"It's important. How did you know it was a sickle?"

Pax paused. The book was evidently every bit as valuable as she had suspected, and if he knew about it he would want it. She lied, "There was a sketch. In the notepad he left on the bar."

Casaria shot her more glances, trying to read her face in brief moments between looking at the road. He echoed her: "The notepad he left on the bar."

"You might've noticed if you hadn't been busy hurting him."

"A sketch." They were statements, not questions. Sceptical statements.

"Yes, a sketch – you want me to go home and get it for you? Let's dwell on that, after seeing that shit! Jesus Christ, did you see what I just saw?"

Casaria nodded, slowing down as he concentrated on what to say next. Pax looked out of the window again, distracting herself with the city. They were passing through Ten Gardens, her old neighbourhood, streets of tall townhouses and warehouses repurposed from working-class slums to chic middle-class hangouts. The next neighbourhood would be the warehouse district, mostly derelict and as good a place as any to kill someone who knew too much.

"Where are we going?" Pax asked, expecting a cryptic answer.

"Someplace safe," Casaria told her, and immediately continued. "I know what you're going through. Eight years ago, I had the same experience. When I'd calmed down, the guy who showed me a sickle gave me the same information I'll give you. The same choice that I am going to give you."

Here it comes. Trapped in a tight space with nowhere to run. Pax had certainly seen too much, and wondered if it was the same for Ronnie Sweet and the others. Sweet had wanted to open a shop under the arches; had he trespassed into their tunnels? Were they all people who had seen too much and decided not to go along with whatever Casaria proposed?

The car turned into the warehouse district. They were travelling east, between the ruins of former industrial plants. The docks wouldn't be much further. Better and better locations to dispose of a body.

"The Ministry has a number of safe locations across Ordshaw," Casaria said. "Places where we can do things in private."

"Things?" Pax spat the word back at him.

Casaria rolled his eyes. "In this case, talking."

"I think I've had enough for one night. Can you take me home?"

He didn't answer, didn't look at her. She had little hope it would work, but it was worth a try. He finally shook his head. "We had a deal. And we're going to talk. Somewhere secure."

"Where no one can hear me scream."

This made him smile again, for the first time since the sickle had appeared. He turned down another road, into another residential area. Old brick houses that didn't look lived in. Pax tried to follow the route, to figure out where they had ended up. She knew the city, and had visited all sorts of difficult locations for games, but she was not familiar with this place. That made it one of the neighbourhoods she actively avoided. The other side of the warehouse district, it had to be St Alphege's.

Casaria pulled over and lifted a hand towards the building next to them, a brick terrace that looked like it should be scheduled for demolition. Pax gave him a nasty glare and he said, "I like your attitude, Pax. It could take you far."

He got out of the car but she stayed, giving the house a hard look. This was it. The perfect place to commit a murder. Willingly travelled to.

Casaria waited patiently at the side of the road.

She could lock the door, start the car somehow. Crack the ignition and spin a few wires together, that's how it worked in the movies, right? But he could shoot her through the glass before she got it going. Unless, being a government agent, he had bulletproof windows . . .

His patience ran out while she considered the full scenario.

"This way," he said, and started towards the building.

She watched him. If his intention was silencing her, he had a nonchalant way of making it happen. Then, wouldn't building her trust in this way make the job easier?

Guessing and second-guessing people was one of Pax's specialities. Bluffs, double-bluffs, triple-bluffs, it was all about thinking a few moves ahead. It was also, after a degree, impossible to truly know what was going on in other people's minds. This wasn't fair, that she had to figure it all out herself. It wasn't fair that she'd seen a dog-centaur with blades for arms, and the only person she could talk to about it was this inherently untrustworthy spook. No. That wasn't good enough. She took out her phone.

Damn Darren Barton and his happy family life, he was gonna tell her something about all this or she'd bring her world crashing into his. She tapped out a message quickly while Casaria had his back to her. Pressed Send. At the least, he would know she'd got more deeply involved in this. Shove that up his conscience. In case she didn't make it back.

Casaria stopped at the door and turned back to her. His face crossed with annoyance when he clocked her still sitting there. "What are you waiting for? *You* asked to come here."

Huh?

Pax checked the surroundings again. Run down. A rough part of town. St Alphege's, he'd said that before. A safe house. They'd come to where he was keeping Rufaizu. She closed her eyes. He'd taken her to the boy. This might work out, yet. She regretted thinking it, the moment the words entered her head.

14

The building was as lavish on the inside as it promised to be from the outside: a desolate shack of dust and decay. Unfurnished, unlit, forgotten. Casaria didn't give Pax a tour, he just walked ahead of her, through to the kitchen, talking as they entered. "The first thing to tell you is that those tunnels spread all across Ordshaw. Further than that, even. The network was built –"

Casaria paused in the doorway to the kitchen, his blue-lit face fixed in steely focus. Pax came up behind him and looked over his shoulder, into a kitchen as grim and bare as the rest of the ground floor, with the exception of its vast fridge. That had been pivoted to one side, revealing a passageway that descended into a luminescent glow.

"Is that a secret entrance?" Pax asked, taking the opportunity to disrupt Casaria in a moment of discomfort. "Who *are* you guys, the Thunderbirds?"

He did not respond, but took out his gun. Before Pax could make a sound, he descended the steps. She listened to his footsteps going down to whatever lay below.

Silence.

Then a loud exhale, and his voice came, almost merry. "Come here. It's your lucky day."

Pax crept through the kitchen and peered down the steps. They ended in a bland corridor below, where the blue glow was brighter. Casaria was barely in view, looking further in. Pax ventured down the stairs slowly, and when she reached the bottom she didn't immediately clock what he was looking at. There were doors leading off the corridor, to the sides, and a single light on the wall, but nothing else.

"Here," Casaria said, pointing at the floor.

Pax followed his gaze to a small object near his shoe. A bug?

She took a step closer and squinted at it. It had wings, and was hardly bigger than a house spider, but it wasn't a bug. Spread out on the floor, it had humanoid limbs. Pax imagined a child dragged down here, dropping their action figure on the way into one of these torture chambers. When Casaria crouched and picked up the figure, however, she saw that it was limp, hanging from the arm he lifted it by.

Pax shifted closer, to get a proper look.

A tiny woman, two inches tall, with lacy wings like a butterfly's. She had fantastically detailed clothing; a white t-shirt with a pattern too small to make out, and small denim shorts with a relatively thick leather belt. Strands of hair in various shades of pink and blue hung across her face. Strapped around her thigh was a minuscule holster, the handle of a pistol sticking out. It was an incredibly detailed and stunningly lifelike action figure.

One of her wings was suddenly snapped from her, jerking her torso as it was ripped out. Pax started in alarm, eyes wide as she looked at Casaria.

"In case it wakes up," he said, holding the freshly plucked wing between the thumb and forefinger of his other hand. He ground the lacy material between his fingers and it split apart and crumbled into the air. "Get one of these things flying around, you'll never catch it."

Pax returned her attention to the tiny woman, still immobile despite the brutal mutilation. Her other wing hung limply to the side, and she wasn't bleeding, the extraction done as freely as it would be with an insect. Pax caught herself thinking – why would a toy bleed?

"What do you mean wakes up?" she said.

"Take it." He held the little woman out and Pax raised her hands without thinking. He dropped the body into her cupped palms. It flopped like a rag doll, making her tense. The little lady weighed roughly the same as a plastic figurine, but Pax could feel the textures of clothing and flesh, and the soft hair.

"This place was only recently rigged to detect things like this," Casaria said, pointing to the ceiling. "Releases a gas that they're highly sensitive to. It could be out for the better part of a day. We'll be rid of it before then, though." With that, he turned to open one of the doors. As Pax stared dumbly at the miniature figure in her hands, Casaria moved into a room and flipped a light switch. He raised his voice as he got further away. "Haven't seen one in maybe nine months, myself. They're masters at staying hidden. But dangerous as all hell. No matter how cute you think it looks, you do *not* want to see one of those things alive, let alone awake."

He reappeared in the doorway, noticing Pax hadn't moved. She said, "What's it doing here?"

"Well, it's no coincidence, that's for sure."

Pax looked up at him, not following, but he didn't elaborate.

"It's good we came across it," Casaria told her. "It's another thing I doubt you'd believe without seeing. There's a plague of these things in the city, but we've never found their source. It's because of their sort that the Ministry does what it does."

"Does what it does . . ." Pax echoed, barely following.

Casaria pointed through the doorway. "Come in."

Holding the small figure out ahead of her, as carefully as if it were a baby bird, never taking her eyes off it, Pax walked after him. In the room, there was a table, a set of filing cabinets, a computer and three office chairs. Casaria indicated one of the chairs, but Pax remained standing, transfixed by what she was holding. He passed her and pointed at a map of the city on the wall. It was overlaid with thick lines, like a maze.

"There's something under Ordshaw, Pax," Casaria said. "A force that makes this city special. I need to get this across to you, straight away, because it's vital. It makes great things possible, but this force comes at a price. Things like the sickle.

Things like this abomination." He pointed loosely at the small figure. "They're the price. We keep them in check. *I* do. I protect ordinary people from this extraordinary world. And I protect that extraordinary world, too." Pax eyed him, sure that he'd said these grandiose words before. Maybe practised them in a mirror. He gestured to her hands. "These things are, as a rule, disruptive and violent creatures. They'd do harm to anything and everything down there."

"So what's it doing *here*?" Pax asked again.

"You want my guess? They're thinking if they get the boy, they make amends for what his father did. His dad got in with them, a long time back, and there's tales he stole something of theirs that could harm everything we seek to protect. It got him killed, but whatever he took never surfaced."

Pax looked from the figure to Casaria, then back to the figure. She swallowed her thoughts. There was a *thing* in this mix-up. He'd said it before, that Rufaizu might have access to things he shouldn't. Things like that weird object she'd taken from his apartment.

Apparently reading her troubled face, Casaria said, "You've always known there's something more than the ordinary world, haven't you?"

"Not like this."

"The details aren't important. You have the right attitude, I knew it when I first saw you."

"The details are a little important." Pax looked up at him again, feeling like she hadn't blinked in a day. "I have a tiny woman in my hands. A . . . fairy?"

"No, don't make that mistake." Casaria quickly shook his head. "That's not a person, and it's certainly not anything magical. That's a vicious little monster. A pest."

Pax took a defensive step back, holding the small figure closer to her. "What are you going to do with her?"

"Not *her*," he insisted. "*It*. It needs to be disposed of. We've got an incinerator not far away."

"No," Pax said, hearing the word come out on instinct.

"What?" Casaria replied.

"No," she repeated, slower, forming her thoughts as she spoke. "You can't burn her."

"Right." He put his hands on his hips. "I told you I'd offer you a choice, Pax, and this is as good a way to do it as any. I can show you a whole new world. Involve you in something that really matters. In order for you to join me, though, you have to be able to accept what needs to be done."

The figure in her hands looked so peaceful, like a sleeping doll. It had impossibly small fingers, tiny boots on its feet.

"You're thinking too much," Casaria said. "Imagine it's a locust."

"Let me take her," Pax said. "I'll take care of her myself. Humanely."

"Not a chance," Casaria replied with a short, sharp laugh. "I have to be sure there's no trace of it. Pax, you have potential, but you've given me no reason to trust you."

"Then . . ." Pax hesitated. The drive to flee she'd felt before, all her fears, were now transferred to the little life in her hands. She could run, bolt for the door and maybe make it back to the car. She could try and push him down, wrestle the gun from him. What other option did she have? She couldn't just let him kill this beautiful creature. She tried to distract him as her mind raced. "You can't burn it. That's horrible. There's got to be a better way."

"Smother it first, then, what do I care? It's already drugged."

"No, let me –"

"There's no way that thing gets out of my sight. For everyone's safety. And now we're on it, you should come with me to the incinerator. We'll do it while the thing's still breathing to be sure this is something you can go through with. In its extreme."

"If I refuse?"

Casaria gave her a firm look. "This is important, Ms Kuranes." He'd brought out the surname. Full sincerity. "There are necessary evils we have to live with, for the good of this world. Hand it back to me, we'll deal with it together."

To hand the small figure back would be as good as committing murder herself. But he wouldn't stop. Wouldn't let it out of his sight. She said, "Hold on, just hold on . . ."

"It's a lot to process, I get that," Casaria told her plainly. "But I'm hoping you won't disappoint me. I thought you had the right temperament for this work. You understood about the Roma boy, after all."

She kept her face straight as that sank in. What did he think she understood about Rufaizu? That she hadn't wanted to help him?

Her only option, she saw, was to play up to this odd impression Casaria had formed of her since he first laid eyes on her. Whatever she had done to convince him of whatever he thought she was capable of, she could use that. If she wanted to avoid being disappeared herself, she had to at least make him believe she was still capable of being who he thought she was. Pax thought out loud: "Okay. I can do it. Not the incinerator, though. Not like that. I could . . ."

It was so small, she could pretend to squash it. Just like palming a card. It wouldn't be hard to slip the figure into her pocket and have him believe she had crushed it. But there would be no remains. He would never believe it. Had to remove all trace.

"I knew I was right about you." Casaria was smiling, confirming Pax's suspicions. "But you'd better let me –"

Pax flung a hand up to her mouth, thrusting the little figure in. It was barely a mouthful, but she made a show of her bulging cheek, holding Casaria's gaze as he started, "What the hell are you –"

She quickly positioned the creature in her mouth, cringing at the feel of the small human on her tongue. Then she swallowed as Casaria yelled in alarm. She gagged, keeling forwards and putting a hand to her mouth, and he rushed to her side, hopping about frantically.

"What the hell!" he repeated, escalating almost to a scream. "What was that?

What's wrong with you? Why would you do that?"

Pax rose to standing with tears in her eyes. She let out a little whimper.

"Jesus Christ," Casaria continued. "I've seen some sick stuff – that takes it. Who the hell does that? Are you out of your mind? Why?"

"I –" Pax went to speak, then swallowed again, putting a hand to her throat and making a show of another little gag. She cringed and said, "I think her gun scratched me."

He stared at her in sheer disbelief.

"I've got the right temperament," Pax croaked. "I . . . couldn't let you burn her."

"That was your solution?" Casaria gaped, incredulous. "Jesus Christ! That's *worse*! That's so much worse!"

Pax bit her lip at him, affecting her best innocent look. He ran a hand through his hair, muttering obscenities. She suggested weakly, "Maybe we should call it a night."

He stopped and stared at her, looking utterly exasperated. Then he shook his head. "No."

She froze. He took a deep breath. It wasn't going to be this easy.

"We had a deal. You won't get another chance."

Pax frowned at the ominous comment, and flinched as he walked past. He ignored her, though, back on his own track, seemingly not bothered if she followed or not. He went along the corridor to the next doorway, then took out a key and unlocked the door. Pax crept slowly up behind him as he opened it, just a crack. Just enough for her to see Rufaizu. He was slumped in a chair, like he'd been drugged too, but the sound of the door stirred him. His eyes shot open and Pax shot towards him, but the door slammed shut again.

"He won't be here tomorrow," Casaria said, as he turned the lock again and whatever the young man called out was muffled. "I shouldn't even be showing him to you here. That's got to be enough. You're satisfied?"

Pax's eyes were wide open but she had no idea what to focus on. In the confusion of the tiny lady she'd forgotten why she was even there, and that brief glimpse had given her no idea whether Rufaizu was hurt or not. He was alive, at least, and Casaria had, for his faults, kept his word to show her so. He was looking at her, even, with an expression of hopefulness.

She nodded and muttered appreciation, and his shoulders slumped with some kind of relief.

"Good," he said, lighter. "Great. What a night, huh? What a start."

Pax nodded again, not trusting herself to say anything, letting him form his own ideas. All that mattered now was to get out of there before he realised the fairy was still alive. And now she'd seen Rufaizu, she might have something to fend off the psycho caller.

15

Fresko watched the pair exit the safe house through the scope of his rifle. The stiff suit and the rough-looking girl, both the worse for wear on the way out. Something had happened and there was still no sign of Letty. He adjusted the scope, tuning his microphone as the pair moved around the car. The man stopped and said something over the car to the girl. Fresko missed it, but got a clear read on the lady's response: "I saw a dog human claw creature and swallowed a fairy, I'll need some time to process."

Fresko sat back in surprise. *What?*

The humans looked at each other gravely enough to suggest it was true. Flashing in anger, Fresko trained the rifle sights on the girl's temple. Finger on the trigger, he gave a second glance to the man. He was behind the car. By the time the shot hit her he'd be behind cover. Fresko couldn't get them both.

The man opened the driver's side door and gestured to the lady to get in. Fresko squeezed the trigger, slightly. Testing it.

Letty always said there were two ways to do things: the right way and the dumb way. It usually followed a suggestion from one of the others. Shooting that girl would be a dumb thing to do, Fresko didn't need anyone to tell him that. He would expose himself and might get caught. It'd inspire the wrath of the Ministry, and do a whole lot more damage to the rest of the Fae. But if what that girl had said was true, something had to be done.

Letty was a handful, an uncompromising badass, but she was *their* badass. For all their faults, she had never given up on any of them.

And he'd let her go in there alone.

Let those monsters get hold of her.

Fresko's finger shook against the trigger.

The lady twisted to his direction before ducking into the car, and he got a good, hard look at her face. Big round eyes, big nose. Big fucking idiot in general, gonna eat a bullet.

Maybe not tonight, but some day soon.

A flutter of wings announced the arrival of Mix and Gambay, swooping onto the ledge next to Fresko. The car doors slammed shut and the engine started.

"What's happening?" Mix asked.

Fresko sat back as the car pulled away. He said, "They were in there. The suit and the girl. Letty was in there, too."

"Where is she now?"

The sniper gave him a cold, don't-ask look.

"If they did anything –" Gambay started, but Fresko cut him off.

"She's toast. We go down there looking, whatever got her will get us too. Listen. Them congregating on this place, with something that trapped her there, it's gotta be where the boy is. There's no way we're getting him out of there alone, though."

"So let's punch a hole in that car and get some human assistance," Mix growled.

"We should be cutting his balls out already," Gambay said.

"That'd be the dumb thing to do," Fresko warned, the car already all but out of view. "This is the Ministry. He's not exactly gonna do something because we ask, no matter how we ask it."

"We need that boy," Mix said.

"We need more men," Fresko said.

Mix stared at the safe house. The other two waited, Gambay grinding his teeth in anticipation. Mix said, "If Letty got in there, then this place is burnt. The girl's new to this, so your man will be getting her out of the way before coming back here to move Rufaizu. We get him then, outside the defences. Get him out the way and take his car."

"He's a Ministry agent," Fresko reaffirmed sternly.

"Who fucked with Letty," Mix snarled. "We don't need to kill him, anyway, just scare him off. Spring the boy, get the Dispenser back. Finish what Letty started. We're supposed to roll over because he wears a goddamned government suit?"

"It could start a war," Fresko stated.

"Not a war," Gambay answered. "A massacre. Long overdue."

Mix nodded agreement. "Yeah. Might be exactly what we need."

The drive to Pax's apartment was even more awkward than the drive to the safe house had been. Casaria chastised her, but tried to stay positive and practical, insisting she check her stool to leave no trace of the bug. She barely responded. He wasn't upset with her; it was tough to be introduced to this world, and she had done better than most when faced with the sickle. Hard-case Sam Ward hadn't been any better on her first outing, vomiting in the gutter, though no one would believe it now. A few hours, maybe a night to sleep it off, and Casaria was confident Pax would be able to see this with the calm and logic it deserved.

Her swallowing that thing was a part of her fear and confusion, that was all. Pax must have had her reasons. Some aversion to fire, a serious need not to drag out what they were doing, *something*. Whatever it was, it must have made sense in her mind in the moment, maybe like jumping into the sea rather than slowly lowering yourself in. She took an extreme course because she was overwhelmed by the choice he'd forced on her. Yes – that made sense.

Her mind was ticking over this new reality, he could see that. She was no longer fighting the urge to run and seemed to have quickly got over any sense of denial. She had also demonstrated some very lateral thinking. He would never have considered such an action, in trying to get rid of a body. It was sick, and strange, but he couldn't deny it was a solution. No, better than fear and confusion, it was a sign that she'd roll up her sleeves and get involved in the dirty work, with gusto and innovation.

The problem was, it left a niggle of doubt that he really didn't want to entertain. It was possible – he couldn't deny it – that it might have been some kind of trick to save the wretched creature. It wouldn't be the first time a woman had lied to him. He took the long route back, driving slowly, to make sure she had enough time to digest the creature, or at least kill it, before they parted ways, in case she planned to throw it up the first chance she got. At least he was certain she'd swallowed it. He had seen the thing in her mouth. He had faith in himself for spotting that kind of detail.

When they reached her apartment, he stayed in the car. As she was leaving, he told her again that she needed to be sure the evidence was gone, and she told him to fuck off.

"I'll check on you tomorrow," he said. "We'll see what we can do about your money, then."

She didn't reply. That aspect of her deal, it seemed, had lost all importance.

Casaria made the return journey in a third of the time, blotting out the thought of Pax Kuranes as his mind shifted back to business. Their safe house had been breached, though the defences had worked. It was one of the more secure ones, totally secluded – that's why he had chosen it. Now it was useless.

Had they been following him? No, then they would have found the place sooner. Were they following the girl? No, the thing had got there before them. Maybe they were just doing a blind sweep of known safe houses in their desperation to find the Roma boy.

Casaria scolded himself: *idiot*. Believing in coincidences was a sure route to failure.

Back at the safe house, he kept an eye on the monitor in his pocket – no sign of any Fae nearby. He headed to the cellar. Rufaizu stirred again at the sound of the door opening, groggy and barely able to speak but conscious enough to move without Casaria having to carry him. Not giving the boy a chance to gather his senses, Casaria hustled him through the house.

He was pushing Rufaizu's head down, a moment from safety, when the monitor beeped. He reacted instantly, shoving the Roma into the car, drawing his gun and dropping to the ground at the same time. The first bullet caught the top of his shoulder; it ripped cloth and drew blood but the sting was no more than a flesh wound. The second shot went clear over his head, splintering the door-frame behind him. The monitor beeped more violently – at least two separate pulses, getting closer.

He fired back without aiming, over the car, into the air, gun emitting fast, wide balls of light. Another shot shattered a window on the far side of the car. The sniper was on the other side of the road.

Shaken awake by the noise, Rufaizu kicked out of the car as Casaria searched the night sky. The Roma screamed, struggling to his feet, but Casaria pulled him to the ground, shouting, "Stay down, you moron!"

Then came a series of gunshots above the safe house, with the volume of firecrackers. Bullets pattered onto the roof of the car and the pavement around Casaria as he rolled out of the way. He returned fire, his gun erupting in a blinding flash, the projectiles fading into the air above. He pushed off with his feet, dragging Rufaizu's flapping body partially under the car as the barrage continued. The attackers were either terrible shots or were aiming to miss.

Casaria reached up to the handle of the car and a bullet struck the back of his hand. He yelled, but kept going, clenching onto the handle and wrenching the door open. As he did, another shot passed his ear. He fired back, this time seeing a shape in the air swerving for cover.

There was a moment of quiet as the attackers regrouped. Casaria grabbed a canister from a compartment in the footwell of the car and hit a button to activate it. Rufaizu rolled out from under the car and half rose. Casaria pulled him back as the gunshots started again, then he threw the canister high above his head.

It made a rumbling noise, and a shockwave spread through the air like a heat shimmer. The wave shot through Casaria with an electric jolt. The canister dropped back to the ground a few feet away, the gunshots silenced.

Rufaizu was gasping, feet randomly kicking. Casaria got a better grip on him, finding the young man bleeding from the neck, eyes wide with panic and mouth voicelessly moving.

Mix rose from the gutter of the safe house roof as the grenade's pulse shot subsided, barely having missed him. He spotted Gambay, falling into a grass patch the next house down; he hadn't been so lucky. Then Mix spotted the blood, streaming out of the Roma boy as the suit scrambled out from under him and put a hand on the wound to stop the bleeding.

"Gambay's down," Fresko said over the radio, factually.

The suit pulled the bleeding boy into the car and pulled the door shut.

"So's Rufaizu," Mix said. Equally business-like. "We're gonna need a new plan."

16

Barton writhed in bed as Holly somehow slept through it.

She always slept through it. He could snore, he could toss and turn, he could watch TV or sing to music, none of it disturbed her once she'd slipped into a slumber. That was what had made it all possible. She was such a deep sleeper he was able to live another life at night without her ever knowing he was gone. It gave him alone time, certainly, but it also meant he had zero support in the darkest hours. He sometimes wondered how different it might all be, if he'd married a lighter sleeper.

He was haunted by imagination and memory, thinking of the things that lurked in the Sunken City and the consequences of their actions. He saw Apothel's face, over and over. Sometimes smiling, laughing and drinking. Sometimes crying, shouting, screaming. Always, in any mood, with that hole in his head. Blood streaming across his eyes. Apothel. He had been so alone at the end.

He saw Rufaizu's face, too, no better. That cheeky child. Full of heart, in heavy supply of smiles. He could only imagine the trials that Rufaizu had been through in his naïve enthusiasm, after he had disappeared from all their lives. Who had raised him? Where had he gone? An orphan at nine on the streets of Ordshaw. Half his lifetime spent without parents, cut off even from Barton, perhaps the only person who knew where he'd come from.

And when he finally resurfaced, what had happened? Barton pictured his face beaten, bruised. The boy tied to a chair in some dark basement, electric probes tied to his bare flesh. Water thrown across his face. Barton spun on the bed, not sure if he was experiencing visions of the truth or nightmares of what might be.

Between the distressed faces of father and son he saw the creatures.

The glogockle's dragging knuckles and clucking cry.

The sickle's gnashing jaws that split its head in two.

The turnbold's tongues as they lashed from under its turtle-like shell.

The wormbird's slashing talons.

All scraping in and out of shadows, one erupting from another and blending back into darkness in the kaleidoscope of his frenzied mind. And behind them all the colour blue. Blue in large, distinct rectangles. Over and over, spinning, splitting, merging and expanding.

Blue screens.

Blue screens everywhere.

He saw the glo, swilling from tankards, rolling off a boat by the barrel-load, disappearing down hungry gullets. Luminescent liquid that opened eyes wider than they were meant to open.

Apothel laughing like a lumberjack, the first time they drank together. Tree-thick arms pointing down the tunnel as he curated new discoveries. Barton swaying on his feet, not sure if he was hallucinating when the helluvian hound appeared. They tackled it together, without explanation; it simply had to be done. They clamped its jaws shut as fire lanced out the edges, and they bound it with fireproof fish leather before thrusting it into a pit. Only after the excitement, after the thrill of the fight and the chase, after the laughter, did they stop to talk. It was almost dawn and the explanation scarcely mattered, then.

The explanation never really mattered. Not once Barton had tasted the thrill.

There were reasons, very good reasons, but they weren't important. What was important was that he was there, involved, doing it because it felt right. He had never needed to explain that feeling to himself. That's what made it so hard to stay away. The logic behind abandoning that life was sound, the emotion was not.

He saw Rufaizu dying, stabbed in the heart and bleeding onto the floor, alone, crying. He saw Apothel's face, blood leaking into the eyes as he tried to blink it out. And what? Wingless hawks flooding out of the rafters like a hail of bats, clawing at them, flying back carrying his family.

His family.

Grace being torn from his arms. Holly screaming.

He thrashed in the bed.

"Take him!" He grabbed Rufaizu's body, throwing it to the hawks. "Take him, not them! Give me back my daughter!"

Barton shook awake, soaked through with sweat, sticking to the bed. He pushed up onto his elbows and looked around. The curtains were open and the sun was up. He was alone, Holly apparently long gone. The house sounded still. He dragged himself to the window and looked out.

Dalford glowed in the morning light, yellow sun bouncing off green leaves. The road wide and clear of cars. As far as you could get from the tight grimy inner-city. Except for one thing. He looked at it, the manhole cover, down the road, like nothing more than a regular sewer entrance. His breathing slowed. He had never been sure why it had been so important to move here, above two houses that needed less work. To be close to that thing. Holly had bought his idea that he wanted a house he could fix up, but that wasn't it. That manhole cover had drawn him here, stronger than anything. There was nothing down there, not this far from the centre, but it was an option, in case he needed it.

No. It was a reminder. A warning that the temptation was close to home; giving in was not an option. Something he could never let himself forget.

He turned away from the window and saw the clock on Holly's side of the bed. 10am.

He scrambled for his clothes. Had to get to work. He flung himself into the bathroom and splashed water over his face, threw on a crumpled white shirt and ran down the stairs as he crookedly buttoned up. He skidded into the kitchen and paused to see his wife perched on a stool, eating a piece of toast. She raised a quizzical eyebrow and said, "Going somewhere?"

"Why didn't you wake me?" he demanded, flicking on the kettle and grabbing a piece of toast from her pile.

She snatched it back at once. "Because it's Saturday. And frankly, you looked like you needed the rest."

Barton stopped, catching his breath. It took a moment to sink in, then his whole body slumped with relief. "Oh thank God."

"Don't thank Him quite yet," Holly said, placing a hand on the kitchen counter. She had his phone. "You're going to wish you were at work in a minute."

He stared at the phone, the possibilities flooding his mind. Had Dr Rimes called him back? He started forming a defence. "Whatever you're thinking, you know I haven't been out."

"I know," Holly sighed. "It doesn't stop it from being a problem."

She passed him the phone and he snatched it, desperate to get it over with. The most recent message was from a new number. From the first line, he realised a call from Rimes would have been better.

Holly said the words out loud as he read them, apparently having studied it enough to know the message by heart. "*I see why you don't want your family involved – but I saw a sickle. You need to talk to me.*"

Barton looked from the phone to her.

"You said you didn't know her."

"I *don't,*" Barton insisted, picturing the thousand things his wife was going to attack him with. "She knew our address, you think she couldn't find my number, too? It's not –"

"Tell me again," Holly said, "about the Layer Fae."

"Don't do this," he answered weakly.

"No, I want to hear it again."

He closed his eyes, preparing the words he'd said to her a dozen times, the story he knew she never truly believed. A story filled with half-truths that she must've been questioning again. He said, "The Layer Fae were a gang, the sort we ran into when everyone else was sleeping. They were the worst of a bad bunch. We avoided them. I don't know why, I don't know exactly when, even, but Apothel started talking with them. He said or did something they didn't like, or maybe they just had a bad day, I don't know. He had a bullet in his head. No trace of who did it. The Layer Fae being who they were, everyone was too scared to go after them for it. Not on account of a bum like Apothel."

"The police turned a blind eye."

"Yeah," Barton nodded. "They said it was suicide. A bullet in his forehead." His voice wavered somewhere between anger and sadness. "Rufaizu was there. He was just a boy. Never should've seen it."

Holly stared at him, letting the weight of his tale fill the room. It had taken three months of degenerate drinking and wallowing, with dozens of fights and accusations and intrigues in between, before she had first drawn this painful explanation from him. She had accepted it, finally, his story that he had only been spending time with drug dealers and gangs, not cheating on her. That he had been partying at night with, essentially, a homeless man. She always seemed to suspect there was more to it than that, though, and he feared one day she would start asking again. For nine years he had been waiting for the probing questions to come back. It had been inevitable, with Rufaizu reappearing.

But she didn't ask any more.

She said "Don't you think you should meet with this girl? Don't let the same thing happen to her."

PART 2:
SATURDAY

1

Grace Barton, at 14 (almost 15), believed she had life more or less figured out. The important thing, which a lot of people seemed to miss, was that you needed to stay positive. No one likes a complainer. A lot of girls bitched about people, and their lives, to be heard. But then you had to think of new things to complain about and new ways to be nasty about other people, to keep things fresh. In the long run, it was easier to be positive about things, and people noticed that instead. Like when Kylie Taylor told the group she was mad at her dad because he'd come home drunk, falling over all the furniture in the house, and she hadn't got any sleep. Grace could've offered a similar sob story. She'd seen worse than knocked-over furniture. But she put a positive spin on it, instead. Alcohol was cool, after all. So when Kylie complained about her bumbling dad, Grace asked if he had any alcohol to share. The girls all laughed, and it was better than complaining. Maybe Kylie's dad didn't do it so well, though. It was easy with Grace's dad, because he was an expert, of sorts, rather than a problem drinker.

"Drink half a litre of water, half a litre of beer and half a litre of whisky," she had heard him say to her mum once, a few years ago, "and see which one changes your life most."

She was not privy to the context of the conversation, or exactly what point he had been making, but Grace liked it. That's why she made a point of sneaking some of his whisky in a flask when the other girls were experimenting with sugary bottled drinks. Kylie had said "You're so classy!", and she wasn't totally kidding. And someone had told Luke Merrick about it, and apparently he'd said Grace was a *legend*.

That was where looking at the bright side of life got you. Grace knew her mum had been upset with Dad about how he used to go out too much, but she just hadn't been looking at it the right way. Mum didn't get that Dad needed a particular kind of stimulation. He loved her, with all his heart, there was no hiding that. You could see it in the way he couldn't leave a room without touching her on the way out, even when he went for something small, like to get a drink. It was a bit gross, but also kind of sweet. And he even seemed to enjoy being told what to do by her, at least a little. But Mum hadn't given him enough of that – enough attention – that's why he went out so much. Once she started caring more, and gave him real specific instructions, he was happy. Sure, he complained a bit, and there had been some pretty big arguments a while back, but he genuinely seemed to enjoy being home, and the most annoyed he got now was when he couldn't do something for them, like buy Grace the best bike in a shop. He just cared, a whole lot, and that was over little things. Grace often thought he must've been sad, like, beyond belief, when his friend died.

No one ever brought that up, now. Even in her head, Grace couldn't put a positive spin on *that*. It was too long ago for her to remember what really happened. When she'd asked him about it, once, all he had replied with was: "Bad choices got him killed. Remember that. He didn't know when to stop."

She did remember it. Like when she drank herself sick in the park once, and she moved on to weak cider for Lonnie's party the next night. And she had a long-term plan. She would cut back around her mid-20s, maybe early 30s. That would give her more time to recover than her dad had, and he was doing fine. With a bit of sensible planning and positive thinking, life didn't need to stop being fun. Not completely. That was Mum's problem. That was most adults' problem. They thought that at a certain age you weren't allowed fun any more. It was like children going to playgrounds. At 14, it was wrong to go on slides and swings and roundabouts, but Grace loved rounding up her friends to raid the parks with the enthusiasm of kids. Fun's for whoever wants it, she said. Adults should go on swings and slides and roundabouts, they'd still enjoy it.

If Mum understood that, Dad would be happier. He was good and settled, sure, but he got a bit vacant at times, didn't he? There was still a little room for more, if Mum only let him loose.

That street lady showing up on their doorstep was a reminder. Grace knew, from the moment she opened the door, that any adult woman dressed in boys' clothes, with almost no make-up, spelt fun. Grace wanted to ask her a hundred questions at once, like what she did for a living and what music she liked, but there was no time. She didn't even get to compliment her on her coat – which was really retro.

Mum was angry, obviously. She'd been angry before the lady showed up, after Dad had been drinking again. The lady obviously wasn't the cause of the anger, and even more obviously wasn't having an affair with her dad, so Grace saw an opportunity where Mum saw a problem. When she found her mum on Saturday morning, stewing over Dad's phone, writing something in a notepad, like she was plotting murder, Grace knew she needed to calm Mum down. Her mum said she didn't understand. Grace said she understood pretty well, actually. Whoever that woman was, she came from a place that her dad knew. He hadn't been back, for a long time, and he was at least a bit unhappy about it. Maybe it was time he got some closure?

The problem was Mum didn't know about it, before. She didn't realise he needed a little something extra in his life. They'd talked it out, sure, and Dad was doing okay – but there'd been fights and arguments and probably ultimatums. What if they looked at it together, now, a bit more relaxed? Couldn't she do that for him?

Mum hadn't said anything. That was a good thing, Grace thought. It meant she was considering it and not just telling her to mind her own business. And with that on her mind, Mum was more positive than before, and didn't grill Grace about the million things she had planned that day. Grace left the house pleased with herself, on her way to the Ten Gardens Arndale.

It was going to be a good day.

2

Pax woke up feeling strangely rested, yawning and stretching her arms. She stood and rubbed her eyes with the backs of her fists, calmly noticing the light creeping in under the curtains. Lit like that, the sun was on the east side of the building. Early morning. She must've had something approaching a normal night's sleep for once. She dragged herself lazily to the window and drew the curtains. She thrust them shut again.

The crack.

She spun to the bullet hole in the wall.

Jesus Christ, she wasn't supposed to be here, with them watching – it wasn't safe. She shook herself wider awake, whipping past the bed to sweep up her keys, her wallet, her phone. She jammed on her boots, scrambled into her coat. Burst out the door and vaulted the stairs, cursing herself. Stupid. What'd she been thinking, letting Casaria drive her home – should've given him an excuse – a late-night game or something – anything to avoid coming back here.

She ran out of the block and down the road, almost knocking a young man off his bike. Squinting her eyes against the sunlight, she shot looks at the nearby windows. They could be hiding anywhere. She hurried into an alleyway between buildings, concealed by high walls, and cut through to the next street. She looked back. No one was following. The Tube station was a block away, she could lose a tail there, for sure.

She paused before exiting the alley.

Why *had* she come back here?

Her mind flashed back to the night before.

Bollocks.

There was a shoebox in her closet with a tiny woman trapped in it. She'd come back because protecting a fairy – *a real life fairy* – had put any thoughts of her unsafe apartment out of her mind. More than that, what with all the frantic energy she'd expended pacing about in despair at what the hell this little woman was, she'd finally just collapsed into sleep, still dressed. She must've been lying around for hours at risk. Idiot – *idiot.*

But wait. She'd been lying around for hours. Nothing had happened.

Was the lunatic caller no longer watching?

She took out her phone. No messages or missed calls. Maybe they were giving her time. And she'd seen where Rufaizu was – when the lady called back, they might be able to work something out. Things might not be so bad, at least as far as being shot in her ovaries was concerned.

On the other hand . . . she was outside, now, she could skip across town to be sure she wasn't being followed, then figure out a proper plan of action. Though that small person would wake up trapped in the dark with only the padded comfort of a scrunched-up t-shirt and a small thimbleful of water. She'd made a prisoner of this small miracle and now she'd abandoned her without an explanation. Could she explain it? Did little insect women speak, or understand, English?

What else could she do? Take the fairy with her, risk dropping it or accidentally sitting on it or something? Take it to a vet? She should find her a bed or a dollhouse or something, at least . . . Pax's phone vibrated in her hand, the surprise almost making her drop it. After taking a calming moment, she read the message. Barton's number.

I'll meet you. But somewhere safe. Don't come to Dalford again.

She reread her own message above his, remembering her desperate idea of dragging this family man back into her mess. She looked back towards her road one last time. Casaria had said the fairy might be knocked out for a day. Maybe it wouldn't even notice she was gone. Shoving her hands in her pockets and pulling up her hood to hide her face, she slunk away towards the Underground.

Weirway Park rose over the city of Ordshaw in the north-west, the peak of its green hill offering a panorama that encompassed industrial warehouses, brick terraces, shimmering skyscrapers and, to the east, leafy suburbs. The River Gader snaked around the base of the hill, in earnest to the north and in gentle tributaries to the south. In the autumn, the trees of the park were a mix of gold and red, and the breeze from the sea was brisk without being outright cold. The hill's peak, wide enough for everyone to spread out and feel alone, felt personal, even with its all-encompassing view. Pax had used it as a thinking spot ever since she moved to Ordshaw. She basked in the quietness of nature while looking over the chaotic city beneath. Apart from it all, but connected at the same time.

"You alone?" Barton asked from behind. She turned and took him in. His scruffy shirt and trousers looked as if they might have been his old work clothes. He had a builder's face, with heavy features, untamed stubble and a few incongruous marks that could have been old wounds or natural defects. He had a big gut, and big arms; probably used to work out but got tired of it.

"Yeah. I mostly am," Pax said. She held out her hand. "We didn't get a proper introduction before. Pax Kuranes."

"Darren Barton." He gave her a short but firm shake, his beefy hand dwarfing hers. He looked around, checking that no one could hear them. The nearest person was an elderly man preparing a toy plane for flight, well out of earshot. Pax was about to start, to reel out everything she'd gone through, but Barton's expression turned serious as he spoke first. "Let's start at the top. What do you know about the Blue Angel? You tried glo yet?"

Pax's hopes for simple answers exploded. She said, "That's the top, is it?"

"Pretty much," Barton nodded, not noticing her lack of understanding. "You met someone from the Ministry, he wouldn't tell you about that stuff. Chances are he doesn't know it. But you need to."

"Shit." Pax's voice fell. She closed her eyes, hit by a wave of exhaustion. She hadn't slept as well as her brief waking ignorance had suggested.

"You come here on the Tube?"

She nodded without opening her eyes.

"No wonder you're tired."

"No," she said, looking at him again. His serious expression had softened, replaced by concern. "I'm not used to being up this early, and I'm kind of up against it right now."

"What happened?"

Pax paused. Barton's eyes told a whole story. They had been mad like a frenzied dog's the day before, but now they had the softness of a worried puppy. The sympathy in his expression was genuine. He was deeply driven by his emotions. Would fiercely protect anyone in need, whether it was his family or a stranger. He had actually come here to help her.

"Let's sit." He swung a hand to a bench down the hill. As they walked, he said, "You didn't run, after what I said?"

"I got curious," Pax said. "Same time the Ministry guy got friendly."

"So you went with him." Barton sounded disappointed. "I told you not to."

"Yeah. I've never liked doing what I'm told. I saw a monster, you know?" As they sat on the bench, she said it again: "I saw a monster. Under the city. Casaria said there's a whole network down there, and it's all fucked up. What am I supposed to do with that?"

"That's up to you," Barton said, not at all surprised. He'd been through this himself, somehow. "You want to get away from it, now?"

"Would they let me?"

"I doubt it," Barton said. "They never approached me. I've never knowingly seen or talked to one of the Ministry myself, but I know people who have. They tend to go missing."

"I heard that too," Pax said.

"Keep them onside if you can. But if you want answers, and don't want to be a pawn in their game, you need to contact the Blue Angel. You got family, friends?"

"No one close. I see my folks, my brother, maybe once a year. That's how I like it."

Barton didn't ask why, and Pax was thankful. He lived in Dalford, he wouldn't get it. "That gives you options, at least. I got involved for my family. I was trying to protect the city, because that meant protecting them, too. Then I realised my kid needed me more than she needed this city."

"I've never felt a special need to protect anyone, or anything, other than myself," Pax said, but his eyes looked doubtful. Rightfully so; even as she said it she imagined Rufaizu strapped to that chair.

"You don't want to walk away, do you?" Barton asked.

"I don't want to get torn up by a monster or shot in the ovaries, that's for sure." She ignored his questioning look. "Look, first off, I lost a big chunk of cash, which is crazy bad timing – I've got rent due and there's this poker tournament – and these people, the things they're doing – I mean . . ." She trailed off, seeing that Barton wasn't entirely following her, and she turned her toe against the ground.

He said, "It's all become background detail, hasn't it? You want to help. You're not even sure why. But trust your instincts. Rufaizu's heart's in the right place. The creatures down there, they're bad news. They've got one big, ugly purpose, hiding a bigger threat. A force that drains people, feeds off this city. Me, Apothel, the others, we wanted to stop it."

"Casaria said there's something good down there."

"What would he know? The Ministry never listened to the Blue Angel, they're clueless."

"What is that? Someone's lofty codename, right?"

This made Barton stop. He said, "I'm not sure if you'll believe me."

"I'm about ready to believe in unicorns, Darren," Pax replied.

"It's a little harder to understand than that. The Blue Angel is someone who told us all we needed to know about the Sunken City. They communicate through blue screens that appear on walls, like projections. Maybe one person, maybe more, I don't know, but they helped us. To a degree. It was never actually enough."

Pax slid down into the bench, legs shifting forward until she was almost hanging off the edge, head lolling into the back. She rolled her eyes to the sky and took her time to release a loud groan. Indulging herself in the frustration of a petulant child. She said, "Fuck me. What do I have to do to go home and forget about all this?"

"You tell me," Barton said.

She met his gaze, maintaining her slouch of discontent. Rather than answer that, citing the kidnapped fairy, an imprisoned youth, the Ministry stalker or her sniper friend, Pax decided to move on to what he knew. "What'd you learn from this Blue Angel?"

Barton continued, "It shared some specifics about the creatures down there, but mostly it pointed us towards glo. Drink glo and you can see everything more clearly. Literally, the Sunken City makes more sense. Most importantly, you can see the minotaur."

"Oh piss off!" Pax sat back up like a shot – that word again. "There's *not* a minotaur down there."

Barton shook his head. "That's what we called it, the thing that sucks the energy out of people. It appeared as something we could see and understand, when we were on glo, but it's made of light, or energy, I don't know." Pax gave him a blank expression and he went on. "I can't describe it well, I'm no poet. It's why I asked about the Tube. It sucks energy from above, but especially from people down there. They blame travelling, don't even know it's feeding on them. What we'd do, we'd go down there and find the beast, and we'd communicate through these blue panels with the Blue Angel, and it'd help move it away from the more populous parts of the city. That's the best we could do. Damage limitation, if not prevention."

"Hold on," Pax said. "How'd this Blue Angel move it? Who's behind these blue screens?"

Barton hesitated, as if he didn't like to admit the next bit. "We never found out. The blue screens were weird."

"Compared to the nightmare monsters?"

He shrugged that off. "To get hold of the Blue Angel, you scratch words into walls. It has to be scratching – don't ask why. We tried pens and other stuff, no good. The answers come back in scratches. We communicated through these screens for years."

"Leaving a trail of love notes on public walls?" Pax said.

"No, these screens cleared up after themselves. Someone, somewhere out there, wanted to help us, but kept it totally secret. And like I said, that help was never quite enough. Sometimes the directions led us to empty glo stashes. Sometimes we'd find the minotaur and it wouldn't get moved. And the Blue Angel never contacted the Ministry, or never got through to them, near as we knew – never persuaded them of the truth of what was going on down there. But still, it was the best we had. I could give you an address where you might be able to find a blue screen, if you want. It's been a long time, might not work."

Pax could see this was a bad start. Barton was a few cards short of the full deck, and his unreliable, anonymous source hardly sounded like a solution. "Who else was into all this?" she said. "You, Rufaizu, and Apothel, right?"

"Not Rufaizu, he was too young. We had a few friends, though. It was stupid, like an adventure club. Some mates get together for a pub quiz once a week, or a game of poker; we got bladdered and picked fights with monsters. We had a scientist helping us, Mandy Rimes. And the filmmaker Rik Greivous. Heard of him?"

Pax shook her head.

"He shot weird stuff. He was trying to get glo to work with his cameras, to record it all. The scientist, she tried to figure out what these creatures were made of, so we could hurt them. The Ministry turned a blind eye as long as we never got near the minotaur. They needed the other stuff culled anyway. I took down glogockles, sickles, the things that they didn't want late-night drunks stumbling across. The minotaur's not like the other creatures, though. It's massive, and not exactly . . . I dunno, physical. Nothing we tried hurt it. No way to record it or study it. You can't even see it properly without glo. Apothel always had some new idea, though, so we kept at it. Until there was an incident with the kids, and I got into it with the wife. Rik disappeared, he had other things going on. Apothel started to run around on his own. We lost touch and he started talking to the Layer Fae. It was bound to go south from there. The Fae hate everything that's not Fae, they're psychotic. I never crossed paths with the little bastards myself, thank God. You wouldn't see them coming if you did."

Mystery psychos you never saw coming. That had been important before, hadn't it, when he gave her that name? You didn't actually *see* the Fae. Little bastards. Pax closed her eyes. The caller had called her "tall". The tiny woman had

had a pistol she'd plucked out of the holster with tweezers. Fae. The word was literal. She said, "The Layer Fae aren't people, are they?"

Barton laughed, bitterly, devoid of humour. "They'd have you think they were. But no, they're not. Again, you won't believe it. They're . . ."

"Fairies."

Barton paused. He was surprised she'd guessed it, but he didn't care to ask how. "Yeah. Nasty, gun-toting little shits. The Blue Angel warned us about them, said they had a long-term interest in the Sunken City."

Pax swallowed. She suddenly didn't feel so guilty about the shoebox. Nor so worried about going back to her apartment, now it was possible it really *wasn't* being watched. She said, "Are there a lot of them?"

"Oh, I think so," Barton nodded. "But they don't work together. Antisocial, aggressive things."

That was the caller all right. That was the lady Pax had trapped. She snapped in another piece of the puzzle. "Apothel had something they wanted, right? Now Rufaizu has it? Or had it."

Barton paused. "Possibly. I knew Apothel was into something with them, and Rufaizu seemed to follow that up, but every plan Apothel came up with was a dead cert, you know? This is the big one, he'd always say. The thing that'll kill the minotaur. You couldn't take it seriously." Barton sighed. "It was me who found him, you know? Apothel. I hadn't seen him in months when Mandy called up, worried he was missing. I had a kid of my own and began to worry about Rufaizu. I found the boy in one of Apothel's half-dozen hiding places. Alone. He'd been locked in a room for days, no food. Piss and shit in a corner."

"My God . . ."

"Finding him was the good news. Apothel was in the loft space above. Rufaizu followed me up there and saw everything. He ran. He ran and I couldn't stop him. I spent weeks trying to find him, chasing up leads with Mandy, to the point that my wife was all but ready to kick me to the curb. The kid had vanished, though, carrying this image of his dead dad with him."

"I'm so sorry," was all Pax could say.

"Still not the worst of it. No one did a damn thing. Police barely opened a report. Said it was just another vagrant gone. The Ministry were covering it up. They got in touch with Mandy and told her to drop it. It wasn't a friendly suggestion. You starting to understand what you're dealing with?"

Pax nodded grimly. "So was it the Fae or the Ministry that killed him?"

"The bullet was a millimetre wide."

Pax tried to picture her wall, back home. The bullet hole. How big had that been? The window was hardly shattered, it was definitely possible it had been a tiny shot. Her thoughts were interrupted when she noticed how Barton's face had fallen. She hovered a hand over his for a second, not sure if this was the appropriate move. She braced herself and took the plunge – placed that hand on top of his. He didn't react. She was left unsure, and after a consolatory pat she took the hand back. She said, quietly, "Thank you, Darren. I know it's not easy."

"I've got a daughter," he replied. Pax hummed appreciation. It was explanation enough. He turned his sad dog eyes to her. "I prayed Rufaizu had escaped it all, and ended up in a normal city, with a good life. But wherever he's been, he's stepped right back into his dad's footsteps. Maybe it's a blessing the Ministry took him, though. That's what I'm telling myself. If they lock him away, at least they'll keep him from getting hurt."

Pax nodded, for his sake, but she knew it was nonsense. There were at least two sides to this thing, and if Rufaizu had picked up where his father left off, then he was in danger from both of them.

3

Letty woke with a dull pain in her back, face buried in material. She pushed herself up with a groan and felt behind her for the source of the pain. The groan turned to cursing when she felt the uneven stump where her wing was supposed to be. She blinked a few times to clear her eyes. It didn't help. The shards of light coming through the holes in the wall barely lit the room. With effort, she moved off the soft bedding, getting momentarily tangled in its folds, and kicked back at it as she broke free. The ground felt soft. Card. The walls, she now saw, looking at the holes, were card too.

There was good news and bad news, she decided. Somehow, the Ministry hadn't got her. They wouldn't have put her in a shoebox. The bad news was that she didn't know where the fuck she was.

She strained to see anything through one of the holes. The box was near a wall. In a closet, perhaps, barely lit outside. She tugged the hole; the card was thick, too strong to rip. Cursing again, she checked the rest of her surroundings.

A small thimble of water. That might work.

She threw the water at the card around one of the holes. It soaked in, a splatter perhaps an inch wide, and she tried to get a fresh grip on the soggy surface. It wasn't enough – the card held firm. She looked at the thimble and considered her other options. She needed a piss, but if that didn't work she'd be stuck in here with the stench of urine.

Huffing, Letty threw the thimble down and looked to the ceiling. The lid. Way out of reach and probably hard to shift. She tried her remaining wing, which flapped, still functioning, but when she tried to fly it spun her out, like stumbling on a bad leg. She hit the wall and rested. Cursed one more time.

Pax resisted the urge to give Barton a hug when they parted ways. The large man spoke with great sadness, and looked at her with such kindness, that she felt an affinity towards him. She could tell by the way he talked that he had lost a dear friend in Apothel and he missed going into what he'd called the Sunken City. But she could also see that he had forcibly put it behind him. The rest of the answers lay with Rufaizu or the Blue Angel. He was done.

The address he had given her for one of these blue screens was on her way home, but she didn't feel ready to engage with that weirdness. If the thing was even still active. Barton and his friends might have drunkenly trusted the anonymous stranger's wall messages, but it hardly sounded like the best contact to her, and the last thing she needed was a third (or fourth? she was losing count) party mixing up matters. Besides, she already had a potentially better source of information in her apartment.

Wary of using the Underground, she rode the bus home, a journey that took twice as long but gave her a rare glimpse of the city during the day. People dressed for the weekend, dipping in and out of shops with bags of junk. Pub tables overflowing into the streets, even this early, with young people laughing over pints. Market stalls with loud vendors offering deals on bananas. She reached her flat with the feeling that she wasn't missing much. Ordshaw was still a vacuous hole of pointless lives, like everywhere else, but it was *her* vacuous hole, all the same. And she liked to believe that she wasn't the only one here who'd step up and do something if they discovered an intangible minotaur was draining the city's energy, or that demonic creatures threatened to rise to the surface if left unchecked.

She returned to the apartment, scanning the surrounding windows. There was no one watching her. It was safe, it had to be. She climbed the stairs, entered her flat and went to the curtains. She stopped there with her hands on the material.

Maybe it was better not to tempt fate.

Leaving the curtains drawn, she went to the cupboard instead. With her hands on the doors, she told herself things were about to get better. She had Apothel's book, and possibly the thing he'd been killed for. She hadn't heard from Casaria today, so he was giving her space. Rufaizu was taken in because he knew about this device, not for knowing about the Sunken City itself, so Pax wasn't necessarily in danger from the Ministry, as long as Casaria thought he was in control of what she learnt. She had enough money to repair the window, as icing on the cake. There was every chance the only serious threat in this whole affair was trapped in that shoebox.

All considered, she was ready to take control.

Letty stirred at the sound of a door slamming. The box shook with the thumps of footfalls. A female sigh. Letty pictured it: a bedroom, a closet.

No prizes for figuring out where she was now.

With the girl not approaching, Letty quickly became impatient. She shouted, "Hey! How about some water! You fucking lummox!"

It took a few more shouts before the footfalls came tentatively closer. Letty got louder, roaring, "Yeah, get down here you giant fucker, I got something for you!"

The cupboard creaked open, and the floorboards flexed as the girl crouched in front of the box. The shoebox walls relaxed from a strain, puffing out as a weight was removed from above. Then stillness, as the girl hesitated.

"It's you, isn't it?" Letty shouted. "The dumpy tomboy?"

"You the one who acts tough on the phone?" Pax's voice rumbled through the shoebox.

"Open up and I'll show you an act!"

"You've lost a wing," Pax reminded her. "I've got your gun. And you're two inches tall. What are you going to do?"

"Fuck you up!" Letty snapped.

The ceiling creaked as a weight rested on it. The girl's hand, staying there a moment, not sure what to do. Letty crouched in preparation.

"Don't try anything, okay?" Pax said. "I want to talk."

The lid opened, slowly, light pouring in, and Letty shot up for the gap. Her single wing was not enough. It buzzed and spun her out, sending her rolling across the floor, unable to steer, let alone fly. She buzzed it again, flapping from one side to another, as the lid was completely removed and Pax stared down at her. Letty came to a halt, punching both fists into the floor with an angry shout. She sat up and swore at the top of her voice.

"It wasn't me," Pax told her. "Before you start."

Letty looked up at her hatefully. Her giant captor's face filled the sky, dark hair brushed back over her shoulder to stop it falling in the way. Letty held up a hand, extended her middle finger. Pax's expression remained blank. She sat back slightly, then her hand descended into the box. Letty rolled aside, yelling, "Oh hell no!", and she tried to crawl away. There was nowhere to go, and no time to get there. Enormous fingers fell around her and as she lunged to escape Pax rolled her into a fist. Feeling the ascent in her gut, Letty kept fighting as the grip tightened.

Pax sat back onto her heels, bringing her hand up in front of her as the fairy used her last remaining weapon, clamping her teeth down onto an exposed bit of flesh. Pax flinched and opened her hand. Letty dropped and started flapping the wing again. She spiralled gracelessly to the floor, hitting the carpet hard and bouncing. Winded, she saw the shadow of the hand descending again and tried to run. Pax closed her thumb and forefinger over her waist and lifted her back up, kicking and screaming.

Letty thrashed violently, but she could no longer get the angle to do any damage. Pax held her in front of her face, staring with fascination, as Letty swung fists in the direction of her nose and demanded, "Put me down, you prick! You've got no idea the pain you're gonna be in!"

"Right," Pax answered. "You need to stop. Calm down."

"Go to hell! You want calm? I'll rip out your heart, show you calm when that stops beating!"

"Jesus," Pax said. "What's wrong with you?"

"Where's my gun? Where's my fucking gun?"

Letty continued to thrash, searching the room for a weapon, even with no chance of reaching one. Pax's apartment was untidy, books across the floor and on the shelves, clothing on the floor. There it was – the pistol barely visible on top of a wooden crate that passed for a bedside table. Pax saw the fairy spy it and lifted her to the side, drawing her attention back to her face.

"You're not getting it," Pax told her. "And you're not going anywhere till we talk."

Letty slumped, at last, energy spent, arms and legs hanging loosely from Pax's grip. She used her last reserves to look furiously into Pax's eye.

"Put me down," Letty said, calmer. "And I'll maybe go easier on you."

Pax twisted on the floor, turning to the bed and sweeping Letty through the air with her. She lowered the fairy onto the bed and let her go. Letty fell onto the duvet with a huff, stood up and patted her clothes down to remove the filth of Pax's grip. She was a long distance from the end of the bed where the pistol was, and there was a big jump if she was going to get it. But fuck it, why not.

Letty sprinted headlong into Pax's palm. She fell back on her arse and rolled aside, tried again, moving to skirt the hand that had fallen in front of her. The hand shifted in an instant and blocked her again, this time joined by the other hand, cupping over her like a dome. Letty punched at Pax, shouting in frustration, but it was no use.

"You're crazy, you know that?"

Letty roared.

4

Cano Casaria had had a long night. His arm needed stitches, his hand was bandaged and painful to use, and the Roma boy was barely clinging to life. He was angry at himself for not having slaughtered all his attackers and that made waiting in the Ministry infirmary harder. He was in no mood to be confronted by two fellow agents this early in the morning. Landon was a portly man who looked like he spent more time eating than breathing. Wisps of grey hair highlighted the unkempt black mop on his head, and the bags under his eyes had folded into bags of their own. The other man was slighter, younger, with patchwork facial hair and pale, blotchy skin that had seen little sun. He wore a leather jacket and a shirt; Landon, a suit, faded, loose around the shoulders and tight at the belly, probably from a charity store. In their own unique ways, the pair of them had tried and failed to comprehend the concept of respectable clothes.

These were the sort of people that gave field agents a bad name. Though Landon had been with the Ministry for decades, Casaria had reached the same level within a year of arriving in Ordshaw. This leather-jacket whelp was Landon's protégé. And they were Casaria's supposed backup.

"Got word from Deputy Director Mathers," Landon said. "You're to stay put, keep an eye on the boy."

"If he needs babysitting, that's a job for you," Casaria said. "I've got real work to do."

"He said you'd say that," Landon replied blandly. "And said to tell you that's why you need to stay here and keep watch."

Casaria imagined Mathers saying it. Another dry husk in this vast bureaucratic machine.

"We've got our best people looking for the suspects," the younger man said. He'd introduced himself earlier. Gum, Gung, Gong maybe? Casaria actively tried to forget his name and gave him the least favourable option.

"The Ministry's best people, *Gumg*," Casaria replied, "are clerks who skim online databases all day. Not fighters. Not *me*."

"The decision's been made," Landon said. "You're grounded."

"They shot at me," Casaria said, standing and wincing as the pain from his shoulder cut through him. He closed his eyes and swallowed. "The Fae are dangerous. We need to act."

He hated himself for letting them get the drop on him. He hated himself for letting the prisoner get hurt and he hated himself for letting them get away. He was fairly sure he had hurt at least one of the monsters, but they hadn't confirmed a single kill.

"What were you doing there, Cano? Your IO-3 was still pending."

Casaria cringed at the mention of the permission slip required to interrogate their prisoner. "Call it a hunch. I thought Rufaizu might have friends looking for him and I wanted to check everything was okay. Rightly so, considering what I found."

They didn't need to know about Pax. Definitely not that he had taken her there to ease her nerves. Looking at these two made him all the more confident that he needed to persist with her. Amateurs and sociopaths, the lot of them. Whatever else had come of the abortive evening, it had felt good to let himself believe, even for a short while, that someone as bright and normal as her might join him. Someone he could talk to without wanting to shoot his own brains out. Someone who wouldn't gravitate naturally to hiding in this office following the whims of stuffy Mathers.

But Pax was hesitant. And possibly crazy. And the Roma boy had got to her, somehow, without Casaria realising. His gut still said she knew more than she'd let on. Casaria asked Landon, "Is it possible Apothel spoke to people we don't know about?"

Landon gave Casaria a disapproving look, then shook his head as slowly as humanly possible. He said, "This was the Fae, and we are on it. You need to stay here, okay?"

The younger man chimed in, in some twisted way hoping to lighten the tension. "I'm sure we'll find a peaceful resolution to all this."

Casaria locked on him, and told him sincerely, "I don't like you."

Gumg's face fell and Landon stepped in front of him. The big guy said, "Take a break, Cano. You obviously need it."

"Shove it up your arse, Landon," Casaria replied frankly. "I think you need that."

Landon chose not to respond, and led Gumg away. Casaria watched them go and looked up at the security cameras. If he so much as stepped out for a cigarette he'd probably get a call from Mathers.

It was three hours before the doctors announced that Rufaizu was stable, another hour before Casaria got a call from Landon saying he was being relieved and it was time to go home. Preliminary reports from the Fae Transitional City were saying that the attack had not been sanctioned. It was a group of rogue Fae, acting without orders. It was unclear what they wanted; the Ministry's Fae contacts denied all knowledge of the group. Casaria left the building sullenly. Just the thought that the Ministry *had* Fae contacts made him miserable. His initial passion had waned, though, replaced by nagging anger at the thought that Deputy Director Mathers had deliberately trapped him there to cool him off. Had Mathers consulted with Sam Ward on that? It was the sort of dirty trick she would endorse. The sort of information and suggestions she'd fed them in her field reports.

Cowards. We don't need cool. We need results.

The Fae *would* deny it, of course. And the Ministry would buy their denial. The cowards in charge would use any excuse not to get into a fight with the FTC. A few lightning balls and a canister of gas and they could exterminate the lot of them, if they were only willing to commit. The inactivity made Casaria sick. As he told them, again and again. But there were fears that the fairies had devastation technology, comparable to nuclear warheads, which no one had ever proven.

It was nearly 8am when he got out of the infirmary, making it too late for his usual recreations. He would have to wait to properly vent his frustrations. Instead, he drove for hours staring at the city, his monitor checking for any hint of the Fae. It was fruitless, though; the insects knew well enough how to avoid people like him. Finally, he went home and sat in the car, hands clenched over the steering wheel as he stared at the parking garage wall.

He considered calling Pax.

The more he thought about it, the more convinced he became that she had actually swallowed that bug. He wanted to believe it. It meant she'd be willing to do whatever it took to get this job done. That she was better than sane. She was like him.

He could imagine the pair of them hunting together. He'd make a comment and she'd reply with something witty. Funny. He wouldn't laugh at first; he'd say they had a job to do. But it would lighten the mood. Make it enjoyable, as it should be. After they tracked and killed some fiend, he would take her to a cocktail bar and they'd share stories about their misshapen backgrounds. How he'd been too busy staying up at nights to ace his exams, though he knew he could've, and how he'd been asked to leave Southampton Uni after hurting that yuppie who'd made fun of his mother. He hadn't wanted to be there anyway; who ever changed the world after graduating from Southampton? Maybe he could open up to Pax about school, too, and how he played trumpet. She'd joke, sarcastically, but deep down she'd understand.

Maybe their hands would touch over the table.

Not straight away. They'd be very professional, they'd make an excellent team, and raise the whole standard of the Ministry. He'd put her off, because he could do better.

But eventually she'd wear him down.

Their hands would touch and she'd tell him everything was okay.

He was okay.

Casaria did not smile at his imagined future. He picked up the phone to make it happen. He caught himself and stopped. This was wrong.

He should go see her in person.

5

Pax knelt by the bed, with the fairy slumped in a seated position on the duvet. Letty had exhausted herself running and fighting and had very well established flying was not an option. Her chest rose and fell with deep breaths, her single wing occasionally fluttering. Vulgar and violent as she was, it was incredible to watch her. Her voice was quiet but easily audible, like a distant TV set. Her fingers were minuscule but slender and fully functioning. There was a subtle beauty in the way her hair flowed. Pax could sit and stare at this marvel for hours. Letty would not let her, though, not for a moment, even finding one last ounce of energy to snarl, "What the fuck are you looking at?"

"I saved you, you know."

Letty glowered at her. Impossibly mustering more strength for insults, the fairy pushed herself to her feet and made a show of curtsying, speaking with bitter sarcasm, "Oh thank you! My hero!"

"You're a dick," Pax concluded.

"Don't like suffering giant pricks, that's all."

"Well, you're here now, and you're not going anywhere. So are you ready to talk?"

Letty slumped back onto the duvet and folded her arms. "Ain't got a thing to say to you."

"Did you kill Apothel?" Pax got straight to the point.

Letty gave her a vicious look, then said, "What's it to you?"

"Casaria says you're trouble," Pax said. "Talking to you seems likely to get someone killed. But when you told me you wanted Rufaizu, it was to get him away from them, right? Am I wrong?"

"Like I said, what's it to you?"

Pax leant in, bringing her face close to Letty, and the fairy backed off slightly in surprise. Pax said, more firmly, "You threatened me, that's what it is to me. You shot a bullet through my window. So how about you answer my questions or I'll crush you?"

Letty did not move. Pax raised a hand, balled into a fist, demonstratively, and put on her meanest face. Rolling her eyes, Letty lay back onto her elbows.

Pax sat back, humming in disappointment.

"Yeah, thought so," Letty laughed.

"Well," Pax said, "I don't have to hurt you."

She lifted her hand again and Letty scrambled back across the duvet, waving frantically and shouting, "No no no, you fuck off with that grabby bullshit."

Pax paused. "Tell me what's going on. What do you want with Rufaizu?"

"He has something we've been after for a long time," Letty said. "Okay?"

"Yeah?" Pax said. "A weapon, right? Something that could be used in the Sunken City?"

Letty paused. She replied slowly, "What do you know about it?" She pointed towards the head of the bed, where Apothel's book sat. "Did he write it up in there? Who the fuck *are* you, anyway?"

"How about I ask the questions? You're after Apothel's son because of that weapon?"

Letty eyed her carefully, then started scanning the room. The fairy seemed to read the book spines she could see, then looked into the cupboard, where the odd brass canister sat. She took a few steps towards it suddenly, trying to see around Pax.

"Holy shit, you've got it?" she said.

Pax looked over her shoulder, then fell back to close the door and hide the contraption. She paused, blocking the cupboard, and looked down at the fairy. Both of them were well aware it had been far too late to hide anything.

"Sweet gangrene." Letty stood staring, strangely calmer. Almost in awe of having seen the device. "You know how long . . . how long I've been looking . . ." She shot Pax another look. "Rufaizu gave it to you?"

Pax answered with a question of her own. "How'd he get mixed up in this?"

"You oughta know. You've got the Dispenser. His daddy's book. What else do you need?"

"An explanation!" Pax insisted, shifting away from the cupboard again. "*Please*. I don't trust this Ministry and I don't like that they've got Rufaizu – but everyone says it's *your people* that are dangerous. Even though you're the only one that's shown an interest in freeing him."

Letty kept staring at her, weighing up her options. She said, "Okay. So you're not all the way on their side, maybe you need some schooling. What's in it for me?"

"I saved your life!"

"Think that makes you hot shit, huh?"

Pax gaped at her. She shook herself out of it and tried another point. "You talked to Apothel before you killed him, didn't you?"

Letty's tiny eyes narrowed. "I didn't kill him." She paced aside, throwing angry looks at Pax, then over to the cupboard. Pax waited. The fairy huffed. "You want to get yourself killed too, is that it?"

"One," Pax held up a finger, "I want to pick the right side in this quagmire. Two," a second finger, "I don't think Rufaizu deserves whatever's coming for him."

Letty kept eyeing her, considering whether or not to believe her.

"Three," Pax leant closer, "Casaria has offered me money – my own money, which I desperately need right now – and my instincts, in saving you, have potentially burnt that bridge. Give me something."

The fairy finally let out an annoyed breath and threw up her arms. "That's a bridge you want burnt! Burnt, ground down and shat on! The Ministry are the vilest, most self-serving, pathetic gaggle of shits this world's ever seen."

"And your people are better, are they? Apothel was shot –"

"Not by me! I told him our weapons would make his dumb prancing around meaningless. All he had to do was wait. I tried to *save* him, from those that thought he needed removing. He went off half-cocked developing his own plan, though. He pleaded – *begged* – me to set up an audience with our great leader, Valoria." Letty spat aside at the use of the name. "They said no, but he'd already gone off, before I told him that. He never gave my people a chance, not really. He snuck in and stole exactly the weapon I'd told him about. I'm blamed. Thank you very fucking much you stupid shit, last time I trust a human. Some prick I thought might be a friend."

Letty stopped and stared at Pax, letting this hang in the air. Pax said nothing, and she continued.

"He turned up dead after *that*. But it sure as shit wasn't me. It was an amateur – didn't even know about the kid. Rufaizu vanished before anyone started looking for him. Meanwhile my crew and I are all exiled. And between then and now, which has been a shitting long time, I've been trying to find that weapon – that thing *you* have apparently just stumbled upon."

Pax crouched in front of her. "You wanted to work with Rufaizu when he came back?"

"I *was* working with him," Letty said. "He resurfaced out of thin air, and told us he'd got the Dispenser. Rats knows where he'd been all these years, we didn't have time to get chummy. We held off flat out handing him over to the FTC, and let him hang onto the device, because he said it needs a very specific fuel – something that can only be found underground. The weapon's no use without it."

"What's the FTC?" Pax asked.

Letty rolled her eyes. "The Fae Transitional City, *obviously*. The great fucking refugee camp we got forced into when the Sunken City got overrun by the myriads."

Pax opened her mouth to ask another question, but Letty bowled on. Now her tongue was loose, she suddenly seemed a lot more comfortable spilling information.

"So, Rufaizu convinces us to go after the fuel before anything else. It makes sense – you need something from the Sunken City to fight whatever's down there – and it goes a ways to explaining why no one's ever made another Dispenser. Except it turns out the fuel is some kind of electric weed, and it's harder to get than you think. Needs someone with serious balls, like Citizen Barton. So Rufaizu tries to persuade the lummox, only my boys get drunk when they should be watching him, and he gets nabbed and here I am. Captured by a giant loser." Letty turned aside and scuffed her boot across the duvet with frustration.

Pax let the fairy stew for a moment as it all sank in. There was much more going on than she'd appreciated, but the bottom line was simple. It all pivoted on the device stashed amongst her dirty laundry. The question was, what could she do about it?

A loud knock interrupted her thoughts, the door shaking with the force of an impatient visitor.

Pax and Letty shared a look of equal alarm.

"Don't you put me back in that box," Letty hissed.

"Pax, you with someone?" Casaria called from the hallway. "It's only me."

"Only me?" Pax mouthed, as though his presence was supposed to be reassuring. Pax shot forward and grabbed the fairy, shoving her into a pocket before Letty had time to complain. Feeling the small lady punching and kicking, Pax closed her hand over her and warned, "He wants you dead!"

Feeling Letty go limp, Pax moved her down into the deeper recesses of the pocket. Pax straightened her crumpled top, pushed her hair from her face, then opened the door.

Casaria immediately strode in, scanning the apartment past Pax.

"Come right in, why don't you?" she said, testily.

"Who were you talking to?" Casaria asked.

"This is my home," Pax snapped. "You don't just barge in here, and I sure as shit don't owe you an explanation as to who I talk to in here."

Casaria stopped in the middle of the room. His jacket was beeping. A low, regular beep, like a quiet Geiger counter. He took out a small device, the size and shape of an electronic guitar tuner. Holding it up, unapologetic, he said, "This detects things from the Sunken City. Fae, among others."

"You checking if I'm one of them?" Pax folded her arms. He came back towards her. The beeping increased the closer he got. She noticed the bandage on his hand and a graze near his right temple. "What happened to you?"

"I'm going to ask you plainly," he said, inches from her face, "do you still have that creature?"

"You saw what I did," Pax answered through gritted teeth. "Think it was a party trick?"

"This doesn't lie." He held the device higher. She stood her ground.

"So you want to frisk me? Or do you think maybe swallowing her got whatever that thing detects into my bloodstream? *Maybe*?"

Casaria paused. He looked from her to the machine, the beeping continuing into the terse standoff. He lowered the device, frowning. Switched it off.

Pax threw a hand towards the door. "Now could you kindly get the fuck out of my home?"

"I..." Casaria hesitated. He ran a hand through his hair, averting his gaze. "This wasn't why I came. I've been searching for them and I came to – not for this – it started beeping."

"You interrupted a call to my mum, you paranoid moron."

Casaria nodded, distractedly backing out. "Not paranoid. They came at me. The little bastards are ready to go to war, I swear."

"The fairies?" Pax questioned. Thinking quickly, she shifted to block his vision, making sure he wouldn't see the bullet mark in her wall. She said, "And what, you thought if they came for you they'd come for me, too?"

This got a smile. His tension faded as he apparently recalled the innocent woman he was dealing with. Arrogant twat. "I wouldn't let that happen. They were after the boy. Trying to silence him, no doubt, seeing as they couldn't spring him. They did a bad job. I'm sorry to worry you."

The danger of the situation caught in Pax's throat. She thought back to Rufaizu, witness to his father's death, kidnapped by the government for trying to talk to her. Not, as Barton had hoped, safe in custody. She asked, "Is he hurt?"

"He'll live," Casaria sighed. "I told you those little shits were dangerous, didn't I? Hence my concern that you did actually do . . . what you . . . you know."

"Yeah. Let's not talk about it, okay?"

"Okay. No. I didn't come about that – I wanted to ask you to join me again this evening. I wanted to give you more warning, after last night. Some time to prepare. I'm going on patrol near one of the Sunken City exits. It could be educational. And, of course, financially rewarding."

"Yes, please, offer me my own money again," Pax said. "Keep forcing shit on me."

Casaria stared at her. The awkwardness of his apology was gone, now, his face serious. He said, "You don't have to come. But it would be in your interests."

Pax did not ask why. There was a thinly veiled threat in his tone.

"I'll be back at 8pm. How's that sound?"

"Sounds like you should go get some sleep," Pax replied flatly.

"So you'll come?"

She nodded. He smiled, genuinely pleased, and apologised once more before going out into the hall. He stopped to say something else, but she closed the door in his face. She rested there with her hand on the handle. Silence beyond. Then footsteps as he left. Descending the stairs.

Pax looked through the spyhole. The corridor was empty. She took a breath and went to the window. She waited in silence. Finally, Casaria emerged in the street below, walking towards his car.

Pax let out a breath of relief, thumping onto the bed and burying her face in her hands. She could feel the adrenaline now. She could act as well as a Hollywood star at the poker table, but the consequences of being caught out in a game seldom invoked the wrath of madmen with guns.

Letty crawled out of her pocket and pulled herself up onto Pax's thigh. She straightened out her t-shirt with a few irritated tuts as Pax parted her fingers to look down at her.

"I think you need to explain to me," Letty said, her voice quietly angry, "what you meant by *swallowing her*." Pax shook her head, biting her lips closed, but the fairy was nodding, "Yeah, that sounds like something I need to know."

6

Fresko leant against the wall with a hand on his upturned rifle, watching Mix across the room. The grizzled veteran was searching through a pile of tools and weapons, discarding handfuls of metal and leather contraptions that didn't match what he was looking for. He'd said he had an idea, so Fresko waited it out. It gave him a moment, at least, to reflect on having left Gambay in the ground, and Letty somewhere far worse. That pair had been a thousand miles apart, a manic liability and their scheming leader, but they were both good Fae, in their own ways. They deserved a vigil, but Mix was racing forwards. Always a man of action.

Probably better that way. Move on, take the next step, avoid dwelling on the dark hanging over them. It'd been bad enough just the four of them, all these years. Just the two of them promised to be worse. Whatever idea Mix was concocting, Fresko was happy to give it a go if it meant taking them that much closer to rejoining the wider Fae community in the FTC.

"You're sure there's nothing we could do for Letty?" Mix asked. There was little genuine query in his voice, but he clearly wanted it repeated, to shirk the responsibility.

"I know what I heard," Fresko said firmly. "There's not many reasons a person would say they swallowed a fairy, is there?"

"Fucking animal," Mix spat into the disparate pile of crap. He'd said it before and he'd say it again. "That's what it's come to, is it? Fucking animals."

"I know where she lives." Fresko had thought about it already, and that was an option, too. "I could plug her from across the road. Didn't look like she's got any friends, no one would find her for weeks, most likely."

"She can wait. We lost Gambay being bull-headed, now we do things the smart way." Mix turned to Fresko like he was expecting a comment. Some allusion to Letty's ideas of what was smart and dumb, no doubt. If she were there, she'd never call whatever idea Mix had smart. The sniper shrugged, so Mix continued, "The way you and me know is smart. You know what Letty's problem was? She thought too much."

"Reckon I think as much as her."

"Yeah but you think about killing. That's smart thinking. She thought about how to please people. How to get Val and the FTC back on side without offending anyone. We never should've cared. Should've been doing what made sense to us — not worrying about wider bloody consequences. Should've been doing shit like this," Mix pulled back from the pile triumphantly, lifting up the device he'd been looking for. It was the sawed-off tip of a human-sized pistol barrel, only 10mm thick but as wide as his chest, suspended in a contraption of shoulder harnesses and spring-loaded levers. He heaved it up with a grin. "She got soft – was scared to let us use this bad boy."

Fresko watched with a neutral expression, still stuck on a response to the reductive summary of his intelligence as being solely focused on killing. He knew about strategy, too; coming at things from different directions. Knew how to make a good rat stew, with the right spices. Knew how to dress so people took him seriously, and all; how to keep a shirt white and uncreased.

Mix tested the weight of the gun-tip as he lifted the device's straps over his shoulders. He pulled a lever and the springs pressed the gun barrel forwards rigidly, supported against his body. A classic Fae device, used to fool a human into thinking they had a gun jammed in them, if they believed someone was standing out of their view. Fresko said, "A guy like Barton knows our tricks, doesn't he? And he's stubborn as a mule besides. You think he'll do anything at gunpoint?"

"You see." Mix pointed a finger his way. "That's thinking too much. You're jumping right into the problems, like Letty did, before considering the possibilities."

"What else are we gonna do?" Fresko said. "The goal's still that fuel, isn't it? And that means persuading Barton."

Mix was nodding. "Sure it does. But we'll do it the way Gambay would've done it."

"Kids?" Fresko frowned, recalling their late partner's frequent insistence that human kids were easy targets. Letty had never liked that suggestion, snarling about how erratic kids were, and how stupid Gambay was. That was their whole relationship right there; cautious and calculating versus brash and mad. Didn't matter now that either was right or wrong. A day had passed and both of them were dead.

"One kid," Mix said, tightening the straps. "Citizen Barton caved for the sake of his dear darling girl before, he'll cave again, won't he?"

Fresko shifted away from the wall as he put together Mix's plan. It was a new angle, one they hadn't needed to consider before. Not when they had Rufaizu to win Barton over. It made sense, though. "Threaten the kid, force the Citizen to harvest some electric weed."

"Damn straight."

Fresko weighed it up, watching Mix scanning the archaic tool. This would definitely put them on the dumb side of Letty's scale, but Mix was right. Plans like this had worked before, and sneaking about talking with humans evidently hadn't. And they needed that weed. Letty had been a bitch, but she'd known where they stood. A thanks-fucking-much for returning the weapon alone wouldn't get them back in. A functioning weapon, maybe the means to make more, that'd set them up. A choice of positions in the FTC, enough wealth to sack off ever working for or with anyone else. Renewed access to the best Fae tailors and cuisine, at least.

"You're worried about going back, aren't you?" Mix asked, into his silence.

"No," Fresko said, but the old mercenary gave a deep laugh.

"Sure you are. It's been a pipe dream for so long. Letty making promises that none of us thought would amount to anything. Now there's a chance we can get back in and you don't know what you'll do when we get there. See women again, real women. Eat proper food. Think it'll be hard?" Mix laughed again, even louder, and grabbed his crotch as he boomed, "Yeah, it'll be hard!"

As his companion kept laughing, Fresko sighed and pushed off from the wall.

"Never bothered me too much, being away," he said. "I just want the choice."

"And this is how we do it!" Mix slapped the gun contraption. "Not through sweet-talking and negotiating. Honest to goodness brute force, that's our way."

Fresko couldn't help but smirk. He said, "Letty never sweet-talked anyone in her life."

"No," Mix agreed. "She wouldn't have loved this, though."

Fresko nodded at the device. "That's because you're half-cocked, like always. How'd you see that playing out?"

"Get her scared, dictate a call to daddy, all done," Mix said, plainly.

"We need more than that. The lummox is a brute, he'd answer a plain threat with anger. We want to put the fear in him, we need to take her away, completely, at least for a while."

Mix's face glazed over with confusion, like there was no other plan possible than simply threatening one of the lummoxes. Fresko checked the room, searching for something among their piles of treasure. Near a wall, a hefty chunk of plastic served as a table for a pile of precious stones, pried from jewellery. It was an electronic device, a souvenir from one of their more ambitious pranks against the humans. Mix followed his gaze and frowned.

"What're you thinking?"

"Daylight robbery," Fresko said, the plan forming even as he said it. "No one's gonna see us, holding that gun to her neck. We lead her to a car, she gets in willingly, we move her right across town and get her hidden. Just need a car that we can control."

"Last time you drove, you hit a damned lamppost."

"Yeah," Fresko shrugged. "But this time I'm sober. All we need is the right motor. We've got an inflatable Joe, don't we?"

Mix looked from the electronic key back to Fresko. As he let the plan sink in, his rough jaw twisted into a leer. He started filling in the blanks, thinking out loud. "Gotta be a recent model, something super fancy, with those electronic controls. Gotta have those dark windows, too."

"Yeah."

"And we'll need gas. Knock-out gas."

"Yeah."

"You see, my man…" Mix walked past Fresko, towards the door. "We put our minds to something, it gets done. We'll get it done damn well. Val and the FTC are gonna squeal when they hear what we've done." He patted Fresko's shoulder, moving out. Fresko followed with his eyes.

Gambay would've loved this, but he would've gone wild with excitement and blown the whole operation. Letty wouldn't have let them anywhere near the idea of kidnapping a lummox, she would've axed the plan before it was one. The pair of them were gone, though, weren't they? It was just them left, and maybe, just maybe, they had a better balance of balls and brains between the pair of them than there had been before.

Fresko followed Mix out of the lair, calling after him, "When we're done, I'm going back for that girl. We'll plug that Ministry man, too. It's what I'd want you to do for me."

"Sure," Mix laughed from up ahead. "We'll slaughter whoever the fuck we have to."

After two hours prowling the Ten Gardens Arndale and a light lunch in a rooftop bistro, with the sun out and a party to go to in the evening, Grace couldn't imagine a better Saturday. She and Kylie Taylor and Jenni With An I had laughed themselves stupid watching a bin-man trying to fend off a seagull. They had raided vintage clothes stores for bargains. They had tossed a bottle of water at a cute street-side coffee clerk and *run*. Grace felt like she was getting wrinkles from smiling too much.

By mid-afternoon, they were languishing in one of Ten Gardens' many parks, a place packed with up-and-coming artists in multicoloured clothing, strumming acoustic guitars. Kylie had persuaded a man coming out of the supermarket to get them a bottle of cider, and they had quickly become merry, rolling on the grass and heckling buskers to take their tops off. A young guitarist did as they asked, to uproarious laughter and cheers.

When the cider rushed through Grace, she excused herself to go to the public toilet. Normally they would've gone together, but Katie was busy chatting with the busker and Jenni was half asleep. It didn't matter – the park's green-tiled outhouse was too small, anyway. Grace squeezed in, sat down and read lewd graffiti as she peed. Guys had snuck in and written nasty sexual stuff, which made her giggle.

Finishing up, she left the cubicle, ran her hands under murky water and gave herself a look in the grimy mirror. The reflection was a metallic blur, but she guessed she looked good. She turned to leave, eager to rejoin the sunny day, and felt the barrel of a gun press hard into the nape of her neck.

Grace gasped as a rough male voice snarled near her ear, "Don't move a fucking muscle."

Sober terror hit her like a slap. She couldn't move if she wanted to.

"We're going for a walk. Don't make a sound. Don't even *think* about running."

Some life came back. Grace trembled, her extremities shaking. Run? Could she run? Just bolt out the door? But it was a gun. What did he want? She blubbed, "I don't have any money –"

"Shut up," the voice said. "Out the door, to the right. Walk real slow, to the gate."

She hesitated, desperate for a solution. If she stalled, someone might come in, save her. She couldn't die – not here – not like this. That happened to *other* people. Oh Christ was it going to happen to her? Was this her life? She'd be a face on the news. Dead in a public toilet because she had been dumb and gone in alone. Everything wasted.

"*Now.*"

She did as she was told, focusing hard on moving one foot after the other, away from the toilet, between the hedges. The people of the park joked and played games together, none looking her way. She pleaded with her eyes, notice me, do something. Don't let them take me, don't let me die. No one saw there was anything wrong, though. Surely they didn't think this sicko was with her? Tears streamed down her face. Another step and she was out of view, almost at the gate.

"Good girl. See that car? Get in."

"No," she whimpered. "No no no please – please – you've got the wrong person –"

"Real slow, calm, how about a smile?"

"Please please I'm only fourteen!"

"Got a lot to live for then, don't ya?" the man growled. "Do as you're told."

She walked to the car, glancing from side to side, this corner of the park opening onto a dead road.

"Open the door."

"Please –"

"Make me repeat myself again and I'm gonna cut your kidney out. Understood?"

She nodded and opened the door. She paused, looking over the car, across the road, as a man turned the corner, walking his dog her way.

"Get in."

"Oh God," she cowered, trying to catch the man's eye. He looked her way, a disinterested glance, then looked away again. Hadn't he seen what was happening? Why wasn't he doing anything? There was a man behind her with a gun!

"*Now.*"

She squeezed her eyes closed and ducked into the car. The gun pulled away.

"Close the door."

She looked out. There was no one there. The engine started and her eyes darted to the front. Her eyes rested on the driver, sat rigidly at the wheel. His skin was shiny and bulbous, like plastic. Unreal. She looked back to the door. There was no one *there*. Where had the man with the gun gone? Had she even heard footsteps behind her? Was it –

Something dropped over her head and the world went black. Material smothered her face – a cloth sack, tugging back. It muffled her responsive cry, then the gun barrel pressed into her neck from the side. The man was back. "Close the door."

She felt sideways, groped for the handle and pulled it shut.

"Good girl. Now go to sleep."

As the man finished his sentence she could already feel wooziness overtaking her. Her body was numb, blending into the car seat beneath her. The car engine was a distant sound, like she was hearing it through water. She slumped down, into sleep.

7

. . . Fae society used to be just unconnected family units and raiding parties. In the middle of the 20th century, the Fae were driven together, maybe by humans coming into their territory, digging underground. In Ordshaw, around the start of World War 2, the Fae built the first Transishional City, an above-ground community. They fite a lot, but have an elected counsel with one main leader. Currently Valoria Magnus, who took over from Retcho.

"Retcho?" Pax commented, looking up from her translation of Apothel's text. The dense pages covering the Layer Fae provided a brief history alongside the basic characteristics of their people: small, winged and difficult to spot. She'd already learnt they were uniformly addicted to a powder substance dubbed *dust*, which had psychotropic effects on nearby people. When Pax asked Letty for clarification on that, the fairy told her to spin on it.

Letty had otherwise been quiet since Pax had tried to explain what had happened in the safe house. The fairy had glared furiously and said nothing, her anger reaching a silent zenith. She barely even protested when Pax lifted her back into the box, though she did later snap that a toilet would be nice. The best Pax could come up with was the plastic lid from a jar of hot sauce. It stopped the complaints, though Pax decided not to check on the results for the time being, instead trying to find something in the book that she could use to relate to the diminutive woman.

Stood over the open shoebox, holding the book, Pax said, "You really had a leader called Retcho?"

"It sounds as stupid to us as it does to you," Letty said. "Big whoop."

"This is incredible." Pax knelt down. "A whole civilisation – a community – right under our noses, and no one knows about it? With your own politics, history, culture?"

Letty gave her a bored look.

"I'm not your enemy," Pax told her.

"You're a dead bitch, is what you are," Letty told her, more factual than insulting. "My boys came for him, they know what happened. They'll know to come for you next."

"So why haven't they?" Pax countered. Letty had no answer for that. Casaria had made it clear Letty wasn't alone in this, and the bullet hole in the wall was a constant reminder of what the Fae were capable of, but it had been the better part of a day and Letty's people hadn't come. "Either they don't know you're here or they don't care?"

Letty glared at her. From the attitude this fairy was giving her, Pax suspected it was the latter. If they were anything like her, their focus would be Casaria. Now that they had apparently tracked Rufaizu, what did they need her for? Pax said, "Well, either they'll come and it won't matter if you talk to me, or they won't and you might give me a better idea of how I can help you." She tapped the book. "There's a comment here, from Rufaizu I think. He says this is inaccurate. Why?"

The fairy couldn't resist snapping an answer. "Because no fucking human should be talking to a Fae, and anyone that writes shit about us is probably making it up."

"But Retcho was real? And the Transitional City exists?"

"Of course it exists," Letty spat. "Nice and above ground where it doesn't belong."

"And your people would prefer the Sunken City for your home?"

"It *is* our home. Those monsters drove us out."

"It didn't look like much of a home to me."

This gave Letty pause. "What do you know about it? Casaria took you down a couple of entrance halls?"

"I saw bare tunnels," Pax said. "Nothing down there but bare walls. Human-sized tunnels, at that. What's so special about it?"

"It's a whole other world," Letty said. "A place where we're hidden from the prying gaze of people like you. A network that takes us everywhere with total freedom of movement – where we don't have to rely on *dust* to stay hidden. The halls are empty because it all got taken from us. Those creatures came in and ruined *everything*. But if you'd seen it in its prime…" Her voice softened, with the fond recollection of a childhood fantasy. "There were vistas of Fae buildings – the sort of architecture that'd make you curl up and weep. Fucking *vistas*. All we've got now is prefab huts and towers that can be dismantled for moving at a moment's notice. They even built 'transitional' into its name."

Pax didn't think it'd help to say the Fae might be equally disappointed with the tunnels she'd seen, so she asked, "Why kill Apothel, then? Even if he stole from you, he did it to fight those creatures."

"What would I know?" Letty said. "He didn't let me in on his plan, did he?"

"But it *was* your people that killed him, right?"

Letty gave her another harsh, unco-operative look. That was a question too far.

"Okay. You've got guns, you built this weapon, what's stopping you from taking the place back?"

"There a section in there on wormbirds?" Letty replied.

Pax sat back to leaf through the book. The monsters got more horrible and unlikely the more she read. She paused on the page about the griffix, which stripped the flesh off its victims while they were still alive. Taken by its disgusting visage, she wondered what she would do if faced with one in the flesh.

Perhaps kneel down quietly and cry.

She continued until she found pictures of winged creatures with tendrils hanging from their abdomens. She showed the fairy to confirm. Letty said, "They lay eggs under the skin of living prey."

Apparently a lot of these creatures fed on living flesh. The wormbird had maggoty offspring, the glogockles fed on flesh where the blood still pumped, the tuckles boiled your unblinking eyes. That was, it seemed, the uneasy truth Letty was highlighting.

"Those things sound bad enough to a knuckle-dragging human," Letty said. "Ten times worse for us. And they come at us ten times quicker. Like they can smell Fae. Guns ain't enough for that shit. The weapons we did develop never got used – we'd need . . ." She trailed off, not wanting to go there. Pax was about to prompt her when she angrily said, "You gonna feed me some time, you crater of filth?"

Pax stared in silence for a moment. She said, "I give you some food, you gonna talk to me? Properly? Without the insults?"

"Oh, poor baby. Didn't realise I'd upset you with my mean words. Here, let me sing it better. Fae are fantastic singers, you know?" Letty began a warbling shout that sounded a little like a tiny dog barking. Pax sat back, waiting for it to stop.

It did not.

When she leant back over the shoebox, her captive was marching in a circle, throwing her arms up and down as she squawked.

"All right," Pax said. "Enough."

Letty started hopping on the spot, though, picking up volume, lost in the moment like a wild child jumping on a bed. Pax gave the shoebox a small push. The movement tripped Letty onto her back. She rolled, grimacing and touching the point where her wing had been severed. Pax shifted with concern, raising a protective hand, but Letty cursed anew: "You goddamned fat stick, I'll cut off your ears!"

"Does it hurt?" Pax asked. "Where your wing . . . I mean . . ."

"What do you think?" Letty snapped. "It's like a dog ice-skating down my back."

Not sure how to picture that, Pax sat back again. She asked, "What do you eat?"

"Human babies."

"That's not –"

"What? You can eat us, we can't eat you? Fuck off. Get me a baby."

"I did it to get you out of there. *Thanks* would do."

"Centuries of coexistence" – Letty waved a hand – "no one gets this sick idea. Then you come along, now people will be wanting to eat Fae all over the shop. I feel so violated."

"Oh, bullshit," Pax said. "You'd have been burnt alive."

"It's a smoking gun, whatever it's called – that thing, where you see a gun in the theatre, someone's gonna get shot. That's what it is. You've said it, now it'll happen."

"Chekhov's gun?" Pax replied with surprise. "You read our literature? I used to study –"

"Look at the space between my fingers and calculate how much I care," the fairy instructed, holding up a middle finger again. The perfect Letty Action Figure pose.

Pax left the fairy to check her kitchen. She had protein bars, cereals, old pasta and some leftover Chinese. Nothing seemed appropriate for such a small person. She broke off a piece of protein bar and placed it in the shoebox. Letty stared at the lump of date and nut, bigger than her head, and said, "Did you literally just hand me a nugget of shit?"

"Take it or leave it," Pax said. Letty did not look up, investigating the food and raising her middle finger once more.

Pax finished the bowl of Chinese, which was close to being too old to consume, then left the abusive fairy sealed in the box while she freshened up in the shower. The sun had gone down by the time she was done, and Letty had gone quiet again. After a few more fruitless questions, Pax settled back onto her bed to continue reading Apothel's book.

She read about munfle, a toxic fungus that grew in the tunnels. Touching it could cause you to shit and vomit for two days straight. Somewhat paradoxically, it could also be boiled for a nutritious soup which could supply your whole day's energy in one bowl. How that worked, and how Apothel had come by that information, was not explained. Perhaps just rumours from the inexplicable Blue Angel.

Pax returned to the large chunk of Layer Fae text. There was a little more about Retcho, the previous Fae leader, who had been a titan of Fae industry as well as a benevolent dictator. His dethroning had led to the closure of many manufacturing plants, and many Fae technologists had been killed. Pax carried the book to the closet and looked at the canister from Rufaizu's apartment. She said, "That's why this is so important? The means of production were lost when Retcho was overthrown."

Letty did not answer. The fairy was lying in the folds of the t-shirt, eyes closed. Asleep and uncombative, she looked harmless, almost sweet. She may have been difficult and foul-mouthed, but however you looked at it there was nothing right in killing her.

Casaria would want to finish the job, though, given the chance.

Pax needed to squash his suspicions and placate him long enough to figure this thing out.

8

Casaria was waiting outside Pax's converted church long before 8pm. He had nowhere else to be, so he parked there and sat motionless. Her curtains were drawn, cutting off any hope of seeing what she was up to, so he occupied himself thinking over the things he could do to the Fae when he caught up to them. Burn their city, crush them, chop them in two. Nothing would be too harsh, not when they'd had the audacity to come after him, one of Her Majesty's finest agents. He was so engrossed in imagining his vengeance that he didn't notice Pax approach. She rapped on his window, snapping him out of the trance. She got in and said, "Looked like you were off chasing bears."

"Huh?"

"Nothing." She held up a hand. "Got something for you."

Casaria frowned, not seeing anything, but put out his hand anyway. She opened her fingers and a metal object a few millimetres wide dropped into his palm. A pistol.

"From my bowels with love," Pax said, and Casaria cringed, almost dropping it. He took a tissue from his jacket and placed the pistol in it, then stuffed it in the cup-holder.

"Can't be good for you," he muttered. "Did you check . . .?"

"I'm not talking about it."

"As far as anyone else is concerned, it never happened, okay? We incinerated that body."

Pax grunted agreement. She said, "You look like warmed up crap. Sure you want to go out?"

"I've got responsibilities," he told her, and started the car. As he pulled out, she started checking the vehicle over, and Casaria sneaked glances at her, hoping she'd be impressed. It was government issue, the Mercedes, but he treated it like his own, washed it and polished it once a week, carpets spotless, nothing she could – oh no. Her eyes fell on an empty can of Monster Energy in the passenger side door and his heart sank a little. He said, in all but a whisper, "Sorry about the mess."

Pax raised an eyebrow at him and he looked away, not sure if she was judging his tatty car, his choice in energy drink or the fact that he'd apologised. To stop her reading too much into it, he quickly took an envelope from his pocket. "This is for you. We didn't discuss any terms last night, so I want to be clear. Three evenings, we agreed to that much – leaving today and tomorrow. You can have half now."

Pax took the cash and flicked through the notes without a word. There was close to £1,200 in there and she barely blinked at it. She really was like him, wasn't she? The money didn't matter – not now. Casaria smiled. She wiped that smile off with a question: "How's Rufaizu?"

Casaria mumbled the answer. "Fine. Recovering. You're not going to ask to see him again, are you? You know that was a one-off. I shouldn't have brought you there."

Pax didn't respond, and looked away from him.

There was still work to do, he could see. He said, "He was lucky I was there, you know. He's unstable, he would've run right into the gunfire. If he'd been out on the streets alone, he'd be in a gutter right now. People like him, they have no idea how much we do for them."

She didn't say anything to that either, but he imagined she was starting to get the idea.

They'd been driving for half an hour with no conversation, which suited Pax fine. Casaria made a few false starts, like he wanted to say something and failed, and she preferred to let him stew in that awkwardness than give him a hand. It was the least she could do to soften her bitterness at having her own money doled back to her in instalments, to say nothing of how far she felt from being able to do anything for Rufaizu. Casaria had given her enough to fix that window and pay rent, though, so she consoled herself that getting through this night might at least keep a roof over her head. The rest was the difference between her getting into the World Poker Tour or not, which didn't seem so important now. Given the mess of the night before and the promise of increasingly threatening monsters, she might even be willing to let that final payment go if the opportunity presented itself. There'd be more tournaments in the future, and anyway skipping it would keep her name from getting too well known.

Casaria pulled up at a derelict building complex with a faded sign, only a few letters remaining of the original *FRITZ DRYERS*. There were massive ventilation ducts rising from one of the low buildings, and dented metal sheet doors closing off a wall, corroded and discoloured from years of neglect. Casaria cut the engine and pointed past a handful of abandoned cars.

"Over there," he said, "is an entrance to the Sunken City. When they built this place, they put in an underground storage room and knocked through to the tunnels. The site was fined for encroaching on government property, a PO-13 violation, and the storage room made off limits."

"Did you close the place down?" Pax asked, imagining Fritz, a plucky business owner with a simple dream of industrial-scale laundry services, thwarted by government fines and regulations. Where was he now, stacking shelves in Aldi?

"This business is still open," Casaria told her. "Contrary to what you imagine, Pax, we're here to help, not ruin, this city. There are dozens of entrances like this across Ordshaw, surrounded by fully functioning civilian operations. We monitor them 24/7, mostly through motion detectors and cameras, but it pays to have people on the ground too. Especially when there've been recent vibrations."

"Which you've had here," Pax concluded.

"Yes," Casaria said. "Something has been circling around this entrance. We might get a glimpse."

"What'd happen if it got out?"

"We'd deal with it."

"Right. And *it* is?" Pax pressed.

"Something medium-sized," Casaria said. "And fast. Could be a hound; it had a strong heat signature last time it came close."

"Like, a stray dog?"

"No, a helluvian hound. They set fire to things."

"Charming." It wasn't one she'd come across in the book. She had been hoping that some of them would turn out to be fictitious, that maybe it was just the sickle Apothel had got right. But no, the opposite was true: there were nightmarish things she hadn't even heard of yet.

Casaria leant over to open the glove compartment and Pax shrank back into the seat to avoid him. He took out a gun with a half-exposed cartridge, filled with long-needled darts. "This neutralises helluvian fire glands. Stops them destroying everything."

"Noted."

"But this will knock it out." He patted the pistol under his jacket. "Permanently."

"And you're allowed to shoot it?"

"Not with bullets. It would explode. No, this has a projectile that's more reliable."

Pax glared at the bulge of his pistol. "A projectile of what? Wizard cum?"

"You can joke," Casaria said simply. She waited for more, but it seemed that was his full response. He indicated the tissue containing the fairy's gun and said, "Before we begin, I want to thank you for this. I didn't like to pressure you, but you understand why it was necessary."

Pax shrugged, not wanting to say anything to suggest she condoned his behaviour.

"I knew you could handle it. The rewards will be great, you'll see. This work gives meaning to this meaningless world. Makes you feel like you have a purpose." He picked up speed, rushing it out like he'd been waiting to say this throughout their quiet journey. "It helps you understand the ignorance of the people around us. Those that walk blindly through life during the day. How could they be anything more than they are, without even knowing there are things they don't know? People like you and me, we know there's more, we know the importance of living that experience. I've had recruits who didn't get it, who wanted to study this like it was some academic project – but I can see you're different. We herd the beasts, and we protect the populace, because they don't understand."

Pax barely took in his soliloquy. From the first words she got the overall gist: *we're better than other people, and fighting these monsters proves it.* However he'd ended up in this position, as a glorified night watchman, he seemed to have gone to great lengths to convince himself it was by choice.

"It's us, the ones who dare to get close, who form the front line of defence for the *praelucente*," he finished, piquing her attention again.

Pax deliberately misinterpreted: "Sorry, did you say something about a placenta?"

Casaria gave her a sideways look. Serious. "The *praelucente*. The force down there. The power base I told you about. Maybe a natural phenomenon, might be a little bit of God, no one knows. Whatever it is, it helps us. The aberrations it creates are necessary for a greater good."

"A *fuck the estates to bolster the banks* kind of thing?"

Casaria gave Pax a sympathetic grin. She gave him an insincere smile in return. He said, "The *praelucente* doesn't discriminate. It moves, constantly, affecting a few blocks at a time."

"You know how nuts this sounds?"

"After what you saw yesterday, you're not willing to open your mind?" Casaria paused. "No, that's a good thing. You think for yourself, I respect that. The *praelucente* is real, though. Look at any great achievement in the city, say an inspired sporting event, or a day that a composer produced a masterpiece. The data *around* that event will show reports of tiredness, weariness, declines in work. But the focal point, the epicentre, that's where the real difference is made. Great things are achieved through this power, even if people suffer on the peripheries."

"If I'm honest," Pax said, "that sounds like an unreliable source of energy."

"We need it." Staring ahead into the unmoving night, Casaria wrung his hands over the steering wheel. "This city is rotten. All the world is. The *praelucente* gives us hope. Gives us something worth fighting for. You'll see."

He rose from the car, swung the door shut and started pacing away. He was not waiting, not even looking back, with his usual tactic of leaving her to make her own choice. It was basic reverse psychology, acting like he didn't care, and she had no desire to play his game. But he still seemed determinedly on Team Pax. He'd given her some space, and returned some of her money; he might be trusted to give back the rest and leave her alone. As if. His interest at least kept the Ministry part of this equation from destroying her life, though, and might take her closer to understanding how to get out from under all this.

Pax caught up to Casaria as he rounded the rusted husk of an old van. Behind it was a knee high structure with doors on the top, like the outside entrance to a cellar. A chain ran through the door handles, locked with ancient padlocks. Casaria took a set of keys from a pocket and started trying one after another. The pause gave Pax a chance to inspect the shadows. She thought back to the sickle. There were tuckles and wormbirds and God knew what else down there, weren't there? Actual, real monsters. Pax said, "How long are we going down for?"

"As long as it takes," Casaria said. "Believe me, this thing will be worth seeing."

Pax bit her lip. "Is it sensible, going down there? Aren't you supposed to be an observer?"

"I never said that."

"Is it really necessary?" Pax continued, warily, "Maybe you could just tell me more about this stuff, I don't actually have to *see* it, now, do I?" Casaria paused with a look of worry. She'd hit a chord, so before he could dwell on it Pax hurriedly continued, "I mean, what if – what if there's still Fae in me? You said the things down there could sense them? Isn't this risky?"

His worry turned to confusion as he tried to recall if he'd actually said that. He shook his head. "I've got the detector on, Pax. You're clean. And we're going in."

9

After a day spent fighting down the memories of the Sunken City, blocking out thoughts of the dangers Rufaizu and Pax might be facing, Barton became gripped with anxiety when he realised his daughter had not come home for dinner. No flying visit to stock up on food, no hour in front of the bathroom mirror. She was a growing girl, increasingly independent, and he'd allowed her to spend a whole day out with a party in the night in the past, once or twice, but they always at least caught sight of her, or received a message. She always replied to messages.

She was off the radar, and, though he was staving off panicking, he sensed that the minotaur and its myriad creatures were responsible. Staring into empty space, he imagined her being dragged into a government vehicle for ruthless interrogation. Worse, being tricked into entering one of the Sunken City's gateways. He had no rational explanation for it, but somehow, something had happened. Rufaizu had come stumbling back into his life. That roguish girl was creating waves, too. His family weren't safe.

During dinner, he sensed Holly watching him coldly, neither of them talking beyond monosyllabic courtesies. She hadn't been satisfied when he told her he had tied things off with Pax, and her face said she was waiting for him to slip up again. Trying to detect his longing to return to his night-time activities. He was careful not to show her where his mind was going, and waited until she was taking a shower to put his fears about Grace to rest. She had lost her phone, or run out of battery, and was eating dinner at a friend's, that had to be it. He called Kylie Taylor. She answered chirpily, "Hi, Mr Barton!"

After a few pleasantries, striving to sound casual, he said, "I was wondering if Grace is with you? She didn't answer her phone."

"Oh? We thought she'd gone home?" Kylie replied with a hint of worry. "I haven't seen her since the park, she left without telling us. She hasn't messaged me – do you think she's upset with me?"

Barton swallowed his tension. What was wrong with her, she'd just let Grace disappear? "When was that?"

"Just after lunch."

"Where?"

"Ten Gardens. Heenway Park, I think. The one with the little fountain, you know?"

"Did you see where she went?"

"No, sorry Mr Barton – we were hanging out on the grass. We – I'm sorry Mr Barton – I wasn't totally –"

"Sober?" Barton asked, carefully. Of course. They were kids, it was so easy to accept random shit when you were drinking for the first time.

"She's not in trouble, is she?" Kylie asked it meaning in trouble with her parents. Oblivious to the idea that some other trouble might exist. "Does it mean she's not coming to the party? I don't want to go with Jenni With An I on my own."

"I'll get her to call you," Barton told her, then hung up. He ran a hand over his head and tried another number. Pax's phone went straight to voicemail.

Barton grabbed his coat and headed to the car, not letting himself think until he was sat with the engine purring. Looking at the road ahead, deciding between turning left or right, he realised he had no plan. It could be the Ministry, it could be Rufaizu's people, it could be something completely unrelated. Maybe Grace lost her phone and was with another friend. Maybe she met a boy and they were making out behind a carwash. Was that any better?

Maybe Pax was a plant. She'd used what he'd told her to get in favour with some other group. Some group that wanted Grace. Or him.

It didn't make any sense.

He punched the steering wheel.

There was one option. He hated it, but he couldn't waste time if his fears were true. He had to get in touch with the Blue Angel. He braced himself and, about to pull out, checked his mirrors. A shape was quickly approaching. His wife. There was still time, she was a few metres away, he could pull out and pretend he hadn't seen her. He hesitated, picturing how mad it would make her, then she was upon him, no way to make it look accidental now.

"Wherever you're going" – Holly dropped into the passenger seat – "I'm coming too."

Her eyes burnt with bottled fury. Barton was speechless.

"So what is it?" Holly snapped. "A pub? A gang meeting? A park rendezvous? Where are we going?"

"I can't tell you," Barton muttered.

Her expression faltered. The sternness and anger weren't enough to hide her strongest emotion: fear. Barton saw it in her trembling eyes, desperately trying to stay strong, to believe he was in control.

"I love you, Diz," she said weakly. "I always will. And I've tried so hard. But there's a line. I'm telling you, this is it."

"Please," Barton said to her. "Trust me. I just need to get some answers."

"Answers to what?"

He couldn't say he feared Grace was missing. That Rufaizu or the girl were somehow responsible. He didn't even know if it was true. "Give me one night, I'll make all this go away. Forever."

"No." Holly shook her head. "You don't get to leave me behind again. You don't get to have secrets. We share this life, that's what you promised me. I don't care what you think's dangerous, there's nothing that can be worse than you not sharing it with me. Nothing."

Barton saw desperation in her eyes, her voice quivering on the brink of sobs. He took a breath. "If I show it to you . . . you'll see why I didn't want you to know. But you have to see it for yourself."

10

The tunnels Pax entered from the empty storage room were eerily similar to the ones from the night before, half a city away. Equally bare and unused, of an almost identical size, with the same occasional faded light boxes, none of which were lit. Equally unlikely as a paradise for fairies.

They travelled along straight paths, intersecting and turning at right angles, occasionally sloping up or down. It was impossible to tell where they were going, or if they had at some point turned in a circle. Pax walked behind Casaria as he lit the way with his blue lantern, checking his monitors for signs of the things that dwelt down there. There were sickles a few blocks away, he said, but it was a distant signal and they weren't of interest. He was tracking something else.

As they descended a set of stairs, onto another unending stretch of tunnel, Pax grew weary of the monotony of their footfalls and the seriousness of the hunt, and she broke the silence. "Are there special laws for your prisoners? Can you legitimately hold Rufaizu for something? Suspicion of possessing a weapon is pretty weak grounds for arrest, isn't it?"

Casaria looked over his shoulder at her, his expression disapproving. "If it was Fae technology, it could do a lot of damage. Unlikely as that is. But yes, we have special jurisdictions. You have no idea of the trouble idle talk could do."

"Who'd take him seriously? My brother used to play fantasy games, you know, and he –"

"This *isn't* a game," Casaria replied shortly, continuing down the tunnel. "Rufaizu stirred those Fae assassins out of their nest, for one."

"You're sure that's what they were? Assassins?"

"What else would they be," he scoffed. Not a question. "You've no idea the complications people have introduced, trying to argue the rights of different animals down here."

"How do you –"

"It used to be simple," Casaria cut in with annoyance. "Fighting these monsters, creating a firm line between the city above and below, preserving the things that mattered. Then people started asking questions, creating absurd diplomatic initiatives for clerks who prefer to sit behind desks than do anything active. Suddenly there's specific words we ought to use, specific protocols to follow when engaging with our enemies, countless regulations they've invented to create meaningless jobs for people enforcing them. There's a lot of ugly ambition in the Ministry, I'm sorry to tell you that. But you stick with me, I'll show you how we can get around it."

They continued in a terser silence, his shoulders stiff ahead. Pax kept quiet, trying to put together the exact issues this loon was dealing with. He cleared his throat and rolled his shoulders to loosen up. Trying to think of something to say, wanting to redirect the conversation. Without looking back, he said, "I used to play the trumpet. When I was a kid."

Pax frowned. Why not. "Yeah? You don't strike me as the type."

"Gave it up when I lost a tooth."

"Was that somehow related?"

"Yeah," he said, but didn't explain. Instead, he said, "I often wonder if I should've got a gold tooth, instead of the white one."

"Would've looked badass. But, like an ex-con. Not really respectable."

"Not like a badass who hunts monsters for the government?"

"No," Pax said. "You'd want a tattoo for that. A coat of arms. Like the SAS."

She could see from his cheeks that Casaria was smiling. Hopefully this nonsense would help when she asked him not to kill her for wanting nothing more to do with the Ministry.

He looked at his monitor and stopped dead. Pax almost bumped into him as he swore.

She spun around, looking back, left, right, above her. "What? Where is it?"

He drew his pistol. "Got behind us. Keep calm, I'll handle it."

They turned and Casaria moved in front of Pax. As he did, the lantern lit up something on the floor that scuttled up the wall, back into the shadow. The alien thing moved with the many legs of a spider or crab. Its claws clicked against the concrete, little green eyes twinkling briefly in the light. Pax froze as Casaria held the lantern higher and revealed it again. It was about a foot wide, five wiry legs joined in a central, round body, which hung under the joints. The body was spiky like a sea anemone, and had a square, toothed mouth in its centre.

The creature paused, seeming to look straight at them, then scuttled into the shadows again, and started moving rapidly away, its otherworldly patter making Pax shudder. Casaria thrust the lantern into Pax's hands and flicked a switch on his pistol, lighting a torch. He ran, gun raised. Pax ran after him.

They caught up to the creature as it turned a corner, two of its queer legs folding as they lifted. Casaria skidded into the open, aimed and fired. A few metres back, Pax flinched as a ball of lightning erupted from the gun like an electric meteor. She turned the corner and saw what was left of the creature charred into the wall, bits of leg sticking out of a smoking black smear.

"That," Casaria said, holstering his gun, "was an Item 13. Scientifically called a *crus adsecula*. Crusad for short."

"It was a giant fucking spider!" Pax exclaimed.

Casaria let out a short laugh. "Oh no. Much worse."

He prodded one of the legs with his shoe. Nothing more than a burnt stick now. He turned back to Pax with a smile, but his eyes widened and his hand fell back to the holster. She followed his gaze to above her shoulder, where a second creature had appeared. Its beady eyes focused on her as it bared its teeth like a dog.

She shrieked and fell sideways as it pounced. She felt the weight of its horrible little body on her shoulder as the talons pinched into her. She shook her shoulder violently and held her arms up and out, trying not to touch it. As she spun, Casaria swore and ran closer. He batted the thing off her. It thumped into a wall, then another thump as it hit the floor. Finally another blinding electric blast and it was gone.

Pax was panting as Casaria helped her to her feet. She looked at the half-incinerated mess of the thing with horror. The shot had torn through it on one side, this time, leaving behind a half-mutilated, twitching monstrosity.

"Holy *fuck*," Pax said. "It was trying to bite my throat out!"

"No," Casaria replied, calm. "Crusads don't eat flesh. It probably just saw you as an easily reachable object to get to the other side of the tunnel."

"Fuck off – it was trying to kill me!"

"If it wanted to kill you it would've used its stinger. You're not hurt, are you?"

Pax quickly looked herself over. She was too pumped with adrenaline to sense any pain, but didn't see any marks. She shook her head. Casaria nodded in approval, then took out his sensors to check for other targets in the vicinity. He said, "Crusads are open season, they need culling. They keep the turnbold population down, but there's a shortage of turnbolds right now."

"That's all right then," Pax muttered, stunned at how this man could talk about hunting an alien spider as casually as if it were chicken farming. Something jarred him out of that calmness, though.

"We need to leave," Casaria said, putting his gun and monitors away. He grabbed the lantern from Pax. She frowned, but he was already striding away. "Right now."

She rushed to match his brisk walk, and asked, "What now? Boar with a chainsaw?"

"Save your energy," he shot back. As he picked up his pace to a jog, Pax's worries grew, aware that serious cardio was beyond her. She tried to keep up without exerting too much energy. Watching his monitor, he cursed once more. His jog turned to a run.

Pax chased after him. He ran and skidded around a corner, and she struggled to keep up, to keep sight of his guiding light. They came to some steps, and as Casaria cleared two or three at a time Pax hit one of the first ones and tripped, falling onto her hand. She cried out and he stopped to look back. As she shoved herself to her feet, he yelled, "Hurry!"

She gave a quick look back to see what it was they were running from, and in that moment was too awestruck to move. Creeping around the corner of the tunnel they'd come down was a branch of effervescent light. It flaked into view like a climbing but crumbling vine, its extremities breaking free with the flutter of autumn leaves. All around the strangely spreading shape was a glow of electric blue.

Casaria's hand clamped on to Pax's upper arm and hauled her up the stairs. He shouted, "Move your damned feet!"

She did as she was told. He dragged her as he ran, and as they reached the top of the stairs she looked back. The glow was floating up after them. Casaria kept going, taking her with him. He was running as though his life depended on it, spurring her into doing the same, charging for the next set of steps, back up into the empty storage room.

They powered through the last stretch together, bursting out into the room, and Casaria slammed the door shut behind them. He rammed the bolt in and brought the barrier down, firmly securing the door. He leant against it, almost as out of breath as Pax.

Breathing so heavily she felt like she was going to swallow her tongue, lungs burning and legs aching, Pax turned to retch. The exertion, the panic and the fear brought up part of her dinner. As she spluttered, she demanded answers, flapping a hand in the direction they'd come. "What the hell was that?"

"The *praelucente*. Part of it, anyway. It shouldn't have been there. The scanners —"

"You said it was a good thing!"

"I *said*," Casaria replied, "it serves a *greater* good. That doesn't mean it's safe." She glared at him as he walked by.

"We're done here."

It was only when she asked that Casaria really thought about how he'd been testing Pax. She wanted to know what came next, and he told her she should rest and think about what had already come. He had established well enough that he could talk to her and that she could behave herself, and she hadn't baulked at the strangeness of it all, or shown any particular need to expose and undermine the Ministry. Or to climb its convoluted ladder. She had also shown enough independent spirit for him to feel he could respect her. He respected so few people. She would be a valuable companion, with a little conditioning. She just needed more exercise and at least a general awareness of how to handle herself in a physical confrontation. If he filed the D7-RRb he was putting off, to make her involvement official, the first step would be a full medical exam.

Running this assessment through his mind, he decided on the next step. Before dropping her off, he said he would see what he could do about getting her some firearms training. She stared at him as though she had just been told he would organise a sex change for her. Nevertheless, she mumbled thanks.

She lingered by the car as he waited for her to leave, clearly keen to ask questions quicker than they mounted in her mind. There was just one point he hoped she wouldn't touch on, and of course, she did: "What's next for Rufaizu?"

She wasn't ready to drop it yet. Watching her reaction carefully, he told her, "It's not up to me now." He held up his bandaged hand. "After the attack last night, the pencil-pushers will take over. In all likelihood, those idiots will turn him loose rather than risk creating ripples."

Another question was clearly forthcoming, but instead Pax held her mouth as though something had risen in her stomach. She retched again, with a nasty cough, but nothing came out except the rancid smell of bad Chinese. Casaria marvelled at how much she'd suffered from such a short run. Perhaps the fairy was repeating on her. "Try and get some rest," he told her.

Waving an irritated hand at him, she spat noisily, then pointed to his bandages. "What about those Fae that came at you? Are they still out there?"

Casaria shrugged. "I might have got one or two of them in the fight, we're not sure. But I'll deal with the others, don't worry."

She nodded.

As Pax left for her apartment, Casaria pulled away and checked his phone for any reports of incidents across the city. Nothing of note. There was no way the administration would actually let him join the Fae hunt, anyway. They resented his enthusiasm for practical activities. Handing over the severed head of a glogockle for examination had once cost him a week of writing reports in a windowless room. Meanwhile Sam Ward got a promotion for conducting a demographic survey. *That* was considered research?

Bastards.

He slowed down at an intersection and saw a man resting against a wall, behind a piece of cardboard declaring his sob story. Young, not yet 30, still strong, though with the vacant look of one who'd lost his intelligence to drugs. If he'd ever had it to begin with.

 Casaria pulled over behind a warehouse, sheltered from cameras. He wove back through alleys on foot until he got to the main street, then approached the homeless man with a smile. "You want to make some money?"

The young man looked up at him, eyes half-closed. He didn't appear to have heard.

Casaria took out a note. "I've got £20 with your name on it. Meet me around the corner. But take that path, don't follow me. It's not a sex thing. And it'll be fair."

The bum couldn't take his eyes off the money. He nodded slowly, not entirely following or caring, then Casaria walked away. The homeless man stood with great effort, then ambled in the opposite direction. The CCTV footage would show this pedestrian in a suit taking pity on the vagrant, leaving him enough money to set him prowling through the alleys for a fix. The homeless man disappeared into an area with no other cameras, where he would be found bloody and bruised late the next day.

When asked who did it, he would refuse to give details.

He'd mumble through his broken teeth that it had been a fair fight. Couldn't fault that.

11

Pax couldn't focus as she tried to find the section in Apothel's book on the *crus adsecula*. It was unlikely to be the name Apothel had used, given the pattern of the others, but it should have been recognisable from the pictures. Her eyes blurred, the detail of the pages hard to make out, and her head started swimming. She felt nauseous, cursing herself for being so out of shape, and twice since she'd left Casaria she felt like she was going to vomit again. It never came, though.

She drank a glass of water, took a few aspirins and sat on the bed waiting for the feeling to pass. She felt the room expanding and contracting like the breathing of some great beast. How long had the fairy been shouting for? The words only vaguely sifted into her ears, and for a moment she didn't understand where they were coming from. She stared across the room to the closed cupboard.

Oh yes.

The fairy.

She closed her eyes, but that made things worse, like she was about to roll off the bed despite sitting still. The shouting continued and she grunted, pushing off the bed and lurching towards the closet. She tried to speak: "Like having a damned pet I never asked for." The words came out like the cries of a dying goat, her tongue barely moving. She opened the cupboard and lifted the lid off the shoebox. Her focus lasted long enough to see the tiny lady looking up.

"You look like shit."

She fell, with just enough time to realise something was seriously wrong.

Letty had pretended to sleep when Pax left, conserving her energy. She had done a good enough job of hiding the tiring effects the Ministry gas had had on her, she felt, but needed to recover in anticipation of a rescue operation. If one came. When the lummox had made a snide comment about no one having come to save her, Letty held her tongue, but there was truth in what the girl said. The boys had not come, and she didn't know why. They had Pax's address, they should have at least followed up on threatening her. But nothing. Letty was alone, out on her arse. Betrayed by those useless pricks.

She was fuming on that when the girl returned. Deciding to vent some anger, Letty started shouting, until the shoebox was finally opened and the girl collapsed with a great crash. Letty took advantage at once.

Using her full weight, Letty shoved the giant t-shirt into the corner of the box, balling it up enough to clamber to freedom. With the lumbering giant felled like a tree, it was a free ride out. Letty jumped onto the cupboard shelf and landed next to Pax's twitching hand. The girl's forearm flopped into the cupboard, her body slumped against it. Her head lolled against the cupboard door, barely conscious, half-open mouth drooling. The arm was a perfect ramp down, which Letty pounced onto, running over the long sleeve of Pax's hooded top. She stopped as she reached the shoulder, though, seeing erratic rips in the terrain, a hole close to the neck. The skin beneath the cloth looked completely wrong.

Letty continued down Pax's back, throwing a few glances back to the wound. She reached the floor and jumped off. As she started across the carpet, its weaves up to her ankles, the fairy slowed down, considering the girl's chances.

Not good, she thought, approaching the looming door. There was a draught excluder at its base, but enough space was left to squeeze through. Letty stopped as the girl let out a groan. She looked like a semi-comatose drunk. Standard human affair on a Saturday night. But there was nothing alcohol-related in Pax's condition. The wound, festering with a bubbling, slightly green tinge, was unmistakably the work of caustic venom. The sort caused by pentanids. It would start with dizziness and nausea, immobilising her and leaving her numb, then the bite would spread through her system, decaying her organs, corroding her bones. The anaesthetic would wear off by the time that happened, when it was too late to do anything about it. She'd suffer a lot.

Which was good, Letty told herself, staring at the massive doomed girl. Teach her a lesson for sympathising with the Ministry and for kidnapping her and tossing her about like a toy.

Pax's whole body shuddered, her upturned hand flapping into the air, and she rolled over onto her back, giving a kick as she lay flat on the floor.

She stank, too, Letty decided. The scent of stagnant sweat all over her.

Pax's foot twitched, near Letty, and the groaning changed to a quiet whimper. Almost no energy left to resist it now.

Letty lifted the draught excluder to form a gap so she could squeeze through. She paused.

There was a problem. Leaving this place, unable to fly and without her gun, she would have difficulty getting back across town. She had no dust on her, so her chances of going unnoticed were slim.

The twitching girl was clearly not well in with the Ministry if they'd allowed her to get in this state. Which made it possible that all her dumb questions were actually geared towards choosing the right side, and she really had saved Letty. Disgusting as the giant's methods were, Letty should never have woken up after taking a dose of that gas.

But it was still a dumb human getting what she deserved.

Letty gritted her teeth.

She swore and marched back across the room. As she got close to Pax, a foot jerked suddenly and the fairy ducked and rolled, barely avoiding the heel crashing into the carpet behind her. "Fuck this," she grunted, and pulled herself forcibly up Pax's trouser leg, to avoid the risk of being squashed. She picked up her pace, running up Pax's body to her neck. Taking a breather, Letty leant against Pax's upturned jaw and surveyed the damage. The toxic green had spread up over the front of the neck, veins coming to the surface in angry colours. Small sounds gargled from Pax's throat. Letty crouched, put a hand to Pax's skin and felt it pulsing with unnatural warmth. She cleared her throat, hoping it wasn't too late, and spat gutturally into her hands.

12

The Whistler Bridge site was not always the most active or helpful spot to visit, but it was one of the closest to Barton's home, so it was his usual port of call when he wanted some quick, simple answers. It was on the remnants of a disused railway, an overgrown ditch that was used by runners during the day and youths smoking pot during the night. A road crossed over the original bridge, and a tight path snaked down its side, through nettles and brambles, to the nineteenth-century brickwork tunnel. Low and concealed, with its surface made fragile by time, this was an ideal spot to write messages.

Barton used his phone light to lead the way, then handed it to Holly so he could concentrate on the writing. Despite insisting that he didn't need to explain as long as she could come and see, she had voiced a dozen barbed questions about where on earth they were going and what on earth they were doing. The first few times, Barton had repeated that she needed to wait and see. Then he stopped replying. He had other concerns. It had been so many years, maybe this site wouldn't work any more. Maybe the Blue Angel was long gone.

He took a lock knife from his pocket, unclipped it and chipped at the brick.

"Oh, you're not serious!" Holly said. "Diz, I swear if you scratch our names into that wall I'm going to slap you."

Barton did not respond, scratching in the two words he needed. His lettering was efficient, a series of quick, sharp lines in block capitals. Holly frowned, reading it as he went.

Where . . .

Impatient, she stirred a foot, checking the old railway. She shone the torch into the tunnel, revealing weeds, empty beer cans and an abandoned tyre.

"On me," Barton instructed. She turned the light back to him as he finished.

. . . Fae?

"Is this some kind of Boy Scout nonsense?" Holly scoffed, and again Barton ignored her. He stood back and waited. "You're right. I wouldn't have believed you if you told me."

It wasn't going to work. It had been too long.

"Honestly, scratching on –"

When the blue screen appeared, Holly clamped her mouth shut.

The wall around the writing changed colour, blending into a foot-wide square, centred on the writing, glowing blue. The deeply etched lines in the brickwork folded in as Barton let out a breath of relief. The mortar reformed, the surface smoothing out. Then new etches appeared, the surface sinking as it created words.

Barton. Why?

Holly took a step back and almost dropped the phone. She pointed with her free hand, finger shaking. "What is that? What did you do? How did you do that?"

As she spoke, the words faded from the brick again, its original surface restored. Holly looked over her shoulder, flashing the torch high and low.

"There's a projection or something? A hologram?"

"It doesn't matter," Barton replied quietly, more interested in continuing the conversation. He used his knife to scratch into the brick again, in the centre of the blue patch.

"What are you doing? Why are you doing that? What is this, Diz? Would you stop that!" She raised her voice sternly. "Stop it at once and tell me what's going on!"

Barton told her, "I am finding out where I need to go. This is what we did. Someone out there wanted to help us, this is how we communicate – they told us where to go."

"Go for what?" Holly cried.

"That comes later," Barton said. He continued scratching. Holly took a few steps around him, looking closer at what he was writing.

Stop them.

"Who's writing that?" Holly asked as Barton's letters faded into the blue. He waited for a response as she continued, "Diz? Who's answering these questions? Where are they writing from?"

"I don't know!" Barton snapped impatiently. He felt ready to hit something, but forced himself to keep calm. "I've never known, but whoever's behind it, that" – Barton pointed at the blue screen – "is the best option we've got."

Holly shook her head. "Don't mess with me. What's going on?"

"Right now," Barton said carefully, "I'm trying to find out where we need to go."

She almost shouted at him, confusion turning to anger. "Why are you asking a bloody brick?"

Barton cringed. The Blue Angel's answer appeared on the brickwork.

Anders Ave.

He took a moment to stare at the address, a little stunned by the importance of what had just been shared with him. Holly must have sensed his surprise, as she asked quietly, "What does it mean? What's wrong?"

"That's where they are. That's where they're hiding," Barton said.

"Who? Jesus, Diz, when are you going to tell me what this is?"

"The Fae. That's where we're going next."

13

Pax opened her eyes slowly, feeling the pain in her shoulder before she saw anything. She winced and blinked to clear her blurred vision. Her throat was dry, and a searing ache ran from her neck down to her left side. She rolled her head to the side and saw the shape of a tiny woman, sitting on a book on the floor, just about eye level. Letty had her arms folded. Her expression said she'd been waiting a while.

"What –" Pax tried to speak, but her voice came out in a rasp. She cleared her throat and went rigid as the pain surged through her anew. She reached for a glass by the bed and took a few gulps of stagnant water, then slumped back onto the carpet. She looked at Letty again, the fairy still motionless. "What happened?"

"You're in a bad way," Letty told her. "Caustic venom in your shoulder. Some nasty fucker in some nasty place gave you a toxic bite."

"I wasn't bitten," Pax whispered.

"You may actually be thicker than you look," Letty told her.

Pax closed her eyes, picturing the encounter in the tunnel. With the prickling of that disgusting creature's many legs, it was possible that one of the touches had been a bite or a sting. In the panic of running away she hadn't noticed a wound. She opened her eyes and said, "You're still here?"

"What can I say, I'm a sucker for a bitch in need," Letty said, less than sympathetic. She pointed at Pax's neck. "That will bore through you, dissolve your insides. I can help, but I'll need assurances."

Pax hesitated. She could move just well enough to call someone. Casaria would know what it was, but he'd see the book, maybe the device. Barton might be able to help. He knew a doctor, didn't he?

"Whoever you think's gonna come, they're not gonna be here quick enough to save your sorry arse," Letty said. "You don't have long."

"What . . ." Pax took in a pained breath. "What can you do?"

"Heal it. It's well within my skillset."

"How?" Pax frowned at the thought of the tiny fairy operating on her wound.

"After I've got your word."

"On what?"

"This thing…" Letty threw a hand around her head, gesturing to the room, the world, the situation, whatever. "This is over. You'll take me out of here. Back to my boys. And you'll keep me safe. And fed. And you'll get me a drink. And I want half your money."

Pax rolled onto her back and looked up at the ceiling. She wheezed, "Your boys . . . they'll shoot me."

"Not if I say not to. I'll be counting on your word, I guess you'll have to count on mine, huh?"

Pax closed her eyes again. Can't get beholden to the psychotic miniature person that everyone says is dangerous. Avoided so many unhealthy attachments, this one has to be the worst. But the pain was real, enough to stop her moving. It burnt, all around her shoulder, as though she were silently on fire.

"Tick tock," Letty said. "It's a good fucking deal."

"You can really heal me?"

"You want to find out? Or just die?"

Pax could feel it moving inside her, spreading down her arm, creeping over her. As though acid was seeping through her veins. Her heart was beating faster, body panicking.

"Do it," she said quietly.

"What's that?"

"Do it!"

"I got your word?"

Pax rolled her head towards Letty, eyes urgent. "I promise. Save me, I'll let you go. I'll take you back. Anything."

"Great." Letty grinned, then held out a tiny hand. "Shake on it?"

Pax stared, unbelieving for a moment, and the fairy started laughing.

"I'm kidding. You're good. Now the first thing to do is go back to sleep. Trust me on that one."

"How are you . . ." Pax started to ask, as the fairy reclined onto the book.

Letty called out in a singsong voice, "Go back to sleep, you big lummox. When you wake up you'll feel a hell of a lot better."

Pax winced as a breath caught her off guard. She held the agony down, clamping her teeth shut, and closed her eyes again.

Think happy thoughts.

Think of staying alive.

Think of all this going away.

14

In the hollow carcass of a once proud building, the walls towering five storeys high, with no floors left to divide them, Barton and Holly scanned their surroundings with phone torches. It was as devoid of life as any place Holly had been, the only structure left standing amongst the rubble of Anders Avenue, in the heart of the warehouse district. The word "avenue" had been used rather liberally, as Holly told Darren.

Still unclear on what they were doing or on whose orders they had come to this impossibly desolate place, Holly secretly let herself enjoy seeing this side of the city. She knew of the warehouse district, populated by these odd relics to bygone industries, from what she had read about the decline of the region, but she had never had any call to actually visit. She imagined, as they crept in through a truck-sized hole in the wall, that very few people did. Even the derelicts of the city didn't camp here, so far from valuables to steal and honest citizens to irritate.

Barton had stayed quiet throughout the journey, ever since seeing the address. It was his *I've got money on this game* face; the one that said all outside influences would be met with wrath until his current obsession was out of the way. She had asked, "Has something happened to that woman?"

"What?" Barton shot back quickly, on edge. He hurriedly shook his head. "No, why would it have? Of course not, she's fine."

He was too insistent, making Holly suspicious, but she took it at face value, at least, that the strange girl wasn't in immediate danger. There wasn't much else worth worrying about, so she decided to let him worry, for a change.

When they'd arrived, he told her to stay in the car. Not on your life, she had told him, and he had, once more, conceded. It made it impossible for her to stay behind, though, when he took the tyre iron from the boot. If there was no immediate danger, he might create some. She considered scolding him for even thinking about violence, especially with her around, but it didn't seem like the right time.

And so they walked through the middle of the vast building, exploring empty corners, looking for God-knows-what, with it more than clear that there had been no people around for the longest time. They traipsed about the bizarre location for a quarter of an hour. Barton studied bricks, stuck his nose in tight cracks, checked behind creeping ivy, all as though he had dropped something very small.

He even shouted a few times, his voice echoing back at them, "Anyone here? We need to talk!"

He finally came to the centre of the enormous space and squatted, thinking things through. Holly tutted. She wasn't sure exactly what had gone wrong, but she was fairly sure he could be held to blame, so she employed a chiding tone to say, "Are you quite done?"

"This has to be the place," he murmured.

"Maybe they were here before," Holly said. She could imagine it would be a good place for burning oil cans, rough sleeping-bag beds, and propped-up Harleys, but she'd seen no sign of a biker gang's footprint.

Barton stood, face fixed in concern.

"It's getting late, Diz," Holly reminded him.

A drum sounded from beyond the walls. A flat, heavy thump. Then another. Holly's superior calm faded.

"What's that?"

The beat picked up tempo, thump thump, thump thump, like a tribal signal. It was getting closer. Coming towards a gap in the wall. Behind the drum was something else – a heavy tapping sound, someone playing coconuts. Holly watched the empty space, dreading the chain-swinging ruffians who might step out.

What stepped into view, though, was a seven-foot-tall, immaculately white horse, thick-limbed and gracefully groomed with a flowing silken mane. It walked into the frame of the gap in the wall, a stick held firmly in its mouth, and as it moved it swung its head in a full, majestic arc, from left to right. The stick slammed into two huge barrel drums, one hanging on each of the creature's flanks.

"Now it makes sense," Holly gasped, taking in the incredible sight. "I'm dreaming. Is that right? I'm dreaming."

The horse stopped in the clearing, letting its head hang for a moment's rest. Then, from above its back, with no apparent source, a muted trumpet let out a few gentle toots. The horse resumed drumming and continued walking. As Holly stared with her mouth wide open, the horse clopped out of view. The sound of its drums diminished as it got further away.

Holly darted forward to get another glimpse of the incredible beast. She leapt over remnants of wall, out into the open, turning towards the horse's departure.

It was gone. She swung her torch around, finding nothing but an empty dirt patch with dry weeds clinging to occasional chunks of discarded machinery. As the thrill of the moment subsided, replaced with disappointment, Barton approached her. He slumped past her, heading the way the horse had come.

"Did you see it?" Holly said. "Tell me you saw that too! I didn't imagine it!"

"It was a drummer horse," Barton said, irritably. He followed the line of the building, scanning the bricks with reduced urgency and purpose.

"A drummer horse?" Holly cried. "As though it's as common as a house fly? That sound – it played that music – and the trumpet. Where did the trumpet sound come from?"

"Invisible proclaimer," Barton said. He stopped next to a small tree that had partly embedded itself into the wall. He brushed the branches aside, reaching through the thicket.

"What are you doing?" Holly ran up to him, giving a few more looks in the direction of the horse's disappearance. "Where did it go? How did it get here?"

"They come when they're needed," he said distantly, "with one simple purpose."

"What? What purpose?"

"To show us where these are stored." He pulled back from the tree, taking something from a hidden recess. Holly lit him with the torch, revealing a metal cylinder in his hand. "This is what got me started. This is what I've been avoiding, since before the Fae caught up to Apothel. Someone's taking the piss, leading me here."

"What is it?" Holly took it from him and he let her. She unscrewed the lid. A liquid rolled around inside, glowing luminescent green. Holly said, "Is it radioactive?"

"Taking the piss!" Barton shouted, almost making her drop the canister. He surged forwards, throwing a punch that clipped the wall. The brick shattered from the force. Holly stared in startled silence as her husband's big shoulders heaved up and down. He looked mad, ready to tear the whole building down.

"Diz . . ." Holly said carefully. "What is this?"

"I don't know," he grunted back.

"Why are we here?"

He slowed his breathing, pushing the anger deep down inside of him so he could look up and meet her eye. He admitted, bitterly, "I haven't heard from Grace. I'm worried something's happened."

The sound of a slap rang down the road, Holly's hand suddenly stinging.

She hadn't realised it was happening until it was done. She stared at his reddening face, holding her open palm out to the side as though considering hitting him again. Barton didn't move. He held her gaze with tired eyes.

"Diz," Holly said through gritted teeth. "If you've done something . . ."

"I haven't done a damned thing," he said, though he accepted the blow as though he deserved it. "I just don't know where she is and it's no coincidence. And this bastard" – he raised his voice, taking the canister from Holly and shaking it to the air – "this bastard is messing with me!"

He was so furious himself that Holly's own anger seemed pointless. She could hear her breathing increasing in speed, not for the first time realising that her husband might be more animal than man. She kept quiet, kept staring. She hadn't heard from Grace either, had she? She'd assumed – she'd just assumed. She squeezed her eyes shut.

"What now, then?" she asked.

Barton didn't have an answer. He just started broadly striding back to the car.

Barton's mind was ticking over the possibilities for the journey home. Holly's eyes were fixed on him, so he avoided looking at her. He needed a solution. Maybe the Blue Angel had hidden Grace to trick him into coming back. Maybe Rufaizu was involved too, maybe Pax. It had worked, after all. Got him riled up blindly following their directions. Exposed once again to the glo, drawn to it like an insect to light. Grace would be safe, though, if it was all a trick. Or she might be with a friend after all. Or she might be genuinely missing, abducted by some other psycho, and the Blue Angel had simply taken advantage of it.

That possibility was the worst.

When they pulled into their drive, he could feel Holly's intake of breath and knew what was coming next. She was going to ask what he was going to do. He hadn't come up with a good answer yet.

But she didn't. She said, "What's that?"

A white envelope sat by the front door.

He knew, the moment it caught his eye, exactly what it was. He rushed out of the car before Holly, hurrying to grab the envelope. He'd torn it open before he had stood up straight.

A simple note, on a small piece of paper, written in large, untrained letters.

We have your daughter. Safe. We'll be in touch.

15

Pax groggily opened her eyes and stared at the horrendous criss-cross of plastering in the ceiling. She blinked a few times, focusing on the pain in her shoulder and arm. It seemed to have subsided to a slight ache, where there had previously been burning agony. She sat up, seeing she was on the floor. She rolled her shoulder. Nothing.

She took off her hooded sweatshirt, heavy with sweat, and threw it aside. She pulled back her t-shirt and looked at her shoulder. A wide bruise surrounded an indentation like a dog's bite mark, which had already scabbed over. Whatever it was, the danger had passed and left a rancid urine-like smell.

Pax scanned the permanent mess of her room. Everything still. The shoebox was open and askew. The fairy had gone. Rather than tempt contact, Pax lumbered to the toilet. She relieved herself at length, with a greatly satisfied sigh, and rinsed her wound with soap and water, before returning to the doorway. There were plenty of places for a two-inch person to hide. She said, "You still here?"

There was a quiet shuffle, a waking curse. She followed the sound to the base of the bed. One of her spotless Nike shoes. Letty pulled herself up over the ankle of the shoe and looked around like a mouse poking from a burrow. She yawned loudly. "You pulled through, huh?"

Pax crouched in front of the shoe and said, "What happened?"

"Saved your dumb life, didn't I?"

Pax picked up the shoe before Letty could complain. She lifted it to her face, the movement knocking the fairy back inside. Letty shot back up the wall of the shoe's ankle and angrily said, "This shit stops, we agreed. You think for a minute to welsh on our deal —"

"Please," Pax said quietly. "It's easier to hear you." She shifted onto the floor and leant against the bed before lifting the shoe and Letty up to eye level. "You slept here?"

"Seemed safe, looks like it's never been used," Letty said. Pax shrugged; it was a fair observation. "Now, you're up. Time to take me to my boys."

"Do you ever let up?" Pax murmured back. "What time is it?"

Pax searched the floor for her phone and picked it up with her free hand. 3.03am. Two missed calls from Darren Barton. She closed her eyes for a moment. It was too late to call him back, wasn't it?

"Hey! Focus!" Letty shouted. "Time *is* an issue here. You heard that prick yesterday, didn't you? Considering my idiot boys never came for me, they're no doubt doing something monumentally stupid right now. And you, you lunatic, you have that thing." Letty pointed back towards the cupboard. Pax followed the small gesture to the odd contraption of Rufaizu's. Apothel's? The Fae's – whoever. "Which means whatever stupid thing my boys are doing is not going to go well."

"Why not?" Pax asked quietly.

"Because my people want the goddamned Dispenser back!"

Pax stared at her silently.

"Thick-shit, it's time to get moving!"

"Give me a *minute*. Are you at least gonna explain what happened to me?"

Letty smiled, proud of what was about to come. "You got bit. I saved you."

"The *crus adsecula*."

"Oh get out. Don't speak Ministry around me, okay? It was a pentanid. They've got a toxic bite with one cure. Similar cure to a lot of the shit in the Sunken City, as it happens. Fae fluid."

Pax blinked and responded slowly, "What fluid?"

"I pissed in the wound, okay?"

Pax kept staring. Not sure if there was a correct way to respond.

Letty prompted her: "Thank you is enough."

"It was spreading through my body, you said – how could you –"

"Oh I'd already done it by then," Letty said. "You gotta get it quick."

"You what? Then that deal –"

"Fucking stands," Letty said quickly. "Don't you dare."

Pax paused, then said, "If I let you go, are we even? I can walk away from the Fae, at least?"

Letty's face hardened. She shook her head. "I can bury a grudge, but you've definitely seen too much. That's your problem, though. Mine is that you get off your arse and take me where I gotta go."

Pax glanced at her phone again, then to the kitchen. "We're not going anywhere, not yet. I'm beat. A drink was part of the deal, wasn't it? We can talk, seeing as you're no longer plotting to kill me."

Letty watched her warily. "You trying to change my mind?"

By way of answer, Pax placed the shoe on the bed and got up. She walked to the kitchen as Letty climbed out of the shoe and watched. Pax grabbed a bottle of beer from the fridge and popped the cap. She turned and held it up for Letty to see. "This do?"

Letty hesitated, clearly not wanting to condone the distraction. She had a thirsty look about her, though, drawn to alcohol. She said, "Got any spirits?"

Pax opened up a cupboard and took out her selection of bottles, one after another, until Letty chose one with a thumbs up. Pax poured a small measure of rum into the cap and returned to the bed. Letty took it in both hands, the cap spanning her shoulders' width. Pax knelt in front of her and raised the beer bottle. "Cheers."

Letty took a big swig of rum, made an appreciative gulp and let out a fearsome belch. Pax cracked a smile. She said, "How are you so loud when you're so small?"

"Fuck you, I'm tall for a Fae," Letty said, failing to answer the question. "This is good. Good rum's rare. Maybe you're not a total idiot."

"I won it," Pax said. "Collateral from a rich guy who ran out of cash."

"Okay." Letty lowered the bottle cap. "I've endured this shit for a full day, so I guess I gotta ask. What's your deal?"

"Huh?"

"This." Letty pointed to the room. "Who the fuck are you? Clearly you don't work or have a life, just dirty boys' clothes and a collection of gambling books. What are you, the thinking man's degenerate?"

Pax reconsidered her surroundings from the fairy's perspective. The clothing, partially strewn about the room and, in many cases, unclean. Then there were the books on poker and psychology, dog-eared from rereading. Plain, bare walls. A stack of empty beer bottles by the sink. There was, at least, one point she could make: "They're all women's clothers, actually."

"You work nights, right?" the fairy said. "Too poor for drugs and no way you're a hooker."

Pax pointed at the books. "Figure it out."

"Card games? Can't be much good, needing to read all these books about it."

"I do all right." Pax caught the defensive note in her own voice and frowned. She looked at the books: the psychology tomes of Herman Lakers and Dutch McRory's *Cash Game Analysis* were genius literature that she treasured. Piotr Venk's *Lockpicking Masterclass* was harder to justify, but everyone needed hobbies. She said, "I'm good enough to have a chance in the WPT next week. I wouldn't expect a psychotic elf to know what that means, though."

"Elf?" Letty laughed without mirth. "Good one. Miss WPT, I could teach you things you can't learn in books. You've only ever played against humans. I'd destroy you."

Pax raised an eyebrow, curious. She said, "How? Physically, I mean. You can't –"

"Oh, we can," Letty said. "Online, for starters."

"You have the internet? On what? Miniature computers? Phones? With apps?"

"Yeah," Letty answered harshly. "We wipe our arses with toilet paper, too."

Pax let out a little snort of a laugh, almost choking on her beer. As she wiped her mouth she commented, "There's an image." She paused, then said, "I don't play online."

"So we use a Fae deck. I can deal and tell you what your cards say," Letty said.

"Thanks but I'll pass."

"You're no fun. Where's your three Fs?"

"What?"

"The things any Fae needs. Fighting, fucking and funnies. You've got none of them."

"Funnies?"

"Shitting with people. Having a laugh."

"I have a laugh," Pax insisted. "My work isn't exactly ordinary."

"Oh yawn. Do you have," Letty asked slowly, giving the question the full weight that it deserved, "any friends?"

Pax drank for a moment, rather than replying. Why was she having to justify herself? "Do you?"

Letty went quiet. She seemed to consider the question seriously. "I played a game with Apothel, you know, where I convinced him to use our cards. He was an idiot. And he raised an idiot kid."

Pax shifted a knee up under her chin. "You were friends once, weren't you?"

Letty hesitated, then said, "Who gives a shit." She took a big swig of the rum. "Good riddance to him. The lot of them."

"Hey." Pax tapped the duvet next to her, drawing her full attention. "What happened between him and your people? Why the theft and why the murder when you all wanted the same thing?"

Letty shook her head. "I told you – he cut me out of that part, didn't he?"

"But you never wanted to know –"

"Forget it. We've talked enough." Letty flung the bottle cap back and chugged down the rest of the rum. The cap finished, Letty threw it aside and stood up. "Time to go."

Pax stared at her. It was a big question mark, and something the fairy either didn't know or didn't want to face.

"We have a deal," Letty snapped.

"You have my word," Pax said, "I'll do what you ask. But the moment I let you go, I'm in the shit, aren't I? And if that's how it's gonna be, I want to be informed and I want to be rested. So I'll give you a choice. Keep talking, let me know everything, or clam up and we get some sleep. Either way, we're not leaving, not yet."

Letty stood silent for a moment. She took a breath and let it out with a loud groan, looking skyward. "Ugh. This had better not be an elaborate Ministry set-up. I swear, I'll cut out your tongue."

The threat made Pax smile. The fairy's tone had changed, no longer fully serious or angry. Letty was ready to work with her.

16

Grace Barton stirred with a splitting headache, groggy and confused. The ground around her was hard and damp, cold. She pushed herself up, blinking and trying to make sense of the murky grey. She looked up, into a wall of eroded brick. Concrete floor. Dust. She murmured to herself, "What the hell . . ."

She rose wearily, back onto her haunches. The only illumination was a sliver of artificial light creeping in through a high window. The ceiling was twenty feet up, rising into corrugated iron, but the room itself was maybe fifteen feet square. There was a single metal door. It was completely quiet, completely still.

"Hello?" Grace called out, afraid of who, or what, might answer.

Nothing.

She put a hand to her head and moaned, trying to figure out what had happened. The last thing she remembered was drinking in the park. No. There had been voices. The press of metal against her skin. Going somewhere by car. A clumsy bit of blind walking. Sitting on a cold floor. Peeing awkwardly into a bucket. She spun around. It was there in the corner shadows. The metal bucket, her only luxury in this room.

They had taken her. *Kidnapped* her. But it was hazy, like she had been only half awake. Which bits were a bad dream?

"Oh, Christ." She put a hand to her head. "How much did I *drink*?"

She took out her phone and saw a number of missed calls and a handful of upset messages from her dad. She tried to call him back, but the phone buzzed off. No signal. She struggled to her feet and swayed on the spot, then noticed the chill for the first time.

It had been ambitious to head out on an autumn day in shorts. Now it was the dead of night and this creep's warehouse had no heating. She wrapped her arms around herself and rubbed them to try and keep warm.

Whimpering, fears starting to fill her mind, she uttered, "Daddy . . . please . . ."

"Oughta have some fun with her, while we can," Mix commented to Fresko on a rafter, as they watched the girl stir. He took out a cigar and lit it with a generous inhale.

"Don't want anything more to do with them than we have to," Fresko replied. "Big ugly beasts, makes me sick that we need them."

Mix allowed himself a small laugh at his friend's negativity. He pointed the cigar down. "At a distance she's not so bad. Imagine she was our size, you'd do her."

Fresko gave him a look. "She's a kid."

"Lighten up," Mix sighed. "This is gonna come together. You make sure her shit of a father does as he's told and I'll tell Val all what we've done. Get some extra hands together to collect the weed and the Dispenser."

"You wanna talk to Val alone?" Fresko couldn't keep the aggravation from his voice. It had been bad enough taking orders from Letty, but at least she thought things through. Mix was a walking heap of hormones, only interested in how best to cause damage. Fresko needed to plan all the details. The simple concepts of bringing the girl round to walk herself inside, of leaving her a bucket to piss in, the idea of leaving a note for her thick-skulled father. Left to his own devices, Mix probably would've knocked the girl out before getting her in the car, even. There was no telling how he'd screw things up during a chat with the leader of the FTC.

"Got a better idea?" Mix sneered. "Think one of us needs to stay and watch her? She's not going anywhere. Or you want me to manage the dad?"

"No," Fresko said. There was no way around it: whatever task Mix was left with, it'd be a risk. "Once we're done with the dad, and done with her, we go to Val together."

Mix went quiet as he eyed Fresko, taking the comment as a criticism. Rightly so.

"Please!" The girl's voice rose from the room. Maybe she'd heard them. She turned on the spot, searching the shadows. The low light bounced back off the tears on her cheeks. "Someone! Anyone! You can't leave me here!"

"All right. Go on ahead," Mix said. "I'll shut her up."

Fresko shot him a look and said, "We might need her."

"Relax. I've dealt with her sort before."

"She doesn't *need* dealing with."

"She will. One way or another. You know that, right? Her, the dad, whoever else. We're not leaving a trail."

Fresko looked down at the girl. She was crying. "My family don't have any money, if that's what this is. And . . . and . . ."

"Leave her be," Fresko said, trying to keep the situation manageable, "until we're done. We don't need complications right now. We need leverage."

Mix let a moment pass.

"We good?" Fresko asked carefully.

Mix nodded, his smile anything but warm. "Sure. But when this is done we need to talk, don't we? A crew of two don't work, does it?"

"No," Fresko said. "All the more reason we need to pull this off."

The girl thumped a balled-up fist into her thigh. "You can't keep me here!"

Mix shouted, his voice booming through the room, "We'll do what we want with you, bitch – get used to it."

Grace went silent, staring up at the rafters, unable to see them. As Fresko watched her eyes quiver with fear, he had to hand it to Mix. The guy had a voice that could contend with the humans.

PART 3:

SUNDAY

1

"Apothel didn't need to die," Letty explained. "There's countless dumb lummoxes that've got in our way before and lived. Draws too much attention to kill them all. It's on me, that. Totally on me."

Pax crossed her legs on the bed, trying to get comfortable as she sat over the small woman, a fresh beer in hand and more rum in Letty's cap. Letty was looking away from her, staring into the memory. She continued, "There was a power struggle going on in the FTC around then, which lasted years. The big leadership contenders were Valoria Magnus and her brother-in-law, your mate Retcho."

"Ah ha."

"Retcho and his followers were developing weapons. They wanted to wage war on the myriad creatures and anyone associated with them. Val had a more academic approach. Believed in improving the Fae supply of dust and laying low, building up the whole community's strength to reclaim the Sunken City later. She also spread word that Retcho wanted to use his weapons on his own people, that his work needed to be stopped. Things swung her way in the end, but it came out, after her big coup, that Retcho *had* been close to completing something that might destroy the berserker."

"That being your name for Rufaizu's minotaur? The *praelucente*."

"Yes." Letty drew this out at length, demonstrating annoyance. "Our name for whatever stupid shit other people call it. It's the beating heart of the Sunken City's disease. Everything else follows it around down there – and that thing, more than anything else, senses Fae presence in the tunnels. Everyone wanted to know about the Dispenser, then. What if it really could secure the Sunken City? A lot of Fae were dead and the functioning of this thing wasn't clear, so Val set the boffins in FTC Uni to studying –"

"There's a university?"

"Crispy geckos, is everything in our fully functioning and technologically advanced society surprising?"

"Crispy geckos?"

"Shut up. Where was I? These boffins were studying this machine, and starting up new studies into the berserker. They realised Apothel's crew of prats could be matched to the movements of the berserker. We'd known about them before, bums bumbling about Sunken City entrances – but now it seemed this merry band of idiots had graduated from drinking funny juice to actively tracking the berserker. And half the time they got near it, the thing moved."

Pax nodded. "Barton said they got instructions through blue screens – they were trying to stop it, but whoever was talking to them was only able to move it around. Somehow."

"Yeah. I learnt that, too, eventually," Letty said. "Most people were pretty heavily against Apothel from the outset. It's a known fact that any human working underground with the Ministry of Environmental Energy's permission is bad for us. And every human underground has to have the Ministry's permission, official or not. The Ministry guard that place like a shrine, and they hate all we stand for. When Val took charge, the FTC had been moved like three times in four years on account of them hunting us. Part of her mandate was keeping that from happening again. Whatever she was up to, developing new tech, sending out scouts, whatever – it worked – the MEE didn't come close to us again. But whatever Apothel was up to, the feeling was that the Ministry benefited, so his people needed to be stopped. My team were sent to do it, and we started with Barton, him being the muscle of the group. Organised a little accident with his kid to scare him out of the game."

"You what?" Pax's jaw dropped open.

"It was nothing, just enough to shit him up. He backed off, and without him the others started to lose their bottle, too. Apothel, though, you weren't scaring that guy off, he was too crazy to worry about his own safety. I came up with the idea of drawing him away; tell him fairies exist and we've got a pot of gold waiting in some far-off country. He seemed the sort to buy it – he was a goofy fucker, acted like everything was a big game – a burly animal with a thick beard like birds could nest in. You saw him in the street, you'd peg him for a circus strongman who'd let himself go. The pair of them, him and his son, first got on our radar when they did over a mansion we were casing, on Friedrich Boulevard, so I knew he had a bit of Fae sentiment in him."

"Wait," Pax said. "A mansion you were casing? A human one? Why?"

Letty stared at Pax as though the answer was obvious. "Anyway. I couldn't help myself, I got curious about this guy. We talked. Drank, too. He tells me how he got started in the Sunken City, after stumbling across this juice that made him see things. He'd found it after burgling some corrupt local governor. Apothel being the sort who'd huff glue, he downed the lot."

"That was glo?"

"Sure, whatever. High as a crow, he started seeing the myriad creatures. He ventured into the Sunken City, found himself a continuing supply. He'd started producing this manual –" Letty nodded to the book "– full of wacky names he'd come up with for creatures we barely knew about. I'd never spoken to anyone who'd been down there, see, and he was eager to share. Then he tells me all about this Blue Angel of his and I realise that all this time Apothel's been thinking he's fighting the monsters. That, if anything, he's on our side. So I come clean with him – I tell him whatever he's doing, it's not working, but if he lays off for a while we can put the Dispenser to use.

"It takes a bit of persuading. He was the opposite of patient, but I got him to calm down while I ran it by Val. Her and her council, they were angry that I'd got familiar with him, but mostly said it was pointless talking to him if we still didn't know how to use the Dispenser. It was too soon, even if we wanted to take that kind of step. Except then it was too late. You know the rest. I didn't kill Apothel, but I *got* him killed, right? All I needed to do was persuade him to leave town. Instead I got him to stay. Gave him the stupid idea to cross the Fae."

"It's not that simple, though, is it?" Pax said. She moved forwards onto her knees, to get closer, and Letty scrambled back quickly, raising her fists. Pax froze. "Sorry. I didn't mean to –"

"Yeah, didn't mean to," Letty hissed. "Story of humans' fucking lives, isn't it?"

"But listen for a second. Apothel followed instructions from an unknown stranger for years, thinking fighting that minotaur was what was best for the city – why didn't he stick to your plan?"

"Because he was an idiot."

"He must've somehow got the idea that he needed to take things into his own hands with the Dispenser. And it sounds like he was partway right – your people weren't ready to work with him."

"He didn't know that."

"He knew something, though, didn't he?"

"Apothel was nuts! You don't get into a vocation of hunting monsters while high on hallucinogenics without being a few bullets short of a full clip. He got his own ideas, he got dead."

"The details are important," Pax insisted. "He died and Rufaizu escaped – and in the time since, nothing's been done to cure the city of what's down there. You're not seeing what I'm seeing?"

Letty stared, refusing to play along.

"Is there any chance that your people didn't intend to use that weapon? And Apothel somehow knew that when he stole it?"

The fairy laughed, nastily, and paced aside. She threw a hand in the air, raising her voice. "Oh, that's rich! Real fucking rich! You have no idea!" She pointed a stern finger. "You, who the hell are you anyway? Fancy yourself smart, sticking your friendless nose in damn books, *talking* your way round things? You're thick as the rest of them – you have *no* idea."

"I can see the way things add up – and the only –"

"I hunted for that device for nine years!" Letty snapped. "I was cast out – and my boys with me, with the whole FTC spitting on everything I'd done! If you could've seen the hate I've seen – the attitude from the Fae – *didn't intend to use it*? Even if Val said I could come back, I wouldn't, not with what my *whole society* think of me – not until I make it right. It's on me, you don't get that? It's all on me."

"Well, it's sprayed me too, now," Pax said, keeping cool. "And for what it's worth, I think you did the right thing. Even if it didn't work out. What I'm trying to say is –"

"You're trying to say shit," Letty said. "Apothel's dead and that weapon's laid dormant when it might've been used a decade ago. The Fae's home might have been reclaimed if I'd stayed the hell out of it all."

"I'm saying," Pax said, more firmly, "it's *not* your fault."

"Well, you're wrong. How'd you think Rufaizu feels now, after he came back to me? And now we've had a chat, you think you'll even survive the day? You're gonna learn, don't you worry – it doesn't pay to be my mate."

Pax didn't respond for a moment. She said, "You can have your Dispenser, and I can help you get that fuel – we can get people outside the Ministry onto Rufaizu's case. But it all starts with deciding who we can trust, doesn't it?"

"There's no *we,* all right? This" – Letty held up the cap of rum – "gets you a little closer to not being dead, but it doesn't make us friends. All *we* are going to do is find my boys, hopefully before they do something catastrophic."

Pax placed her empty bottle down. She said, carefully, "Thanks, anyway. I'm glad you talked to me, even if you've got a habit of getting people killed."

Letty went quiet, staring like she was trying to figure Pax out. The usual look. Pax smiled at her, then pushed herself up off the bed with such force that the mattress bounced and Letty was knocked off her feet. As the fairy threw insults, Pax went towards the washroom, holding up her middle finger.

2

Come to Galley Road station now or she hurts.

That was all the confirmation Barton needed that the Fae were behind Grace's disappearance. He knew enough about them to know they couldn't explore that nest themselves. It wasn't where they had taken Grace – there was something there they wanted, which they needed him to get.

Galley Road connected the heart of Ordshaw with the docks, but the Underground station of the same name sat in cold neglect halfway along it, a long way from anything useful. The station was notable for having four platforms serving a single train line, the spares allegedly built to serve a line that was never completed. The empty platforms were sealed behind temporary metal walls that had sat chained and bolted for over thirty years. People had heard and seen things moving in the shadows behind the barriers, and Galley Road station frequently made lists of Ordshaw's most haunted places.

Darren Barton and Apothel had known better. Galley Road station was actually near a nest of glogockles. They lurked close to the abandoned platforms, drawn to the lights, and sniffed around the edges of the barriers looking for a way in. They retreated at the sound of people, though. The superstitious station workers avoided the area, but Barton and Apothel had seen a dozen of the sickly creatures lurking there.

Barton drove there alone, with the sun still rising. Whoever had left the second note had to be nearby, but he knew better than to waste time looking for them.

He hated doing as he was told. He hated that he had a cylinder of glo in his hands again, tempting him towards the bitter unreality of its influence. He hated that the Blue Angel had led him to it, instead of helping him. The only positive he'd had was that in her nervous exhaustion Holly had fallen asleep shortly before the second note had been delivered. She would wake up and find him gone, and she would know why, but she would not be able to follow. By the time he got home, he'd either have saved Grace or had something truly terrible happen, and whatever that meant to Holly now was a very minor concern.

The hate helped. Barton knew that when he reached Galley Road, whatever else was going on, he'd have a few glogockles to use his hate on.

Barton stopped at the corner as he walked the final distance to the station. It hadn't changed in fifty years, an arch of concrete with basic, faded lettering chipped into the header. The metal shutters obscured half the entrance, where they got stuck on opening. Barton walked in, down the steps into the green glow of the station's belly. A few men in shirts were hovering around, waiting for what must have been the first train of the day. They were yawning and stretching, barely keeping their eyes open. On a Sunday morning, they must have been going to church or coming home from a bad night. It had to be a bad night if it had ended anywhere near here.

Barton passed them, went into the dividing corridor and made his way to the dead end of two of the metal walls, ready to punch something. The makeshift door in the barrier, a smaller bit of metal that had been hung on hinges, had its chains hanging loose. There was a padlock on the floor. Someone had come here before him. He pushed the door aside, creating an opening big enough to get through. Beyond the metal, there were no lights, only a dark cavern. There was a piece of paper hanging on the door. He took it off and found the same abrasive writing that had been on the previous notes.

Bring us the electric weed and you get her back.

Barton frowned. He looked into the darkness. They'd come down here, and the place wasn't crawling with monsters, so the station itself must've been safe from the minotaur. The little bastards must still be hanging around to watch him.

"Face me like a man," he growled. "I'm not doing shit until I know she's safe."

There was no answer. He looked around: no movement in the tunnel behind him and nothing in the darkness ahead.

"Forget it." He turned away. He was halfway back to the other platform when a whistle caught his attention. He turned back but there was still no one there.

"Up here, numbnuts," a sharp voice said, and he looked to the ceiling. Near the metal barrier, a tiny figure sat on the edge of a luminescent light. The rifle in his hands targeted Barton. The man, in the white shirt and suspenders of an '80s financier, had one eye fixed to his scope, hands not moving as he said, "Need me to explain what happens now?"

"Where is she?" Barton snarled.

"Safely waiting for daddy to do as he's told."

"If you've touched her –"

"Get to work. Or you join Apothel, and your sweet little daughter takes your place."

Barton fought the urge to charge at the fairy. He'd never clear the distance, and probably couldn't reach the light anyway, but he wanted to hurt him, bad. The sniper told him, "I know, I know. Now be a good boy."

All he could do to show his discontent was to walk by very slowly, glaring at the little man all the while. The thing was wearing a tie, even. What kind of fairy was it? Barton stopped at the entrance to the platform, then went in. It was colder on the other side, as though the darkness had sucked the heat away.

"What am I looking for?" he called back through the door.

"Electric weed. You'll know when you see it," the tiny man said.

Barton resisted the urge to make more idle threats. He'd learnt long ago to save his energy for when it was needed. He walked over the empty platform until his feet touched the rippled edge. He took out his phone and lit it up. The unevenness of the floor was apparent in the pit ahead, but there were no tracks. This part of the station wasn't even half-finished.

He climbed down and checked in either direction, then started walking. The tunnel to his sides and above was too vast for his torchlight to reach its edges. The sounds of his footfalls rolled back towards him. A sound ahead told him he was close. A stone knocked loose or a claw scratching the ground, indicating one of the myriad creatures lurking in the shadows. He slowed down, searching for all the precious little detail he could make out.

Another scuffle, like a fox picking through junk, and his eyes fixed on its location. He shone the torch at it and the creature shied away – slightly. It crouched into the shadow, then rose out of it, pincer-jaws snapping in his direction. Though it was a foot shorter than him, it was still a big one, its rocky flesh lighting up as the veins that ran through it glowed peculiar green. Its gangly arms flopped to the sides then drew in, tensing, the claws clicking together. An extra appendage sprang forward over its left shoulder like a scorpion's tail.

Barton stared it down, unafraid.

"Come on you bastard," he said, putting his phone away.

It thumped a flat stump of a foot towards him. Then the other one. Each step sent vibrations through the room to help it sense where he was. Its edges lit up enough to create a pool of light around it, giving Barton all the visibility he needed. He raised his fists defensively, preparing for its charge.

The glogockle clicked like an oversized beetle, gnashed its mandibles, then ran at him. It was an ungainly creature, listing from side to side as it moved, but its power was unmistakable, a wall bearing down upon him. Barton let it approach, not moving until the last second. It swung both clawed arms towards him in a windmill arc. He ducked, the grab going over his head, and he jabbed the thing's gut. Its flesh cracked and erupted around his punch, green light spilling out of it as the glogockle howled. Not finished, it slashed its claws at him. Barton lunged aside and threw a flurry of punches into its side, finishing with a punch to where its kidneys would be, if it had any. The glogockle could not turn quickly enough, the strength of the punches and the force of its own momentum making it trip over itself and roll into the wall. It crashed to a stop, twitching, a pool of luminescent blood spilling out around its legs.

Barton stood over it, shaking his hands off at his sides, breathing deeply.

Not quite fit enough for this.

A series of clucks chattered behind him. He turned and saw the rest of them, thumping into the tunnel, claws pinching and jaws clicking. The flank of glogockles shunted into each other as they formed a mob of brightly lit monsters. To the left, where the first one had been sniffing around, he saw what the fairies were after. A patch of moss with a neon blue light sparking around its tips.

Barton stared at the monsters, unflinching. He reached into his pocket for the cylinder of glo. He opened the cap. The smell, the flavour and the burning brought back memories of another life, a decade past.

At least he could tell Holly he didn't have a choice, this time.

3

Rufaizu woke with a tube down his throat. Teeth clamped onto a chunk of plastic, mouth forced open and impossible to move. He gagged, panicking, but gagging did nothing. He tried to sit up, but his arms were bound, giving only an inch of movement. He shook the shackles, arms and feet, then threw his head from side to side to see where he was. The tube ended in a large machine with some kind of artificial lung, its accordion plastic slowly rising up then falling down, each breath met with a muted beep.

On the other side of him, a man sat staring.

Another suited cog in the Ministry machine.

This one had been more volatile than the others Rufaizu had encountered. His eyes were fiery, and vanity seeped from his pressed suit and well-groomed hair. He had the aura of a hunter who did it for sport.

Rufaizu grunted, tried to demand he take the tube out, release him, anything. The man took the maximum amount of time possible to fold away the newspaper he was reading. He watched Rufaizu buck, and said, "Don't waste your energy."

The man scraped his chair closer, leaning in.

"You won't be able to breathe for yourself for a while. What with where the bullet hit you. You're lucky to be alive."

Rufaizu glowered back at him.

"What everyone's asking," the man said, "is why you'd come back here, and reconnect with the Fae, considering their history with your family? I mean, surely you saw this coming?"

Rufaizu tried to snarl, baring his teeth. The man sat back, offering a pitying look.

"You really are animals, aren't you." It wasn't a question. "You couldn't pose a threat to anyone. But here we are, the biggest news in a decade. A feral boy scrapping with the fairies." The man glanced to the door, checking they were still alone. He lowered his voice. "You can nod, or shake your head, so you can answer me. Do you even know why the Fae tried to kill you?"

Rufaizu fixed his eyes on the man, making every effort not to move.

"They *did* try to kill you, you realise that? They sure weren't shooting at me. I was in the open, wasn't I? An easy target, really. No, they were 100% on you, didn't particularly want to hurt someone from the Ministry. You need protection. Without my help, they could still finish the job."

Rufaizu narrowed his eyes in what he hoped was a piercing look, to say: *you're wrong*.

The man's mouth twisted with satisfaction. "You're genuinely not afraid of them? They must've convinced you they were your friends. Maybe you had something they wanted? You know your dad thought they were his friends, too."

Rufaizu twisted away from the man, trying to hide his face.

"The thing is, the FTC say that the Fae you were involved with were known deviants. Bad eggs. Yeah, we've had word from them. These creatures you were dealing with are the sort of Fae" – the man held up his left hand, bandaged around the middle – "who would risk crossing the Ministry. I can only hope you're smarter than the facts suggest – that you'd know better than to talk to the sort of maniacs that killed your dad. You were running a con with them, weren't you? Looking for revenge?"

Rufaizu looked back at the man, then, and shook his head.

"Oh please. Kid somehow returns from hiding after his father's murdered, what else is he gonna have on his mind? Hell, *I* would go after whoever killed my dad, and I didn't even like my dad." The man placed a friendly hand on Rufaizu's shoulder. "I want justice, the same as you. Help me help you."

Rufaizu looked at the man's cracked knuckles, oddly blemished compared to the rest of his smooth skin.

"You know where I can find them," the man said. "Just give me an address."

Rufaizu kept staring. Even if a word this guy said was true, he was still a suit in the system. If the Fae couldn't be trusted, he was no better. Silence hung between them for a moment, then the man closed his grip on Rufaizu's shoulder and the boy tensed, pain shooting through his body. There was a wound there he hadn't noticed before; it lit up with fury. The man held on tight as Rufaizu squirmed, screams muffled by the tube in his mouth.

"They did this to you," the man told him. "This and the one in your neck."

Rufaizu dug his teeth into the tube, as his eyes streamed. The bonds that held him dug into his wrists and ankles as he struggled.

The man released his grip suddenly. "Are you gonna help me help you? You want me to stop those animals, once and for all?"

Rufaizu nodded quickly, urgently, his body forcing the answer out even as his mind tried to resist. The man sat back. Rufaizu slumped, shuddering, fighting back sobs.

"See, we can co-operate. You're gonna write down their address, aren't you?"

Rufaizu eyed him again, regretting his moment's weakness. But he remembered, now, they were shooting at him. Those *were* Fae gunshots. They could've shot the suit and they didn't. And the implication was clear enough. If he defended them, after what they did, he was going to suffer, one way or another.

The man spoke softly: "These creatures want you dead, Rufaizu. They're a menace. You're going to give me an address, and you'll be doing the whole world a favour."

Rufaizu closed his eyes, preparing himself for it. It wouldn't matter anyway, would it? There was no way Letty and the others would've stayed in their hideout after firing on a Ministry agent.

*

Casaria straightened his jacket and tie as he left the prisoner's room. Just being close to that homeless urchin made him feel dirty. He paused as the door swung shut behind him, finding Landon and Gumg waiting for him in the corridor.

"You got something from the asset?" Landon asked.

"The asset?" Casaria scoffed at the attempted sincerity. "He's got a tube in his mouth, what could I get from him?"

"Wherever he sent you, we're going with you."

"He didn't send me anywhere. Go in and ask him yourselves – I'm going out on patrol."

"I've been doing this job a long time, Cano. I know you want the Fae. The Ministry know it. You can pretend to patrol for a few hours, and we can watch while you do it, or you can cut straight to the chase."

"That's a go-ahead, is it? I can do my job as long as you come along to stop me from doing it?"

"We'll make sure," Landon said plainly, "that whatever is done is done right."

"You don't have a choice," Gumg said, confirming the initial dislike that Casaria had felt for him. Casaria shook his head dismissively at the pale man. Gumg wasn't deterred. "We've got our orders."

"All right," Casaria said. "Come along. Give the Fae someone else to shoot at. Maybe I'll get lucky and see them castrate you."

"We're not looking for a fight," Landon warned.

"Don't be naïve. Whether these Fae were under FTC orders or not, the fight's already begun."

4

Pax took in Riley's Bettor Off with a mixture of awe and disgust. It cut a fine example of everything that was wrong with West Farling: a betting shop for the middle classes, taking all the grittiness and danger out of gambling to make it safe, bright and friendly. The shopfront of beech wood and clear glass looked in on low armchairs and coffee tables. Its flat-screen televisions were framed like antique pictures, and the tout's counters had been fashioned in the style of an early-20th-century bank. This sort of innocuous spectacle of vice made West Farling an area Pax despised, even as she used it regularly for games. The rich businessmen around here enjoyed hosting her crowd as a challenge, when their games weren't being done via the safety of the internet or as part of an off-limits millionaire's club.

She watched a young man in a two-tone shirt ask a patient teller for the odds on some race or another. Letty was up above in the eaves, a perch that Pax had barely been able to reach. Pax was not sure if the fairy was coming back, and was even less sure she should want her to. They might return in a whole pack, after all. With guns. She was confident she'd made progress with the tiny lunatic, though, and that there was a solution they could work out together. In the meantime, she was content to watch the affluent losers placing bets on a Sunday morning, and told herself this calm was awaiting her when she was done with the Sunken City. Letty would be free, the threats cancelled, and she could tell Casaria to stuff it. Rufaizu's release would be a more long-term, administrative interest, which could wait until after she'd turned the money she had recovered into something workable.

Her phone started ringing. She took it out quickly, hoping to see Barton returning her call.

It was Casaria.

"What?" she answered abruptly.

"Where are you?" he replied, equally blunt.

"Somewhere I'm supposed to be?"

"You're not home."

"And you're not welcome to go looking for me there," Pax said. "Do you even get what I do for a living? *Why* I do it?"

"Of course I do. The same as me. And you can have all the time and space you need to do whatever you want. *After* we know we can trust each other."

"So . . ." Pax felt her patience wearing to breaking point. "I need your *permission* to go out now? Can't go to the shops? Visit a friend? I didn't ask for any of this."

"Is that what you're doing? What friend?"

Pax barely paused. "You want me to put her on? She can tell you to fuck off, too."

There was a sharp intake of breath on the other end of the line, Casaria biting back his irritation. "I wanted you to join me for something. It's important." His tone sounded forced through his nose, his jaw clamped shut.

"Take a day off."

"That won't work."

"Make it. Look, I'm busy –"

"I really think you should tell me where you are."

"And I really think you should back off. We had a messed-up night last night, that's two nights running. I need a break. If you don't give me some space, I'll snap, I swear."

Casaria was quiet. Hopefully feeling admonished. "I'll give you today. Tomorrow, we'll pick up where we left off. No fooling around."

Before she could respond, he hung up. Pax looked at the phone for a moment, rolled her eyes and put it away. As she did, another unwelcome man came towards her. Curly locks of hair, unnaturally broad shoulders, a gleaming white grin that drew attention to how narrow his mouth was. Milton Tran was an insufferable card player who wore suits in an impossibly unlikeable array of colours. Today's choice was the off-mauve of a pensioner's hair overdue for dyeing.

"Pax? I thought it was you!" Tran went in for a strong, uninvited hug, the sort that had probably been practised to show off his firm chest. It made Pax wince. She didn't return the hug, and he didn't notice, letting go with a look of satisfaction. He said, "What are you doing here? At this time of day? I thought you only came out at night."

"Catching some Vitamin D," Pax said. "You live here?"

"Two blocks over, you know that," Tran laughed. She had no idea where he lived; if he had ever told her, she hadn't listened. "Come to bet on the nags. Got a sure thing, want in?"

"Not my thing," Pax replied.

"With this tip, you should make it your thing. Say, though, what are the chances – we've got a game this evening, if you're up for it. I'd pay money to see my alphas lose a hand to a girl."

Pax frowned, not sure whether to be offended or flattered. "How much?"

Tran laughed. "Oh not literally. You'd do well though, I'm sure. Bankers from the city."

"As opposed to rural ones."

He laughed again. "Shoot. How long's it been? Three months, at least. I've missed you, Pax. You hanging around? I'll buy you lunch."

"Already eaten," Pax said.

"Coffee, then."

"How about you place your bet, and we can talk at this game of yours later?"

The rebuttal made Tran stop, losing some of his cheer. He said, "Okay. Guess you've been up all night again, am I right?"

"Yeah," Pax replied without conviction. "You have fun now."

"I'll message you the deets. If you change your mind about the coffee, I'll be here."

He ducked into the shop, looking back at her, a little wary now. Pax gave him a one-handed wave, basically telling him to piss off. He turned away, and Letty called from above, "If you're done flirting, can we go?"

Pax looked up to the tiny lady standing directly above her, on the edge of the shop's sign. She had a bag over one shoulder, and was clearly alone.

"You gonna catch me?"

Pax nodded and the fairy jumped without warning. Pax quickly raised her hands. With Letty's weight, the fall was gentle, and she landed in Pax's cupped palms with a little thump. Pax immediately closed her fingers over her as she took a step back, looking into the shop to see that one of the punters was watching and frowning. Tran, beyond the man, noticed the strange look and stared at Pax himself.

"Where are your guys?" Pax asked quietly, backing off.

"Gone," Letty replied. "Taken their stuff, which means they're already trying to pull off a scheme. Which means they've entered a world of shit. There's half a dozen places they might've gone. We can start by heading to Hanton."

"As a random option?" Pax said. "How about we start by you thinking a bit more clearly about where we *need* to go, rather than keeping us moving out in the open where someone might notice us?"

"Someone being . . ."

"Who do you think?"

Letty went quiet, staring at Pax while apparently considering her options. Pax turned on the spot, though, checking up and down the road.

"Take your time," she said. "We're getting a coffee, at least."

5

Mix and Fresko had never had much use for ceremony. When Valoria Magnus approached them and the nearby Fae guards stiffened to attention, the pair merely stared, unimpressed. She was a large lady, prone to indulgence and inactivity, and the act of travelling out of the Transitional City to meet them appeared to tire her. Her expression said she was angry before she had said a word, her footfalls shaking the corridor as she approached.

"Where's Letty? She has a lot to answer for."

"Letty's gone," Mix replied.

Fresko added, "So's Gambay, before you ask."

Valoria slowed down at this news. She settled her attention on Mix, deciding he was the leader. "What happened?"

"The Ministry," Fresko said coldly. "Some new girl, they got her to do it. Don't like to say how."

Valoria kept her eyes on Mix. "Was this before or after you imbeciles tried to start a war?"

"Letty was trying to make things right," Mix said. "It got her killed. Since then, we've done things our way, and got results."

"Results!" Valoria let out a humourless laugh, a sound that came from the bottom of her gut. "You got the MEE hunting for us. The FTC is on high alert, ready to evacuate."

"It'll be worth it," Fresko said. She still did not look at him, eyes boring into Mix.

"I'm aware that you failed to release, or silence, the boy. The popular feeling is that the Fae responsible should be executed. That the Ministry should be placated. Tell me what you could possibly have that would make me even consider letting you go."

"We needed the boy to get fuel for the Dispenser," Mix said. "He was gonna persuade Citizen Barton to help. We found another way to persuade him." Mix left a meaningful pause, savouring the surprise in Valoria's face. "So, you want to make idle threats or you want our results?"

Valoria checked around her, the half-dozen guards appearing completely disengaged from the conversation. All of them had to be listening, though.

"Yeah." Fresko followed her thoughts. "Maybe we should talk in private?"

The pair of mercenaries escorted Valoria and her single most trusted bodyguard down the steps of the emergency tunnel and out to the widening cavern of a human room. There, on the floor of the empty room, lay a large plastic bag, filled with what looked like a pile of dirt lit in blue highlights by occasional lightning sparks. Overcoming her initial surprise, Valoria flitted over to the bag with a few beats of her powerful wings. She landed next to it, hands greedily running over the moss. The men followed at a slower pace.

"Where did you find this?" she asked.

"Where Apothel said it was," Mix said.

She turned back to them, face steely. "And what do you expect us to do with it?"

"Use it, what else? The boy *found* the Dispenser. We know where he left it." Mix walked past her, throwing a hand up towards the bag. "But we knew better than to bring it back without power. It's worth at least a big fucking thank you, maybe a sorry or two along that road."

Valoria stepped back, taking in the crackling pile of dirt for a moment longer. "Do you have any idea what this means?"

"Yeah," Mix said. "It's means we're back in FTC favour, ain't that right?"

Valoria held his gaze. "Did the boy talk to you about it? Did *he* know what it was?"

"He knew," Fresko said. "We also know it was worth killing humans for before, so we figured you'd forgive a few casualties now."

This finally drew her to look at Fresko, her voice becoming more severe. "You need to learn your place. I never much liked Letty, but she at least had more sense than to antagonise the MEE. So don't think you are entirely in the clear. This is merely a step in the right direction. I'll send a team with you to collect the device."

"Tell us what it's worth, first," Mix said.

"And demonstrate that gratitude," Fresko added.

"I will arrange for your pardons," Valoria said. "Believe me, that is more than generous."

"We can take this to Retcho," Fresko warned. "See how he defines generous."

Valoria's face turned to stone. "You people bring shame to our society. To even suggest such a thing."

"We're businessmen. Same as you."

Valoria grunted, looking from Mix back to him. Mix looked no better than a thug for hire, but Fresko saw Valoria's eyes, scanning his shirt, his tie. Now she'd deigned to look, she knew he was something else. She said, "Very well. There are other rewards we can arrange." She stepped back from the moss as it sparked again. She frowned. "How did you get Barton to do this?"

"We didn't exactly negotiate," Mix said.

"Then I assume you cleared up after yourselves?"

"We left him to rot. The daughter, too. No sign of Fae interference."

Valoria raised an eyebrow. Without asking for details, she said, "That sounds far too vague. I don't want them *left* to do anything. I want the job finished. I don't reward incomplete work."

"With respect, he might still have his uses," Fresko said, though Mix gave him a look that disagreed. "How else are we gonna put the Dispenser to use?"

"That's not your concern," Valoria said. "All I need from you right now is their silence."

6

There was a ferocious knock at Dr Mandy Rimes' door. Any knock was usually enough to startle her into dropping whatever was in her hands, given the infrequency of visitors, but this was a particularly severe knock, causing her to scatter a project all over the worktop. She fussed towards the door with tuts, pushing her welding goggles onto her forehead, and called out, "Who's there?"

"Me," came the gruff reply.

She opened the door. It was just as well she'd recognised his voice, because she wasn't sure she would have recognised his face in that state.

"Oh heavens!" she cried, reaching towards Darren Barton, then taking her hands back. She stepped back, then out towards him, utterly at a loss for how best to respond.

"Water," Barton said, one shoulder digging into the wall for support. "Please."

Rimes scurried away with mild curses, knocking over a pile of metal on the way. She stopped to pick up a piece, then left it be, and spiralled back towards the tap to get water. In the time it took her to find a glass, Barton had managed to drag himself to one of her many cluttered work surfaces and had sat on a high stool. He leaned to one side, blood dripping from his forehead onto a gutted watch mechanism.

"What happened?" Rimes asked, forcing the glass of water into his hands.

"The Fae," Barton said. Cracked blood ran down one side of his face, while the other had swollen like a balloon. One of his eyes was halfway closed, and his sodden ear was out of shape. Perhaps there was a piece missing. The rest of his body was little better, but it was so dark with blood that it was hard to see where the injuries lay. "It's their technology."

"What is?" Rimes replied.

"The plans you said Rufaizu had. It was a Fae device. That's what Apothel stole. And it's got them after me, got Grace . . . Grace kidnapped. You need to tell me how I can find them."

Rimes blinked behind her thick glasses. "Darren, you need medical help –"

"So give it to me," Barton said. "Then point me to the FTC."

Rimes gave a quick hum, hesitating between questioning him and helping. She chose the latter, scurrying to a small medical kit at the side of the room. She rummaged through the supplies, saying, "Are you sure they have Grace?"

"Sure enough."

"They did this to you?"

Barton shifted with effort and pain. "More or less. They needed electric weed. Needed me to get it. From a glogockle nest. There was . . . ten of them, maybe."

"It's a miracle you're alive."

"No miracle, just a necessity. They came in. Took the weed from me and drew the myriad towards me. But I got out. They didn't give me enough credit. You know where they are, don't you?"

Rimes paused, holding a gauze pad to a gash on his forehead. "No. But I have been testing a device that might help. It's a bad idea, though. The Ministry –"

"Can rot," Barton rumbled. "I'm getting my damned daughter back, and I'm burning them all to the ground."

Rimes backed off, too chilled by his rage to argue. As he calmed, Barton fished in his pockets for something. He said, "There's something else. Tell me what you know about this."

He pulled out a crumpled sandwich bag, faded in parts as though plucked from the gutter. He placed it on the table, its contents partly spilling out. It looked like a clump of earth. Rimes frowned, coming closer to it. The dirt suddenly glistened, bright blue in places, as though sparking energy, making Rimes jump back in surprise.

"You held some back?" she asked.

"Seemed damned important. What do you know about it?"

"I only know *of* it. I've never seen electric weed in the flesh. As it were. I'm not sure anyone has. Darren. It's a very strange power source. What did you say it was for?"

Holly was barely surprised to see her husband was not home when she woke up, late. She was mad at herself for letting it happen. She was no kind of mother, being able to sleep at a time like that. But they had called all Grace's friends, they had notified the police, they had driven through the streets, what else was there? Barton had done it all convinced this was no ordinary disappearance, and now he had gone, leaving Holly, in the new day, to think of her own solution. Fighting down the anger and the fear and the confusion, she forced herself to be calm. Told herself, in no uncertain terms, that this was a time to think rationally. The best way forward was to write a list of problems and possible steps she could take to overcome them.

Daughter missing.

Husband missing.

Possible supernatural creatures responsible.

Police no use?

Each point seemed to present an impossible task, so instead of solutions she started to come up with more problems.

Husband still lying.

Possible relapse to radioactive drink.

Horse playing a drum.

He had taken whatever that infernal liquid was with him and buggered off back into his mystical world, alone, but she at least had a firmer grip on what it was she should be annoyed at him for. And that was partly satisfying. No more fears for his unfaithful gallivanting, though the fear that he was involved with unruly gangs was heightened. How could he have got Grace mixed up in it?

The thought of Grace distracted Holly from her useless list of problems. She picked up a photo album she had created when Grace had been young. She smiled at how healthy and happy they had all looked. It was easy to create that impression in front of the camera. The memories were less than perfect. There were photos of Grace in Darren's car. A photo of her sitting amid a pile of cables from some computing project he'd clearly botched. Then one with her grinning happily at the filthy bandage around the top of her head. She'd even looked happy then, after the accident. Daddy's tough little girl. Darren hadn't been so happy. Holly had been positively livid.

That was the last time Holly had felt so afraid, she realised. Not just for Grace's safety, but for her own. She had known, when Darren had told her their daughter was hurt, that his attention had been divided. He had somehow let it happen. He could not be trusted to be left alone with her.

Holly looked at the injury in the photo and Grace's unflappable spirit, and realised that she didn't know the truth of what had happened that day. Darren said she had fallen off a stool. From what Holly had seen the night before, though, anything was possible. Had she been trampled by a riderless horse? Slipped on poisonous goo? What?

Holly slammed the photo album and huffed.

There *was* something she could do. She had always been vigilant, and kept careful note of the new numbers in Darren's phone. She said it was in case of an emergency; there was no telling exactly who she might need to call, if something terrible should happen. But there were lots of types of emergencies, and that included the sort that required her to keep track of strange ladies Barton be in touch with.

It was a line to cross, though. He had gone out with a plan, surely. He might come back, before she opened this particular Pandora's box.

Taking a rueful glance at the clock, gone 11am, she poured a glass of red wine to help make the decision. People were out of church by now, and *they* must have had a drink, so screw it. After the first few sips, she was already confident in moving forward.

She scrolled through to the number she had resisted calling for years. She had contemplated deleting it so many times, but she'd kept it for the extra special days when she thought nothing would cheer her up more than shouting at someone who truly deserved it. Now, though, she hoped that the lady on the other end of the line might be able to help her. The one whose name she had cursed like a voodoo doll. She dialled Dr Mandy Rimes' number.

A mousey-voiced woman answered. "Mrs Barton. How can I help you?"

Holly paused a beat. She'd expected at least some surprise. "Have you seen my husband?"

A pause. "No." Rimes answered too carefully. She clearly wasn't used to lying.

"Is he there now?" Holly demanded, firmly.

"He is not."

"Then where is he?"

"I don't know. He's trying to save your daughter."

Holly froze. So it was real, then. The doctor knew about the threat. Darren was out there fighting. Something, somehow. Holly squeezed her eyes closed. "Tell me you know something. Tell me there's a solution."

Rimes paused again. "Your husband is possibly the strongest man I know. If anyone can get your daughter back, he can."

Holly caught the trailing off of the final word, and prompted, "But . . ."

"Strength alone is rarely enough."

7

Pax sat on the upper floor of a minimalist café with cheap plastic seats and coffees the price of a meal. No wonder it was empty. Her back shielded her from the room so Letty could sit on the table in front of her, unseen. The wide window had a good view of the street, opposite Riley's Bettor Off, from the junction to the right to the Tube station to the left. The pair watched pedestrians as Letty mused over locations they could go to, spread across the city.

"There's a water tower near the river," she said. "Good place to hide a human. But you'd have to get them up the ladder." The fairy muttered something else, dismissing the idea.

"You honestly think they'd try and take Barton?"

"Try and fail, probably. Yeah. But it's gotta be somewhere they could hide him."

Pax inhaled deeply over her coffee. Alcohol would've been better, but it'd do. She took another bite of croissant as Letty mumbled random curses to herself. Pax broke a bit of pastry off and put it down next to her, saying, "You eat pastry?"

Letty gave the croissant a glance, then twisted to look up at Pax, ready to come out with another insult. She resisted, though. She tore off a flake and took a bite. Chewing with her mouth open, she said, "Better than nothing."

"You're welcome," Pax said. Watching a local walk by, she tried to lighten the fairy's mood. "Were you guys out here enjoying the company of high society? I made a grand playing a game run by a dentist out here once. He told me his shirt was worth more than the pot on the table. I won it off him. The shirt off his back."

Letty gave Pax a look like she wasn't sure why she was being told this. She swallowed another mouthful of croissant and asked, "Was it?"

"Huh?"

"Worth more than the pot?"

"No idea," Pax shrugged. "Even if it was, who was I gonna sell it to? I gave it to Bees as a thank you for getting me in on another game. Never saw him wear it."

"Bees," Letty echoed thoughtfully. She looked back out the window. "Yeah, we didn't camp out here by chance. We took these pricks for everything they were worth."

"How?"

"Every way you can think of. It's a whole neighbourhood full of marks."

Pax smiled at the thought of these violent fairies somehow mugging the oblivious rich fools. "My mum, she used to send me property suggestions for out here. *If you've got to live in that god-awful city, you could at least move to a nice area.* My dad told her to stop encouraging me, though."

"Your dad. Was he a bit of a prick?"

"Still is."

"Wears a suit and has a number-plate with something vaguely close to his initials?"

Pax laughed. "That's about right."

"Dumb fucking humans."

"Yeah?" Pax shifted over Letty, getting more comfortable. "Your parents were perfect? Assuming you're not hatched from eggs or something?"

"Ha ha," Letty replied dryly. "My dad was a lunatic. He got in fights with literally every person he spoke to, like other people being alive just pissed him off." She trailed off into the memory, her voice almost fond. Pax smiled at the fairy again.

"I'm Pax, by the way. Since you never asked. Pax Kuranes."

"Jesus," Letty laughed. "Your dad didn't give you a chance, huh?"

"It comes from the Roman goddess of peace."

"Except that's not where *you* got it from. It's not enough of a prick move for your dad."

Pax raised her eyebrows. "You're good, you know? No, he took it from his university motto. *Pax et Lux.* You know the worst part? They weren't even the first to use it. They copied it from a research centre in America."

Letty laughed harder, coughing out some croissant. "Classic. All right. Let's do this. I'm Letty." She held up her hand and Pax stared for a second. Minuscule as it was, the gesture was important – she took the tiny hand between her thumb and forefinger, as gently as possible, to shake it. Letty seemed satisfied, twisting away. "That doesn't make us mates, though. You know, with the whole eating and kidnapping shit."

"I'd call it rescuing," Pax said. "And don't knock it yet. In other circumstances, I think we'd get along."

"In other circumstances?" Letty straightened her face, giving Pax a mock scolding look. "In other circumstances, I'd have taken you for everything you were worth."

"Sure," Pax said.

Letty flapped a dismissive hand at her, turning back to the window. She paused, though, a thought hitting her. "The research centre. That's a possibility."

"What?"

"For my boys. We've got a big room there. A good place for dealing with humans. But we haven't used it for ages because . . ." Letty gave Pax a serious look. ". . . it's not far from the FTC. In the circumstances, and being a dumb bunch of fucks, the boys might think that's a good thing."

"Near the Fae city, whose location is a fiercely protected secret?"

"Yeah, there."

"The sort of place the Fae might consider shooting a person for getting too close to?"

Letty nodded.

Pax was about to suggest trying the water tower first when a movement below caught her attention. She hunched down suddenly, slamming her hand down in front of Letty to create a barrier before the window. Letty shot to her feet, shouting, "Are you fucking –"

"Quiet!" Pax hissed. "They've seen me."

Casaria disliked West Farling. It was full of people who had graduated from the bohemian seeds of Ten Gardens into thriving better-than-thou wretches, looming over their inferiors with roots dug deep into the city. In the shiny SUVs and cashmere-scarved dog-walkers of West Farling, Casaria saw people immune to speeding tickets, who walked away from charges of sexual assault by virtue of importance.

Sam Ward lived somewhere in the neighbourhood. When he'd dropped her off after work one night, he'd asked why she didn't live in Central, like him, in the action. She'd given him a pitying look, and hadn't even bothered to answer.

That said it all, didn't it?

Casaria wished he could fight these people, knuckle-to-knuckle out on the street. But there were cameras on every street corner and Neighbourhood Watch everywhere. He had devised a thousand plans passing through here, from a staged road rage assault to a simple balaclava mugging, but there were always flaws. The best he could do, instead, was to make sure any assignments he had in West Farling were taken slowly, to maximise the opportunity for the side effects of the Sunken City to deliver some damage to the area. With the help of an able partner, he mused, maybe he could come up with a better plan. Pax was bound to hate these people as much as he did; they clearly represented everything she opposed. But then, she was hardly full of enthusiasm for continuing their training.

He put it out of his mind as he swung the car onto a high street's overly high curb, across double-yellow lines. There were enough people here that if there was trouble with the Fae, he might be able to draw a few bystanders into the fray. Discretion was the Ministry's principal watchword, but if it was a matter of national security, it might be possible that someone would get shot, or at least punched, for being in the wrong place at the right time.

He was smiling at the fantasy as he got out and surveyed the betting shop, not listening to Landon's complaints about the antagonistic parking job. Rufaizu had given Casaria an accurate address, as far as the shop name and street went, and there was the Underground station he'd indicated in the childish map he'd scrawled. The boy hadn't taken much persuading. Maybe it was an old Fae hangout and he thought it wouldn't do any harm. It was a start, though.

Landon gave up huffing and ambled away to check the area.

"Mr Casaria!" Gumg shouted over the roof of the car.

Casaria turned to him with a severe look.

"I asked if I should check over there." He was pointing across the road, to a hair salon, a café and a clothes shop that looked like an art gallery.

"Considering the boy gave me the exact address of this betting shop," Casaria said, "what would you hope to achieve by volunteering to search a different location?"

Gumg shrank in shame, but Casaria froze, spotting a flash of movement in the window above the café. Gumg and Landon followed his gaze. Too late to duck out of view, Pax merely stared back.

Pax tucked Letty into her inside coat pocket and hurried down the stairs to find Casaria and his two goons in the door. Casaria stopped rigidly, the leather jacket and tatty suit pair behind him forming an impassable wall. The clerk behind the counter opened his mouth to welcome the men but said nothing as the strangeness of the scene grabbed him.

"It's more than a little worrying to find you here, Pax," Casaria said.

"You've got to be kidding," Pax started indignantly. Her instincts took over. "You came looking for me after what I said? Seriously?" She pulled towards him, fists clenched, every bit the victim of a stalker. "I told you to leave me alone. How'd you find me? Have you been tracking my phone?"

"Please, Pax," Casaria answered. "They might buy it, but I'm no idiot. Meeting a friend, were you?"

"You need to step the fuck back." Pax raised her voice. "And what's this?" She gestured to the two men, aware of the counter clerk watching them. "Backup, in case I didn't want to come with you?"

"Excuse me…" The clerk tried to intervene, his voice cracking at a high pitch, as though he'd chosen that moment to hit puberty.

Casaria glanced at him, affecting a forced smile. "She's unstable. We'll take care of this."

"What is this, Casaria?" said the bigger man, in the threadbare suit. "Who is she?"

"Apparently she's our ticket to the Fae."

"Am I shit," Pax snarled. She took a step towards them, making for the door. "You need to leave me alone." The two men instinctively stepped aside, but Casaria stood his ground, and moved to grab her shoulder. She jumped back, raising a fist. "Don't touch me, you prick!"

"Where's this friend of yours?" Casaria said confidently. "Too small for us to see?"

Pax kept her fist raised.

"Landon," Casaria said. "Got your faeometer on you?"

"Over there." Pax pointed past Casaria's shoulder.

"Huh?"

"My friend. *He* is over there. In the betting shop."

The others followed her gesture, but Casaria stayed fixed on Pax. "I thought you'd be better at bluffing, given your –"

"Tran!" Pax shouted, waving. Casaria turned, spotting the man leaving the shop on the other side of the road. Tran waved heartily back as he ventured into the street, his golden hair flopping about his face. With Casaria momentarily dumbstruck, Pax pushed past and ran out.

"You're still here," Tran said merrily, approaching her.

"Yeah," Pax said. "Ran into some acquaintances." She lowered her voice. "Not exactly welcome." Tran frowned slightly.

Casaria and the other two edged out onto the pavement behind her, Landon rummaging in his pockets. Casaria was sizing the man up. "Good friend of Pax's, are you?"

"Sure." Tran grinned, showing his bleached teeth. "And you are . . . ?"

"I really do need to go." Pax smiled sweetly at him, the sort of smile that crossed her face only when she was working. "Send me that address and I'll see you later."

"Definitely, most definitely. You run along."

"You start to get the idea," Landon said in a disgruntled tone, shuffling around the group, "that this is why you needed help, Casaria."

Casaria looked from his colleague back to Pax, his eyes saying he hated every inch of human fibre that surrounded him. "Pax, you can't just –"

"Leave me the hell alone, all right?" Pax snapped, and moved to leave. The moment Casaria took a step after her, Tran stepped in the way and placed a hand on his chest. Pax kept going, giving them a backwards glance to make sure this played out.

"There a problem, pal?" Tran asked. He was taller than Casaria by a head, wider by a shoulder, and open to dealing with troublesome squirts. Casaria was grinning, though, like he welcomed the challenge.

"It doesn't concern you."

"Leave them alone, for Christ's sake," Landon said, starting to cross the road. He had a tracking device out, like Casaria's from the day before, and he was shaking it to get it to work.

Pax continued, heading for the Underground station. She heard Casaria move, and Tran moving in step with him. The guy in leathers suggested, in a nasal tone, "Maybe we should get back to it, huh?"

The tracking device beeped.

Pax stopped in the middle of the road, everyone going quiet behind her.

It beeped again.

Pax didn't look back. They'd be exchanging concerned looks. It beeped again and she took a step away. Careful. Then another. A gap in the beeps this time. Slower.

"I knew it," Casaria said quietly. "She has it on her."

Pax ran.

"Stop her!"

Hearing the footfalls of Landon close behind her, she flung a fist back without looking and connected with his face. He stumbled and grunted a curse as she broke away. Pounding over the pavement towards the Underground, she heard the leather jacket shout, "I got her!" She threw a quick look back and ducked as she saw the gun, the man's legs spread ready to shoot. Someone screamed. Casaria bowled into him from the side, throwing his aim off. The shot went high and wide, the noise sending bystanders diving for cover. Pax watched in shock as Casaria chopped the leather jacket's neck. The man fell down in splutters.

Pax was all but at the Underground station now. Landon was steadying himself in the middle of the road, clutching a bloody nose, any semblance of giving chase gone, and Tran was next to Casaria, startled still. Casaria gave Tran a sideways look, then his eyes rested on her again. He raised a pointing finger. "Pax! Stop!"

"No, you stop!" Tran shouted stupidly, leaping at him. Casaria ducked the hulking man's grasp and swung a punch into his temple. The blow knocked Tran onto his delicately chiselled teeth. Pax winced as he rocked back onto his knees, upright just in time for Casaria to catch him with a punch square to the other temple. This one toppled him.

Pax bolted, all but diving down the Underground steps. She shoved through a gathering of people hiding from the sound of the gunshot. She vaulted the barriers and glanced back as she sprinted onto the platform. A train was rolling into the station, and Casaria hadn't caught up.

8

Pax struggled to breathe as the train moved, sinking deep into the seat and closing her eyes as she panted. Sweat dripped down the back of her neck. No chance of showering that off any time soon. Letty shifted in her pocket, and Pax quickly checked for fellow passengers: an older couple stared unashamedly her way; a young man was listening to a stereo a few seats down; a man in a shirt was checking out a girl standing further down the aisle, over his magazine. Pax opened her coat and whispered, "Not here . . . too many people."

Letty shoved the pocket opening outwards slightly so she could see up, her face stern. "Get off this fucking train," she hissed. "Right now."

Pax covered her mouth and ducked. "They'll catch up at the next station."

"You brought a Fae underground, we've got bigger problems than those arseholes!"

Pax pulled her coat closed again, putting a hand to her chest to hold Letty closer to her, muffling her protests. She looked up and around. The next stop was a five-minute drive for the others, at most. How dangerous could it be to keep going? As she thought it, the train slowed. The lights dimmed, then came back brighter. They dimmed again, almost to darkness, as the train screeched to a halt.

The other passengers looked around, more curious than concerned. The older couple turned their attention away as the man mumbled about forgetting to water a hydrangea.

Pax stood and walked down the carriage, brushing past magazine man and moving close to the door. Looking back, she saw the other passengers starting to yawn. The lights came back up, a little brighter, and there was a spark of blue light somewhere outside. The sort that railways randomly throw out, she told herself. She flinched as part of Letty's tiny form jabbed at her through the pocket, punching or kicking at her.

Blue light flickered at the end of the train carriage with a cackle of sparks. Pax jumped back, remembering the thing that had chased her and Casaria, earning a disapproving look from the magazine man. The other passengers had slumped, eyelids drooping. The young man with the stereo rolled his head back against the seat. The lights went out.

"Oh bollocks," Pax uttered.

"Happens all the time," the magazine man said. Was that supposed to be comforting or scolding? The lights came back up as she glared at him; he caught her eye and looked away.

The train started moving as the blue lights flickered around it again. It continued rattling along the tracks, too slow for Pax's tastes. It rolled into the next station, the platform opening up in light. The moment the doors opened, Pax charged out, glancing back only briefly to see the tunnel flickering as though lit by vast blue candlelight. No one else noticed or cared.

She sprinted out of the station, up the stairs, through the barriers and out onto the street, a carbon copy of the place she'd left behind. Checking for Casaria's car, Pax turned away from the road to run down a side street. She went on for two more blocks before turning again, into an alley that cut towards an open green area, then she finally stopped.

She leant forward, gagging on her own saliva, put her hands on her knees and cursed. As she hung in exhausted relief, the fairy in her pocket started shoving at her again. Pax half walked, half swayed to a bench and slumped down. There was no one else in the park, but Pax wasn't sure she cared anyway. She lifted Letty out of her pocket and opened her hand in front of her face. Letty clambered to her feet and steadied herself in the middle of Pax's palm. Her fists were balled tight and her eyes bulged with anger.

"Don't you ever do something like that again," the fairy said.

Pax spat out some phlegm. "What? Save you from those nutters?"

"What'd I tell you about the Sunken City? We go down there, the creatures come at us in an instant. The berserker could've travelled the full length of Ordshaw to get to us just there."

"It didn't though, did it," Pax said. Letty folded her arms. "Get us, I mean."

"They knew where we were," Letty huffed.

"But they weren't expecting us," Pax noted, before the fairy could blame her.

Letty nodded. "Rufaizu gave the place up. Guess I should've expected it, given how much of a louse his father was."

Pax took that in. At least that meant Rufaizu was okay, if he'd been able to tip off the Ministry to the Fae's location. He was alive, anyway. He was safer than her. She said, "They know where I live, too. That makes me homeless right now. Homeless and an enemy of the state. Fuck. My cash is in the apartment, what am I supposed to do?" In her frustration, she shifted on the bench and Letty had to steady herself on Pax's hand.

"Oi! Settle down!" Letty said. "You're gonna take me to my boys, that's what you're gonna do. Figure yourself out after."

"Figure myself out?" Pax gaped at her. "That's all you've got?"

"Sorry I don't have plans for hiding humans from the Ministry. In case you didn't notice, I'm out on my arse with a wing missing, which gives me bigger problems of my own."

"I'm in this mess because of you!"

"Oh please. You'd be *dead* if not for me. Here's what's gonna happen. You're gonna jump on a *bus* to the warehouse district, I'm gonna tell you where to get off, and we're gonna check the abandoned research centre building."

"And then?"

"We part ways. Most likely, you start hightailing it as far from Ordshaw as possible."

"Hightailing it?" Pax shot back. "All right. Counter-offer, we go back to mine and you sneak in to get my cash for me. Then we figure out a plan *together*."

"Not going to happen. They're looking for me the same as you."

"Except you're decidedly less conspicuous. And seeing that I'm your ride around this city, I don't see you having much choice."

Letty held her gaze, testing her, seeing how serious she was. She nodded slowly and crouched down, opening the bag that she had taken from the betting shop. As she delved in, she said, "Okay. Here's my final offer." She drew back holding a chunky metal pistol. Chunky compared to her, at least; it was the size and shape of a plug fuse. "You take me to where I've got to go and I don't scatter your brains."

Pax didn't respond at once. It was hard to feel threatened by such a diminutive figure with such an insignificant weapon, even with the strength of Letty's conviction. "You realise you're standing in my hand, right? I could squash you like a bug."

"Bet you all the cash in Ordshaw you're not quicker than a bullet."

Pax paused again. "And I'm supposed to believe that thing works?"

"You believe Apothel's dead, don't you?"

"Right." Pax tried to think quickly. "So shoot me, where does that leave you?"

"Without having to worry about loose ends, for starters." Letty toed the bag at her feet. "I got all I needed at our stop. Even if I can't fly, I've got dust, I can stay hidden. I don't *need* you, Pax. But if your life's worth something, you *can* still help me."

"Just like that?" Pax said.

"Just like that," Letty replied coldly.

So much for bonding. Pax said, "And when you get to where you're going . . ."

"I'm good for my word, same as you. You can walk. But that's where this ends. Now get moving. I'll have this on you every step of the way."

Pax took a deep breath, eyes fixed on the fairy. She said, finally, "For such a small person you're a massive bitch, you know that?"

Along the quiet journey, on more than one occasion Pax considered taking her chances. With Letty in her pocket, she could slap a hand against her and potentially incapacitate her. But all the fairy had to do was pull the trigger. And Pax also suspected that Fae people were stronger than they looked. Their small size did not necessarily make them frail; it didn't seem to have the expected effect on the volume of her voice, after all.

Having spent most of her physical energy running from Casaria, and her mental energy on fresh feelings of animosity towards her companion, the effort of sparking a new fight with Letty didn't seem worth it. A few bus rides and she would be rid of her, no more fuss. With that resolved in her head, she tried to plan her next course of action.

They would definitely be monitoring her apartment, but whatever she wanted to do she needed her money. And her passport, if it came to that. Why couldn't they be like all the other government agencies she knew of – slow and ineffective? The government agents she crossed had to be the ones who carried guns and shot people to solve problems. Whatever happened to receiving a strongly worded letter in the post ten weeks after an infraction?

Her mind was wandering. She looked out the window and saw that they were passing through Ten Gardens. It wouldn't be far from here.

The most sensible option was her original plan, which she resented Letty for not going along with. If an inconspicuous patsy could get into her apartment for her, she could avoid the Ministry and get away safely. And go where? Back to London? Abroad? Home for a thick slice of humble pie? She sighed. Home might not be so bad after all this. At least she'd see Albie again. He'd appreciate what she'd been through. He might even believe it.

Passing the ivy-dotted facades of renovated townhouses, where a group of eclectic adults were making music from pots, pans and a guitar, Pax swallowed those thoughts. She didn't want to leave Ordshaw. It had been her home for long enough that she felt she owned a piece of the city. It was hers. From the abandoned industrial behemoths to the allotment shacks, part of it belonged to her, and part of her belonged to it. It didn't matter that she woke as the rest of the city slept, or that she followed her own path while they slaved within the system, she was still a part of it all, in her own way. She wanted to stay a part of it. And she wanted to protect it, if that's what it came to. The words slipped out of her mouth: "I don't want to leave."

She felt Letty shift in her pocket, but the fairy said nothing.

The bus passed a street vendor trying to convince a smartly dressed couple to buy a ceramic pig. They didn't look interested, but he was giving it everything he had, hands waving and mouth flapping.

There was another option. The money in her apartment wouldn't get her far, but the device that the Ministry and the Fae were willing to kill for might.

Pax took her phone from her pocket. A present from Bees' friend, Howling Jowls Jones, who'd insisted it was untraceable. That had been important to her once, probably for imaginary reasons; it was a godsend now. It was unregistered, contained none of her personal details and used a series of masking programs to access calls and the internet. She brought up Bees' number and hesitated before ringing.

Was it safe?

"Letty?" she said quietly, not caring that there was a handful of other passengers who might or might not be able to hear. It would look like she was making a call, and given the fairy's small voice, it would sound like her responses came from the phone. Letty didn't answer. "Letty? It's okay to talk."

"Is it fuck."

"I'm on my phone."

"They can trace that shit, you idiot."

"That's my question. How did you get my phone number?" Silence from the pocket. Pax kept staring at the phone. "It's not registered."

"We followed you home. After that prick took Rufaizu. Then we used a scanner on your building. Yours was the third number we tried."

Pax imagined the fairies threatening two strangers before getting to her. She said, "A scanner gave you my number?"

"Quick tip," Letty said. "Assume, at all times, that Fae technology is at least a few years ahead of yours. We know everything you've got, we deconstruct that crap and make use of it when we need to. Only we've got our own stuff, too. So, yeah, we did that. With a cheap bit of kit."

"There's a lot we could do, working together . . ."

"No. There's a lot we could teach you. What would *you* offer *us*? Ignorance and idiocy?"

Pax went quiet again. They were back to this. She kept staring at the phone.

It could wait.

They alighted near an anonymous series of buildings that could once have housed entire businesses, with a look from the driver that said no one ever got off here. The surrounding streets appeared to have lost their names, and many of the buildings were without roofs. Pax waited until the bus was out of sight, then crouched and took Letty out of her pocket. She held her up and asked, "This it?"

"Over there." Letty pointed. "The hexagonal building."

Pax walked towards it, taking in the strange complex. The paint was cracked around it, some of the windows were missing, and someone had scrawled graffiti on another wall. *COCKS*. A faded sign on a wall read *Innovation Centre*.

"Holds a certain subtle irony, doesn't it?" Pax commented. Letty didn't answer.

The glass entrance door was open, the building inside abandoned. Pax followed Letty's instructions through a network of halls to a corridor that left the offices behind. Past a few more doors, Pax came to a metal bulkhead with a five-inch metal contraption over its lock, blinking with a red light. Some kind of electronic lock.

"Fucking knew it," Letty commented as Pax came to a stop.

Holding the fairy in her fist, as Letty took in the door, Pax considered her options again. The gun was still there, vaguely pointing in her direction, but Letty was distracted. A quick squeeze might –

Letty's gun went off. Pax flinched, tightening her grip, and Letty spun to her. "Watch it, fuckwit!"

Pax loosened her grip as Letty shoved against her fingers. The fairy gave her a mean look, gun raised, and Pax took a moment to figure out what had happened. Letty had shot the lock. The red light was now dead and the metal box gently smoking.

"Open her up," the fairy instructed.

"Yes, master." Pax rolled her eyes. She pulled the door towards them and looked in. Then she froze. "You've got to be kidding."

"Fuck," Letty snarled. "Worse than I thought. Useless fucking morons."

They both stared in silence as Grace Barton kicked away into a corner, too scared at their entrance to say anything. She had one arm raised defensively, covering her face.

"Close the door," Letty hissed. "Close it now."

"Are you serious – we can't – "

"Close the fucking door!" Letty snapped, rattling her gun. Pax did as she was told, not arguing now she'd seen what the pistol was capable of. Grace found her voice as the door was sealed. "No, don't leave me in here!" It was a dry, desperate plea, accompanied by the scuffling of her feet. She was cut off by the door thunking into place.

"Right, to the FTC, then," Letty said.

"Your men are clearly –"

"They're not here. They would've made it known if they were. Back the way we came."

"We can't just leave her here."

"Why the hell not?"

Pax raised Letty to her face. "Because I'm not a monster!"

"Look like one to me." The pistol was aimed right between her eyes.

"You're not either, I don't believe that," Pax said, undeterred. "You never would have talked to Apothel if you were. Never would've shared a thing with him if you didn't think there was some hope in it. And you wouldn't have spent all these years trying to get that Dispenser back if all you cared about was yourself. You never would've talked to *me*."

"Bullshit, you don't know me. And this is *not* a discussion. You oughta be thankful I don't involve you in this, because in all likelihood that girl's gotta go now."

"I'm not letting that happen."

"Well *I* am, so get the hell out of here."

Pax flexed her fingers on the fairy. Letty's eyes dared her to make a move, the pistol unwavering.

"This doesn't have to end badly for you, Pax," Letty told her. "Just walk away. I can have my people take back the Dispenser before you get home, and you can forget any of this ever happened. That's what you wanted from the start, isn't it?"

Pax growled, finding words failed her. She couldn't argue with the pistol. She turned from the metal door, striding back the way they'd come. Letty told her to walk carefully, but Pax only moved more quickly through the building, up the road and along the block. Away from the offices and on towards the empty warehouses. She came to a half-crumbled wall and thrust Letty down onto it, the fairy stumbling to regain her balance on a dislodged brick. Letty spun back and aimed her gun at Pax, but Pax had already stepped away, hands on her hips. "This far enough for you?"

Letty checked her surroundings. She eyed Pax, but didn't complain. "I suggest you walk that way. Steer well clear of where I'm going. Don't even look my way. Twenty minutes or so you'll hit the edge of Ten Gardens."

Pax followed her gesture. It all looked the same, brick walls after brick walls. She said, "Do what the hell you want, I'm not leaving that girl behind."

"Well. Good luck with surviving the day."

"And you know what, I would've taken you back here. Whatever else we did, I was gonna keep my word. You didn't have to pull a gun on me."

This gave Letty the briefest pause. "Yeah, well, you're still a fucking human."

Pax shoved her hands deep in her pockets and started back towards the Innovation Centre, Letty's directions be damned.

"Hey!"

Pax turned, the tiny person barely visible. "What?" Letty hesitated, couldn't bring herself to say what was on her mind. Pax huffed. "Whatever. Have a nice life."

She kept walking, not looking back this time. She took out her phone and dialled Bees. He answered on the second ring. "So they didn't disappear you."

"Not yet," Pax said. "But they tried. I need some help."

"Thought you'd never ask," Bees answered brightly.

9

Barton pulled his car to a stop at the edge of the warehouse district, swaying in his seat like a drunk. Rimes' vague hunch to come here was hardly the most inspiring start to a city-wide search, but her hunches tended to be better than most. If the Fae city was anywhere in the sprawl of Ordshaw, it made sense that they'd use the abandoned warehouses. And maybe the Blue Angel hadn't been entirely wrong before, maybe there'd just been a mix-up.

He stared at the decayed industrial buildings. Big enough to hide whole streets, tall enough to build rockets in. Wonders of human engineering rendered useless, now that born labourers like him spent their days pining over numbers and computer servers. If he'd had a life in the factories, however hard it might've been, maybe it would've satisfied that part of him that always wanted to get out and do something physical. He reflected only as long as it took to recover enough energy to get out of the vehicle. Light-headed, he almost sat straight back down.

Barton took out the device Rimes had given him: a scanner with an archaic black and green display and two pointed antennas. He was sure she'd designed it for kitsch value as much as practicality, such was her way. He switched it on and held it high. It made a slight buzzing noise, hard at work, but that was it. No change on the display, no sign of life.

He walked away from the car, turning on the spot to scan the area. He moved in and out of a few derelict buildings. Finally, returning to his car, he took out his phone and cringed at the number of missed calls it showed. They weren't all from Holly, but at this point he couldn't see Pax being anything better than a distraction. He brought up Rimes' number. She answered straight away.

"It's not doing anything," he said.

"No beeps?"

"No."

"No blinking light?"

"Nothing."

"Then they're not there."

Barton looked at the canister of glo on the passenger seat. "Any chance it just doesn't work?"

"It should work. In theory."

"You ever actually tested it?"

"The Ministry wouldn't allow it. They hold the Fae's privacy in high regard, Darren. I've been trying to tell you – it's complicated. There have been discussions. Agreements. Diplomacy."

"Give it a rest," Barton told her roughly. "My daughter's out here somewhere."

"I don't know what to suggest."

Silence as Rimes waited for Barton to come to a decision. He studied the green liquid in the canister. Its thick warmth would comfort his throat. His angry thoughts would dissolve in the liquid. It had all happened too fast in the tunnel. He didn't get to enjoy it. "If they're nearby, I can pick up the trail."

"Darren? If you mean glo, that's not a good idea. The medicine I gave you —"

"Mandy. I know what I'm doing."

The doctor hesitated. "Of course."

A few moments later, Barton had his phone in one hand and the glo in the other, as he toyed with the idea of taking the drink. He dreaded pressing Call just as much. The nastiest creatures of the underworld couldn't make him shake like this. He gritted his teeth and did it.

The phone rang. A painful series of beeps with no answer. He closed his eyes and realised the one thing worse than having to explain himself was the thought that she might not answer. Holly's voice interrupted his fears. "Darren?"

"Holly," he said, voice hoarse.

"My *God* Darren, you bastard, you tell me you're safe. Tell me Grace is safe."

"I'm fine," Barton lied. "And I'm close to her. But there's something I have to do."

"Where have you been?" Holly's voice rose. "You tell me where on earth you've been!"

"There was another note. I did what they said, now I'm following them."

"Call the police! Get someone else involved! Are you out of your goddamned mind?"

"There's no one else who can do what I need to," Barton told her.

"Is there hell! This is our daughter —"

"I need to go . . . back down the hole. I wanted to talk to you. Wanted to let you know. I've hidden it all for too long. And this time . . ."

"Darren . . ." Holly's anger was subsiding, replaced by fear.

"Holly," Barton said, "it'll be okay. This is just something I need to do."

"Where are you? Let me come and help. Let me do something."

"The best thing you can do" – he took a breath – "is stay safe. Don't worry. Don't . . ."

He trailed off, looking into the drink. Holly waited only a moment before starting up again. "Darren Barton, you listen to me. I am not impressed. I am not happy at all. You tell me where you are this instant, and I will come and I will —"

"I love you, Holly," he said, quietly. The quiet *I love you* of a man who was afraid he might not get to say it again. Holly's voice quivered in reply.

"I love you too, Darren," she said. "You come back to me. You bring our daughter back, with you, or I'll never forgive you, you hear me?"

"I hear you," he said, then hung up.

He lifted the canister and took a hearty swig. This sweet, vile drink had taken him many places in the past. It was time it took him to the one that had got his friend killed.

10

Pax was relieved to find Grace where she had left her. The poor girl hadn't even tried the door since they'd gone. Checking the rafters to make sure there was no one else around, as though she could even see the tiny people, Pax raced to Grace's side. She put an arm around her and Grace flinched away. "Please don't hurt me please don't hurt me!"

"Everything's going to be okay," Pax whispered, more to herself than Grace.

Hearing her voice, Grace lowered her arms and looked into Pax's face. She was stuck halfway between relief and renewed fear. "You? Did you . . . are you . . .?"

"Oh God, no!" Pax waved a hand towards the door. "I'm not a part of this. I'm getting you out of here. Taking you home."

Grace nodded quickly, and Pax helped her up. Grace asked, "Is my dad here?"

"I've got no idea where your dad is," Pax said, taking stock of the girl. Her bare legs were turning blue. She'd suffered the night in this place. "It's okay. I know someone else who can help us."

The steel door slid open a few inches with a piercing screech. Bees poked his head out and stared at Pax as though her presence was a complete surprise. Then he saw Grace and his eyes relaxed. He was wearing a white apron and face mask, sprayed up and down by barely dried blood. His neutral voice betrayed nothing as he said, "It's cold, you shouldn't be out dressed like that."

Grace merely lowered her gaze, meekly, as Pax led her into the building. Bees closed the door behind them.

"Got any food?" Pax asked, rubbing her hands together.

"Yeah." Bees pointed. "Got a blanket in the office too, for the little one. Do us a favour and don't look into the main room. Save you asking questions and save me giving answers." He regarded Grace. "You sure she should be here?"

"No choice right now, no time to piss about," Pax said, and Bees nodded. That was that. He walked ahead down the corridor, and Grace gave Pax a nervous look. A mechanical drill, or a saw, or something, whirred somewhere in the building. Pax fought the urge to turn in the direction of the sound, to where the building opened up to some kind of factory floor. In her line of work, avoiding seeing certain things might help you live longer. A tip, she realised, which she should have given herself a few days ago.

Bees led them up some stairs and into an office. After Pax and Grace entered, he closed the door and went to the fridge. He gestured to a dusty couch, and they planted themselves down as he took out a tray of sandwiches: a variety of flavoured triangles, such as might be found at an academic conference. He tossed the tray onto the coffee table, then threw a heavy blanket to Grace and took out a can of beer. Pax turned down a beer herself, but started shovelling small sandwiches into her mouth. Grace was more hesitant, but once she got her first bite she quickly overtook Pax, famished.

Bees watched the pair patiently.

"I think my apartment's burnt," Pax started explaining, finishing a messy mouthful. "The Ministry guys chased me out of West Farling, and they know where I live. But I need to get something out of there. Fast."

"Who's the girl?" Bees nodded to Grace. Grace paused mid-bite, frightened.

"Separate problem," Pax said. "Kind of. I'm taking her home."

"What happened?"

"Basically…" Pax sat back. "I saw too much."

"Think they're gonna kill you?" Bees asked, as though asking about the weather.

"I think they'd like to question and torture me first." Pax saw Grace hadn't moved, shocked still. Bees nodded, though, like that was a good thing. "I've got nowhere else to go, Bees."

"It's just the MEE. We can put feelers, see what it'd take to get them off your back."

Pax stared at him for a moment. Of course, Bees would come to her rescue, digging in the hooks of debts. She took another sandwich while she chewed the prospect over. He looked like he could wait a decade for an answer. Grace still hadn't moved.

"I've got no intention of owing you," Pax said. "Or your boss."

"Didn't think you would," Bees said. "There's options, though. You want money, we could stake you for a cut, no debt involved. I can vouch for you. But you're not *that* good, so you're not going to find the terms favourable."

"It's not money I want right now."

"Indeed. Option two would be more interesting to both of us." Bees took a deliberate sip of beer. The drill in the factory below got louder, then skipped a beat, followed by a loud curse. He ignored it. "I value information. As does my boss and as, I'm sure, do you. You've got information people might kill you for. See to sharing that and we can make other arrangements."

"They'd come after you, too," Pax replied.

"I can handle myself," Bees said, and she didn't doubt it.

"Right." Pax took another moment. Faced with the prospect of sharing the secrets of the Sunken City, she realised again how important that information was. She studied the office, appreciating exactly where they had ended up. The desk was thick with dust, likely never used for paperwork. The real work was done below. Work involving aprons and masks and blood. Bees and his associates were the least responsible people she could involve in this. But she needed help.

She cursed Letty for abandoning her. Just when it seemed like she had an ally. However vicious the little woman was, Pax felt there was something good in her.

Or at least some affinity with hers. But she was gone now. And this was her backup option. The fruition of friendlessness.

If she could keep Bees just far enough from the truth, she could work it out. Letty and the Fae couldn't be trusted to do anything good; even if they put an end to the minotaur, which she doubted the would, they weren't saving Rufaizu. They weren't looking out for Ordshaw. The sole means to turn the whole situation around sat in Pax's apartment, in her cupboard. She frowned, uncomfortably acknowledging these weren't thoughts that would get her free and clear.

"I trust you, Pax," Bees said, seeming to respond to her uncertain face. "Enough that I'd tell you what's going on downstairs and know that information would be safe. You can trust me just the same. You want us to help you, we need to know what we're dealing with."

Pax bit her lip. There'd be no going back from it.

There was a shout below. A door slammed and heavy footfalls rang through the building. Bees' companion burst into the office, announcing his presence loudly. "Snapped the bloody saw head. That's two this morning. This guy must've –"

Howling Jowls Jones was halfway across the office, headed straight for the fridge, before he noticed Pax and Grace. He paused as Pax gave him a light, nervous wave. Dressed in overalls like Bees, he also wore plastic gloves and a hairnet. There was little white showing around his bloodstains, though his cheekbones were sharp and high enough that Pax could make out his smile behind the mask.

"Good to see you, Pax – to what do we owe this pleasure? And who's this young dear?"

"She's in trouble with the MEE," Bees explained.

"The MEE?" Howling Jowls let out his trademark whoop; it was a wolfish sound that Pax suspected he practised. He turned to the fridge to get a beer, pulling his mask down. "So that's why Bees has been waxing lyrical about them. Chewing my ear off about this theory and that theory – why there's no methane in the sewer system, why the skyscrapers in the CC1 postcode have green antenna lights, cover-ups and conspiracy on a national level. Ain't that right? I've heard it all and it all sounds like shit, but here you are." He opened the can. "It's you that's been digging up dirt about them."

"Something like that," Pax said.

"I was telling her," Bees said, "we might find a way to get her clear of a predicament, if she happened to let us in on the details."

"Now there's a proposition," Jones swung his beer can around. "I'd be game just to shut him up. There's no aliens in Ordshaw, are there? Or is it a water supply scandal? Give me *strength*." He spun away from Pax, letting out another whoop. He was going to keep talking, that's what these guys did. But time was an issue. "It'd be fun if I didn't already know no government ministry ever did anything more interesting than filing shifty budgets. The MEE. Give me *strength*."

"They're hiding a secret network of tunnels." Pax rushed it out. Jones froze with his eyes and mouth equally wide open.

Bees placed his beer can aside. "What kind of tunnels?"

"Ones that run all over the city. They're extremely dangerous."

"Dangerous structurally, or some other way?" Bees asked.

"Some other way."

Jones turned to Bees and they exchanged a look. Jones cleared his throat. "Pax, you're bright, we all know that. If you're talking about a network of tunnels that might get us from A to B unseen, you'd be talking about something our boss would take a *real* strong interest in. You'd know that, wouldn't you, before bringing up a thing like that? You'd need to be thinking that this is something you *really* want to share."

"I think it could get you in a lot of trouble," Pax said, "but if you can help me out, you're welcome to the problem."

"You got a map?" Bees asked.

Pax shook her head. "I know where a couple of entrances are."

"Monitored by the MEE?"

"Yeah," Pax said. "They're not so interested in the tunnels as in what's down there."

Jones let out a loud, heartfelt laugh. "Stop being dramatic. What's down there?"

"That's as much as I'll give you right now. Here's the cut." Pax stood up, to firm her point. "There's stuff I need from my apartment and I don't feel safe going back there. I need it yesterday, because there's other people after it. Not the Ministry – they might be watching the place, but they don't know what's there. You help me and I'll tell you where to find an entrance to these tunnels. I'll give you some idea of what's down there, but you need to see it for yourself. And I want to be 100%, before we start this, in saying I think you should *not* go down there. Got it?"

"All right," Bees replied carefully. "What's this stuff you need?"

As they walked away from their factory, Pax let out a breath of relief, freed from the stress of being in the same room as the two bloodied men. Grace asked, quietly, "Who were they?"

"Just friends."

Pax didn't like the answer herself. Too many of her suspicions about them were being confirmed, a step beyond imagining she lived in a dangerous world to knowing it for sure. Contrary to what they had said, she did not know exactly why their boss would be interested in the tunnels, but the best case scenario involved contraband. The very best case. She might have just contributed to a criminal enterprise, but it had to be better than whatever was already down there.

"I'd really like to go home now," Grace said.

Pax gave her a smile. "That's exactly what we're doing." The teenager did not look convinced. This detour probably had her questioning whether she had even been freed. Pax's smile faded. "I'm not a part of the bad stuff. Honest. I need those guys to help me the same as I'm helping you, that's all. You'll be fine."

Grace nodded, clearly filled with doubt.

Pax sighed and kept on walking. She checked her phone and saw a missed call from an unknown number. It gave her pause. Had Letty changed her mind and wanted to get back in touch? Maybe she would help out after all, and she could call off Bees and protect the secret of the Sunken City. But the voice she heard when the voicemail clicked on was not Letty's. It was a woman who sounded equally hostile.

"This is Holly Barton. You spoke with my husband. I'd like to speak with you myself. Call me back."

Pax turned to Grace. "See. That was your mum. She's waiting for us."

11

Letty was received without the flanking honour guard that typically shielded the Fae leader; Valoria had chosen discretion above safety now, and only her bodyguard Hearlon attended their meeting. The brick-headed goon strode into the dugout room, a cavity in the concrete walls, and all but pressed into Letty in the tight space. When he moved to frisk her, she raised a warning finger.

"You fucking dare."

Every time they met, he backed down with an expression that said he'd like nothing more than to punch her face off. The feeling was mutual. Hearlon stepped aside, settling for the threat of resting his hand on the handle of a pistol, holstered at his shoulder.

Valoria squeezed into the room and looked Letty up and down. "There were reports of your death."

"Guess they exaggerated," Letty replied dryly.

"You were in a Ministry compound," Valoria continued. "You know our thoughts on Fae that leave Ministry compounds alive. My council would have you shot on sight."

"Good thing you know better, huh?" Letty replied, sarcasm dripping off the ceiling. "Guess you're just too damned curious about that Dispenser, aren't you?"

The governor kept calm, making a clear effort to tune out Letty's attitude. "Of all the Fae I know, I'd imagine you to be the least likely to be turned by the Ministry. But yet, I must ask." She didn't.

"The fuck do you think?" Letty said. "As to what they got from Rufaizu, though, I couldn't say. Your people haven't taken care of that, have they?"

"The Roma's fate is uncertain."

"I can certain it," Letty said coldly. "He's alive enough to have ratted on me."

"That's disappointing. But your team hardly helped matters."

"No? Seems to me they've made some kind of progress. Seems to me it's something we need to discuss. In pretty serious terms. Things are moving forward, Val. At long last. You know what we've uncovered, right?"

Valoria fixed her with an icy stare, designed to make Letty uncomfortable. Letty didn't get uncomfortable about people's looks. She stared right back.

"Do you expect me to be impressed?" Valoria said, each word thick with bitterness.

"Are you on the cusp of getting the Dispenser back or what?"

"No thanks to you."

"No thanks to – are you fucking serious? I'm the one that got Rufaizu onside. It was me that organised to have –"

"It was *you* who got it stolen in the first place. And from what I can gather, your men used their own initiative to get it back, not yours."

Letty could feel the colour rushing to her cheeks. "If they had followed through with my plan, you wouldn't have had this human collateral to deal with right now."

"Nevertheless, the Dispenser is all but secure. And your . . . boys' . . . security has already been negotiated. It did not involve you."

Letty's eyes bulged with hate. "You know it was my project, those are my –"

"You dealt with humans without our go-ahead, you led an attack on a Ministry compound, you got yourself injured, if not caught – there is nothing in any of this that suggests you deserve a reward, Letty. Your team performed better, and quicker, without you."

"This is bullshit and you know it."

"This was *inevitable* and you know it. Your back-street diplomacy got you nowhere and your half-measure violence threatened us all. So here you are, where you belong. Outcast."

Valoria turned on her heel, as though that was all there was to say. As she moved away, Letty surged forwards to curse and throw fists and shoot if necessary. Hearlon moved faster, though, pistol drawn and aimed at her chest. Letty stopped, but wasn't done.

"This is *bullshit*!" she repeated, louder. "You're bullshit! How are you gonna use the Dispenser without human help? You need me if you want the Citizen onside, at the very least! You can't keep forcing a brute like that!"

"It's time you left," Hearlon told her.

"You can't keep me out!" Letty roared at Valoria's retreating back. "I know how to make things work with the humans! I've got friends!"

Valoria paused. All but out of view, she turned back but kept her distance. "We don't need human friends, Letty. Why did you never understand that? Your *friends* give us all the more reason to keep you away."

"You honestly think we can reclaim the Sunken City without at least a little human help?" Letty growled, but as she said it she saw that there was no question in Valoria's eyes. Letty frowned, thinking of the dumb questions Pax had raised. Was there a chance the Fae didn't want to use the weapon? Did Apothel know something she didn't, when he stole it? "Do you even want to take it back?"

Valoria gave her a slight smile, not deigning to answer. Letty saw what it meant, with such surprise she had to look to Hearlon to share it, no one else to turn to. "You know what's going on here?"

Hearlon said nothing, trained to lack emotions.

"You never belonged here, Letty," Valoria concluded. "You never understood. Our relationships are nuanced, our place in this world layered – you cannot shoot your way through everything."

"What the *fuck* are you saying?" Letty snapped. "You've got the whole of the FTC waiting to reclaim what's ours, who gives a shit about nuance?"

"I'm being incredibly generous not punishing you for what you've already done," Valoria said, the first strains of impatience entering her tone. "Keep talking and you'll leave me no choice. Walk away, Letty. Let it go. It's probably better that our people still think you're dead."

Letty bared her teeth. "Where are my boys?"

"They won't want to see you," Hearlon answered.

"Who the fuck asked you?" Letty shouted. "Are they in the city? Are they still working? Fucking give me something! I'm out here with one goddamned wing!"

"They're putting everything you started to rest."

Letty looked from Hearlon to Valoria, neither giving anything else away. She shook her head, saying, "Out of order. You're bang out of order."

"This is the first and only lesson you need to learn, Letty," Valoria said. "They're only humans."

Letty backed off, still eyeballing them both. Without another word, she turned and ran.

Mix and Fresko were, at that moment, standing side by side in the rafters at the Innovation Centre. Both regarding the emptiness of the room. The lock had been shot by a Fae gun, but there was no sign of violence. Mix lit his cigar, speaking through the side of his mouth. "What do you make of it?"

"I don't get the why," Fresko said. "Must've been Fae, someone who knew we'd been here. Don't see what they'd gain from boosting her. Or why they'd do our job for us. Doesn't make sense. But we need to be sure, don't we?"

"How's that?" Mix took a deep puff, blew smoke in Fresko's direction.

"We go to her house and check she hasn't escaped."

"To her house," Mix repeated.

"Yeah." Fresko shouldered his rifle. "Either someone already did away with her, and we got nothing to worry about, or someone helped her out. And took her home."

"One of our own?" Mix raised an eyebrow.

"We can figure out the why of it later," Fresko said. "Right now, let's finish the job."

Mix grinned and slapped Fresko's back. "Now you're talking my language."

12

Pax and Grace had made it to a street corner in Ten Gardens by the time Holly caught up to them. Though her energy was waning, Pax wanted to keep moving as long as it took to put a distance between herself and the Fae, and the sight of clean streets and stoop flowerpots was welcome. As they waited for Holly, Grace struggled to make conversation, with meek questions about how Pax was feeling and how far they had to walk, too tired for anything else. When Holly skidded her car up next to them, Grace's energy barely came back. She mustered a smile and a hug for her fussing mother, but that was all. She crept into the back seat and all but fell asleep.

Holly stayed out of the car, halfway between scolds and blessings. "Oh thank God you're all right. You had me so worried! What were you thinking? I'm so glad you're safe!" She turned on Pax. "What happened? Where's she been?"

Pax took a moment before responding, partly from the force of this sharp woman, partly from confusion at her attire. Holly was dressed in jeans and a t-shirt with an important-looking crest and the words *Professional Wine Taster – Free Consultations Offered*. Not taking Holly for one with a sense of humour, Pax took a moment to realise that the t-shirt was a joke, by which time Holly was ranting on. "Speak, would you? You don't think I'm owed an explanation?"

During their walk, Pax had thought about what she might say or do when Holly arrived, and now it was time to put it into action. Rescuing Grace wasn't just a means to do good; it presented an opportunity. She needed somewhere to lay low while Bees did his bit, and no one was likely to go looking for her in the suburbs. She said, "I'll explain what I can, if you take me with you. I'd like to make sure Grace is okay. And . . . to see your husband."

Holly gave her an uncertain look. She quickly made the decision, though. "Get in." She rushed back to the driver's seat. Pax scanned the road, as though they might be under surveillance already, then she got into the car. Holly spun the tyres pulling out, and started throwing looks back to Grace, who was curled up like a child trying to sleep on the sofa.

"Young lady. You tell me what's going on."

"Someone with a gun," was the best Grace could offer. "A man. I never saw him."

"Where? How?" Holly asked urgently, but her questions came too quick to answer. She turned on Pax. "You know who it was?"

"Kind of," Pax said.

"Kind of? My daughter's been kidnapped and the best you can do is *kind of*? That's not good enough. We're going to the police."

"No!" Pax said firmly, imagining the police handing them straight over to the MEE. "They'll only get worse people involved. Trust me – the best thing for us right now is to get you both home."

"Are you out of your mind?" Holly thumped a hand into the steering wheel. Pax gave her a moment to calm down. Holly took a deep breath, in through the mouth and out through the nose, as though she had been trained to do it. She said, "I just think that when a teenager has been abducted by a man with a gun, the police are the logical people to get involved. Don't you?"

"I would," Pax agreed, "if it was a man that did it. They weren't men, though. Not as you understand the term."

Holly glared at Pax, doubt in her eyes. She knew there was more to this. Yet she ventured, hopefully, "Transvestites?"

Pax shook her head. "Is your husband home?"

"He went looking for Grace. You haven't seen him?"

"No. I tried to call him."

"I'm going to give him such a talking to when he gets back, don't you worry. Damn all of this." Holly frowned. "How did you find Grace?"

"It's a long story," Pax said, quietly.

"You'll tell me, though. Someone has to tell me something or I'm going to do something terrible. I'll drive this car straight off a bridge, or I don't know what. He is going to get *such* a talking to!"

Pax stared at the side of her head. There was no way for Holly to cope. Raise your family, live your happy life, get your ducks in a row and finally have your daughter kidnapped by something that wasn't a man. Suddenly you have no reasonable way to deal with it.

Holly gave Pax another questioning look. "Who *are* you?"

"No one," Pax sighed. "A card player." It was an answer that never failed to pique people's interest, and even Holly's hard façade softened in surprise.

"That's . . . all you do? I mean – your work?"

"Yeah. Pretty much."

"And . . . Darren plays?"

"No," Pax said. "He doesn't know me. Honestly."

Holly concentrated on driving for a minute longer, apparently deciding how to continue. "My husband has told me very little about all this. I need to know more. Why was my daughter taken? Why on earth won't the police do something about these maniacs?"

"I can't pretend I know everything. But what I do know is hard to believe."

"I saw a horse playing a drum, with an invisible horn, and I saw a blue square writing things on a wall. I'm willing to give you the benefit of the doubt." Pax frowned. The descriptions sounded familiar. Things from the Miscellany. In her pause, Holly bowled on. "I can pay you."

"Excuse me?"

"Cash." Holly offered it quickly, as though the thought was dirty. "I can pay you to tell me, just say how much."

"I don't want your money."

"Then what *do* you want?" Holly's voice rose. "Why are you here? Who *are* you?"

Pax stared ahead, looking through the world as she asked herself the same questions. The answer seemed obvious, though, now that she was delivering this innocent girl back to her family. Now that she had sent gangsters to square off against the Ministry, and liberated a fairy who wanted, in her own way, to fight the monsters. Now that she seemed further than ever from being able to help Rufaizu. She wanted her part in this madness to mean something. "I fell into this the same way your husband did. I avoided an ordinary life long enough for the extraordinary to corner me. Now I'm trying to do something about it."

"About *what*?" Holly implored. "My daughter was kidnapped. My husband ran off after Grace with a vile liquid that looked like something a cartoon villain would use to kill rabbits. He's been talking with that blasted woman again and he's been running off talking to this" – Holly threw a hand towards Pax, suddenly speaking as though she wasn't there – "this younger, mysterious woman, and I don't know if I should hate him, and I'm scared." Holly took small, sharp breaths. "I'm scared, for myself, for him, and for my daughter, and I don't want to lose them."

Without saying anything, Grace sat up and shifted forward, apparently having been listening. She put an arm around her mother and rested her head on her seat. Holly fought back a tear, and in a flash, on and off, offered a thin smile. She took one hand off the wheel to pat Grace's arm and whispered, "Thank you, dear."

"It's okay," Grace said softly. "I wasn't hurt. Just frightened."

"That's hardly the point," Holly huffed, coldness returning. "Honestly, you've been missing for a day and all you have to say is you weren't hurt? I despair, Grace, I do. Now, please…" She turned to Pax. "Tell me what you know."

Pax took a breath and began.

Holly listened to the account of Rufaizu, and Apothel's book, and the notes that pointed to Barton. Of the Ministry, and then the tunnels, and the monsters that Holly had no reason to believe in. She responded by mentioning what she had seen herself. The horse and the blue square again, writing on the walls – something Pax realised she understood now. The Blue Angel, communicating as Barton had described it. And it had misled them, only confirming her initial instinct, and Letty's insistence, that whoever was sending those messages was not to be trusted.

Finally came the fateful question. "Who, exactly, took my daughter? What kind of gang are the Fae? Is it something to do with that liquid? Drugs?"

"They're not a gang," Pax said. "Not exactly. And there's a good reason Grace never saw them, even if I don't quite get how they pulled it off."

Holly slowed down as they turned into a familiar street. Pax went quiet as the green of the Bartons' neighbourhood glided into view. Grace pressed towards the window, smiling at her home, no doubt sensing the nightmare was over.

"Don't worry dear," Holly assured her. "You're safe now. We just need to figure out where your father got to." She turned to Pax. "You'll stay with us, won't you? You'll help bring this to an end?"

Pax nodded. Let's settle into this paradise, she thought. Have a cup of tea, put on the gas fire and wait for Barton to come home. Wait for the bad men to finish whatever needed to be done across town. Worry about how she was going to use the Dispenser when it was back in her possession. In the meantime, she could try and explain why the Barton family were in the crosshairs of two-inch-tall psychopaths.

Why not.

13

Casaria split his attention between watching Pax Kuranes' church apartment block and flashing nasty looks into the rear-view mirror at Gumg. The younger agent's face had swollen where he had been struck, taking on a satisfying tinge of purple, and every time he met Casaria's eye he looked away. It was a good way to pass the time, Casaria had discovered, inciting unease by staring at this subordinate clown. He needed the entertainment to take his mind off Pax's betrayal. She had promised so much but, like him, she was too rebellious. Quite the opposite of Sam Ward's stuffy ministerial ambitions, Pax was actually showing loyalty to the monsters. She might still see the error of her ways, but it was unlikely. The damage was done and he'd have to take care of her. To save the thought, he distracted himself by glowering at the moron in the back of the car. Landon was handling the real work, after all, by motionlessly watching the building's entrance. He was built for this kind of job, silently fixing his eyes on a point and doing the sweet sum total of piss all.

"What?" Gumg snapped, at last.

"Huh?" Casaria feigned innocence. "Something wrong?"

"What's your problem?" Gumg shifted in his seat.

"Easy," Landon warned in a monotone, not looking back. "We're here to do a job."

"No," Gumg insisted. "He's messing with me. Trying to get a rise, dammit!"

"Looks like it's working," Landon answered tiredly.

"He oughta be sent home," Gumg continued. "You saw what he did. He's mad."

"Have you taken him down the tunnels yet?" Casaria asked Landon.

"Hey, I'm talking – you hear me?" Gumg said. "You're a lunatic! This is assault, I'll –"

"Have you?" Casaria pressed. Landon turned slowly to him, then gave a disinterested glance back to Gumg. "Didn't think so. You can see it in him. Green as the grass."

"Green?" Gumg protested. "You think anyone *needs* to go down there? We've got databases – hotlines – diplomacy for crying out loud. You're a gatekeeper, man – that kind of attitude – that – it's no wonder you're still out on street patrols, instead of doing things that matter."

Landon raised an eyebrow, making Casaria smirk. This hotshot thought he was on the fast track to a better position in the Ministry, didn't he? Like all their worst recruits. Landon didn't say anything, but Gumg caught the look and cooled off. He said, "Are you gonna report him? Because I will."

"Oh, I'd love that," Casaria said. "Tell Mathers exactly what happened. How are you gonna make firing a gun across a crowded street sound like something that *doesn't* warrant quick preventative action?"

Gumg glared back. He gritted his teeth. "What about the man you beat up?"

"Beat *down*." Casaria grinned, entirely unapologetic. "Have you ever seen a sickle?"

"Stop avoiding the question."

"Hesitate with a sickle and it'll tear your arms off," Casaria said. "I've seen it. I know how to avoid that sort of thing. Whether it's a sickle or a man on the street. The Ministry respects that kind of decisive action more than your ability to file reports."

"The Ministry would prefer to keep things calm," Landon said, though his attention remained on the church. "For whatever reason you think they let you get away with this stuff, it's only because we're understaffed."

"Like hell. I've got a specialist skillset."

"Disparaging as this recruit may be," Landon said, too dry to even bother looking at Gumg, "he's right. You're not supposed to go into the tunnels. You don't need to fight a thing. Quite the opposite. You should be more discreet."

"It's people like you that let the Fae get the drop on us, that let this happen." Casaria held up his bandaged hand.

"As far as I'm aware," Landon droned, "you poked that hornet's nest yourself."

Casaria met his eyes with contempt. He left it there, deciding this waste of fat was not worth convincing. Gumg was right about one thing: *these* agents were nothing more than glorified zookeepers. One with aspirations to follow in Sam Ward's desk-bound footsteps, the other with no aspirations at all. They didn't understand that there was a delicate balance that could only be maintained on the ground level. That the Ministry needed the likes of Casaria to do the unthinkable in times when no other option remained. Landon and Gumg didn't understand the Sunken City. Rufaizu probably knew more than they ever would.

Landon nodded towards a white van. "There's two men over there, waiting to go in. Recognise them?"

Casaria followed his gesture. It was a rusty Vauxhall, no windows at the rear. Both men were larger than average, one darkened by stubble, the other sporting greasy golden curls. They looked like people you might regret hiring to evict squatters, when they accidentally crippled a harmless student.

"Couldn't see Pax hanging with their sort," Casaria decided.

"They're looking at us like we should be looking at them," Landon said.

"How long have they been there?"

"About as long as you've been patting yourself on the back for being a loose cannon," Landon replied, without any humour. Casaria wondered, in that moment, if he could contrive a way to cut his heart out. "Looks like they've had enough."

The van doors opened and the two men got out. They were both easily over six foot four, burly though neither in especially good shape. In their workmen's boots, ragged dungarees and shirts patterned by incongruous stains, they belonged at a roadside diner. They stared at Casaria's car as they walked purposefully towards

Pax's apartment building. Their unblinking looks were a challenge, daring the agents to follow them in.

"Here's what's going to happen," Casaria said. "We're going up to her apartment, and when they give us trouble, we're going to give them trouble back. If either of you has a problem with that, I'll do it alone. But say it now, because I'm not having you get in the way."

"Maybe they're not connected to her," Gumg suggested, anxious.

"They bloody well are, and they *are* going to cause trouble," Casaria replied firmly.

"We should call for backup," Landon suggested warily. "Or just follow them."

"*You're* the backup," Casaria hissed. "Come or don't, but don't get in my way."

"It was on the radio," Bees said, climbing the stairs as he continued the conversation from the van. "Back in the '80s, a sewage worker found it. He was curious about this smell from the drains, see. Knew how the system worked, so looked into it himself, and what did he find? A whole bloody tunnel that wasn't on the maps."

"You're confusing it with the Fallout Train," Howling Jowls Jones replied. "There's a system in the south-east of the city that allegedly connected directly to London, they set it up during the Cold War. That was what the sewage worker tapped into, and they blocked it all up because it wasn't safe. I took that to Mr Monroe once. He said his people already tried it, but it didn't go under the city, just touched the south-east corner."

"*I'm* his people that told him that," Bees said as they reached the third floor landing. He lumbered towards Pax's door and took out her key. "I'm not talking about the Fallout Train, this was something else. Listen, see, on the radio, when they interviewed this guy –"

Bees stopped, key in the lock, and turned around, with great deliberation, towards the movement he'd seen from the corner of his eye. Jones turned with him, folding his arms as he stared at the man in the suit that had followed them up. Leaning against the wall, Casaria smiled, pearly white, straight-cut teeth.

"Not subtle, are you?" Bees said.

"Look who's talking," Casaria replied.

"We're picking up some things for a friend. No business of yours."

"We all know that's not true."

"Whatever," Bees said, turning back to the door. He opened it and looked into the apartment, then back at Casaria. The suited man hadn't moved. Bees said to Jones, "Wait here, yeah?"

"Yeah," Jones replied, eyes locked on Casaria. As Bees went inside, Casaria moved to follow him and Jones stepped in the way, a mass that almost filled the door. "Invitation only."

"I'm sorry," Casaria said. "You don't know what you're getting involved with here. I've no doubt you're not close enough to Pax that you'd risk your lives for her."

"Who's risking their life?"

Bees only vaguely listened as he opened up the cupboard and scanned for the things Pax had wanted. The little money safe, the book too. The mechanical device was strange. He'd have a think about that later.

"You're not taking anything away from here," the guy in the hall was saying.

Bees took a moment to give the apartment one last look. He wasn't sure if the spare clothes he'd collected were clean or not, but that didn't really matter. It might be an idea to discuss a few matters of personal hygiene with Pax, anyway. She'd seemed to have been keeping a pet in a shoebox lacking amenities, and all. As he lumbered back to the door, he found two newcomers standing in the stairway entrance, behind Casaria, both hesitant to move into the corridor.

Casaria stepped back, smiling wider than ever, and his jacket fell open to reveal a pistol.

"He's got a gun, Bees," Jones commented. "Says he can't let us leave."

"That's a shame," Bees replied. He drew his own pistol from the back of his trousers and held it up. It was a large revolver, the sort that looked too heavy for the average man to lift. Usually enough to convince people to rethink their life choices just by looking at it. He twisted it from side to side as the two new arrivals backed into the wall, stunned. Yeah, these weren't the sort that were used to having someone tell them *no*. To drive his point home, Bees said, "I've got this, see, and I don't think I want to let him stop us."

"You poor, clueless morons," Casaria said, the smile still fixed on his face but the humour gone. Bees' gun was out while the agent's was still deep in its holster. The suit had balls, you had to give him that.

"Ministry of Environmental Energy?" Bees said, looking from one man to another.

Jones commented, "Seems to me civil servants shouldn't be threatening the public on matters of picking up things from a friend's apartment."

"Maybe you fancy yourselves as special kinds of civil servants?" Bees said.

"Casaria," the bigger man warned, as close to the stairs as he could get without moving down them. He had the right idea. "Perhaps we should let the gentlemen –"

"Don't be a damned coward, Landon," Casaria replied. "We're not going anywhere until I see what's in that bag."

Bees shrugged. "You're welcome to stay."

"Here's what I suggest," Casaria said. "You leave the bag and go on your way, with the knowledge that you're still intact and did the right thing. No one needs to get hurt on Pax's account."

"Oh, that sounds lovely," Bees replied, his gravelly tone suggesting the opposite. "Only we already told Mr Monroe we were coming, and he'd be very disappointed if our deal fell through. Unless you yourselves wanted to give us what she offered us?"

"What did she offer you?" Landon asked suddenly, concerned.

"We're not giving you anything," Casaria said. "And neither is she."

"Awful shame," Bees said, turning the gun in his hand again. "Awful shame."

Bees lifted the revolver, but before he could make any further threat Casaria sprang forward. For a relatively slight man, he moved with tremendous speed and force, his full weight meeting Bees' chin headfirst as the gun went off. Bees snapped back into the wall and flopped to the floor, eyes losing all focus. As Jones tried to draw a weapon of his own, Casaria drove an elbow into his ribs.

Jones stumbled aside but was not down. With a few feet between himself and Casaria, he raised both hands in guarded fists. Bees blinked heavily, trying to clear his head, his own hands limp against the floor. The scuffle before him was a hazy blur; Casaria skated around the hallway, light on his feet, laughing excitedly. Jones took a swing, missed. Casaria swung back and connected. With Jones momentarily stunned, the smaller man started pounding at his body, but Jones recovered and returned the punches. It was like watching a fox attack a bear. They scuffled around each other, exchanging short, nasty strikes, before separating and stumbling apart.

Bees pushed himself back against the wall and up to his feet, checking the floor for his pistol. He looked up as Casaria moved away from Jones, touching a hand to a bleeding lip, head shaking.

Jones flexed, rolling his muscles, inviting another bout.

"Don't move!" Landon shouted from beyond them. Jones looked sideways, finding the agent's pistol trained on him. Landon was nervous, hands shaking even with both of them clamped on the gun. It was the sort of nervous that could see a gun going off.

Casaria deflated, saying, "Seriously? *Now* you do something?"

"That's enough, Casaria, you damned lunatic," Landon snapped. "Just get the bag."

Casaria glared at Landon, apparently upset about taking orders.

Bees spotted his gun, way over in a doorway. He exchanged a glance with Jones, who was shaking his head. They were covered. These guys were too erratic to test. A more professional bunch of spooks would've been easier to take down. Bees glowered at Casaria.

"We'll come after you," he said. "Mr Monroe doesn't like to be disappointed."

"Mr Monroe can sit on a rusty dildo," Casaria snorted. He picked up the bag from the middle of the hall and looked inside, frowning at the contents. He pulled out the mechanical device, regarding it with an expression that said it was a mystery to him. As he put it back in the bag, he gave Bees and Jones one last, questioning look. He didn't ask, though, and went towards the stairs. "Let's go."

"What about them?" Landon said. "They attacked an officer of the –"

"You want to arrest them?" Casaria called back, already halfway down the stairs. "Be my guest!"

Bees glared at the overweight man as he and his young, terrified colleague gave them worried looks. The older one shook his head, backing off after Casaria, and offered a moronic parting comment. "You boys stay out of trouble."

14

Barton scanned the red-brick wasteland, holding up the useless instrument Rimes had given him and still getting nothing that resembled a response. It didn't matter. He was confident that it didn't work, now that he could see the trails of colourful light hanging in the air. The pain from his injuries had gone. His niggling doubts and fears, too. The drink gave him focus: a narrow, sharp mind to follow the trail and do what needed to be done.

Destroy them all.

He had picked up the trail easily after swigging from the canister of glo. He could sense the flutter of wings and muted voices from half a mile away. He blundered towards them. Then he saw them emerge from between the abandoned buildings, talking in hurried tones. "Let the FTC sort it out, we take care of ourselves first."

They flew between the buildings like a pair of dragonflies, black shapes against the sky that would not usually have warranted a second look. Barton was used to the tricks of the Sunken City, though, and knew not to trust his eyes. When he squinted he could see through the mirage. The insects flickered like a heat ray, not entirely solid, though he couldn't see what was hidden underneath. There was no doubt they were fairies. They darted off through the sky, leaving a trail behind, fresh and thicker than the others. The clear glint of gold in the air gradually faded to the pink he had followed to get there. He watched them go, high above the buildings, making a beeline towards the city.

Barton did not follow them. He turned in the opposite direction, continuing along their earlier trails, the ones that were slowly dissipating. They didn't lead to the FTC, he could sense that. He continued until it took him back to the dusty remnants of an office complex. The trail led into a building, and back out. They had made a stop here. He crept inside.

There, in the back room, he found a very different energy. The dull grey cloud that glo revealed as human. Someone had been here. More than one person. It was hard to make out, much less distinct than the trails that fairies left. Frustrated, Barton picked out the pink of the fairies again and followed them back out into the road. From here they might have gone to their camp. Maybe the FTC itself.

The trails ahead were fading. He picked up his pace and clambered over half-fallen walls for the quickest route, and less than a block away he started to see more colours in the sky. Different paths crossed over the pink, some stronger, some weaker. Greens, blues, yellows. Other fairies, heading to a central location somewhere behind the buildings ahead. Was this the hub? The Fae Transitional City itself, up ahead? He dropped Rimes' device and cracked his knuckles. No idea what he would do when he got in there, only that someone was going to answer to him. He took a heavy step forward. A female voice came from somewhere up above.

"Wouldn't do it if I were you."

It had taken Letty longer than she'd have liked to get mobile again, and the result was hardly impressive. After a decade operating outside the FTC, it was little difficulty for her to locate a mechanic in the periphery of the city, but it was another matter to trade for the specific and expensive piece of machinery she needed. Fae disabilities were a niche market that demanded high prices; while alternatives to wings and limbs were available, sometimes even superior to the originals, the funds she had taken from their Bettor Off hideout were scarcely enough. Only through her fiercest haggling was she able to get the minimum equipment required to puff through the sky, with a tractor-engine hum. The fan stabiliser on her back was the flying equivalent of a leg crutch.

At least she was able to move again. She needed to concentrate on matching her surviving wing to the erratic stop-start of the artificial engine, but she could still cross the city quicker than any human.

She headed straight for the Innovation Centre, hoping to catch her boys returning to the hostage before they discovered Pax had screwed up their plan. Assuming they hadn't already done the unthinkable and gone after Barton. Had her leadership really been all that was keeping them from murderous idiocy? Mix, she could understand, he liked to solve things with his guns, but Fresko was at least a little brighter than that. The pair of them must have known that Barton, even if he was a dumb lummox, was not their enemy.

She flew to the research centre and found it empty, the girl long gone and no sign of Pax or her boys. That meant going to the Barton household. On her way out, though, she spotted a suspiciously human shape leaning around a wall, looking in the direction of the city. Given his attempt to hide and his focus on the sky, he was searching for something particular.

Letty floated towards him with a sigh of relief.

Finally, she told herself, some good fortune.

Barton slowly looked up at the voice, fists ready.

"You're incorrigible, aren't you? Gonna punch the sky?" The fairy settled on a windowsill above his head. Barton put a hand over his brow to block out the sun's glare, trying to get a better look at her as she studied him. He could see this one alright. Maybe because she was closer, maybe just not as well masked. She rested the pistol in her hand on a knee. "Shit, what happened to you?"

Barton hadn't got any cleaner since the morning. He had seen his reflection on the way over, skin caked with dried blood and coloured by bruises. So what, he had no desire to speak to this little nightmare creature. He stepped out, preparing to launch at her.

"You wouldn't stand a chance," Letty said. "And what the hell were you thinking to do in *there*?" She screwed a thumb in the direction he had been heading.

"Improvise," Barton said, barely opening his mouth beyond a snarl. The fairy smiled.

"Well, now you don't have to. You can thank whatever God you jizz over that you ran into me. I knew Apothel, lummox. And I know you. We can help each other."

"You *killed* Apothel."

"No. He betrayed me, actually, if you care."

"I don't. Should've come for you people years ago. You've crossed a line now. My daughter. My goddamned *daughter*. Where is she?"

"Last I saw," Letty said, "she was safe. If you're lucky, she's on her way home. We have a mutual friend that was trying to help her."

Barton frowned. "Who? Why?"

"The card player. Except going to your home does not mean safe, right now. The bitch in charge has given orders for a clean-up. That means you, your family, whoever else has touched this."

Barton's face brimmed with anger, his eyes running from the fairy to the direction of their city. "Not if I tear your whole world apart first."

"If I hadn't seen you," Letty told him flatly, "you'd have been shot the moment a scout spotted your face. Still a long way from the FTC. I'd rather keep you alive."

"What's it to you?"

"You know what Apothel was killed for, right? You know why Rufaizu came back?"

Barton glowered at her, echoing the words. "What he was killed for? What *your people* killed him for? Trying to *help* you?"

"Something like that. I just had a very interesting conversation that might've shed some light on that. Some people..." The fairy looked aside, seeming to reflect on her distant, hidden home. "*My* people, have an idea of what's possible. What the device Apothel took can do. And they don't all want to do it."

"What's it matter now," Barton snarled. "You went after my family, you're all –"

"Are you listening to me?" Letty snapped. His response had angered her, causing her to swoop down towards him, and he took a step back as she buzzed in his face. "You want to help your family, you need to do as I say!" He looked at the odd contraption slung over her shoulder, as a single wing flapped at the other side. She wasn't normal, this Fae. "Your family are in the firing line now – Pax too – all because there's people that don't want us to succeed in the Sunken City. Actively fucking sabotaging it. *Listen to me* and we can take them out *together*."

Barton took a breath. He asked, slowly, "Like I said. What's it to you?"

"They fucking cheated me. They're cheating them-fucking-selves. Now, you're gonna take out your damned phone and make a call."

*

Watching through his scope, Fresko could see activity in the house, but it came to a halt in the living room area. They were exchanging pleasantries or something when the roughly dressed one received a phone call. The others stopped when she held up a hand for quiet.

"Something's wrong," Fresko said.

The one on the phone waved at the others. The mum rushed to the window and drew the curtains, cutting off their view.

"Shit." Fresko sat back from the gun.

"They're going for the blinds," Mix said, pointing. "Take them out."

"I'd get one of them, maybe, then the others go to ground and we have to go in there. No. They think they're keeping safe in there right now. Means we can still do this slow and simple."

"No, numbnuts," Mix said, "it means Barton's alive and he's coming back."

"Can still make it look like an accident." Fresko checked through the scope as the younger lady pulled a blind down over another window. "Set some charges."

"Why bother?" Mix snarled, drawing his pistol. "Let's do this the old-fashioned way."

Fresko hesitated. It was unlikely that Barton could stop them if he did come back, but he added an element of uncertainty. If it was even him they were waiting for. It was the card player who'd taken the call, and she had to have her own plans. She'd found the girl somehow, after all. Fresko thought out loud: "It'd take us five minutes to set the charges."

"And it'd take us ten seconds to shoot the pigs."

"The Ministry can't know it was us."

"Fuck the Ministry," Mix grunted. "Let Val worry about them. Come on, are we Fae or what?"

All the windows of the house had been covered, now. The women inside had to be hunkering down in fear as they waited for their slovenly hero to return. Idiots and cowards. "All right," said Fresko. "It's not every day we get to have some fun. Let's go in."

"Yes!" Mix let out a booming laugh. "I knew you hadn't gone soft!"

15

"What did he say, *exactly*?" Holly demanded as they pulled the last blinds closed.

Pax was moving in a flurry, running from one room to another, checking the walls for holes, any ways for the smallest of creatures to get in. She replied, without looking at Holly, "Lock the doors, close the windows, he's coming back soon and he's got help."

"What help could he have? That mad scientist woman?"

"I don't know, I just know we're not safe," Pax said. "Do you have a chimney?"

"A what?"

"A fireplace, somewhere Santa could drop in!"

"No, we have gas –"

"Vents? Extractor fans? Any gaps in the walls at all?"

"This isn't a country pub, for heaven's sake!" Holly said. "What exactly are you expecting? Rats? Snakes?"

"Worse." Pax stopped and gave her a level look. "Fairies with guns."

Holly held the look for a moment. Grace, hovering at her shoulder, paused too. After processing the word, the mum let out a shrill laugh. "You have got to be joking."

"I said you wouldn't believe it." Pax turned away to keep checking the house, scanning the awnings, the corners. Her urgency, she felt, made Holly pause and take note. "Block any holes you can. Nothing so big as a mouse can get in here. And don't worry, as long as we can keep them out we can work through this. My people are going to bring me something we can use to negotiate."

"Negotiate with fairies?" Holly laughed again, this time without humour.

"Believe me, we need to."

"In there, the toilet." Grace pointed helpfully. "There's a fan above the mirror."

"Thanks." Pax hurried through to the opening. She took off the extractor fan's grate and shoved a hand towel in, blocking it tightly.

"Grace, don't listen to this nonsense," Holly said.

"It's not *nonsense*, mum!" Grace protested. "You don't have a better explanation!" Holly went quiet as Grace dogged Pax's heels. As Pax backed off from the toilet, she bumped into the younger girl, and Grace whispered, "I love your coat."

Pax paused, taken off guard, and checked her tatty fleece-lined jacket. She couldn't help but feel a little warmth at being validated by the teenager. As she muttered, "Thanks," a window smashed.

They all froze, locking eyes as the sound came again, in the living room, followed by glass shattering against the floor. Grabbing Holly by the wrist, Pax pulled her into the bathroom with Grace and shut the door.

"What on earth –" Holly spun back, but Pax kept hold of her, shooting a finger to her lips for quiet. They all listened in deathly stillness. Something moved into the corridor, with the flutter of a tiny bird.

"All right," a man's voice said. "Light up the closet."

"Get down *get down!*" Pax shouted, pulling Holly and Grace to the ground, with not a moment to spare before an eruption of gunshots. The door burst apart in miniature explosions of splintering wood. The sink cracked as though hit by a lightning-fast ball bearing. Grace screamed.

Pax kicked the door out, counting on catching the fairies in the tight space of the corridor. The gunshots paused as she caught the blur of one of them flying to the ceiling, the other twisting around the door.

"Move, quick!" Pax yelled, sprinting for the front door. The two fairies quickly recovered and started shooting as she crashed a shoulder through the plate glass of the door and rolled outside, the wooden frame exploding around her in tiny gunshots. Holly and Grace came out shrieking under the gunfire, ducking the shots that were meant for Pax, and before the fairies could adjust their aim they were outside, too. On her way through the door, Holly dragged the coat rack down and a mess of jackets flapped behind them, bullets tearing through the down of a winter coat.

Pax tried to stand and winced, something stinging her leg. She rolled aside with a cry and landed on the grass, both hands grabbing at her calf where something had gone through. It was at the very rear, her jeans lightly ripped; close to the surface, but a bastard all the same. Warm blood rushed over her hands as she clutched the wound.

"Son of a bitch!" Pax screamed back at the doorway.

"To the car, the car!" Holly cried, taking Grace by the hand. She skidded next to the vehicle, patting her pockets. No keys.

All three of them looked to the front door, as the tiny attackers navigated their way through the mess of coats. Grace let out another scream and picked up the nearest object she could find, a ceramic plant pot. She hurled it.

"Back!" one of the men shouted, as the plant exploded over the entrance. In the mess of shattered pot and scattering earth, one of the shapes appeared to spin out of control and hit a wall.

"More, more!" Holly encouraged her daughter, picking up another pot and throwing it. A short barrage of plant pots followed as mother and daughter threw every unfixed piece of the front garden back at their unseen attackers, creating a cloud of debris.

Pax pushed herself up and limped away from the house. In the momentary respite from the gunshots, Holly took out her phone and started dialling. Pax bowled into Grace and Holly together and pointed down the road, shouting, "Keep moving! Head for the manhole!"

Without questioning her, the two women sprinted. Holly was already shouting into her handset, "Yes! Police! I need the police!"

"No!" Pax yelled, slapping the phone out of her hand. "Just run!"

The gunshots started up again from the doorway. They were more than a building's length away from the door now, though, and the first shots went wide.

"Stay low, Grace!" Pax warned, as she raced past the teenager to the manhole cover in the road. She threaded her fingers into the holes and hauled for all her worth as the gunshots stopped, the fairies either reloading or repositioning.

"What do we do, what do we do?" Grace pleaded.

"Help me!" Pax commanded, and suddenly Grace and Holly were at her side, all three of them taking a grip on the cover and heaving at it.

As the metal shifted, Holly demanded, "How is this going to help?"

An immediate answer came as Pax pivoted the cover behind them and a bullet twanged off it, the makeshift shield protecting her chest. She gave herself only a moment of surprise, then pointed into the opening. "Get in there, now!"

"The *sewer*?" Holly exclaimed.

The gunshots picked up again, another bullet hitting the manhole cover, one scratching the tarmac nearby. Grace and Holly threw themselves into the dark hole. Pax dropped down after them, hearing the man's voice as she fell. "You done preening, get after them!"

Pax's feet found the slippery rungs of a ladder and she dug her heels in as she put all her strength into hauling the manhole cover back over the hole. It shifted and almost swung onto her, making her let go and drop. She fell ten feet onto hard concrete, with a thump and a light splash of surface water. Looking back up, she could see the light of day through a crack in the cover – it hadn't quite fallen into place.

Holly and Grace came to her, trying to help her up, as the small silhouette of a man appeared at the cover's edge. He had a pistol in his hand, which he aimed down at them.

Pax rolled aside, just as the gun went off, its sound echoing through the arched chamber. The three women sprang up and started running again, Holly directing this time. "Over there!"

They ducked around a buttress, falling into shadow. The sound of their deep breathing filled the void, guns quiet.

"Did you see that?" Holly hissed. "It was a – he was small – you'd think the detail to mention was the fact that they're the size of doorknobs, wouldn't you?"

"Not that they've got fucking *guns*?" Pax snapped back at her.

The men's voices filtered down. "Get in there."

"It's no sewer," a second voice said, a higher-pitched one.

"You think I'm stupid?"

There was a pause, and Holly looked questioningly at Pax as they held their breath. Pax crouched slightly, touching a hand to the wound on her leg and flinching at the pain.

"My dad is going to kill you!" Grace suddenly shouted as she leaned around the buttress. "As soon as he gets back, you'll be sorry!"

A gun went off and Grace slipped back into the shadows with another scream, a fraction of her t-shirt tearing as the bullet struck her. Holly screamed too, seeing a dark stain of blood rising to the surface of the material. She slammed a hand onto it, the pair of them ducking back into cover. Pax stared, at a loss for what to do.

"Clipped her," the second man said.

"All right," the first snarled. "Let's cave the place in."

Grace whimpered as Holly dabbed the wound with her torn t-shirt. The hole was clean, like a needle mark to the top of the teenager's shoulder. Bleeding but not severe. Watching them, this innocent mother and daughter, nothing to do with any of this, Pax shook her head. Not right. They shouldn't be here. She shouted down the tunnel, "They don't know anything! All Barton ever wanted was to protect them from it!"

While the fairies paused, Pax took out her phone and rushed through the numbers. She rapidly wrote a text: *In the Sunken City. Fae on us.* Clicked Send.

"Send them out," one of the men replied. "Promise they can go, unharmed."

"They'll kill us," Holly stated, simply. Pax nodded. She looked at the phone again. The message blinked with a cross. Failed to send.

"No signal," Pax said.

One hand on her wound, Grace stood uneasily, Holly helping her. She looked at the phone and suggested, with a pained voice, "You've got one bar. Use the GPS." Pax gave her a confused look and Grace insisted, "Share your location!"

Pax nodded and did as she was told, bringing up the contact.

"It'll show us at home, what use is that?" Holly said.

"They'll be ready for your husband no matter what," Pax warned, "but there's someone else who can help." She clicked Send, sharing her location, and the phone pinged. Success.

"I'm coming in," the rougher fairy shouted. "You know what that means?"

"He's going to shoot us!" Grace cried. Holly held her close, looking desperately at Pax, but Pax was shaking her head.

"No. They can't follow us down here. It'd just . . ." She stopped. She knew exactly what it meant. As one of them descended into the tunnel, the sound of fluttering wings getting closer, something groaned loudly, far away in the tunnels.

The weary squeak of an ancient pipe brought to life.

Grace whimpered. "What is that?"

"You got a choice," the fairy said, closer still. "Come to us, or stay here with them. I can at least promise to make it quick."

"You were with Letty, weren't you?" Pax shouted.

The fluttering paused, but when his voice came it was even more fierce. "Don't even say her name. You goddamned animal. She was a thousand times better than you. I oughta cut your hamstrings and make sure you suffer."

Pax went quiet. They didn't know. She said, "I didn't hurt her. She's *alive.*"

The fairy hesitated again.

Another groan. Louder, not so far away.

"You're a liar," the fairy decided, then fired a shot in their direction to end the conversation. The bullet twanged into the brickwork. Pax wanted to argue, to make them see sense, but the fluttering wings retreated. She leant out and saw the blur of the fairy speeding towards the tunnel opening.

"Letty's alive!" Pax shouted. The fairy flew through the crack in the manhole, out of view. "We were helping each other! We tried to find you, at the betting shop!"

There was silence above.

If the fairies had any response to make, it was cut off by the rumbling of monsters. The pipe groan was met by an intense, high-pitched clicking, and Grace's whimpering picked up volume as Holly offered comforting words. Pax looked at the ladder, their only way out, guarded by the fairies, and considered making a break for it.

The higher-pitched one said, "All right, say she's alive. Come back up here and we can talk it through."

Not even halfway convincing. Pax cursed, pushing an angry hand against the wall, and turned to the endless dark of the tunnel ahead.

"Pax?" Holly said, voice strained as she struggled to keep strong. "What are those sounds?"

Pax listened. The tunnel started shaking as though a train was passing by. The clicking noise came again, closer than before. Another groan. Maybe all from one direction.

"What is it?" Grace sobbed.

"This isn't a sewer," Pax said, keeping her voice as steady as she could. "And those sounds aren't natural. We have to move, this way."

"What do you –" Holly started to question, and Pax shoved her, shedding her calm voice. It wasn't going to work.

"There's no time! Run!"

16

"I don't know how she did it," Casaria said loudly, finding it difficult to keep his voice level in the face of Deputy Director Mathers' nonchalance. "But this changes everything. This is a Fae weapon. It could be *the* Fae weapon. You know what it means as well as I."

Mathers was staring at the device on his desk, like he was unsure exactly what it was or where it had come from. He had the same vacant expression as Landon. Another moron who didn't get it. Casaria was sure, though: his instincts had told him the moment he set eyes on it, and a closer look had all but confirmed it. The metal was too intricately crafted to be of human origin. It made sense of everything: Rufaizu hadn't been running a con. He had the weapon all along, the same thing Apothel had been killed for. Something that could do serious harm to the Sunken City. No wonder the Fae had attacked him.

"It could be anything," Mathers mumbled. "Could be a factory part."

"Could be a water filtration system," Gumg offered from his corner.

"No one's killing people to stop them talking about a damned water filtration system!" Casaria said. He took a breath, brushed his hair back into place and shot Gumg an insincere smile. "Sir, I'd like to request that this waste of space be banned from speaking."

Mathers eyed Casaria, then Gumg, unimpressed. He sat back in his leather chair, netting his fingers behind his head. "We'll send it to the lab and have it tested. Then turn it over to the IS Relations Initiative."

"What for?" Casaria exclaimed, voice coming out higher than he'd intended. The mention of Ward's team was like ice down his neck. He made every effort to sound calm. "With all due respect, sir, Sam Ward's diplomats are the last people you want dealing with this. They'll want to talk it over – they'll give the Fae a chance to cover it up, or replace it – or worse."

"The FTC have always denied something like this existed, I don't –"

"Exactly!" Casaria caught himself again. After a pause, he continued, "Either they've been lying all this time, or they didn't know it was still out there. Either way, they want it back now."

"That's for the Initiative to decide."

"You know where we can find the FTC, don't you? Give me a team of ten men to block off all the exits to their hole and we can gas them once and for all."

"No one is entertaining that thought," Mathers replied blandly. "If there *was* a case to be made for exterminating the Fae, it would still rely on an IS analysis, and would require at least four levels of approval beyond that. And that's *if* a case could be made."

"Oh my God…" Casaria dragged out each word. "Don't give me ten men – give me a canister of gas and give me *permission*. I'll do it myself!"

"Why is it so important to you?" Landon grunted. Casaria shot him a look that warned him to be quiet or face violence, but the heavyset agent continued. "What've you got against the Fae? They stay out of our way, we stay out of theirs."

"You ignorant whale!" Casaria surged towards him. "They take advantage of us – because of apologists like Sam who want to *talk* to them. They shot at me! They're murderers and thieves who'd do anything to wipe us out, given the chance."

"No," Mathers said.

Casaria paused, a foot from Landon, and let his fists drop. "Excuse me?"

"I said no."

"No what?"

Mathers tapped the desk near the metallic device, face blank.

"No they wouldn't," he said. "If this weapon is what you think it is, they didn't use it when they made it. They have never claimed to have a weapon that could damage the *praelucente*, but they have made claims of equally important things. The truth is they choose not to use such technology. If it even works."

"The weapon was stolen!" Casaria protested. "That gypsy took it. They've been hunting for it ever since! We thought he was working with them, but he genuinely tried to screw them!"

Mathers' expression finally shifted, looking uncomfortable. "That really is an ugly word, Casaria. We can't have representatives of Her Majesty's Services referring to people as *gypsies*. It wouldn't do."

Casaria froze, mouth open in surprise. It was all he could do not to explode.

Mathers continued. "Now, as for this, it's a matter for diplomacy, Casaria. Civilised discussion. It's not a case of everyone wanting to kill each other, is it? The Fae speak English, for heaven's sake. The IS Relations Initiative has made excellent inroads with their representatives."

"The Fae speak English," Casaria repeated with disbelief.

"Of course. And we have enjoyed mutual existence for a long time, now."

The deputy director said it as though this was obvious, but Landon and Gumg joined Casaria by frowning at the idea that diplomacy between their species had been so successful. Fae crimes had declined since the Initiative had started, but the thought of them actively working with the MEE was unheard of.

"What exactly are you saying?" Casaria said.

Mathers pointed to Landon and Gumg. "You two, give us a moment."

Gumg wanted to protest but Landon shook his head at him, gesturing to the door. As the pair left, Casaria stood rigid, unblinking, as he glowered at Mathers.

"I'll telling you this because you need to stop," the deputy director said. "You're a night watchman, Casaria. We value your work, you're an effective agent, but know your boundaries. What goes on in the Sunken City at night, and with rogue Fae agents, is not the same as what goes on in the management of the Ministry during the day. There are trade talks, negotiations, politics. Now, I know what it meant to you when Ms Ward was moved up, but it was because she understood all that. You never have. Perhaps it would be best if you talked to her again, I know she'd –"

"This isn't about her," Casaria answered through gritted teeth. "Everything I do down there is to protect our work. For the good of this city – does no one else see that? Seriously?"

"It's for the good of this city," Mathers continued, keeping impossibly calm, "that we don't rock the boat. We don't want to hurt the Fae and they don't want to hurt the *praelucente*."

"You *cannot* trust them. Whatever they tell you –"

Mathers waved a hand for silence. "Calm down. You couldn't understand, not from your position. Let me make this plain for you. Stop this maverick nonsense. We cannot have you assaulting your colleagues and members of the public. Talking about inciting violence, consorting with civilians without proper clearance."

"This was a special –"

"Casaria," Mathers said, more firmly. "Not another word. I want you to stop, right now, or you'll leave me no choice but to suspend you."

"Are you completely stupid –"

"Casaria," Mathers snapped. "That's enough. I'm suspending you for a week. I know you've had a tough few days, so be thankful it's not worse. You're not to set foot in the Sunken City, or anywhere near its entrances, until further notice. Hand in all your weapons and relinquish your vehicle."

"You're making a mistake."

Mathers stood, fastening the buttons on his jacket. He wasn't going anywhere; it was just his signal for Casaria to leave. "I think not."

"Sir." Casaria held his gaze, his passion subsiding as the deputy director's sincerity sank in. He fought the urge to beg. He squeezed his lips shut and asked in a muffled tone, "What about the device?"

"IS will look into it. You have done well and there will be results, don't worry."

"And the girl?"

"She'll be brought in. You will have nothing to do with it."

Casaria left the building flushed with anger, desperate to punch someone. It took all his willpower not to throw Gumg's satisfied face through a window as he passed him on the way out. He stormed onto the street and paced back and forth. They didn't deserve him. They were patsies to the fairies, after all. Sycophants, company men, cowards, bastards. And Sam Ward was their chief agent. It was his biggest mistake, bringing her in.

He'd go through St Alphege's and find someone to take his anger out on. Maybe two or three of them. Maybe he'd track down Mr Monroe and ask for a rematch with his men, they'd be game. Those big bastards could put up a fight. He needed it.

Pumping up, he walked briskly down the road.

He'd use the Tube. For the first time in God-knows-how-many years. It might tire him out slightly, and he was already running on steam from the night before, but a little more tiredness wasn't going to hurt. Why not flirt with the monsters, what difference did it make now. He'd go to the warehouse district and ask for Mr Monroe, that was as good a place to start as any. Then he'd figure out a plan. Get to those fairies, do it for himself, if they weren't willing to take action for the country.

As he marched towards the Underground, his phone beeped. The message stopped him cold.

PAX KURANES has shared her location.

17

The three women hurried down the tunnel, tripping over themselves as they reached out in front of them. The sounds were drawing in, becoming more horrific and unnatural the closer they got. Grace couldn't help but cry more loudly, panic overcoming her. Pax drew alongside her, felt her way to putting an arm around her and whispered, "Keep quiet, it's safer."

Grace choked back her next sob, and Pax felt her tensing in her grip, her head moving, nodding. Her next few breaths were strained, holding back whatever sound was ready to burst out. As they sped along, their footfalls splashing through puddles, a birdlike trill rolled past them.

"Use this wall!" Holly whispered, somewhere to the side.

Pax followed her voice, taking Grace with her, free hand reaching out until it touched brick. The wall curved upwards; it was a small tunnel, after all.

"Light," Grace said. She broke away and raised her voice. "There's a light! Look!"

Pax squinted. Was there something there, or just a trick of the darkness? It looked like a pale line. Grace's feet pattered ahead. Holly started running, too. As Pax got closer the line got bigger. It was definitely a light, a fluorescent one. She slowed down, recalling when that electric force had chased her before.

"Wait, wait!" she shouted, but Grace and Holly were moving away.

"It's another tunnel!" Grace shouted. "Lit up!"

Pax stopped, the light silhouetting the other two as they rushed towards it. It wasn't flickering. It was a clear, solid beam. She took a deep breath and committed, sprinted.

The trio turned into the next tunnel together, finding a long, empty corridor stretching into the distance, lit by occasional luminescent bulbs. They took a moment to stop and stare. Far down the corridor, new bulbs were coming on, one by one, extending the view, as though the system was just booting up.

"There's a door," said Holly, pointing.

"Go for it," Pax said, and Holly and Grace ran ahead. She hesitated, though, looking back the way they had come, towards the approaching sounds. A light came on just above her, making her flinch. Another one came on further back, lighting part of the path they had followed, a wide floor with a film of shimmering water across its surface. Another light, further back, then another. Pax was transfixed, for a moment, by the gradual progression of the lights towards the sounds. Another light, and she gasped. A beast reeled back with a hiss as the light hit it, eyes flashing at her. The light barely stopped it, though. Slowly, inexorably, it dragged itself towards her, filling the tunnel.

Pax ran.

She followed Holly and Grace, who were quickly approaching the doorway. Her heart was swelling as her mind tried to conceive what it was she had seen.

There was another hiss from the tunnel behind, almost upon them.

Holly rattled the door, but it wouldn't move. "It's locked!"

"I can do it, I can do it!" Pax panted, pounding towards them and fumbling a hand into her jacket pocket. Pins, metal pins somewhere in there. Grace and Holly watched with terror, checking in the other direction. Pax made it to the human-sized entrance and its heavy metal door. It had an archaic lock that made her heart sink; there'd be no technique involved here, just trial and error. She started rifling through her picks, thrusting one then another into place, as Holly said, "We can keep moving, this goes on –"

"We get through here, it'll cut off half of what's following us," Pax said, trying another pick. It stuck, jamming in place as though connecting with something. The lock didn't move.

"They're getting closer!" Grace cried.

Pax fumbled, dropping one of the picks. Rather than pick it up she moved on to another one, trying to keep calm. Can't use force, need to feel it out. She shimmied, this way and that. Not working, try another.

Grace screamed and Pax dropped another pick. She looked down the tunnel. The beast had made it to the turning and was coming their way. This tunnel was smaller than the first, it seemed, and their pursuer fully filled it.

"Come on, Grace!" Holly said, pulling her daughter's arm.

"No!" Pax yelled, picking up her pick to try again. "It won't fit through here!"

Holly tried to move but Grace stood fast, staring horrified at the creature.

Pax gave it another glance.

It was a bulbous mass of pulsating flesh, its many folds sucking away the light. What was illuminated was wet with thick slime. Somewhere in its amorphous shape, claws occasionally protruded forwards, dragging it down the tunnel. Towards the centre of its mass, surrounded by blinking golden orbs of eyes, it had a circular maw, an open hole that blew out steam. It moved slowly, its mouth hissing and puffing, claws scraping against the brick, but it was approaching them nonetheless.

"Grace!" Holly shrieked, pulling her daughter again. Grace stumbled towards her, into motion, and the pair were about to move when the door clicked. Pax shot a hand up, dropping more of her picks to catch Grace's other wrist before she moved out of reach. She hauled the teenager towards her, the sudden motion catching Holly off guard and tripping her. As Holly let go, Pax thrust Grace through the doorway, then grabbed Holly under the arms and dragged her in too. She slammed the metal door behind them, just as a jet of steam shot past them.

Beyond the door, the sound of the monster's approach continued, the tunnel creaking under its weight. Behind it, the high-pitched trill and the clicking resumed.

Holly had fallen by the side, sat on the floor staring back at the door with eyes wide in alarm. Grace ran further into the tunnel, hand over her mouth to hold in more screams, as Pax stood dumbly, turning on the spot. The new tunnel descended a few steps into another empty passage, narrow and square this time, lit by smaller and less frequent lights.

The door shook behind them, the beast trying to move it. The hinges shifted, coughing mortar. Pax helped Holly to her feet. "The door won't hold. We need to keep moving."

"What was that?" Holly asked. "What was it, what was it?"

Pax didn't answer. It didn't warrant a name, and a witty response was not forthcoming.

18

Letty had flown ahead, moving as quickly as the artificial wing would carry her. As the central apartments and offices fell away below her, giving way to increasingly spread-out suburban houses, Barton's car trailed behind her. He was driving like a maniac, weaving between cars, swerving around oncoming traffic and running red lights, and she was put-putting through the air like a bloody mechanised blimp. Pathetic.

She was barely ahead of him when she reached his street and saw the mess Barton's home was in. The entrance was caked in soil and broken pottery, glass scattered across the path. Letty searched for signs of life and spotted the manhole cover askew in the middle of the road. Had this arsehole moved his family near one of the Sunken City entrances? She torpedoed down. As she reached the road, car brakes screeched nearby, Barton turning the last corner to get there. Daylight was fading, and his headlights bounced erratically over the street. Letty checked her surroundings: no sign of her fellow Fae.

"Where are you fuckers?" Letty shouted, but the sound of Barton's engine muted her efforts. His car skidded towards her, smoke erupting from under the tires. Barton jumped out, turning towards the devastation of his house, and Letty sprang into the air. "Take cover, you oaf!"

He ducked, dipping behind the car door.

Nothing happened.

Letty flew onto the tip of the door, searching the street. It was empty, the other humans quiet in their homes, a few lights on but no one looking. Barton watched her cautiously.

"Where are they?" he said. He stood away from the car, spotting the manhole cover. A man appeared in an upstairs window opposite them, but when Barton looked his way he ducked back inside. Barton was flicking glances between his home and the manhole cover, torn between them. Letty's eyes were drawn more to the Sunken City entrance.

"That's what I think it is, right?" she asked.

He grunted an affirmative.

Nothing good was coming from this, but the writing was on the wall.

"They're not here," Letty said.

Barton thumped over to the manhole and grabbed the cover with both hands. He gave it one short tug and sent it clanging onto the road. Letty saw the nosey neighbour had re-emerged to watch. Still no one else showing an interest.

Another engine approached, making Barton look up. His car was blocking the road, door open. Letty watched him carefully as he climbed into the hole, no hesitation there. He said, "Guess we part ways here. Do me a favour and piss off."

Letty didn't reply, turning from him to the other car. As Barton dropped out of view, a light flashed on her eyes, from the side, and she followed the glint to a muddle of tree branches. It flashed again, a red light, scanning across her eyes. A signal.

"Oh shit," she said. "Barton! It's a trap, don't –"

Too late.

With a blast and a thick puff of brick and mortar, the manhole collapsed. The road fell into the entrance, like a sinkhole, fissures spreading across the tarmac as the street shook. It had come down directly on top of Barton. He was gone beneath it, no sound as the dust settled. The approaching car skidded to a halt. The man in the house flapped his frightened hands and was joined at the window by an equally shocked woman.

"You fucking idiots!" Letty roared, buzzing towards the tree. She sped through the leaves, to where Fresko was drawing his rifle back up against his shoulder. As she got closer, his satisfied expression contorted to surprise, reading her anger. He stood. "It *is* you. We thought –"

She didn't let him finish, slamming into him. Fists balling over his shirt, she lifted him up off the branch, through the air, and drove him into the next branch up. She pinned him there with her full weight, wing flapping and artificial engine whirring, forearm shoved into his throat. "What the fuck were you thinking?"

Fresko's face flushed red, then blue, blood restricted. He struggled, but the initial impact had knocked him weak.

"You fucking idiot!" Letty shook him. "You fucking moron!"

She turned and shoved him back down. He landed on another branch, a foot below, falling too quickly to catch himself. Winded, he tried to push himself up. Letty dropped down next to him, pointing at the road. "You know what you've done? Do you?"

"Val," Fresko wheezed, struggling to recover his breath. "Val's orders."

"Fuck Val!" Letty shouted. "We need him!"

Fresko rose onto his hands and knees. He stopped there to glare up at her without apology. Letty's arms shook with tension, ready to hit him again. She shot another glance to the road, the cloud around the hole dispersing to reveal the shattered mess the tunnel had left. The other car driver was approaching it. A house door opened nearby.

"Pax," Letty said. She spun back to Fresko. "Where's Pax? What did you do with her?"

"The girl?" Fresko said, sitting back onto his haunches. "The Ministry one?"

"Yes, the fucking girl!" Letty launched at him again, one fist raised as the other closed on his tie. He scrambled back, gagging, as she tightened the tie around his neck. "What did you do?"

"She must be dead!" Fresko flapped his hands weakly, failing to break free as Letty sat on top of him, pulling even tighter. Letty shoved him down, pressing his face into the branch.

"Must be? You don't know?"

"She went down there, didn't come back!" Fresko said. "We left them to it!"

Letty let go, turning to face the road. The driver was waving at the people across the road, his back to the tree. He was calming them down.

"How long ago?" she asked.

Fresko coughed, nursing his neck. "I don't know. Half an hour."

"Because Val told you to."

"Because I thought she killed you!" Fresko replied forcibly. "I heard her say it!"

Letty shot him a vicious look. "Where's Mix?"

"Gone to the nearest entrances," Fresko said. "To make sure they're not getting back out."

"You bloody idiots," Letty said. "I was gone for two days. Two days and you screw the whole thing up."

". . . no, that's fine." The car driver's voice got louder as he went to the manhole cover. Taking charge of the situation. "You stay inside, there could be fumes."

Letty paused, pricking up her ears.

"Val said this was it," Fresko said. "We've got the weed. There's a crew going to the boy's hideout to collect the Dispenser. Barton, his family, they just needed to disappear. We're back in, Letty. We can put all this behind us."

"Val can burn," Letty told him quietly, her mind tracking away from the Fae situation towards what was happening below. The guy in the suit had stopped by the caved-in tunnel with his hands on his hips, but he wasn't surveying the damage. He was looking up towards the sky. "You sent Pax down there. You utter prick."

"Aren't you listening to me? We're back in. This ends it – we're done with the Dispenser."

"No." Letty shook her head. "I'm not done. *She* understood."

"That fucking human?" Fresko snapped, and she sparked into action again, kicking down at him. She caught him unawares, boot cracking into his chin, but he'd regained enough energy to react. He rolled aside, one hand to his face and the other whipping to his back, where he had a pistol holstered. He ended on his back with the gun aimed at Letty as she stood over him, aiming her pistol right back at him. "I won't let you screw us on this," he said.

"You did this, not me," Letty snarled. With her eyes locked on his, she raised her voice to shout sideways, "We're up here!"

Fresko's eyes widened, and he shot a look to the side, to the man in the road. He lost his focus in his surprise, the man in the suit looking up at them, and Letty quickly jumped aside, out of the firing line and up next to him. With Fresko's pistol still aimed forward, hers was at his neck. She growled, "All right, drop it."

"Pax's friends, I take it?" Casaria called up from the road.

"Something like that," Letty replied, staring Fresko in the eye. He was shaking his head, appalled. She said, "We're gonna make this right. And that starts with getting Pax back."

19

"Mum," Grace bleated. She hadn't stopped making little noises of suffering since the fairies' assault, and Holly and Pax had started to simply accept them. They must have travelled a mile through the featureless tunnels, through a handful of doors and around a number of turns that betrayed no logic. For the most part, they walked in silence, to conserve energy and avoid alerting any more lurking creatures, and though Grace had whimpered Pax was impressed at her attempts to keep quiet. Now that the horrible clicking had faded behind them, and the high-pitched trill hadn't sounded for a while, the teenager seemed ready to speak louder. "Mum. Mum?"

"What is it, dear?" Holly replied wearily. Fatigue had calmed her: she sounded as though she was busy reading a newspaper, not fleeing from hellish monsters. "Can it wait?"

"Mum, no." Grace came to a halt. Pax stopped and turned back. "My feet. I can't go on."

Pax frowned at Grace's dirt-encrusted feet, not having noticed before this moment that the girl had made the whole terrifying journey barefoot. She had never had a chance to put her shoes on when they raced out. Her soles were red around the edges, swollen and maybe bleeding. Holly stared without an answer. She looked to Pax for guidance.

"Here." Pax started undoing her laces. "Take my boots."

"They won't fit," Grace said.

"You can try," Pax said, but Grace was firm. "No, I can see. You've got tiny feet, and mine look like balloons. Can we just rest? Can we stop and rest, please? I'll be okay."

"Dear." Holly's lip trembled. She swung towards her and held her in a loving hug. Pax saw her eyes welling with emotion. "My brave little girl. My poor little thing, I'm so sorry."

"It's not your fault," Grace replied, but her voice caught with emotion too. "I should've told you where I was going. I should've stayed home. I'm so sorry I went to that park, Mum!"

"No no no." Holly rubbed her soothingly. "This isn't your fault."

Pax stared at them silently. She tried to steel herself. It was like watching a board pair against your flush, with all your money in the pot. You didn't give in to emotion, no matter how unfair or irrational or dangerous the world became. You couldn't betray signs of weakness. Crying could come later. She looked away, the mother and daughter hug shifting up a notch as they both started crying.

"Are we going to die, Mum?" Grace asked.

"No, of course not, it's okay," Holly said, but clearly didn't believe it herself.

"I think there's some steps ahead," Pax said. "We can sit down."

Her sober voice cut through their emotions, tearing their attention away from each other. There was a little shame in Holly's face. She nodded and guided Grace onward, towards the steps. Back the way they had come, something clicked, a sound like a bird pecking wood. Pax tried to ignore it, sure it was far worse than any bird.

The steps led up to a small enclosure. The trio climbed into an unlit room, only a few metres square, a secure hideaway. Grace shuffled into a shadowy corner and sat down. Pax joined her. Taking the load off, she realised now how depleted she was. There was barely any sensation left in her legs and her chest was tight with pain. The moment she slumped against the wall she wondered if it would even be possible to stand again.

"Why aren't there any exits?" Grace asked, with a child's curiosity.

"There are," Pax told her. "We just haven't found them yet."

"What else is down here?" Holly asked.

"A lot," Pax said. "But as long as we see them coming, we'll be okay." Even as she said it a voice in her head disagreed; if they saw a sickle coming, they wouldn't be able to outrun it.

"You're tired," Holly noted. Pax frowned. She'd done nothing to betray it, she thought. "And your leg's hurt. It looks safe here, you can rest. I can go on, I can find a way out."

"No." Pax shook her head. "We can't split up."

"You can't keep going, either of you. I can cover more ground alone."

Grace wasn't arguing, too worn down to talk. Her bright eyes stared hopefully at her mother. Pax hardly had the energy, either. She said, "You'll get lost." Holly had no answer, so Pax took out one of her lockpicks and scraped it against the wall. It was hard enough to leave a scratch. She held it up. "Take this. Mark your way."

Holly nodded. She hesitated in the entrance to the room and then jumped on Grace with a hug. "I love you. Don't forget that."

All Grace could muster in response was "Mum", and with that Holly ducked out of the room. Pax shifted closer to Grace and put an arm around her, awkwardly stiff. What the hell did she know about comforting people. She said, "She'll be fine. We're the ones in trouble, waiting here."

As she heard her own words, she knew it was both unhelpful and true.

She rested back against the wall and allowed herself a moment to reflect on how monumentally she had screwed up. In the space of a few days she had discovered terrible things about this terrible place no one was supposed to know existed, and rather than escape it all, or so much as lend a kidnapped young man a hand, she had got herself and an innocent mother and daughter trapped there, facing imminent demise at the hands, or claws or teeth, of the most ungodly things imaginable.

This, she told herself, was why she did what she did. Connecting with other people led to trouble. Arguments at a wedding, accusations of shoplifting, monsters in a tunnel – it was the same old story. You get involved, you suffer.

Holly's footsteps faded into the distance, leaving quiet in their little room. The sounds of the myriad creatures did not seem to be any closer, though they occasionally emitted unsettling chirps or groans from some unknown distance away. Grace had calmed down, at last, in her exhaustion, and snuggled up against Pax like a puppy searching for comfort. Pax held her stiffly, unsure what to do. She gave Grace a little pat on the head, then rested her hand on Grace's shoulder and sat uncomfortably still.

Pax and Grace sat listening to the drips and scratches, hoping for Holly to rush back with good news at any moment. Holly did not return, though. The minutes had stretched ever longer between the sounds of the Sunken City. Pax considered the worst. What if Holly had run into something? What if she couldn't find her way back? What else could they do? They couldn't move, in case Holly was trying to find them. And what about Barton? Had he made it home yet?

What did it matter. The fairies would not let them out, however lucky they were in escaping the creatures. And even if they did, what then? The Ministry were out to get her, the Fae were out to get her, by this point Bees and his employer probably thought she had betrayed them, too.

Something scratched down the hall, much closer than the previous sounds, making Pax jolt upright. Grace stirred with a little murmur, seeming to wake from sleep. Pax put a hand over her mouth and listened. Another scratch. It was in the tunnel, moving nearer. It chirped, like wood tapping together.

Grace started with surprise. Pax held her tighter.

"Not a sound," Pax whispered. "Not a movement. They sense vibrations."

It scratched closer, claws dragging against the brick. They held their breath and watched the room's opening with unblinking eyes. Another tapping sound signalled it was just outside. Even though she knew what was coming, the sight of it made Pax cringe.

The sickle moved into view slowly, its smooth head twitching from side to side as its vertical jawline snapped open and shut with another chirp. One of its gangly claws traced along the wall with a chalkboard screech as its canine body moved into the open. Pax felt Grace swelling in fear, and could almost hear her eyes bulging.

The beast paused in the doorway, its claw dragging to find the entrance. It tapped with its clawed feet, feeling for the steps.

Keep going keep going keep going, Pax prayed.

The monster reached a claw in towards them. It ventured up the steps. In the tight space, with it closing in on them, there was zero chance it wouldn't feel them sitting there. Pax and Grace were rigid, as the ungodly animal rose into the shadow of their room, mantis arms reaching around them. The claws rose over their heads, scratching the wall above, just missing their hair. Its wrinkled face tilted towards them, jaw opening and closing as though tasting the air. It stopped and let out another chirp.

Something in the pause told Pax it had found them.

"Run!" she screamed, and as the sickle reeled onto its hind legs she followed her instincts, same as facing any late-night predator. She drove both her fists into the creature's groin. Grace scrambled past, rolling out of the way of a flailing claw, as Pax punched and clawed at what felt like some kind of thick genitalia towards the base of the beast's torso. Whatever she got a hold of, it had the desired effect, as the sickle let out an ear-splitting shriek and fell to the side, arms curling around its face.

Pax followed Grace through the doorway. The teenager was already running, headlong down the tunnel, the wrong way.

"Grace! Here!" Pax shouted after her, waving a hand. In the room behind them, the monster was quickly recovering, its claws tapping against every wall as it tried to steady itself. Pax took a few steps in the opposite direction to Grace, seeing Holly's first scratch on the wall, but Grace was pelting away, shrieking, "No! No no no!"

The sickle emerged into the tunnel, turning towards Grace's yells. Without thinking, seeing its back was turned to her, Pax jumped onto it before it could give chase. She brought it to the floor, its stumpy dog legs unable to hold her weight, and as she slammed a hand onto the back of its head she saw that its claw arms couldn't pivot to the rear. It scratched around her, slicing at the bricks and gnashing its teeth, but for all the strength of its splayed limbs and bucking torso it couldn't reach her. She held on tight, pinning it down, and rammed its head into the floor. With sheer animal drive, she shoved its head into the floor again, momentarily weakening it. It stopped bucking long enough for her to adjust her grip, and with both hands she clutched the thing's twitching skull.

Grace had stopped, far down the tunnel, and she turned back to watch. No helping it, Pax thought – let her see, as she cracked the beast's head open against the floor.

20

"Take out your phone," Letty instructed as she glided down in front of Casaria. He looked at her uncertainly. "Take our your fucking phone so these prats watching don't think you're talking to dragonflies." He reached into his pocket, but Letty waved her pistol. "Ah ah, slowly."

He slowed down but continued, lifting the phone to his ear before responding. He put on a smile but spoke with a hint of aggression. "You're the ones that shot at me, aren't you?"

He turned back towards the couple in the nearby house, back inside, looking worriedly out through the front window. Whatever they were seeing, it wasn't the little people he saw, else they'd be doing more than watching. That was how the Fae worked, wasn't it? Shrouding themselves from onlookers. Casaria was better than that, though. He saw. He gave the couple a friendly *everything's okay* wave.

"You're the one who tore off my fucking wing," Letty snarled. She looked over her shoulder to Fresko, lingering in the air nearby. "Amazing how much damage you've managed to do without harming this greaseball."

Fresko did not respond. Being stripped of his weapons had left him grumpy and mute.

"How'd you know to come here?" Letty asked.

"Pax messaged me," Casaria said. "I take it things didn't work out between you. No surprise."

"Seriously?" Letty shot another look to Fresko. "You let her bring the Ministry to you, too, you prick."

"What did you do to her?" Casaria asked.

"Not me." Letty shook her head and pointed at Fresko. "Him. She's down there. And you're going to help us get her out. Where are your goons?"

Casaria looked to his empty car. "I work better without them. They'll follow me soon enough, though. What direction did she go in?"

Letty paused, studying him. "I don't even need to persuade you, do I? You're so sweet on her, you've run off from work to find her."

Casaria's smiling eyes suggested there was truth in it, but he didn't admit it. "The situation's complicated. Let's say we've got unfinished business."

"Then you can help me out."

"Why would I do that?"

"My people put her down there," Letty told him. "And they're not gonna let her back out. I don't see you being much use against my people on your own."

"And you're not going down there to get her out yourself," Casaria said, completing her thought. "This won't end well for you, you realise that? Even putting our differences aside for the moment."

"Doesn't matter," Letty said. "It's the way it is."

Casaria nodded slowly. He gestured to his car. "There's something I want from you, first."

"This is hardly the time for a fucking negotiation – we –"

"It's important." He was already walking to the car. Letty shot Fresko an uncertain look, but he shrugged. The pair hovered above Casaria's head as he pointed through the passenger window to the device lying on the seat. The metal and glass canister was instantly recognisable to them.

"How the hell did you get that?" Fresko asked.

"Doesn't matter. I need you to tell me how it works. And why it's never been used."

"Spin on it," Letty said.

"Do you even know the answer?" Casaria said, patiently.

Letty met his eyes angrily, but resisted the urge to insult him as his words hit her. His smug, knowing expression. He wasn't saying it like *he* knew, though. Letty thought of Valoria and her indifferent attitude to the device, and realised that the question Casaria was asking was the same one she had. Not the what of the machine, but the why. There was confusion on both sides of the divide. Pax had said it, hadn't she? Talking to these assholes might fill in the bigger picture.

"That was designed to destroy the berserker," Letty said. "Do you know that much?" Fresko opened his mouth to protest, but she flapped a hand at him and continued, "Not a word. Apothel stole this thing. All we needed was some electric weed to fuel it, and he took it away."

"All you needed was some electric weed?" Casaria replied sceptically.

"What'd I just say, Agent Orange?"

"Right." Casaria was smiling again. This time genuinely pleased, as though everything had been answered. He moved to get in the car. "Let's deal with it after saving Pax, shall we?"

"What? What the fuck are you smiling for? You think this is funny?"

"No." Casaria's smile spread. "I just get the idea that your people have been about as honest with you as mine."

Letty and Fresko flew in silence above Casaria's car as he left Dalford for the heart of the city. The next entrances to the Sunken City, their only hope, were the ones to the south. If the girls headed north, where the population got sparser and the Sunken City less developed, the nearest exit was over three miles away. It would be impossible for them to find it, let alone reach it, before the monsters caught up to them. The exits to the south were a mile at best, three of them with a network of winding tunnels that rose up and down between them. Then, whatever direction they went in, it would be perfectly possible to go by all the exits without ever seeing one, continuing towards the caverns of central Ordshaw.

Passing into a more built-up area, Letty shot Fresko disappointed, angry glares. He was trying to avoid eye contact, but eventually he responded, raising his voice above the sound of the wind. "Why are you doing this?"

Letty gave him a look to say the question itself was insulting.

"You know as well as me," Fresko said, "that everything we've done, ever since Apothel, has been to mend this rift. Leave them down there, ice this fool and take the Dispenser back, and it's done. We're done. You wanna throw that away for some fucking human? What happened to you?"

"It's not about some fucking human," Letty said. She paused, thinking it wasn't *just* about some fucking human. "Something major is off with Val. She isn't interested in stopping the berserker."

"So what?"

Letty slowed down to give him a severe look. "*So what?*"

"It's not our job to care," Fresko said. "We're tying up loose ends. We were supposed to recover the Dispenser, not use it. Wasted all our damned time drawing the Citizen back into this, just to dot all the Is – if Val isn't interested then we wasted time, that's all."

"Well, shit." Letty spat at him. "Sounds like you're okay with the Fae Transitional City being transitional forever? Leave the whole Sunken City to the abominations?"

"Why not?" Fresko said. "They feed off the humans, not us. What do we need the Sunken City for? We're good as we are. Or were."

Letty glided closer to him and swiped out, cuffing a hand across the back of his neck. She kept close, face near his as he tried to move away. She shouted, "That human down there, she got it. You don't leave the world to rot when you can do something about it. And she's my friend, and she fucking matters, okay?"

Fresko's eyes were fixed with shock. "You've lost it, Letty. Listen to yourself. The Council, the Dispenser, the berserker – none of that's our problem. None of it was ever our problem, not until you made it our problem."

It was hopeless. Him and the rest of them.

Letty picked up speed, moving ahead, just to put some distance between them.

"Casaria."

"Where are you?" Landon demanded through the phone. Casaria checked his mirrors, in case he was being followed. Didn't look like it.

"I'm driving," he said. "Not the best time."

"Yeah, I can hear that," Landon said, actually sounding annoyed. Good for you, Casaria smiled, finally emoting. "You were supposed to hand in the car. And why am I hearing reports that you've turned the power on across the Dalford sector? I'm assuming it was you that breached the Dalford entrance?"

Casaria considered channelling Pax's spirit for the correct response of *fuck* and *you*. Resisting long enough to think of the task ahead, he decided there was a better way. "There's some civilians in the Sunken City. The Dalford entrance has been destroyed."

"What?" Landon gasped.

"It's the Fae, Landon," Casaria continued, almost singing the words in a delighted I-told-you-so. "They went after Darren Barton's family and dropped half the road on him. Now there's three people down there, four if Barton's alive. If *any* of them are alive, they're running from the *praelucente*."

"Jesus Christ."

"You want to know what you need to do?"

Landon said nothing for a moment. "Where are you?"

"I'm heading for the entrance on Pestfax Road. I've got a couple of fairies with me – Sam Ward would be happy to hear that. But there's likely to be some Fae ordinance on the other entrances, one of the Fae is going Rambo on them. You want to know what you need to do?"

Landon paused again. In a small voice, he answered, "What?"

"Send people to Dalford, see if you can dig out Barton. Send people to Old Fairbrook and Pointing Avenue, check if those entrances are safe. Watch out for Fae traps. Send people in if you can. I'll take care of Pestfax. In the meantime, get Mathers, tell him to get me some electric weed, whatever it takes, and ship it up to Pestfax Road. If it comes to it, I want to have a fighting chance."

More silence.

Casaria waited, then said, "Landon, you still with me?"

"Yeah."

"You gonna do all that?"

"Yeah."

The sun had ducked behind the buildings by the time Casaria pulled up near Pestfax Road. He left the car a block away and approached the entrance painfully unarmed. It had been easy enough to steal back his own car, activate power switches and take the Fae device under the guise of courier work, but there'd been no way to get his weapons back.

This entrance was at the back of a dive bar; a heavy door sunk four feet below the street, like a tunnel for deliveries. All the neighbours assumed it belonged to someone else. Casaria entered the alleyway, shining his torch along the walls that flanked it. The problem with this city, he reflected, was that there were countless places that a two-inch fairy could hide. Especially with the dusk light casting shadows. And it looked like he'd lost the pair that were supposed to be supporting him. Flakes.

He shone his torch up and down the cracks of the entrance, over the hinges, around the handle. It was an old door, metal mottled in places that had taken on too much water, green paint cracked all over. Infinite possibilities for a tiny trace of Fae explosives to be hidden.

"Back off," a rough voice said, somewhere above. Casaria turned to face the man. Of course, a miniature thug in the denim guise of a biker, sitting on the alley's rear fence. Mix had a pistol in each hand, pointed his way. "It's not meant for you."

"I'm guessing this isn't the only one you've rigged," Casaria said. "You realise the night patrols will be starting soon. Did you intend to warn *everyone* not to go in?"

"Consider yourself the lucky one. Walk away, Ministry man. Quickly and permanently."

Casaria didn't move. The gunman was too far away for him to do anything, but he was damned if he was going to back down and do what he was told.

Mix looked away, though, eyes or ears picking out something that Casaria had not sensed. The other Fae, somewhere in the sky. Casaria looked up too. It was too dark to make anything out. The buzz of that odd machine on Letty's back got closer, louder.

"Never had any goddamned sense, did you!" Letty shouted.

"Letty?" Mix said. "You're alive?"

She dropped down next to him, her pistols raised, and he understood the threat immediately. Mix jumped off the fence, wings carrying him up and along the wall. Casaria watched as the pair squared off, spinning through the air like tiny fighter planes.

"Take the explosives off the damned door!" Letty commanded.

"What for?" Mix shot back, spiralling above Casaria's head, keeping his distance.

"If she's hurt I'm gonna gut you!"

Mix made an angry noise from somewhere deep in his gut. "Soft on a human? You're a disgrace, Letty. Would've been better if you *had* died."

Letty opened fire without warning. Mix twirled to the side, the bullets missing, and he started firing back. The pair of them flitted from side to side, four pistols blazing as they avoided the shots. At about two metres apart, it seemed neither could get a good shot on the other in flight. Following them with his eyes, Casaria sidestepped to the bins against the opposite wall and took off a large circular lid. When the two fairies had gone through the first clip in their pistols, they each threw a weapon aside to reload the other, never slowing down. Mix flew into a wall and used his legs to spring back off it. Letty somersaulted through the air to avoid his counter-attack. They started shooting again, flying in zig-zags. The chase had reversed, Mix going after Letty now, and she led him down, skating towards the ground.

Mix flew head on into the bin lid, the force of the blow sending him slamming into the wall, pistol flying away. He slid to the floor, wings twitching, as Letty doubled back. She fired at his almost motionless body. The shots glanced off the concrete next to him and her gun clicked empty as she sped towards him. Reaching Mix, she skirted suddenly to the side. Stepping over them, Casaria saw he had drawn another pistol, which he fired straight up. Casaria dropped back as the bullet glanced off his chin, shooting up the full length of his face along the cheek and catching his eyebrow. Casaria yelled, clutching a hand to his face, as Letty jumped onto Mix and kicked the gun from his hand.

The fairies grappled on the floor, exchanging punches. With the height advantage, Letty used her wing to rise above Mix's flailing fists. Then she sank back down to punch his face, again and again, and he finally fell back. She grabbed a knife from his leg sheath and twisted it back to stab him.

Fresko pushed between them.

Letty was thrown sideways, spinning again. She stopped, furious. Fresko had Mix up under an arm. He growled, "You've lost it, Letty. He's one of *us*!"

Letty panted, looking back at him angrily, but the fight was over. With Mix barely conscious, Fresko was shaking his head, disappointed. He carried Mix's weight, beating his wings to propel himself up towards the darkening sky. He shouted, "Enjoy your life with the fucking humans, you've earnt it!"

Casaria edged away from the wall, one hand supporting himself and the other applying pressure to his bleeding wound. He watched the fairy glide down to retrieve her guns, apparently not interested in pursuing her colleagues. He said, "You should've killed them."

21

Barton's ankle was stuck under a chunk of concrete, his left arm hurt all the way up and the impact from the fall had potentially shattered something. He reflected that he had otherwise been fortunate. His ears were ringing and his head throbbed worse than a hangover, but the rest of his body was apparently unscathed, other than a few surface wounds. The bulk of the blood was coming from a reopened wound on his head. It had bled enough for one day without killing him – not worth worrying about.

Using the light of his phone, he searched for something to use as a lever. Roads and tunnels had iron bars and that crap sticking through them, didn't they? You always saw shards like that in the rubble. Not here, it seemed. He had to get his hands underneath the concrete block instead, and put his back into heaving upwards, knowing this stupid movement was going to haunt him for life. It didn't matter, though, just another pain to add to the collection. He groaned and tugged and shifted the weight just enough to wriggle out. He gave the busted ankle the briefest look. It was limp and thick with blood. Examining the damage wasn't going to help.

Barton clambered up, falling against the wall and taking his weight on his other foot. He shone his phone up the tunnel. The lights were working up ahead, that was something. He took out his hip flask and swigged what was left of the glo. Barely a mouthful. It would do, though, for a short while. He let the flask drop with a clatter. Dead weight.

He waited a minute, while his head partially cleared and his eyes started to refocus.

The trails began to appear in the air before him. The colours of the myriad beasts, hanging like slug paths. So many of them. He took a few limping steps along the wall and peered ahead, to where a thick purple line led up to a doorway. A tuckle had come through here. Tried to smash through the door.

As the glo took control, he saw the rest, too. Hounds and sickles. A turnbold in the mix, with its multiple skeletal faces. A horde of creatures. And at its centre, the minotaur.

Pax was desperately trying to recall the floorplans of the Sunken City from Apothel's book, but even the sections she could picture seemed, in her recollection, to be random lines. Uneven, probably not to scale and completely useless. There were names of entrances, but it was no help to know that one of the tunnels came out near the Morricone Theatre. That might be a two-mile walk away, it might be five miles. And it might be in any direction.

She had given Grace her coat, which the teenager draped over her shoulders after a hug of gratitude. Pax let her believe it was a gift of kindness, not just because the murderous grapple with the sickle had unbearably raised her body temperature. Grace was still soldiering on barefoot, though, which worried Pax. How far could they go before she collapsed?

The noises were behind them but getting no further away. Occasional new chirps and clicks kept startling them. Whatever was out there, of which there seemed to be an awful lot, was still following them. Equally daunting was the fact that after the very first tunnel they had lost Holly's scratches on the walls. Maybe she hadn't made them clear enough, maybe she had simply given up on the idea, maybe something worse. Yet Pax told Grace they were going the right way, with nothing whatsoever to base that on, and the girl seemed to believe her.

Eventually the tunnels got wider and more complex. One or two expanded to the width of a narrow street, with platforms at the edges, like walkways. Some resembled railway tunnels in size and shape, though without any of the fixtures to suggest rails had ever been laid there. It was remarkable, and Pax started to get an idea of the magnitude of this place – and how much vaster and more incredible it would seem to the Fae. These tunnels led to even wider rooms, with one large enough to house a truck, its ceiling over twenty feet high. It had four exits, one on each wall. They chose one that was up a small flight of steps. The lights were less reliable in these greater expanses. Some of the rooms were too large for the small lights to reach their corners; others, including whole corridors, did not have their lights activated. Pax assured Grace that there was nothing in the shadows, well aware it was nonsense.

When it was starting to seem like they would never encounter another living being in this nightmare maze, and would be doomed to walk its halls forever, a movement cut across the tunnel ahead. Another human. Pax and Grace stopped dead.

"Mum?" Grace asked hopefully.

Am I a bad mother? Am I a bad wife?

The two questions kept circling around Holly's mind as she picked her way through the tunnels. She had left what she thought was an admirable trail of scratches along the wall, but she was grimly aware that she had also left her only daughter behind her with a miscreant poker player, in an underground system teeming with monsters. She was also grimly aware that her husband had been dealing with all this for many years and had never once thought she could handle the truth of it.

Am I *that* hard to talk to that he couldn't trust me with this?

She had travelled through what seemed like a dozen narrow tunnels without getting anywhere, finding two doors that were locked and one set of stairs that led up to what seemed to be an exit, but turned out to be an impassable brick wall. She could swear that she had walked down some of these tunnels before, but her scratches were not on the walls. Whoever built the place must have produced an awful lot of identical mundane passages.

At least the sounds of the creatures were dying down. The birdlike noises and the caustic barks had been starting to grate on her. She kept calm by convincing herself that even here there must be some pathetic little man at the top of it all who could be told off. That would make her feel better when she got out. Locate the fool in charge and watch him shrivel up in the knowledge of his ineptitude.

If she could escape.

She turned a corner and finally saw a break in the monotony. The walls, for so long, had been nothing but tired concrete and brick; now, there was another texture, bumps in the shadows. Roots. Plant life. Something was growing out of the corner of a wall at the far end of the long corridor. It gave her hope. She hurried towards it, finding renewed energy to pick up her speed.

It was about the height and thickness of a sunflower, with large green roots tangling around its base and snaking up one wall.

As she got closer, she slowed down. Something about the plant wasn't right. There was a strange smell in the air, something she couldn't quite place but that made her nostrils wrinkle. A few more steps and it became too noxious for her to continue, a vile smell. She covered her nose and mouth and studied the plant. It was moving. The head on its thick green stalk swayed from side to side, while its centre, a broad brown circle, bubbled with a gooey liquid. Around its roots she noticed more liquid. The thing was secreting slime. One bubble expanded and then popped; with it came a rush of gas. Holly gagged and covered her face. She quickly backtracked, disgusted.

Reaching a corner, looking back down a tunnel she knew she recognised, Holly froze. The wall was bare. She looked closer, ran a hand over the brickwork. Her scratch had gone.

"Oh no," Holly gasped. "Why . . ."

She scanned the walls, searching for any blue patches. There was nothing there, but she knew in her gut what had happened. She ran back down the tunnel, tracing her fingers along the wall, searching for her markings.

They were all gone.

She took the lockpick and hurriedly carved into the wall: *Why?*

She stood back and waited, looking up and down.

It appeared, rising from the floor, the flat shape of a blue screen. The blue rectangle moved over her words and rested there. The brick distorted, the indentations turning in on themselves, healing before her eyes.

A moment of inactivity, then new letters formed, carving themselves into the brick.

Ugly.

Holly stared at the letters, shocked. She put her full indignation into a one-word response. "*Wow.*"

The word slowly faded again.

She thought for a moment, then scraped into the blue rectangle: *Way out?*
Her words faded and new letters appeared.
Myriads coming.
She put her hands on her hips and relented at the useless nature of this communication. How had Barton let whoever was hiding behind these flat squares tell him what to do for so long? She listened, though, and the sounds of the creatures were indeed getting nearer. There was another groan, like the movements of a pipe they had heard when they first came down here. Making a quick decision, she turned away from the antagonistic blue thing and took an alternative route into the next tunnel, away from the flower.

Pax and Grace hurried after the shape, turning a corner and seeing whoever it was disappear into another doorway. Grace shouted, "Mum! It's us! Wait!"

Pax grabbed Grace's arm and pulled her back. Grace tried to break free but Pax held her fast. "I don't think it's your mum."

"Who else would be down here?" Grace replied hotly.

"Grace, wait," Pax said forcibly, pulling her still. "That might not even be a person."

"Get off me! You're not helping!" Grace shoved Pax and turned towards the shape. She shouted again, running down the tunnel. "Mum!"

Pax watched her, thinking of the unthinkable act she had already done in protecting this girl from that dog demon. She could leave her, save herself. Grace was stumbling like a drunk goat, her feet barely functioning. She was so skinny and clueless, she wouldn't stand a chance against anything down there. Pax's mind ran back to her diminutive fairy friend, her ability to let all this go. Friend. That was rich. She was better than Letty, she'd already made that decision. Given the choice, she had to do the right thing. She charged after Grace. It took no time to catch up.

Pax skipped ahead of the hobbling girl and checked through the doorway into a cavernous expanse. As Grace drew up next to Pax, they both came to the same conclusion. There was no way Holly would have run into a room like that.

"The other way," Pax said gently, nodding back up the tunnel. "Whatever it was, we have to get away from it."

As she spoke, a light crept into the vast room, capturing their attention. On the far wall, a high-up doorway glowed faint blue. The light grew stronger, flowing like water, its source slowly moving into the room. Its growing flicker revealed a cathedral-like expanse with a domed ceiling. The pair were halfway up in their entrance, on the edge of a ring walkway that ran around an open centre, a drop of ten feet or so to the ground.

Pax had no name for the spectre they had followed, but she realised its purpose. It was designed to lead them to this place, and the thing that was entering it. A sound like a thunder crack came from the far tunnel.

"That way." Pax turned out of the room, but far down the corridor a shape had already appeared. Another canine centaur, its claws stretched ahead of it. It was searching the air, unaware that they were up ahead. Pax spun in the other direction. A dog was sniffing at the opposite end of the tunnel. Its flesh was smoking.

"Shit," Pax uttered under her breath. Grace moved close to her, more terrified than ever. They both looked back into the vast room, the brilliant blue growing ever brighter. Shards of electricity licked into the room from the distant doorway, like lizards' tongues. The room was otherwise empty, though, and there were at least two other doorways. Dark voids, but possibilities nonetheless.

They had been running from it since their arrival, but somehow they had arrived at the heart of their pursuer's domain. The myriad creatures surrounded it, but did not come close to it. Their best hope, Pax saw, was to get close. To go through the middle. No one understood it, after all. The Fae said they hated it but they hadn't gone through with stopping it. The Ministry wanted to protect it. There was a chance. The slightest chance that they might be able to brave it.

She took Grace's hand and looked her in the eye.

"I need you to trust me," she said, and pulled the teenager into the room.

22

Descending into the Sunken City, Casaria searched the walls with torchlight for any more fairy welcome presents. Down the steps and to the right, the lights were on. Letty was left watching from outside. Casaria turned back and said, half serious, "Not coming?"

"I got you in," Letty replied. "You get them out."

He nodded, creeping further into the tunnel. Unarmed. The fairy clearly had no idea that this was not what he usually did, but he felt naked without so much as a gun or a knife. All he had was the Fae device, which clearly had no fuel.

"Don't worry," Letty said. "I'll keep watch. In case my boys come back."

Casaria hummed. That wouldn't be much help if he ran into a griffix, would it?

He kept moving, into the featureless abyss of one of the Sunken City's anonymous tunnels. He took a breath. The Ministry would soon catch up to them with real weapons, but he'd be kept out. Likely as not, they'd have Sam Ward along, saying he was unfit for a sensitive rescue operation. But it had to be him down there, getting Pax out. Not them, not those glorified crossing guards.

Why? Why did it matter? He gave one final look back up to Letty. She was floating around at head-height, arms folded. He knew. It was the same reason that this ridiculous little creature had come to help.

Pax did not deserve to be down there, and for it all he could not bring himself to stop caring.

He pocketed his torch and waved the fairy off. "Just keep this door safe."

The pain in his ankle had all but subsided as Barton pressed on through the tunnels. He didn't think about the damage he might be doing to himself; the important thing was that he couldn't feel it. He picked up speed as the trail became clearer, the walls covered in claw marks. He was getting closer, but the horde was still moving, otherwise he would have caught up to it already. That was a good thing. If it was moving this quickly, it had to be still giving chase.

There were too many colours of creatures in the air for him to discern what he was going to come across first. Glogockles, turnbolds, sickles and perhaps another tuckle. They would be moving separately, different spokes of the minotaur's wheel, but they were close enough together that he might see one or all of them at any time.

It didn't matter.

Nothing mattered, he kept telling himself, other than getting Grace to safety.

The glo had given him strength. Bring on the beasts.

*

Pax and Grace sprinted through the domed room, in a low defensive crouch, for all the help it would afford them, as the electric arms of the berserker lashed into the room, lighting their way in a dazzling blue. The thing was moving into the open like a collection of lightning whips, swinging in and out through the doorway as the central body, still approaching, got brighter and brighter. The pair followed a slope down, below the tunnel that the thing was coming through, and they bolted for an arched opening on the opposite side, tucked under a concrete walkway.

As they reached the exit, one of the flashing limbs of the berserker crashed through the walkway, its tremendous power shattering the concrete. The pair staggered with a shared scream as the destructive limb rested there, pressing against the wall ahead. As it touched the bricks, sparking offshoots dug into the bricks like clawing fingers.

Pax pulled Grace towards the next doorway, glancing back at the tunnel. The monster was emerging, finally, its long electric limbs pulling the rest of it in like a kraken. Pax held up her hands to shield her eyes from it, the flash blinding as it came into view. As it revealed itself, though, the light faded, diluted by the size of the room. Grace was stone still, mouth wide open, and Pax had to shake her by the shoulders to get her moving.

"Look at it!" Grace gasped, but Pax was more interested in surviving. She shoved Grace ahead, towards the next opening. Grace tripped, distracted, and Pax heaved her back up. She pushed the girl into the tunnel, just as another electric limb cracked into the floor. A shockwave jolted through the ground and the walls, throwing Pax off balance. She fell into Grace and they tumbled down together, half-turning back. Multiple electric limbs were striking the floor behind them, pounding it like a stamping spider.

"There!" Grace pointed into their new tunnel. She scrambled out from under Pax and ran. Beyond the entrance Grace was going for, there was another small shape ahead, a low, sniffing creature. Two of them. Small smoking dogs. They looked up and bared their teeth. Twenty metres ahead, perhaps, beyond Grace's target door.

Pax jumped up and sprinted as Grace charged at the door fearlessly, seeming to not even see the dogs. The dogs started barking and Grace shrieked. That made them run; two hounds pounding towards her. Grace slammed into the door and rolled through, but the dogs were close, about to leap as Pax got there. They stopped, skidding to a halt with a whine just before her. Pax froze too. The dogs backed off, growling and snapping, puffs of smoke coming out of their mouths, and other orifices, and hovering over their fur. Pax turned a slow look over her shoulder. One of the electric limbs was snaking into the tunnel, still coming after them. Pax jumped through the doorway and slammed it shut as the dogs ran yelping in the other direction.

There was no light, but she could hear Grace nearby, panting and slapping the bricks, feeling for a way forward. She cried, "There's no exit! We're trapped!"

Pax turned back to the closed door. The light from the searching limb came through the edges of the door, giving the room a dull, eerie glow. Grace was right: it was an alcove with no exit, a tiny circular room built of brick, with a domed ceiling and no breaks in the walls. Pax leant against the door, out of options. She thought of Holly, somewhere out there, perhaps their only hope, and chose to deal with her distress through indignation.

"Why the hell did anyone even build this room?"

Barton was closing in on the sounds; he recognised the probing click of a sickle. Another twenty-metre tunnel and he was sure he would get to them. The clicking became frantic, though, and suddenly drew nearer. It was on the move. The pad of its claws across the floor was rapid, a pursuit he knew all too well. It had found a target. Had it somehow sensed him? He braced himself, spreading his arms, waiting for its approach.

The monstrous shape burst across the end of the tunnel and continued, gone in a flash.

Barton frowned as the sound of the monster died down. It was replaced by footsteps ahead, and the chatter of two men.

"Told you, just a sickle," one of them said.

"No, I've still got a reading. To the right."

Barton braced himself again; the two men stepped into view at the end of the tunnel. One of them had what looked like a radar dish out in front of him. The other, more tense in posture, had both hands on a pistol held at his side. One thick, one thin. The one with the scanner lowered it and waved towards Barton.

"There he is!" he said. "Hey, you there! We're here to help."

Barton looked back the way he'd come, then towards the men. They were approaching him.

"Christ, are you okay?" the thinner one asked, gawking at Barton's injuries.

The glo was fading. Barton's focus was growing weaker, the sounds less clear. Now that he'd been reminded of his state, and seen two ordinary people from the ordinary world above, all his strength and resolve seemed to be fading. He heard himself murmur, "My daughter . . ."

"Yeah, we're getting them all out, don't you worry," one of the men assured him.

Barton shook his head. They wanted to stop him. To take him out. He tried to move away from them but swayed. One of the men shouted something and he lashed out. Suddenly they were both on top of him, trying to hold him still. He threw a punch that connected, but it wasn't enough. They were swearing, flapping at him as he broke free. He made it two paces, maybe more, but the effort made his head spin. He fell to the side, hand on a wall to support himself. Then he slumped forward, crashing into the floor. As his consciousness faded, he heard one of them approaching. "Christ, we need a medic."

*

Holly heard a commotion somewhere ahead and paused. If those were shouts, her daughter might be in trouble. Or it might be something else, drawing her into danger. She started to skirt the sound, through tunnels that seemed to run parallel, without getting too close. She listened carefully for more.

At a doorway that ran towards the noise, she stopped and found a drop, a ledge looking over a brick courtyard below. There was a sound below like a pig sniffing for truffles. A large creature shuffling about. She leant into the room, looked down and immediately regretted the decision.

A creature that looked like a four-foot hairless man with spiky bones exposed along the length of his spine was crouched over something else; a heap of gore and fur that might once have been a creature but that was, in this instant, nothing more than a bloody mess. It was still moving. A pawed foot twitched and a round eye, part of what must have been its head, looked fearfully up towards her. The thing crouching over it was feeding, its snout rooting into flesh, splashing blood to the sides.

A hand clamped over Holly's face and pulled her back, held her tightly enough that her scream was muffled. A man's voice whispered, "Best not to disturb it, come."

He frog-marched her down the tunnel without removing his hand. She did as he bid, stiffly walking, eyes ahead. They reached a corner and he said, "I'm going to let you go. Can you be cool?"

She nodded.

He released her and she jumped away and turned back in one motion. Her index finger was up and pointing, ready to scold. Casaria's usual charm was somewhat diminished by the blood caking half his head and shirt. Still, when she saw his smile Holly found herself conflicted, halfway between fear and thankfulness.

"Where's Pax?" he asked.

Holly resisted answering, with questions of her own. "Who are you? What happened to you?"

"I'm here to help," he said, then repeated, "Where's Pax?"

Guilt suddenly rolled over Holly and she threw her hands up, despairing. "I don't know! I don't know where I am, or where anyone else is – I left my daughter, I wanted to help – but I left her, oh God, I'm a terrible person –"

"All right, all right." Casaria closed his eyes. "Let's get you out of here, at least. Christ."

He gestured for her to follow, with a dirtily bandaged hand, and walked ahead. She rushed to his heel as he continued without looking back, barely seeming to register her presence. He knew these corridors, she could see. She asked, "What are you doing down here?"

"Came to save you, didn't I?" he replied, though he hardly sounded happy about it. "When did you lose the others?"

"Ages ago. I left markings in the walls, but they disappeared."

Casaria hummed, not surprised.

"There are things down here," Holly told him. "Terrible things, lots of them. We need to be very careful."

"Sure. We don't have far to go."

"Thank God."

"Casaria?" A portly man in a tatty suit plodded into view, low on breath, unsurprisingly considering the state of him. A young fellow in a leather jacket appeared behind him, looking miserable. "You found another one!" The bigger man hurried towards them, waving his free hand; Holly saw he had a pistol in the other. She took a step behind Casaria for cover. The man huffed, looking at his gun, "Oh, don't mind this, ma'am, it's for your protection. Casaria, what were you thinking, coming down here?"

"Doing your job for you, evidently," Casaria said. "Now you can take her back to the surface and I can keep going."

"Absolutely not. You need to get out of here, now. You're in enough trouble as it is. What happened to your face?"

Holly frowned at Casaria, not liking where this was going. She reflected that the filthy bandaged hand and bloody face might have been clues as to him being bad news.

"Worry about it later," Casaria said. "Did you bring the weed, Landon?"

Holly was about to exclaim in shock; none of them looked like pot-heads. Maybe the younger one. But Landon thrust his hands onto his hips, puffing himself up, and said, "You're out of your mind if you thought Mathers would even entertain the idea."

Casaria gaped at him. "They're in the heart of the thing. And I have something that can help. You want them to just outrun it?"

"You couldn't have seriously thought it was an option," the leather jacket sneered. "Even if we knew what the machine did, why would we risk damaging the *praelucente*?"

"Because we need to!" Casaria snapped, marching towards him with his finger stiffly pointing. The young man retreated, fumbling for his gun, a moment from lifting it.

Landon stepped between them. "You need to *leave*."

"So you can do what? Create a distraction by wobbling your lard?"

"We already found a man, we're pulling him out. Given his state, I'd say it's a big gamble that the others are even still alive."

"They are!" Holly blurted out. "My daughter – and the girl. You have to find them!"

All three men turned to her. Their expressions said her desperation was clear.

"This is a mess," Landon said.

"Take her out of here," Casaria said, "and give me your gun."

Landon eyed him. His hesitation was enough for Casaria to take charge. He ripped the pistol from Landon's hands and turned back the way he had come. Landon watched and didn't protest. He turned to the young man and, in an attempt to save face, snapped, "Go with him, I'll take care of the others."

The leather jacket hesitated, too, but rushed after Casaria.

"This way, ma'am," Landon said, holding a thick arm up. She followed, with one final look back towards Casaria. Landon's laboured breath got heavier as he walked, from discomfort, it seemed, as well as poor health.

"Will they be okay?" Holly asked. He did not reply.

They turned a corner to where Barton was lying. Landon started, "You can help me –"

Holly shot ahead with a cry, running to her husband's side. "Diz!"

23

Pax and Grace pressed themselves up against the far wall as more light seeped through the cracks around the door. Something thumped against it, like an enormous beast knocking to get in.

"What are we going to do?" Grace whispered.

Pax was out of ideas. The monstrous electric creature was filling the tunnel beyond their only exit. Even if they could get past it, there were creatures surrounding the whole thing. Had they been in its inner circle ever since she killed the sickle? Had they run the wrong way, and cut a path towards the inevitable ever since?

The door banged again, shaking on its hinges. Sparks of electricity flickered through.

"It's not going to hold," Grace said.

"It'll hold," Pax told her. "It has to."

She knew it wouldn't, staring at the shaking door. And no one was coming to save them. The only option was for one of them to save the other.

A plaintive howl rolled past Casaria and Gumg.

"We've saved two people, isn't that enough?" Gumg said, struggling to keep pace as Casaria strode ahead. Casaria did not reply. "We can get all the information we need from her, leave the others down here, deal with the aftermath when the horde has moved on."

Casaria kept his eyes ahead, only walking faster.

Gumg broke into a trot to catch up. "He had this on him, might interest you." Casaria gave Gumg a look as the younger man pulled a bag from his pocket. They stopped. Casaria stared at the glowing sack of mud. He reached, but Gumg dropped back, keeping it out of range. "Government property, now. You want to see what this is capable of, we take it back to the Ministry."

"You're raising your own bar in stupidity. We need that right now," Casaria said. "Where did you even get it? *Who* had it?"

"The other one we found. Barton, I guess. Don't know what he was up to but if you'd seen the state of him. Man, you're not using your head. This girl isn't worth losing your job over. Or worse." Casaria raised a fist, but Gumg was ready. His pistol was up, and though he took a fearful step back, he was resolute. "I'm doing you a favour. Think about it. You're not following protocol, breaking half a dozen rules with no upside for the Ministry. With this, with that machine, you can actually get ahead. Just play ball. What's this girl worth?"

Casaria turned away again; there was no time to argue. "We need to keep moving."

The sounds of the myriad creatures were getting closer.

"I oughta leave you down here with them!" Gumg called out. He could not, though, and Casaria knew it. The younger man rushed after him, but was not giving up. He said, "We can go as far as the break line. Hit a few of the creatures and give you an idea of how bad this is. But that's it. Then you have to admit it's over, turn back. Even if we *could* get them out, what'd be the point? The Ministry won't let them walk away."

Casaria gave him a sideways look. He wasn't sure, now, if he had an answer himself. Gumg was right. Saving Pax, and trying to free her, could spell the end of his career. It would lead to questioning and imprisonment, at best. In all likelihood, she would have to disappear. The thought of her ever joining the Ministry, after what she'd already done, was impossible. And even if she escaped their wrath, what then? She'd betrayed him from the start, and she was dangerous to the Sunken City. What use was she? Why did he care?

He shook the thoughts from his head. He cared precisely because she didn't. She'd defied the Ministry. And she'd reached out to him for help. He cared because this was his domain, and he was the sheriff down here. He wasn't going to let these monsters, or Ministry bullshit, get in the way of him doing his job and saving her. He'd figure the rest out later.

Turning another corner, they were both struck momentarily still by a tremendous fluttering, as though a cluster of bats had just taken flight. The noise grew louder, rapidly approaching.

"What is that?" Gumg asked.

"You should know," Casaria replied, readying both hands on the pistol.

Gumg cleared his throat before venturing a guess. "Wormbirds."

They flew into the tunnel, a flock of skeletal creatures with jagged, leathery wings. They fanned out across the ceiling, knocking into each other, ferociously swarming towards the men. Their curved bone-like beaks snapped with a war cry sharper than a pack of dogs barking.

Casaria stood his ground and started shooting, the pistol erupting in electric blasts that disappeared into the flock with explosions of feather and bone. Gumg looked over his shoulder, ready to run. Casaria shouted, "Stand your ground!"

Gumg did as he was told and started shooting too.

There were dozens of them, spread too wide for each shot to catch more than one or two at a time. As they got closer, the dark flock's detail became more apparent, white eyes flashing and tendrils dangling from their bellies, their noise roaring into a din. Gumg let out his own escalating shout of defiance. When the flock flapped within a few metres of them, Casaria saw Gumg's foot shift, the young man ready to run. Casaria turned his gun. One quick blast to the younger man's knee.

Gumg looked up in disbelief, more shocked by the betrayal than the pain. His leg was all but severed below the knee as he crumpled to the floor, mouth dumbly open, asking *why*? Casaria snatched at his pocket to take the bag of electric weed and leapt out of the way as the birds descended.

Gumg screamed under the attack. The wormbirds covered him, in a formidable cluster, too many for Gumg's final few shots and flapping hands to fend off. Their wings enveloped him, beaks pecking him into submission with sharp jabs. As their talons gripped his flesh and they settled, the belly tendrils stretched towards him. More and more piled onto Gumg, until he was completely hidden under the writhing mass. The whole flock was united, their flapping wings cloaking the egg-laying taking place underneath.

Casaria adjusted the setting on his gun and aimed down at the mass. They were all so concentrated now, the task was easy. Three shots of the wider, short-range charge and the mass was obliterated.

The pile of bodies smouldered on the floor, the stench of burnt flesh filling the tunnel. A few wings flapped up and down for a moment, and one or two of the birds fled back down the tunnel, having survived the final scorching.

Casaria stepped over the mangled remains and continued, giving the carnage no more than a cursory glance. As he walked, he threaded the pistol through his belt and lifted the Fae device, looking for a way to open it and fit the weed inside.

Holly's heart lifted as they broke free of the noxious underground, with Barton dragged between her and Landon. The fresh air filled her lungs as Landon needlessly helped her up the steps, out into a grotty back alley. They laid Barton down, groaning, on the concrete. Holly took in the surroundings. There was no one else there. An army of police cars and ambulances would have been nice. Fire trucks even, blaring red and blue lights and horns. Instead she had a man who looked like an overweight office worker with a beat-up saloon car parked beyond some overflowing steel bins.

"Where's the help?" Holly demanded. "My daughter is still down there, my husband is in" – she threw a frantic arm towards the bloodied, swollen mess of Barton – "*this* state. And you're all we have?"

"We'll take you back to the office," Landon mumbled, putting even less effort into talking than he had into carrying Barton. "He'll get the attention he needs. Help me lift him."

"He'll get help in an *office*?" Holly said, incredulous. Landon didn't appear to listen, puffing over to the vehicle and opening a door. "And the others? Are you going back down there?"

"It's under control," he said.

Holly stomped a foot. "My daughter is trapped down there. With monsters chasing her. *Chasing* her. If this is your department then you *must* go down there and help. Understood?"

Landon scratched the back of his head. "I can't leave you."

"I'm fine, as you can very well see. And I can keep myself more than occupied by trying to tackle whatever horror has befallen my husband. You, however, can help below, can't you?"

Landon grunted, then nodded. "Okay. Yes. Of course. After we get him into the car."

She watched him as though searching his face for some guarantee that he would help, and in return he gave her a weak smile. She sighed and did as she was asked. Together, they lifted Barton and heaved him, with all their combined strength, up onto the back seat. As Holly got in and dragged her husband further in, his blood smearing across the leather upholstery, she fussed, "This is highly unorthodox. An ambulance would be more appropriate."

"We've got the best doctors in the city," Landon assured her. He closed the door behind them. Holly took Barton's head on her lap and scanned him up and down, as Landon took something from the trunk of the car. Some of Barton's wounds, Holly could see, had already been treated, with stitches and dirty bandages covering them. Many were fresh, though; cuts and bruises over his upper body. His unthinkably distorted ankle. She tore a length of her t-shirt off and tried to reach the ghastly thing. At least tying it off might help. She paused and looked through the window. Landon moved as slowly as physically possible, back into the maze entrance, a long gun hanging by his side now.

She was still staring when a tiny lady dropped onto the window in front of her. Holly fell back in surprise, then scrambled for the other door. She grabbed at the handle but it wouldn't open. There was no button to unlock it. She looked to the front. A grid of metal separated her from the driver's area, like the rear of a police car. Spinning back desperately, she found the tiny lady waving, her voice barely audible through the window. "I'm taking out the glass!"

A small firecrack sounded: a pistol blast that shattered the glass in front of the fairy. Holly froze in fear and awe as she watched Letty hover into the car, pistol in her hand. Her heart pounding in her ears, it took Holly a moment to acknowledge the fairy's words.

"We need to get you out of here."

Holly stared at her untrustingly, her hand probing behind her for the door handle. She subtly, quietly, tried again. Definitely not moving. From one world of monsters to another. She put on a brave face and turned back to the fairy. "Get away from me, you little devil!"

"Where's Pax?" Letty asked, ignoring the threat.

Holly steeled herself, gritting her teeth. She said, "Safe from you, at least."

"I'm trying to help," the fairy snarled, fluttering closer and making Holly flinch. "I heard you before. You said the things were following you. What things?"

"The worst! A whole army of them. Isn't that what you wanted?"

"Not me," Letty said. She looked at Barton. "Is he gonna make it?"

Holly hesitated. Was this thing asking so she could kill him? It sounded like concern, though. "I – I think he's okay – just his leg –"

"Okay. I need you to listen to me. It's not safe for you here. The guys who forced you down there – *not* me – they'll be back. The guys who helped you out, they're no better. I'm gonna unlock this car and get it ready for you to hightail it out of here, you got me?"

Holly shook her head. "My daughter – I can't just –"

"Don't worry. We're not going anywhere till the others get out."

"All right," a man's voice interrupted them. They snapped their attention back to the tunnel entrance. Landon was back, shotgun raised and aimed at the car. "Knew I shouldn't leave you."

Letty met Holly's gaze, dropping down into the car. The fairy whispered, "Don't let him know I'm here."

24

The electricity bled through the bricks around the doorway, though the monster's limbs could not seem to penetrate the door. It was trying to suck energy from their room, the same way it sucked energy from the city above. The mortar between the bricks lit up luminescent blue, which spread along the walls and slowly crept closer.

"What do we do?" Grace cried, tightening her grip on Pax.

Pax hesitated, deciding on her final plan. She'd spent all her life running from responsibility but she was better than that. She was not like the fairies or the Ministry. And this time she'd do something before it was too late. She closed her eyes and said, "I'll draw its attention. You run for another exit."

"What?" Grace yelped. "No – you can't –"

Pax moved Grace away from the rear wall, as the threat snaked through the brickwork and along the floor towards their feet. She said, "On three, I'm leaving. You go the opposite way. Stop for nothing. You understand?"

Trembling uncontrollably, Grace nodded, eyes fixed on the blue light.

"One . . . two . . ." Pax grabbed the door handle, braced herself. "Three!"

As the door opened, the blinding light flooded in. Pax ran headlong into it. She met no resistance, only the warmth of this creature, crackling from all directions. Thrusting her hands over her ears, Pax aimed for the large room, ducking under the centre of the beast of light. She screamed, "Go, Grace! Go!"

The blue light retreated from the walls, from the room, as Grace flashed through it. Pax rolled out into the massive room and the full force of the lightning creature followed her, its electric limbs licking over the walls and slamming into supportive positions. Pax scrambled across the floor, away from it, but one of the limbs dropped onto her, pinning her down. Her breath was punched out of her as she shouted to Grace, "Get out of here!"

Grace had stalled in the middle of the room, staring horrified at Pax. The shout triggered her, though, and she sprinted for a set of steps, the monster ignoring her. Pax twisted back to face it, as shards of electricity wrapped around her like a hundred fingers. The light surged, another blinding flash, and her whole body convulsed. The energy pulsed out of her again, preparing for another surge, and she slumped.

Pax watched the light shift above her, the beast settling with its tentacles of light rooted in the walls. Where the limbs touched the walls, they spread out, flowing into large rectangles of light. More limbs extended above, an array of reaching arms clambering into the roof, pressing towards the city above. As it jolted through her again, with the force of an electric shock, the whole thing began to pulse. It was feeding. As it was draining her, it was pumping energy down from above, too, all surging into its core, making it brighter. But it didn't stop there. The energy kept going, flowing through the lower limbs, back into the walls. Back into the rectangles where it was connecting.

The pulse slowed again, leaving Pax gasping for air.

As Pax lay helplessly, two horrible truths gripped her. First, the beast looked nothing like a minotaur. Barton and Apothel and the rest had been completely duped. Second, whatever energy was draining from her was not fuelling the beast. It was being siphoned elsewhere. Towards whatever it was that had supposedly been helping them.

There had to be a way out. Pax had to tell them. Had to tell someone. They were wrong about it, all of them. None of them really understood what this thing was, or what it was doing. She had to get out.

The monster waxed in luminescence once more, the glow signalling its next surge. Pax gritted her teeth in anticipation of what might be the final shock.

Casaria slammed into Grace as she ran out of a doorway and almost knocked him down. He pushed her against a wall as she shrieked. Aware of the blue glow ahead, he shouted, "Is she in there?"

"Yes!" Grace cried back. "She saved me!"

"Stay here!" Casaria ordered, and turned to the domed room, hefting the Fae device up. He entered on a high walkway, the *praelucente* below, filling the space in its full electric glory, limbs spread to the walls and above, all glowing a dazzling blue, near white. He had to shield his eyes from the brightness, spying movement below. It was on top of her, her limbs flapping amid the chaotic sparking.

Propping the Fae device against his hip, the thing now filled with dirt, Casaria spun the cogs that would spin and pressed a finger to the only button that he was confident would actually do anything. The weapon seemed to be reacting to the movements ahead, vibrating with a magnetic pull, emitting its own contrasting glow.

Pax screamed. He saw her face, writhing out from the chaos, and was shocked still. In her agony she caught Casaria's eye. Then it moved, a sudden shift, and Casaria let out an involuntary sound as he saw the central shape of the creature turning his way.

"Shoot it!" Pax gasped up to him, barely able to form the words.

He didn't think, couldn't think, merely clung to the sound of her voice and did as he was told. He pressed the button, and the monster's blinding light met with an even stronger flash from the Fae device. A terrific roar shook the walls and ceiling. The crackling and groaning and clicking of the monsters was overtaken by its sound, the world filled with light.

Then the beast retreated.

Quick as a spider, it sucked its tentacles back into the furthest exit, the room dipping into instant darkness. The roar decreased in volume as the creature moved further away, leaving behind a gentle rain of dust and mortar, a terrific ringing in the ears, and the vile smell of burnt flesh.

25

The trio made their way back through the tunnels without talking. Pax and Grace had no energy left for conversation. It was all Pax could do to use Casaria as a crutch and carry herself out. Casaria clearly knew the way and the creatures were gone, the horrible sounds of the Sunken City silenced. There was nothing else to discuss. They made no comments, not even when they passed the charred corridor of mangled bird corpses, with its steaming pile of bones and feathers that seemed, somewhere underneath, to contain human remains.

When they reached the surface, there was no sound of beasts pursuing them. It seemed, as they took gasps of the air above, that they had all been holding their breath. The moment they exited onto the alley, Grace crumpled and started sobbing. Pax followed her quickly, touching her shoulder and wanting to tell her it was okay, they were safe now. She didn't manage to say anything, just groaned.

"I know," Grace wept, tears streaming. The emotion flowed out of her, the despair she had been pushing down throughout the ordeal. Pax fixed Casaria with an accusing stare. She wasn't sure exactly how or why, but she needed him to know this young lady's suffering was his fault. He hardly looked bothered, regarding the pair of them, instead, with a quizzical eye. Pax must have looked frazzled, hair singed and clothes charred. Casaria gave her a shrug as he ran a hand through his slick hair and took out a cigarette. As he lit it, he looked around the alley, up to the windows and roofs.

"You still here?" he called out. The answer he got surprised him.

"Of course," Landon said, drawing all eyes to the alley entrance. He was next to a car, the rear window smashed, a shotgun in his hands, aimed in at Holly. Sat in the car, she looked petrified. In their elation at getting out, none of them had heard Holly's attempt to call to her daughter, or the agent's snarl for her to be quiet and stay put.

"Good to see you're with us, Landon," Casaria said flatly. "Don't know what we'd do without you."

"Where's Gant?" Landon said.

Casaria held the cigarette in his mouth for a still moment. Landon's former nonchalance was gone, his mouth tight with focus. He didn't need to voice the obvious conclusion.

"I need all of you over here," Landon said. "Join the parents."

As Pax stood up, Grace stopped crying, unable to comprehend who this newcomer was or what he wanted with them. She met Holly's worried gaze and her mother gave her a smile filled with relief. Grace struggled upright too, as Holly nodded to inside the car. Something for Grace to see. The bulk of her father was lying across the back seat with her.

No one moved towards Landon. Grace looked to Pax for guidance. She, in turn, looked to Casaria. He had set off the Fae device, and he and Landon hardly seemed to be on the best terms. Casaria kept smoking. He said, "Did you see where the horde went?"

"Gone," Landon said. "They came this way, but moved off. Quickly. Your doing?"

Casaria held up the weapon he'd set off.

"You maniac," Landon said. "What have you done?" He didn't wait for an answer. "We'll figure it out at the office. All of you, to the car."

It was time to test Casaria. Pax said, "I'd rather walk, if it's all the same to you." She nodded to the broken window. "Doesn't look safe."

"It's not all the same to me," Landon said irritably. "You'll all give full statements. And you'll need to fill in a W6-DPe, Casaria. Explaining *exactly* what happened to Gant."

"I've had a long day," Casaria said. "The forms can wait."

Landon turned the shotgun from Holly towards them. "It's not a choice."

"What's wrong with you?" Grace's voice quietly interrupted. Landon's face softened slightly at the sight of her. Her face dirty and bare feet black with blood, her round eyes shining in the encroaching dusk, pleading for everything to simply be okay. "After what we've been through. How can you point a gun at us? How could you point a gun at my *mum*?"

"Good question." Casaria tossed his cigarette butt aside. "How's that necessary?"

"She was trying to get away," Landon said, glancing to his vehicle.

"The glass was smashed from the outside," Pax pointed out, frowning.

"Look –" Landon started, but stopped as Casaria took a step towards him.

Pax put a hand on Casaria's arm, brushing close to him. "Don't."

"It's okay," Casaria told her, determination in his eyes.

Exactly what she needed.

"You're being an idiot, Casaria!" Landon said, bumping into the car as he raised the shotgun. He did not fire. Casaria closed the distance between them and pushed the gun to the side. He threw a punch square into Landon's jaw. The bigger man smacked into the car but didn't go down. He was stunned for a moment, unbelieving. Then he fought back. He swung the gun at Casaria, and Casaria grabbed hold of it. They grappled away from the car.

Pax took Grace's hand. "Come on!"

"Here, here!" Holly called, bursting out of the car but immediately dropping into the driver's seat. Pax and Grace rushed around her, the sound of the men's struggles rising from strangled grunts to a flurry of thumps and flapping jackets. They broke away from each other and started swinging punches. Pax shoved Grace into the back of Landon's car, then scrambled for the passenger seat as Holly shoved the door open.

The slamming car doors and the starting engine drew Casaria's attention away from his fight. He let out a "Hey!", enough distraction for Landon to recoup, and took a punch to the gut.

Holly hit the accelerator hard and they lurched forwards, out onto the street and almost straight into another car. She swerved, and they were away. Pax twisted back to see Casaria thrusting Landon across the alley, taking control once more. He turned away from his stumbling adversary and ran after them. When he reached his own car, he stalled as he patted down his pockets. Pax held up his car keys for him to see, and smirked at his bemused face, just before they turned a corner.

"Oh thank God you're okay," Holly said quickly, clutching the steering wheel tight. "Thank God thank God thank God."

Grace clambered forward to hug her mother as they sped down a main road. Pax sank into her own seat. She rolled her head to one side, impressed. "You stole his keys, too?"

"No," a familiar voice said from above. Pax's eyes widened at Letty, perched on the rear-view mirror. "I did."

26

Interrupted by the theft of his car and the continuing betrayal at the hands of Pax Kuranes, Cano Casaria's passion for defying the Ministry and pummelling the sense out of Landon left him. Landon had pulled himself to his feet and recovered the shotgun by the time Casaria returned to the alleyway, but he, too, was uninterested in continuing their fight. He used the gun to support himself as he gave Casaria an *I-told-you-so* sneer. They waited for a Ministry pick-up then drove back to the office together. Casaria considered, on the way, that it might be best to tell the whole Ministry where to shove their regulations, but he was weary and had done enough damage for one evening. That could wait until the next day, when he had more time and sense to weigh up his options.

When he stopped to think about it, Casaria realised that he had lost blood from the Fae gunshot and had taken a few blows from Landon, who was heavy, if poorly trained. He had also suffered some kind of impact from enduring the blast of the Fae device. Put it all together and he should receive some sort of medal, if he could make the story sound heroic enough for the powers that be. Never mind that Gumg (Gant?) had died and he'd had a hostile encounter with Landon; he had come face-to-face with the *praelucente* itself, and any divergent behaviour could, perhaps, be explained by that. People simply did not survive getting close to that thing.

By the time they reached the Ministry building, he had slipped in a brief apology to Landon, with a winning smile, saying he was not sure what had come over him and perhaps he had simply gone too deep into the Sunken City. Landon had no choice but to accept the apology; Casaria knew, after all, that his fellow agent had hardly shone in the crisis himself.

There was, indeed, a furious meeting with Mathers, who promised extended suspension without pay, but for all his bluster the deputy director could not hide his curiosity about the encounter with the *praelucente*. And he had to admit at least a little responsibility for neglecting the Fae threat. Casaria had warned them it would happen. He did not go into detail about exactly how the *praelucente* encounter had played out, though. Casaria started to warn Mathers about the apparent effect it had had on Pax, but Mathers shut him down. He didn't want the burden of that particular truth. Not at this juncture.

Casaria would give a full debrief in the next few days, to a council organised by the IS Relations Initiative. Just what he needed; a grilling from Sam Ward over his conduct in the field. The suspension was nothing in the face of that worse punishment. And before going home and taking his unpaid leave, Casaria had the added wound of needing to fill in a mountain of forms.

An R42, to give a general account of how Pax Kuranes originally came into contact with the Sunken City. Likewise, R42s accounting for Grace and Holly Barton's knowledge of the Sunken City. One wasn't necessary for Darren Barton, as his was already on file, but an R46b was needed to explain why he had resurfaced after a nine-year hiatus.

A series of F67s, one to record each encounter with the Fae.

A D7-PR for each and every civilian involved, including any notable encounters in the West Farling incident and the apprehension of Rufaizu. These would be supplemented with a D7-PRe each for Pax, Grace and Holly, to be shared with local and national law enforcement agencies who would be on the lookout for them as persons of interest.

A D7-X to notify local law enforcement of the stolen Ministry equipment, one car. Even though that should've been Landon's to write up.

A W4-SoI, describing the circumstances that had led to the civilians entering the Sunken City. Followed by a W4-SoE for each notable event within the Sunken City.

Then of course there was also the W6-DPe, explaining the exact circumstances and nature of Gumg's death, and a series of W4-GIs and MC12s that would explain anything else that had happened or been encountered over the course of this madness. The W6-DPe was particularly frustrating, as Casaria was well aware he would need to fill it in a second time after spelling Gumg's name wrong.

These forms were a living hell about one rung below the thought of repeating this information to Sam Ward in person, with each minute that Casaria spent writing seeming to stretch for an hour. Still, the more he wrote, the more he appreciated the situation, and the easier he imagined it would be to throw his successes in Ward's face. For all the trouble she had caused, Pax Kuranes was exactly the breath of fresh air he had hoped for. She had brought the fairies out of hiding and she had delivered Fae technology to the Ministry. With the destruction of a Sunken City entrance, one of their own agents dead and confirmed Fae shots fired at him, Casaria saw an unavoidable conflict on the near horizon, with Ward's Initiative in tatters.

It made him smile. There were precious few soldiers in the Ministry's ranks; they would need him when the Fae came. They needed him a lot more than he needed them. He concluded one document with every intention of being provocative, not caring how close to the truth he was:

The weapon that has fallen into our hands is what they are willing to cross the line and kill humans for. It cannot be questioned that it has the potential to harm the praelucente and change our world. It is the opinion of this agent that this is the first real evidence of the bigger plans of the Fae population. Their interests in the Sunken City are not, as MEE canon dictates, historical – these interests are current and dangerous.

Casaria left the office shortly after midnight, satisfied that some clerk would be suitably frightened into encouraging a superior officer to do something. He walked the short distance home, enjoying the night air and imagining the future. He would see the Fae and the Ministry clash, he would see blood in the tunnels of the Sunken City and he would be given permission to lead a force against the Fae Transitional City. His own initiative.

And he would see Pax Kuranes again.

They would argue and fight, and she would insult him and he would laugh, and they would be forced to join forces and he would channel her passion towards his own agenda. Maybe they would sleep together, he hadn't decided on that, yet. The more he saw of her the more tempted he became, despite himself. Maybe, he decided, she was more an 8 than a 7.

Beaming at his imagined future, Casaria approached his apartment block and stopped across the street. His smile disappeared as he felt, all in an instant, the trepidation and urge to run that he must have so frequently bestowed on others. He let it pass, forcing his smile back onto his face and walking towards the entrance.

The two large men he had fought in the afternoon were waiting with metal bats in their hands. There was no shame in their stance, even though they were loitering by the door of a wealthy apartment block in one of central Ordshaw's most prestigious neighbourhoods. Between them stood a shorter man, more discreet but menacing in a different way. He was round at his waist and cut a contrast to his goons in their labouring overalls, with his brown woollen suit – something he had clearly chosen with an eye to personal preference, rather than style. As Casaria approached, the man stepped forward.

"Mr Casaria." He had a rough west Ordshaw accent, the sort that intimidated people from out of town. "My name's Stacy Monroe. I believe you had a disagreement with my men today."

"I thought we'd settled that," Casaria replied.

"No. We're about to."

Casaria scanned all three men, particularly focusing on the bats. They were making a statement, bringing bats instead of guns. And he had already established that at least one of them was no pushover. Tired and injured as he was, it was unlikely he could take on all three of them. He kept smiling, though, thinking it was still worth a try.

27

Pax got out of the car for some air, finally clear of the centre of town and, apparently, not being followed. Letty flew out to settle on the car roof next to her. Pax rested an arm on the car, with barely the energy to keep standing.

"You got a new wing," Pax observed tiredly, mustering the strength to smile.

"Of sorts. You got all beat up."

"Kind of," Pax said, nodding.

"Reeling with regrets?"

Pax looked into the car, at Grace hunched exhausted across her defeated father's slowly breathing chest. She scanned over to Holly, who was stretching her legs, staring out at the city skyline. On this hillside road, the view was spectacular, all the skyscrapers and low houses coming together in a chain of yellow windows reflected in the calm river. Pax said, "Nah. You?"

Letty followed her gaze to the skyline. She took a breath. "Not especially."

"I hoped you'd come back," Pax told her.

"Yeah? *I* hoped you'd get yourself killed." Pax reached out to poke her, her finger all but knocking the fairy down, and Letty batted back at her. "Oi. I'll tear it off."

Holly turned back to them, no humour in her face. She had developed lines of exhaustion over the space of the past few hours. She gave Letty an odd look, still unsure quite how to reconcile the existence of such a small person. Rather than dwell on it, she turned to Pax. "Where do we go? I have a sister in Manchester."

"I'm not sure that's safe," Pax said. "I wish you hadn't become involved yourselves."

Holly nodded. "All this . . . it's unnatural. Not for normal people."

"I've got some people that we might contact. They're not normal." Pax pictured Bees' warehouse. He might still be there at this hour. Even if he wasn't, they could hide inside, it wouldn't be difficult to find a way in. Though given that Casaria had turned up with the device instead of them, and her phone was fried so she couldn't call ahead, that avenue looked hazy.

"My husband has a friend, near Long Culdon I believe," Holly said. "The inventor. She knows what we're dealing with, at least. And she's kept herself hidden from it, all these years, somehow. I think she could help him, if we can't go to a hospital."

Pax considered it, thinking out loud. "Mad scientist versus possible gangsters. Some choice."

"That settles it, then," Holly said firmly. "You didn't mention your friends were criminals."

"Ah." Pax lifted a finger, about to protest, but realised there was no point. "Okay." Holly nodded and went to get back in the car. Pax said, "Mrs Barton. You did well."

Holly gave her a short nod. "Thank you for keeping my daughter safe."

She sat back down in the car and turned to her family, whispering assurances to them.

Letty lolled onto her elbows and let out a big sigh. She said, "So you great lummox, what now? Now that there ain't no one wants to resolve this thing but us."

"Whatever that thing is down there," Pax said, "it's doing more damage than I think even your people realise. Or care about. And it's more complicated than you realise. It was feeding the thing that I think was giving Apothel orders."

"His Blue Angel?"

"Yeah. Its screens can do way more than communicate messages. Whoever or whatever's behind them, I think it's *their* monster. Why did they make Apothel jump through those hoops? Why did they encourage him to get your device if it could harm this thing that they're somehow connected to?"

"To remove it from the equation?" Letty replied. "Apothel *died*, remember."

Pax frowned. She drummed her fingers on the car. "Whatever he was doing, it wasn't what he thought it was. Right?"

"Yeah." Letty yawned. "I need a fucking drink. So do you."

Pax nodded. She imagined going back to the Sticky Tap, and putting a full stop in the craziest weekend of her life. Have a drink, pat herself on the back. They'd all got away more or less safely, at least. But that only reminded her of Rufaizu. He must've known what Apothel went through, having come back from wherever he'd been. And she hadn't done a thing for him, even as she'd risked everything to save this family. Hadn't done a thing for him *yet*, she told herself. She said, "We can figure this out, Letty. We want the same thing, don't we?"

Letty stared at her, like she was studying her anew. The fairy said, "Close enough."

"That'll do," Pax said. She laid her hand down for Letty to hop on, and the fairy regarded it oddly. She didn't need the help any more. But she shrugged and stepped up anyway. As Pax lifted Letty and moved to get back in the car, she said, "We've still got a few days until the WPT. Think we can save the city by then?"

Blue Angel

An Ordshaw Novel

Phil Williams

PART 1:
MONDAY

1

Electric soldiers marched across her vision.

Between them and an abyss of black stood legions of unnatural things. Alive but unmoving, familiar but obscure. A blur of animal parts and humanoid shapes, sharp and soft, solid and fluid, all writhing together. Things that should not be, amassed in the darkness. Each was individual, but all combined into one whole.

The electric soldiers formed a cordon. Managing, monitoring, watching, silently. Their limbs spread out and drew the world in. Their lightning flashes snapped against the features of Ordshaw. A wall of tall bricks, lit blue. A concrete pillar, before a body of still water. A weather-worn bridge, arching like a wave. The grimacing face of a statue – a fountain. Black metal stairs, a scaffold of steps. A small hall, cracked as though lashed by a tremendous whip. A high point, atop a tower looking down on the sleeping city. Each thunderous, flashbulb moment, connected somehow to a central crackling ball of light.

They were drawing together.

Her heart burnt and pressed against her ribs, drawn there too. With each beat, the creatures were lit in fearsome poses, baring teeth, watching her, hating her. The electric soldiers watched too. Monitoring. Monitor. Minotaur.

The jaws of the beast ripped through it all.

Pax Kuranes jolted awake. She put a hand to her chest, taking gasping breaths as the feeling faded. Some old machine rumbled in mechanical stops and starts on the other side of the room. She frowned. Had that woken her? Created images in her dreams?

There were no monsters, nothing to be scared of.

She rubbed her eyes and took in the dusty floor she was sitting on. Dirty plastic trays teetered over her, atop a table and bench, and the scent of a harsh chemical made her nose crinkle. She recalled where she was. An old telegraph station in Long Culdon, the home and workplace of Darren Barton's doctor friend. A doctor who ran experiments on unusual plants and creatures. Possibly monsters.

There *were* monsters. Lots of them.

Pax leaned against the wall. Her back ached, but her outstretched legs felt fine. She flexed her feet, trying to remember why that mattered. There was a rip in her jeans, stained dark from blood. She touched a finger to a tiny but deep scratch. It had scabbed over, and it hurt like a dull bruise. She'd taken a bullet there, from a fairy gun. A fairy bullet.

What else?

She ran a hand through her hair, pulling it out in front of her face. Frizzy, smelling like she'd rolled in burnt animal fat. The edges of her jeans and her hoodie were marred with scorch marks and concentrated filth. She picked up one of her boots. The treads had warped as though left on a hot plate. For six years, these unbranded boots had been a comfortable constant. One thing in her life unaffected by the march of time or the turns of a deck of cards. Victim, at last, to an intangible electric beast.

The minotaur. An underground monster, formed of light, that looked nothing like its namesake; a ball of electric limbs that had pinned her to the ground and tried to suck the life out of her. All because she'd tried to save Barton's teenage daughter, Grace, while Barton himself, actually eager to fight the monsters, had succumbed to terrible injuries elsewhere in the secret labyrinth that was the Sunken City.

It had been an interesting night, hadn't it?

Pax took out her phone to check the time, but that was warped too, screen cracked and unresponsive. Her coat was balled up on the floor. That, at least, looked unharmed. Pax bent over it and whispered, "You in there?" No response. "Letty?"

"Screw off," a little voice replied from somewhere in the folds.

"Hang on," Pax said, scooping the coat up. The voice started to complain, but Pax warned, "I'm taking you outside – you're the one that wanted to stay hidden, remember?"

The voice went quiet.

Pax scanned the rest of the room as she stood. It was filled with laboratory equipment and overgrown plants. There was a corner sectioned off by frosted glass that formed a makeshift testing chamber, where the machinery sounds were coming from. The doctor's vaguely scientific tests suggested she was some kind of botanical scavenger, collecting weeds, perhaps living off worms. The sort of person you could make a documentary about, if anyone realised she existed. Pax had barely spoken to her, in the drama of their arrival; the doctor had avoided eye contact and flitted off to her experiments as soon as she was sure Darren Barton wasn't going to die.

He, presumably, was in the bedroom with his family, where Pax had left them.

Pax stepped into her boots and tested the uneasy balance of their soles, then navigated a corridor of roots to get outside. The building's surroundings mimicked the wildness of the interior, with trees reaching towards the porch and invading the lumpy track that led away. Pax spotted a sliver of light through the thicket, morning threatening to break through.

Her coat emitted a muffled snarl.

"Wait," Pax warned. Letty burst out of the coat pocket and circled in the air. The two-inch fairy drew level with Pax's face. She had a single beating wing and a contraption strapped over the opposite shoulder, which whirred and distorted the air like a heat shimmer.

"You mountainous turd, you wake me up by picking up my fucking bed?"

With her miniature t-shirt and shorts, colourful hair and holstered pistol, it remained a marvel that a creature so delicate was so vulgar.

Pax swung the coat on. "Let's get clear of this place so we can talk."

"Talk, hell," Letty said, but she was already away, gliding through the trees. Pax followed. Thick as the trees were, they soon ended, abruptly, at the edge of an empty expanse of grass. The sky was a blanket of steely white beyond, muting a curved landscape of peaks and valleys.

"The Drumdon Hills," Pax said. "I never realised they were so close."

"Big whoop," Letty said, landing on her shoulder. "A whole lot of nothing."

"You have to stand there? Want to give me a crick in my neck?"

"Yeah," Letty said. "Maybe it'll break."

"Not a morning person, are you?"

Letty snorted. "Thought we had that in common."

The fairy had a point. The sun's glare sat low in the clouds. This was three days in a row that Pax had risen before lunchtime. A personal record. She said, "Something woke me. Didn't feel right."

"Baby had a bad dream?" Letty responded harshly.

"You blame me?"

The fairy paused, finally taking stock. Her voice softened. "Where's it hurt?"

"It doesn't, actually. Which isn't right, is it? I got *shot*. And that thing got me. It felt like I was being skewered by light. Or raped by a river."

"That old feeling."

Yet there was no pain now. Only the echo of that other feeling. The burning in Pax's chest, and the sense that she was being pulled towards something.

"You touched it," Letty said, following her thoughts. "Who knows what kind of effects that'll have on you. I wouldn't let *her* know, though." She indicated the doctor with a nod in the direction of the telegraph station. Surrounded by trees, it was the sort of place where a prowler would invite gullible college students and play disco music while he sawed them up. "You'd wake up in a white room full of tubes."

Pax agreed. The unreal creatures in the city's hidden labyrinth had powers she didn't understand, beyond the knowledge that one of them was sucking energy from oblivious Underground commuters and the buildings above. Reaching that understanding had driven her into financial ruin and potential homelessness.

Revealing to a scientist that she'd touched an intangible creature and *might* be suffering side effects wasn't going to make her life easier. She rocked on her heels. "My boots are screwed."

"Good luck shopping," Letty said. "The Ministry will have eyes on every camera in the city. If this hill-dyke doctor doesn't turn you in first."

"We lasted the night."

"And now it's time to leave town and join a travelling rodeo."

Pax considered the hills ahead. In their folds, she could see a small hamlet. The government wouldn't have surveillance in places like that. She *could* start a new life. All she needed was locals with spare cash and an affinity for gambling. She could conceal herself in a blanket of countryside or hide in the crowds of another city. But it'd taken years to build her life in Ordshaw, and that had only just started taking shape. "How do I go back to how things were a few days ago?"

Letty laughed. "Unsee everything you saw? Hope the Ministry forget you exist?"

Pax hummed. No. The Ministry of Environmental Energy weren't going to leave her alone. And if they didn't hunt her, then the fairies – the Layer Fae – would, for the things she'd seen. Those miniature maniacs were as keen on protecting the status quo as the MEE. "So. We've got my government protecting a monster because they think its weird aura benefits people. Your government think it's all better left alone. Neither of them are aware that this thing isn't just a parasite, it's connected to something else. Someone needs to open all their eyes."

"Uh-huh. Except there's no one but us to do it."

"Yeah," Pax said. They had themselves, the painfully normal Bartons and a reclusive botanical scientist. And Rufaizu – she couldn't forget Rufaizu. The young man had been abducted by the MEE. *He* was interested in the answers, and possibly had a few of his own. "You know where the Ministry are based, here in Ordshaw?"

"Yeah," Letty said. "Cheap ugly building in Central. Labs, cells, a right little den of intrigue, all sandwiched between a bunch of offices so you wouldn't know they're there."

"Could you sneak in?"

"Sure," Letty said, in a tone so light Pax knew a tirade was coming. "If you turn off the Fae detectors and knock-out gas and get their access codes and make them look the other way. Use your book-brain, Pax, they've got ways of killing us that would make you shit kittens."

"I don't like leaving Rufaizu locked up in there," Pax said. She wasn't sure if it was thoughts of her brother Albie, or her struggle to keep Grace alive, but she couldn't quench the protective flame that had been stoked in her. Whatever miracle might see her clear of this, it wouldn't be enough if Rufaizu was totally abandoned. To justify it, she said, "He must know things that could help."

"Seriously," Letty said, then yawned loudly. She stretched her arms up, an almost inaudible click coming from her back. "You'd need an army to go up against the MEE. Your best and only chance to get that boy out of there was before he got put *in* there."

That would have meant crossing Cano Casaria, the Ministry agent who'd drawn Pax into this. The unstable oddity who had tried to induct her into his way of life, threatened to arrest her and, finally, broke rank to help her. Pax had left him stranded with another agent who wanted to take them in, so it was likely he had his own problems now. Sighing, she said, "You got any ideas yourself, or just more problems?"

Letty shrugged. "Already gave you one: get out of here."

"Are *you* going to run?"

"Hell no," Letty snorted. "But it's not like this is your fight."

"It's my city," Pax replied defensively. It was her home, her poker circuit, her heart that burnt uneasily in the night. "I can't let it be overrun by mythical monsters. And if I left, what'd happen to you? And the others?"

"Me, I can hide a hell of a lot easier than you. Now I know for sure that monster can be hurt, we can find another way to destroy it. I can take the Sunken City back myself. I could be queen all on my own, my people be damned. As for *the others*, who gives a shit? Think they'd stick around for you?"

Pax was fairly sure Barton would do anything to protect anyone in need, even a stranger. And she suspected Letty might too, despite her words. But the mention of Letty's people made her pause, as she recalled Letty's past speeches about reclaiming the Sunken City for the Fae. The Fae Transitional City, or FTC, existed because the minotaur and its minions had driven the tiny race from their territory in those underground tunnels, long ago. Letty still referred to the Sunken City as home, and directed every atom of her considerable will towards getting the Fae safely back there. Pax said, "Aren't there other Fae who think like you?"

"No one thinks like me," Letty said, informatively. "I'm a superstar."

"Ones who *sympathise* with you. They can't all be happy living in the FTC, peace or not. Surely others want to reclaim the Sunken City?"

"Definitely, but I'd be caught trying to get anywhere near them. And they'd have to be willing to defy our governor. A crew like that takes a lot of time to find."

An army of Lettys was a troubling thought, but it might be just what they needed. "There aren't others already in exile?"

Letty screwed up her face, uncomfortably. "Yeah. The sort I would avoid myself. But now I've got a few choice things to say about the great governor Valoria Magnus, we might find ourselves on more equal ground. Yeah. Rolarn comes to mind."

"Roland?"

"Ro*larn*," Letty corrected. "Fat fucker out in Broadplain who controls one of the best bits of Fae real estate you'll find. Best for *you* – you'd actually fit in there. Personally, I think it's a dump. He's a difficult, irritating loner, but he harps on about the old guard, dreams of putting the FTC back in the hands of someone willing to stand up for Fae rights. There's a chance I could get him on board."

Pax raised an eyebrow. "You got his number?"

"You don't have conversations like that over a phone," Letty said. "I can get over there in no time, check in with him while you wrap things up here. Or do you wanna come, sneak off before the others wake up?"

Pax shook her head. "The doctor and Barton have information to share, this —"

A noise from the woods cut her off. A dog-like growl, feral and angry. It recalled the low and terrifying sounds that had haunted Pax through the tunnels of the Sunken City. She stared in its direction, wide-eyed, but the sound didn't come again.

Letty hopped off her shoulder, into the air. "You oughta be more scared of that doctor and this place. While you're sharing information, make sure her experiments are locked up safe."

2

"Something's happened, across town," Holly Barton announced, as Pax returned to the telegraph station. Holly had positioned herself at a chunky laptop near the centre of the scrappy workspace, and Pax took more interest in her than the news. After surviving Ordshaw's tunnels, Holly had driven them here, negotiated their stay with a woman she disliked, and single-handedly dressed her husband's wounds. She'd even remade the hot chocolates, after spitting out the doctor's brackish first attempt. Pax had last seen her sitting by the bed, where she might have stayed all night. Now she was wide awake and presentable, her shoulder-length hair free of tangles and her clothes oddly crisp, despite her t-shirt being stained and torn.

"I've only been gone a few minutes," Pax said. "How did you . . ."

"I heard you moving," Holly said. "And I saw this antique out here last night. I thought I'd check if we'd made any Most Wanted lists. But this came up. It's literally just happened."

Pax came closer, sensing before she saw it that this news was somehow connected to them and what they'd been through. She leaned in to read the headline: *Breaking – Five Injured as Burst Gas Main Shakes Ordshaw.*

"It's on the BBC," Holly said. "National news. We were near there last night, weren't we? And look – right here –" She searched for a line. "*Potentially caused by a trespasser in the sewer system.* Did we cause some kind of structural damage?"

Pax stared at the photo on the article, showing stricken residents recovering in the street, and got an unsettling sense of déjà vu. She recognised the face of a young dark-skinned man, but she couldn't place him. Had she played Hold'Em in that area once? At least passed through? A name came to mind – Greg? The memory felt intangible, like she'd seen it in a dream. Perhaps the dream she'd woken from, with the electricity, the monsters, that feeling. "When . . . exactly when did this happen?"

"It's just breaking," Holly said. "Couldn't have been half an hour ago. Probably less. Don't suppose we could've felt the tremor at this distance, but I bet we would've felt it back home in Dalford."

Pax was wary that she *had* felt something, waking in that panic. "Does it say anything about us?"

"No. Which is rather odd. You'd think our names and faces would be out there."

"They want us found but not seen. Or heard. Or whatever."

Holly made a frustrated sound, scarcely believing the nerve of these people.

"I've spent my life accepting that the government do good work. I *happily* pay my taxes."

"They had us at gunpoint."

"I *know*. Darren told me in the night, *stay off the phones, don't send emails*. Like this Ministry could pick up our scent on radio waves. It's madness and I've been racking my brains but I can't figure it out. What are we going to do?"

"Did Darren have any ideas?"

"Oh, he was rambling like a loon. We don't have phones, anyway – only Darren had his on him and it's dead. All *I've* got is this." Holly handed over a piece of paper and Pax scanned the elegant handwriting.

Problems:

Husband mortally wounded.

Government can't be trusted – ergo police/hospitals/ communications unsafe.

Monsters under the city.

Fairies = real – also want to kill us.

Solutions:

Contact the Evening Standard.

"The Evening Standard?"

"Yes," Holly said. "They ran an excellent exposé on a pothole scandal in Ten Gardens. Those roads are now being fixed and the culprits are facing jail time. This isn't much different, is it?"

"There was a fifty-foot electric octopus thing," Pax said. "It's a little different."

"The principle's the same," Holly insisted. "The papers could offer us protection, surely. We need help of some sort – Darren needs to get to a hospital. I'd rather hoped for more, visiting a doctor." Holly glanced towards the thickets of plant life that surrounded them, like she held this botanical recluse personally responsible for not having a medical degree. "But now we need to rethink – and the newspapers seem as good an idea as any."

"Except," Pax said, "all we've got is a story."

"We've got your friend?"

Pax met her eye and checked the room with concern that the doctor might be nearby. Something moved behind a wall of overgrown ferns, a few tables over. Pax willed Holly to be more careful keeping Letty secret; the fairy had rescued her from the Ministry, after all. "Her people stay hidden for a reason. But you're right, we need more options. I'm hoping the doctor might present some."

"Oh, good luck. She's been lurking," Holly warned.

Pax moved away and found the doctor standing aimlessly behind the ferns, thin hands clutching a steaming tin mug. Under her tent-like lab coat and dungarees, she seemed skeletal and birdlike, and was most definitely lurking.

"Doctor," Pax said. "How are you?" The doctor nodded awkwardly, the worry in her eyes intensified by thick-lensed glasses that covered half her face. Pax's gaze tracked to a large glass jar hanging from the ceiling, the grime on the outside obscuring whatever floated inside. The machinery noises, she realised, had stopped. "You experiment on things from the Sunken City, right?"

"When I can," Rimes said. She lifted a hand to a potted tree with warty bark and mottled brown leaves. "There are . . . fascinating specimens down there."

"A regular horror show," Pax agreed. "We weren't properly introduced, were we? Pax." She held out her hand. "Thanks for taking us in." The doctor took a halting step forward, almost spilling her drink in surprise at her own movement. She gave a bony shake.

"Dr Mandy Rimes."

"With what?"

The joke met with silence.

Pax continued, "You're friends with Darren?" Another nod. "And Rufaizu?"

"I knew his father," Rimes said. "I hadn't seen the boy since he was little, though."

"Hadn't?"

"Until last week."

Pax waited, but there was no elaboration. This woman might have been the only person to actually talk to Rufaizu before he was abducted. "Did he tell you anything? About where he'd been, where he was going? Anything he'd learnt?"

"No. Not really. Just checking if I was still here. Ready to help."

"I guess this isn't the sort of help you had in mind. Bunch of maimed strangers with the Ministry breathing down our necks?"

Rimes' shoulders bunched up weirdly, her nose scrunching, and it took Pax a moment to realise she was amused. "It's exactly the sort of help I had in mind," the doctor said. "This is a safe house. It always has been. *Especially* from the Ministry."

That was to say, it was a safe house for Apothel's team. Their fight against the monsters had ended nine years ago, though, after Apothel's assassination at the hands of an anonymous Fae. Yet the doctor was still here. Pax said, "Do the Ministry know about you? That you're out here? That you knew Darren?"

"Oh yes," Rimes said. "Since Apothel – ahem –" She went quiet, as though the death of Rufaizu's father was taboo. "They came after Apothel left us. I consult on their research, now."

"You *what*?" Pax started in alarm, almost jumping into the ferns.

"I consult," Rimes repeated, completely unapologetic. "I had to agree to it. Otherwise – otherwise they would have shut me down."

"You can't be –" Pax began, but saw the doctor's innocent smile. She had seen enough poker faces to know when someone's emotions rested on the surface; Rimes genuinely didn't see a problem. "Does Darren know?"

"Of course," Rimes nodded quickly. "We've been very careful – but really, we parted ways before Apothel's . . . incident. And the Ministry understand Apothel was in the past. They never come here. Even if they did . . ." She pulled her thumb and forefinger across her lips to show they were sealed.

Pax stared. This was a bad start. But she'd said it herself: Rimes hadn't turned them in so far. "What if they do come?"

"Ah. They usually send me samples by courier. Or I collect from the Long

Culdon Post Office. They don't like to visit, because of the security system."

"A security system that keeps the government away?"

"Oh yes," Rimes said. "An alarm, the dogs. Then the beacon. A combination of blinding water and a flock of ether bats."

"Blinding water and ether bats." Pax could not recall these oddities from the nightmare creatures she'd first read of in Apothel's book.

"A powerful deterrent. I have various ways to reveal Sunken City secrets to the wider world. Otherwise the Ministry might have just – well – you know."

Pax did know. They might have killed her and disappeared the body. Yet something about the doctor's manner, living in her own world, suggested Rimes hardly took the Ministry threat seriously. "Why haven't you revealed these secrets anyway?"

Rimes gave an awkward shrug. "You experienced some things down there, yes? We disagree on some of our research, but the Ministry are right to be cautious. Widespread knowledge of that world could be very dangerous."

That was true enough. A little knowledge had turned Pax's life upside down. "There's a lot you must be able to tell me, though. Can I ask you some questions?"

The lower half of Rimes' face fixed tightly. "Questions?"

"About the creatures – what Apothel called the minotaur, and the blue screens on the walls, the ones he used to write messages – what? What's wrong?"

Rimes was shaking her head. "No. Can't talk. I don't know you."

"I came here with Darren, we're –"

"The Sunken City," Rimes said, almost in a whisper, "is not to be discussed."

"You trust Darren? What if he tells you it's okay?"

Rimes shot a look towards the bedroom. "He's hurt."

"Yeah," Pax said, "and he's not getting help if I can't figure something out."

"I can help him." Rimes' eyes were still on the bedroom door, away with her thoughts. She hadn't helped last night; if she was hiding some medical talent when he'd lain bleeding and broken, then she was a bigger mess than Pax thought.

"How?"

"I've got some glo," Rimes said. "Not much, but it should do."

She pointed a shaky finger to the far side of the room. Pax spotted the unnaturally glowing bottle of liquid partially hidden behind a stack of translucent containers filled with either old stew or preserved animal organs. She knew a little about glo, the potion which had given Barton and Apothel the ability to see the creatures in the tunnels. "How's that supposed to help?"

"It accelerates the healing process. One of its many charms. If he has no serious problems, the body will heal itself, with glo's help." Rimes smiled with a twitch. "If his wife will let us. She's a *stern* woman."

A light, surprised cough, behind the plants, revealed Holly had been listening.

The bedroom had an atmosphere like a candlelit vigil. Cardboard boxes and rags littered the space around the bed, making the room dark and impossibly tight.

Darren Barton lay across one side of a rusty cot, his skin blue with bruises where it wasn't black with scabs or hidden under darkening bandages. His daughter, Grace, lay alongside him, curled up with her bare soles raw and swollen, flesh hard and dirty even after she'd spent half an hour scrubbing.

Holly perched on the rusty metal chair where she'd spent the night. She took one of Darren's beefy hands in both of hers. "Diz, dear. Are you awake?"

He clearly wasn't, so she leant closer and asked again, louder. He stirred with grumbles. Rimes crept into the room, ahead of Pax, the jar of bright liquid cradled in two hands.

"What's happening?" Barton moaned. He tried to push himself up.

"Stay put, dear. We just came to check on you."

His eyes scanned the gathered trio and rested on Rimes. "Wasn't a dream . . ."

"No," Holly said, more patronising than comforting. "Your family *did* get molested by monsters you neglected to tell us exist. And tiny people and government agents *do* want to kill us."

"I remember," Barton said, pulling free from her and sitting up. His face creased with pain as his leg shifted, and his strangled curse woke Grace with a moan.

"Bloody hell," Barton heaved, staring at his ankle. "How bad is it?"

"Apparently," Pax said, "it's outside all our expertise."

Barton kept staring as Grace shifted up onto an elbow. "Oh, Daddy . . ."

"No hospitals," Barton said gravely. "No phones."

"Yes, we got that," Holly replied. "How about no foot?"

"Darren?" Rimes said, simply, holding up the glo.

Barton's expression grew graver. Holly said, "I told them we're a few furlongs short of experimenting with magical elixirs. But obviously the choice is yours." Her tone said it really wasn't.

He waited long enough to suggest he respected her view, then said, "I need it."

"Darren –"

"Give it to me."

Rimes looked to Holly for guidance, and Holly held off for a few seconds, mouth tight. Pax asked Barton, "Can it really do what she says?"

"Of course," he told her gruffly, and Pax felt a little hope, however unlikely it was. It'd be an early win if they could get Barton walking. He could share the burden. Except he complained, "Is that all we've got?"

Rimes was about to answer, her sad face confirming it, when a car engine growled outside, wheels rumbling over the uneven road. The doctor's eyes broadened in alarm, magnified by her thick lenses. Pax cursed under her breath. "Where's your defence system?"

The doctor said, "No – it's not active, not while we're in here!"

Pax's fists clenched. After finding this reclusive hut and the doctor who'd just admitted to working with their enemies, what did she expect besides a useless security system? Should've gone with Letty when she had the chance. She didn't need to ask to know no one good was visiting. "You have to get rid of them."

3

There was no chance of moving Barton unnoticed, so Pax urged Rimes to greet their guests and keep them away from the bedroom. Pax went with her, wary of the doctor's inability to lie and her possibly split allegiances. Fortunately, the chaotic mess of Rimes' workroom was packed with hiding places, including a roomy desk space near the entrance, draped with hanging plants whose leafy branches created a curtain.

A man coughed outside, louder than was necessary, signalling to the world that he was irritated. Pax imagined the cloud of dust their rapid approach must have stirred; she'd coughed on it too, when her group had arrived in the night.

The walls were thin enough for her to hear the men's approach. The first one spoke in a deep, aggressive tone. "Seriously expect me to check the perimeter? I didn't pack *galoshes*."

"We'll see what's necessary," the second man replied with a younger, more reasonable voice. "She's one of us, right?"

"Look at this place. The only thing she is, is abnormal."

Definitely Ministry. Pax leant out to watch Rimes' face as the doctor stood by the door. She had a claw-like hand near the handle, unblinking face tight with nerves. Dammit, she was going to give them away.

"Dr Rimes?" the low-voiced one shouted, apparently not one for knocking. "You in? We've got some questions."

Rimes cleared her throat, eyes fixed on the door handle.

"She's in. Car over there, no way she owns more than one."

Pax tensed at the mention of the car. They had stolen the distinctly old Cavalier from an MEE agent. It was concealed under a tarpaulin, between the trees, in case the MEE had satellites or something looking for it, but all these men needed to do was look under the sheet.

"Rimes!" the boorish one called out and pounded on the door. The doctor jumped back, before composing herself and opening up. Pax ducked under the desk.

"Finally," the man snorted. Almost definitely a terrible person. "Agent Farnham, Agent Devlin. We wake you?"

"No," Rimes answered quietly, then cleared her throat and tried again, with all the flatness of someone trying too hard. "No, not at all. I've been working since sunrise."

"You know what's happened in town?"

Rimes didn't say anything, no doubt affecting an innocent, ignorant look. Pax prayed these men would see her as eccentric rather than untrustworthy.

The loud one, Farnham, huffed and raised his voice as though talking to a simpleton. "Not got a radio out here? Some way to hear the news?"

"I have the internet," Rimes replied, matter-of-factly. "Even on my phone now. I check my emails twice a day –"

"Dr Rimes," the younger one said. "Is it alright if we come in?"

Rimes scuttled away from the door. "By all means, by all means."

The floorboards groaned under the men's weight; at least one of them was carrying more than his share of bulk. Pax could guess which. They continued between the workbenches, scanning the room.

"This place is a dump," Farnham concluded.

"Dr Rimes," Devlin said, "there's been a number of incidents in town. It started Friday and came to a head last night. You haven't heard anything about it?"

"I didn't receive an email," Rimes said. "Or a call."

"This was on the local news."

"National news, now," Farnham corrected. So they had connected the gas main incident to them. As he creaked through the room, Pax curled tighter into her hiding spot. "You heard from Darren Barton lately?"

"Darren?" Rimes said, with a peak of volume. *Too* surprised. "No, not in many years. He cut off all ties with me, you know. He left it all behind him. Everything."

Pax squinted through the leaves at the shape of the man passing the other side of a bench. He was big alright, and had a great curly beard like a Viking. He moved towards the bedroom.

"No visitors lately?" he asked. Rimes laughed nervously. "Something funny?"

"No – well, yes. I don't *get* visitors, Mr Farnham. Who would come here? I don't even see *your* people. But – do you want to search the grounds? Do you think someone could have sneaked in?" Her voice rose with worry. Pax hadn't given her enough credit; Rimes didn't just sound convincingly scatty, she was playing on Farnham's clear reluctance to be here.

"It's *Agent* Farnham," he replied bitterly. He moved away from the bedroom, back through the room, and Pax let out a quiet breath of relief. The other agent started moving, closer to her. His legs came past the desk, right in front of her, and she held her breath again.

"We've got reason to believe Darren Barton is active," Devlin said. "You will tell us if you hear from him, won't you?"

"Oh." Rimes affected even more surprise. "Active how? His wife would *kill* him."

Devlin scratched a smart shoe down his calf, smearing mud on the suit trouser. Not used to being outside the city. "You're aware of the rumours that the Fae once had a weapon that could affect the *praelucente*?"

The MEE's word for the minotaur.

"Rumours," Rimes echoed, dismissively.

"Seems someone had access to something like that, and it got set off last night," Devlin continued, getting a snort of disapproval from Farnham. No doubt angry that it was one of their own, Casaria, who had activated the weapon. "The *praelucente* is behaving somewhat unusually this morning. Possibly after-effects from the device."

"You got any ideas about that?" Farnham said, accusingly.

"I'm not sure I follow," Rimes replied. "I haven't done such research in almost a decade. My primary concerns are in testing Sunken City flora. Do you know I've been running some very interesting tests on wading moss –"

"You used to do other things," Farnham pressed. "Back when you worked with that bastard Apothel. Before the MEE educated you about the *praelucente's* net benefits, right?"

Casaria had used the same phrasing; the MEE's dogma that the minotaur, on balance, offered some force of good. Rimes didn't answer at once, which Pax realised was a genuine falter. Whatever work she'd done with these people, the doctor didn't believe the minotaur was a good thing. Rimes said, a little testy, "Apothel never found a way to hurt it. He never even got close to it."

The Ministry men let that sink in. Farnham was right on the other side of the room now. Near the cloudy-panelled corner space. He said, "What are you working on here?"

"Oh, that." Rimes cleared her throat again, quieter. "A weed."

"Why's it glowing? Put some kind of dye on it?"

Pax tensed. Was it electric weed? The fuel for the Fae weapon? Christ, that would do it – moments from exposure. She could grab Devlin's shins and yank; in the cluttered confines he might hit his head, be knocked out cold. Break his neck even – shit, why not bite out his Achilles tendon while she was at it, if she was considering murder.

"It's – no – it's –" Rimes pattered towards Farnham. She bumped into something and a glass broke, making Devlin move quickly to the side, out of range. So much for ankle-biting.

"What is that?" Devlin demanded.

A noxious smell caught Pax's nose too, and she threw a hand over her nose and mouth to avoid gagging. It smelt like a broken sewage pipe.

"Bloody hell!" Farnham shouted, marching across the room. "Are you serious?"

"Ah – oh my –" Rimes said, metal and glass tinkling as she ineffectively dealt with the breakage. "It's quite harmless but – oh, it smells –"

Smells was an extreme understatement. Stinks didn't cover it either. Pax squeezed her nostrils closed but even the traces of the odour made her stomach lurch. As something rose up her throat, a second from betraying her position, Devlin gagged, too.

"Open a window – Christ!" Farnham boomed.

Devlin ran groaning for the door.

"Quite harmless!" Rimes reminded them. Farnham ran, too.

As the agents got outside they inhaled big, deep breaths of fresh air. One of them coughed and spat noisily.

"Bloody loon!" Farnham complained. "Living up here among that crap!"

Devlin was too busy spluttering to agree. Rimes walked after them, unaffected by the smell. Pax's eyes were tearing, the fumes working through her hand, clamped over her mouth and nose. She needed to run, it was choking her. She'd get caught, reeled in, disappeared – after everything – all because of a smell.

"You do that on purpose?" Farnham demanded. "I swear, you fucking –"

"Easy," Devlin said, hoarsely, then started coughing again.

"That smell gets in my suit," Farnham continued, "in my *hair*? Bloody hell."

"I'm so sorry," Rimes started, anxiously. "But this is – well – I don't get visitors! Please, wait – let me make a tea? You say something *affected* the minotaur? We can talk –"

"Fuck this and fuck you," Farnham spat, storming away.

Pax curled over, all but burying her head between her legs. About to explode.

Farnham stopped, his heavy footsteps coming back. "You're a goddamned mess, woman. Waste of all our energy, having you out here."

"Please . . ." Rimes replied, sounding genuinely hurt.

Pax's mouth forced itself open, trying to inhale, but she resisted. There'd be no coming back from a mouthful of that gas.

"Disgrace," Farnham growled. "For Christ's sake. Come on. We've got real work to do."

More hurried footsteps, the car doors opening. The engine started. Pax's vision blurred. Tears flooded her face, seeping through her fingers. As the car pulled away, she let go, taking a quick, sharp breath in – a vile mistake. She gagged, loudly, and coughed it back out, reeling forward. She hit her head on the desk and fell onto her hands and knees. Scrambling up, she shot out, running for the open door in a half-crouch, choking, nose streaming.

Pax burst through the doorway, shoving Rimes out of the way, and inhaled with a great gasp. Again, again, rolling her eyes back to the sky. Shit, shit. She leaned forward again, hands resting on her knees, and hesitated to look up at the Ministry car.

The cloud of dust lingered in the road, blocking her view of the men's exit. She froze, staring as the dark shape of the vehicle turned through the trees. Heading back down the hill.

They weren't stopping, weren't coming back.

They hadn't seen her.

"My," Rimes commented lightly, at her side. "That was fortunate."

Pax straightened up, taking in the frail recluse. She wasn't sure if Rimes had deliberately broken that canister, but she could draw two conclusions. The doctor was on their side, but Letty was right about this place. They were free from neither prying eyes nor Rimes' experiments.

And if they were going to move, they had to risk Barton using that glowing liquid.

4

"Tell me again," Sam Ward said, chair legs squealing against the floor as she sat, "what you thought you heard."

The man across the table, Malcolm Joseph, looked nervous.

He was a few years younger than Sam, dark-skinned and, from the broad curves of his upper body, likely spent more time in the gym than reading. He folded his thick arms over a stained grey t-shirt, hiding Mickey Mouse's face, and said, "I panicked, okay? But I'm cool now. When can I go?"

Sam clicked her pen and wrote the date in the top corner of her writing pad. Then the time, 09.32 by her watch. Malcolm Joseph, IP-6, AGa-26. Was this office designation 26 or 27? She turned to Hail. "Is this AGa-26?"

Hail nodded, standing rigidly by the door. She ignored his look that said she should know. He was hardly one to judge professional standards; he hadn't even combed his mop of ginger hair.

"Sorry you've been kept waiting, Mr Joseph," Sam said, unapologetic. She was feeling, she imagined, more put out than him. She was three days late to all this. Saturday night, she had endured a date explaining why he had fallen out of love with eight different women. Sunday, she had watched Attenborough documentaries and eaten ice cream. This morning, even, she'd taken an extra ten minutes for her run. Meanwhile, the Fae had fired on humans in two separate incidents, an untested weapon had been set off, and now this. No one had told her about any of it until she got into the office. She wasn't sure if it was the weekend staff's incompetence (they were only in it for the overtime) or the general fear that her involvement created more work for everyone (because, oddly enough, she noticed details that others missed). Thankfully, Malcolm's case had given her a rare, if tenuous, opportunity to broaden the scope of her department, InterSpecies Relations.

"You can go as soon as we've covered a few questions. You did agree to be interviewed, didn't you?"

"Sure, well – of course I want to help, but it's been hours, see – and this is pretty strange. Are you people even legit –" He cut himself off as Sam offered what she hoped was a friendly expression. Not a smile, as you had to be taken seriously, but a calming look.

"What he *heard*," Hail said, impatiently, "was the sound of –"

"Thank you, Agent Hail," Sam said. She'd heard Hail's take on the way over, and he was toeing the Ministry line: atmospheric sounds caused by the movements of the *praelucente* and the creatures surrounding it (caused by a broken pipe, as far as the public was concerned). But in the online video of his outburst in the street,

Malcolm Joseph had used words to describe those sounds. "I'd like to hear it from Mr Joseph."

Malcolm shifted in his seat, almost unfolding his arms then quickly folding them again, remembering what he was wearing. He must've grabbed the t-shirt in a hurry; it didn't match the work he'd put into his physique. He started defensively, "I'm a COO, you know. Gold Hat Enterprises. Public-facing and B2B relations, tech and PR management."

Sam guessed he managed a couple of clients, if any. She knew the smell of embellishment; the Ministry was full of people who described work rather than did it. "You ran out into the road shouting that you heard something. What happened?"

"Okay," Malcolm said. "Here's why I did that. The building was shaking like an earthquake. Woke me up. The wall cracked, there was dust, a sound like everything was falling apart. This big chunk of ceiling almost hit me on the way out. I didn't know what was going on. It happened fast, everyone was panicking."

"You felt light-headed? Did you smell anything?"

"Smell?"

"Gas?"

"Is that what it was? I mean, I don't remember a smell – but that'd make sense, wouldn't it? Because what I heard, I know what it sounds like now, but at the time it shit me up." A hand shot to his mouth. Even strangers were cautious in front of Sam. Was it her fringe? Too square? She didn't actually begrudge cursing; should she swear more herself, to relax people? "Sorry," he went on. "I was in a strange state, that's what I'm saying."

"Yes, I've seen the YouTube video," Sam said. "You shouted that it spoke to you. Gave you a rather specific message?"

"Um. It started like a groan. Then it sounded like speaking. Like words, almost, but all twisted, distorted." Malcolm slowed down. "I – I know how it sounds. What I said before, I mean, that's just what it sounded like."

"*A dinosaur trying to speak*," Sam quoted his own words back to him.

"Hey, it was nuts. I was half asleep?"

"A gas pipe burst, under the block. Is it possible that caused the sounds?"

"A splitting pipe?" Malcolm exclaimed. "Making *those* sounds?" The instinctive response showed he'd heard something unnatural, even if he quickly changed tack. "I inhaled some gas, is that it? Makes sense."

"I'm interested in exactly what you heard," Sam said.

"I wasn't with it, was I? I was high as a kite –"

"Please, Mr Joseph, what did this voice say?"

"Kind of…like…'Greg . . . you lost.'"

"*Greg you lost*. You heard these words distinctly?"

"Yes. Well, no, they were kind of rolled together, but that's what made sense, I guess? It seemed important at the time. I must've inhaled some fumes."

"There someone called Greg in your building?"

Malcolm took a second. "Not that I know of."

"Friend of yours?"

He shook his head.

"Does it mean anything to you? Half-remembered from somewhere?"

He shook his head again. "I mean, it might not have been quite *Greg*, just a noise like that. And it sounded more like . . . *locks*? Maybe? But that wouldn't make sense, would it? Grammatically."

"Since when did dinosaur speech obey grammar," Sam replied, knowing all too well the creatures of the Sunken City had a scant disregard for English. She wrote it anyway. *Locks*, not *lost*. Hail would've let that go.

The details were necessary to understand the Sunken City, but even more necessary to justify her work. She could help the whole organisation run more efficiently if they only *listened*. That was the great irony of them all thinking she was trying to make life more difficult – her advice, and interference, would *reduce* work. A misreported audio reading had led to six days of wasted manpower in June when agents were searching for a sickle instead of an *effundo porcum*, but Management ignored her suggestion of implementing validation checks. Iron out those niggles and they could afford the manpower to do real work, like developing a relationship with the Fae.

"So what's the deal?" Malcolm interrupted her thoughts. "Is my block safe to go back to? Do I need a check-up or something? Only, I've got a presentation on Wednesday, and I've already lost half a day here."

Sam gave him a wan smile. It was impressive, half a day lost before 10am. "You'll probably be allowed back in by lunchtime. The fire service are still running safety checks. You should rest, though. And I'd recommend you be careful how you talk to people about this. The video, I understand, has already been seen by a few thousand people, and I wouldn't want any undue embarrassment for you."

"Seventeen thousand," Hail said. "Last I checked."

"Of course," Malcolm nodded quickly, not questioning why they were monitoring it. "You think I wanted that uploaded? If the press asks, I'll give it to them straight. Wasn't thinking. Inhaled gas."

Sam stood, then paused. "Did you happen to *see* anything, Mr Joseph?"

"Oh yeah," he said. "I told you, cracks all up the wall. It was crazy."

"Anything else?"

"Like the gas?"

He asked like it was a possibility. Had he seen the fumes from a *bufo cloaca*? The blue glow of the *praelucente* itself? "Yes, like the gas. A haze in the air, anything near the ground level?"

Malcolm considered it, then flashed a pearly white smile, "I was off my face, I guess – I didn't notice anything but the sound, and had my eyes on where the door was."

With the hallucination excuse in place, it was unlikely he'd say anything useful now. That was rather the point for the Ministry, but not overly helpful for Sam. Then, they'd always cared more about keeping the public quiet than doing a good job.

But if the creatures themselves were becoming more noticeable, especially if there was a chance the noise had come from the *praelucente*, then she could use this. She could break free from the box they'd put her in, and make Management take notice. Today, she told herself, InterSpecies Relations was going to matter. *She* was going to matter.

5

From the slack expression on his face as Barton wriggled his toes, Pax could see the liquid had started to take effect. Holly was right that it didn't look safe to drink, but a more natural glow was returning to Barton's skin. In a matter of minutes, while Rimes rustled up some tea, his bruising had lightened. Pax willed it to work faster, so they could get away. The lab's ventilation system had quickly cleared the stench, but with animal noises outside and potential Ministry visits, nothing about this place felt safe.

"How much longer?" Pax asked, hopefully. "You'll be able to walk, right?"

"After that much? No," Barton said. "But it'll do for now."

"It'll do?" Holly said. "A painkiller won't stop your foot from needing amputating."

"It's not a painkiller," Barton said. His eyes drifted to Pax and suddenly widened.

Pax tensed, wanting to hide or at least avoid his gaze, but it was too late. He fixed on her with deep creases of concern as she huddled up self-consciously. After the confusion of his pain and all they'd been through, he probably hadn't remembered exactly who she was yet. He was nothing if not protective of his family, and she was the stranger who'd put them all in danger. Pax cleared her throat and broke his gaze, ready to apologise, but he spoke first. "You touched it? The minotaur?"

Pax paused. Not what she'd expected. She met his eyes again. His stare was intense, but concerned, not angry. She said, "Well, *it* touched *me*."

He scanned her up and down, like he was able to see into her. Did he know, somehow? About the weird dream? The unsettling feeling? "How do you feel?"

"Fine." Pax shrugged. "Better than I've any right to, actually."

"Fine? You touched it . . . no one's ever touched the minotaur. Never got close enough. Never risked it."

"Yeah, about that," Pax hurried on, to shift attention away from her. "It didn't look like a minotaur. More like an electric kraken. There was a ton of messed-up stuff down there, nothing that looked like a minotaur."

Barton kept staring. Had he even blinked? "You didn't have any glo?"

Pax shook her head. "Can't imagine it would've helped."

"It would. It reveals things . . ." Barton was high on the stuff. Were his dilated eyes seeing things now?

"And it emits a pheromone," Rimes elaborated, joining them with a tray of steaming ceramic mugs. "It keeps some creatures away, attracts others."

Pax took a mug; the tea was two quite different shades of brown. An earthy contrast to the liquid they were discussing. She said, "This magical glo, does it make your farts smell like roses, too?"

"Oh," Holly joined in, "perhaps it could solve the Israel-Palestine conflict?"

"No," Rimes said, seriously.

Barton looked unamused, still staring at Pax. "You're seeing the effects, aren't you?" He *did* know, didn't he? But he lifted his leg, swollen foot on display as it rotated at the ankle. He took a sharp breath, still hurting, but said, "It works. If we had more, I'd be up in hours."

"You could say the same of opiates," Holly said.

"It's not a damn painkiller!"

Grace almost flinched off her perch at the corner of the bed. Barton reached towards her. "I'm sorry – honey –" He lowered his hand when she didn't come closer. He breathed deeply, calming down. The outburst, at least, had drawn his attention from Pax.

"But the bottom line," Pax said, "is you're not going anywhere fast?"

"And your *friend*," Holly added hotly to Barton, "is working with the people after us."

"She turned them away, didn't she?" Barton replied, his protective streak shining through. "Mandy does what she has to, God knows she has no one else. And the research she offers the MEE can only help open their eyes – it's *not* a betrayal."

"Absolutely not," Rimes said quickly. "Just – just last month I submitted findings on wading moss that indicate a need for better air circulation around the Tupsom tunnels. The gaseous build-up there could put the city above at risk."

"There's a lot more going on in the Sunken City than our problems," Barton said. "And there is some *good* in trying to understand it. Glo, for instance, we've proven to work, repeatedly."

"Indeed," Rimes said. "It's not my speciality, but the Ministry measure an energy they call *novisan* – which I believe might be affected by glo. The same energy the minotaur uses. But measuring novisan is complicated. There's nothing you can see or weigh. It requires systems of deduction – they've never given me the means myself."

"*Novisan.*" Pax tested the word. The best she had been given before was Barton's tales of people getting tired in the Underground. She had seen it herself – heads nodding, briefcases slipping from lifeless hands, as blue light flickered in the dark tunnel outside the train. "That's the energy this minotaur is draining and manipulating? Some kind of mystical life energy? Paired with a minotaur which doesn't even look like a minotaur."

"I'm so glad," Holly said, "that you're here to witness this. I'm sure if it was me, on my own, suggesting they were bloody fools, *I* would be the unreasonable one."

"Holly," Barton said, bristling. "I didn't want to return to all this. It's what I always tried to protect you from." He reached out to Grace again, this time squeezing her dainty hand. "But you can be damned sure I'll kill those monsters once and for all, for all of us."

"How?" Pax said. She had never learnt what he had been through to get in his current state, but she was fairly sure, from their own experiences, that it hadn't been especially helpful. "What'll you do next time, jump in front of a bus?"

Barton glowered at her. "You brought those bloody Fae to my home, I could've –"

"You could've what?" Holly cut in. "Last I checked Pax brought *our daughter* to our home. Those psychotic fairies already had her! No thanks to you!"

"I was doing –"

"Stop! Stop it!" Grace jumped to her feet, wincing as she did. Her voice was high and desperate. "Stop fighting! We're alive, aren't we? I thought you were going to die, Dad! I thought we were all going to die!" She moved closer to Pax in solidarity, squeezing uncomfortably close. "You need to listen to her. Pax knows what she's doing. She's smart and she's quick and she's tough and she sees things better than the rest of you!"

The expectant gazes of Holly and Barton rested on Pax. Even Rimes' googly eyes had grown larger with anticipation. Pax wanted to be somewhere else. Grace smiled encouragingly, and Pax quietly told her, "You're going to break so many hearts when you're older."

"Pax," Barton said, letting out a big breath. "I *am* grateful for what you've done." But his stare was heavy again. "What did you see? Are you really okay?"

Pax hesitated. It was an invitation to explain the dream. Her burning heart and the electric soldiers and the foreboding feeling she'd had. And then what? Make this family pity her and argue about whose fault it was she'd been electrocuted? No, describing the dream wasn't going to help. They had bigger concerns. She said, "I saw those blue screens, connected to your minotaur, when I was down there. What Apothel called the Blue Angel – whoever or whatever used those screens to send you messages – it's the root of all this. How much do you know about it?"

Barton was frowning even harder. "I told you everything, more or less. We shared messages, scratched into the walls on those blue screens. Messages were scratched in return. The screens came out of nowhere and disappeared again. Apothel named the contact the Blue Angel because of this divine bloody intervention. But the Angel sometimes pointed us to glo, sometimes to nothing, wasting our time. Likewise, when we relayed the minotaur's location, he did something to slow it down. Sometimes he did nothing."

"He? You had some idea who this was?"

"No," Barton said. "He, it, they, whatever."

"Let's assume nothing then, okay? This Angel, *it* didn't give you anything else?"

"Some information. A lot of what we know came from the Blue Angel's messages."

"The turnbold's weakness for zinc," Rimes offered. "For example. I extrapolated advice about concentrated oyster brine from an Angel message."

Holly stirred at the idea. "Is that so? That wretched blue square sent us on a wild goose chase! And one underground wiped away my marks on the wall! Your

Angel wanted us trapped down there.”

“He – *it* – wasn’t consistent,” Barton said, “but it helped us stay alive.”

“Because it needed you,” Pax said. “*Not* for what you thought. It connected to that minotaur somehow, through those blue screens.”

“You’re sure that’s what you saw?” Barton replied warily.

“No minotaur,” Pax said. “No drink-induced illusions. Just an electric monster surrounded by blue screens.” She held Barton’s questioning gaze to drive home her sincerity. “I’m telling you, the Blue Angel is the crux of all this. If we want to figure out the Ministry’s angle and get ahead of it all, we need to figure out the Blue Angel.”

“And how do you expect to do that?” Barton said.

“You tell me,” Pax said. “You must’ve done *something* to explain who was sending the messages? Where do we start?”

There was silence at the weight of the question. Barton looked like his cogs were turning at half-speed, while Rimes sought distraction around the cluttered room. Grace, bless her, had an expression of tense concentration, doing her best to think of a solution.

Barton spoke first. “Only me and Apothel ever saw the screens, not even the rest of our group. Whenever Rik or Mandy got near, they didn’t show. The Ministry don’t even believe they exist.” He looked at the doctor. “Assuming that’s still true?”

Rimes nodded, replying in a quiet tone, “Yes.”

“You could point me to the blue screens, at least?” Pax asked.

“Yeah,” Barton said. “There’s about a half a dozen locations where they showed. All near Sunken City entrances.”

“We saw one under a bridge,” Holly volunteered.

Pax gave her a conciliatory smile, then flashed on the images from her dream. The bridge, the body of water, the fountain. Pointless coincidence, she told herself. The city was full of bridges. “The Angel didn’t give you a clue to where it was writing from? Something in the way it wrote?”

“The messages were simple,” Barton said. “Not even full sentences.”

“Could Apothel have known more that he didn’t tell you?” Pax turned to Rimes. “He double-crossed the Fae; was he talking with his Blue Angel when that happened?”

“I don’t know,” Rimes said. “We lost touch.”

“We *all* lost touch,” Barton clarified. “If he’d told me, I could’ve helped.”

“But Rufaizu . . .” Rimes said, but stalled.

“He said something?” Pax pressed, hopefully. The doctor shrank with nerves.

“He said he had help. He came back to kill the minotaur, he was excited, and he said he had *new* help. Someone who would fight with him. That and – and he thought he had a solution. That was all he said.”

The solution Pax already knew about; Rufaizu’s return, drawing her into all this, spiralled around the discovery of the Dispenser, the Fae weapon that could injure the minotaur. The new help, she suspected, was a reference to Letty.

Holly, apparently, made the connection, too: "It was the fairies, isn't that right, Diz? The *Layer Fae*. You told me all about them, without telling me a damned thing. *Fairies*. They killed your friend Apothel and they" – she spun a hand in the air – "dragged us into all this!"

Barton didn't answer. Rimes replied mournfully, "If that's true then no wonder Rufaizu got caught. The Fae can't ever be trusted."

Pax said, "What makes you say that?"

"The Blue Angel, of course," Barton said. "But you've had first-hand experience of the Fae, haven't you? Where is she?"

Pax felt Rimes' curious eyes on her, and gave Barton a warning look. "She's exploring our options elsewhere. Can we stay focused? The blue screens."

"I can give you their locations," Barton said, "but I wouldn't bank on them showing, especially not if you think you've rumbled the Blue Angel. You might as well watch our videos and get the same experience of not seeing them."

"Videos of what?" Pax said. "The Sunken City?"

"Yeah." Barton gestured to some of the stacked boxes. "They're in here somewhere, shot by a real pro. Experience the Sunken City without ever having to go down there."

Pax scanned the clutter around them. Footage of their experiences, she realised, was preferable to actually encountering that dangerous world. "Show me."

6

Most Mondays, Sam Ward came to work feeling reinvigorated. She was rested, freshly reminded of the banality of home life, and ready to make a difference. Some people hated coming to the Ministry of Environmental Energy's offices at 14 Greek Street, with its jutting buttresses and narrow slits of windows. Sam saw it as a place of opportunity and brought a new Big Idea every Monday. By Wednesday or Thursday, it would hit a wall of some sort and she'd start to slump. By Friday she'd have another new Big Idea, which she'd refine over the short break, ready for Monday.

She'd engaged in this cycle for three years, since the Ministry's governing board, the Raleigh Commission, had accepted her proposals to establish an InterSpecies Relations initiative, to (quote) *create understanding of and foster dialogue between those creatures that demonstrate communicative capabilities*. She'd been taken off the streets and given her own office and two members of staff. Then she had been more or less cut off from the rest of the Ministry, and she slowly realised the appointment was designed to keep her from creating ripples.

Before she'd started, it was clear the Raleigh Commission had already had contact with the Fae Transitional City. The Ministry had made peace with Valoria, the Fae leader, and her council a decade ago, though it hadn't led to open communication. The MEE knew roughly where the FTC was located and mostly left its inhabitants alone. Some field agents still believed the Fae were a threat, and there was a plan – Protocol 21 – to eliminate them, but it wasn't something they discussed seriously. The Fae hadn't interfered with any MEE business in years. Given their reputation for disruption, that proved the existence of a mutual understanding between the two governments.

Sam imagined herself codifying that understanding, laying out regulations and proposing diplomatic missions, encouraging new levels of co-operation. The technology swaps and cultural exchanges could hugely improve efficiency and decrease MEE patrols, to say nothing of the wider effects these learnings could have.

Except it turned out neither Management nor the Fae wanted this. As countless phone calls and emails went unanswered, and meetings were postponed or cancelled, Sam learnt the Ministry weren't interested in change. She discovered the same situation in the Ministry's Support and Operations departments: Doctors Hertz and Galler, respectively, conducted research into Sunken City biology and technology that was kept entirely in-house, despite having potentially world-changing implications.

The point of the MEE, Sam realised, was to maintain equilibrium. It was more true in Ordshaw than anywhere else, because the unusual elements under Ordshaw had extra potential to generate change. As far as she was aware, no other UK city had a subterranean labyrinth of monsters. But then, no one much spoke to her, so they might.

This belief made her ineffective position especially uncomfortable. Sam had resigned from her previous job at Lyndale Finance specifically to get away from the repetitive chores of completing spreadsheets, filing reports and silently enduring circular meetings. Such mundane work made her entertain the idea of joining the MEE. Managing the Sunken City demanded innovation, and she *enjoyed* being innovative.

Having been left with a dead duck in the IS department, Sam tried to find ways to extend her jurisdiction. She proposed language analyses, worldwide surveys and behavioural studies to better understand animal behaviour in the Sunken City, amongst a few hundred other ideas. The answer was usually the same: the MEE didn't have specialist analysts or field agents to spare, as (in spite of their vast resources) they rarely hired new staff, due to trust issues.

Still, she tried. Four years at Lyndale Finance had taught her that this was simply the way the world operated; you had to make small changes where you could. At least in the MEE she had a title, and her own office, and a good wage. She didn't want to rock that boat. It would just be nice to feel like her work mattered.

So, each week started with a new Big Idea. Last week, she had focused on the return of the vagrant boy Rufaizu, who was rumoured to be in town, even if no one could place him. He was of interest because his father, Apothel, had explored the Sunken City before his death nine years ago. She had canvassed the various locations Apothel had once frequented and suggested a handful of pubs and bars worth monitoring. Management accepted her suggestions with no enthusiasm, and explained that the search for Rufaizu had nothing to do with her. She sent a disagreeable email explaining that if Rufaizu had direct contact with the myriad creatures, it *was* of interest to IS. That email had gone unanswered.

By Friday, she had devised an idea for a funding application for improved phone lines in the office, assuming all communications came under her Relations title. This Monday, feeling fresh from her pre-breakfast run, she was going to nail it.

But she found a markedly unusual atmosphere when she came into the office.

Most Mondays, the bullpen on the sixth floor of 14 Greek Street, consisting of five rows of computers, typically staffed by no more than four people, was a slow-moving hub of chatter about the weekend's television. Sam was usually one of the first in, giving her time to share pleasantries with the secretary, Tori, and to start mentally preparing her new ideas. This Monday, the analysts' eyes were glued to screens and Tori was frantically fielding phone calls. People were *busy* and *focused* and it felt like Sam was *late*.

A rushed field agent told Sam that Rufaizu had surfaced on Friday. Surfaced, been captured by the MEE, shot by the Fae and finally hauled into their med bay on the fifth floor of Greek Street (a floor otherwise used for storage). The shocks stacked up from there, culminating in the dual disasters of a Ministry agent being killed in the Sunken City and a novisan energy surge, around 06.42 that morning, hitting a building with enough force to convince the residents it was an earthquake.

Sam had been a little slow to react herself. Her first (unvoiced) question was why on earth no one had told her about any of this. Admittedly, IS Relations had taken her away from questions of novisan, the largely unexplained energy source that the MEE struggled to measure across Ordshaw. But the questions novisan raised affected all of them. It was, after all, the driving force of the *praelucente*; it was the energy they used to keep track of its location, and to identify when it might have produced a positive surge. Her thought, as usual, was that something affecting the Sunken City in general *had* to involve IS Relations.

When she took it to her boss, Deputy Director Mathers brushed her off, saying she should wait for correspondence from the Fae Transitional City. Which would never come. Dr Galler, Support's tech guru, said no, she could not look at the Fae weapon, not until he had done a detailed analysis. The Ministry were concerned that the morning's surge might have been a reaction to the weapon being set off – possibly distressing the *praelucente*. But, just to doubly frustrate her, they couldn't actually confirm it was a *Fae* weapon yet (let alone the rumoured weapon they called the Dispenser), so it shouldn't concern IS. Dr Hertz, their biologist-slash-physician, meanwhile, said no, Rufaizu was in no fit state to talk. Her last hope had been to talk to the agents involved in the Sunday night events, but they had, incredibly, been sent home.

Mathers said he would get them back in, although he noted the agent who'd been closest to the action was Cano Casaria, and didn't Sam have history with him? As if she needed reminding. She left it with him and studied Casaria's reports about all that had happened.

That had occupied Sam until she noticed a couple of analysts laughing over an online video. Malcolm Joseph's panicked charge into the street, claiming something *spoke*, gave Sam, and InterSpecies Relations, an excuse to actually do something. The interview itself, granted, wasn't promising, but she was working on it.

On the way back from the discrete site of Maclolm Joseph's questioning, Sam rehearsed in her head what she was going to say to Deputy Director Mathers. This was a major crisis and the exact words of what a civilian had heard were important. She needed to be allowed to expand her investigation, as they might be dealing with something new, or a sound emitted by the *praelucente* itself.

Sam stopped herself at Mathers' door, nails digging into her palms.

She could organise a team to properly collate the weekend's findings, to identify and keep track of this new sound. Then she would have the opportunity to explain the source of the morning's tremor. They might, after all, be taking for granted that it was caused by this unusual weapon. She could do this faster and better than Operations or Support – she'd proved that often enough (in her own head, at least).

Sam knocked and waited for a response.

She knocked again.

"Yes, yes, come in already!" Mathers called out, as though she should've guessed.

He looked like he hadn't slept, tie half undone and a few strands of greying hair loose across his brow. With him was a bulky field agent in a tattered suit. Landon. The agent's over-large brown jacket was ripped and his shirt crumpled. His hair was thinning, and his skin textured with the gristle of age, making it unclear if his swollen nose and red eyes were injuries or the result of an unhealthy lifestyle.

"Agent Landon," Sam greeted him. "Is Agent Casaria in yet?"

"Probably sleeping," Landon said.

"I'd really like to talk to him."

Landon didn't seem interested, looking to Mathers to move things along.

"You can start with Landon," Mathers said, reclining in his large leather chair. "I'm expecting a call from London, it'd do well to have Landon on hand for it."

Sam was wary of her uncomfortable smile as she considered a tongue-twister involving Landon and London, to avoid getting annoyed at the promised phone call. In MEE parlance, London translated to the Raleigh Commission. Lord Tarrington, the Commission chairman and the titular director of the Ministry, liked to waste time brainstorming over the phone. He was one half of the Commission's two permanent peers. The other, the elusive Lord Broderick Asquith, frustrated the office in a more novel way, by rejecting modern technology and insisting on sending faxes – faxes! – to issue ill-informed but highly disruptive orders. Alongside the two permanent peers, the Commission had a rolling membership of some five to seven other government bigwigs who cast long-distance votes on things they had no expertise in. One of Sam's unsuccessful proposals had been to limit the Commission's ability to directly interfere with the day-to-day running of the Ordshaw office.

"Right, well," Sam said, trying to recall what she'd planned to say. "Before we begin – about Malcolm Joseph. I established –"

"We've all seen the video," Mather said. "I'm not sure you needed to meet him."

Sam was momentarily stunned. *Of course you're not, you haven't given me a chance to explain.* "Um. Malcolm thought the words might have been *Greg, you lost. Or locks.*"

The men stared with equally empty eyes. Mathers said, "What I need, Ward, is for you to send another message to the FTC. Include whatever you think you've learnt this morning if you think it will help."

"But it wasn't about –" Sam started to explain.

"Shall we go through last night, then?" Mathers turned to Landon. The field agent gave her a look, checking she was done.

Sam revised the explanation: *It was clearly a distinctive sound, enough for Malcolm to spot a difference in syllables. Something we should investigate fully as –*

"We secured the device from the girl's home," said Landon, interrupting her thoughts. "The girl Rufaizu had contact with. Casaria had met her but hadn't reported it. The girl –"

"This is Pax Kuranes?" Sam said. "The gambler?"

Landon nodded and continued, "Yeah. The girl –"

"Twenty-seven years old?"

"If you say so." Landon didn't see the relevance.

Sam thought accurately identifying the suspect might be important for finding her. Referring to a grown woman as a girl might send the wrong message. She didn't say so.

"This girl had been talking with the Fae," Landon went on. "We caught up to her yesterday, Casaria, Gant and me. My faeometer went off."

"Did you see it?" Sam asked, worried he might neglect details there, too.

"No, I did not," Landon said. "I saw the readings on my faeometer, and the girl ran, making the Fae presence seem likely. I saw the Fae weapon recovered from her apartment." Landon straightened his shoulders, resisting looking at Mathers. Clearly they had discussed this next bit in advance. "There were no Fae at the Sunken City when I got there. None helping Casaria or the civilians. Whatever happened with them happened earlier in the day. The latest problem is unlikely to be connected to them."

"Huh," Sam said. In other words, no reason to involve her, even if everyone was talking about the damage a potentially Fae weapon had done. But she had expected that. "What Malcolm Joseph heard this morning – what if it's a noise created by the *praelucente* itself?"

Mathers digested that. "That's a question for Support."

"Does it not –"

"We're understaffed, Ward," Mathers told her. His get-out-of-anything card. "Trust that their work is being prioritised properly. I believe *you* have plenty to be getting on with."

Sam's frustrated smile threatened to return. "Certainly, but my team can work –"

The phone chimed and Mathers put the call on speaker, waving at Sam to leave.

"Two incidents in the space of a week," Director Tarrington said, not bothering to introduce himself. He had the drawn-out baritone of the eminently well-educated, a voice that sounded bored and disappointed at the same time. "It's not on, is it?"

"Sir, thank you for calling. I've got –"

"It's not a social call, Mathers, your city is on the national news *again*. You understand that babysitting the Ordshaw MEE is *not* my full-time occupation?"

But it *should be*, Sam thought. Nowhere was the MEE's work more important than in Ordshaw, and their own director had a part-time attitude.

Mathers said, "Sir. I've got Sam Ward and Agent Landon here."

"Ah, Ward," Tarrington said. "You've had contact with the little wretches behind this mess?"

"Director Tarrington," Sam said. "Sir, good morning."

"Yes, yes," Tarrington replied. "What are the buggers saying?"

Sam thought, *you'd know better than me.* She said, "They claim no knowledge of the device and no knowledge of the Fae behind the attacks."

"Unlikely. But we're not looking at all-out war? Buildings collapsing and all that?"

She found Mathers and Landon watching her expectantly. "No sir, it seems the Fae weren't responsible for what happened this morning."

"Very well. You're a bright lass, so what's your take? The *praelucente's* unstable, is it? Anything we can take from it so far?"

"There was a sound –"

"It's possible, sir" – Mathers cut her off – "that we heard the *praelucente* itself make a noise." Sam stared, aghast. "It may have been caused by an injury, after the weapon was discharged. Our working theory is this morning's surge was an attempt to recover."

He'd been paying attention, at least.

"Excellent, Mathers, now that's something I can sell. Things are back on track with the bonus of new observations. Good thinking."

Sam blurted out, "We're also exploring exactly what Agents Landon and Casaria saw for more insights."

There was silence for a moment. Sam looked at the toes of her shoes.

"Casaria." Tarrington tested the name. He must have known it from past HR crises. "Is he there?"

"No, sir," Mathers said. "He was dismissed before the latest crisis."

"For Christ's sake, Mathers," Tarrington huffed. "The man isn't even on site?"

"Actually," Sam said, not daring to look up but forcing the words out, "I was about to propose to Deputy Director Mathers that I retrieve him, seeing as our Operations team are fully occupied."

Another stiff silence. Sam could feel Mathers' unappreciative eyes warning her against this sort of initiative. To save face, he said, "A reasonable idea, sir. I'm happy to send Ward out into the field. Agent Landon, you're without a partner, aren't you?"

Landon and Sam locked eyes. It was a cold thing to say, knowing Landon's partner had died only the night before, though that barely seemed to register on the big man's impassive face. He was staring at Sam like he'd rather it be anyone else. The look she got from most of the office. Most of the time. She smiled back.

7

Barton's idea of videos was actually a pile of movie reels requiring an ancient projector, which had been buried under crates of stones. Pax and Holly heaved the lot out of the way without receiving an adequate explanation for their existence. Once they'd dragged the projector back to the bedroom and left Rimes to tinker with it, they turned their attention to a map of Ordshaw that Barton had found in a box near the beds.

Pax spread it across a too-small table that would have been best cleared with a broom. The map was crumpled, beige, and faded, and smelt vaguely of urine. It was marked with fifteen circles drawn with a big red marker pen, and seven crosses in blue. They were spread evenly across the city, with more blue in the east and red in the west. The prospect of travelling through Ordshaw hardly filled Pax with glee, but she was willing to consider it as an escape from the looming threats of probing Ministry agents, unsavoury experiments and Barton family tension.

"The crosses are contact points," Barton called out from the bedroom. "The circles are where we were sent for glo pickups. Mostly beyond Ripton and around Nothicker."

"First point being," Holly said, "this liquid turned up in the worst parts of town."

"There's one not far from you," Pax said, noting the circle in Dalford.

"Whistler Bridge," Barton called through, then continued like he knew the map by heart. "West of that you've got the Weirway Reservoir. Below that, a subway near the east side of Lyle Square, that's an active one. Then . . . central New Thornton, that was under a fire escape by the Portrait Gallery. One south of central in Tupsom. The one out west, the closest one to us here, that was by a laundromat in Ripton."

"Who knew you were so well-versed in the lay of Ordshaw," Holly said, to silence from her husband. Her malice hung in the air worse than the smell from Rimes' broken jar.

Studying the points on the map, Pax pictured the locations. A bridge, a reservoir. The large bricks of the gallery wall. They were all strangely familiar. It gave her the same uneasy feeling she'd got seeing that dark-skinned man's face in the news article; a dreamlike memory, or understanding, of something she'd never seen. Dreams worked that way, didn't they? Maybe Barton had mentioned these places to her before?

It didn't mean anything, not if she didn't want it to.

Pax stood back and her own smell wafted up at her. She flapped her t-shirt to clear it. Shifting boxes hadn't made her any cleaner. She ran a hand over her face and turned to the bedroom. She asked Rimes, "You got any spare clothes?"

"Oh yes," Rimes nodded happily. Then paused. "Not really for women, though."

Pax gave her a dumbfounded look, but Barton explained from the bed, "The spare stuff was meant for us, in case we needed to regroup here. Apothel, Rik, me."

"And did you?" Holly asked bitterly, joining Pax in the door. "Regroup here?"

"Not often," Barton said, quieter. "Grace, honey, check those boxes over there. Rik was slim, some of his stuff might fit you. Must be some shoes or something?"

"Perhaps," Rimes said, focused on trying to spool the movie reel.

"You didn't have digital back then?" Pax said. "Or video, at least?"

"Not as effective," Rimes explained. "The atmosphere played havoc with Rik's equipment, so the more basic the better."

"Rik, Rik," Holly said. "Who, pray tell, *is* Rik?"

"You don't know?" Rimes gave her a surprised look. "Rik Greivous?"

"The filmmaker?" Holly exclaimed. "Excuse me, no. My husband was friends with Rik Greivous? I'm sure he would've told me *that*." She glared at Barton, and for someone so big he managed a great feat of shrinking into the bed. "Ludicrous. You're telling me this boys' adventuring club included one of the great film auteurs of our time?"

"I'm sorry," Barton said.

"Who's Rik Greivous?" Grace asked.

Pax wasn't sure who Greivous was either, but recalled what Barton had told her before: "He disappeared?"

"Mysteriously!" Holly said. "He was a genius loner, famously avoided social contact, but *my husband* somehow got to be friends with him? Possibly the most interesting detail of your life and you kept it from me?"

Her voice was rising, so Pax tried to intervene: "I'd say the more interesting detail was getting drugged up to fight monsters."

"He kept that from me, too!"

"What choice did I have!" Barton answered loudly. It was only getting worse. "It wasn't a damned public meeting group, we needed to keep our work quiet!"

"Oh, your *work* now, is it. Your secret *career*!"

"Besides," Barton growled, with the sense that this next barb was going to be particularly fierce, "you met him."

Holly froze and Pax cringed. This same scene had been played out a thousand times in her youth. Sarcastic sniping leading to defensive shouts, to screams and the eventual slamming of doors. An occasional smashed plate. People who spent too much time together to know *that was the problem.*

Holly stared daggers at Barton until he explained.

"Grace's third birthday. You shook hands. He left a gift. You spent most of the day bitching with Fiona Antwerp that I hadn't trimmed the hedge."

She put a hand to her mouth. "That shady young man?"

"And I would've brought him round again, but he *disappeared*," Barton said, his voice wavering with upset. "He had his own projects, he left us for them. Then he was gone altogether. We were left guessing like everyone else."

Holly's mouth was open like she realised her husband wasn't too happy, either.

Rimes brightly ignored the tension to say, "His house burnt down, you know?"

"You think it was something to do with the Sunken City?" Pax asked.

"Oh no," Rimes said. "Rik had urges I don't think most people could understand. Artistic ones, I mean. He gave up on us before he went missing."

"Months before," Barton said. "Said he couldn't do it any more, there was something else up. The general theory is suicide, isn't it?"

"But they never found . . ." Holly started, clearly aware of this legend of Rik Greivous, but hesitating as she acknowledged it was personal, now.

The Sunken City had left Pax with her uneasy feeling; perhaps Rik hadn't been able to live with the memory of its horrors. She said, "Did he touch anything down there?"

"No," Barton said. "He observed. Recorded things, rather than get his hands dirty."

"What if the Ministry –"

"It was nothing to do with the Sunken City," Barton growled, the memory clearly a painful one. Wondering if it was worth coming back to later, Pax let it drop rather than risk angering him. He was sure, for whatever reason, that Rik had followed a different path.

"The videos were really starting to come along," Rimes said, and flipped a switch. The projector whirred, a flickering bulb lit up the wall and the image stuttered into grainy life. "Rik was trying to combine the cameras with glo when he left . . ."

She trailed off as the image focused. The camera barely picked out the shapes from the shadows. Pax and Holly shifted closer together and Grace scooted up next to Barton as the outline of a tunnel became apparent, highlighted by a couple of dancing torches.

"There's no audio," Rimes whispered, as the whir of the machine and the tick of the spinning reel had already made clear. "We attempted that separately."

There were two people in the image, big silhouettes in front of the bobbing lights. The image jumped unsteadily, picking out a wall, then the shape of the tunnel again, the two men moving ahead. One of them dropped back and turned towards the camera, his torch lighting his face. His rounded but sturdy physique was unmistakable. Younger Darren Barton smiled awkwardly, for the camera, then continued down the tunnel.

The man in front waved a hand above his head. The cameraman bobbed, hurrying to catch up. The image steadied again with three shapes ahead. Barton and the leader, surely Apothel, panning across a wider space. Beyond them was a third figure, a man bigger than them.

No, not a man.

It was humanoid, but there was something wrong with it. A bump, something extra. As the camera got closer and the focus shifted, Barton and Apothel moved to flank it, spreading their arms. The third figure moved and the bump stretched over its shoulder. An extra limb, rising like a scorpion's tail.

"What on earth," Holly uttered.

"A glogockle?" Pax recalled the pictures from Apothel's Miscellany.

It suddenly lumbered towards Apothel. As all three figures moved rapidly, the image became a mess of blurred shapes.

The camera spun suddenly, and everyone but Barton jumped at the hint of a tooth or claw flashing across. The image spiralled, then stopped, facing a wall lit by the camera's torch. A shadow danced across the wall then was gone. A moment later, it went black.

The doctor gave a light laugh. "They used to enjoy watching that one."

"What on earth," Holly said again.

"What *was* that?" Grace asked, fascinated.

"Glogockle," Barton confirmed. "And that's as good as the footage got."

Pax shook her head. What were these fools doing? Videoing fights with demons and chuckling over them while swigging beers? "Anything recording the Blue Angel's messages? Or at least the locations?"

"Nothing useful," Barton said. "But you might like the chapel. You got that one?"

Rimes nodded, already feeding another reel into the projector.

The image flickered into life again, opening on a wall that appeared to have been clawed by some ferocious animal. As the focus adjusted, the scratch marks became identifiable as writing and crude images, like the cryptic symbols from Apothel's book. A childish depiction of a minotaur and a savagely scratched lightning bolt. Other nonsensical shapes. The camera dwelt on them briefly before turning away, to Young Barton, sat on a barrel. He gave another sheepish smile, then chugged on a can of beer.

"Called it," Pax muttered to herself.

Behind Barton, the room stretched far back into deep corners. A circle of light obscured part of the image, a lantern on a distant table. Apothel moved by the other wall, something in his hands. He turned towards the camera and the lantern lit him from one side. He fit the descriptions Pax had heard well enough. Big, bearded, and friendly, even in this poor resolution. He waved, but the camera spun back to Barton.

Barton's mouth moved, responding to something Greivous was saying. From Barton's tight shoulders, the cameraman was teasing him.

"His idea of fun," Barton mumbled. "Bothered me more than Apothel."

"I can't even," Holly said, and Pax saw the concern in her face, watching her husband in this unfamiliar terrain. "This whole other *life* . . ."

"Where was this?" Pax asked.

"The Ripton Chapel," Barton said. "It was like a meeting hall. Apothel had a few places like that across Ordshaw. Squats. That was one of his favourites; he laid out a lot of ideas on those walls. Can't make them out here, can you?"

Pax squinted at it, as if that would help. "Is it still there?"

"I haven't been back in nine years. The only place I revisited was the loft in Hanton, where . . ." His eyes rested on Grace for a moment, as he thought better of saying it. Where Apothel was killed. "I checked other places, looking for Rufaizu, but half of them had been boarded up by the Ministry within a week. The chapel included."

In the video, Barton crushed his can in one fist before tossing it towards the camera. The image jolted as Greivous ducked, then it started shaking up and down. The cameraman was laughing.

Clueless fools. They'd blundered into something big enough to affect the whole city, and then sat around boozing and making home videos, while the doctor conducted brazenly unscientific experiments. No wonder the Blue Angel had taken advantage of them.

Pax said, "How'd it work, then? You waited for a signal from the Blue Angel?"

"No," Barton said. "We usually only went to those blue screens for glo. The Angel gave a street name, where we looked for a hiding spot. If we found it on our own, fine. If not, the Invisible Proclaimer came."

"The prancing horse playing an invisible trumpet?" Holly asked.

"The horse beat the drum," Barton corrected. "The trumpet –" He stopped as Holly intensified her glare. "Essentially, yeah."

"A horse and trumpet that appears and disappears out of thin air."

"So did the glo. The weird thing –"

"Not the horse with a drum or an invisible rider? That wasn't the weird thing?"

Barton's eyes hardened, but he didn't bite. "There were times that the glo appeared in spots we had already checked, even within minutes of returning to them."

"An invisible delivery man, too," Pax said.

"Something like that."

"Or a teleporter," Grace mused, a hand tucked thoughtfully under her chin.

The room went quiet, because there was no way to reject that suggestion without admitting there was no better one. Pax sensed they were missing something. She watched the projection as the camera twisted again, running over the writing on the wall. True enough, it was illegible in this low-lit, shaky recording. But Apothel had preserved ideas in that room, as he had in his book. What else was there?

"The Ripton Chapel isn't far from here," Barton said, watching Pax's face. "Relatively, at least. There was a blue screen near there, the laundromat one. I could try contacting the Blue Angel. It might not suspect me. At the least, it might give us more glo."

"Don't be ridiculous," Holly intervened. "You're not going anywhere, you're practically disabled. And you've all been preaching about this Ministry – they'll spot any one of us with facial recognition traffic cameras or something, won't they?"

"Actually," the doctor ventured, "I've – well, my understanding is that they have the technology. Certainly. But. Well. They can't monitor *everything*."

"What's that mean?" Barton frowned. "We know what they're capable of. Remember the Misty Cellar? A barman there heard noises behind the walls. Apothel found him when tracking a slather ghast and barely convinced him to share what he'd heard. The guy told *no one* else, he was scared he was going mad. The Ministry caught up to him all the same. Disappeared. No more Misty Cellar."

"Ah, yes." Rimes smiled at the curiously dark memory. "Though they may have been tracking the slather ghast, don't you think? Remember, they needed *me* because they don't have much staff. I have – I don't believe they can monitor everything."

"They certainly weren't out in force last night," Pax considered, recalling the two inept agents who had joined Casaria in his search for her.

"Well, that's just typical, isn't it?" Holly turned this on Barton. "You always just *assume*, don't you? We could be on a train to Manchester – we could be talking to –"

"No we bloody couldn't," Barton snapped. "Even if they can't watch the whole city, you think they won't have eyes on major transport links? They'll have the police looking out for us, at the least."

"Maybe . . ." Rimes started, but stopped.

"Just say it, Mandy," Barton grumbled.

"They may be distracted. With the news this morning. You – you heard them, visiting, yes? They were more interested in the *prael* – the minotaur – than you. Now, I have my scooter – the scarf would hide your face."

"Look at him!" Holly cried. "He's not going on a bloody scooter!"

That silenced the doctor, but Pax's mind was ticking. This cramped room was only going to get tenser, and she needed answers. She needed a sign that the answers were out there, at least. And if there was no way to get to Rufaizu, yet, then maybe she could bridge the gap between them with what his dead father knew. She sensed she might regret this, but what the hell, it hardly seemed safe here. "There might be a blue screen at that laundromat. And Apothel's place, if it's still there, might be unguarded. That's good enough for me. I'll go."

8

After Rolarn didn't answer her shouts, Letty started rummaging through his stash, searching for ammunition and food. His hiding place, in a human security safe, was a nice two-tier setup, with a lounge and living area on the shelf and stacks of weapons, supplies and treasures on the bottom. The safe sat behind the counter of an absurdly large human shop, long since closed down and abandoned, itself covering three empty floors; a vast open space that Letty had cautiously flown through, expecting all manner of traps. A couple of electric lanterns flooded the safe in yellow light, wastefully left on while Rolarn was out, but there was no other sign of life. If he was off raiding, it might be hours before he got back, days even.

Letty wasn't sure if she should be annoyed or not at Rolarn's absence. She had little interest in connecting with a Fae activist; they tended to believe the war for control of the FTC had never ended, and that glory there – the overthrow of Valoria – would revive the fight with the humans. As they couldn't get near the FTC, it typically resulted in violent infighting; Rolarn had forcibly taken this hideout in Broadplain from a gang called Vagnam's Reds on the justification that it was of historical significance and belonged in the hands of a patriot. Really it was just bigger than the shoebox he'd been living out of. But it was an insanely big space for a single angry Fae.

Letty had half-filled a bag with dried meat and bullets, and was moving towards the Fae dust, to give her fuel for the journey back to Pax, when a knock made her spin towards the open safe door. Her pistol was drawn, cocked at her hip, but the man had a shotgun on her, two fist-sized barrels, big enough that he held it in both hands. He was rotund, with a round, red-cheeked face and a comb-over of thin, straight hair that barely concealed his baldness. With his grease-stained beige suit and ruddy face, he looked like a failing shop manager who didn't understand smiles.

"You've put on weight, Rolarn," Letty said.

Ignoring the comment, he said, "This goes off, it takes the room with it."

"So lower it," Letty said. "I come in peace."

"Doesn't look like it." Rolarn's stare was unsettlingly steady, his beady eyes dark.

"You heard what I've been through this weekend? I figured you'd sympathise."

"I heard," Rolarn said levelly. "And I got warned you might come here. Seemed unlikely, since I also heard you got eaten by a human."

"*Clearly*, no damn human ate me." She straightened up. "Not that they didn't try."

"I'm glad," he said, flatly. He nodded to her pistol and she nodded back. Together, they slowly lowered their guns. "There's been all sorts of talk over you and your crew."

"That so?" Letty said. "Does that talk involve how the Ministry of Fucking Energy stole the Dispenser?"

"No. The *talk* is that the Ministry took something inconsequential, which you and your boys were trying to flog."

"Sack of fucking lies. I recovered it – a marvel of Fae engineering, our best hope of taking back the Sunken City. Apparently Governor Val doesn't *want* to take it back, though, sitting pretty as she is. I figured that'd be something you understood."

Rolarn kept staring with his dead eyes. "You lost a wing. How did that happen?"

Letty scoffed, holstering her gun and turning back to his lair. The Fae dust was out in the open, a waist-high sack leaning against a stack of human coins. "I lost my wing trying to get help with the weapon. Trying to take back the place that's rightfully ours." Letty picked up a bag and started filling it without asking. It was only polite to share with a Fae in need. Rolarn didn't react. Letty tied off the bag and shoved the takings into her backpack, then said, "My own boys came gunning for me last night. Val wants me dead. She wants the Dispenser buried."

"Val the Peacemaker?" Rolarn replied, with the clearest hint of sarcasm his dull tone allowed. "Promiser of everything the Fae can dream of?"

"As long as everything is contained in the fake city she's built," Letty snarled. "Turns out she wants to preserve the FTC forever."

"So your eyes are finally open."

Letty curled her nose at him. Activists like Rolarn had a range of personal reasons to hate Val, but most of them stemmed from resentment that she was in charge and they, or their bloody-minded mates, weren't. Still, she and Rolarn had common ground now. "How about you pass me a phone while you explain where we stand, then."

Rolarn hesitated, then gave a slight nod. He ambled to one side and rifled through a pile of small electronics, saying, "All this talk, it suggests you were working with the humans." He held up a phone but kept it back. "Did you give them our tech yourself?"

"Sound like something I'd do?" Letty said, struggling to keep her voice calm. "I spent nine years looking for that fucking weapon." She snatched the phone. Rolarn let her.

"You're not co-operating with the Ministry," he said, "but not eaten, either. My guess would be you're friendly with someone useful, but lost our technology on account of incompetence."

"Try backstabbing and betrayal," Letty snapped.

"With the rumours circulating," Rolarn continued, "I've seen a few old faces floating around Ordshaw. Unexpected ones. I've got a truce with the Tupsom Trawlers right now."

"Arnold's lot?" Letty frowned at the name. The Trawlers were a low-rank street gang from the south of the city, the sort of thugs who slashed human tyres in the name of Fae supremacy. Gutter trash lacking Rolarn's more idealistic politics.

"A mutual benefactor brought us together," Rolarn said. "Someone come back from abroad. As it happens, it's someone who didn't believe all this talk out of the FTC, either. Someone interested in meeting you."

"Fucking say the name already."

"No," Rolarn said. "Not without a meeting."

Letty held back, sensing the gravity of his caginess. When you didn't want to throw a Fae's name around, it had to mean a very high price on their head. Valoria's team of exile hunters, the Stabilisers, were expert at picking up on such names. So Rolarn had the ear of someone dangerous, who had both the funding and the charm to bring together the likes of Rolarn and the Trawlers. Maybe exactly what they needed, maybe the exact opposite. Letty said, "And what's this someone gonna want from *me*?"

"That depends on your connection," Rolarn said, "to the human."

Letty hesitated, instinctively keen to keep Pax away from such a Fae. "This mythical human I'm friendly with? Responsible for losing our tech?"

His face didn't shift, stoic as a statue.

"This feels like bullshit," Letty said, shouldering her backpack over her artificial wing. Now she had two constricting straps on her chest. Great.

Rolarn stepped out of her way, wordlessly inviting her to leave if she didn't like it.

"That's it, you're letting me walk?"

"You're the one that came here," Rolarn said. Way too fucking sure of himself.

"Say there was a human," Letty said. "Say she helped me out. She'd be just about the only person who has. I wouldn't be inclined to get her in trouble, would I?"

It wasn't something a Fae should admit to, in front of a Fae patriot, if she wanted to stay alive. Yet he said, "No."

"She's good people," Letty reaffirmed. "The sort we need."

"Then we're on the same page," Rolarn replied dryly. "You captured the FTC's attention. Everyone's remembering how dangerous the humans are, imagining how monstrous it was what happened to you. Presents an opportunity."

Letty could see where it would take them well enough. Use Pax as some kind of totem, get the Fae's blood up. A great excuse to attack Val and her council. She said, "I'm not here to bring down the FTC. The Dispenser is the opportunity. We use it to take back the Sunken City, Val and her refugees can spin on it."

"Sure," Rolarn said. "But one thing doesn't exclude another. And you need protection." He paused, reaching a particularly complex conclusion. "Bring the human here, and I'll bring my chief. We'll figure something out."

"Tell me who your chief is and I'll think about it."

"That's not my offer," he said.

Letty had an urge to smash in his unemotive eyes, make her own offer. Only he was right, even if her instincts warned her off. She'd come for help, and this place was big enough to hide the humans. "I don't want to incite chaos. If that's your idea, or your chief's, you can fuck off right now. Understood?"

Rolarn was frozen, like someone forgot to pay his meter.

"Say something, you walking roulade."

"Bring the girl, talk with my chief."

"Give me your number," Letty conceded, but repeated, "I'll think about it."

9

Sam found Casaria's building porter housed near the bottom of a stairwell, in an office barely big enough to fit his chair and a mop and bucket. It was a stark contrast to the hallways she'd navigated to find Casaria's apartment, with their waxed floors and leather-bound entrance doors, but it suited the building. The obnoxiously tall half-glass tower lorded its wealth in contrast to its surroundings, all looks over practicality. The soulless interior made Sam happy she'd never visited when Casaria invited her. She could still see his face, the smile when he tried to hide his disappointment at her rejections, and she disliked being there now.

One of the few comments Landon had made on the way was to double-check that she was sure she wanted to see Casaria. Of course, *she* didn't bear the man any ill will. It wasn't personal when she reported him. Realistically, it could have helped his career if it set him straight. Though she couldn't deny the slight relief that he hadn't answered his door while she was alone. She hoped Landon would find a parking space and catch up to her before she caught up to Casaria.

After a quick knock on the porter's door, she said, "Apartment 1302. I need to get in there."

"Excuse me?" The porter looked up from a moisture-warped book. A smutty romance, by the cover. He had a face like a sick horse and an overlong neck, sticking out of a doorman's suit two sizes too large.

"I need to get into Cano Casaria's apartment. Do you know him?" The man stared, so Sam prompted, "Handsome, wears a suit, looks Latino but he's not."

"That's about half the people that live here."

"Only comes out at night."

"Ah." The man gave a one-sided smile. "Hunts undesirables for the government?"

"He told you that?" Though they were strictly forbidden to mention the Sunken City to civilians, and trust was the foremost reason that the MEE didn't hire more people, there weren't specific rules about what agents *should* tell people. Mostly because it was bloody obvious they shouldn't allude to the truth. This was hardly a surprise, though: for his faults, Casaria trumped most of the MEE with his enthusiasm. Sam had never had to wait for him to find a parking space, and it was pride in his work, after all, that had led to him engaging her after only a single drink. Which had led to a welcome career shift from Lyndale Finance, even if it had come with a misguided mentor.

If only he could iron out the niggles, such as looking for trouble, Casaria could be a very effective agent. That was what her report had meant to highlight. But there'd been no anger management classes or more conscientious partner pairing, only Casaria going back on patrol after a short reprimand. In the rare moments between night and day when their paths crossed in the office, his previously awkward small talk was replaced with silently malicious glares. She had, for some time, hoped to better explain how he might channel his potential. But that would've meant talking to him.

"Fun guy," the porter said. "We got to talking when I made a comment about his clothes, dressed like he's going for a business meeting in the dead of night. He said I didn't know what he did for this country."

"Okay. Did you see him come in this morning?"

"Nah, but he often slips in while I'm doing the dawn rounds."

"Can you open up his apartment for me?"

The porter rolled his mouth around uncomfortably, like he knew he should kick up a fuss. But he also knew Casaria and understood some things weren't worth questioning. "I assume you've got some kind of credentials?"

"You can assume that, yes."

"Always the ones that look tightest, isn't it?" the porter commented, as he stood behind Sam in Casaria's doorway. How the man would think Casaria, never seen without a hair out of place, was secretly filthy, was beyond her. This was clearly a crime scene.

There were clothes all over the studio apartment, pots and pans out in the kitchen, paperwork scattered across the floor. The place had been searched, thoroughly and methodically, from the neatness of the papers. It was too tidy for a robbery; someone had been looking for something. Sam checked the documents. Utility bills, bank statements. Not much in his account, which was unsurprising considering the rent here.

Had the Fae come and taken him, wanting their weapon back? If it really was their technology, their *Dispenser*, even, then it'd be hugely important to them. But if they were aware the Ministry had the Dispenser, they surely would have realised it was impounded in Greek Street. If they wanted to strong-arm Casaria into recovering it, why the search? And shouldn't Casaria have had a Fae detector in the flat?

"Sorry it took so long." A huffing voice made Sam turn. "It's a –" Landon stopped, breathless, in the doorway. The agent's expression supported her conclusion, but he said it anyway. "They came for him?"

"What?" The porter started. "You mean –"

"Where do we start?" Sam asked Landon. She wasn't going to pretend she knew how to handle a crime scene. Landon hesitated, not trusting himself with the responsibility either, so she raised her eyebrows for him to get started.

He turned to the porter, saying, "You've got security cameras here?"

"You mean –"

"Go down to your office, retrieve whatever footage you have from last night. No one's to come up until we say so, understood?"

"Should I call the police?"

"We'll take care of it," Landon said. "Go." The porter nodded and scampered away. Landon turned back to Sam. "This is exactly what Casaria said was gonna happen. Should've known. The Fae are out of control."

"We don't *know* it's the Fae," Sam said.

Landon frowned. "Who else?"

"I guess we find that out?"

They walked in together.

"Everything's been moved," Landon said. He pointed a thick finger at the carpet, indentations near the faux leather sofa's legs. He nodded to a hanging picture, where a sliver of discoloured wall was visible along its edge. Landon voiced the question that was forming in Sam's mind. "Why would they check there? Only a few places their weapon could've been."

"What else would they be looking for?" Sam asked.

"From the looks of it . . . whatever they could get."

"Uh-huh."

In the elevator down, Sam processed their initial inspection, leaving Landon to continue searching. If this was the work of the Fae, she could definitely involve IS now – but Casaria *did* have Fae defences, and they were still active. And logically, any information the Fae could get off an agent like Casaria would be trivial. Her gut said it wasn't them, even if that meant she'd be taken off this case. But who else? It couldn't be a random burglary: nothing appeared to have been taken. As Landon had pointed out. He had also answered her unspoken concern, which must have shown on her face, that the Ministry themselves would never leave a scene like this. Their incompetence lay in the bureaucratic realm; leaving such a mess after disposing of a liable agent was unthinkable.

Sam found the porter reading again, as though nothing had happened. He looked up curiously. "Find anything?"

"The security footage?" she said.

"Oh, that." He took his feet down off the mop bucket. "Yeah. It's a no."

Sam paused. "It's a what?"

"No. There's no footage."

"What's that mean?"

"It's blank," the porter said. "Didn't record."

Sam almost laughed. "You're serious?"

"As a beef dinner," the porter said. "I'll show you if you like? It's just a blank file."

"How?" Sam could scarcely form a sentence, stunned.

"Happens sometimes. It's all digital, automatically loops to a new recording. Every now and again it glitches and does the wipe but doesn't restart. You have to hit record manually. We check it at least once a week. Guess Larry missed it yesterday."

"Once a week?"

The porter's crooked face suggested he'd seen how hard she was taking this. "It's not as useful as you think, you know. When there's like, six, twelve hours of footage to look through, most people say forget about it."

Sam swallowed her agitation. There were a hundred responses she might say, chief amongst them being *are you a complete imbecile* and *does doing a job* ever *actually matter?* Instead, she said, "Have you got anything else that might help? It's a new building, do you track who comes in the door? Anything like that?"

The porter's pitying expression said no.

"Anything at all?"

"Oh. There was something, don't know if it'd be connected. Few hours ago I had to scrub up something outside the main doors. Might've been blood?"

Sam smiled into her disbelief. If Casaria were here, he'd assault this man. But that was the difference between him and her, wasn't it? She dealt with her emotions calmly. Through the gritted teeth of her uneasy grin, she asked, "How *much* blood?"

10

"Alright four-eyes," Letty said into the phone, "put Pax on."

"Um."

"*Today.*"

"It's – it's for you," Dr Rimes stuttered. Letty waited for them to swap the receiver as she buzzed over a neighbourhood of square terraces, various shades of red and grey.

"Hi?" Pax said, cautiously.

"I'm done. What's the plan?"

Pax paused, probably needing a moment to remember that Fae could use phones. She asked, "What do you mean *you're done*?"

"I met with Rolarn. He's got a place big enough for all of you, better than that Ministry haven you're in now. But I get the impression things have been moving quickly in Fae circles. He's in league with someone, and that's not normal. He wouldn't tell me who, which is extra bad. So tell me you've got a better plan than relying on my people."

Pax paused to digest that little nugget of essentially bad news. "Well. There's somewhere Apothel used to go with the others, seems he clawed shit in the walls, the same way he did with the book. You know it?"

That brought back memories. Letty said, "Half his crazy hideouts got locked down by the Ministry. I spent months, years, searching the crap he left behind for clues to where he dumped the Dispenser. What makes you think there's anything left now?"

"This one was in Ripton," Pax replied, like that mattered.

Letty slowed down. "His chapel. One of his favourites. I went there once. Got a good enough look to know he didn't leave anything behind. The place was empty, even the cellar. We watched the MEE board it up; all they took out was junk furniture. You want to get yourself on the Ministry's radar for what, to feel his aura?"

"The writing on the walls, maybe he left something."

"What writing? The guy was nuts. He left nothing remotely legible."

There was movement around Pax, in the background, suggesting they were already underway on this dumb plan. She said, "I'd still like to give it a go. Barton said he contacted the Blue Angel nearby, too."

Letty tutted. Stubborn as a damn squirrel. "And you reckon you can do the same?"

"I'm going there to find out," Pax said.

*

Pax cut the engine to Rimes' scooter and allowed herself a few moments of deep, relieved breathing, squeezing the handles to keep herself from trembling. Driving was as terrifying as she remembered, especially on this exposed little vehicle. The one saving grace of the bike was how small it was, so she didn't have to guess how close she was to hitting obstacles. She could feel it. She'd flinched every time she passed a vehicle, even the parked ones, and a blaring car horn had almost knocked her off.

Pax took off her vintage disguise of a leather helmet and rust-framed goggles. They matched the scooter's cracked leather seat and duct-taped mirrors perfectly.

"Didn't realise you were coming in fancy dress," Letty said, as the fairy appeared between Pax's hands. "The Ministry have a blind spot for 1920s aeronauts?"

Pax smiled, her tension defusing at the sight of her tiny companion.

"Thing like this?" Letty stomped on the bike. "Gun it hard enough, it could make you cum."

"Is that how you get off?" Pax gave the fairy a questioning look.

"It's the doctor's, right? Would explain a bit, wouldn't it?"

Pax smirked but left it at that, not wanting to insult Rimes when the doctor had taken them in and given her the scooter and a surprisingly modern smartphone for use as a satnav. Rimes hadn't even pressed for information about Pax's *friend,* who no one was pretending wasn't a fairy.

Pax took the phone from the frail mount in the middle of the handlebar, making Letty skip out of the way. The building she'd arrived at was a square launderette with a yellow-on-blue sign: *Suds Fun!* It sat between a convenience store and a closed flower shop, the rest of the street a line of brick townhouses with white-framed windows. The area was small-scale and grimly unimaginative, with no trees or bushes, just the occasional weed poking through a pavement crack. Typical Ripton.

"The blue screen," Pax said, "should be around the corner."

She stood, opened the seat of the bike and squeezed the helmet and goggles in, then paused. Now the tension of the bike ride had passed, she realised her fingers were tingling and her heart felt oddly warm. Somehow bigger, notably present in her chest. She had the same feeling she'd got looking at the points on the map or the face in that news article about the burst gas main. The feeling she associated with that bizarre dream. What if the minotaur had permanently damaged her somehow? Messed up her whole central nervous system? As the sensation faded, she looked up and saw a couple of women walking towards them, one pushing a pram.

Pax quietly told Letty, "You might want to lay low."

"Bollocks," Letty said. "No one's gonna notice me unless you draw attention."

"I see you well enough."

"Because you're *you.* Keep quiet, let them pass."

The woman approached, chatting loudly: "Don't advertise it that way, that's all I'm saying. Wherever I got it, the coupon's valid, ain't it? You gotta honour it."

They eyed Pax as they passed, but kept talking. "By rights, it was my bloody burger, wasn't it?"

"By rights. No doubt."

As they moved on, Pax's eyes ran to Letty. They hadn't noticed her at all, stood right there on the bike. Even if they'd thought she was a toy, wasn't that curious?

"Okay," Pax whispered. "What the fuck?"

"They're talking about McDonald's," Letty said.

"Huh?"

"Cheated out of a 20p burger saving or whatever. Dumb fucking humans."

"How does it work?" Pax asked.

"The bitching or the neediness?"

"Them *not seeing you.*"

"Dust." Letty shrugged, like it was nothing. The fairies' mysterious drug of choice.

Pax said, "I see you perfectly. I saw your men when they came to attack us – Holly and Grace saw them too."

"Dust gives you energy," Letty said, and lifted off towards Pax's shoulder with her auxiliary wing whirring. "You can use it to power a fake wing or go wild in a fight. Same energy creates a haze like heat-shimmers, making mirages."

"But *I see you perfectly*!" Pax protested. "They went right past."

"Something their brain can't comprehend, they don't see it. Know what I mean?"

Denial was something Pax understood well, but it still didn't make sense. How did taking a drug affect *other* people? As if she didn't have enough questions already.

"Come on," Letty said, "what are we doing here?"

Pax pointed and started walking to the side of the laundromat. "If there's a blue screen here, I grill it, we go home with questions answered." There was the wall Barton had described, a five-foot structure enclosing the three shops' commercial bins. Pax checked the empty road, then used the scooter's ancient key to scratch the brickwork: *You here?*

She backed off and watched the wall carefully, studying the greying bricks.

With nothing happening, she looked at Letty.

The Fae wasn't just a tiny person, she was conspicuous in her grungy style, too. Frayed vest and shorts, messily coloured hair, a chunky holstered pistol; even the bulky, metallic strap of her artificial wing crossed her chest like a punk fashion accessory. Maybe her extreme appearance made her harder to believe. Pax said, "I knew a guy, Georgie Weyland, doorman in the West End. One game, he went to take a big pot after I showed a winning flush. I laughed, before I saw he was serious. Big George was glaring at me like I was mad. I said, 'Look at the cards. Take another look at the cards.' I kept saying it, over and over, before he got it. Then he went quiet as a mouse, finally seeing the hearts. Left the game shortly after, barely showed his face around me again."

"Sounds about right," Letty said.

The bricks weren't changing. No blue anywhere. Pax's scratched words stood out plainly, permanently. She said, "What'd happen if a human took your dust?"

"Want to try?"

"Would I be the first?"

"Maybe." Letty hovered up, scanning the wall closer. "There's nothing here, Pax. Or it doesn't want to be seen. Big surprise."

She was right, but Pax kept waiting. "What's the connection between dust and glo? Dr Rimes said their drink has an energy they couldn't explain, too."

"No connection I know of," Letty said. "Ours has a number of highly beneficial properties, *theirs* is basically psychedelic booze."

"Where's dust come from?"

"State-controlled production. Val's people have run it since long before she took charge. Her people own these big vats on the edge of town. Sealed off in ugly square buildings. You can hear the machines through the night from two blocks away."

"Humans don't hear that?"

"FTC blocks, idiot. All within the confines of the FTC. To you, I guess it'd seem *small*." Letty made it sound like an insult.

"And these vats and machines do what, exactly?"

Letty scoffed. "Something hidden. Ancient family recipes and state secrets and that shit."

Pax scratched a nail over the marks on the brick, picking out the reddish-grey dust. "So. A mystery substance that messes with people's heads."

"Don't fucking go there," Letty warned. "The secrecy in dust is deliberate. Mystery adds class. Exclusivity. That's all."

"It stops people asking questions. You're honestly telling me that's all the public knows? Vats and state workers doing *what*?"

Letty grunted. "Well, there's the stories you're told as a kid. Starts with peepy-tales about ground-up animal bones, or beans gifted down by giants, that kind of shit."

"Peepy-tales?"

"Peepy-tales, yeah," Letty said. "You know, the peeps, fantastic stories about magic and heroes and giants and nonsense like that. Tansel and Gretel, the House of the Human, all that."

Pax tripped on the interplay of the familiar and random. "And when you get over the . . . peepy-tales?"

"You realise the stories hide the boring truth about them fermenting some kind of fungus. It first came over from a Fae colony in France or something. Up in the Alps. Our people don't travel much, so who'd check?"

"A mystery fungus, then. Even if it's not the same as glo, you don't see a parallel?"

"I see you trying to shit on a world you know nothing about. Dust has been a part of Fae society forever. Your monsters and conspiracies have only plagued Ordshaw for fifty, a hundred years max? Spin on it."

Pax went quiet, seeing that she was only making Letty defensive. She'd put it out there, anyway. The fairy could stew on the idea.

Letty pointed at the wall and angrily said, "How long you gonna stare at this?"

"Barton said it'd be practically instant," Pax sighed. "Or nothing."

"Could've told you it'd be a bust," Letty snorted. "And don't expect anything better from the chapel. This way." She flew ahead, and Pax followed, with one last glance to the wall. It'd been a long shot, but there was definitely nothing there now.

They continued down the side street, around a turning and past another row of near-identical houses. Letty floated closer to Pax, saying, "Apothel suggested it once, trying dust. He stabbed me in the back before he got round to it. Don't know of any other human that's thought it'd be a good idea. You've got a lot in common, you and that lummox."

"That makes my day," Pax said.

"When we're done with all this, we could give it a go."

Letty drifted ahead to a squat single-storey building with a peaked roof. The windows were boarded up and the entrance hidden behind a chunky steel panel and door. A wooden sign hung over the entrance, most of the letter's gone: *St. J . . . n's . . . ion . . . F. . t.*

Pax suggested, "*St Julian's Zion Fart?*"

Letty snorted a little laugh. "Pretty sure whatever this was wasn't religious. Else someone would've cared about it."

The steel seal bolted over the entrance was smooth despite its evident age, with wires of weeds rising up one side and rooted into the brickwork above. Pax pushed the metal door. It didn't even move on its hinges. When they sealed the place, the Ministry had made sure no one could squat there again. She patted her coat pockets, looking for her lock picks. All gone? "How do we get in?"

"Easiest way?" Letty flew higher, up past the sign. "There's a hole in the roof."

"You gonna carry me up there? Tell me you have ant-like super-strength."

"Comparing me to a fucking ant, now, you want your jaw broken?"

"It's a *positive* comparison. You prefer a rhino beetle?"

"I'd prefer you shove it," Letty drifted back down. "I'm *Fae*, not an insect. And even my one shitty wing *could* lift a lot more than you'd think. Just not your fat arse. There's a bin out back. Can you climb? You people are like monkeys, right?"

Pax rolled her eyes at the attempted retort. As she followed Letty down to where an alley cut between two townhouses, though, she wasn't sure she actually could climb. When was the last time? She'd broken the low branches of a tree in her childhood garden, once. Climbed on top of a wall when she was drunk at university?

She found herself at the end of the alley, before a walled gate.

"Boost yourself over here," Letty said.

"Wait." Pax looked back down the alley, "this is someone's home."

"And? Coming here was *your* idea."

Pax gave her a wary look, then pulled her hood up. Great. Add suspicion of burglary to whatever else the MEE might pin on her. She dug the tip of a boot into the brickwork, got a foot onto the gate handle and hoisted herself. She just about had the strength to pull herself up, but her chest landed heavily on top of the narrow wall. Flopping like a beached whale, she looked into the overgrown dirt patch to one side. Half a dozen rusty gardening tools were piled against the far wall.

"You stuck?" Letty asked, buzzing near her ear. Barely keeping the laughter from her voice. Pax flapped a hand her way but realised the effort had left her breathless.

"I've got some good news," Letty said. "You won't need the bin."

Pax pivoted on the wall gracelessly. Unfit. Not recovered from the Sunken City. Shouldn't be climbing walls. She followed the fairy's gesture. In the other direction, a narrow ledge ran behind the next house, to where the roof of Apothel's chapel banked down to only a few feet higher. With a little more scrambling she'd be able to get up there. In the middle of the slanted roof was a hole, just as Letty had promised. Boarded up like the windows out front.

"You know how high that is?" Pax said, rising unsteadily. "If I can even get in, how am I supposed to drop down? How am I supposed to get back *out*?"

"All your thinking is exhausting," Letty said. "No wonder you're puffing over a little wall."

"I'm not enjoying this," Pax said. "Not one bit."

11

"Proximity alert," Landon said, studying one of his various electronic devices. Phone clamped to her ear, Sam frowned at him to be quiet. He ignored her. "A site in Ripton. Motion sensors say there's been disturbances at the door and the roof. AGe, number 218. I should go."

"What's he saying?" Mathers asked, on the other end of the phone line.

"Nothing, sir," Sam replied, trying to keep his focus. So far, Mathers had shown little interest in her account of Casaria's disappearance. "Should we wait for a forensics team? There were signs of a struggle."

"Outside the building? On a street used by hundreds every day?"

"His apartment's been searched – I think –"

"He might have been bleeding, you know?"

Sam paused. "Isn't that the point, sir?"

"His *existing* injuries might have come unstuck. There are perfectly logical explanations we might look to before diverting attention from the very real problem of managing this morning's crisis, Ward."

"What logically explains Casaria tossing through everything he owned and disappearing?" Sam said, before she could filter that one. She cringed into her boss's unimpressed breathing, as Landon gave her a surprised look.

"Alright," Mathers said, and Sam closed her eyes with relief. "When Dr Hertz is done in New Thornton, perhaps he can swing by with the police." *Perhaps* was no good. Dr Hertz might be no good either; the Ministry's catch-all member of medical staff could analyse Sunken City samples and treat wounds, but she doubted his talents stretched to forensic science. "Time you came back. I believe your team have drafted some correspondence for you to check over."

"But sir," Sam started, without knowing what to say. Going back would mean getting bogged down in paperwork. Sidelined. To say nothing of the fact that Casaria was *actually missing*. As Mathers waited, Sam clicked her fingers at Landon. "There's something we need to follow up." She mouthed at the agent: *Where is it?* "Agent Landon has an alert."

"Yes?" Mathers replied warily.

Landon gave Sam an uncertain look. He said, "AGe. Site 218."

The designation for a civilian location, above ground. Most likely a cat rubbing up against a shop the Ministry had closed. Sam told Mathers, "It's a site breach near here, while we're in the field. An AGe alert. Operations are all occupied, aren't they?"

Mathers' slow breathing betrayed that once again he felt agitated about Sam making her own plans. "Landon can go alone, you can walk in."

"Sir, he just lost his partner . . ." Sam said, trying to sound caring.

Another pause. Mathers conceded, dryly. "Be back within the hour." He hung up before she could respond, and Sam found Landon staring at her, unconvinced.

"Proximity alerts are serious," he said. "We are going there."

Sam expected as much. At least it'd give her a chance to think. She might even work on this drone, get him to open up. She asked, "So where's the car?"

It took a lot of shoving and ungainly levering, but the ragged planks over the hole in the roof finally snapped and fell into Apothel's Chapel. Pax scooted back from the hole and the tiles creaked dangerously underneath her. Sliding onto her belly, spreading out her weight, Pax peered over the lip. It was dark inside, bar the empty pillar of daylight she'd created. The floor was maybe fifteen feet down, with nothing near the hole to climb onto.

Letty stood on the far side of the hole, hands on her hips. "Rather you than me."

"I can't get down there," Pax said.

"Don't be hard on yourself, you'll fit."

Pax narrowed her eyes. "*I* don't have wings."

"A little drop like that? Come on. They're gonna know someone's here, we don't have all day."

Pax dipped her head over the edge. A fog of dust partly concealed the open space, but as it turned and settled she saw there was nothing to conceal. Her eyes adjusted to the low light and she saw the shadowed corners; the hall was completely empty. Except . . . no, there was a radiator against one wall.

"You said there's a cellar?" Pax asked.

"At the back. A side-room and a little kitchen unit, too, all empty. You think the Ministry were gonna leave stuff behind for any muppet to find?"

"I can't see the walls. Are his markings still there, at least?"

"Here." Letty rifled through her backpack. She pulled out a tiny cylinder and twisted it. It flared at one end like a Roman candle. Letty tossed it through the hole and it fell slowly down, burning brighter as it went. The flickering light revealed the far walls in white flashes. A network of scratches ran over the surfaces as if a ferocious beast had been caged there, clawing to get out. The marks were random, nothing like the coded symbols of Apothel's book. They ran in deranged lines to impossible heights, scratched deep from the skirting up to the ceiling.

"Jesus Christ," Pax said, imagining Apothel hacking at this mad mess while perched on a ladder. She leant further in as the roof flexed under her. Everywhere she looked was the same. "This isn't like the video."

"Guess he revised his notes," Letty said. "To reflect his idiotic state of mind at the end. Seems representative of what was going on in his head."

"You came here after he died, you knew it was like this?" Pax asked.

Letty shrugged. "Yeah. I *said* it was all scratched out."

Pax let out a deep breath. Was it her fault for not listening properly, or the fairy's for failing to communicate it? She'd assumed Letty couldn't interpret it, not that the writing was gone. "There must be something . . ."

"Sure, insist hard enough, that'll make it real."

Pax ducked down again. There *had* to be something. She was tingling again. The heat in her chest was tickling her ribs, and something told her this was the right place. Had it been in the dream? The claw marks on the walls? There was something in this she couldn't rationally explain, but she didn't need to. The same way you knew when you'd sussed your opponent's cards. You had to trust your instincts. She slid around the hole as the flare dimmed. In the final splutters of light, she saw letters.

A single word. Spread sideways, near a rear door.

The light went out.

"There's something there," Pax said. "You got another flare?"

"Not worth it."

"You need to go down there, check it out."

"*You* go down there."

Pax glared at the fairy, but Letty had her arms folded, resolute. "By the far door, there's something written. Anything that survived this vandalism has *got* to be useful."

"If there's anything to be done, which there isn't, it's on you."

"Why'd you even come?" Pax said, struggling to keep cool.

"To keep an eye on you. The Ministry has defences specifically designed to screw with the Fae. Remember how we *met*? Fuck off, me going in there."

Pax hesitated. She remembered well enough, finding the tiny woman unconscious on the floor. Knocked out by a Ministry trap that released a Fae-paralysing gas. "I'll keep a hold of you, how's that?"

"How's that?" Letty echoed with alarm.

"You can get closer, and I can pull you out if anything happens, Ministry defences or whatever you're scared of."

"Are you fucking –"

Before Pax could overthink it, she closed a hand on the fairy. Letty started roaring curses as Pax quickly shifted forwards and hung her hand into the room. "I'm sorry – I'm sorry – but just have a look – see if there's any other way down and I'll go!"

Letty swore at the top of her voice, twisting in Pax's grip. Definitely couldn't let go of her now, she'd be liable to murder.

"You're in already, no use –" Pax said.

"I'm gonna tear you apart!" Letty snarled.

"After you've had a look!" Pax insisted.

Letty thrashed a moment longer but started to calm.

"There's nothing, is there? No Fae defences? You're alright?"

"I'm gonna gut you."

"*After* you have a look."

Letty snarled, but Pax felt her relaxing slightly in her grip. The fairy twisted around. "I can't see shit, not any better than you. Gonna get yourself killed over nothing."

"Should I let go?"

"Yes you should fucking let go."

Pax released Letty. The fairy shot out of her grip, and Pax winced, fearing a reprisal. Letty hung in the air below the hole, glaring up like she was about to explode. Pax waited, holding her gaze with what she hoped was blameless innocence. The fairy huffed and gave the hall another look. She pointed a finger back up. "You're gonna regret this." But she dropped into the dark.

Pax crouched to watch Letty fly. "Further that way."

A tiny light came out ahead of Letty, some kind of torch. From a phone? It lit up an impressive circle of wall, a few feet wide. Letty hovered up and down, searching.

"Probably seeing things, weren't you?" Letty said.

She kept moving and the letters came into view. A single word, as Pax had thought. Angular Latin script, not Apothel's coded symbols. A name? Letty hovered in front of it and said, "What the fuck's that supposed to mean?"

"You don't recognise it?" Pax called out. She squinted to read it herself, but the shadows were deep and long. *Gruswlock?*

"Fuck this," Letty snapped. Her light went out, pocketed, and she sped back up to the hole. As she cleared it, she drew her pistol.

Pax held up her hands and affected her most disarming smile. Seldom before had she seen such fury as in that tiny face, though, and Pax accepted it had been another terrible idea. Letty swept in close, tensing like she wasn't sure herself what to do. As Pax backed off, the fairy pulled up level with her eye, drew the pistol back and cracked it into Pax's brow. Pax winced to the side as the blow lanced like a paper cut.

"Shit!" Pax put a hand it. "You little shit!"

"Don't!" Letty snarled, gun aimed at her eye. "Don't test me, fucker."

"Alright!" Pax raised her hands again. "Okay. I deserved that."

Letty hissed. "You're lucky you've still got a hand, grabbing me like that."

"*Okay*," Pax said. She felt blood trickle into her eyebrow. Pistol-whipped by a fairy.

"Worth it for one of Apothel's dumb fucking words?" Letty said. "*Grugulochs* is what it said. Insane rambling *shit*."

"Grugulochs," Pax said. She hadn't come across it in the time she'd spent going through Apothel's book. But if he'd erased everything else in the chapel and left one word, it had to mean something. Her gut *had* been right.

A nearby car engine broke her concentration. Letty went quiet, listening too. The car slowed as it got closer. Then stopped. Right outside.

The doors opened.

"A homeless guy hid out here once," a man's voice said. Deep, slow and familiar. "It's been quiet for a long time."

"A homeless man?" A woman. "Anyone in particular?"

"Yeah," he said. Definitely familiar; the big guy in the cheap suit, the one whose car they'd stolen, who'd wanted to take them in. The one Casaria had knocked down. Apparently he wasn't being helpful, not explaining this was Apothel's place. "I'll start the scans."

Letty drifted near Pax's ear and whispered, "Happy now?"

"Clear of UE-r, checking for FT."

Something beeped below. The newcomers said nothing. It beeped again.

"Meaning . . ." the woman, said, carefully.

"Shit," Letty hissed, recognising the sound.

"It's the faeometer," the man said, like a bomb disposal expert realising he had seconds to live. The woman cleared her throat, calculating how to react.

"You have a . . .there's a key to this door?"

"Yes, hold on." Fumbling movements below. The beeping continued, steady. "It's not moving. Probably inside."

"Are you armed?"

A pause. "In the car."

Their footsteps, and the beeping, moved away. Pax held Letty's eyes.

"They can't keep up with me, even with this shitty wing," Letty said. "I'll lead them away and send help. Find you later."

"Send help? No –" Pax started to complain, but the fairy shot up into the air. Letty flew higher and higher, nothing but a speck against the sky. The faeometer beeped slower. Then created a different sound. A drawn-out warning tone.

"It's moving," the man called out. "That way."

"Follow it!" the woman said.

"Okay." The man was less urgent. "Take this."

There were scrambling footsteps, a jingling of keys, then the car doors slammed shut. The engine started and the wheels screeched as the car pulled away. Pax waited, not daring to breathe. The street fell deathly still.

She slid over the tiles, hoping the far corner of the roof would be low enough to drop down to the street without her needing to climb over any more walls. Twisting awkwardly around, she poked her head out.

The woman was still there, a large ring of keys held in one hand. She was sharply dressed in a pantsuit, with a short bob of precision-cut hair around her mousy face and a mole high on her left cheek. Their eyes met before Pax could back off.

Pax said, "Would you believe . . . this has nothing to do with me?"

12

"You're Pax Kuranes?"

Neither woman blinked. The newcomer looked as startled and uncertain as Pax; they hadn't come looking for her, this agent wasn't prepared.

"Ms Kuranes, I'm sorry you got involved in this – I know Cano Casaria. I've been there myself. Whatever's going on – wherever he is – I want to help –"

"Thanks." Pax sat up onto her haunches. "But I've got plans."

"Wait!" The woman put a hand up. "Please. I'm Sam Ward, did he mention me? I run our InterSpecies Relations Initiative. We manage Sunken City communications."

Pax was fairly sure Casaria hadn't said anything about this woman or any Ministry work involving diplomacy. She said, "You sound like a business report."

Ward stared searchingly, clearly trying to figure out a way to connect. Pax waited for the attempt. The Ministry can protect you? The Ministry are your friends? I like your coat? Ward said, "Casaria is a very particular person, I know what he's like. He scared me, too."

Ah. The scared woman angle. Pax said, "Good for you, bye."

She moved back in a crouch as Ward protested. Best just to leave, don't let them try mind tricks or play for time. She moved a few paces across the roof. There was a sharp crack. Tiles and wooden supports snapped beneath her, the floor suddenly gone. Pax yelped as she dropped into the darkness.

She was airborne for a second before landing, hard, debris scattering around her. Pax rolled to the side, wheezing; she'd flopped onto her back but taken some of the fall on her legs and one arm, the wind knocked out of her.

Behind her, there was a bang on the door. Ward shouted, "Ms Kuranes! Are you okay?"

Pax sat up, rubbing her back. It ached like she'd been hit with a hammer. Bits of the roof were still settling around her in a gentle rain of splinters. She shook them off, as Ward pounded harder.

"Please talk to me!"

Pax rose unsteadily, and the pain hit her again. In her chest, it throbbed, and she gasped – this wasn't from the fall. It was as if the jolt had revived that waking feeling of uneasiness, but worse. She took deep breaths until it subsided, leaving her to look, more closely, at the sinisterly carved walls. Ward was trying the keys, cursing. She rattled the door. No good. Pax took a step away from the entrance, towards the back wall, and another pain shot through her thigh.

"I'm your best hope!" Ward pleaded, pausing her attempts to find the right key. "When the others get here, they won't listen – they'll just lock you away, at best."

Good to know good cop/bad cop was still alive and well, Pax told herself. Even with only one cop present. She limped to the rear door, through to a short corridor, two doors, one open on a sink. Pax went for the other one.

"No one called me on Friday!" Ward shouted. "I can create a bridge between us and the Fae – they don't want me to!"

Pax gave that a moment's attention. Her instincts told her that Sam Ward was a rather sad and lonely individual. Perhaps genuinely sympathetic. Or perhaps saying anything to trap her. The key-jangling resumed frantically. Pax continued into the dark. She took out Rimes' phone and lit the area with its screen. There was a panel in the floor with a metal ring. Down on her knees, Pax ran her hands over the trapdoor, testing the ridged gap. She pulled and the trapdoor shifted slightly. She tugged again and it popped up, another waft of dust making her cough.

Ward had gone quiet, her keys still. The shouting piped up again. "Ms Kuranes, are you hurt?"

Ignoring her, Pax heaved the trapdoor fully open and shone the light down a set of wooden steps. It meant going underground again, not a day after last time. She took a breath. It was this or get locked up by the government. At best.

Pax swivelled round and probed the steps with her feet, then shimmied down on her backside. She pulled the trapdoor down after her as she descended. Such a bad idea, stupid as hell. The stairs led into a narrow room, barely high enough to stand in. She scanned the phone from side to side, revealing a couple of wooden beams and four bare brick walls. A few metres of space. Nothing else.

What was worse than stumbling back into the Sunken City, Pax realised, was stumbling into a dead end, when all that woman above needed to do was find the right key. She gritted her teeth, listening for Ward. The agent had stopped pleading, which meant she was focusing more determinedly on getting in.

Pax scanned the walls again and realised her fingers were tingling hard. Her chest was heating up. There was no way this room was connected to the Sunken City, or anything else, but she had a strange sensation that it wasn't just a cellar. There was something nearby. Behind her . . .

Pax turned, eyes widening. It wasn't there before. It couldn't have been, she'd have seen its light. A foot-wide square on the brickwork, bathed in a soft blue glow.

Pax's mouth dropped open as she moved towards it. This *was* where Apothel's secrets lay – she *knew* it – Letty could apologise later. But she didn't like the irrational way she knew it. The blue screen was connected to the thing that had tried to drain her. These ominous panels had sucked energy through the underground chamber as she'd writhed in pain on the floor. Were the weird feelings of the morning *real*? A connection on some level?

Pax raised a tentative hand, drawn mindlessly towards the blue patch.

When she touched it, the screen moved, and she jumped back with a gasp. It had vibrated, she was sure. Up and down, maybe just an inch, but definitely a response to her touch. It was still again. But the brickwork under it shifted. There was a sound like nails on a chalkboard as a deep scratch appeared. It grew, a line scraping down. Then up, at an angle. Slowly spelling out a letter. A childish scrawl, angular and lopsided.

Who?

It was communicating with her. Apothel's Blue Angel. And, in that instant, it didn't *know* it was communicating with her.

The brickwork shifted again. The lines closed up, the old brick reforming like it had been unchanged for decades. Just like Barton had described. You needed to scratch into the blue screen yourself to communicate. Another message formed as Pax watched.

Everyone gone

Was it a trick? Holly Barton said they had encountered a screen, so the Blue Angel must've known Barton was still around. Though it might not have realised he survived the night, after the various problems they'd all run into.

There was one other person the Angel might believe was out there, though, who it might be willing to do business with. Pax took out the scooter's key and lifted it to the blue screen as the second message faded into nothing. Her hand shook as she scratched into the bricks. A messy line, followed by another.

Rufa . . .

Before she could finish, her letters disappeared. The response formed.

Taken

So it knew something of current affairs. But it couldn't be the Ministry themselves, could it? It would've known Barton wasn't *gone*. She took a chance, quickly scratching in her answer.

Escaped

Her letters faded, leaving the brick blank again. What could she ask to trap this Angel? To figure out who or at least where it was?

A noise came above, a metallic rattle, followed by a curse. Another failed attempt from Ward. The bricks shifted.

Why here?

The words faded, and Pax sucked her lower lip. Only one way to get the Angel talking, most likely. Play the same game they'd always played. She scratched in:

Help?

The words faded. Come on. Give me something.

Ward shouted above. Back to trying to reason with her.

The Blue Angel's response formed slowly as Pax watched:

Chaucer Crescent

Pax frowned. Directory enquiries, like Barton had said. It was offering her glo? What did it expect Rufaizu to do with that? She quickly scratched a response:

Why?

Her word disappeared but no answer came. Something squeaked, loudly, above, and Ward's voice came through again. Closer. She'd got in. Her footsteps thunked through the hall.

Pax took a step back, eyes on the ceiling. If she waited for the right moment – if

Ward went into the other room before checking here – she might slip past. She moved to the steps and paused, noticing new words had appeared in the blue screen.

Not him

She stared at the fading words. It took a moment to appreciate the weight of the message. The blue screen vibrated. Whoever it was had figured her out. Before she'd scarcely processed that, her vision suddenly blurred, a hot pain flaring in her chest. A jolt shot through her and she gagged. Her vision went white before blazing with a waking dream of rapid images. Tunnels, brick walls, metal rails – sparks of lightning – she closed her eyes fearfully, almost falling to a knee. Was it the screen itself? Sending out some psychic attack?

She took a step back and her hand found the stairs, supporting herself from falling. The images kept flashing behind her eyelids – jumping shadows, splitting metal. They faded as quickly as they came, but she understood them. Something had happened – she was *seeing* it happen. Or feeling it, at least. She even knew where. Not exactly, but the direction. Across the city. Somewhere south?

Ward's voice came desperately above, closer. "Where are you?"

Pax tried to focus on it, blinking heavily. The pain diffused as she refocused on the cellar's shadows. The faint blue glowing square on the wall. It was responsible somehow, it had done this to her – the timing wasn't a coincidence. As she stared, the feeling subsiding, the screen made a noise. A hiss, like a valve opening.

Her eyes opened wider, and her heart pounded – this time from simple fear. Something was coming *out* of the screen. A dark shape, rolling over itself. Oozing like an oily custard, with a rotten egg stink.

She backed further around the steps.

The glutinous mass twisted in the shadows, pivoting from where it was attached to the wall, rearing its slimy front up like a worm testing the air.

Pax dived up the stairs, slamming her head and shoulders into the trapdoor. It flew up and bounced back, catching her on the head again, and she slipped on the steps. As she glanced back into the gloom, the phone light caught the top edge of the sluglike creature, on the floor now. Sliding towards her.

13

Sam tensed as Pax Kuranes shot out of the dark in a cursing panic, running from something. The woman skidded to a halt, clocking the open door and Sam before it.

"Wait!" Sam shouted, as Pax bolted. Sam was nearer, quicker, and threw a hand ahead. As Pax reached the doorway, the steel bulkhead slammed shut. She smacked into it and grappled with the handle as Sam jammed the key in. Pax's fingers clawed at her as she turned the key, but the lock clunked into place. Snatching the keys back, ducking away from Pax's grabbing hands, Sam took quick steps back. Now to take charge –

"You lunatic!" Pax shouted. "Open the fucking door!"

Sam held up Landon's fistful of keys like a weapon. "Ms Kuranes, you need to –"

"You're locking us in with it!" Pax pointed sharply, baring her teeth. "*Open the door.*"

Sam looked from the shadows back to Pax. The woman was a poker player, an actor, of sorts. "I can't let you leave. You need to answer some questions."

"Questions?" Pax threw the word back at her. "There's –"

Something squeaked and both women froze. Pax's eyes found the rear door, and Sam followed the glance. There was nothing there. MEE-cordoned properties were cleared out, sealed off. No matter what had been here before, this place *had* to be empty. The squeak came again, with a light bang, a door rattling on its hinges. Low, at ground level.

"There's no . . ." Sam started, but couldn't say it out loud. An entrance to the Sunken City? Something coming *up*? That wasn't possible. But Pax was here for a reason.

"Give me the keys," Pax said, pressed against the door, hand outstretched.

"What is it?"

The door beyond moved again, pushed up and bounced back down.

"Give me the fucking keys!" Pax shouted.

"Tell me what you're doing here!" Sam spun on her. "Do you have *any* idea the trouble you've caused?"

Pax's face expressed a primal rage at the mere suggestion of answering questions. Sam didn't falter. This woman *would* explain.

The trapdoor squeaked again, and this time didn't bang back down. It landed on something soft. Whatever was underneath was finally pushing out. The floor groaned as something slid heavily over it.

"Look," Pax said, urgently, "there's a blue screen, in the cellar – it released something –"

"Blue screen?" Sam said. The phrase fired up a memory; something from old Sunken City lore, to do with Apothel. He'd made claims about blue screens, hadn't he? He wrote on walls, with no evidence of anything writing back. One of the many reasons the MEE brushed him off as mad. But there was definitely something moving. Coming closer.

"Get us out of here!" Pax roared, slamming both her hands into the metal and making Sam jump as the slap rang through the room.

The sliding drew closer, out into the corridor that connected the hall to the back rooms. The light from the hole in the roof gave the scantest outline of something shifting in the shadows. Low but thick. Rolling like a tiny stream of molten lava.

"What is that," said Sam, gaping. She'd seen nothing like it in the MEE databases. As it crept into the hallway, it was slowly revealed. A foot high, maybe a metre long, pulsing along the floor. Sam barely had time to react when she heard Pax move. The other woman slammed into her, and she hit the floor hard as Pax grabbed at the keys. They flew from Sam's hand. Through the air, down with a clatter, sliding right up to the approaching shape.

Pax froze, straddling Sam. They stared together, breathing deeply from the brief scuffle. Reacting to the sound, the thing changed direction, slightly, to roll into the keys. As its molten flesh touched the metal, the keys steamed and hissed and started melting.

"Jesus Christ," Pax gasped.

"What – what –" Sam stuttered.

The shape moved over the keys' remains as they bubbled down like boiled butter. It was coming closer again. Pax kicked off Sam and scrambled to a window. Sam pushed herself up, darting her eyes between Pax, clawing at the window frame, and the sliding shape. It had changed direction again, slurping towards Pax.

"Fucking do something!" Pax screamed at Sam.

"I can't!" Sam screamed back, moving towards a different wall. She didn't have a gun, didn't have anything. She wasn't supposed to be here.

The sludge kept advancing, backing Pax into a corner, inching closer and closer.

"Get away from me you fucker!" Pax roared.

The sky seemed to open on Pax's command, with a crack of thunder that shook the room. Sam threw her hands over her ears, screaming again. The creature exploded in a cloud of black powder, which hung in the air like flour. Sam lowered her hands, ears ringing, as the powder settled on the empty floorboards. Part of it was still there, a shadow of twitching ooze, but the majority had been vaporised.

Sam looked questioningly at Pax, mouth open. Pax was looking up, though, towards the hole in the roof. A muffled voice came through the ringing, and Sam shook her head to try and focus.

"Oh my God," she gasped, spotting the two-inch figure perched on the edge of the roof, a miniature man silhouetted against the sky. Heavy-set and oddly inelegant. The long, thin object sticking out from his side smoked like a used matchstick.

"Now, here's what's going to happen," a male voice came down, a dry monotone; small, but clear even at this distance. "The young lady's going to exit freely, and come with me, and you'll stay right where you are."

Sam looked to Pax, who didn't look convinced herself. Finally calm for a moment, Sam studied her face, in the dramatic half-light from the hole in the ceiling. Pax had big staring eyes and softly rounded features, countered by a boyish grubbiness and dirty skin. A tatty imitation leather coat, faux fur lining. She looked defiant rather than defeated, after their panicked scuffle. She must've fired up every cylinder of Casaria's weird interests; the sort of tough, night-dwelling person Casaria had once imagined Sam to be. Pax had been dragged into this by him, but she was here on her own initiative now. Provoking things under the ground. Sam's eyes shifted back towards the remains of the creature, as Pax said to the Fae, "Letty sent you?"

"She called," the man replied. "The door . . ."

"It's locked."

"Lady, hand her the keys."

"I guess you got here too late to see the keys get liquefied? So unless you've got a ladder . . ."

"What –" Sam started. Her hand was raised, shakily pointing at the black smear on the floor. "What was that?"

"Co-operate," the fairy said, "or you join it."

Pax exhaled a curse. Sam's eyes ran dumbly from the tiny shape back to Pax. She had her arms folded – regaining her composure and apparently none too pleased about the fairy's threats. She suggested, "How about you use that thunder-stick to blow out a window?"

The fairy considered it, then said, "I'll handle it." He popped off the roof and glided into the room. Sam stared with awe. Though he was rotund, and his small wings looked inadequate for his weight, he moved as weightlessly as a bee. He flew between Sam and Pax, down to the handle of the metal door, where he landed.

"Got a name?" Pax said.

"Rolarn," he answered.

Pax hummed satisfaction. She turned to Sam, as though she wanted to share something, but changed her mind when she met the agent's eyes. The fairy fluttered off the handle and inspected the keyhole. He rummaged in a pocket.

"Um…" Sam took a tentative step forward. Her hands were still shaking. Her voice shook, too. "Excuse me – my – I'm Ward. Sam Ward – I've been –"

The man stopped. "One step closer and you lose your knees."

Sam looked down at her legs. She didn't doubt the gun could tear her in half, from what it had done to the molten creature. The casual way he said it made it all the more threatening. All the emails she'd sent – all her ideas, her dreams of creating a dialogue – now she had finally met a Fae and this –

"Stand clear," the man said, and gave them no time to react. There was a bang, the volume of a firecracker, and white smoke poured out of the keyhole. The fairy flew up and away.

"Try it."

"Wait!" Sam blurted out. "You can't just go!"

Pax's hand drifted towards the door handle, slow and deliberate. "And yet . . ."

"You're with the Fae – this is huge – I've been trying for *three years* to create a dialogue –"

"So take a hint," Pax said, opening the door.

"I believe you, okay!" Sam hurried to say it. "You saw a blue screen down there, okay! Whatever you're doing, we can work together! Look at this place." She gestured to the hall with its horrible lattice of mad scratches. "You're trailing Apothel, he wasn't well."

Pax gave Sam an assaying look. "And you would know?"

"Please," Sam said. "Whatever you're up to, however you've hooked up with the Fae, I need to –"

"What you need," the tiny man hovered up with his gun across his waist, "is to be quiet."

Sam held her tongue. She'd got funding for IS on the theory that the Fae weren't as violent or unreasonable as rumour had it. Maybe they were.

When Pax swung the door open, a gust of air stirred the dusty remains of the molten creature. Pax stepped out with the fairy, and Sam moved after them for one last plea. "Do you know where Casaria is? Tell me that, at least!"

Pax looked back, surprised. After a moment's confusion, she said, "I haven't seen him since he helped us last night. If he's got any sense he's a long way from you."

Sam shook her head, "He came in – was debriefed –"

"That's enough," Rolarn cut in.

With the shotgun aimed at her head, Sam didn't say another word.

Pax had paused. "You took him back in, and now he's missing?"

Sam nodded, barely moving.

"And you're asking me? You people are bullshit. I saw the thing you call the *praelucente*, sucking energy. It tried to drain me and an innocent damn teenager. It drains people as they travel on the Tube, it drains them in their own homes. But you believe sometimes – somehow – that's helpful. You're ignorant of the fact someone or something is using that energy, *moving* that energy, and until you admit that you don't get to ask me another fucking thing."

Sam stared, silent, and the fierce look on Pax's face said she'd given up all that she was willing to. She shook her head and ducked out into the daylight.

14

It was all very well that Darren and Grace were idling in bed, but Holly was fit and ready. She regretted that she hadn't simply gone with Pax on the ropey scooter. The next best course of action hardly felt as adventurous: trawling the internet for information. She'd gone from learning precious little about the supposed gas leak, and precious little about the supposed government ministry, to exploring the origins of the Ordshaw Underground. She had discovered the K&S Line had an eccentric history traceable to the end of the Victorian era, and started scribbling down ideas, when a high-pitched bark made her sit up straight. It was close: the other side of the wall.

Holly called to Rimes, who was clattering about in a corner, "Do you have a dog?"

The doctor went still. Her voice came out uncertainly. "No."

Holly huffed. There was another bark.

Like hell she was going to sit here and be lied to. She stomped outside. Along the rickety porch and round the side. The hedges and trees thickly encroached on the building; a few more years and the roots might drag the doctor into the mud. If they were lucky. Holly continued past a tangle of brambles.

"Mrs Barton! Hold on!" Rimes' voice came behind her.

Holly flashed her a glance. Rimes waved a bony hand, half-hidden around the corner of her house, not daring to come closer. Her white lab coat was splattered with a violet liquid. Holly raised her eyebrows, waiting for an excuse or an explanation.

"I don't think – that is –" Rimes was struggling. "Darren thought –"

"What Darren thought about what I should or shouldn't know is beyond immaterial," Holly said. Quite calmly, she thought. She continued and Rimes rustled through the leaves after her.

There was a shed, nearly five foot high, the open front barred with a grid of metal. Something growled within. Holly walked towards it; no dog her arse. The hut shook as the animal jumped out of the shadows, crashing against the bars. Holly shrieked, a hand at her heart. The thing dropped back before doubling its efforts, hurling its weight against the fencing, big slobbering jaws snapping. The wooden slats barely shuddered, suggesting the innocent-looking hut was reinforced.

Its eyes were alive, glowing red and flickering. Smoke poured from its jowls, its ears, even from spots across its skin, like it was on fire under its ragged, charcoal fur.

Holly flinched again as it threw a paw. Three-inch claws lashed out between the bars. It bared its teeth as it dropped back.

"A helluvian hound," Rimes explained, apologetically.

"Why?" Holly demanded. The dog snarled and bit again, and Holly saw fire in its throat. "Why is it here?"

"Our security measures –"

"My daughter is in there! She's supposed to be safe and *this* is out here? This *monster*?"

Rimes made defeated whimpering sounds. A fast movement drew Holly back to the hut. The creature had disappeared back into the shadows, flickers of smoke lingering where it had been. The growls sounded far away. This opening led to a larger domain. "What else is down there?"

"Just that," Rimes said. "One dog."

"How? Who *built* this?"

"The hut . . ." Rimes cleared her throat. "Darren. And the others. The tunnel was left from the war."

Holly imagined Darren up here, covered in sweat and dirt as he put together an impenetrable dog crate. Was it because she'd never let him have a dog of his own? "How much time did he spend here?"

"Oh..." Rimes' voice was quiet, regretful. "Not much. The men brought supplies, occasional samples. Mostly they grouped together in town. Without me."

The doctor was careful to make that point. She clearly knew there'd been friction about her, in the Barton household. Holly sighed at the dumb simplicity of Darren's deceit. He'd wanted to hang out drinking and fighting, like most uncivilised males. It just fumbled him into an unholy underworld. "Why *are* all these things under Ordshaw?"

Rimes gave her a nervous look.

"Who built those tunnels? Where does it *come* from?"

Again, Rimes looked uncertain. She smiled awkwardly and said, "The helluvian hound has more in common with a lizard than a canine; possibly it has reptilian ancestry. My speciality is the flora, though. Adapted to survive without sunlight. Some of the strains – the plant life – there's nothing like it in the UK. One plant – its closest relative is found on a little-known Pacific island."

Holly raised an eyebrow. "So it's not just Ordshaw?"

"Maybe." Rimes shrugged. "If not, it's a secret elsewhere, too."

Of course. Likely there were countless remarkable, otherworldly phenomenon, institutionally hidden by organisations oblivious to each other's existence. And secrets upon secrets because husbands thought their wives couldn't handle the truth.

A phone rang inside.

Out here in the woods with a fire-breathing dog, it seemed almost surreal. It rang again. The chime of an old phone bell. And again. Rimes didn't move, looking terrified, and needed Holly's intervention as a trigger. "Shouldn't we answer that?"

*

The fear of pursuit made it easier to traverse Ordshaw's traffic. Pranging the bike or breaking the Highway Code no longer concerned Pax. She had to get out of the open, into the (supposed) safety Rolarn claimed was waiting in Broadplain Plaza. Broadplain was where Letty said his hideout was, wasn't it? She'd said she'd call someone, and used his name earlier, so this was all good, Pax told herself. Never mind that he hadn't relaxed his grip on his gun and was completely stand-offish in his manner.

Pax tried not to think beyond following road signs. Only once she was safe, and reunited with Letty, would she let herself worry about other Fae. Or the fact that the Ministry had almost snared her. Or that the Blue Angel's slug-like emissary could have killed her. Or that the encounter with Sam Ward had raised questions about Apothel – the one man who might've known what she herself was going through, labelled as mad. And then there was also the question of the trouble Casaria was in. And, worst of all, the physical response she'd had when the Blue Angel had caught her out. The same feeling she'd woken with, when the building had been quaking on the other side of Ordshaw. The same feeling, she considered, as when the monster had shocked her, under the city.

All that could wait. It had to wait, while she focused on the signs pointing towards Broadplain. She weaved between slow-moving vans on a four-lane road, skirted the south side of Old Ordshaw, passing cobbled lanes, and finally left the glass skyscrapers of Central Ordshaw for the concrete squares of Broadplain, a commercial district that had been poorly preserved over the years.

Broadplain Plaza was impossible to miss. The shopping centre was a windowless eyesore that spanned three streets with variously sized cubes and walkways. Its single defining feature was its name, hanging on one wall in giant metal letters that must have once stood as proud, angular white monoliths. They were now greening relics, cracked but too sad for even weeds to come near. The outward-facing shopfronts added to that tired image, mostly boarded up, but the area was still busy with people milling through the plaza doors carrying overstuffed carrier bags.

Pax kept her head down, passing spiked security camera poles, to ride into the covered multi-storey car park. After hiding the scooter in a corner, she followed Rolarn's instructions through the building, the fairy appearing out of nowhere to tell her to turn left or right, then disappearing again.

Pax continued on autopilot, trying to suppress the feeling that something was seriously wrong with her. She followed a path overlooking scores of stores. The complex space of the fluorescent-lit halls, tiered walkways and distant ceilings with mossy skylights made the individual shops seem like minor glitches in an otherwise abandoned labyrinth. The shoppers were eerily quiet as they filled the complex. A group watching TVs through an electronics shop window did so silently. Pax frowned. Were they gathering around some breaking news?

It was time, now. They had arrived and she had to admit that when she'd faced that blue screen she hadn't had a simple panicking spasm. It wasn't just the screen somehow attacking her, either. Something had happened, she'd *felt* it happen.

"This way," Rolarn said, near a turning.

Pax said, "There's something going on. Can you go check it out?"

"Mm."

"Mm *no,* or mm *yes?*"

He didn't clarify. Which made it a no.

"Christ." Pax took out Rimes' phone, to find the answer herself.

"You want to keep stopping," Rolarn warned her, "we're gonna have a problem."

For someone supposedly there to help, he was determined to make life difficult. He also still had that gun out. Pax risked activating the phone anyway, figuring he was, after all, sent to save her. There was no internet connection. Predictable, inside this concrete temple. There was one bar of phone signal, at least, so she said, "I've gotta make a call."

"You tell anyone where you are, we're gonna have a *big* problem. Human." Rolarn made the last word bite, his attitude feeding into Pax's instinctive dislike.

She gave him a careful look. Rolarn had on a faded yellow shirt, collar open and crumpled, half-untucked from loose beige trousers. His gut hung over his belt and his head folded into his neck, with a bad comb-over and an unhappy, impatient scowl up top. Pax concluded, "You look like a shit lawyer. A tiny shit lawyer."

"With a gun."

"Congratulations. Listen, I'm not gonna give away your home, but I *need* to make a call." Pax thumbed through the contacts on Rimes phone. Five names. There had to be someone with the number for the telegraph station, so she could get in touch with Barton and the others. *Apothel*, well he was dead; *Darren*, his phone was dead; *Ministry,* go to hell; *Rik*, missing. That left *Ruth*. No home number. Great. Pax called Ruth and spoke to Rolarn as it rang. "You can relax. You're mates with Letty, right?"

"Letty doesn't have mates."

"Are you *associates*?"

"Mandy?" A mature woman answered the phone. "What's wrong?"

"Not Mandy," Pax said. "I've got her phone, have you got her home number?"

There was an awkward silence. Ruth said, "How did you get her phone?"

"Found it in Asda, in Long Culdon," Pax lied. "Please, if you give me her number I can return the phone."

Another wary pause. "Hold on." The woman shuffled about briefly, but gave Pax the number. When she had finished, Ruth said, "Before you go, give me a moment. You be polite with Mandy, you hear? She's been through a lot. It'd be better she lost her phone than had another episode."

Thank you, Ruth, for making things more complicated. "Episode of what?"

"Just be gentle," Ruth said. "Good day."

She hung up. Pax chose to ignore that detail as she dialled the new number. As the phone rang again, she asked Rolarn, "You know what that thing was, back in the chapel?"

"No."

"It came out of the wall."

No response. There was a better analogy than shit lawyer, Pax imagined. Beat-up church janitor? Sexually-confused shoe salesman?

"Hello?" Rimes answered, a cautious whisper.

"Dr Rimes," Pax said. "Can I –"

"Pax?" Holly cut in, wrenching the phone off the doctor. "Pax, is that you? Did you know there's a monster *dog* on our doorstep?"

Ah. The strange noises, the security system. Pax was happy she'd left *that* behind. "Yeah. Holly, I . . ." Pax paused, not sure how to describe the feelings she'd had. *I'm concerned something's happened because I can feel the minotaur in me?* At best it'd make them worry. And saying it would make it real.

"Are you okay?" Holly asked. "I was thinking, we haven't even contacted your family, surely we should? Somehow?"

"If you want to make a bad day worse."

"Pardon?"

"Nothing," Pax said. "No, it's fine. Look . . ." She slowed down, dreading the answer. "Has there been anything else in the news? Another incident?"

"Hmm?" Holly said. "Not that I've noticed. Why?"

"Do me a favour and keep your eyes on it? I've got a bad feeling, but I've got to keep moving right now."

"I've had a bad feeling since Friday, it's understandable."

"Yeah. This is worse." Pax paused. "Another thing, Holly. Can you put something to Rimes and your husband? Ask them if those blue screens have ever done anything more than communicate."

"Like what, play the bassoon?"

"Like if anything's come out of them."

"What sort of things are likely to have come out of them?"

"Just…" Pax realised she couldn't describe the sludge creature any more easily than she could describe her internal strife. "Maybe they *were* moving glo around, like Grace guessed. Maybe they can move other things. Crazy as it sounds."

"I see," Holly replied, slowly. "You know, I was thinking about the tunnels themselves, personally. Who built them?"

Rolarn hovered a little closer to Pax, his scowl hinting at her to finish. Pax scrunched her nose at him, hinting that he give her a damn second.

Holly continued, "It took twenty years to construct the Central Line, after the war, and fourteen for the K&S Line, earlier. The chap who designed the K&S Line, Frank Trellis, started on another line, too, but nothing on the scale that we saw. He ran out of funding – probably fell out of favour with the royal family."

No, these were not details worth riling the fairy over. "Holly, can we do this when I get back?"

"I do have a point," Holly said. "How could you hide the resources required for such a thing? I'm looking at these monster dogs and thinking of these secrets, and thinking it must've all been concealed very long ago, to be that well hidden."

"The Sunken City has concrete and brickwork, and electric lighting –"

"One thing you've made painfully clear," Holly said, "is that ignorance is our biggest enemy here. The means to create all this have clearly stayed hidden, whatever they are, and must be something worth finding, don't you think? It could be anything. Dwarf gold-miners, giant worms?"

"We *saw* a giant worm," Pax said, wishing it wasn't true. "Anyway, we'll ask the Blue Angel the rest of these questions when we find it, won't we? I need to go."

"Where exactly are you?"

Rolarn's face grew grimmer, so Pax said, "Someplace safe. I'm done with the chapel, nothing to report yet, but I'm with another fairy. Rolarn."

"Roland?"

"*Rolarn*. Not as fun as he sounds. Take care, Holly – let me know if anything hits the news."

"Certainly. It'll –"

Pax hung up and raised her eyebrows at the fairy. "Was that so hard?"

He turned away without comment and floated towards a corner. Dragging her heels, Pax followed him, into a wide dead end where half the lights weren't working. The shopfronts here had been partly painted over to hide stacked rubbish. The single surviving shop, on the floor below, boasted crystals, dragon statues, and no customers. The far wall hosted three tiers of store space hidden behind whitewashed boards. One massive, forgotten department store. This, she sensed, was their destination.

Pax narrowed her eyes at the ghostly outline of its long-removed name.

"Where once was a Debenhams," she said, "now there are Fae?"

Rolarn reacted blandly. "See the entrance?"

There was a door-shaped crack in the emulsion ahead. No sign of a lock or handle. It looked like no one had been through it in years. As Rolarn hovered ahead, Pax watched him uneasily. She wished Letty was there, to offer some kind of reassurance this place was safe. But he'd saved her, hadn't he? These Fae were the help they needed . . .

15

Sam shone a torch over the rough markings on the 'chapel' walls, crisscrossing one another with grooves so deep the lines looked black. There were only the barest hints of plaster left between the gashes. Apothel must have done it possessed by a wild energy, using an axe, or a spade, or a hammer and chisel.

Now she realised exactly where she was, Sam recalled the Ripton Chapel was well known in the MEE; its rabid markings were all the argument the Ministry needed when anyone entertained thoughts that Apothel had been underutilised as an asset. The man was not in full control of his mind. Whatever he had written, these walls proved he disagreed with it himself.

It gave Sam a chill. Even with the field agents coming and going, taking photos, running their different scanning devices, the place was grimly lifeless. The word left on the rear wall stood as a sinister, singular epitaph.

Sam couldn't recall it being mentioned in any of the files about Apothel, or the stories she had heard about this place. Had whoever sealed up the chapel neglected to record it? A nonsense word to some, no doubt, but painfully relevant, now.

Grugulochs.

The sound Malcolm Joseph had heard when the Sunken City shook his home.

By the time Letty circled back to the Ripton Chapel, the road out front was packed with vehicles. A dented grey Transit van, two dirty Astras and a little Hyundai. The dilapidated, nondescript cars of the Ministry might have looked like civilian vehicles if they weren't parked by an abandoned building surrounded by men in suits.

Letty watched from the steeple of a church two blocks away, where only a finely targeted faeometer would pick her out. Tucking her knees up under her chin, pistol in hand, she wouldn't be averse to bleeding the lot of them if they'd hurt Pax. Even if the lummox had the gall to grab her like that.

Letty checked her phone again. No updates from Rolarn, but he might be on the move.

She watched some goons exit the chapel in white plastic suits, like the place was toxic. The one in front tore off his outfit and tossed it to a waiting attendant. He was tall, ginger-haired, and carried himself like he was in charge. Behind him was the lady who'd rumbled them. A humourless-looking bitch, all right angles. She was talking. Ginger didn't answer back, apparently not as high-ranking as he wanted to be.

Their discussion was cut short by the return of Agent Landon, the Ministry's chief ape. He took about a million years longer than necessary to straighten his car against the curb, with the crowd watching, before he got out and Ginger barked some angry words at him. Landon replied huffily. Letty could imagine the conversation perfectly:

"You didn't catch that super-cool Fae, you giant sack of lard?"

"No, but I did better than you would've."

"You idiot, your breath smells!"

"That's because I eat shit!"

The square woman steps between them and addresses Landon.

"It's okay, you tried. She was just too super-cool for any of us."

Landon makes a face like he's farted.

"And you –" The woman turns to Ginger. "Your breath doesn't smell so good either."

A silent acceptance of the truth.

"What are all these people doing here?" Landon says. "I've gotta shit."

"Obviously," the lady answers, "we needed a hundred people to go over this empty building and make sure it was empty. We're still not sure."

Ginger gets his phone out. "It's the head office. The tests are in. We *all* stink."

The lady looks stunned by the results, she might cry. "Not *me!*"

"All of us," Ginger assures her.

"Well we're not getting clean here," Landon says, waving a hand over his head. He's older and fatter than the others so they take notice, time to pack up. The first couple move towards their cars. Square lady gets a final word in, really taken by the phone call, but no one's listening.

Landon confides in her: "You *do* stink. Same as the rest of us."

"I know." She looks between her feet, sad as a short giraffe.

And then they're all leaving.

Someone started locking up the chapel again, adding a chain this time. Letty sat forward, confident that Pax was long gone. Hopefully in Broadplain by now, free as a Fae. Unless Ginger just got a tip on where she was.

Letty sprang into the air and rose above the buildings, keeping one eye on the Ministry cars as she tried to spot any dumpy lummoxes tumbling over garden fences.

The Ministry goons all headed in the same direction. Southwest.

With the street empty, Letty glided over the next road and realised the MEE vehicles weren't the only ones gone. No sign of Pax's crappy scooter, either. She'd better follow this Ministry horde in case they had a bead on her. But as she flew higher, watching the convoy, something else caught her eye.

Across the city, a cloud of smoke was rising.

Sam braced a hand against the dashboard as Landon took them through the city, on course for the Bristol Street Underground station and the reports that there had been another quake, this time causing (or caused by?) a Tube accident. Landon drove with remarkable efficiency for someone sticking solidly to the speed limit, narrowly skimming through gaps in traffic and barely slowing for corners. However quickly he got them there, they were already too late, Sam knew that.

Having come face-to-face with Pax Kuranes, she understood that whatever the civilians and the Fae were up to was more important than the after-effects of what had already been done. The noise the *praelucente* was making and the word on the wall, Pax's claim she'd seen a blue screen, the simple fact that Kuranes was following Apothel's example with the help of the Fae. It all added up to an underlying issue that the Ministry were missing. These civilians had recovered that unusual weapon, after all. They had somehow damaged the *praelucente* and possibly caused today's surges.

"We're chasing symptoms," Sam told Landon. "Apothel understood something about the *praelucente*. Pax knows something. That word on the wall is important in explaining what's going on with it, and we're spending time chasing the results."

"Explaining words is *your* job," Landon replied. The hint of bitterness in his tone was standard street-level Ministry fare. They knew how ineffective IS was, though they had no idea why and she wasn't going to waste breath explaining.

Sam said, "Could Pax have taken Casaria?"

Landon grunted at the question, seeming to disapprove of thinking about her. Between his and Casaria's reports, Sam had developed a quick impression of Pax as a victim in this, and she'd felt for her, recalling how Casaria ensnared her in the same way. But Pax knew the Fae, somehow. What if she knew Rufaizu, too? Landon said, "She already used Cano. He's weak in a lot of ways, did stupid things for her. He attacked me, you know?"

The agent said it like a point of curiosity, no animosity in him. Something about his dull nature shielded him from that kind of emotion. He saw Casaria's instability as an unfortunate flaw, not something to be scorned.

Sam said, "But *he* approached *her*."

"Maybe they planned that."

"They being who?"

"The Fae, or those thugs we ran into at her place?" Landon suggested. He was referring to the two men they'd reported at Pax's property the day before, Ordshaw locals who had been after the Fae weapon, seemingly on Pax's command. One of them had carried a gun. That didn't sit well with Sam; the MEE's files showed Pax led an unusual life, but there was no evidence she was a criminal.

"What possible reason," Sam said, "could *anyone* have for kidnapping Casaria?"

"He took the Dispenser from us before," Landon said. "Hit me. Then came back to us with his tail between his legs, saying it was a mistake. She made a fool of him. Maybe she didn't want to risk him coming after her? One way or another, Casaria got himself all tied up in knots with this girl."

"The *praelucente* did, too," Sam thought out loud. "Whatever she's up to, or connected to, is dangerous. And it connects to that word, and Apothel, and that

Fae weapon."

Eyes on the road, Landon didn't look convinced. He said, "What do I know, I've barely slept." Sam paused, realising he'd had his own problems. He took his confrontation with Casaria stoically, but he'd barely mentioned his partner being killed. His eyes said he was thinking about it, and didn't like what had happened, even if his flat voice betrayed little. "Gets you thinking about yourself, you know."

Sam didn't know. She had never known anyone who was killed violently, nor been in situations where it might happen to her. When Casaria had put her in danger in the field, she'd outrun the threats before they properly manifested. She said, "I hope you don't think I'm speaking out of turn if I say this whole situation has been handled badly. From the top down." The usual way.

Landon grunted again. Either he agreed or thought she was part of the problem. He ran his hands over the steering wheel. "Got a better car out of it, anyway. The Cavalier did the job, but I always wondered how a Ford drives. It's smooth."

This was good, something more personal. Sam had been surprised when she'd read in the report that the Ministry-issue car stolen from him was over twenty years old, and said so. "You should've had an upgrade years ago. Better-equipped staff do a better job. That's the sort of basic logic we're lacking."

He gave her a third non-committal grunt. Accepting, or thinking she was over-complicating his simple pleasure?

They drove in silence, but she felt him glancing over. Like he wanted to say something but didn't know what. The MEE only had a handful of female field agents across the UK, so it was likely most of Operations hadn't shared a patrol car with a woman before. And if they had, they wouldn't choose her.

"It was your first time," Landon said, finally, "seeing one of the little people."

"Yeah," Sam admitted. "And it wasn't really positive."

"Not sure that Casaria was far wrong about them."

"Absolutely not. They're capable of rational discourse."

He was quiet again, and she knew it had come out too severe. And too lofty; this was not the environment for words like *rational discourse*. Confirming she'd ended their conversation, Landon turned the radio up. Middle-of-the-road country music, exactly what she'd have expected.

As they went through a set of traffic lights, Sam spotted a sign for Bristol Street station. "You've never seen that word before, Agent Landon? 'Grugulochs'? It was the noise this thing made during the building quake this morning."

"Not one I recall." Landon lazily turned the wheel.

There was a police cordon ahead, tape across the road, civilians standing on tiptoes trying to get a look. Beyond all the hubbub, the street was partially concealed by dusty smoke, thick and motionless in the still air. A fire engine's blue lights spun. Landon slowed down. "Lot of things make noises down there. Apothel wrote a lot of mad words. Doesn't all mean something. This, though" – he pointed ahead – "is important."

She followed his gesture. Smoke piled out from the Underground entrance beyond. Firemen were barking at one another, the danger apparent. A woman pushed through the police line, wailing and clutching her head. Blood streamed through her fingers. A policeman rushed to her, putting an arm around her. There was nothing Sam could say without sounding dispassionate. The same as ever; there was always something that made it hard to speak, in the halls of the Ministry, in the conference calls, in superiors' offices. The general public needed protecting, and that made most of her concerns moot.

You couldn't ask difficult questions when they detracted from the suffering public.

Landon unbuckled his seatbelt, struggling to navigate it around his gut. "I'd better get down there."

Another car pulled up beyond them and two men in suits started flagging down the police. She recognised the bearded one. Farnham? He looked like he was in his element, almost smiling as he issued orders to the police. The Operations team would lock this down, quieten the story and keep whatever had happened under careful wraps. They'd brush over the difficult questions to make sure life rolled on as usual.

Sam took a breath.

"I'm coming with you."

16

Rolarn lit a torch as Pax followed him into the cleared-out shop, nothing but occasional pillars interrupting its dark expanse. The floor was thick with dust. A card display lay on its side, the light revealing a smiling woman pointing at something. A frying pan?

"That way." Far across the empty floor was a motionless escalator.

"You know," Pax said, "there's people in New Thornton who pay a grand a month for a shoebox to live in? And here you've got this massive waste of space."

"This place thrived, once."

No doubt, if the Fae were here. It would be an even greater expanse for them. "What did your people do here?"

Rolarn didn't answer, as a small shape fluttered out of the escalator opening. This one had a slender body and an overlarge head.

"This is her?" the newcomer shouted. A female voice, with a smoker's huskiness.

"This is her," Rolarn said.

"Down here, then," the fairy said, then flew back the way she'd come.

Pax followed the tilt of Rolarn's gun to the top of the metal steps, where he aimed his torch down. Was she about to see one of the hidden marvels of the world, a civilisation of miniature people hiding in the wing of a shopping centre?

Making her way down the steps, she found the next floor as drab and empty as the one before, with the exception of a counter along a far wall. The female was there, by an electric camping lantern that lit a grey hunk of plastic that must have been one of the earliest digital cash registers. Another fairy stood by the register. A light shone out from behind the counter, towards floor-level. Their camp, apparently.

The fairy by the register was lanky, square-shouldered but thin like a stick-insect. He was tall for their kind, pushing three inches, and wore a tatty bomber jacket, the sleeves rolled up. The woman sat on the edge of the cash register, one leg hanging and a knee up. She had well-fitted flared white trousers and a wide-collared white jacket, with two pistol holsters hanging over her chest and one around one leg, all piped with silver. Her head wasn't overlarge, after all; she had a great body of auburn hair, swept into a blow-dried mane. A picture of disco fashion done right. With added firepower.

There was tension in the way they all looked at Pax, and she wanted to break the silence. She addressed Rolarn: "I'm guessing she's the leader, on style alone."

No one responded.

"Looks like regular human scum to me," the tall one said, predictably gruff.

"As opposed to the special kind?"

The Disco Killer said, more erudite despite her huskiness, "You're the oaf that recovered the Dispenser?"

"Wow. I've been called some nasty things in my time – *oaf* takes it."

"What do you think, Arnold?" The woman dipped a hand into her jacket, deliberating, and drew out a miniature hip flask. "Am I seriously gonna talk to a human?"

The tall one, Arnold, grumbled wordless dissent. They weren't off to a good start; even if Rolarn had saved her, they didn't seem too happy to see her. Pax said, "I'm told I'm easy to talk to. Just don't ask Leonard Holland. He's been bitter since I bluffed him out of a massive seven-card-stud pot. Makes it easy to keep beating him, if I'm honest."

"What's she talking about?" the woman asked.

"Playing cards," Rolarn said.

"*Why* is she talking about cards?"

"I tell you a bit about me," Pax said. "You tell me about you. You get comfortable enough to explain why we're gathered in an abandoned Debenhams."

The Fae all continued to stare.

"She's got a mouth," Rolarn concluded, "but she's co-operated so far."

"Thanks," Pax said. "So you people want to tell me who you are?"

The male Fae both looked to the Disco Killer, who took a long pull on her flask then put it back in its pocket. She stood and patted down her immaculate clothing, her body swaying at the hips with the fluidity of inebriation. If she was drunk, it didn't show in her voice. "She calls us *people*, that's a start." She pointed at the tall one. "He's Arnold. Chief of the Tupsom Trawlers, who you're probably familiar with. I'm Lightgate."

"Scourge of the Grit Plateau," Arnold added.

Pax stopped herself from questioning either fairy's ambiguous title. She indicated Rolarn. "And him?"

"He," Lightgate said, "is the owner of this fine home."

"Wonderful," Pax said. "So where's Letty?"

"You tell me," Lightgate said. "Aren't you like that?" She crossed her fingers. Her tone suggested she didn't entirely approve.

"We've found humans and fairies *can* get along, I guess."

Arnold tensed and Lightgate said, "Fairies, now. Not so civilised after all."

"The F-word's taboo?" Pax replied with surprise. Letty hadn't shown special exception to *fairy*, had she? But then, Letty showed exception to everything.

"How would you know," Lightgate sighed. "Human ignorance is immortal. But I figured it was worth a talk with *you*. First time for everything."

"I've talked before."

A hint of a smile teased Lightgate's mouth. Finally ready to engage. "Okay. Let's start with the Dispenser, then. A lot of Fae don't even believe it exists. How'd you get it?"

It sounded like an accusation. "I didn't. I came across the guy who did. The

MEE captured him. And they have your Dispenser, now. My turn? What's it to you?"

Lightgate held her gaze for a lingering moment. She shrugged, at last, with one shoulder going nearly to her cheek. "You know what it means to our people?"

"The opportunity to take back your home."

"That," Lightgate nodded, "and it'd piss off the Ordshaw MEE. You dislike them, don't you?"

"Your man just used a shotgun to get me free of them."

"Did you hurt anyone?" Lightgate turned this to Rolarn. He shook his head. "Why not?"

Rolarn held her gaze uncertainly, a chink in his armour as the question confused him.

"Never mind. Next time. Let me set the scene, human."

"Pax," Pax corrected.

The fairy echoed her in a mocking tone. "*Pax*. Ten years ago, most Fae were focused on taking back the Sunken City. Not just for a place to live, but a place to fight from. Then this humourless mare Valoria Magnus came in, preaching peace. Fae killed each other on her command. The worst of us were driven away, or faced death at the hands of her Stabilisers. Some peace, right?" Lightgate paused to let out a loud yawn, then shook her head as though trying to stay awake. She continued. "Friday night, I'm running diamonds in Hungary and I hear the FTC back in Ordshaw finally has serious human concerns again. There's a story about an MEE lummox doing something unspeakable to a Fae. Letty, no less; someone most Fae know about. For negative reasons. You're following me?"

Friday was when this had all begun for Pax, and she doubted there were many other women who'd had encounters with fairies that night. The unspeakable act had to be her pretending to eat Letty, to trick Cano Casaria. "How'd this story reach your people? You –"

"Those dullards are *not* my people," Lightgate cut in. "*I* was in Eger."

"Hungary? Smuggling diamonds?"

"It's good work," Lightgate confided. "But low-key. No setting anything off with a bang." She went quiet, reflecting on that, before finding her place again. "There was a sensationalist article on the internet, that's what reached me. The Fae remembering that the MEE are, and always have been, our enemies. At that point, I thought I might be forgiven for hurting you."

"Until," Pax ventured warily, "something told you I didn't do what they said I did?"

"Lucky for you." Lightgate gave an unconvincing smile. "Now, while I was travelling, the FTC was panicking, like old times. There was talk of relocating, in case your attack was just the start. Quite a response, right? The soft FTC, determined to sit on their arses indulging in" – Lightgate let out a fake yawn this time – "*peace*. After years of Val's drivel, they forgot we came from somewhere better. They forgot there was a time when we *fought* humans, instead of negotiating or running.

"But talk of a human *eating* a fairy –" Lightgate paused, something rising in her throat. She held up a hand for patience, the other hand over her mouth. Pax frowned, not sure if she was performing some sort of imitation, but the fairy swallowed and shuddered like a ghost ran through her. No, it was a drunken tremor or something. Lightgate continued like it hadn't happened, but took her hip flask back out. "Some people in the FTC had a wake-up call, at least. Started asking if it wasn't better to stand and fight. Some started questioning Valoria."

"Finally," Rolarn said, a touch angry.

"Yes." Lightgate pointed a finger back at him. "Fortunately, there's still exiles alive who *never* trusted her. When I made it back to Ordshaw, I found these good, honest men" – Pax noted the miserable faces that looked neither good nor honest – "itching for a plan. Alongside voices in the FTC who weren't happy, either. Things were looking very interesting. Until last night. Then, the Fae media say Letty is alive, shooting up human neighbourhoods after a deal gone bad."

"She was known for doing bad deals with humans," Arnold commented, as Pax imagined the Fae media. Tiny reporters in fedoras, punching at typewriters?

"But we've seen the results," Lightgate said, "with a tremor underground, and the berserker behaving strange. Like someone hurt it. The Fae media say it wasn't the Dispenser. They claim Letty lost a useless bit of Fae tech, not this fabled weapon of old."

"It *was* the Dispenser," Pax assured her. "I saw it."

Lightgate took another swig from her flask. "Val's persuaded everyone that the MEE aren't out to get them, that this weekend's fear was a big misunderstanding caused by Letty, up to her old tricks. An easier story to digest." Lightgate paused, looking at Pax's navel. "No pun intended."

Pax covered her stomach defensively with her hands. "But the Ministry took your weapon. And hurt Letty. Get the Dispenser back and you can prove Val's been lying."

Lightgate took one more swig from her flask, then beat her wings and flew off the counter. Pax drew her head back as the fairy came level with her face. Lightgate hovered from side to side, studying her, before grinning, a sinister expression in the limited light. "I had a feeling about you. With Letty causing havoc, reports of a psycho human, I knew I had to meet you. Maybe you're a human that could actually be useful, with ideas like that. That's *much* better."

"Why?" Pax frowned. "What was *your* idea?"

"Sigh…" Lightgate actually said the word. She exhaled loudly, making Pax's nostrils curl at the whiff of ethanol, potent even at this woman's size. "It required help from the FTC Council, but they've lost their bottle. There are weapons at their disposal, still, despite Val's promises to disarm them years ago. *This* situation was the perfect opportunity to use the turnbold."

"The what?" Pax vaguely recalled the name from Apothel's catalogue of hideous beasts. It was not something she'd studied or, she felt, encountered.

"The – turn – bold," Lightgate raised her voice, speaking slower, as though talking to an idiot. "Before Val took over, Fae scouts lured this beast under the

Ministry offices, ready to take them down at their source."

Pax stared dumbly back. "How? Fae can't move under the city without drawing the minotaur's horde to them, can they?"

Lightgate took another drink. "It cost a few brave lives. But it got forgotten because it was such a low-tech, basic idea. A simple bit of monster-baiting and some old-fashioned explosive charges under the building. The idea being to blow a passage through the floor, into their filthy offices, and this beast climbs up and decimates the Ministry." She pulled the corners of her mouth down. "Ministry gets unhappy. Understand?"

Pax's dumb stare hadn't left her. It sounded like the sort of bluntly destructive plan she'd come to expect from the Fae.

"It *was* audacious." Lightgate apparently read her thoughts. "But it went against the principle of fighting without being *seen* to be fighting. Ordshaw Fae always want to stay hidden. Even before Val took charge, it looked unlikely anyone would go through with it. When she started her peace talks it was totally dismissed. Except" – the fairy held up a triumphant finger – "while most of our weapons were dismantled, in this case, it would've cost Fae lives to remove the explosive charges. So they're still there. Ten years later. And the Council still has the codes to set them off."

Pax found herself shaking her head, "No – surely the Ministry –"

Lightgate pre-empted the question. "They don't know about the charges. The MEE know the turnbold's there, but not that we put it there. Having it settled under Greek Street is good for them. A turnbold can stay put for many years at a time, waiting for food to come to it, keeping the area quiet. But given what the Ministry's been up to, with this woman eating a Fae and the Dispenser locked up in their offices, I thought some of the Council might finally be persuaded to use those charge codes. Only now Val's worked her magic. Leaving" – Lightgate screwed a thumb back towards Arnold – "his boys to sneak back into the FTC and find those codes themselves. No small task."

Whatever a turnbold was, this plan sounded like a great way to kill a lot of innocent people. Rufaizu included. Lightgate seemed like a relatively reasonable, intelligent fairy, so Pax chose to be honest with her: "It lacks finesse."

"It's a wrecking ball." Arnold chose to answer this. "And when the Ministry retaliate, the FTC will see what Val's peace is worth."

Each word he said sounded angrier than the last. Lightgate grinned eerily at Pax, eager for her response. Clearly Pax had come at the right time to defuse this. "Do you guys still believe in the Sunken City? Settling back down there?"

"That comes with time," Rolarn said.

"It's something the FTC have forgotten," Arnold grumbled. "They call themselves Fae, they've got no right."

"Yeah," Pax said carefully. "But convincing your people humans are dangerous, and removing Val, doesn't get you the Sunken City back. Listen, I want rid of those monsters. I want the Ministry to back off. But random monster attacks are only going to make things worse. There's people in that building with answers.

And the Dispenser is in there, too. You want to hear my take?"

"Yeah," Lightgate said. "I do."

Pax took a breath, not sure what she was going to say but sure she had to come up with something. She couldn't exactly promise them the Dispenser, but it went hand-in-hand with getting Rufaizu back from the Ministry. She was about to say so when Rimes' phone chimed in her pocket, a high-pitched note that rose and fell before tinkling into something like a Japanese folk song.

Pax took out the phone as the fairies watched. The telegraph station's number was on the screen. "Sorry – I've got to take this."

"Pax?" Holly's voice, anxious. "I couldn't get through –"

"Can I call you back?" Pax said, not wanting to leave the Fae with any doubt about the madness of their plan. "I just need to –"

"You were right. How did you know?"

Pax's stomach lifted in concern. "About what?"

"A train crash. Well. Technically *two* train crashes. Four dead and at least twenty injured. So far. It's the same thing, isn't it? That monster down there, it did this?"

Pax couldn't speak, though she knew the answer. She'd experienced it, face-to-face with the blue screen. It had communicated it to her as it launched its assault. Possibly done it *because* of her?

Meeting Lightgate's eyes, looking for someone, anyone, to share the horror with, Pax knew more than ever that she had to get a handle on this. Her own body was being affected, and she was surrounded by war-mongering fairies. Whatever had happened, she had to cut through this bullshit.

17

Bristol Street station was barely visible through the thicket of smoke and the foggy lenses of Sam's gas mask, the concrete pillars like sentinels in the torchlight. The volume of her filtered breathing partially blocked out the sounds of panic. When a shape shot out of the smoke, Sam jumped with a cry. Landon put a hand out, either to stop her or reassure her, as a fireman passed with a civilian draped over his shoulder.

As the rescuer faded back into the smoke, Sam watched Landon continuing, his hand on the pistol under his jacket. There was nothing down there, the preliminary scans had already shown that. The myriad creatures never crossed into the Underground stations; it was like there was something in the walls of the Sunken City that confined them to its corridors. But then, the Fae were supposed to leave people alone and the *praelucente* wasn't supposed to cause earthquakes. Everyone in the Ministry knew that: as it moved across the city, it caused residual fatigue in the Underground and in the city above, while also inspiring certain positive results. That was all. Otherwise, it roamed under Ordshaw without impact. But Pax had called that analysis ignorant.

Something is using that energy, Pax had said. *Moving it.*

Did the *praelucente* hide a threat the Ministry didn't understand? These surges suggested so, even if they had somehow been caused by Pax and her cohorts. Such a secret would make it a ticking bomb.

Passing into an open space, Landon waved a hand in an attempt to clear the smoke. It did nothing. Sam followed a trail of bloodstains with her torch. Cracked tiles. Shattered glass. Then the twisted, ghastly mess of the crumpled train. The shapes of a handful of firefighters moved around the wreckage.

Landon nudged Sam and pointed to the side. Down the platform, away from the action. He continued without looking back, and she forced herself to do the same. Glass crunched under her shoes. Probably shredding the soles of her flats, which were not suited to this. Like her.

At the end of the platform, the train carriage had risen off the track and wedged itself against the broken wall. Landon crouched and shone his torch through a gap.

"You're not going down there?" Sam asked, which came out as a plastic mumble.

Landon nodded, then lowered himself onto the floor and wriggled through the hole. Sam came to his side, looking back to the firefighters. Did none of them care that some suited fat man was scrambling under the unstable ruins of this disaster? Apparently not.

When she turned back, he was gone. Sam stared with concern. Should she follow? His hand shot back out and Sam jumped. The palm was flat. Telling her to stay put. She nodded, as if he could see it.

As he made his way into an abyss, Sam watched two figures exiting the train, the limp form of a body draped between them. Small, frail, head lolling. An old woman? Sam wanted to look away but couldn't. They all evaporated into the smoke.

This was all wrong. None of the Ministry's spreadsheets extolling the cost-benefit analysis of the *praelucente* factored in people dying. Not like this. Working in the office, Sam had distanced herself from the possibility that her organisation was shadily silencing serious security breaches, but assumed that meant dealing with opportunists who couldn't be persuaded to keep quiet for the greater good. These were unassuming innocents.

Sam closed her eyes. Why did she come down here? She was *right* to keep her distance from all this. Objectively, the figures would still make sense. If someone had meddled with the brakes of these trains, it would be no different: you wouldn't blame the trains for moving too fast, you'd still support the concept of the Underground. The Sunken City was no different. Casualties happened.

Something groaned in the middle distance and she opened her eyes again.

Another noise, a whisper behind the chaos.

Will you say it to me. Like it means something, like it can help make sense of this. Make it more than just an excuse to get out of the office. Grugulochs.

Whatever it was, the groan was rendered inaudible by the painful creak of metal being forcibly separated.

Their lights flashing over Letty's face, the ambulances and fire trucks started to leave. The injured and the terrified had mostly been removed. That just left gawking bystanders, some police around the perimeter and a smattering of journalists. A bunch of Ministry shills deflected questions from all of them. Letty listened in on numbers of dead and injured, and accusations against the rail company, the station manager and the city council.

The berserker had sucked out everything some of these saps had, Letty could see it in the colour of their skin. Like faded denim. She heard a Ministry goon whisper, "That was no heart attack."

The monster was preying, hard enough to wreck a train or two. Maybe it felt bitter about Pax getting away. Maybe she'd given it a taste for more direct feeding.

"It's as I'd expect." Landon's voice. Letty watched from a building's moulding as he strode out with the square lady. "Nothing crossed into the station, so the train must've been affected before arriving. My guess, the driver lost his senses."

"You didn't hear anything?" the woman asked.

"Not your area, is it? All this, I mean."

The square turned on him, eyes level with his chest. "My area is wherever I'm needed. I want to know whatever sounds have been reported."

Landon didn't look impressed, probably aware that the only way she could threaten him was if she jumped and rammed her head into his chin. "Protocol is to limit discussion. Discourage any thoughts of what these people might've seen or heard."

"You don't think that might stop us from doing our job?"

"We've got rules for a reason."

That aggravated the woman. "Yeah. So you don't have to use any initiative."

Landon paced up to her, a nerve touched, too. "You hang on a second. I do plenty for this city. For this country."

She stared for an uncertain beat, then plucked up the courage to puff up her little chest and say, "I'm sure you do. You just don't think for yourself."

"You know, for all the stink you made about him, you sure sound like Casaria."

Her face was aghast. "Exactly what do you mean by that?"

"You think it's any wonder they keep your hands tied when you keep stirring the pot? You'd give the game away, have these people cementing ideas of what they've seen. To say nothing of what you'd do talking to the Fae, whatever."

"What about doing a good job?" she said, voice getting loud and surprising herself. She lowered it again, overcompensating. "Opening more liberal communications channels with the Fae has always been the right move. Figuring out what these people saw and heard is the right move. Especially when it's written on Apothel's wall."

Letty cocked her head. A *clue*?

Landon looked away to grumble something, the coward.

"What's that?"

"You don't know what you're doing. You want to risk repeating this word all over the place. The last thing we need's the media picking up on a pattern."

"The pattern's already here, with things erupting underground! I need to know what that word, or sound, means – what Pax *wants* and *knows*, what Casaria saw, why he's missing – I need you to help me, Landon!"

"We ought to get back to the office –"

"Don't! Take a moment, please."

Landon bunched up his mouth like he'd just smelt shit.

"Think. This noise, this word, it could explain something about the *praelucente* itself, and that'd explain their plans, and this threat. Where do we go with that?"

"Back to the office," Landon said. The woman was about to throw her knickers at him, but he held up a chunky hand. "You're desperate to talk, try the kid."

The lady stared at him, blank.

"Rufaizu."

"He's not talking, is he?"

"He spoke to Casaria, yesterday. Before everything got turned upside down."

She looked stunned again. "Has anyone else spoken to him?"

Landon shrugged.

"I don't know if I should be shocked or pleased. Thank you." The woman lifted a hand to pat him encouragingly on the chest but didn't quite make it, seeming to remember they weren't that close.

Letty watched them climb in the car. She'd love to sit in on that conversation, but there was no way she was getting near the Ministry offices. And she had pretty well confirmed no one had caught up to Pax, not with this distraction and no better mention of her. Time to head back to Broadplain.

18

"Seven humans dead, now," Lightgate reported, poring over her phone as she paced around near Pax's feet. "Probably more by the time they're done."

Her back against a pillar, sat on the floor, Pax had the same thoughts looping in her own head. *I'm connected to it. I can't be connected to it. I'm sick. I'm tired. This has to stop.* She looked at her hands hanging over her knees, not sure if she could trust her own flesh. Did it work the other way, could the minotaur sense where she was? Worst of all, did she *cause* this?

"Why," Lightgate said, "are you so upset?" Pax frowned at her. The flamboyant drunk spread her arms in a questioning manner. "Excuse me, human? Are you unwell?"

"No," Pax said. "I ran into your berserker last night, it's . . ." She stalled. The Fae hated the creatures of the Sunken City. She couldn't explain to them that she might have formed a bond with the biggest, baddest thing down there. "The Dispenser made the minotaur unstable. That makes this my fault. I can't take a moment over that?"

"I'd rather you didn't," Lightgate answered candidly. "I came back for a Fae-eating monster, or a human sticking it to the Ministry. Doing away with one of them, even. *Yes.*" She shook her head. "But this? Total lack of enthusiasm for the turnbold idea, legs going to jelly at the thought of humans dead? You're a bit . . ." Lightgate searched for the best word. "Sad?"

Pax opened her mouth to rebut her but paused, realising what Lightgate had just said. "*Doing away with one of them?* What are you talking about?"

"You thought we didn't know about Casaria? Tell me he's dead, please, I'm starting to think we gave you too much credit."

Pax shook her head, slowly, unable to blink. She'd last seen Cano Casaria watching her in angry confusion, face painted with blood, as they made a getaway in his colleague's stolen car. Sam Ward had said he was missing; Pax had barely had a chance to consider his fate since then. She shifted forward, sliding a knee under her. "You know what happened to him?"

Lightgate looked to Arnold on the counter, who stayed quiet. When she turned back, she shared Pax's confusion. "You got rid of him?"

"I haven't done shit! Bloody hell, what else has your Fae media been saying?"

"Not the media," Arnold said. "We saw it ourselves."

Lightgate explained. "Arnold's men checked his place, thinking to pick him up when he got clear of the security. Another angle we were testing. He was gone, the place had been turned over."

"The Ministry –" Pax started.

"Not their style. They like things neat and tidy."

"Other Fae?"

"I would know about it," Lightgate said. "It had to be you."

"Do I look like some sort of vengeful thug?" Pax said. Lightgate gave the question a little too much thought. With her loose clothing and arguably masculine occupation, Pax was used to certain assumptions, but this was an extreme. "How would I even do something like that?"

"I did my homework," Lightgate said. "Some FTC drones paid a visit to your place yesterday, when they were looking to recover the tech Letty lost. They found security footage of what happened. The sort of friends you keep."

Pax's eyes widened. They were talking about Bees. The thinly-veiled criminal she enjoyed cards and conversation with, who she'd tasked with recovering the Dispenser from her apartment. But Casaria got it first; he'd turned up with it in the Sunken City. Had their paths crossed? Bees had been heavily suspicious of the MEE, without much concrete knowledge about them. If he had discovered the identity of one of their agents, would he have followed it up?

"Ah," Lightgate said. "You didn't even know you'd done it?"

"Wait." Pax held up a hand, wanting this to slow down. Stop, if possible. Bees and his cronies might have followed Casaria, but they wouldn't touch him, would they? They kept a low profile, and crossing the government was as far from discretion as you could get. But Bees put a premium on information, and his employer, Mr Monroe, was eager to learn about the tunnels. She hadn't established exactly why, but they most likely wanted to smuggle or store contraband under the city. Had they cut her out and gone to a Ministry source? If so . . . Pax concluded out loud, "If it's them, those men wouldn't have killed him. They'd want to learn as much from him as they could."

"And kill him after?"

"I don't know. You didn't track them down?"

"It wasn't a priority. But it's not rocket science." Lightgate touched a hand mournfully to her hip flask. "This is a massive bust, isn't it? You're not who I thought *at all*."

"Hey," Pax said, firmly. "I might not be a murderer or a thug, but I *can* disrupt this. If Casaria's with those men, I can get him back. I can get him onside, he can help."

"Come on. Casaria is known to the Fae. He's everything that's wrong with the MEE."

"Listen." Pax shifted closer to the fairy. Lightgate took flight, a metre back by the time Pax realised she'd startled her. Pax froze, aware that Rolarn's gun was aimed at her head. "Sorry. I didn't mean to –"

"Watch yourself, human," Arnold rumbled from the counter. Lightgate had one hand on a pistol but hadn't drawn it.

"Sorry," Pax repeated. "I wasn't thinking." But she saw a chance to respond to Lightgate's doubts. "Sitting up doesn't normally threaten anyone."

Lightgate's slight smirk returned. "Careful. You're a big target."

Pax held her gaze, and decided it best to move past the playful threat. "Casaria. He came into the Sunken City and set off your Dispenser – him, of all people. He did it for me." *And I fucked him over.* Never mind. "If my friends have him, then I can get him back. We can use him to get into the Ministry. Get Rufaizu and your Dispenser out of there, without any explosives or turnbolds. That'd be enough to cast doubt on Val, wouldn't it? You could get the FTC listening without sparking a war."

Lightgate was unmoved. "What about crippling the Ministry?"

"Rufaizu knows things. Casaria, too. You can damage the minotaur and take back the Sunken City – that's a blow to them, you said that yourself. Meanwhile, I can figure out the force *behind* the minotaur. Something Apothel called the Blue Angel, it's pulling strings none of us knows about. You keep the Fae and the Ministry off my back and I can blow this puzzle wide open. It's safe here, right?"

Lightgate looked up to Rolarn and he answered plainly, "There's tech in these walls that'll keep the Ministry from finding us. But I'm not running a hotel, definitely not for humans."

"Be nice," Lightgate said. "It's one human, you've got space."

"No, not just me," Pax said. "There's others that need protection too."

This piqued Lightgate's interest. "What others?"

"Darren Barton, his –"

"Citizen Barton." Lightgate said the name with wonder. "His wife, that kid – *they* got mixed up in the fighting yesterday?"

"You know them?"

"Of course." Lightgate smiled. "All the FTC know about Citizen Barton and the Apothel Five. Or at least they used to. The stories we had. The Slippery Stone, the – what was it?" She clicked a finger at Arnold. "That story about the sickle?"

"The Apothel Five and the Sliding Stone," Arnold corrected, his voice losing its hostile edge for the first time. He recited what sounded like poetry: "Two score beast clashed in the pen, Amongst them stood five humen. Be they fang or be they claw, Aren't they all of . . . of . . ."

"The same fucking thing," Rolarn finished, impatiently.

"There's no way that was the rhyme," Pax commented.

"There were lots of these stories," Lightgate said. "Bloody, gruesome adventures, with essentially the same moral."

"Peepy-tales?"

Lightgate paused, looking a little impressed. "Similar. These stories said there were humans in the Sunken City as violent and dangerous as the monsters."

"Clearly you've never met Darren Barton," Pax said, picturing that gentle giant of a man.

"No," Lightgate said. "I would like to. Bring everyone here, we can defend them." Rolarn made an irritated noise, but Lightgate shot him a look and he kept quiet. "And Casaria. If you can charm him, I'd like to see that, too." She actually sounded enthusiastic. "I *knew* it was a good idea to come back."

Pax felt herself smile. "And you can call off this turnbold plan?"

"It's going nowhere anyway." Lightgate fluttered into the air. "This calls for a drink." Flying over to the counter, she said, "Lighten up, Arnold, she's only human."

"Pax!" A voice came from the floor above.

Lightgate spun back, hands on her pistols.

"Pax, you'd better fucking be here!" Letty's voice got closer, descending the escalator gap. "Tell me you got her, Rolarn, you doughboy fuck!"

"Perfect." Lightgate's hands relaxed off her guns.

Pax's heart lifted as her tiny friend flew into the middle of the room with the whir of her artificial wing going into overdrive. Letty glowered at Rolarn. "You can't answer your fucking phone?"

As Pax climbed to her feet, Lightgate drifted through the light of the lantern.

Letty stopped dead in the air. "Lightgate?"

Lightgate spread a hand to one side and gave a wonky curtsy.

"Fuck." Letty took a breath. She shot Pax a worried look, then shot an accusing one at Rolarn. Pax offered a light wave and an awkward smile.

"Good to see you, too, Letty," Lightgate said. "It's been a while."

19

"I can *not* believe you," Letty hissed, as they approached the scooter in the dark of the car park. "Talking to any old Fae now? Making deals with lunatics? Promising shit we all know would be best avoided."

Pax hadn't been aware how tense meeting the new Fae had left her, but Letty's admonishing tone made the stress nice and clear. It was a relief to close the conversation with Lightgate and her ominous minions onside, though Pax wasn't sure she wanted the drunkard along on her search for Casaria. At least she had a moment alone with Letty while Lightgate instructed her minions, though.

"We've got a way forward," Pax said. "You didn't hear *their* plan."

"Did it involve brutally killing everyone?"

Pax paused. "Pretty much, yeah."

"You don't have any idea who they are, do you?"

"Sure I do," Pax said. "That was the magnificent Lightgate. So called because she walks softly?"

"What's that supposed to mean?" Letty spat.

"Light" – Pax enunciated more clearly – "gait. The way she walks?"

Letty looked ready to bite her eyes out, not in the mood. "She's a nasty piece of work."

"Uh-huh," Pax said. "Scourge of the Gritty Plain, I heard."

"The Grit Plateau, you arsehole. And Arnold, from the shit-sack Trawlers, he's the head rat in a pack of them. Him and Rolarn are dangerous on their own, but put *Lightgate* in charge . . . by the manes of lizards, you're lucky they know me – I can't believe they talked to you."

"You see how well she's dressed? How bad can she be?"

"Very bad, alright?" Letty snapped. She landed on the bike between Pax's hands, making Pax shift out of the way. "And you're talking about Casaria like you're old pals. Your instincts were right when you left him in the lurch. You want to know what happens when you bust him free? If he's even alive? He hauls your arse in, that's what."

Whether he helped them or not wasn't even the issue, was it? Pax couldn't leave him in whatever hellish situation she'd put him in. And that aside, getting him back *was* a way forward, which was better than brooding. "If I rescue him from gangsters, he'll jump back on Team Pax."

"And you know what they say about *ifs* and *buts* and ducks and sluts."

Pax frowned. "No. What do they say?"

Letty gave her an unappreciative look. "It amounts to *don't be a fucking idiot*."

"Okay. One" – Pax held up a finger – "that sounds like a saying I need to know in full. Two" – another finger – "he's already screwed the Ministry once, so there's hope." As long as this didn't get her killed. "Bad things have been stacking up today, Letty. If I can do something good by the day's out, I have to do it. And whoever these Fae are, they're with us, aren't they? That feels like a win to me. I need a damn win."

"Whoever they are?" Letty gave a humourless laugh. "Lightgate should've been executed decades ago. Would've been, if anyone had the balls to go after her."

Pax was familiar with other well-spoken, deadly people, but it was particularly hard to take the threat of that tiny, finely-dressed woman seriously. And it was clear they weren't running from these apparently dangerous Fae. "But you're still mates, right?"

"She doesn't *have* mates." That sounded familiar.

"Associates?"

Letty finally slowed down. "Look, she'll do what she says – and she's definitely someone you want on *your* side – but she's wired funny. Last I saw her must've been six years ago. She made fleeting visits into Ordshaw after she was cast out. We helped her clear out a human shed, in Hanton. A good little shack for a hideout. Me and my boys, and her, we scared off some human kids, got them convinced it was haunted, so they'd sooner kiss a clown than go back in there. She paid us off with a heap of dust. Then she set fire to the fucking shed."

"O-kay…" Pax drew out the word. "I'll admit that's troubling."

"That's *nothing*. That's the shit she gets up to during peacetime. The things she did during the coup – the things she was responsible for. Landed on both sides of the conflict, day to day. Lot of Fae dead, Pax. And you've promised to fuck up the Ministry for her? You'd better deliver."

"Well," Pax said, "we're not going to fuck them up. We're going to get Rufaizu back, and she can have the Dispenser, and they can raise questions about your leader without anyone getting hurt. We have to do it this way – *our* way."

Letty groaned and rubbed her face, clearly still stressed at having found Pax with them.

"I'm sorry," Pax said. "I would've run a mile if I'd known they were trouble. And, you know, if I was capable of running a mile. But I thought it went well . . . and we *need* them onside, not just for our own sake. To stop them doing something else. She set fire to this shed after paying you, didn't she? And this war of yours . . . you must've forgiven her that, working with her since?"

Letty offered a vacant look, delving back into that memory. "No one stayed innocent, back then. But she was so *good* at it." She took a deep breath, trying to let it go. "It was a long time ago. They *can* help us, now. But you didn't know that. I don't like going to any of them. They're all fucking rogues."

"Like you."

Letty gave that a second. "Worse than me."

"Rolarn saved me. Even if he looks like he would drown puppies."

"I just don't want you going the way of Apothel."

"You and me both," Pax said, checking back across the garage. No sign of Lightgate yet.

"And that was a great idea with the fucking chapel, by the way. Next time remind me to be more forceful in telling you *no*."

"I got something, though," Pax said. "There was a blue screen in the basement."

"Frozen donkeys!" Letty spun back. "You went in?"

"Not by choice. It *was* too high to jump."

"What happened?"

"This Blue Angel gave me an address. Chaucer Crescent. Then it figured I was bad news and spewed out some ungodly slug monster that tried to acid me. If Rolarn hadn't shown up, I would've been melted."

"Chaucer Crescent and a slug monster. Fantastic."

"We're wading through the same shit that dragged Apothel down, aren't we?"

Letty considered it. "This is way worse than the shit he stirred. You heard what happened? Across town?"

Pax nodded. More than heard it, she wanted to say. But her jaw stayed shut.

"It's fucked," Letty said. "I went and *saw* it. The Ministry don't know what the fuck they're doing. I heard that Ministry bitch talking, though. Might be something in that. She had ideas about that word, grugulochs. Reckoned the berserker's making noises while it goes apeshit. Reckoned that's the name of the berserker itself." Letty put her fists to her hips, proud at her reconnaissance. Pax smiled. Apparently it wasn't convincing, as Letty snapped, "Well it's better than Chaucer fucking Crescent."

"No, it's good," Pax said. "Apothel was onto something when he was killed, why else leave that word behind? Think he got close to understanding the minotaur? The Blue Angel?"

"Grugulochs. Commander of the blue screens."

"Galactic warlord."

"Apothel through and through," Letty said. "The names he came up with. The clutterbattem, you know how he figured that? Only ever saw them in areas *cluttered* by debris, *battering* things about. He'd be made up knowing people used his stupid terms, Ministry included. Tuckles, sickles, all him."

"But 'grugulochs' comes from the sound?"

"He named the glogockle that way."

"The minotaur never made a sound when I saw it." Pax recalled the snaking, twirling limbs of the electric beast. It had floated down the tunnels after her. It had surged through her, pinning her in place, tearing chunks from the brickwork of the Sunken City. It had snapped against the walls with whip-cracks of lightning, but it had never growled. "I'm not sure it's a creature at all. I didn't see anything resembling a mouth."

"Maybe that shot from the Dispenser gave it a voice."

Pax paused. "Then when did Apothel hear it?"

"There you go needling again," Letty huffed. "Maybe it's not the berserker — maybe it's a fucking safe word that gets all this to stop when you say it twirling in a pink tutu. Point is we have *something*. You have to pick at the details till our ears bleed?"

"Yeah. You're right. It's a start."

"You're still here?" Lightgate interrupted, gliding towards them. She stopped in an action pose, one elbow and one knee cocked. Oozing style despite a slight drunken waver. "I've refuelled and given Arnold a dozen places to be. *You* should be halfway across town by now."

"We were waiting for you," Pax said, and opened the scooter's seat to start assembling her helmet and goggles disguise. Aware that the Fae were regarding her clothing with distaste, she tried to show some appreciation for fashion: "Who tailors your suits?"

"This?" Lightgate held out her arms and turned them over, like the jacket was some old rag she'd forgotten she owned. "Guy in Japan, goes by K-Zero. Want me to put in a word?"

"Fetid lizards," Letty snorted, "get a room. We've got a Ministry psycho to save."

Pax murmured agreement, her focus shifting back to Casaria and the path ahead, which ended in Bees' undesirable neck of the woods. Having Letty and Lightgate for backup was small comfort. For the moment, concentrating on having a finely tailored suit to call her own helped. She wondered whether K-Zero was human or Fae. As she considered it, her stomach rumbled. That was another distraction, to put off the danger they were wading into. She said, "I've gotta eat before we get there."

"Don't look at me," Lightgate chided. "You wouldn't like how I taste."

There was a sound like a hammer hitting an anvil. Agony seared through his head, bouncing from one temple to the other. He blinked to clear his vision, but it didn't help.

The hammer again, increasing the throb of his headache. He gritted his teeth and threw himself back in the chair. Arms and legs held fast, chair itself fixed in place, couldn't move any more than to twist from side to side. A few metres' space on either side, and ahead. No windows, only chipped grey brickwork. A little light came through a hole in the wall, near the ceiling.

The place stank like rust on a hob, making his nostrils curl. From the itch under his nose and the sting around his eyes, he guessed the smell actually came from him.

Another hammer blast, metal on metal.

He pulled at his restraints, first with his wrists then with his legs. A sharp pain stung his foot. A scream came out that sounded too high, too girly, to be his. But his eyes were watering, and he was the one hurting. And that was his foot, bound in a sodden bandage, black at the point of the toe where he'd bled the most.

Tears streamed down his cheeks as he clenched his jaw against the pain.

The hammering stopped. They'd heard him.

He sniffed, hard, as his face leaked more weak, pitiful fluids.

This was nothing, he told himself. Just the body betraying him. False signals, indicators of pain that didn't really matter. Nothing to fear, nothing really at all.

He forced himself to smile. Nothing at all. Enjoyable, if you let it be.

Something squeaked behind him, the hinges of an old, heavy door. Footsteps thumped into the room. The slow, low voice of the animal that had brought him here. Dry, emotionless. "Ready for more?"

He started laughing, head bowing forward, and as his body shook pain shot through him again. He flinched and shifted his foot. The bad foot. It produced another agonised shriek. But he was still laughing, louder, manic. No way anyone's gonna know the difference, a scream or a laugh.

Between his wheezing chuckles and behind his tears, he heard the goon say, "Fuck's sake, this again."

20

Sam Ward watched the artificial lung working alongside Rufaizu. In the two days since he'd been interred in the Greek Street med bay, no one had done much to make the young man clean or comfortable. His bright turquoise coat was draped over a chair, darkened by patches of blood, but there was no sign of his other clothes or possessions. He lay in a beige hospital smock, restrained by thick leather straps at his wrists and ankles, with two tubes sticking out of his arm, one connected to a drip, the other running into the machine. She had no idea what it was doing; certainly not pumping air into him. The lung moved with a clattering, unsteady noise that suggested, along with the tarnished bed frame and the scuffed seat of the chair, that the MEE's medical facilities needed updating.

Whatever the case, Landon had been mistaken. The young man was very much unconscious, and hadn't responded to her various attempts to stir him. She'd opened an eyelid and found his eye rolled back in his head. Casaria was the only one who had talked to their most valuable lead. Maybe the only one who'd seen the boy awake. That was probably his intention, from the haphazard way that Casaria had reeled the boy in, holding off bringing him here to enact his own personal investigation. It wasn't clear exactly what was wrong with Rufaizu now, other than the patched-up bullet wound on his neck, and Dr Hertz wasn't around to ask. No surprise there; with dusk setting in, most of the Ministry staff had left the building, patting themselves on the back for a good day's work. A member of Support's night team would drop in on Rufaizu every few hours, with alerts for emergencies wired to a computer upstairs.

The latest incident was in hand, with the media briefed and all casualties accounted for. Support had tracked the *praelucente* towards the southwestern districts of Ordshaw, most likely under Nothicker, where building fires and accidents were a part of everyday life. As Nothicker was unlikely to make the news, everyone could go home. They'd received a fax from Lord Asquith on the Raleigh Commission, congratulating the office on a good day's work: *Back to normal tomorrow, the world stops caring overnight!* Something about his communication encapsulated everything that was wrong with the Ministry. The affirmation of an out-of-touch pencil-pusher, a generation removed from reality with his bloody printed messages. Never mind his actual message, in what world did he find a fax better than their countless other options? Near as Sam was aware, it was just a slower email that required printing. Of course, he was afraid of change. Doing things the way they'd always been done, the same mentality that got people going home when the bell went.

If I was in charge of this office, Sam told herself, everyone would've been in on

Saturday morning and no one would've gone home yet. If she could live without bad dates and learning about marine life in South America, they could live without their pubs and reality TV shows. The monsters would be fully monitored, her questions answered, and this boy would have medical care 24/7. At the very least the supervising doctor – their *only* doctor – would leave a chart by the bed detailing exactly what the problem was. The W4-MS filed in the weekend's reports said Rufaizu had been shot and placed under guard, but the details were scant and written in what looked like purposefully obtuse handwriting.

That was another thing: all handwritten reports should be legible.

The door opened and Landon entered, holding two disposable cups, their contents steaming. Sam caught the scent of chocolate from the murky brown liquid he offered her. His, she noted, was black, strong coffee.

"Thanks, but I don't drink milk," Sam said, taking the cup anyway.

"It's done with water," he said. Sam didn't bother explaining the concept of powdered drinks. It was a nice enough gesture, and they'd enjoyed at least an amicable kind of silence since Bristol Street station. She regretted raising her voice at him, but it must have made an impression, as he'd made no more fuss.

"Shouldn't you be heading home?" Sam asked.

"Got a shift starting in twenty minutes," Landon said. "Might as well slog through."

"But you've been in all day?"

He shrugged. Perhaps his disengaged style used so little energy it could be sustained indefinitely. "You need a ride home?"

"No. I'm not happy with where we've got to."

"Plenty of avenues to try tomorrow."

"And this evening. I intend to search our files for a reference to this grugulochs. To see what was written about the Ripton Chapel. Maybe look deeper into Pax Kuranes' known contacts. Who's on the Support night shift? I want to ask about Pax's question, too, about where the energy goes."

Landon had an almost sympathetic look on his face.

"You honestly don't see why it's useful?" she said.

Landon was ready to move on. "Word is," he said, pointing his cup towards Rufaizu, "he's been out since yesterday. Operations have been waiting for Hertz to declare the kid stable before anyone questioned him."

"How bad can it be?" Sam said. "A Fae bullet surely doesn't leave that much damage. How can he lie half awake for two days then slip into a coma?"

"I don't think it's a coma," Landon said. He indicated the drip. "He's sleeping."

Rufaizu was certainly in something deeper than sleep, but she'd assumed that bag was feeding him vital nutrients. "They've drugged him?"

"Not unusual. We're not running a hospital, or a prison. You get someone difficult, it's easier that way, till we can decide what to do with them. Chances are Casaria's interview got him agitated and made it more necessary."

"Can we disable it?" Sam said. "Wake him up?"

"Without a signed AO-31, no. You'd need director-level clearance for that, to override the doctor's orders."

"Then let's get Dr Hertz on the phone."

"I tried. Three times."

Sam gave Landon a surprised look. It wasn't good news, but at least he was trying.

She studied Rufaizu again. What a life he must have led, hiding so effectively that their organisation had believed him dead. He was so young, not meant for the abuses of someone like Casaria, or the Sunken City. It was dumb luck that he'd been picked up by Casaria rather than someone more professional. Could they have avoided this if her search plan had been implemented properly? Sam said, "How exactly *did* Casaria find him?"

"Only way Casaria ever does anything effective. Coincidence. Rufaizu frequented the sort of dives Casaria ducks into himself."

"It wasn't Operations following my guidelines? Checking Apothel's old haunts?"

Landon gave her a look that said he had no idea what she was talking about, so that was a no. But Casaria didn't get things done by coincidence, Sam knew that. He got things done by forcing them. Ignoring the rules. In this case, maybe he had taken her plans on board, even if the rest of the team hadn't. Sometimes, uneasy as it made Sam to admit it, his ways worked. What choice did you have in an office that made you fill in forms to open a door? There was a reason Casaria was the only person to speak to Rufaizu. The same reason he'd got close to Pax Kuranes and whatever she was involved in. Maybe the same reason he was stuck in a low-end position all his life, too. Never mind.

Sam said, "Are the sedatives monitored? Would it raise alarms if we cut them for a few hours?"

Landon's face fixed in discomfort, but he said, "It's a bag of liquid – you could drain a bit in the sink if you wanted the levels to read right."

He'd surprised her again, and it made Sam smile. "And the machine?"

"Measuring novisan. Kind of."

Sam arched an eyebrow, unaware that it was possible to directly measure the strange energy in people. Though Landon's *kind of* suggested it wasn't.

"It won't be affected by removing the drip," he added.

"Show me how."

Landon did so without question or pomp, waddling to the drip and disabling it at a tap in the middle. He disconnected the cable, slid a bedpan out from under the bed and left the tube hanging in, liquid oozing out. He paused a moment, studying his work, then walked to a small unit of drawers and searched for something. He came back with another bag of clear liquid, which he hooked up alongside the original, and plugged this into Rufaizu's arm. "To keep him hydrated. I'd give him a few hours, at least. But that'll do it." Landon nodded satisfaction, then said, "Got something for you to look at in the meantime. Upstairs."

She gestured for him to lead the way, and gave the sleeping youth one last look before following Landon out into the corridor. She glanced over her shoulder, in case anyone was watching, feeling naughty.

"There's been no signal on Barton's phone," Landon said, as they continued towards the stairs. "Support's done limited checks into surveillance footage for the Bartons and my car, but they hardly had the manpower for it. It's just Roper on it this evening."

Roper. Sam pictured him; usually found in the hours when the more competent workers had clocked off. He was pushing retirement age, always wore woollen tank tops and made coffee at a snail's pace.

They climbed the stairwell to the sixth floor, the main office. The lights were dim, desk lamps glowing where Roper and a younger analyst were working, two aisles apart. They were staring into their screens like zombies. Sam asked Landon, "Has Mathers left specific orders for the overnight search?"

"Watch the figures, that's all."

"And you're going back out on patrol?"

"Not right away. I've got a waterway sighting to follow up on, but that can wait. Here, what I thought you might be interested in. We recovered this from Ms Kuranes' apartment when we got hold of the Fae weapon." Landon guided her to one of the side-desks, where a massive leather-bound book lay, an ancient tome like something out of a centuries-old monastery. Its title was viciously scratched into the front.

Apothel's Miscellany.

"We're in luck," Landon said, opening it and tapping a piece of paper inside. Crumpled but white, much newer than the book. There were lots of similar leaves sticking out. "Seems Ms Kuranes did a job of translating it."

"All of it?"

"A fair chunk."

Sam turned a few pages, glancing from cryptic symbols and sketches of savage monsters to the rounded lettering of Pax. The existence of this book had been rumoured for years, but, like the Fae's Dispenser, no one thought it had survived Apothel. The state of the chapel suggested he would have destroyed it, in his descent. She'd ignored it in Casaria's reports herself, and a quick scan reminded her why. Between the things they knew to be true, such as the sickles and the wormbirds, were creatures of pure invention and wildly inventive maps with no resemblance to the world the Ministry had charted.

"Until the boy wakes up," Landon said, "I figured this might be useful."

"Has it been analysed?"

"No one's had time."

Sam settled on a drawing that had to represent what Apothel believed about the *praelucente.* It showed a trainload of commuters, their souls being sucked out of their bodies, with the margin notes labelling it as the *minotaur's grasp.* And the title, in large symbols, was paired with Pax's handwritten translation.

Grugulochs.

That same word, written on the chapel, and heard, in some form, by Malcolm Joseph that morning. The Ministry were wrong to discount Apothel and those connected to his legacy. Sam called out across the room, "Roper? Are you busy?"

The old man was startled, as if he'd not realised there was anyone else there. The night staff were typically engrossed in piecing together the various energy readings that could indirectly measure the more mysterious force of novisan; they didn't often need to interact with real people.

"I need you to look into the novisan levels across the city," Sam instructed. "See if there's any suggestion that the levels don't merely decrease with the *praelucente's* surge, if they change elsewhere at the same time. Agent Landon, I'd like very much if you'd find –"

"Excuse me," Roper responded, turning quizzically in his chair. "Who are you?"

Sam paused in disbelief.

"Damn it, Roper," Landon grumbled, "you don't know the Head of IS? She's our ranking officer right now. And she just gave you a damn order."

Sam felt her cheeks flushing. This was it, then, her chance to do something useful with the office, if only for one night. Between Landon, this old man, a dusty book and a drugged youth, maybe she could resolve the crisis by the morning. She completed her instructions: "Agent Landon. Please find Casaria."

21

Pax tied the bike helmet's straps around the handlebars, taking in her target warehouse against a sky painted purple by the setting sun. The workhouse, as Bees called it, was a huge brick cube with high latticed windows and a couple of chimneys out back. It would have been an eyesore elsewhere, but it blended in to the widely forgotten warehouse district.

Letty pushed out of Pax's coat pocket and flew to head height. "Looks like a fucking abattoir."

"It might've been," Pax said. In a way, it still was; she'd heard drills and saws and seen bloodied aprons in there. It was possible they were butchering illegally imported animals. But not likely. When Bees brought morbid hypotheticals to the poker table, the topics tended to turn towards getting away with crimes or getting people to talk. Everyone laughed it off as dark humour, and Pax hoped some of it was. Bees and Mr Monroe were not bad people, even if they operated in a bad business. Not like Jack the Tee, a volatile poker player who you wouldn't dare look in the eye. Surely?

Pax's stomach turned at the thought of going in there, and she wondered if picking up a burrito on the way had been a mistake. Would projectile vomiting in fear serve as a good distraction if she needed to escape?

"You'll come with me, right?"

"Yeah," Letty said. "I'll go through the roof."

"Pocket's not good enough for you now?" Pax half-joked, wanting her closer.

"Pocket's not good for any Fae," Lightgate said, descending with the grace of an angel. Holding her refilled hip-flask. She pointed it at Letty. "You ought to be ashamed."

"Spin on it," Letty replied. "Let's rip your wing off and see how you travel. Besides, didn't you always say we oughta make slaves of the lummoxes?"

Lightgate looked away, uninterested, to let out an unashamed belch. "You know we *could* get Casaria out of there without the human."

"What?" Pax exclaimed. There was no way that would end well, considering Lightgate's turnbold plan. "No. They're reasonable guys, I can talk them around."

"Reasonable people who abducted a government agent?"

"*If* he's here. Just lay low," Pax said. "Let me handle it." Lightgate gave an unconvinced *your funeral* shrug, so she added, "We're mates."

"Unless you say the wrong word by accident," Letty said. "If these pricks are the sort of people that hang around here, icing them *might* be the best move."

"Shouldn't one of you be the good conscience?" Pax said, looking from one bloody-minded little angel to the other. "Neither of you think I can resolve this peacefully?"

"You're a human," Lightgate sighed. "I assume the worst."

"I can do it without making a scene," Letty said. "Blow off some steam."

"Please don't," Pax said. "Besides them being, as I said, *mates*, I'm pretty sure their roots run deep in this city. There'd be consequences."

"For you," Lightgate said.

Pax gave Letty a sideways look, asking her to settle this. Letty said, "Fine. But we'll be ready."

Taking a deep breath, Pax started walking, hands deep in her pockets. The two fairies took off towards the sky as she approached the warehouse's massive sliding steel door. No sounds of drills or saws, at least. Maybe they weren't in.

She knocked, and the metallic ring bounced into the distant valleys of buildings. Almost immediately, the door squeaked open on rollers.

"Pax," Bees said, unsurprised to see her. In his filthy apron again. His grey face had taken on a little colour, the skin almost black under one eye, surrounded by purple and yellow. The white of one eye was tinged red with blood.

"Jesus, did you nut a girder?" Pax asked.

"No," Bees said. "I've been trying to call you. Better come in, hadn't you?"

Bees stepped aside and Pax entered after the briefest hesitation. Something in his face, and that response, told her their assumption was absolutely right. He'd gone after Casaria and he knew where he was. Bees dragged the squealing door shut and moved towards a corridor. Pax followed cautiously. The place seemed empty and inactive. She glanced back to the door. Probably too heavy to open if she had to run.

"You been busy, Pax?" Bees asked. "How's everything going? With the spooks and that."

Pax chose not to get into it, and instead asked, "Is he here?"

Bees gave her an appraising look over his shoulder. "Last I checked, there's in the regions of 7.6 billion people in the world. Roughly 50.4% of whom are male. An ambiguous question like that offers an approximate 3.83 billion choices for me to answer. If you include animals and other personified objects, a lot more."

Pax let him talk, imagining he'd practised this speech. He led her into a room lit with the greenish-yellow buzz of an ancient bulb. An antechamber with three metal doors and a drain in the centre, fed by gutters between the tiles. If it wasn't an abattoir, it did an excellent imitation.

"First off," Bees said, and put a hand in his pocket, rummaging. He seemed huge in this tight space, with the room making threats for him. Pax cringed at his minty fresh breath, which was somehow less pleasant than the halitosis his appearance suggested. He drew out a bunch of keys. Her keys, her casino-chip keyring; the set she'd given him when sending them to her apartment. She took them as he said, "Sorry we didn't deliver, you're probably aware we had complications."

"Yeah. I'm hoping I can help you with that."

"Help me?" Bees' eyes smiled. "At this moment, knowing me, and my talents, as you do, do you think I'm a man in need of help?"

"Bees," Pax said. "If you're stepping on the toes of the Ministry of Environmental Energy, then yes you need help. If you don't think so, then you *definitely* need help. You don't know what you're dealing with."

"Not knowing," Bees said thoughtfully, "is rather the point. I wasn't sure you were coming back and we had some questions that wanted answering."

"Did you find any, turning over his place? Bringing him here?"

Bees gave her a thoughtful look without denying it. He answered carefully, "No. We didn't find anything turning over his place. Hence we're here now." His eyes fixed on a door and Pax followed his gaze. It had great rusted fixings, a cell fit to cage a bull. "It might be best if you walk away, Pax. We talk much more and you'll become complicit."

Christ, had they killed Casaria in this vile dungeon? She answered quietly, "Whatever you've done, or are doing, it's no worse than the secrets I've already got."

Bees kept staring, giving nothing away. He moved towards the door, and Pax swallowed as he opened it. "This way, then. "

Fresh air swept in, the door opening onto a long, cracked path that led to a single-storey brick office, tiny against the surrounding warehouses. The lights were on, windows yellow.

"The boss is in session," Bees said. "He'll want a word."

Pax followed him across the open court, scanning the sky for the fairies, but finding no sign of them. They reached the squat building and Bees led the way inside, voices audible from somewhere beyond. He wiped his hefty boots on a mat and called out, "Mr Monroe. Got someone eager to talk to you."

A rough voice shouted from the next room, "Come on through."

It was Monroe's broad Farling accent, Ordshaw's answer to Cockney.

Bees and Pax passed the desk and chairs of a waiting room. A noticeboard with yellowed posters. *Fagan's Falsies - You'll Never Know They're Not Real*. A middle-aged lady grinning for England. Pax muddled through the slogan. Was this an old dentists' surgery? She followed Bees to a staff room with built-in cupboards and shallow sofas. A blond hulk lurked by a counter with a can of beer: Howling Jowls Jones, grinning at Pax. The boss put down a cup of tea – china, saucer and all – and stood from his sofa. He straightened out his woollen suit jacket.

"Pax, right?" he said. He had a round, rugged face with a receding hairline buzzed short. Deep lines of experience creased his brow and cheeks. "We played together at The Grand?"

"Once or twice," Pax said. The boss offered his hand and Pax noted he was barely taller than her. His firm, businesslike squeeze reminded her his personality made up for his height. The sort of old-school criminal who considered it gentlemanly to use *darling* and *love* as forms of address. His palm was damp.

"Sorry." Monroe gave a warm smile, patting a handkerchief over a sweat bead on his forehead. "Afraid we've been busy."

"Getting some exercise, I swear." Jones laughed, then rubbed his square jaw like it hurt. His skin had taken on new colours, like Bees'. Casaria's doing?

"Yeah." Monroe had guessed her question. "We've got you to thank for this particular situation, ain't that right?"

"I didn't mean for . . ." Pax started, cautiously. They definitely had him. They were men capable of kidnapping a government agent. This was real.

"It's alright," Monroe said. "Been a pleasure, if I'm honest. I could use a man like him, in other circumstances. Got a lot of fight for a civil servant."

"He's a bit more than a civil servant," Pax warned.

"Indeed." Monroe picked up his tea again. "Where's our manners? Three ugly men and a pretty young lady and we ain't even offered you a cuppa? What'll it be? Got a feeling you don't take sugar."

Pax frowned, not sure what that was supposed to mean. "No, thanks, I'm fine. You know what this is about?"

"These boys had their theories, but they always do, don't they? Shit, you know them. Your tight-lipped pal, he's not been particularly helpful either." Monroe took a sip from his dainty cup, a crack of culture in his otherwise boorish facade. Pax watched his little finger, hoping he'd stick it out like royalty. He didn't. "You want to enlighten us?"

She didn't want to tell them anything, now that he asked. It would hardly help her case with Lightgate and the Fae if she opened the doors of the Sunken City to more violent humans. But his boys had their theories already; her best bet was playing on their paranoia. "I crossed paths with this Ministry of Environmental Energy a few days ago. They're shady bastards. The resources they've got at their fingertips – city-wide surveillance, phone tapping, satellites, heat sensors. All to protect the tunnels I told your guys about yesterday."

"Yeah," Monroe said. "The tunnels. I thought these boys were shooting the moon. Should've taken it seriously, shouldn't I?"

Like kidnapping a government agent over it wasn't serious? Pax said, "The tunnels are real, the MEE's power is real, and they defend this kind of knowledge with a vengeance. I need to get the Ministry to back off, and Cano Casaria is my best option."

"Hear that, boys?" Monroe turned a look to his goons, and Pax realised how quiet both of them were. Possibly the longest she'd seen either of them hold his tongue. "She's looking to back off a government ministry. All by herself?"

Jones broke his silence, "Pax is a sprite, boss. First time I met her, you know what I saw? She folded second nut to that florist fuck from Wong's Tuesday Hold'Em game. Lost a pot that'd make your nose bleed, folded second damn nut. She took this guy's needling for *two months* of games before making this monster call and busting his *arse*." Jones whooped. "I *swear*. It was, what, King, Eight –"

"Cute," Monroe murmured, to avoid the full details. "So you're a girl who plays the long game. Who thinks she can back off the government."

"Yeah," Pax said. No sense in being shy about it. "Minus the *girl* bit."

"Pax?" Jones laughed, loud, eyes wandering to her crotch. "I had no *idea*. How –"

"She's talking about respect, moron," Monroe said. "I apologise, darling. Anyone can see you're a lady." Pax gave a slight smile. The important thing was *he* thought it was an improvement. "Respect is why we're here right now. Your tunnels, all that aside – this government agent, he showed up my boys. That's bad for my business. My men" – he nodded to them each in turn – "look visibly worse for wear, don't they?"

"You're concerned about losing face? To the Ministry? They're a government –"

"We're at *war*, Pax," Monroe explained. "Not one you'd hear about, but a war all the same. It's bloody. You know what it is we do?"

Pax shook her head, really preferring to keep it that way.

"Doesn't matter. What matters is there's others that want to take over from us. Heard of the Seventh Street Regulars? Yardies. Jamaican kids with attitudes and guns. We didn't ask for any of that shit in Ordshaw."

"You're losing me," Pax admitted. The last thing she needed was another secret war on her conscience. "What's a gang war got to do with the Ministry? With Casaria?"

"We're not violent people," Monroe said, perhaps the least believable comment Pax had heard in a week spent learning about fantastic monsters. "They forced this on us, the Yardies. We gotta protect what's ours, don't we? You ask me what it's got to do with your pal Casaria – that's twofold. First, those tunnels of yours, if they exist, they'd help us *avoid* violence. Imagine us operating under these Yardies' feet."

"Can't fight us if they can't see us, can they?" Jones contributed.

So it wasn't just smuggling contraband they wanted the Sunken City for. They had more enemies than the law. But that wasn't all.

"Second, these Yardies get wind of my boys taking a beating, especially if they hear it was some skinny suit that did it, that gives them a laugh, doesn't it? They think to try their own luck. A message needs to be sent, Pax."

Pax exhaled, wishing that at least one step she took would lead to simplifying her life, rather than making it more complicated. "This message . . . is it something Casaria can walk away from?"

"You want him to?" Jones said, grin returning. Pax gave him an unimpressed look.

"*He* created this situation," Monroe said. "We got what we needed going through his place. Didn't even need him to talk. We only needed to return, in kind, what he did for my boys."

They already knew something about the Sunken City? Pax started, "You got what –"

Bees interrupted. "He's one of those people you hear about that takes pleasure in bad things, I reckon. Tendency to escalate things unnecessarily."

"Son of a bitch *wanted* a fight," Jones said. "Left us no choice."

"Wherever that's left you," Pax said, "you *don't* want to provoke this Ministry."

"I believe you, Pax," Monroe said. His eyes hadn't left Pax, unsettlingly steady. "With this talk of tunnels and things shaking up the city today, we kept a careful eye on the news. Don't take a genius to see your Ministry pals might actually control a certain amount of power, putting out what – ambiguous explanations at best. No, we didn't want a part of that party. But we had a little brainstorm about that, didn't we, boys?"

"Certainly did, boss," Jones said, proudly. "And Bees came up with a pretty fine idea, if you ask me. Pretty fine *indeed.*"

Pax gave Bees a concerned look. "Don't underestimate these people. They have –"

"I always put stock in what you say, Pax," Bees said, flatly. "I guessed these people were dangerous. *You* say it, we're all listening. Doesn't have to be a bad thing, though."

"No?" Pax asked, dreading the reason.

"We'll kill two birds with one stone," Monroe said. "We make this man answer for his actions, saving face, and we invite his Ministry to return fire. Only, not in our direction."

"You want to hurt Casaria and blame the . . . Yardies?"

The room was quiet, confirming she'd reached the right conclusion. Jones put his beer can down, no sign of a smile now. Monroe watched Pax, and she stared back. Looking away showed weakness, Christ knew she'd learnt that enough times in poker games, and here the stakes were much higher than a pot of cash. These people were as bad as Lightgate – did everyone solve problems around Ordshaw by sparking conflict?

"That's a hell of a risk," Pax said. "However good you are at covering your tracks, the Ministry could figure it out. They're thorough, they've got ways of . . ." *Killing you that would make you shit kittens* came to mind. It didn't seem appropriate. "They'll come for you, no matter how well you think you can pin this on someone else. Please tell me you haven't already gone too far to call this off."

"How'd you define *too far*, exactly?" Jones asked.

"The point at which Casaria can't be convinced to let it go. The *only* way you walk away from the Ministry is if they say so."

The silence returned as the men seemed to be questioning whether or not to believe her. It gave Pax a second to appreciate her own statement; she needed Casaria for exactly the same reason, didn't she?

Bees said, "Their whole purpose is keeping secrets, isn't it? I'd say we're well beyond negotiations there."

"He told you something about the tunnels?" Pax shot him a look, this idea again.

"Didn't need to." Monroe offered a proud snigger. "Thank fuck. We got his measure pretty quick, he might *never* talk. But the moron's phone was full of GPS locations. A Google Maps history with half a dozen frequently visited back alleys and dead ends."

"Entrances to your tunnels, right?" Jones clarified.

They already knew. They could go down there, it was already too late.

Pax's mind was racing. They'd be torn apart at best. At worst, they'd unleash the monsters on the city, encounter the Fae – so many opportunities to cause chaos.

"The beauty is," Jones continued, "he doesn't *know* we know. All the time we've spent tenderising him, setting up our story, he's been thinking it's because we want him to talk."

Pax blurted out, "They're not safe. You can't go down there."

Monroe replied slowly, "Come again?"

Pax closed her eyes. Had to come up with something fast. "You want to know everything? I'll tell you. But you *can't* go down there. There is a tunnel network running all over Ordshaw, like a disused train line. These guys ran experiments down there – in the sixties, seventies, something. Now it's like – dead, and deadly at the same time. The Ministry contain it, they're monitoring every access point, hiding all evidence of it. Like an underground Pripyat."

"A condom?" Jones contributed.

"Pripyat, not prick hat," Bees said. "The city by Chernobyl."

"Oh, *that*. Sure, I know it. Evacuated the afternoon of –"

"Alright," Monroe said. "These tunnels are radioactive?"

"Worse," Pax said. "I don't know *what* it is, and that's the point. They don't either, not exactly. It's totally unmanageable – their best bet is to pretend it doesn't exist."

Disappointment set into Monroe's face. Buying it. He glanced at Jones. "It's always the same shit with you two. Bloody 28 Hunters Drive all over again."

"28 Hunters Drive *looked* stable," Jones protested. "You got to imagine it with a bit of work, I swear you could've –"

"Enough!" Monroe snapped, making Pax jump. He followed the outburst with a much smoother tone. "Hunters Drive was lined with asbestos. Head to toe. The things we did to secure that deal, before I found out. Fucking property investment 101 there. And now it's nuclear tunnels? Nuclear fucking tunnels?"

"I know a guy," Bees proffered, "can get us Soviet-grade hazmat suits at a discount. Built to withstand anything."

"It's not nuclear –" Pax started.

"Save it," Monroe said. "Nuclear, gaseous, leprous, *whatever*. I get it. A lesson in the old *too good to be true*, right?"

"Stay away from them," Pax asserted, "for your own good. You do that, no one needs to know you've had anything to do with the Ministry – you said Casaria doesn't even know you got those locations. No one will come after you."

"Love," Monroe sighed. "I appreciate the warning, but you think we're chatting for no good reason? We're already in motion, we're not going back."

"Let me talk to him. Please. If I can persuade Casaria to go along with your story, he could take it to his people himself. He'll do it, if you let me talk to him. If you let him walk away. We all win, don't we?"

Monroe eyed her warily. He screwed up his face for a moment, the turning cogs behind his eyes practically visible.

She threw in some icing: "All except the Yardies, I guess?"

That got the start of a smile. "Fuck it. You can have a shot."

22

The lock noisily turned and Casaria struggled in his restraints. Again he was held fast, and again the effort shot pain through his whole body. He twisted his head from side to side, trying to see the doorway as light poured into the room.

"Jesus Christ," a woman's voice. Pax? It couldn't be.

"He's alright." The cocky blond guy, with the punchable face. Footsteps came into the room, a big shape blocking Casaria's vision. "Only a little superficial damage. Not all our doing, even, truth be told."

"Fucking hell," she said, suddenly close, breath hot on Casaria's face. Her hand closed on his shoulder as she looked at him. Her big eyes filled with concern.

She cares. Of course she cares. He knew she did.

"You came for me," he tried to croak, but phlegm caught in his throat and made him cough. She reeled back, avoiding the spit.

"Would you look at that," the blond said. "Is this guy smitten, or what?"

He tried to buck, to curse them. They had no idea who they'd crossed. When he was free, they'd be ashes, he'd take off their heads –

A hand gripped his jaw. "Hey, Furious Fred? You ever give it a fucking rest?"

Something hit him in the temple, his vision pulsing black for a second. He bared his teeth and snarled.

"Enough!" Pax said. Not afraid to stand up for him. "You want this to work or not?"

"Look at him, didn't I tell you?" The other brute, the ugly ashen one, somewhere way behind the chair. "He loves it. Got a complex of some sort, isn't it. Not right in the head."

"He went for us like a goddamned wolverine," the blond said. "And started bawling his eyes out later. Next minute he's laughing like a jackal."

"So now you tell me," the midget leader said, with an air of finality, "if there's any chance he'll walk away?"

Silence.

Casaria slowed his breathing. She was looking down at him, arms folded across her chest. Worry on her face. Worry for him. He smiled, a hint of laughter creeping up.

"Here we go," the blond said.

"Casaria, you hear me?" she asked.

He nodded.

"I need you to promise me something. Can you do that?"

"I promise." Casaria tasted the words, spit hissing between his teeth. "I'll bury these motherfuckers."

"I need the opposite," Pax said, levelly. "Keep calm. They're willing to talk, understand?"

Casaria narrowed his eyes. Keep calm. It was always *keep calm*. Cowards kept calm. He opened his mouth to say it but Pax went first.

"I need you, Casaria," she said. "I really fucking need you, so *please* think before you say something we're all gonna regret."

He didn't speak. His eyes were wide. She needed him. But he had his pride. He had his honour. He growled, "I won't tell them a damn thing."

"I know" – Pax hurried it out – "and they know, too. You didn't talk, you won't talk, we all get that. But . . . can you keep *this* quiet?"

He held her gaze. "Why would I?"

"Because I need you to."

That was all? He was supposed to walk away from thugs who'd attacked him outside his own home? Chained him to a chair and cut off his damned toe?

"There's no one else who can help me," Pax reaffirmed.

Casaria took a deep breath, sending pain through his lower ribs. He grinned into it. "You see what they did to my toe?"

"Jesus. Yes."

"Actually, the story is, the Seventh Street Regulars did it," the ugly one said, like it wasn't him who'd levered those rusty secateurs. Casaria twisted but couldn't find his face, so turned back to Pax. Surely she wouldn't believe a lie like that? Her face didn't shift as the brute continued, "Second toe on the left foot, always. Seventh toe, if you're counting right to left; that's the message."

"You had to go that far?" Pax replied, disgusted. So. They were carving him up to make it look like someone else's work and she knew about it. She wasn't happy.

"This particular storybook" – the leader crouched in front of Casaria, looking him dead in the eye – "started before we got him, with that knife wound on his face. We were just completing the picture. The Seventh Street Regulars love their knives almost as much as their guns. Show her one."

"See this?" The blond again. "This kink in the blade makes it so when you pull it out the wound splits wide. Dead hard to stop the bleeding, you can take my word on *that*."

"Filthy weapon used by filthy people," the leader said. "No honour, not if you measured all their blood from here to Jamaica. And they wouldn't flinch at making a corpse of a powerful government man. But, Pax, the question is, this man wouldn't talk for us. You honestly believe he's gonna talk for you?"

She didn't say anything. Quietly horrified.

"I know your faces." Casaria couldn't help himself. "Your fucking names."

"He knows our faces," the leader echoed. "Our names. What about that, love?"

"Give him a chance." Pax pushed past, to look into Casaria's eyes. "Look, I don't know what happened between you guys, but I'm guessing you got the drop on them before, didn't you? You took that weapon from my place."

Casaria forced a smile. That was a fond memory at least, taking down these thugs. They'd got lucky the second time, catching up to him after an exhausting night.

"You did that to their faces?" Pax said. He couldn't see them, but he imagined it well enough. Cut up and bruised, weren't they? "I've never seen anyone hurt these two before."

"Nutcase," the ugly one commented. "Came at us both at the same time."

"That true?" Pax looked into Casaria's eyes again.

Yeah, it was true. They could cut him, they could take his toe, but they weren't undoing his victory over them. He said, "I could've killed them. Landon got in the way."

"It's why you're here," Pax said. "Do you even realise that? You shamed them."

Casaria paused. No. They had been in his apartment, looking for information. They demanded answers. Who did he work for? What did he do? Like hell he'd ever speak.

"They did their homework," Pax said, reading his face, "to try and explain why some civil servant was able to take down two of their finest. All these two found out" – her eyes locked on his, begging him to go along with this – "is you're just a dangerous nobody. You've been punished, right? This can end, now, if you accept that. They're satisfied, as long as you're willing to drop this."

Casaria couldn't respond, her face inches from his. Drop this? Whose pride would be more injured, here?

"Fuck!" She slapped the arm of the chair and he flinched. "Say it! You understand, don't you?"

Casaria nodded quickly.

"Say it!"

"It's what I do, isn't it!" He let it out louder than he intended. "Keeping secrets – spreading lies. It's what I'm good at!" He looked past her to the men. "You think I want anyone knowing about this?"

No one responded, their faces confused. Like it wasn't obvious how pathetic this was, him cornered, captured, humiliated in this chair. Like they expected him to run crying to the first authority figure he could find. The leader got it first, and his face softened in satisfied smugness. Casaria wanted to tear his skull out.

"This guy's something else," the man said.

"And?" Pax stood up straight again.

"I actually believe you, love. This nutter genuinely might not talk. But I didn't get where I am taking chances. You want him, he comes with the message. Bees, Jones, make the arrangements."

"What's that mean?" Pax said, with alarm.

The leader walked away. "Turn him loose in Seventh Street territory. Then he's your burden. Good luck, Pax. You tell us how this all works out for you. And if he gives you a lick of trouble."

The blond one moved in front of Casaria, wearing that stupid grin. "Ah hell. Didn't I always say it? Women are the *real* torture. Pax, we could put you to *work*."

*

Pax sat squeezed between the two massive men in the bench that formed the front seat of Bees' van, leaving the warehouse district for ever-more-threatening locations. She recognised some of these streets from when Casaria had first driven her to an MEE hide-out. Either St Alphege's or the rough neighbourhoods that flanked it.

The men hadn't said much while tying Casaria and flinging him in the van with her scooter. Jones had given Casaria a stack of photos of dark-skinned faces, telling him to identify them as the ones that hurt him. Casaria barely registered the instructions, face full of malice. He was a mess, and Pax had no idea if he could be trusted, but this was working. She almost let herself believe she'd performed some kind of miracle, though Monroe clearly wasn't bothered if Casaria lived or died, as long as the taint was far away from him. But it was clear that Casaria's anger was mixed with shame. He was likely to keep this quiet for the sake of his pride; Monroe had seen that.

"How much further?" Pax asked, as they drove down an unlit street. She feigned searching for lights in the dead buildings, actually checking for a sign that Letty was nearby.

"Border of West Quay, that'll do it," Jones said. "Somewhere along the viaduct. Jerry Rise, maybe? What do you think, Bees, we gonna go as far as Jerry Rise?"

"Sounds good to me. It's a small jump to the hospital from there."

"I go to a hospital," Pax said, "I get picked up."

"Give them a fake name, say you lost your ID, who's gonna know," Jones said. "And do us a solid, get in the A&E *screaming*, say you fought off some psycho Yardie bear to get this guy safe."

"I'm not gonna do that."

Bees gave her an uncertain look. She avoided his gaze. Casaria's toe was cauterised and, as they'd said, everything else was superficial. Chances were no one was checking the wounds to see what knife had been used to cut them. They could keep their gangland narrative. Her only goal would be to get far away from West Quay. People only passed by its pebble-dash estates and razor-wire-lined storage facilities to catch a boat, and that was limited to industrial-scale shipping.

"You'll be doing the whole city a solid," Jones said. "About time the Quay got shaken up. It used to be real cosmopolitan out there. Shipments coming in from the Baltic, the Atlantic, sometimes the Med. I mean, we still get them, but now the docks are staffed by a particular kind of person, *real* particular."

"Linked to the Seventh Street Regulars," Pax guessed.

"Among a few others," Bees said. "Outsiders. Lowlifes, dragging our whole city down. You know what I read a few weeks back? This article, see, said people are calling Ordshaw *Gun City*. I never heard anyone say that, did you?"

Pax didn't answer. He'd keep talking anyway.

"Apparently North Ordshaw General Hospital's got the highest incidence of gunshot care in the UK. More than a lot of Europe. But there's a fallacy there, right, because in NOGH we've also got the best gunshot wound specialists, don't we? People chopper them in knowing that. It's all a bit chicken and egg."

She was only half listening, waiting for this particular chapter in her nightmare to close, so she could take Casaria back to the safety of Broadplain Plaza and start persuading him to work on resolving *her* problems.

"Those tunnels would be damn helpful, I can tell you." Jones changed tack, drawing Pax's attention again. "Imagine us being able to get in under their feet. Get *around* the shipping channels. We can't get boats *through* no more. Man, with tunnels. The things we could do with tunnels. Damn shame they're polluted, I say."

"Damn shame," Bees agreed.

Both of them, Pax feared, sounded unconvinced. She said nothing, hoping the topic would fade away. She expected their friendship might, too.

Bees pulled the van over at the base of a steep hill of houses, the black brick viaduct rising ominously over the road. At least there was a light under that, deep yellow and casting grim shadows. The big men got out and led Pax to the rear of the van, where they hauled her scooter onto the road. Bees rubbed his hands together as Jones bent in around the sliding door, fussing with Casaria's restraints.

"The hospital," Bees said, pointing, "is that way. Hit the main road and you won't miss it for signs. Or if you want to call an ambulance, you're at the south end of Jerry Rise."

"I'll make do," Pax said. Jones pulled Casaria to his feet, and Pax leant around Bees to see. The agent looked terrible, but he was upright, with colour in his face, and his expression was at least less than totally violent.

Jones straightened him out, big hands on his shoulders, saying, "Now you remember, we know who you are. We know where you live. Hell, you *know* what we know."

Jones gave him a sick grin and shoved past to the van.

"And remember those faces," Bees said. "You want to tell anyone who came for you, it was them. And no hard feelings, hey?"

Pax frowned at the last comment, directed at her, and caught a glint of light reflecting from inside the van, where Jones was drawing his arm back out. She met Bees' eyes, begging it not to be what she thought. He stared back impassively, unapologetic, as Jones turned on Casaria, knife in hand. Of course – this had been too easy.

"No!" Pax yelled, but she hit a wall as Bees' arm blocked her. Casaria hissed like a cornered cat, moving to evade, not quick enough. As Jones lurched at him with the curved knife, a gunshot sounded. The van twanged. Another shot sparked off the curb. Bees and Jones were down, crouching, both familiar with gunfire. Jones rolled into the van's open door. "Fucking Yardies, go, go!"

Bees scuttled like a crab, hands over his head as a shot hit the tarmac and another glanced off the van. Pax flattened herself against the road, twisting to see where the shots were coming from. A wing mirror shattered.

"Drive, drive!" Bees shouted, pulling himself into the passenger seat, big legs flailing. The engine shuddered as the van careered away. The gunshots stopped.

Pax sucked in breaths as shadows moved in the windows, hunched shapes of people peering out.

Casaria was down, both hands pressing into his gut where Jones had stabbed him, blood oozing through his fingers.

"Fuck fuck fuck!" Pax pulled herself across the ground towards him.

"Some fucking friends!" Letty said, from above. The fairy buzzed into view, expression grim.

Lightgate joined her, a pistol in each hand, white suit glimmering like a star against the sky. Smiling, she said, "I don't know, I kind of liked them."

Pax pressed her hands onto Casaria's seeping wound, putting all her weight into it. He stared, teeth gritted. Too much pain to get a word out. How deep had the cut gone?

23

Holly brought the barest satisfaction to the day by producing a stew that replaced the telegraph station's aroma of stagnant mould with a more hearty scent. She had little faith in its nutritional value, as the tinned food's labels had faded, but it was a distraction, at least, especially when paired with the riddle of finding space in the cluttered workspace to sit and eat. They gathered, in the end, around the small table with the map spread on it, which worked as a lumpy tablecloth, covering bulky objects underneath. For a few minutes, she was treated to the satisfying hungry slurps of her family (and the thin sips of Rimes), and reflected that despite everything, they were doing okay.

Watching Darren eat, she couldn't deny his bruising and swelling had reduced. Some minor cuts even seemed to have disappeared. Holly wondered if she was being a bad mother by refusing Grace the same toxic-liquid treatment. The girl's feet had been rubbed raw journeying into the sewers. But Holly suspected offering her daughter that liquid would make her a worse mother. And besides, they didn't have any more.

Darren sat back from his meal with a deep noise of pleasure, and his eyes fell to the map between them. A wistful look crossed his face as he let himself slip into the memories of his adventures. He looked up, seeing Holly staring. She folded her arms and said, "What did you think I'd say if you revealed all this madness to me? Did you think I'd kick you out? Scream?"

"No," he said. "I just didn't think you'd understand."

"I don't understand why you watch football, I don't understand why you drown yourself in beer. So what?"

He had sad eyes, like he wasn't sure of the answer himself. She suspected she knew, even if he didn't. He wanted something to himself. A break from the life they'd created. Their happy, ordinary, comfortable life. Why else?

"I've made mistakes, Holly," he said. "A lot of them. And I'm sorry. But it always felt right, fighting for our city. And it always felt right to shelter you from that. To give you one less burden."

"Having a deceitful husband is worse," Holly told him, plainly. "You could've died, and I never would've known why. Your daughter would've been left in a broken home." Grace looked up from her stew with surprise, not expecting to be drawn into this.

"That's why I stopped."

Holly narrowed her eyes. "After it became too dangerous."

Darren took a breath, and Holly waited. "I'm sorry I kept it from you, but I'm not sorry for what I did. I know you don't want to hear it, but I shouldn't be sitting here, I should be doing what I'm good at. It should be me out there, not someone like Pax."

"Someone like Pax?" Holly arched an eyebrow. "Seems to me you barely survived last night, while she came away unscathed. Perhaps she shouldn't be out there, but by heavens neither should you." Holly held back for a moment. "What really hurts, Diz, is that you didn't think I could help."

Darren had the barest second to register that, as if the revelation of this thought might have made sense of the world. Then the phone rang.

"Jesus Christ, Jesus Christ," Pax cursed, tying one severed sleeve of her hoodie tightly around Casaria's gut to pack the other sleeve into the wound. The pressure she'd applied was enough to stop the bleeding, following Letty's quick instructions, but Casaria's eyes were rolling about aimlessly and he wasn't supporting himself or speaking words that made sense. And there was a lot of blood on the pavement. A lot of blood.

Lights were coming on up the street. The siren of an emergency vehicle was approaching. Pax got under Casaria's arm, heaved him up onto her shoulder and pivoted him onto the scooter. It threatened to topple, dragging both of them down with it, until Pax got a scrambling leg either side of the vehicle.

A window creaked open nearby. Had someone finally got up the courage to help? "Fuck off with your colours, we don't need it here!"

The window slammed shut again, leaving Pax unsure what that meant.

"You've got about two minutes," Lightgate called from up high.

Pax pulled Casaria's wrists around her waist, trying to tuck one hand under the other like tying a sweater. The warmth of his wound pressed into her back, and his weight threatened to pin her to the handlebars, making it even harder to start the bike. As if she knew where to go. The hospital would ask too many questions, no matter what Jones said. Those two fuckers didn't care, as long as this got pinned on their rivals. How could she have been so stupid? This was why she didn't have friends. Fucking Bees.

What else? A private doctor? There was Dr Merriweather, from the poker games in West Farling. But he was a massive twat, which Pax vaguely connected with him being a cosmetic, rather than actual, surgeon. And despite the name, West Farling was right on the east side of the city. No one useful lived near West Quay. She cursed again. "Those pricks. Utter pricks."

"Humans for you," Letty said, landing on Pax's shoulder.

Pax turned the key. "You got anyone can help him?"

"It'd take a Fae javelin to stitch that," Letty said.

The scooter came to life and Pax breathed relief. Casaria's fingers wriggled against her gut, limply groping for a hold. She swatted one off then pulled his hands together, interlinking his fingers. His face pressed into her shoulder and he made an indecipherable comment. Pax gave Letty a look. "So where to?"

Lightgate floated down beside them, hip flask out as though she'd been spectating. "Leave him to bleed out, there's always Plan A."

Pax gave her a disapproving look.

"Time's a factor, Pax. *My* ideas want to happen *yesterday*, and this gentleman's not opening doors any time soon."

Pax hoped Letty might defend her, but the other fairy hummed agreement. Letty didn't know about Lightgate's turnbold, did she? Pax said, "The wound's not too deep – we get him help soon, he'll be fine."

Casaria gargled something that sounded offensive.

"Save your energy," Pax huffed. She gunned the bike and steered away from the viaduct, back towards what she hoped was the city proper. After a few streets of wobbly riding, she listened for the siren and found it wasn't getting any closer. She kept going until it was all but a whisper, then pulled over again.

Pax wrestled Rimes' phone from her pocket and shakily dialled.

"Dr Rimes' residence," Holly's voice answered, as prim and formal as an answering service. The two fairies hovered down, listening.

"Holly, I need Rimes."

"Oh!" Holly answered. "There's *definitely* a joke in there."

"Not now," Pax said. "I need to know if there's any way – anything there we could use, anyone we could ask – to treat a knife wound?"

"Oh my God, Pax, what happened?" The receiver was jostled. "No – get your –"

"Pax?" Barton said. Sturdy, awake. "Where are you? I'm coming for you."

For a beautiful moment, Pax found a second's hope. Then she remembered his situation: "You can barely walk."

"She's been *stabbed*!" Holly's fearful voice cut in.

"No! Not me! I've got Casaria, the MEE agent."

"You've *what*?"

"He's injured. Don't think it went too deep, the attack got thrown off, but he's bleeding a lot. Can Dr Rimes do something for him?"

There was silence, except for Pax's worried breath coming back to her. Holly asked a muffled question in the background. Pax could imagine Barton's hand over the receiver, making demands of Rimes, sheltering in the distance. Barton came back: "If it's bad enough for you to ask, then no. And we don't have any more glo."

Glo. Pax hadn't considered that. Barton was up and talking, and he'd been through something as bad as this. If it worked, it offered discretion and speed.

"Drop him at the A&E," Barton said. "Let his own people take care of him."

Pax shook her head, unseen. There was another option. "You know Chaucer Crescent? Is it somewhere you used to pick up glo?"

"No. Why?"

"You didn't always go back to the same places, did you?"

"Pax" – Barton hesitated – "where's this coming from?"

"I've gotta go."

"Have you had contact with them? You have to –"

"I'll explain when I get back," Pax said, hurriedly. "Chaucer Cresent's on the way." Before Barton had time to issue a warning, or something, she hung up. Letty eyed her as she straightened out the bike.

"You're nuts, you know that?"

"The Blue Angel gave me that address before it realised who I was," Pax said. "There might be something there we can use to help Casaria."

"This *Blue Angel* again?" Lightgate said, amused rather than curious.

"The Angel's had plenty of time to spring a trap since then," Letty said.

"Why would anyone think I'd be crazy enough to go to that address, after that encounter?" Pax said. "And besides, I've got you guys for protection, don't I?"

"Why would this Angel offer you *any* glo when Apothel's been gone for years?"

"It thought I was Rufaizu," Pax said, revving the engine, "and it blindly led Barton to glo before, recently, Holly said so. Maybe it's trying to keep up the pretence that it's on our side – it doesn't *matter* – it's our best hope of keeping him alive."

24

Roper knocked tentatively at Sam's door, holding up a manila folder. He could have been a librarian, with his plastic-rimmed glasses and tousled white hair. "The numbers you were after."

"Please tell me you've got something," Sam said, as Landon appeared by the man's shoulder, watching as though wary of the technician.

"Not what you're hoping for, I think," Roper hummed, leaning into the room and stretching out his hand, afraid to enter. Landon took the folder and passed it to Sam.

"A list of numbers," Sam said, leafing through pages of large figures. Only the date column was obvious. Many rows had been highlighted with fluorescent yellow marker, some in adjacent blocks. "What am I looking at?"

"Novisan levels within a mile radius of the *praelucente*, during different surges, broken down over ten-metre squares. That is, the energy fluctuations it causes. The highlighted rows are abnormal troughs and spikes. Mostly troughs."

"So they are happening in more than one place," Sam suggested, hopeful that the multiple highlighted rows would clue them in to Pax's hint.

"No, these are figures during different surges," Roper said. "Where you see a whole lot of dips at the same time, they're next to each other. A wider radius, not different locations. A surge can see reduced novisan across as many as ten areas. Though a spike, with higher levels, only ever occurs in one focal point. The epicentre, directly above the *praelucente*."

Sam sighed. Basically, these reams of pages showed what everyone already understood of the *praelucente's* surges – they reduced energy levels in a wider area and occasionally produced a beneficial increase.

"You may recall the Stray Symphony," Roper said, helpfully. Sam already knew the story, the classic example everyone in the MEE used to justify the Sunken City. Staring at the numbers, she let him continue anyway. "Sebestyn Furedi's masterpiece, composed in one inspired night, Thursday 21st November, 1997. There was a novisan spike under his apartment building in Ten Gardens that evening, during a surge that reduced novisan across the two surrounding blocks."

Sam turned through the numbers that Roper had wasted time printing out. "Bottom line is, novisan levels are only affected around the *praelucente*?"

"Within the mile radius that we measure, yes," Roper said. "There was one exception, during a surge in Ripton, on page four." He waited while Sam looked for herself. A single yellow row in the middle, another highlight towards the bottom. "There was a slight increase in Hanton at that time. Not significant, within the realms of standard deviation."

It was hard to say if it was significant, Sam pondered, as these numbers said nothing about the actual locations, above or below the city. "Where exactly in Ripton and Hanton were these?"

"You mean street names?" Roper replied uncertainly, unprepared to offer real-world details. Just bloody numbers. "I'd have to cross-check against a map."

"Please do," Sam said. "And what about elsewhere? Outside the mile radius?"

"That would take a long time to scan," Roper said. "We don't have the server power or the manpower."

"You've got twenty computers out there that no one uses," Sam replied.

"None of them powerful enough to run the scans," Roper explained patiently. "Only the Castle, downstairs, can combine the results. We cross-reference readings from half a dozen simultaneous measurements to estimate novisan. They need to be inputted individually, and someone has to update the scan twice an hour. It takes six hours to process the data within a mile radius alone. For a period of twenty-four hours."

Sam couldn't respond at once, torn between questioning *why on earth it was so inefficient* and admitting that it sounded like a long and difficult task. No. This was her office, this evening. She wanted answers. "Why does it take *that long*? Why can't the input be automated? Why can't we split the task over multiple spare computers?"

Roper's face suggested he'd been caught unawares. "Who would implement that?"

Sam shut her eyes. It was Asquith and his fax machine all over again: why risk change. "Do we have historical records for other locations? Could we do scans retroactively?"

"In theory," Roper said. "Measurements are *recorded* everywhere, but they need to be processed. Covering one mile for one 24-hour period would take –"

"Yeah, I got that," Sam said. "We don't need a 24-hour period, though. We can focus on a single historical moment, when we *know* there was a surge. There was one this morning, wasn't there? When that building started shaking. You could check other locations for exactly that time."

"Yes, but it would take time . . . what do you hope to achieve, Ms Ward?"

Sam gave him a look that said it wasn't his place to ask.

"It's just…" Roper cleared his throat. "It's a serious appropriation of resources. There are always anomalies in the numbers, that's why Support exist – we look for *important* deviations. Otherwise you'd be knee-deep in tangents. Perhaps if you told me exactly why you think novisan spikes would occur elsewhere, I could help explain it?"

Sam continued to glare at him. As if anyone ever deigned to give her explanations. "I'm just following leads. Thanks for your help, Roper, let me think on it for now."

"You know where I am." He turned to go but paused in the doorway. Sam looked up, hopefully. "Can I bring you another coffee?"

"No," she said, deflated. "No thank you."

Roper nodded and ducked out, leaving Sam alone with Landon and the pile of paperwork on her desk. She raised her eyebrows to the agent for his report.

"Fairly sure I found him," Landon said. His tone sounded no more confident than Roper's, so Sam sat back deep in her chair to receive the news. "Got a white van on double yellows around the corner from his building, on a traffic cam. Three men entered it a bit after 6am; can't make out their faces but one was dressed in black, flanked by two bigger guys. Right sort of build for the pair we ran into yesterday. Looks like your instinct was right."

"Damn," Sam said. Her instinct, though, said this wasn't as simple as it sounded. Pax had fled from Casaria, why go back for him? Who *were* these people and what did they want? "Can you find them?"

"I tracked back to when they arrived – the van was there since midnight. I couldn't trace the direction they came through the traffic on the ring road, though. Tried to follow them leaving, driving across town. Caught the van on an intersection out of Central, and a flyover near Ten Gardens. Then lost it. Could be anywhere west of the Gader, unless they doubled back."

"Can you check the –"

"Number plate? Already done. The van's registered to a fish and tackle business supposedly based in the Net. Fairly sure it's a front. Phone number goes to an answering service, company's registered address is a PO box."

The Net was about as far from civilisation as you could get within Ordshaw, sitting towards the city's northern limits, opposite the Gader from the warehouse district. It mirrored that area's penchant for sparsely populated industrial properties, though the Net was alive with failing, shady or unsavoury businesses. "Any guesses who these guys are?"

"Two other cameras around the building had been erased. Between all that and the little performance they gave us yesterday, I'd say they're career criminals."

"We might find their faces in the databases, then."

"The images aren't clear enough for our recognition software – I tried that. But I might find the faces in the files myself. If that's where you want me."

"Yeah. Good work so far. But come here a second, first. I could use your input."

Sam's eyes ran back to the paperwork on her desk, hoping this, at least, might produce results. Around Apothel's Miscellany, she'd arranged historic reports on the Ripton Chapel, questioning why the word *grugulochs* was important. According to the files, the chapel had been sealed about two weeks after Apothel had been murdered, along with five other locations. The inventory of recovered items from his lairs included alcohol, pages of scrawled notes, and the barest essentials for living: electric hobs, tired clothes and stacks of tinned meat. There were also the ashes of small fires that had been used to burn other papers. Apothel covering his tracks.

None of the other locations had been marked in the way that his chapel had been. The claw marks that covered its walls had been notable enough for the investigating agents to photograph and describe in their written reports, but prompted no further investigation. The best-quality photos, which were woefully lit and grainy, revealed hints of words that hadn't quite been scratched clear. Clusters of letters that hinted at creature names: *-ckle*, *gl-*, *ven*. But none of the photos or notes referenced the one clear word that remained. Most of the images weren't clear enough for her to tell if they were the wall she'd seen, but the chief reporting agent, Jelani, had starkly written: *No legible text remains. Clear the civilian hoped to conceal his legacy.*

Had they actively hidden the word "grugulochs" from the report?

"Were you based in Ordshaw when Apothel died?" Sam asked Landon.

"Yeah," he said. "Strange time."

"You knew this guy, Jelani? I've never come across him."

"Sure. Good man. Black. Got moved to London." Sam sat back from the report to question why *black* mattered, but Landon went on, eyes resting on Apothel's book, open on the page about the Layer Fae. "You getting anywhere with that? The note in the margin said that bit was inaccurate."

"I saw," Sam replied. "You think the rest is?"

Landon shrugged. "I only had a little scan." He turned the pages to a section headed *Bunch Spider*. "From what I read, that one's roughly true, about tackling one of them. If you had to face one hand-to-hand. There's other things I couldn't say either way, creatures I haven't encountered."

"Or don't exist," Sam said, voicing the MEE's agreed line on Apothel's anomalies.

"Yeah. And there's other things we've updated the research on now. Particularly the plant life, as we've worked with Dr Rimes since then."

Sam froze at the name. The doctor on the hill. That unconventional recluse beavering away outside their tight budget. When they first enlisted her help, after Apothel's group disbanded, she must have verified many of Apothel's claims. "Has anyone contacted her to cross-reference the information? See how much of it is fiction?"

"I don't think we've had the time," Landon said. "Like I said, no one —"

"She worked with Apothel, back then," Sam thought out loud. The doctor's place had been on Sam's list of locations to check in the recent search for Rufaizu, which Operations had ignored — what else had they ignored? "If Pax is following his trail, maybe the doctor would have an idea why? The *praelucente's* actions today, she might have input on that? Has someone at least checked if the civilians have been in touch with her?"

"Yes." Landon confirmed this one proudly, something he could finally answer positively. "Farnham and Devlin checked on her this morning, no one had been there. She seemed clueless as ever, they said."

"And we're satisfied with that? Did anyone ask her if Rufaizu or Barton had been in touch before all this kicked off?"

Landon said nothing. He stared into space as though the suggestion of missing something so obvious had shut down his mental faculties.

"Landon?"

"I don't know. Probably."

"That sounds like a no."

"I'll check." Landon went to the door, and Sam looked to the book again. A darkly etched image of an embattled, gorilla-like creature. Why was she poring over Apothel's wild drawings when she could ask his scientist friend directly?

"Wait," Sam called out. "Get me her number. I want to talk to her myself."

25

On the north side of Ripton, Chaucer Crescent took Pax a mile south of her apartment. She tried not to think about home, easing Casaria down against a tree. He had regained some focus after the initial shock, eyes following her, but his teeth remained gritted in agony.

Pax assured him, "I'm gonna get you help. Just hang in there." She walked briskly down the road, scanning semi-detached houses, ignoring his moans and muffled grunts that might have said *hospital*.

The homes were masked by weeds and scaffolding, or otherwise had building supplies in their drives. A suburb for people aspiring to better lives, who didn't have the time or money to complete their projects. Not that Pax could judge. She wasn't sure if her home was even *hers* any more. It was almost certainly being watched.

Fuck.

She turned back towards the bike, to Casaria, and realised for the first time that he had no shoes, and his bandaged left foot was bleeding. And she'd brought him here, to a crusty dead street for the promise of, in Holly's words, a magic elixir. His eyes met hers imploringly, but he'd stopped complaining, a hand pressed into his side as he waited for her to save him.

Christ, even if she stabilised Casaria, saved Rufaizu and pinned the chaos on the Blue Angel, did she have anything to go back to? Letty was right: she had seen things she couldn't unsee. Monsters, not just under the city but in her limited personal life, too. She'd been *happy* playing cards. She'd been *happy* wandering Ordshaw at night, not knowing what lay under the surface. She didn't need this.

"Regrets?" Letty asked, dropping down from the sky.

"Huh?" Pax shook out of her thoughts. "You see anything?"

"Definitely more than you, staring off into la-la land. There's a spot about halfway up the road. Building gutted by a fire or something. Would bet your mum on it being the place. If you thought Apothel's chapel was something, you're gonna love this."

"Show me." Pax gave Casaria a thumbs up and started away.

She felt an odd sense of foreboding in her gut. Another dreary location, drawing her into trouble. It had a direction; she sensed exactly where they were going before they reached the site. Her fingers tingled as the dread built. Was something happening again?

No, it wasn't like before. Just a slight burn, a subtle pull. But it *was* something. Simple anxiety, perhaps?

Pax stopped as Letty drifted up to their target building, the nervous feeling only getting worse as they got closer. Maybe she felt the glo itself, if it was connected somehow to the energy of the minotaur?

The rough shape of the building matched the others, but the roof was mostly missing, the windows were boarded up, and the entrance was blocked by a chain link fence. Unlike the chapel, it wasn't secured. The fencing could be moved, and the boarding was weak chipboard. Some kid had graffitied it with an illegible green tag. Letty perched on the fence as Lightgate joined them.

Pax asked, "Can you go in and scope the place out?"

Letty didn't answer at once, likely recalling their disagreement at the chapel. "What's it worth?"

"I'll pay you," Pax said. "Tenner?"

"How about you owe me," Letty said. "Pretty sure you're no good for cash."

Pax flipped her a middle finger and Letty buzzed to a gap in a window frame.

Lightgate hung back. The Fae's hip flask was out again, another swig. Had she been drinking ever since West Quay?

Pax turned to check the street again. A few neighbours had lights on but their curtains were drawn. The sounds of bad television came through too-thin windows two houses down; loud voices followed by a cacophony of either laughter or cheers.

Sure she wasn't being watched, Pax crept into the driveway of the ruined building and took out Rimes' phone to use the torch.

"You've got something going on here, don't you?" Lightgate said, suddenly a foot from Pax's head. Pax suspected the fairy had tried to make her jump. Not this time.

"Me and Letty?"

"You and Letty. You need to be careful."

"Thanks, but I trust her."

"I'm not talking about *her*. Neither the Ministry nor the Fae look kindly on mingling. It's one thing we have in common. And you're making it worse." Lightgate gestured back up the road to Casaria. "This pot you're stirring had better taste good."

"Like I have a choice," Pax said.

Rimes' phone buzzed in Pax's hand, making her start. An unknown number; eleven digits that could have been anyone. Pax had come to fear mystery callers since her first terrifying conversation with Letty.

"You're in luck." Letty swept down from the sky. "This is going to be a –" The fairy paused, seeing the ringing phone. "What is it?"

"It's not my phone," Pax said.

"Want me to talk to them?" Lightgate offered.

"God no."

"Just answer it or I'll give you a slap," Letty said, and Pax did.

She said nothing, as the caller was already speaking: "– not on silent."

The caller went quiet for a second. A woman. Holly?

"Dr Rimes? This is Sam Ward from the Ministry of Environmental Energy."

Pax shot her hand up to hang up, but Letty waved urgently. The fairy put a finger to her lips for quiet, then mouthed, "Let her talk."

"Dr Rimes, are you there?"

Pax cleared her throat, and Letty nodded. Pax croaked an ambiguous, "Yes."

"I'm the head of IS Relations," Ward said. "We spoke once before, about two years ago, if you recall."

Pax gave a muffled, "Mmhmm."

"I'm sorry about the time. I believe you spoke with our agents this morning, and I expect you've heard what's happened today?"

"Yes . . ."

"Could I ask you a few questions? If it's not too much bother?"

Pax hesitated, searching down the road for Casaria, as though he might help. Letty got in her way, nodding encouragement. Pax spoke in her best mumbled mimicry of the doctor's voice, "Go on."

"The *praelucente*, or something very close to it, was heard to make noises today. They match a word Apothel wrote a couple of times. Did he ever mention this to you?"

"What . . ." Pax kept her voice quiet. High-pitched. Lightgate stifled a laugh, earning a fierce look from Letty. "What word?"

"Grugulochs."

Pax frowned, as Letty gave her an *I told you so* look.

"I'm looking at Apothel's diary, the Miscellany, as he called it. There's a page on what he labelled the minotaur, titled 'Grugulochs'. Did he connect the two words with you?"

"In his book?" Pax croaked.

"Yes, in his code. It's been partially translated by a civilian."

"A civilian . . . wrote that word?"

"Yes."

That hadn't been in the Miscellany when Pax had read it. She would have remembered if Rufaizu's notes included it, and she certainly hadn't written it herself. This didn't add up. Had someone doctored the book? Was it a trap?

Ward continued, "Is it a word you're familiar with?"

"No," Pax said.

Ward gave that a moment. "I wonder if you might come to Greek Street, Dr Rimes? We could benefit from your particular viewpoint."

Pax grunted dismissively.

"If I'm honest, I'm concerned. We've missed some important details, and an outside perspective would be welcome."

Pax opened her mouth to say no. But this was an opportunity for information. If they were going to cross the Ministry, she had to know it was worth it. She spoke slowly, sure her cartoonish voice would be discovered. "Ms Ward – do you have Rufaizu?"

Ward didn't answer at once. "It'd be best if you came to Greek Street, then we could talk in person."

"I'd like to see him," Pax told her. "But not there. I don't go there."

"Why don't we –"

Pax winced, suddenly, and let out a short shriek, the phone dropping from her hand as pain shot down her lower back. Not *now*. It knocked her to a knee, one hand slamming into the pavement. The pain pulsed, her heart lurching, the same electric jolt.

The same feeling as when the trains had crashed.

But no images – just black – burning black – the monster moving – feeding – doing *something*. It was close. Very close.

Pax gritted her teeth, trying to move away from it but paralysed by the pain.

"What the fuck?" Letty demanded, flying in her face. "You having a stroke?"

"Dr Rimes?" Ward's voice said from the phone on the pavement, loud with concern.

The pain gave one more pulse, then left as quickly as it came. Pax dropped onto her haunches. Her jaw slackened and she uttered, "Bloody hell."

Then it was all over, with no sign it had ever happened bar breathlessness and the position Pax found herself in.

Letty hissed, "You got some kind of illness I should know about?"

Pax shook her head, grabbing the phone. Ward wasn't talking. Pax affected Rimes' voice again, "Sorry, I –"

"Ms Kuranes? Is that you?" Ward said.

Pax froze.

"Why do you have Dr Rimes' phone?"

Pax's mouth dropped open. This was bad. Very bad.

"Let me." Letty flew below Pax's nose, to the bottom of the phone. She raised her voice, and said, "Rimes is dead and you'll join her if you keep this up. Understand, fuck-bucket?"

Pax stared, aghast, and imagined Ward reacting the same way.

"Fucking hang up already," Letty snarled.

"Who is that?" Ward spoke urgently. "Pax, are you with –" She was cut off by someone in the background. A panicked man. "Not now! Pax – please –"

"I said step the fuck off, desk-jockey!" Letty shouted. "Or you wanna learn what InterSpecies Relations really means?"

"Wait!" Ward said. "You can't –"

Pax ended the call and glowered at Letty. "What the hell was that?"

"You tell me, you're the one on the floor!"

"No, that!" Pax held up the phone. "You just –"

"She made you! Better to give her the fear."

"Absolutely," Lightgate agreed, grinning at this whole exchange.

The phone started ringing again.

"Ditch it," Letty commanded. "We need to move."

Pax looked over to Casaria, in shadows with his head resting back against the tree. Had he passed out? She stood quickly, cutting off the caller, and brought up Rimes' home number. She nodded to the ruined building. "The glo's in there?"

Letty hovered upwards, "In the kitchen, straight through. I didn't see anything else."

The phone was answered: "Dr Rimes' residence –"

"Holly, you need to get out of there."

"Pax?"

"I got a call from the Ministry. On Rimes' phone. They know. I'm sorry."

"What do you mean –"

"You need to leave, now."

"And go where? How –"

"Is that the Bartons?" Lightgate appeared alongside the phone, eyes suddenly bright with excitement. "I can take them to Broadplain."

Pax needed only the briefest pause, her instinct flaring against leaving Lightgate responsible for anyone's safety. "I'm sending Letty to get you, she'll take you somewhere safe. And . . . I'm sorry, I need to lose this phone."

She hung up as Letty said, "Get this fucking liquid and we'll go together."

"You said there's nothing dangerous in there. Go, meet me back at Rolarn's place."

Letty looked from Pax up to Lightgate. "You gonna watch her?"

"While you're on a collision course with the Ministry?" Lightgate's hands dropped to her pistols. Holding them like handles. "No chance."

"Both of you go if you have to," said Pax, raising her voice. As the fairies started to move, she looked at the phone in her hand. Rimes had said they couldn't track everything, but they'd surely be after this now. "Can you take this with you? Dump it somewhere."

Sam swept her jacket off the back of her chair as Roper blocked her doorway. She started dismissing him before she'd met his eyes. "We're on our way out – what's wrong?"

"There's been another incident," he said, cheeks flushed red. "In Nothicker."

Sam stared. They couldn't waste time cleaning up after the *praelucente* – not now. Pax was with someone – it had to be one of the Fae, they'd referenced IS – and she'd done something with Rimes. The doctor *had* been involved with whatever Apothel knew. Even if Pax wasn't a criminal herself, her thuggish connections or the Fae were. She said, "I need to find this woman – can you run a phone trace?"

"*Now?*" Roper exclaimed. "Ms Ward, we've got a major crisis!"

Sam bit her lip. Fine. She had to move fast. Whether Pax had hurt the doctor or was working with her, chances were they'd been to the laboratory on the hill, and would be covering their tracks. Maybe they'd been hiding there all along. Had Casaria there. Was Pax there *now*?

"Get Mathers in," Sam told Roper, quickly. "Use the agents near Nothicker."

"Devlin's been alerted," Roper said, "and the deputy director. But –"

"There's nothing I can do," Sam said, briskly. "We've got to go."

"You're the ranking officer!" Roper insisted. "Someone needs to call through to London, and file an LR-58 –"

"Not *now*!" Seeing his stunned expression, Sam struggled to keep her voice reasonable. "You can open the LR-58 yourself. London can wait. *Please* step aside."

"I'll handle it," Landon volunteered, drawing a hopeful look from Roper.

"No!" Sam insisted. "I need you with me."

"Ms Ward . . ." Roper started. There was no time: Pax would know Sam was on her way to Rimes' place. She barged past the analyst.

"We've got a lead on the root of this problem," she said, for her own benefit more than his. "All this chaos started with Pax; she's got information about the *praelucente's* instability – meaning she can help us *stop* it or she could make it *worse*. We have to find her, we have to understand what she's up to." Sam turned back to give one final, firm reason. "And she might have Casaria."

Roper responded with weak, stuttering complaints. "But the LR-58 – street-level – *what if the papers call?*"

"Don't answer!"

26

"Why were the Ministry calling you?" Holly demanded, storming after Rimes like a woman possessed. "You turned them away, didn't you?"

Barton hopped after her, trying to get in the way, barely able to keep up. He should have seen this coming: Holly must've been waiting for a chance to rip into Rimes.

"They work together," Barton said. "Keep your enemies close, Holly, that's basic –"

"The only basic thing here is your thick skull!" Holly snapped. She turned on Rimes. "Do you have any idea the trouble you've caused?" Rimes refused to meet her gaze, receding into her own flustering attempts to organise a stack of petri dishes. Holly circled a workbench, trying to get in front of her. "What are we supposed to do? We're not using that stolen car, are we? Do you have some form of transport besides rusty scooters?"

"They don't come here," Rimes answered quietly. "They can't come here."

"Are you hearing me?" Holly raised her voice. "How do we get out of here?"

"Mum!" Grace cut in, loud and worried enough that Holly paused. Bless her, Barton thought. She could calm this beast.

"Grace," Holly faltered. "Best get your things together."

"What *things*?"

"I don't know!" Holly exploded again, hands in the air. "Find some!"

"There's a tunnel . . ." Rimes said. "Then a boat, or a path along the river. But the Ministry aren't going to –"

"Get your head out of the clouds!" Holly commanded. "Where's this tunnel go? What then?" She spun to Barton. "Do you know about this?"

Barton nodded. The old escape plan, which they'd never needed. How many times Apothel had insisted the spooks would come for them, and none of them had really believed it.

"I can talk to them," Rimes said.

"I bloody doubt that," Holly said. "Do you have money? We'll get to a train station, that's what we'll do. Go to Betty in Manchester, as we should've done in the first place."

"They have people in Manchester," Barton said.

"So where *can* we go?"

That was the part Apothel's plan hadn't accounted for. Escape, fine, but then what? Barton said, "They have people in every major city. Across Europe, too. We're better off in Ordshaw."

Holly snarled, "In places like this?"

"Mum!" Grace cried again, stomping a foot. "We need to work together!"

Holly paused, but her gaze was no less fierce. Rimes turned without another word and pointed at the edge of a trapdoor, beneath a crate of metal piping. She crouched to start shifting the crate, and her face strained, feebly. Holly shoved her aside. She used all her weight to move the box herself, and it scraped over the floorboards with a piercing sound, tearing up the woodwork. Holly thrust the trapdoor open.

Grace took Barton by the elbow as they got closer, the pair of them ambling like they were shackled. He could feel his ankle straining, but couldn't let it show. The look on Grace's face gave him strength. She was ready, eyes determined, filthy t-shirt and shorts partially concealed under a tatty leather raincoat she had found. She'd found some slip-on shoes, too. Barton whispered, "We'll be okay, honey."

Rimes stood beside Holly, frightened eyes absurdly big in those glasses.

"A light would be nice," Holly said.

Rimes fussed to the side and thrust a torch into Holly's hands, then took a few quick steps back. Holly regarded the torch oddly. "You first, I think."

Rimes did as she was told, climbing nervously into the tunnel. Twenty years Holly's senior, but following her orders the same as everyone else. Barton came to the ladder next, as quick as his aches would allow. He said, "You go, both of you. I'll activate the defences."

"Oh rot," Holly snapped. She told Grace, "Hurry on down, dear, we're right behind you."

Grace jumped forwards, embracing her in a hug.

"I love you, Mum."

Holly swallowed the lump in her throat. "Get along."

As Grace climbed onto the ladder, Holly turned to Barton. "Are you going to get your fat gut down there, or what?"

"The defences . . ."

"Tell me what needs doing." She helped him onto the ladder, carrying some of his weight.

"There's a panel," Barton said. "Near the window. Throw all the switches up." He paused and warned, "We've never had to do this before. Never tried it."

"Right," said Holly, determined. "All the switches are going up."

Pax crept quickly through the burnt-out building. Letty's assurances hadn't made the place feel safe, given the sharp edges of its scorched fixtures and the lack of clear light. Had the Blue Angel chosen this place for a drop-off after learning about the fire, or had it started the fire to create a drop-off point?

Was this her over-thinking, like Letty said?

Entering the kitchen, Pax was drawn to dim green light. The cylinder sat in the middle of the room like a fluorescent camping lantern, the love child of a masonry jar and a nuclear reactor. Behind it, the remnants of the outer wall stood two feet high; chipboard and tarp covered the space above. To the right, a charred star emanated from the skeleton of cabinets and hinges. The source of the fire. At least Pax had solved one mystery: some prat had failed to use an oven properly.

Pax moved closer. No sign of hideous clawing in the walls. No electric squid limbs. Didn't look like the ash-dusted tiles were going to break apart and reveal a pit of teeth.

She approached the jar and scooped it up. Just as she turned to leave, *crack* – the floor broke apart around her boots. She shrieked as she dropped, plunging into something. She heaved at her legs but both feet were stuck. Regaining her balance, clutching the glo, she looked down and swore.

Not teeth, but scarcely better: where there'd been tiles before, there was a dark, pulsating mass. Like the acid slug from the chapel, it moved fluidly, bulging undulations illuminated by the liquid's light. It was wrapped around her boots, up to her ankles, and tightening. Pax heaved at her left leg, leaning into it, but it wouldn't move.

"Get the fuck off me!" she yelled, but it closed tighter and sucked down. She was being dragged into it. Pax shifted the jar under one arm and threw the other out, looking for something to grab hold of. She twisted, clawing at the tarp and boarding of the broken wall. The thing sucked at her calves like living mud. She swore again, getting a fistful of tarp, but the material ripped, high up, and fell on her like a drape. She flapped it frantically out of her face and grabbed out again, but her fingers scraped against the boards, nothing to hold onto.

It had pulled her down to her knees, enveloping her. She planted her free hand on the floor, pushing back against it. Barely slowing it. It kept sucking, pulling her further – into what? An expanding, moving, squeezing mud.

Should've seen this coming, she told herself. Did see this coming. Stupid, stupid.

She checked the doorway, the shadows. The living mud squelched up around her thighs. No one was saving her this time; no fairy entourage, no Casaria with a miracle weapon. She took deep breaths, gritting her teeth and pushing harder against the floor.

And all for this dumb fucking liquid.

She looked at the jar. They'd said ridiculous things about it, hadn't they? It helped Apothel's fight. It brought Barton back from the brink. It gave them eyes in the Sunken City. Pax gave a last frantic look around the room. No other options.

She twisted off the cap and lifted the jar to her lips. The vile sludge gave another hard tug, swarming up to her waist. She gulped down a mouthful of the glowing liquid and gagged noiselessly as it burned its way down. The warmth spread through her as if it was whisky, but bolder, surging into her limbs. Filling every vein. Right to her fingertips. Her vision blurred and pulsed in a kaleidoscope of colours.

For a moment, time stopped. The sludge wasn't pulling. She wasn't breathing. The air was still. In that frozen second she placed the jar slowly, calmly aside, and blinked heavily, once, twice. The room twisted then came back into focus with clear grey lines, the shadows gone. She could make out *everything*.

She looked down, to where her lower half was being consumed by darkness, and it sucked at her again, wrapping around her hips. She raised both fists in a defiant cry but held them there as she saw the sludge for what it really was.

Under its thick black skin a network of arteries was moving, manoeuvring the creature in multiple directions at once, twisting around her legs. They lit up like a purple X-ray image. The arteries fed back, in a complicated, vascular pattern, to low-down masses of light: throbbing internal organs.

There was something Pax could grip onto.

It sucked at her again, and she screamed as she punched a hand into the writhing mass, aiming for a gap in the arteries. Her fist went straight through, all the way down, and the sludge separated around her as she bent into it, driving her hand in. Her scream turned to an animal yell. She flexed her fingers as she continued, parting the mucky flesh, stretching, finally, to the nearest of the bulging organs. Her fingers closed around it, texture like liver. And she pulled back.

The arteries lit up red as she squeezed, and the whole shape pulsed outward, stricken. Her legs were released and she fell back, lower back hitting the edge of the hole in the floor but her hand still squeezing. The mass of sludge throbbed up, out, bulging in all directions as she twisted her hand and kept pulling, putting every ounce of her strength into shifting this thing. She kicked at the same time, getting a foothold in the struggling monster and pushing herself out of the hole. Another kick, another push, the thing in her hand all the time. She heaved herself away and rolled off, through the ash, finally letting go of the creature's organ.

Gasping, her back muscles burning, Pax rolled over and looked back as the creature released a piercing hiss. The parts of its sludgy mass that had spread out into the room flopped to the floor, and the whole thing slowly slid back into the hole like a deflated balloon. The crack in the tiles steamed like a geyser. Light bounced off the gas, the red of the arteries turning purple again, then dimming. Pax blinked, not sure what was real, what was the effects of the drink.

She raised her hands in front of her face, and saw the light there, too.

Her own veins, glowing through the flesh. Electric blue.

Pax fell back with another small shriek and shook her hands to get it off.

No no no, fuck that.

She scrambled to her feet, swept up the jar and ran.

Pax slowed down as she reached Casaria, skipping on the uneven kilter of having only one boot. Someone was silhouetted in the window of a house opposite, watching. Pax pulled her hood up and ducked. A neighbour shouted, uncertainly, "I'm calling the police!"

She ignored the threat, hoping that's all it was.

Casaria stared at her warily, still leaning against the tree with his hand pressed into his wound. As she crouched and opened the jar, he tried to speak, "Pax . . . what are you . . ."

His eyes ran to her clothes, her trousers sodden with slime. No sense trying to explain. She tilted the glo towards his lips. "Drink this."

Casaria's eyes shot open and he jerked his head away with a curse. He struck the tree behind him, and Pax thrust her other hand out to hold him still. He was weak, thankfully, and only half awake; she held his neck firmly and rammed the jar into his mouth. He tried to spit the liquid out but she clamped her hand over his mouth and hissed, "After what I just went through, fucking drink it."

In his struggle, Casaria gulped, swallowed. Pax saw the change come over him in an instant, recognising what she'd felt herself. He had to blink a few times, and as his eyes got wider his pupils narrowed. His mouth dropped open as he focused horrified eyes on her.

He was seeing what she'd seen, wasn't he?

Pax slowly removed her hand from Casaria's mouth, ignoring the blue light under her flesh. There was no similar glowing under *his* skin. She stood, uneasily. It was bad. This liquid's power was starting to fade, already, her vision going back to dreary normal, the blue in her veins dimming, but it was too late to ignore it. Casaria clearly saw it too.

His face relaxed, somewhat; his jaw unclenched, like the pain was lifting. His hand holding the wound slackened. But he was staring at her with a knotted brow.

She'd taken more from the minotaur than psychic fits. Something was inside her. She didn't want to know what.

"Get up," Pax said, breaking Casaria's gaze. "We've got to go."

Casaria said nothing, still staring, transfixed by what he was seeing. But he stood.

27

"We're getting close to something," Sam told Landon. "I know it."

As they sped through the suburb of Long Culdon, Sam scanned the changing scenery. The houses were small, cheap and quiet. A retirement community, if there was any community at all. It had been one of her options when she moved into the suburbs last year, but she'd opted for Geeside in the east; slightly younger, if further afield. Seeing how quickly Landon had got them here, she wondered if it had been the right choice.

As they climbed the hill, a bigger question occupied her mind. Would Landon be able to handle what they found here? The decision hadn't come easily for him, ignoring the duty of cordoning off another accident in favour of a fugitive chase. She hoped his uncertainty about helping her came from his reluctance to break the rules, not because he was afraid. Pax Kuranes was an enigma and Darren Barton was known to be dangerous, if he was with her. To say nothing of hired thugs and Fae. Landon carried a gun, but how well could he use it?

Either way, in a few turns they'd reach the approach to Dr Rimes' shack, alone.

"Gonna be interesting," Landon said, so dry she doubted he meant it. "They don't like us coming up here. Never been myself."

"Another problem we've been avoiding," Ward said. "I understand them letting Dr Rimes continue her work, but didn't she warrant close scrutiny, rather than being kept at arm's length? Did Devlin and Farnham even search the place this morning?"

"Easy to say after the fact," Landon replied. "She's not an effective asset."

Sam didn't reply. She'd complained about the Ministry's sponsorship of this unregulated civilian before and been ignored. As usual.

Landon turned another corner and pulled up at the end of a long, tree-lined road. Skeletal branches reached overhead, with no sign of houses either side. Sam said, "This is it?"

"No," Landon said. "Short walk. Better they don't hear the car coming."

Sam got out. "Do you think they're still here?"

Landon gave her a lazy look over the top of the car. He offered his slow, professional opinion: "No. Apothel's whole crowd were always good at hiding."

He started walking. The incline got steeper before the peak of the hill, and his breathing grew deeper. Sam fell back, contemplating that the one thing a field agent should possess, at the least, was a moderate level of fitness. But she scolded herself; that wasn't fair. He was all she had. And he'd been doing a good job today.

They turned another corner, and there was the doctor's shack, down the end of a dirt track. It looked like a scout camp or a hostel, forgotten in the wilderness. One small square window was lit from the inside.

Landon drew his pistol, checking the trees left and right, as though he could see anything in the dense shadows. He pointed at the cracked paving under the dirt. "Road surface hasn't been repaired in decades."

Sam looked. Was it important?

Landon stopped walking and lowered his pistol to his side. He let out a relieved breath as Sam saw the object in the undergrowth. A car – hidden by leaves and a tarp, but still recognisable. It had to be the Cavalier that Pax's group had stolen after Friday's debacle in the tunnels. The Ministry might pat them on the back for recovering that, at least. And make an example of Farnham: how the hell had he not checked *that*? But Landon's shoulders tightened with apparent realisation. Of course, the car meant Pax *was* here, and so too might be her criminal friends or the violent Fae.

"Stay behind me," Landon said. He continued towards the shack, crunching over brittle leaves with no care for subtlety.

Despite the light in the window, the building looked empty. Sam wanted it to be empty. She didn't want to test Landon, or to have to make decisions resulting in violence.

They reached the porch and Landon gave her a look, deferring for instructions. She stared at the door, a flimsy wooden thing. They didn't have a search warrant, but in the course of Ministry duties that wasn't necessary. The presence of the Cavalier gave them all the right they needed for Landon to break in, and more, and his eyes said he was prepared to do whatever she said. Sam hesitated. She took out her phone and whispered, "I'm calling it in."

As she dialled, Landon narrowed his eyes. Concentrating on something she hadn't noticed. He raised a finger to stop Ward making a sound. Scanning the trees, he shifted forward. His foot snapped a twig, loud enough to make Sam cringe.

The snap was answered by shaking branches.

Their eyes shot to the noise, and Sam saw the outline of the squat dark creature, just inside the treeline, a moment before it growled. The drawn-out rumble of a furious dog. Another rustle as it moved a paw closer.

"On my mark." Landon straightened up, fingers teasing his pistol grip. "You run back the way we came. Don't stop. Could be more of them."

"What . . ." Sam said, barely able to form the word. The growl revved like an engine.

"Get to the car." Landon rested onto his back foot, raising the gun, and broke another twig. The dog darted forward. "Go!"

Sam sprinted as Landon stepped in front of it, raising the pistol and spreading his legs, making himself a target. She shot a glance sideways and saw the animal moving her way. After her, not him, peeling to the side with a – there was light around it. An orange mist, caught on wisps of smoke streaming from its flesh. Not a dog.

Sam yelled, sprinting for all she was worth, but it kept pace, flanking her. Landon shouted, "Dive left!"

She did so without thinking, throwing herself to the side as the thumping paws drew level with her and crashed through the trees. She sensed it rising from her side, the ferocious dark shape of a predator in flight.

Its snarl was cut off by a gunshot – an explosion a split second later.

Sam rode a wave of fire, into the trees.

The Bartons and Rimes were on the river when the blast shook them. The ten-foot boat listed, from the tremor and their collectively turning towards the sound, and they braced themselves against the light vessel and each other. With a steep tree-dotted hill rising behind the mouth of the cavern they'd exited, there was no way of seeing what had happened, but the sound was tremendous. Rimes made an upset noise, and Holly felt a pang of guilt. Had the booby-trap she'd activated destroyed this hapless woman's home?

"Damned fools must've shot a dog," Darren said.

Holly eyed him. "Those dogs *explode*?"

"Very volatile," Rimes said, voice cracking. Something twigged in her mind, and she darted a look to the sky. "Now we'll see the blinding water. The ether bats."

They stared at the opaque clouds.

Nothing happened.

Rimes' expression shifted, a little confused.

"We never tested those things . . ."

"Great," Holly said. She looked from the nothingness above the hill to the water around them. The boat sat low in the stream, an aluminium basin surely unfit to carry this many people. It could have been paired with the scooter in some kind of art collection. Derelict Vehicles of the Impoverished. The engine at the back was pocked with green mould, almost certainly useless, though they had agreed not to use it for subtlety's sake. Her hulking husband heaved on two rotten oars, with the scientist twitching in the corner and Grace shivering with nerves; hardly a romantic trip.

"Where does this take us?" Holly asked.

"Down the River Drum," Darren said, citing the city's second large tributary, which ran through the slums of Nothicker before joining the River Gader. Decidedly *not* romantic. Did junkies mug people on boats? "If we get off in Nothicker, we can cut through to our nearest hideout."

"The Den?" Rimes replied with surprise. "Oh no. That's no good. The Ministry found the Den shortly after Apothel . . . you know."

"They knew about the Den?" Darren eyed her.

Rimes looked away. Her gaze settled on Grace, apparently the least threatening audience member. "They knew most of our locations. I didn't tell them. Well. Except about the pack of ravishers near the room on Mercer Street."

"You told them about *Mercer Street*?" Darren slowed his rowing.

Much as Holly liked the idea of this odd woman being tossed in the river, it was hardly the time for Darren to start questioning her. She said, "Presumably, then, you can tell us which hideouts they *didn't* touch?"

"That I know of," Rimes replied quietly, "the game room in West Farling. Maybe the apartment in East Farling."

"On the other side of the fucking city," Darren scoffed.

"Diz!" Holly hissed. "In front of your *daughter*?"

"It's fine, Mum," Grace said.

"It's *not* fine, Grace. Your father –"

"That apartment's not gonna have stood idle for ten years," Darren continued, seeming not to have heard the interruption. "The game room, maybe. But we'd have to use the Tube." He said it with a distaste that Holly realised, now, was not entirely caused by his affinity for cars over public transport.

A voice came from the gunwhale: "I've got a better idea."

Seeing Letty perched near her hand, Holly jumped off the bench, rocking the boat and drawing a squeal from Grace. "Heaven and hell – how did you get here?"

"Helicopter, what the fuck do you think?"

"I don't think –"

"Alright, shut up." Letty flew to head height. Darren tensed, squeezing his fingers into the oars. "Pax sent me to get you lummoxes. You're gonna come with me to *our* hideout, in Broadplain."

"I'm not putting my family in the care of fairies," Darren said, without hesitation.

"Excuse me," Holly said, "you were *just* saying we have nowhere to go."

"Broadplain's worse than nowhere," Darren countered. "Their sort fester around there. They came to our house, Holly, blew a hole in our street –"

"Chew a sock, shit-tower," Letty said. "That blast must've jogged the bit of your memory where I was *helping* you."

"Trouble is," Darren growled, "your help comes with other Fae attached."

The fact that Letty didn't deny it outright said Darren's fears weren't unjustified. She even looked upwards, seemingly to confirm it. They followed her gaze to another small shape floating a short way off. A white dot in the sky.

"The Ministry aren't gonna stop coming for you," Letty said, more calmly. "My people can hide you."

"I've had it in the ear from every direction how dangerous this Ministry is," Holly said, eyes on Darren. "Considering what I've seen of your efforts so far, Diz, I'm inclined to go with the fairy."

"Pax will be there?" Grace chimed in.

Darren went quiet and merely looked to Rimes. She was staring at the Fae, fascinated, making it no mystery where her interests lay.

"That's sorted then," Letty said. "Next on the agenda, I've got a name and it's not fucking *fairy*."

28

Pax's fear and confusion abated with the distraction of Casaria, sitting close behind her, shifting from his numb trance into more conscious stiffness. As they shakily swerved through Ordshaw, she felt Casaria leaning self-consciously away from her, his touch easing off from her waist. The liquid had worked, and he was regaining his senses, but it reminded Pax who she was dealing with. Hitting the ring road, she drove faster than was safe for the bike, nuts and bolts rattling, to end this closeness.

Pax parked a short distance from the shopping centre, leaving the remains of the glo in the bike's seat, with Casaria on it, rather than stop and talk to him. He called out, "What are we doing here?"

He'd got his voice back.

Pax stopped across the road from the first gloomy walls of Broadplain Plaza. The shutters were down on the ground-level shopfronts and windows, the doors chained and padlocked. No sign of the Fae welcoming her in. She searched the gutters for scrap metal to use as lock picks.

"You fed me those vagrants' hooch," Casaria scolded, catching up.

"I'm trying to focus," Pax told him. He watched silently, his energy not totally returned, until she found the little shards of metal she was looking for – one the bent arm of a brooch, the other some hair clip remnant. Bless Broadplain for its unclean streets.

As Pax settled into picking a lock, Casaria decided to speak again. "*Never* do that to me again. You know that stuff rots minds?"

That was good, at least; whatever he'd seen, Casaria was likely to dismiss it as an illusion. Never mind that the glo had clearly worked unnatural wonders, relieving his pain and leaving him walking and talking like he hadn't just been stabbed.

"You were laid out dying twenty minutes ago," Pax said.

"Twenty minutes ago," he echoed, as though that was explanation enough. Suggesting he'd rested it off, riding on the back of a scooter? Pax gave him an incredulous look; was he *that* delusional? He continued, "They were rank amateurs – it took three of them to capture me. And they botched a *stabbing?* And who did they think I would talk to. To report *what?* I've had more trouble with drunken brawls."

Pax probed silently at the lock's mechanism. If that's how he wanted to see the day, who was she to stop him.

"You came after me, though," Casaria said, raising his voice. Christ, the liquid had done a full job reviving him. "You realised you need me, right? After running off into the night. But I set that weapon off. I did that. No one's ever faced the *praelucente* like that before. I injured it."

"You pulled a trigger," Pax replied. "*I* faced it."

His reply came slowly, "And what did it do to you?"

"Hurt like hell."

"Afterwards," he said, tone hinting he was questioning his hallucinations after all. "The power of that thing – you must have felt –"

Pax said, "Stop. Talking."

He did, for a moment, and she realised his line of questions sounded like Barton, when he'd drunk the glo that morning. He'd seen it too, hadn't he? Thankfully, Casaria changed the subject. "They talked a lot, your gangster friends. The talk of morons is a particular kind of hell. Good thing they didn't realise that."

Pax ventured a glance at him. From the way he was standing, the knife wound really wasn't bothering him. She couldn't see any fresh blood. His foot was still a bloody, bandaged mess, though. "How bad is your toe?"

"I've got others. It was nothing."

He was smiling. His false smile, the street light bouncing off those straight white teeth. His eyes told a different story, discomfort biting at their edges. He'd make light of it, even find pride in enduring it, but he had suffered.

"I'd never have talked," Casaria continued scornfully. "People like that are the reason the Ministry exists. They could use those monsters. Breed them, unleash them."

"*Make* them dangerous?" Pax said. "Your *praelucente* is already hurting this city."

"Please. You've been poisoned with the lies of psycho Fae and driven to the Ordshaw mafia, what do you know?"

Pax gave Casaria a severe look. "The Fae saved my life today. Yours, too."

Casaria paused, for a second seeming ready to flat-out deny it. But he said, "You might think you and me are even, but –"

"We're a long way from even."

Casaria's expression softened. Surprised. "Well, that's a start."

"That wasn't an apology, you prat. You took my money. Kidnapped Rufaizu, stole things from my apartment –"

"Saved your life? While you lied to me, stabbed me in the back, left me to hang."

The padlock clicked open and Pax stood. She pulled the chain away and opened the door, then replied, "You *didn't* hang, I notice. You ran back to the Ministry, right? Did they take you in with open arms? After what you did?"

"I convinced them it was momentary madness," Casaria said. "Manipulated by a woman. Who, it would seem, is trying it again."

"I never fucking manipulated you. Listen. We're gonna get safe, and we're gonna have a proper talk about who's been stabbing who in the back, okay?"

She entered the unlit expanse of the plaza and stopped, checking for an alarm. A light blinked green in the distance. A smoke detector.

"What a dive," Casaria said, walking past her, scanning the dead shops. "This the sort of place you shop?"

"What do you think?" Pax said, closing the door behind them. She scanned the upper walkways. "This way."

"You never answered my question," Casaria said. "What's in here?"

She still didn't tell him, heading towards the dead-end of the Fae's hideout. She reached the department store and climbed the stairs to the gap in the boarding. Coming up behind her, Casaria announced, "I know this place." He laughed like he'd just got the punchline to a joke he'd heard long ago. "They came back here? The arrogant little shits."

"Keep it down," Pax warned. "What are you talking about?"

"The Fae," Casaria said, voice suddenly nasty, accusing. "You brought us here for the Fae. What's the plan, deliver me from gangsters to be sacrificed to insects?"

"No," Pax told him, "the plan's for you to live long enough to do the right thing."

"The only right thing for the Fae is burning them all to ash."

"I need you to rein that right the hell in," Pax snarled. "Keep talking and you're gonna turn this opportunity into a bloodbath. Your choice."

He was grinning, enjoying the suggestion of trouble, but he didn't answer back. For all his bluster, Pax sensed the day of torture had humbled him.

She turned back to the store entrance and paused. This place was supposed to be safe from the Ministry. "How did you know the Fae were here?"

"I've seen photos," he said. "From before my time. I never come this way myself – patrols in Broadplain tend to be restricted to the west side, around the storm drains – but this was once the site of their gypsy city. The MEE tracked them here. The bugs evacuated before we could snuff them out. And now they're back?"

"No," Pax said, "there's no city here. Just a few sympathetic souls. Why didn't the Ministry keep an eye on this place?"

"What would I know?" Casaria's mood shifted again, bitterness redirecting. "Apparently what the MEE do with the Fae is not my concern. Maybe Sam Ward ceded Broadplain to the insects when she started sucking up to them."

"I don't think so. I've been told her department hasn't had much luck with the Fae." A mix of pleasure and confusion passed across Casaria's face; happy to hear of others' failings but curious about this unexpected insight. Pax said, "You've got layers of misinformation within the Ministry, haven't you?"

"No. Management think they're better than us on the ground level, that's all."

"Management being?"

"Bureaucrats behind desks, men with no connection to the real world."

"Uh-huh." Pax appreciated the irony. "I've got an idea it's more complicated than that. Come in." She moved into the empty store and scanned the area with the phone torch. Bare and desolate as before. She continued to the escalator and searched the darkness below. No lights, no sound of movement. She called out,

"You guys here?"

No reply.

"I can't believe –" Casaria started, but Pax clicked her tongue for quiet. She went down the steps. The lantern was off, the light behind the counter too.

"Guys?"

By the counter, the shadow of a fairy came around the till. The rounded bulk of Rolarn. He said, blandly, "So this is the corrupt agent? Our key to the Ministry?"

Pax gave Casaria a glance, finding him staring with tight-lipped anger. "Casaria, this is Rolarn. He saved my life earlier today, same as you did last night. You're more alike than you realise." Both violent creeps, for starters. Casaria looked too livid to respond. She turned to Rolarn. "Arnold not here?"

"Arnold," Rolarn scoffed, leaning on his shotgun as if it were a crutch. Apparently they weren't close. "Lightgate's had his crew running errands all day. With luck they won't be back. Bad enough I'm putting up humans, I'm not taking in Fae garbage, too. The shit I'm doing. Look."

Rolarn turned the lantern on as Pax moved around the counter. She discovered a remarkable stash of human produce that Rolarn had apparently amassed alone. Wrapped sandwiches, bottles of water and bags of snacks, stacked to knee-height. Behind that, a pile of blankets, packaged fresh from a camping store. These Fae definitely had their uses – and despite Rolarn's words, this stockpile showed empathy for human needs.

"How did you get all this here?"

"Carried it."

Pax whispered, "Like rhino beetles."

Casaria loomed over the counter from the other side, keeping his distance. He said, "Carried it from where?"

"No one's going to trace it," Rolarn said.

Pax noticed the safe. She crouched by the sturdy metal box, its door open. The two-tiered Fae hideout contained worn dollhouse-sized beds and armchairs, surrounded by piles of trinkets: jewellery, credit cards, a torn family photo. At the front, a barrel of powder that had to be Fae dust. Enough to dip a whole fairy into. The stash suggested the supply stockpile might have more to do with Fae hoarding instincts rather than empathy. And if this little camp was anything to go by, the Fae city had to be a sight worth seeing. Pax stood again, hearing Casaria's voice getting more aggravated: "*Illegal* isn't measured by whether you can get away with it. I didn't think you were actually a criminal, Pax, even if you associate with them."

"*You* stole from me."

"In the interests of national security."

"Bollocks." Deciding not to fuel his hostility, Pax turned her attention to the state of her clothing. She asked Rolarn, "You do requests?"

Casaria tutted. "Add more theft to your willingness to work with these vermin and we're getting into *seriously* dangerous territory."

Pax bit back the need to reply. Barely interested, Rolarn said, "Lightgate says you get whatever you need."

"Have you heard from her?" Pax said. "Are Letty and the others okay?"

Rolarn shrugged, his nonchalance as irritating as Casaria's hostility. "Sure."

"You can carry a human blanket but you can't string a sentence together?"

"I can get it to talk," Casaria said. "Ask me to get it to talk, Pax."

"Yeah, Casaria" – Pax gave him a scathing tone – "I want you to hurt our only allies. That's why I risked everything to get you back. You wanna park the macho for a minute and let me tell you what I *do* want?"

Casaria gave quiet assent.

"I want to figure out exactly how the minotaur and the things surrounding it are fucking us all."

"It's good for Ordshaw –"

"Get bent. You talk about protecting the city; after you shocked the minotaur, it started tearing through Ordshaw. Popped up at least twice to feed. People *died*."

Casaria hesitated. "Impossible. It would never –"

"It *did*. At least seven dead in an Underground accident caused by the minotaur. And it's only getting worse."

Unsettled, Casaria's voice broke slightly. "I'm sure – then the Ministry will deal with it. Our analysts monitor the net benefit, and if it crosses the point where it stops being useful, the MEE have protocols to take care of it. We have –"

"Bullshit," Pax spat. "You have no idea what it is, how could you possibly know it's got a *net benefit*, let alone deal with it? I saw it attached to the blue screens, and I saw a half-formed slug monster come out of one of them today."

"There are no blue screens," Casaria said, automatically. "Apothel invented –"

"They exist!" Pax replied, firm enough to startle Casaria into quiet. "I saw them myself! And there's *definitely* something operating behind them, the thing Apothel called his Blue Angel. It's capable of more than scratching on walls – these screens can move things, I saw an acidic slug creature come out of one – something else" – she pointed, indicating back where they'd come from – "at that glo drop-off. The Blue Angel controls these screens, and somehow uses this energy. I saw the screens connected to your *praelucente*. Whatever's behind them is behind *everything*."

"What *everything*?" Casaria said. "We have undesirable creatures surrounding a single desirable phenomenon. There's no conspiracy –"

"There's nothing *but* conspiracy!" Pax said, exasperated. "The creatures protect the minotaur, keeping us and the Fae away, so this Angel can keep using the energy it sucks from *us*. The Ministry are acting like game wardens – preserving the minotaur without properly understanding it. Fuck, Apothel did the same thing, even if his heart was in the right place."

"Apothel," said Casaria, pronouncing the man's name like a curse, "wanted to destroy the *praelucente*. He was out of his mind."

"Beside the point – he *didn't* destroy it. He spent his time tracking it, telling the Blue Angel where the minotaur was, with no result. The moment he got his hands on a weapon that could make a difference, he died. And now *you* do his job instead, tracking the monster, protecting it."

"Because we have data proving its worth, not because anyone tricked us."

"Data that tells you *what*?" Pax said. "You don't know what the minotaur is, do you? You have this idea of – what's it called – novisan? Life energy? But you don't know what glo does, or how the blue screen works. You don't even believe they exist. But look at yourself, you're standing, talking, after what you went through? *Think* – the truth of this whole mixed-up energy source is being hidden by this anonymous Angel, with powers beyond our understanding. It's messing everyone around; it needs the minotaur, but it needs people watching it, too. The Blue Angel is using the monsters but they are not in its control. See the danger?"

"I see conjecture and paranoia," Casaria said. "You think you're the first person to ask these questions? Pax, I'm glad you're invested, but the MEE have –"

"No," Pax said, quickly. "Your people aren't playing with a full deck. And maybe I'm not the first to ask, but I'm trying to get all sides of the story. It sure as shit feels like I'm the first to talk to the Fae without losing my head."

"The Fae can burn in –"

"They used to live in the Sunken City!" Pax said. "They know things we don't! Apothel died for these questions. People killed to silence the answers – *your* people continue the tradition."

"I do what's best. "

"Yeah? Where the fuck is Rufaizu?" Pax's voice rose again.

Casaria stalled. "It wasn't safe having him free to share what he knew."

"And what *does* he know? You've got all that from him now, have you?"

Casaria frowned. "Pax, he's an aberration, like his father. Look, this isn't you. You aren't like *them*. You're smarter than that."

"Fuck you," Pax spat. "You don't know me." She moved closer to him and thumped a hand against her chest. "This is me, standing up for my city." She tapped her temple. "Using my fucking brain. Talking with other people, even if they're homeless or tiny or just *different*, because they've got different pieces of this puzzle. I *am* like them, because I'm willing to fight a good fight. What are you?"

Casaria leant away, intimidated by her proximity. The muscles around his mouth tightened. He was digging deep, for whatever justifications helped him sleep at night. He wanted to argue back but no words came. Finally, he gave in, breaking her gaze. "Whatever. Go steal some clothes."

"That's all you've got? Ignore the problems? I need you to help me, Casaria. *Do* you know what Rufaizu knows?"

Casaria reluctantly shook his head, and Pax saw the doubt in his eyes. Of course, he wanted answers, too. He hadn't taken Rufaizu in straight away, when she first met him – he definitely had questions of his own. She pushed: "You didn't let your mate in the Ministry take us in. You know we're on the right side of this. Are you gonna help this city? Or do you want to go back to being part of the problem?"

He replied, with a tone meek enough to say he was ready to really listen, "What would you have me do?"

29

Sam was vaguely aware of a bright light flashing back and forth across her vision. A male voice asking her questions, fast but concerned.

"Ms Ward, can you hear me?"

She nodded numbly. Trying to look past the emerald blur of his bulky uniform. There was a crowd down the road. A fire-extinguisher hiss.

"Can you tell me what day it is?"

"Monday."

"You remember what was in the news this morning?"

"In the news?" She batted his hand away as his fingers touched her head. It hurt. Stinging above her temple. Something warm trickling down.

"I'm just going to dab it, this might sting. It's nothing serious."

She winced as cloth touched the wound with an acidic bite.

"You saw the news this morning?"

"Yes, it was a great way to learn what I should've already known."

She tried to stand and her knees buckled, almost sending her down again. The man caught her, hands firm but gentle. Surprised by her vulnerability, Sam looked into his eyes. He was tall, broad, kind-faced. From what she could see behind the thick ginger beard. More hair on his chin than his scalp.

"You took quite a knock back there," he told her. What was the accent? Scottish, Glaswegian? How does someone from Glasgow end up in Ordshaw?

Irrelevant – Sam brushed his hands off and took a step aside, testing her legs again. They worked, after all. The pain was restricted to her head. "Just need an aspirin." She lifted a finger, but he took her wrist and lowered her hand.

"You'll need a couple of stitches, I can do it in the van."

She looked aside, noticing the spinning blue lights for the first time. A massive, luminous yellow and green ambulance. Next to that a black Mercedes, and behind that a fire truck. A couple of firefighters stood chatting with a policewoman. No one seemed in an especial rush to do anything. One of the firemen was smiling.

Sam turned the other way. Towards the house.

Between the walls of trees, the road was blanketed by smoke. Another fireman was wandering along the tree-line with a fire extinguisher, searching for something to douse. Half a tree lay smouldering across the road. Beyond that, the doctor's telegraph shack was patterned by torchlight. People moved in the windows.

"Excuse me," Sam said. The paramedic blocked her path with a soft smile.

"Best you get some rest, Ms Ward. We'll take care of that cut."

"Give us a minute," Landon said, approaching from the side. He looked severe, his face and cheap suit charred. He eyed the paramedic like a protective parent willing a suitor out of his daughter's bedroom. Sam allowed herself a snigger. Landon put his hands on his hips as the paramedic reluctantly moved away.

"You alright?" It sounded like an order.

"He seemed to think so," she said, lightly nodding towards the medic.

Landon continued brusquely, "They're gone. But they *were* here, all of them – Barton and the others too, by the looks of it. And there's no sign of trouble. Rimes must've been working with them. We could've had them."

"At least we got your car . . ."

Landon snorted, "Not after that blast."

"Ah." Sam paused. "There was a flaming dog –"

"*Canis inferorum*," Landon corrected. "Apothel's people must've dragged it up here. They were here, and we should've known. You were right; Apothel's crew getting back together has to present a danger to the *praelucente*."

The trees nearby pulsed and blurred in Sam's hazy vision. She took her time. "Maybe now Mathers will listen. Divert some resources where they're needed."

Landon didn't look happy. "Mathers is under pressure from London. They'd rather these people be silenced than given a chance to spread whatever they know."

"Silenced?" Sam's jaw dropped open. "Without understanding their angle?"

"Containment is the top priority, with the media already circling around Ordshaw," Landon said. "But I agree, it's shortsighted."

Sam stared at his grumpy face, his eyes averted from hers. She knew – of *course* she knew – the extremes that the Ministry went to to protect the Sunken City. But in her mind that meant transporting derelicts far from the city. Using violence only against the most unreasonable lowlifes. She had met Pax, who almost seemed reasonable. And the Bartons, if they were still together – they were an innocent family. Suddenly Sam wondered it was a good thing the dog had exploded around her, if it gave the civilians a break. She said, "So we're searching for them, now?"

"Not yet," Landon said. "What you see here, that's what we've got. A couple of agents going over the place, but they're due in Nothicker after. The search for the civilians can resume in the morning."

"In the morning?" Sam exclaimed. "They could be out of the country by the morning!"

"We're lucky to have what we've got, here." There was gravity in the way he looked at their surrounding support. "Things are worse in Nothicker."

"What happened?" Sam asked, realising she'd completely abandoned all thoughts of the latest surge.

"It brought down a squat. An old library building, might've been thirty people in there. Most of them got out, but we can't be sure, no proper records. The building's gone. Flattened. The media are crawling over it, even out there. The country's watching us, Mathers says, so it's all hands on deck to keep things quiet."

Sam paused. "But Pax and the others could indicate where this is going next."

"Mathers won't hear it. He's not happy you left the office."

"Even if we almost caught up to them?"

"I get it," Landon said. "I agree. For what it's worth. But Mathers says if you go off the book again, you'll face suspension. Or worse."

"Mathers wouldn't suspend me," Sam said. "There's no one to pick up the slack. We have to keep going, forget his threats. What's in there?" She pointed to Rimes' shack. "Tell me there's some clue to where they've gone, something telling us what they got from Rimes."

Landon paused. "They left a map out, with location markers. Not Apothel's known locations, at a glance. It's something, maybe, but we don't know what. We can't go and check the sites out, not with Mathers on our case."

Sam huffed at the thought of their guileless leader, blocking the way to progress. "We have to go around him. We'll put in a written request to the Commission; they can't ignore it in writing. Email – hell, a *fax*. Go straight to Lord Asquith, explain where we are, the potential implications. We can demand he intervene, at least let me direct IS towards this investigation."

Landon didn't disagree, which she took for support.

"In the meantime, Mathers has to sleep. We'll wait for him to leave the office, then continue our work."

"*You* ought to rest," Landon said, like she needed to consider it very carefully.

Sam scanned the ambulance again. The protective paramedic was leaning against it, watching her from a distance. She remembered being airborne, surrounded by heat. Hit something hard and flopped down like a tossed doll. And that was the result of her being saved. If that dog had caught up to her . . .

Landon must have been reading her thoughts, because he said, "You took a knock. These lads can fix you up and take you home. I can pick up the slack."

"You barely slept *last* night. I don't want to –"

"I'll get a few hours on a sofa in the office, once I've got things rolling. I'm used to nights, you're not. You said it yourself: better equipped means more effective. Same with being rested. I'll organise everything, giving you something to work with in the morning. Starting with that map."

"And the novisan scans –"

"I'll take care of it," Landon said, firm enough to be final.

Sam nodded, silently, worried that if she said anything more it would come out emotional. Unprofessional.

Landon gave her an understanding nod and turned back to surveying the scene. "This didn't go well. But we made progress. My work doesn't usually involve progress. I think we'll do even better tomorrow."

30

Pax's mood improved once she'd got the rancid smells of sweat and slime off her, using the shopping centre's public toilets. The clothes Rolarn procured, though not remotely her style, were also a blessed change from her ripped, sodden jeans and her sleeveless hoodie. Things were on the up, relative to where she'd been an hour ago, and the sounds of people arriving in the abandoned Debenhams only added to her eagerness. Voices – familiar voices. Barton grumbled something hoarsely. They'd made it, in good time. Letty answered teasingly, "– racks for organ harvesting, wait and see. You can build a whole industry from a single human kidney."

"Cut that shit out," Barton snarled, "or I'll deal with you, understand?"

"Take a day off," Letty said.

"Letty?" Pax called, bounding up the dead escalator.

"Damn straight," Letty shouted back. "You good, Pax?"

"More or less." Pax swung her light their way. Holly raised a hand over her eyes, with Barton propped between her and Grace. Rimes lingered like a shadow behind them. "Thank God – you're all alright?"

"Physically," Holly answered. "But I think everyone's had quite enough." She toed the old bit of advertising board on the floor. "We're setting up camp here, are we?"

"Yeah," Pax said. "We've got food, blankets, come see."

Pax waited at the lip of the escalator as they filed past her, each giving her tired smiles. She couldn't help smiling back. Letty hovered up to her as Pax said, "We made it through another day, huh?"

"Yeah," Letty said. "And these pillocks set the woods on fire. Ministry almost had them. What the fuck are you wearing?"

Pax gave the clothes another look as Grace passed. New jeans (too tight), tennis shoes (too *light*), and a long-sleeved top (striped white and blue). Was it that bad?

"You look like a catalogue model for sad single mums," Letty confirmed. "Revelling in mediocrity."

"I think it's good," Grace whispered, in an uncertain voice that hinted the opposite. She hesitated in front of Pax, worried eyes wanting for something, and Pax gave her another smile. Awkward this time. The teenager jumped forward and hugged her. "I'm so happy you're okay."

Pax seized up, looking at Letty over the girl's shoulder. The fairy smirked at her discomfort. Grace let go and quickly continued down the stairs.

"*Are* you okay?" Letty said. She'd last seen Pax keeling over outside the burnt house, hadn't she? As Pax struggled for how best to explain, Barton's booming voice saved her the trouble.

"We have to share breathing space with *him*?"

Casaria replied with something Pax didn't catch. She gave Letty a shrug and raced down the steps to intervene. The Bartons had bunched at the bottom of the escalator, blocking her way.

"Alright, he's with us now!" Pax insisted, pushing through. "Come over – sit down."

Casaria leered as he leaned against a pillar, seeming to enjoy the concern on the Bartons' faces. He looked sinister, between the light of Rolarn's lantern and the unnatural luminescence of the jar of glo Pax had retrieved from the bike. Pax directed the Bartons to the blanket padding she'd arranged on the floor, away from Casaria, as Letty hovered above, eyeing him, too. Pax asked, "Where's Lightgate?"

"Who?" Barton said. "How many of these bastards have you been courting?"

"Don't insult me," Casaria said, "by association with these wretched insects."

Pax tried to move swiftly on. "Lightgate is another Fae, with concerns about the Ministry and the Fae leadership. She's working with Rolarn here – it's his place. There's Arnold, somewhere, too, but apparently he's busy. Which is no great loss." Pax gave Rolarn a knowing look. The plump fairy shook his head. "Anyway – they can protect us."

"If you can help us fuck the system." Lightgate's voice came from the escalator. She floated into view with her hands on her pistols like a Wild West sheriff looking for trouble. Her focus rested on Barton. "Welcome to my sanctuary." She flew through the room, looking over each human in turn. "You will be fed. Sheltered. And you will *like* it."

She landed on the till, staggering a few steps on the landing, marring the smooth entrance. As she pivoted on one leg, for a moment it looked like she might fall over. But she steadied, spreading her arms like this display was something to be proud of.

"Jesus Christ," Pax said, under her breath.

Rolarn, stood by the lantern, watched Lightgate with unhappily folded arms. This was, of course, *his* sanctuary. But he didn't complain, letting her continue, "And yes, Arnold and his boys won't be joining us. Hopefully we won't need them, because Pax has a plan. Don't you?"

The Bartons were watching her, with Rimes awkwardly looking for a space behind them. Letty settled onto Pax's shoulder and said, "It's like you've rustled up an ensemble superhero team. Except made up of the shit heroes licensed in the public domain." She shifted closer, lowering her voice. "And you need to tell me what's up with you."

"I'm fine." Pax forced a smile, and Letty stared up at her, looking for more. Now that they were all here, waiting for her plan, it was no time to explain her psychic spasms, nor that she'd seen herself glowing. It'd only distract them. They needed a way forward. She did too. She said, "We'll talk later, okay?" then turned to the others.

"Okay," Pax said. "For starters, we are safe here. I think." She gave Rolarn a look, and the fairy nodded like it was obvious. "And the next bit doesn't need to involve any of you. This man here has agreed to help us." She gestured towards Casaria.

The Bartons regarded Casaria with wary scowls, even Grace, as Casaria smirked back. None of them said anything, apparently trusting that Pax knew what she was doing.

"We're gonna get Rufaizu back," Pax said, then pointed to Lightgate, "and the Fae weapon, too. With what Rufaizu knows, we'll figure out this Blue Angel, and with the Dispenser, Lightgate and her people can convince the Fae that we're not their enemy."

"How?" Barton said. "The Fae leadership wanted us silenced."

"It's high time the Fae people questioned the leadership." Lightgate rolled a hand to one side. "They lied about the weapon. That's the point. Right, Letty?"

Barton slowly took his distrusting gaze from one fairy to settle equally suspiciously on the other. Letty regarded Lightgate warily, but said, "If you say so. It's here nor there. We get the Dispenser back in our hands, we can end that fucking berserker."

"This is going be fun," Lightgate concluded.

"Sorry," Holly cut in, "but that's our plan? Relying on her, who – no offence – I have no idea who she is, and" – she eyed Casaria – "relying on *him*? I thought he was stabbed?"

"It was nothing," Casaria said, lifting his shirt to demonstrate the grim mess of his crudely sealed knife wound. Grace gasped and Holly shielded her daughter from the view.

Pax tapped the jar of glowing liquid on the counter. "This helped, apparently."

"Or not," Casaria said. "I probably could have walked it off."

"With all the effort in the world," Pax shot back, "you might've crawled into a gutter." She hurried on, "But he's up, as long as this liquid isn't a temporary fix. Your foot's alright, Darren? Not gone black and dropped off?"

Barton lifted his injured leg, outstretched on the floor. The bandaging was dark from being dragged through Ordshaw, falling apart at the seams. "Still there."

"Is it magic?" Grace asked, fully serious, and Holly responded with pity, "Honey."

"Accelerated healing," Rimes said, her voice distant. She was engaging on some kind of autopilot, while her eyes fixed with unblinking wonder on Lightgate and Rolarn. "The body can heal itself, given the right conditions. You were able – able to stuff the wound." She nodded to Casaria's hideously soiled shirt.

"Yeah," Pax said, as Lightgate blew Rimes a kiss. The doctor flinched.

"You'll need more," Barton said.

"I'm not touching another drop of that poison," Casaria replied at once.

"That 'poison' gives us the means to stop what's going on in the Sunken City," Barton said. "Without it, we might as well rely on the Ministry; they can't see the world for what it really is, and it's left them doing the exact opposite of what's necessary."

"Actually," Pax said, "I'm leaning towards Casaria's view. I'd rather not rely on this liquid, not knowing exactly what it is or what it does."

Barton gave her a cold look. "It makes sense of all that's down there, that's what it does. Even the Fae – their trails light up in the sky."

"Trails?" Letty said, spinning to jab her arse his way. "You see any trails? We look like slugs? Fuck off."

"Take a sip, you don't believe me," Barton said.

"I believe you," Pax sighed, though she wished she didn't. "It works. Doesn't mean I trust it. Or the things it helps you see."

Barton's glare softened. "You tried it yourself?"

"Yeah," Pax said. "I had a bit of trouble pulling it out of Chaucer Crescent."

"You what?" Letty said. "There was nothing there!" She shot a look to Lightgate, as though the other fairy could back her up. "I checked –"

"There was something there," Pax said. "I dealt with it."

"I knew it'd be trouble," Holly piped up. "I knew you shouldn't have –"

"I dealt with it," Pax repeated. "But I used that liquid, and I saw what it does. If the Blue Angel manipulated the things we think we know, couldn't it manipulate this liquid too? Maybe corrupting what it reveals?"

"What did it reveal?" Barton asked, cautiously. He was looking at her with the same look as when he'd tried the glo in the morning, which made total sense now. Casaria was, too. Yes, they'd seen the same damned electric veins she saw.

"Enough for me to escape something," Pax said, avoiding the issue.

"Well, we certainly shouldn't be going on any more dangerous wild goose chases for it," Holly said, shifting onto her haunches. "You ask me, it's all sorts of suspicious. These blue screens always being so far away from this liquid is weird on its own."

Pax paused. It was a curious detail, especially if they considered the screens themselves might have transported the glo. "I'd still give you good odds on there being screens near those glo drop-offs," she said, addressing Barton, "but you just never saw them. The Angel wanted to hide the pattern." She recalled the feeling on Chaucer Crescent. The feeling in the chapel basement. Not the pained pull of the surges, but the way she'd sensed something was there, beforehand. She took a breath. "My theory is the Blue Angel's using those screens for more than just communicating. It sent a creature to attack me in the chapel. It put this jar," she pointed, "in Chaucer Crescent. And there was another creature there, like before." She twisted to Letty. "There's every chance it *wasn't* there when you checked. And an equal chance a blue screen *was*."

"So," Barton said, starting to get angry, "you're saying *everything* connected to this drink, everything we saw, everything we did – is mixed up in their trickery?"

"Possibly," Pax said. "But it's not all a lie. This liquid works. The Blue Angel needed to give you something that worked so you could survive the Sunken City and herd the monsters. You just weren't herding them the way you thought. You were reporting to the Blue Angel so it could keep track of its monsters." The word *herd* called to Pax's mind exactly what they were doing. "When you told the

Angel where to find the minotaur, it used its blue screens to suck energy for itself. It was milking that thing, and you were its farmers."

"Yeah?" Barton held off accepting it on principle alone. His accusing eyes fell on Casaria, a way to process it. "And now the MEE do the same?"

"Yeah," Pax said. "Maybe. There's only one thing that I'm certain of about the Blue Angel. Its highest priority is to stay hidden. If the Ministry are helping it, chances are they don't know so, either. Agents like Casaria, even their InterSpecies Relations division, they don't even know the screens exist. I think that's something we can use. They'd be less inclined to kill us if we could explain what's really going on."

Lightgate made a sound that could have been amusement. She said, "You like to make things complicated." Pax glared; it was the second time today she'd been accused of that. "If the Ministry's a bit corrupt or a lot, they're still a plague, aren't they?"

"They *think* they're doing good work. The Ministry believe the minotaur has a positive effect on the city. They're trying to preserve that effect, securing and hiding the Sunken City. They aren't fully aware of how fucked up it is."

"That's generous," Barton said, and gestured to Casaria. "You're getting this from him?"

"Partly. I ran into a woman from InterSpecies Relations, too, and she –"

Casaria grunted like a pig choking, making Rimes and Holly jump in surprise. He coughed, putting a fist to his mouth to conceal his alarm. "You spoke to *Sam Ward*?"

"Yeah, her," Pax said. "She's been hounding me. But I get the idea she was questioning where they're at, the same as us. Why, what's wrong with her?"

"She sold me out," Casaria snarled. "All she's interested in is climbing their ladder."

Aware his judgement of character wasn't entirely trustworthy, Pax said, "Is there anyone in the Ministry you *would* trust?"

"I work alone for a reason," Casaria said. "That way no one can let you down."

"Except yourself," Pax pointed out, to a few murmurs of agreement.

"Unlikely," Casaria huffed. "You've done well to rely on me, Pax, don't worry. I'll get that boy out of there alone, we'll beat answers out of him if we –"

"No!" Pax exclaimed.

"You try it and see what I do to you," Barton threatened.

It only made Casaria's eyes light up. He said, "Oh, I'd like that."

"No," Pax repeated. "Absolutely *not*. We want to help Rufaizu, for fuck's sake."

Casaria went quiet, but his eyes narrowed like he was picturing violence.

"Damn, Pax," Letty said. "How you gonna stop him from killing the kid before we get a chance to talk?"

"Sorry," the agent said, "I just assumed that as you've thrown your hat in with these *monsters,* anything goes."

Lightgate sprang into the air faster than anyone could track. She reappeared a metre in front of Casaria, pose squared-off elegantly with a bent knee and a straight, outstretched leg. She had a highly polished pistol, glistening in the lantern-light, aimed towards Casaria's face. He looked at her cross-eyed, his surprise shared by the rest of the room. The speed of her movement was counterbalanced by her slow voice, as she said, "Why don't I make this easy and suggest you leave the necessary violence to *me?* Then you can focus on doing . . ." She paused to give Pax a thoughtful look. "Whatever she tells you to."

Casaria's concerned eyes ran to Pax. Pax was frozen herself, for the first time appreciating this fairy might be as dangerous as her reputation suggested.

"All clear, now?" Lightgate asked. He didn't respond, which she seemed to take as acceptance. She turned in the air to question the others, all too startled to answer. Grace alone offered a nervous nod. Lightgate turned back to Casaria. "You're boring me, and we've already established the plan, yes? I suggest you all sleep on it. I've got better places to be, now."

"What?" Letty jumped off Pax's shoulder. "Where?"

"Places." Lightgate paused and yawned loudly. "Places *you* can't come. Fun as this is, I've got other plates spinning. You need anything . . ." She waved loosely Rolarn's way. "My butler can assist you."

"What other plates?" Letty called out, but Lightgate drifted towards the escalator with a dismissive wave. She veered from side to side, as though she couldn't pick out a straight line. Pax gave Letty a concerned look, suddenly feeling Lightgate was more complicated than she seemed.

Once she was out of earshot, Casaria commented, "Useless fucking fairies."

"Whatever, she's right," Pax said. "It's time to get some rest."

She turned away and exhaled her own relief that this hadn't devolved into arguing or fighting. The others sounded like they were relaxing behind her, too, whispers passing between the Bartons and Rimes. Letty flew close to her, though, and quietly said, "So? Shall we?"

"Tomorrow," Pax said, almost inaudibly. "Let's talk tomorrow. I need to take a break. More than you can believe."

Letty didn't argue, but her eyes said an explanation would be necessary soon. Pax wanted one herself. But she wanted to sleep more. She wanted, at least for a little while, to pretend everything would be okay.

PART 2:
TUESDAY

1

Casaria watched them sleeping. An innocent family huddled on blankets, in desperate need of protection. Half-innocent, anyway; the bruiser of a father was at least partly responsible for their problems. The ratty doctor was hardly innocent, either. She looked like something found caught in the sluice gates of the River Gader. It had taken him a little while to realise who she was; he had met her once, when the MEE sent him to deliver samples. Once was enough. She was plainly as loopy as Apothel, but Management deemed her worth keeping around. Then there was Pax, sleeping apart from the others, near the counter, closer to the Fae than the humans. On her side, arms and legs folded gently, breathing lightly. Almost delicate. In need of protection, too, even if she commanded this group like she knew what she was doing.

If she knew what she was doing, there was no way she'd be able to sleep.

No way any of them would.

They were in a lair of villainous insects who'd done precious little to prove their worth. The one called Letty, of course, had a thing for Pax, but that would prove fickle. Casaria understood that Pax had a strange effect on people. Like most women that drew you to their will. When the dizzying effect wore off, the vile little creature would turn on them. The other two might not even wait that long.

The plump one with the simple aspect, he was the worst.

Casaria had noticed him watching, not sleeping either, sitting on top of the till. Murderous, looking for a chance to strike. Casaria stared, making sure the Fae saw the white of his eyes in the dark. Bad things might happen if the Fae thought he was asleep.

Just as well Casaria didn't need to sleep. He'd rested when strapped to that torture chair, and even more during the lengthy bike ride across Ordshaw, even if he'd been too close to Pax for comfort. His wounds weren't troubling him now. Much as he despised the drink that had been forced on him, it didn't seem to have had any ill effects. And he'd been careful to keep hydrated, the large bottles of water his single concession to Pax's stolen goods. That and the shoes. He could hardly function without shoes. He would return money to the shop they came from when all this was over. If he could find it.

With the stealing, and the Fae, was Pax any better than that gypsy boy? Why was Casaria still here, waiting on her, involved in this? Who was *she* to decide such things as the fate of the *praelucente*? This gambler, this thief, this friend of animals.

She rolled over, away from him, soles of her feet facing up. Wearing fresh socks, at last. The new clothing was a step up; at least she was no longer dressed like a derelict. It was easier to take her seriously, now.

And some of what she'd said, difficult as it was, needed serious consideration. The MEE had agreements with the Fae, Mathers had confided that. The creatures down there were dangerous, no one could deny that. And he'd seen what the *praelucente* had done to Pax. What it might have continued doing, if he hadn't been there to help.

What if it happened again? What if it did get worse?

His eyes ran back over the room. There was no choice, really. If the *praelucente* was dangerous, someone needed to do something about it. It wasn't about her, it was about saving Ordshaw. It was about him doing what others couldn't. The Ministry weren't prepared to get their hands dirty enough.

He was. He could do whatever was required to stop the monsters once and for all. Even if it meant co-operating with Fae scum. And when he did, Pax would see it. A hand on his arm as he stood over the bodies of their enemies. A whispered thanks in his ear.

Excuses, like propping him on that bike, excuses to get close to him.

She couldn't do this without him.

His eyes fell on the till again. The little man might have been looking his way, or might have been asleep sitting upright. No, he had to be awake. Casaria pointed a finger at him, to let him know he knew. The shape moved, offering a gesture in return, impossible to make out at this distance.

Casaria imagined the coming glory. He'd grill Rufaizu for whatever he knew, as he had intended to do before the Fae's Friday ambush forced him to bring the boy into the office. And he'd play the Fae before he let them play him. And what of Pax drawing Sam Ward into this? Yes. He would approach her with the truth of the trouble the Fae had caused. She'd see him for what he was, and she'd know the futility of her work, defending these bastards.

The little shit was just sitting there. Staring.

"What the fuck do you want?" Casaria hissed, making Barton's teenager stir with semi-conscious mumbles. She blinked. It was too dark to make out anything but her doe-like eyes, wide and fearful. She was as bizarre as the rest of them, really. A girl that beautiful coming from that ingrate father? It didn't make sense. He could scarcely bear to look at her. He whispered, averting his eyes, "Don't worry, miss. Everything will be fine. I'll make sure of it."

He could feel her, still staring, like she needed to process it.

On the till, the tiny silhouette hadn't moved either. Casaria glared at him again.

Let them look. Let all of them see what he could do.

*

There had to be thirty. At least thirty.

Like stars in the night, isolated, moving through an abyss. But connected. Electric current flowing between them. Fizzling, snapping, cracking, communicating wordlessly. Burning with unified purpose.

At least thirty.

Lightning lances shot between them, connecting, combining. Meeting in the middle. Liquids bubbled from the force. Vats overflowed with sizzling sludge.

The beast exploded, the blinding beast, rising, roaring, glowering, snorting.

Eyes of a dragon, horns of a bull.

Its skin shimmered with blue fire, growing then waning. There a second and gone the next, an illusion, but a ferocious one, a terrifying one. Watched by thirty hungry eyes.

Messages passed between them, in words that didn't exist. And they were everywhere, watching, talking, feeling each other's needs and pains and ideas. She rolled to avoid the closing walls. She whimpered and shielded her eyes from the light.

The lightning came from her fingers, before her face. It jumped through the darkness and touched them. They glowed brighter as they registered her.

Her eyes shot open and Pax found herself breathing sharply. Looking into the vague silhouettes of the old shop, nothing more. She blinked but kept still, trying not to disturb the others.

Letty walked across the floor a foot from her face, her artificial wing and its hefty strap absent. The fairy folded her arms, staring with concern, as unreal as the dream, this shadow of a miniature single-winged woman on an empty shop floor.

"Having a bad dream?" Letty whispered, voice tiny. "Your man hasn't slept. He's still watching."

"Mm," Pax replied, trying to pass it off as a snore.

"You're gonna tell me what's going on, aren't you?"

Pax nodded, slightly, but said nothing, waiting for Letty to take the hint: Later.

The fairy sat on the floor, crossing her legs. Pax rolled her eyes to the side, indicating Casaria, as the fairy had said. Not in front of him.

"You spasmed like that fucking thing still had its claws in you," Letty said.

Pax inclined her head, another little nod. That pretty much summed it up.

Letty kept staring. She must have suspected what Pax had been going through. It didn't help, though, did it? There wasn't anything she could do.

"I'm right here, Pax," Letty said. "I can't help if you're gonna keep shit from me."

"It's an aftershock," Pax whispered, as quietly as she could, "that's all."

"And if it's not?"

Pax offered a slight smile. All they could do was stop the Blue Angel, anyway. Letty kept staring, clearly with some inner turmoil of her own. She pointed at Pax's brow, to where she'd hit Pax with her pistol at the chapel. "I'm sorry, okay?

I should've been more willing. Don't freeze me out thinking I won't help. I will."

Not waiting for a response, or not wanting to deal with one, Letty turned and lay on the floor herself, facing away. Going back to sleep, or at least pretending to. Pax watched her tiny form, how delicate and peaceful she looked now. Yeah. Better to keep at least some of the pressure off her.

2

Having forced herself up at the sound of three different dawn alarms (just in case), Sam only fully awoke when she saw Landon waiting for her in Greek Street. Impossibly, he looked no more tired than when she'd left him, insisting a few stolen kips on Ministry sofas had recharged him. Leading her through the building his mood bordered on excitement, as he explained that he'd corralled help after Mathers disappeared around midnight. The lightness in his tone told Sam that, despite appearances, he definitely needed some sleep. He'd sent a fax to Lord Asquith and persuaded Roper to look into Dr Rimes' map as soon as it was clear that there were no residual effects from the disaster in Nothicker. They'd also traced Dr Rimes' phone and found it rapidly moving out of the city – a satellite image picked it out on the roof of a lorry before they wasted more time on that. As if that wasn't enough, Landon had even got another member of the IS team, Ryan, to come in early and monitor for any correspondence from the FTC, freeing Sam of her responsibilities. Whatever she planned next, she'd need to be quick, he said. Asquith was yet to respond and Mathers might be in any time now.

Sam thanked him and told him to go home, suspecting his exhaustion under the surface. He said no – not until she'd seen what they'd found.

In the bullpen, Roper sat at a cluttered desk with Rimes' map spread amongst reams of number lists like the ones he'd shown Sam before. Another analyst joined them, along with a field agent – Devlin? He had wide eyes, a high voice and a thick head of black hair. Tori the receptionist stopped, too, on the way to drop off some mail.

Based on Sam's questions about the energy from the *praelucente* being transferred, Landon and Roper had gone back to six major novisan surges over the past twelve months and cross-referenced them against the marks on the map. Each time the *praelucente* had drained novisan, small spikes had occurred over some of the marks. Even the single anomaly Roper had previously found matched a circle on the map in Hanton.

Sam wanted, deeply, to go back to their records for the night when the Stray Symphony was written, to see if the spike attributed to the masterpiece was matched with *another* spike somewhere else in the city. That would get people's attention, wouldn't it? Bring their all-encompassing anecdote into question.

It wasn't a simple correlation, though: with each surge, the spikes hit only a limited number of marks on Rimes' map. And never any of the marks within two miles of the *praelucente*.

"And there's no difference," Sam asked, as the analyst's report concluded, "between the surges? Nothing to suggest why some are marked with circles and some with crosses?"

"Not that we've found," Roper confirmed. "More or less equally spread."

"Plainly," Sam said, carefully, "the *praelucente* is redirecting novisan, somehow, to different spots in the city. It's doing it well outside our typical range of observation. The question being, is it a coincidence that we've narrowed our focus that much, or are these energy transfers designed to avoid detection?"

"No one has *forced* us to keep a narrow focus," Roper said. "Spreading a wider net would've been folly, given our resources – but even if we had, the likelihood of noticing this as a pattern would've been negligible. These minor surges are scarcely hitting the same location two or three times in the space of a year."

"Okay," Sam said. "But how did these *civilians* know about these hot spots? And why did they differentiate between two kinds?"

No one answered, but Sam had a partial idea herself, recalling Pax's panicked words. The Ministry had laughed off Apothel's claims as tantamount to admitting a belief in Bigfoot or alien abductions, but what if he wasn't mad? He had talked of things they'd never seen, spread all across the city. "Do we have a record of where Apothel claimed the blue screens were?"

She met with uncomfortable silence, so she looked to Landon in particular. "Not to my knowledge," he said. "Apothel was known for creating distractions."

"You know about the crocodile?" Devlin chipped in.

Sam gave him a confused look, fairly sure Devlin was too young to have been around when Apothel was. The lift pinged, someone else entering the office as they all waited for more.

"It was one of the only times we caught up to Apothel. He took an agent to West Quay, to check out a loading bay with a supposed creature above the surface, something we had no records of. Crocodile with hands or something."

"Hands and eyes on stalks," Landon confirmed, as the newcomer approached their group. "And a lizard tongue. Half a day, they searched for it, and found no trace. Apothel slipped away during the search. Exactly the sort of distraction I'm talking about."

An irritated voice cut in: "Which he appears to have succeeded in beyond the grave."

It was Mathers.

Everyone straightened up, squaring shoulders, faces serious, searching for something productive to look at. Devlin and Tori scuttled off, muttering comments about their work. Roper hunched over some papers, pretending to read. Mathers' face was as angry as Sam had ever seen it. She said, "Sir, I think you need to hear –"

"A building came down last night," Mathers snapped. "Untold casualties. Seven dead yesterday. Ordshaw's all over the papers. You have *one job*, all of you. Whatever else you think you're doing here. You have *one* job. Keep a lid on the Sunken City. I need focus now more than ever, and I find this? The whole office exchanging rumours about a man long dead?"

"This map –" Sam tried again.

"In my office," Mathers ordered. "Now. Everyone else, back to your damned jobs, while you still have them."

Fists balled tight and braced at his sides, he marched away. Landon gave Sam a concerned look, wanting to help. She shook her head. It was up to her.

Every movement Mathers made was angry. A heavy thump into his chair, the forceful opening and closing of drawers, slapping a piece of paper onto his desk, deep, frustrated breaths. Even his blinks were angry, pointed breaks in his search for something. Sam watched in silence, waiting for the conclusion.

A suspension form, an AE-12? Or the AE-54, discipline for insubordination?

Sam squinted at the first lines of fine print. It was a WP-SoE, and it had already been filled in. He stabbed a finger at the text, searching for a particular line, then quoted, *"Showing a marked lack of respect for protocol . . . Direct dismissal of MG-7b, using inappropriate terminology . . . Direct dismissal of MG-7d, assigning time to unauthorised tasks. Multiple details not accurately recorded in W4 forms."*

Sam frowned. She had written it herself, three years ago, regarding Cano Casaria's behaviour. He had been flouting Ministry guidelines to conduct his own personal crusade against the myriad creatures, enjoying himself too much and failing to do the MEE's work properly. Mathers sat back and glowered.

"This is different, sir," Sam said.

"I thought you, of all people," he said, "understood the chain of command. Imagine me hearing that *Sam Ward* had destroyed the home of our civilian asset – and worse –"

"I didn't destroy –"

"*And worse,* appears to be distracting everyone with some mindless boondoggle!" Mathers waved her report in the air. "The same Sam Ward who gave me this?"

"The map –"

"I know what that blasted map is!" Mathers raised his voice, making Sam jump. A vein throbbed in the side of his neck, and his eyes looked ready to pop out.

She replied in a disbelieving squeak, "You do?"

Mathers let out a noxious breath. "In what world did you think it wise to go over my head? In what world did you think the Commission weren't fully behind my decisions here? To say London are unhappy is an understatement." Sam cringed at the realisation, and knew his scathing tone was justified. How stupid she had been to think Lord Asquith would care. "The only saving grace in this mess, right now, is that we somehow kept the explosion in Long Culdon out of the news. Chance alone, it would appear, prevented Dr Rimes' other defences from being activated. You're aware that she could've utterly exposed us?"

Sam said nothing.

"No, you weren't, and you know why? Because your *job* is InterSpecies Relations, not whatever desperado quest you've been on!"

Sam opened her mouth but didn't know what to say. *Someone* had to ask these questions – if it wasn't her job, whose was it?

"Exactly." Mathers read her face, wrongly. "You had no idea, and no authorisation. And now I find you distracting my whole office with nonsense we fought for years to keep out of the MEE. Apothel was mad. Verified so by a hospital in Reading, which he *set on fire*! There were times when our productivity ground to a standstill with agents chasing Apothel's fantasies – we cannot afford to do that now."

"Respectfully, sir, the marks on that map correlate with the surges. There's –"

"I *know*," Mathers said. "You honestly believe we limit our monitoring activity due to computer processing power? You think no one's noticed patterns before? They drive people to *distraction*. They're residual effects, with nothing there. They are *not* important."

"According to who?" Sam asked.

"According to the Raleigh Commission," Mathers answered heavily. "Who else?"

Sam held his gaze. It wasn't enough to say it didn't matter. Not when Apothel's people had come across this information on their own. Mathers had to know it. But he was taking the easy route and blaming London. "When did they decide it, sir?"

"You're one of our best people, Ward," Mathers replied without answering. "You know I can't afford to lose you, especially not over something trivial. But heed my words when I say that our work in Ordshaw is *carefully* regulated. With the limited staff we have available, distraction is our single greatest enemy. Coincidental novisan surges are the height of it. Do you understand?"

"I do, sir," Sam said, tersely. "But there's a detail here that I don't see how we can possibly ignore."

"Trust me, there are no details that have not been considered."

"How did Apothel's people know about these locations? These novisan spikes?"

"I fail to see how that affects your work."

"It affects *all* of our work –"

"Your job," Mathers said, "is to be accountable for the *Fae* involvement in this. Where are you on explaining who is responsible for their weapon?"

Sam froze. Her anger at him demanding a patently impossible task was shadowed by a realisation. He didn't want the complications because London did not want them. They wanted to police the Sunken City in the same blinkered way as usual, while they concentrated on their more central interests. Interests outside Ordshaw, whose unnatural phenomenon was, for some reason, not the most fascinating thing in their arsenal. It was the same for the *praelucente* as it was for the Fae: the Commission had more answers than they were giving. Sam made the same request that she had made a hundred times before: "Sir, I respectfully request to speak with the Raleigh Commission on that matter. I believe they have contacts of their own that we might use."

Mathers' anger dissipated as this shifted into familiar territory, with her asking rather than doing. He rolled a hand towards the door, repeating his usual stance: "Put a request into writing and I will relay it. And stop getting in the way."

Sam nodded. Exactly back to normal. She turned for the door.

"Ward?" Mathers relaxed slightly, the tension past. "Where on earth did you see this going?"

Sam hesitated. "Back to the *praelucente*, sir. We're being exposed to how unstable, and dangerous, it is right now. My concern is that it's no longer viable."

Mathers was cold in the face of that shattering observation. He said nothing, merely gestured again to the door.

3

After enduring brief farewells from the Bartons, Pax and Casaria climbed the escalator to the exit. Following in the air nearby, Letty said, "I still say the stuffy mum should go. She can drive a getaway scooter."

"It's on me," Pax said, holding up a hand for Letty to land on.

Letty gave her a look that said she still wanted to know why, but the fairy didn't ask. They'd prepared for the day without any more discussion of Pax's fits or dreams. She wanted to explain, but didn't know how. All she knew was that it was all connected. She had to go with Casaria because it had to be her that rescued Rufaizu; there was no guarantee how far they'd get, and she needed to see him, even if only briefly. For her own sake, if not for the whole city's. Letty must have sensed the truth, somehow, because she wasn't probing.

The fairy said, "We'll have a proper talk when you get back."

"For sure," Pax said. She wished the fairy could come, but there was no way they were leaving the Bartons alone in Rolarn's care. That, and Letty didn't want to miss Lightgate, who had been absent since the conclusion of their discussion the night before. Still, Pax said, "Wish me luck. I'm noticing every time we part ways shit starts to turn dramatically worse for me."

"That's sweet," Letty replied. "Just keep yourself away from the MEE building and let him handle himself." She gave Casaria a sneering look and he scowled back. "Ditch him if you have to."

"And I'm the one you don't trust," Casaria said to Pax.

"Still say you should wait," Letty said. "Lightgate must be up to something, what with Arnold at work out there. We'd do better to hear from her before you go knocking on doors."

"She could be hours, if she even comes back," Pax said, picturing her either drunkly passed out or stirring up more angry fairies towards senseless violence. "And I can't see her making it easier to get into that office."

"You should at least get hold of another phone."

"We're already late," Casaria grumbled. "The office gets busier as the day goes on."

"Alright, we're going," Pax said, then offered Letty a smile. "Take care of them, and yourself."

Letty shook her head, arms folded, unconvinced. "You're the one that's in trouble. Take my number, anyway."

As they approached the scooter, Casaria broke the silence with the purposeful tone of a man who'd long been considering offering stern words. "You got an easy ride yesterday, on account of my condition. But I'm rested now. You can't honestly expect me to go near that thing."

Pax stopped at the bike. "You're too good for it, now? Take a look in a mirror."

A few days earlier, granted, there would have been a marked contrast between his expensive suit and her motoring equivalent of a stack of used toasters. But he hadn't changed in two days, and the dust and blood and grime had solidified into hard patches. His slick hair had lost its sheen and hung in greasy shards. The wound on his face had scabbed over from his jaw to his brow, crossing one eye, and a bruise was going from purple to yellow just below his ear.

Casaria said, "A temporary setback. I've no intention of touching this death-trap and I've no intention of returning to the MEE offices without going to my place first."

Pax watched his eyes stray to the side, willing her not to press more. He was stalling, after all his insistence on getting a move on. "You said the Ministry took you back in. You *can* return, can't you?"

"Of course," Casaria said, haughtily. "I'm the best they have."

"But you don't want them to see that you got beat up, is that it?"

"As if," he snorted. "It'd do them well to see what real field work looks like. It'd just be easier if I was able to blend in. Especially going in during the day."

Looking at the blood on his shirt, and the flecks around his jaw and neck which he hadn't bothered to wash off, Pax suspected he probably quite liked the look himself. Meaning he was thinking of someone else's opinion, for once. Between his reaction to Sam Ward's name last night, and what Ward had said herself, it was an easy guess. "Can I give you a hint as a woman? Whatever you think your co-workers think of you, your immaculate appearance is *not* the issue."

His eyes narrowed. "It's a matter of going unnoticed."

"They know you were abducted," Pax said. "Better if you look like you've just fought your way free of captivity than walked away, isn't it?"

"No one's been looking for me," Casaria said. "I'm telling you –"

"Jesus Christ," Pax said. "I didn't realise it was pity o'clock. For your *information,* it was *her* that was trying to track you down. Sam Ward. And she seemed pretty concerned." He looked surprised, for a brief moment, before scowling.

"You've already proven yourself a liar, Pax," Casaria said. "She's an ice queen."

"Uh-huh. When you were working together, did you pull her hair?"

"What?"

"Call her smelly, laugh at her for having fruit in her packed lunch?"

"What are you –"

"It's okay if you like her, and it's shitty if she hurt you, but I'm pretty sure she took it with a little less scorn than you. Give her a break."

Casaria had the same sort of half-angry, half-confused expression he'd worn when he realised Pax was working with Letty. The same expression as when she'd stolen his car keys. Like the thought had never crossed his mind. "You don't know her."

"No," Pax said. "But I'd bet a golden squid I know her better than you."

"She's played their game since she first met me," Casaria said. "Not interested in the Sunken City itself, only how she could fatten her pay cheque."

"Except she suggested the idea of talking to the Fae, right? Sounds good to me."

Casaria scoffed. "An empty gesture. High in principles, ineffective at actually getting anything done."

"Listen: you see her in there, be civil, and if anything see if she can *help*. Now get on the bloody bike."

She jumped on and started the engine without looking at him again. It would be interesting to see how awkwardly he'd handle sitting behind her now that he was fully conscious. She considered warning him not to get an erection, but didn't, in case the warning made it more likely.

Casaria walked into the MEE building with more anxiety than he felt the place had a right to elicit. He didn't intend to run into anyone, but they had cameras, and people were moving in the halls, more so than he was used to. The daylight zombies came to work in force while the sun was up, getting in the way.

Still, he'd get in unseen and do what he needed to on the fifth floor, where the med bay and inventory were secluded from the worker drones on the sixth floor. He'd slip in and out, as easy as when he took the fairy weapon before.

The idiot guard on the front desk watched him go in with a stunned look. Yes, this is what real work looks like. Some fool from another office was too afraid to ride the elevator up with him. Rightly so.

Casaria marched proudly to the infirmary door, unhindered by a single MEE contact. A quick, simple job – show Pax how a professional worked, even if she hadn't given him the chance to dress like one. He keyed in the door code. Maybe he'd requisition some car keys from Inventory while he was here, get a better vehicle. It was demeaning, perching on the back of Pax's rusted hobby-horse. So close to her. She probably enjoyed it, practically rubbing against him.

His face turned at the thought, imagining her mocking, smirking face, if she felt his body react. You couldn't control that. He hadn't let it show, of course, but give it time and it might. Then he'd be the one in the embarrassing situation, when she was enjoying it. Disgusting.

There was a beep. He put in the code again and frowned at the red light.

The damn lock wasn't working.

That'd be right, wouldn't it? They'd chosen to change the codes now, after years without so much as considering the weakness of their security. Oh well.

He would put in an appearance upstairs after all.

Maybe Sam Ward would be there, so what. It'd serve her right to see him like this. Maybe she'd finally feel some guilt.

*

Mid-morning, and things were settling down in Greek Street. Sam kept half an eye on the monitors of Ordshaw's topography, which showed a heatmap of amorphous red and yellow shapes moving ponderously east. The *praelucente*, and its horde, circling the city with their usual speed and trajectory. No more destructive surges, no abnormalities since the night before. Operations were moving ahead of the horde advised by Support's standard alert monitoring. Another Tuesday morning in the MEE.

London would be happy.

As long as Pax and her friends were kept at bay, perhaps the *praelucente* was safe after all. Everything could continue as before. People had died, riding the train to work or sleeping rough, but they'd be written off as opportunity costs in the grand scheme of Ordshaw's gift.

The best option, for Sam, would be to keep playing the game and hope to gain some kudos for the little assistance she had offered. She could report, at least, that she'd actually spoken with one of the Fae now. Yes, he had threatened to shoot her and aided in a fugitive's escape, but she could describe other things besides, like his general appearance, accent and patterns of movement. She could spin it to garner some validation for IS Relations, maybe give talks in London. Maybe spearhead similar initiatives in other cities. Istanbul had a Fae population, and the lesser-known city of Guadaleizam in Mexico. Imagine instructing a team of Mexicans – she could say things like, "I need you to be a Mexican, not a Mexican't."

Was that racist? She'd email Jen in HR to check.

Anyway, if she wanted to get her career back on track, that's what she had to accept.

Keep things simple, don't rock the boat, don't aim for change.

Except.

Except she didn't *want* to accept that. She couldn't shake the wish that these resources be put to proper use again. In the briefest moment she'd had charge of this office, she'd exposed something that she *knew* had meaning. No matter what Mathers said. What was really going on in those pockets that the Commission deemed irrelevant? What did Apothel's people know and how could they use it? What had actually caused the previous day's devastating surges? And there had to be a reason that novisan was affected in different parts of the city to the *praelucente* – there had to be a result.

Sam found herself hovering by an analyst's shoulder. As he stared at a stream of ever-growing numbers, she considered how vital it was that they monitor novisan *everywhere*, with the unsettling awareness that the levels around Dr Rimes' map coordinates were only affected when the *praelucente* was far away. But of course she couldn't redirect Support. She scanned the office. Landon had gone home to rest, at last, but maybe when he got back in there was another option. Someone watching one of these markers might take some readings on the ground. Did Operations have equipment for that?

The lift beeped, beyond the reception desk. The doors opened, and Tori's surprised jump alerted everyone else to their visitor.

Those other questions could wait.

Casaria stepped out, grinning as usual, reminding Sam in an instant of how he made her skin crawl. But his suit was torn, his shirt filthy, his face bloody. She'd been right to be worried.

"Casaria? Are you okay?" she asked loudly, pacing across the office.

He waved a hand dismissively, purposefully ignoring her as he approached the secretary. Tori shot Sam a worried look, no doubt intending to buzz Mathers immediately. Sam shook her head, making Tori squirm.

"Agent Casaria," Tori stuttered, "are – are you hurt?"

"I expect you heard what I went through on Sunday?" Casaria said, nonchalantly. "It's nothing, but I'm taking some time, of course. I just needed to check something."

"You were suspended, I can't . . ." Tori said.

"He was *missing*," Sam said, surely the more pressing matter than his employment status. There was no way his condition was caused entirely by the events in his reports; he'd been in more trouble since Sunday, for sure.

"Yeah." Casaria winked at Tori. "So, I need the new security codes, I left something downstairs."

Reminded of his arrogant manner, Sam sensed the sympathy she'd felt for him dissolving. She moved closer, hissing, "Where have you been?"

He leant around Tori's desk and lowered his voice. "Miss me?"

"I'll get Deputy Director Mathers," Tori decided, fumbling for the phone.

"No," Sam said. "I've been looking for him. I'll take care of it, and report to the deputy director myself." Tori regarded her sceptically, but Sam kept her eyes on Casaria, in case he disappeared again. He was still smiling. "Agent Casaria's input directly affects the work we're doing in IS."

That worked – the smile skipped like a hiccup.

"We'll use my office," Sam said, but paused. She checked him over again, realising they had an excuse for greater privacy. "Unless you need to go to Medical first?"

Casaria looked at his own bloodstained clothing, then the bullpen, and came to the same conclusion. "You know, that's a great idea."

4

Rolarn hadn't taken his eyes off the humans, and the longer Letty watched him the stranger she thought it was. The guy wasn't interested in a game of cards, or shooting the shit, or anything, it seemed, other than staring like a creep. The humans felt it, too; whenever one of them looked his way it was with the uncomfortable awareness of having a nasty spider on the wall, hoping someone else would remove it. There'd been no hint of Lightgate coming back, and Letty was getting tense thinking about her other plans when a visitor arrived.

Rolarn suddenly stirred from the counter like a dog sniffing the air. He lifted off without explanation and flew to the escalator. The Bartons went quiet, watching him, and, after a moment of surprise, Letty launched after him, calling out, "What're you doing, lardo?"

"Wait here," he said, continuing up to the next floor.

Like hell. Letty followed Rolarn up to find a man near the top of the escalator; a thin Fae in a grey suit, waistcoat, tie and all. Before Rolarn could greet him, Letty shot ahead and demanded, "Who the shit are you, Lightgate's accountant?"

"Letty, is that you?" the man said, with surprise. "I was hoping to meet you."

She slowed down; he didn't look like an exile. Not in those threads, with that educated accent. He adjusted his little glasses and offered her a smile, holding out a hand. Letty looked at it like it might kill her.

Rolarn said, "You alone?"

"Yes. I didn't want to waste time, not once I heard – well, how everything's going."

"How what's going?" Letty said, accusingly. "Who the *fuck* are you?"

"Edwing," the man said, lowering his hand. "You weren't expecting me?"

Rolarn answered, "I was. You're here to see the humans?"

Edwing gummed his lips for a second, in anticipation, a glance down the escalators. "They're down there?"

"You're some FTC toff?" Letty demanded. "What are the humans to you?"

Edwing eyed her warily. "I'm here on Lightgate's invitation. You *are* aware of the messages Lightgate relayed to the FTC?"

"You think this is my fucking *aware* face?" Letty advanced on him.

Rolarn gave her a fierce look. "This doesn't concern you –"

"Are you fucking kidding me? You and Lightgate are bringing FTC pricks in here to gawk at *my* humans and it doesn't concern me? You want your own fist rammed down your throat, Rolarn?"

The heavyset Fae swelled, ready to bite back, but Edwing intervened. "Sorry – I'm getting in the middle of something here. But we're on the same side, Letty."

"That'd be why you're tiptoeing around?"

"I'm on the FTC Council," Edwing said, like that explained everything. Letty's scowl didn't shift. This was where Lightgate had gone? Rustling up a shit-heel from the FTC?

Letty said, "If you've sold me out to Val –"

"No," Edwing said, insistently, "quite the opposite. Many of us in the FTC fully sympathise with your intentions, Letty – creating dialogues about the viability of relocation and the Sunken City, human interaction – long-buried issues. But it would be political suicide to publicly suggest such things without a *very* convincing argument. I understand the Dispenser has slipped away from us again – but your humans present other opportunities. If I can see them…"

"My humans," Letty said, "are not fucking zoo animals. What're they to you?"

"Lightgate presented various ideas," Edwing ventured carefully.

"Which ought to stay between you and Lightgate," Rolarn said.

"No, he'd best keep damn talking," Letty snarled.

Rolarn's shotgun swung her way, his expression warning her off. "We'll talk. Once he's gone."

The two Fae squared off in tense silence, neither blinking.

Edwing looked from Rolarn to Letty hesitantly, deciding who was the more dangerous. "Yes, I think you *had* best talk yourselves. I've seen enough. The general sentiment is that Lightgate's not there yet. This rather confirms it."

"Not there yet?" Rolarn growled. "We've got a damn Ministry agent and Citizen Barton himself. What's not ready?"

Edwing adjusted his glasses. Fair play to him; for a frail-looking suit he kept his composure. "You have components, not a cohesive whole. This" – he gestured to Letty, indicating the confusion between them – "is clear enough. Tell Lightgate I'll be in touch."

Rolarn glared at him angrily. A more extrovert Fae might have railed at Edwing with righteous vitriol about whatever they were scheming. He only nodded towards the exit. "Get, then."

Edwing said, "Good to meet you, Letty. I hope we'll speak again."

Letty stared at Rolarn as their guest sped off towards the exit. Her hand itched over her pistol. "After the shit I've been through, you think I'm gonna let you drag me into an FTC-sponsored –"

"Relax," Rolarn said, his own voice strained. "Lightgate's got a good thing going."

"So good you didn't want me to know?"

"So you could fuck it up like that? It doesn't involve you, Letty."

"That," Letty hissed, "pretty well looked like it involved me."

Rolarn gave her a grim look. "Alright. Imagine the Dispenser resurfaces, we can call Val a liar, say she did nothing to get it back. But that's ignorance, she can weather that. Now imagine she did something to actively conceal it. Something serious."

"The fuck are you talking about? With the Dispenser, we don't *need* Val –"

"What if she'd done something against her principles?" Rolarn finished. "Like murdered humans to cover up this weapon. Citizen Barton, of all people. A celebrity."

"What?" Letty said, incredulous. "You want to finish what Val started? *Because* it's a psycho move? We've got witnesses – we can *tell* people –"

"Tell hell," Rolarn snorted. "Actions speak louder. Dead bodies speak loudest."

"You bloody idiots," Letty snapped. "It's *not* happening. I'm taking the humans."

"No you're not."

"You're gonna make me hurt you?"

"You got close to that girl for whatever reason, fine. But the rest of them – you must value your life over them? You must value the restoration of the FTC over *them*."

Letty glanced downstairs. She'd seen enough from these hapless humans to know they weren't scum. The women were bloody bystanders, and Barton was ready to blunder into any old shit for a righteous fight. She locked on Rolarn again, ready to shoot him down. Except his shotgun was on her; it'd only get her dead. She said, "What's the plan, then? String them along until we've got the Dispenser, then stage a slaughter?"

"Something like that," Rolarn said. "Edwing and his sort might have given us more support. Can't say I expected much from him, though."

"More support with what?"

"Other pies," Rolarn said, blandly.

Letty kept staring. Definitely ready to hurt this bastard. "Where's Lightgate now?"

"Couldn't say," Rolarn said.

"Arnold?"

He shrugged.

"I'm gonna go find them."

"No. You're staying here. Might be best you hand me your gun."

"You can take it when I'm dead."

Rolarn held her gaze, unmoved and not moving. He curled his upper lip like it wasn't worth it, and said, "So keep it. So much as think about drawing it and I end you."

Her head clear after a little sleep on the hard floor, Holly was eager to take action. Pax would return with more answers, and she would be ready to take the baton from there. She'd take them from inactive hiding to a complete, workable plan against the government. Starting with legal counsel.

To prepare, Holly continued trying to gather information. Darren and Rimes were reticent about their pasts, but she drew dribs and drabs from them, mostly through the art of flattery. By thanking Darren for his attempts to protect them, she got an idea of the time frame he'd operated in; exploring those tunnels from shortly after Grace was born until she was almost three. It was awful to hear, yes, but she avoided criticising him. At least for now.

"And it never struck you to work with these little people before?" Holly asked, an eye on the fat fairy on the till. Letty was standing angrily apart from him. She always seemed angry, that one.

"We heard stories about them," Darren said, but did not elaborate. Despite her efforts, he still expected her to trap him.

"Have you studied them, at all?" Holly asked Rimes. The doctor was surprised to be addressed, and anxiously shook her head.

"I would love to. I'd never *seen* one –"

"None of us had," Darren said. "Not until Apothel did. It killed him."

Holly could see this going down a road they'd trodden before, so she sighed and stood up. Clearly it would be best to get everyone talking, to get over *that* hump. She approached the little people on the counter. "We could do with some more water, couldn't we? I can bring us some more."

"You don't have to do anything," Darren said. "Just rest."

"What about food? We'll get on to lunch before long." She turned to Rimes. "Do you have some money?"

"Me?" Rimes started patting her pockets. "Yes – that is – I think so –"

Holly turned back to find Rolarn and smiled. "Aren't you hungry? I can do a run."

"Best not," Rolarn said.

"I'd like to pull my weight. Being idle doesn't suit me."

"It does when the MEE are watching."

"I hardly believe they've got eyes on every CCTV screen in the city. I saw a WH Smiths downstairs, I'll drop by there."

"You'll sit back down."

Holly frowned. This wasn't the bridging exercise she'd had in mind, and that sounded decidedly like an instruction. She looked to Letty. "You think it's not safe, now?"

Letty held her gaze but said nothing.

Rolarn said, "She thinks you'll sit back down and wait."

Holly blinked at him, hard. His tone had barely changed, but that was a threat. Darren had heard it too; he shifted behind her, making the unhappy noise that came with him preparing to get confrontational.

"For your own good," Rolarn said, a little testy. Holly frowned at his infernal gun, glued to his hands.

"Leave it, lardo," Letty said, savagely, "let the lady go get some water."

There'd been no issue when they'd been escorted to the toilets, with the Fae keeping an eye out for cleaners and whatever. Something had happened when they'd gone upstairs, leaving them in this tense state, Holly was sure.

"If it's all the same," Holly said, slowly, "I think I'll be okay, and could certainly use a little break from this room." She held the tiny man's gaze, aware that the issue now was not what she planned to do, but whether or not this fairy would permit it.

"Sit down," he said, settling *that*.

"What the hell are you –" Darren started, going to stand.

"Don't," Rolarn said, voice raised just enough to say any further movement might lead to violence. Holly glanced over her shoulder. Darren was in a half-crouch, supporting himself on his hands, furious eyes locked on the counter. Grace had stirred behind him, sitting up alongside Rimes, both markedly worried.

They were all, of course, thinking the same as Holly. Were they prisoners, now?

Rimes spoke into the tension. "Darren . . ." She managed to squeeze a lot of terror and confusion into that one word.

"I'll make this clear," Rolarn said. "You all need to stay put."

"Well," Holly said, "you can't –"

"You don't need to stay alive."

Holly clamped her mouth shut. Rolarn's shotgun faced her gut. He was actually pointing a gun at her, what was that weapon capable of? Letty was on her feet, a hand on her pistol in its holster, too. Except she was turned side-on to Holly. Facing Rolarn.

"Darren," Rimes whimpered again, and was joined by a bleat from Grace, "Dad."

"It's okay, keep calm," Darren replied, waving one of his big hands but otherwise not daring to move. "Holly. Come back here."

Holly was rooted to the spot. Her family hadn't braved a labyrinth of unholy monsters to succumb to a miniature gunman. She'd failed to do anything about them last time, when they invaded her home, but she had no idea they were coming, then. This was just one man – a tiny bully – within arm's reach. Her daughter was here, her husband.

"I don't like it, I don't like it," Rimes said, voice teetering. "This isn't right."

"Mandy, please," Darren said. Grace whispered something to the doctor, trying to comfort her.

"Shut her up," Rolarn said, "and sit *down*."

"Rolarn," Letty said, his name a warning on its own. She wasn't on board with whatever these people had planned, and that meant Holly had to act. He had the bigger gun, and he was the bigger fairy by a long way. Holly was close. She could do something. No one expected it from her. Useless, uninvolved Holly.

"There's no protection here!" Rimes cried out, suddenly. "Worms!"

Holly didn't dare turn, no matter the rising madness in the doctor's voice. Rolarn and Letty weren't moving.

"Ah, ah, ah..." Rimes started shaking her head.

"Are all your human friends insane?" Rolarn demanded, with a sideways look at Letty.

"Must be," Letty grumbled back, "trusting me."

"Ah ah ah!"

"Shut her up!" Rolarn was losing his cool, at last.

"Let me –" Darren reached towards her, but Rimes moved suddenly, up on her feet, throwing both hands over her ears. Grace scrambled away with fright.

"Not safe, never safe!" Rimes started raving. "Worms return, between bricks between soil under earth –"

"Mandy! Look at me!" Darren raised his voice.

Rolarn's hands flexed on the shotgun, his face steeling with irritation.

"She's not well," Letty told him. "For crying out loud, give it up."

Rimes stepped away from the blankets, shaking, starting to wail. Darren winced onto his bad leg, trying to follow her, nowhere near. Holly glanced back as Rimes pointed suddenly at Rolarn and shrieked, "Not with the worms, never under earth!"

And she made a dash for the escalator.

Rolarn launched off the counter, booming, "Stop!"

Rimes didn't hear him in her panic, stumbling with flailing limbs towards the stairs. The shotgun went off, the blast tearing through the metal of the escalator and eliciting a startled scream from Rimes as she fell to the side. Darren was up, flinging his big body over the falling doctor. Rolarn turned in the air, gun swinging back around, past Holly, towards Letty. She was in the air, too, pistol firing. The gunshots snapped like small fireworks. It happened so fast, Holly moved without thinking, trying to follow Rolarn as he zipped through the air avoiding Letty's shots. But her bullets were small – Holly's hand was much harder to avoid.

The impact made a dull slap, followed by the clatter of Rolarn's gun skating across the floor and, a moment later, his own bump and grunt. He skidded to a halt near Holly's feet, a crumpled mess of splayed limbs and ripped wings. She kept her hand up – the shocked pose that always follows an instinctive slap – had she *killed* him? A living, talking –

Rolarn moved, a hand twitching to some other part of his body, and there was another, final gunshot that caught him in the centre of his bulbous chest. His tiny body convulsed once before going still.

Letty buzzed near Holly, pistol aimed at the other fairy's body. Her arm was scratched and bloody where a shotgun blast had glanced her, but the worst of Rolarn's shot had been deflected by the dented and scratched metal strap of her artificial wing. She spat down at him, with a simple epitaph, "Prick."

Slowly, the others came back to life. Rimes cried in thick sobs, her panic replaced by a more muted despair. Darren pushed himself up onto his hands and knees with laboured breaths. Grace was breathing heavily, too, on the verge of tears.

"I don't understand," Holly said. "I didn't – *why* did he –"

"They're screwing us," Letty said. She holstered her pistol and put her hand up to the wounded arm. Peppered with red scratches, bleeding. "Or more specifically, *you*. They wanted to complete what my boys started. You have to get moving. Now."

5

Casaria sat in the office's smallest med bay, Rufaizu two doors down. Sam Ward had left to find Dr Hertz, who was no doubt out on a cigarette break, as usual, leaving Casaria exactly where he needed to be. He could kick in the next door, drag Rufaizu to the lift and run. They wouldn't have the Dispenser, but that hardly mattered. He could beat the answers they needed from the boy, prove or disprove Pax's theories and settle everything. He had to admit he wasn't so sure which questions exactly needed settling or why Pax had put such stock in the boy – but those answers would come, too.

Anyway, it'd save the MEE a lot of embarrassment in the long run. When Casaria reported their findings – *if* he reported back – they'd court him for promotion. Set up his own initiative, even. He smiled.

No, thank you.

Yet he was sitting by an empty bed, waiting for Ward to come back. The smile left him. It'd been all work, from the moment she set eyes on him, exactly as he knew it'd be. Promises of reporting to Mathers, comments about completing forms. Sam Ward was as company-focused as ever. Still, she was here, now, and he could prove it to Pax. He could lay out their situation, and Sam would turn her nose up. Then he'd have to restrain her. He'd have an excuse. She couldn't get in the way.

But Sam had said it to the secretary: *I've been looking for him.*

I, not *we*. And she'd seemed worried about the cuts on his face. Maybe her efforts to find Dr Hertz showed genuine concern, rather than a desire to get him back to work.

The door opened and Ward entered alone, checking the corridor one last time. "I think he's out to lunch. It's not even midday."

"Lunch isn't a time," Casaria told her.

She leant against the door, as far from him as possible, face hard to read. Plotting how much trouble she could get him in, no doubt. He'd let her scheme, then pull the rug out with what he now knew.

"You look bad, Cano," Ward said. "You should've gone straight to a hospital."

"I can handle a few scrapes," Casaria said.

She kept staring. With mild disgust? "It's not about handling it; I'm sure you could grin and bear bleeding to death. Where *were* you?"

"Taking care of our interests, where else?"

"Why did they take you?" Her voice went up a pitch. "Can you just tell me what happened?"

Casaria smirked. He'd forgotten how good it felt to get under her skin. She did care. She'd always cared and she couldn't stand it. "It wasn't related to what's been going on here. I dealt with it."

"By the skin of your teeth, from the looks of you."

"You're not so hot yourself, you know." Her disgust intensified, but Casaria only smirked. It was true. There were messy stitches on her forehead and dark rings under her eyes. While she struggled to find the words to respond, he said, "I missed some fun yesterday. What's the feeling in the office, with the damage that's been done?"

"Right now?" She shook her head, disappointed. Always disappointed by everyone else's work. "It's calmed down, so it's no longer an issue. Heads back in the sand."

"I heard you've been hounding fugitives," Casaria said. "Getting out there, for a change. Seizing whatever opportunity arises, huh?"

The disgust in her face was replaced by confusion.

"How do you know about all that?" she said.

"My job requires observation, you know. How's it working out for you? They gonna give you a more expensive desk –"

"God *dammit* I spent the whole day looking for you! I almost got blown to hell! Stop pissing around and tell me where you've been!" She stamped a foot. Fists clenched at her sides. Tears sheened across her eyes.

Had he gone too far? Forgotten she was sensitive?

Casaria stood, swallowing hard. He held a hand her way. Should he offer to hug her? There was anger in those teary eyes, though. He said, "Are you okay?"

The anger intensified. "Why are you *here*?"

"The *praelucente's* dangerous, isn't it? That must be clear by now. There's difficult questions that Management aren't willing to ask. Are you willing to ask them?"

Sam glared and he expected another emotional response. Flat-out refusal. But as his words sank in, something shifted behind her eyes. Curiosity, the look of that naïve woman he'd first drawn into this game. She said, "She's turned you. Is that it? Pax lied – she *did* take you and she turned you –"

"Forget Pax," Casaria said. "*I'm* asking questions. The Sam Ward I recruited, I thought, would've asked these questions, too. The answers" – Casaria pointed aside – "are with that boy. I need to take him out of here."

"Have you lost your mind?" Ward replied, her emotional roller-coaster taking her, finally, into numb disbelief. "Even you know better than to suggest working outside the Ministry."

"I never should've brought him here. There's – wait, where are you going?"

Ward had her hand on the door. "I shouldn't be alone with you, this is more –"

Casaria's hand slammed past her, closing the door, creating a barrier. His face was suddenly inches from hers, her frightened breath on his cheek. So this was it. Just as he'd predicted. She didn't speak, but the fear in her eyes said enough. There was no way she was coming with him – no way he could persuade this company girl.

Only what needed to be done.

*

At the perimeter of Broadplain Plaza, Letty whistled for the lummoxes to stop and fluttered down onto Holly's shoulder. She checked up one street, then another, seeing no signs of pursuit. She took out the phone she'd recovered from Rolarn and started thumbing through it. It wasn't much better than the burner he'd given her, but this one at least had internet access. While its browser loaded painfully slowly, she took stock of the humans watching her. Rimes was a shuddering mess, pale and frail as a skeleton, but barely scratched by Rolarn's shot. Barton was limping determinedly with support from his daughter. Holly's face looked like it might recede into her neck; she drew away from Letty like she had some kind of deadly disease. It made Letty snigger, noticing that the woman was rigid as a brick. She'd quickly got used to using Pax as a landing platform, and forgotten this kind of proximity was unusual for Fae and humans alike.

Her smile disappeared as the Fae news website loaded on the phone.

"Ah fuck. Not good."

Barton shifted closer. "What?"

It was headline news: *Sunken City Catastrophe as Apothel Five Resurface.* The information was basic but the intention clear: the FTC media were reminding the world that Barton existed. Had Lightgate manipulated this, priming people for a high-profile murder? Letty held up the phone, as if Barton had any chance of seeing it. "These bastards are setting you up."

"Who? Why?" Grace contributed, desperately confused. "What's happening, Dad?"

"Explain," Barton rumbled at Letty.

"Right now, the FTC have been led to believe the Dispenser has *not* resurfaced, and that *you* have been disrupting shit in the Sunken City. Playing on what we all know about you as a lunatic monster-baiter."

"But –" Barton started to protest, but she carried on.

"They plan to kill you and make it look like Val did it, set that up alongside the Dispenser, and your intentions to use it. Completely discredit her."

"Who's *Val*?" Holly asked.

"The Fae governor," Letty said. "Rolarn, Arnold, Lightgate, they want to fuck her over, they don't give a shit about us – or the Sunken City."

Barton brimmed with anger, fury preventing him from responding. That was for the best, because his ideas were bound to be stupid. Letty tried to think quick, her priority to keep these fools alive, to at least thwart that part of Lightgate's plan. "I've got someone else who can hide you. You get away from here, keep safe – I'll deal with this."

"The hell you will," Barton said. "If it's my name they're dragging through –"

"Look at the state of you!" Letty said. "You're not doing shit."

"He might not be able, but I can –" Holly started.

"You?" Letty almost laughed. "You realise you just swatted a vicious killer out of the air? That's great and I love you for it but the Fae media is already focusing on human threats so *you need to lay bloody low*."

"While you do what?"

Letty hesitated. She needed to face the other Fae before they realised they'd lost the Bartons, that was all. "Whatever Lightgate's up to herself, she'll have people coming here. I'll deal with them, make sure they don't follow you. You go to Nothicker, find the derelict sandwich shop on Dresden Street. Ask for Palleday and wait there."

"You're serious?" Barton said. "Walk into another Fae trap?"

"You got somewhere better to go?" Letty snapped, gesturing to Rimes. "*Her* place was hardly much better!"

"We're in the east already," Barton answered readily. "If we can get to Apothel's game room – if it's still there –"

"Because the Ministry won't think of that? My people won't think of that? You need to hide, not be in the most obvious bloody place imaginable!"

Barton went quiet. His wife looked at him uncertainly and cleared her throat. Letty turned on her, ready to argue another dumb lummox down. Holly said, "Your people lost us underground, before. You can't go down there?"

Letty frowned. "You're nuts, the Sunken City –"

"Not *those* tunnels. What about the Tube?"

Letty paused. "Not totally dumb, but hardly a long-term plan."

"We can ride the Central line. It's circular, and it's not part of the monster network, is it?"

"The minotaur drains people down there," Barton said. "It'd take energy –"

"It can't drain every train, can it?" Holly said. "People survive the Tube every day. And surely tiredness is better than bullets and monsters?"

"Two trains dead," said Rimes, shaking her head. "That big accident – it's not safe –"

"After an accident?" Holly said. "Those drivers will be more focused than ever today. It's the *safest* time to travel." She looked at Letty for confirmation. "How long do you need?"

Letty eyed her, impressed by the woman's willingness to put her family in harm's way so soon after they'd survived the Sunken City. As a temporary solution, it was better than trying another potentially compromised hideout. If Pax was at the Ministry already, and she could deal with Lightgate's people here, it might all be over soon enough. Letty said, "You keep moving. If you have to get off the train, do it far away from here. I'll give you my number, keep me updated."

"You can come with us," Grace suggested.

"No, I can't."

"You *have* to," the girl insisted, probably more afraid for them than for Letty.

"I *can't*," Letty replied, equally forceful. "Aside from not being fucking able to, I have shit to take care of. You're all liabilities. Easy fucking targets. Now get the hell out of here and keep your heads down so I can deal with my people."

6

Pax marvelled at how ugly the MEE's building was. The unpainted block came from the era of architecture when angular concrete was deemed attractive in a way only council buildings and municipal courts aspired to. From the looks of the humourless people coming and going, it did a fine job of making life miserable. There was no obvious name or title to the block, besides the great brass number 14, and a stack of name-plates near the double-door entrance suggested the MEE shared the place.

Pax wondered if it was wise to stand close.

After hiding the scooter around a corner, she had scouted the area for a newsagent's, hoping to revise the previous day's news, but there was nothing within the closest few blocks. Curiosity had got the better of her as she questioned where this shady organisation operated from, and she doubted anyone was watching the building itself, not while they were chasing across the city for her.

"Not going in?"

"Jesus *fuck*!" Pax spun, fists raised at the empty air. A flutter of movement drew her eyes up. Lightgate settled onto a slight protrusion in the brickwork above Pax's head. "I'm gonna hang a cowbell round your neck."

"You're waiting for Casaria?" Lightgate asked.

Pax followed her gesture to the Ministry building and answered sarcastically, "No, I'm hoping to get spotted. Where've you been?"

"Busy," Lightgate said. "Good to see you didn't waste time. How long will he be?"

"How would I know?"

"Best get him to hurry up."

Odd remark. Pax paused, turning back to the fairy. "What are you doing here? You shouldn't be anywhere near a Ministry property, should you?"

Lightgate held Pax's gaze for a few ponderous moments, then finally answered, "I might have got lucky, and wanted to give you a courtesy call, in case you were still here."

"What? Have you done something?"

The fairy gave a blameless one-shoulder shrug. "An opportunity presented itself."

Fuck. Pax spun back to the MEE building. She concentrated, imagining the possibilities. Blown-out windows, a rain of rockets? The sewers, the trains, the tunnels, so many choices – and she felt it, then. Something down there. She closed her eyes, recalling her first conversation with Lightgate. The Fae charges under the building, that hidden monster, ready to burst up and savage the Ministry. Was the feeling imaginary, knowing something was down there because she'd been told so? The turnbold, as Lightgate called it – was it there, big, lurking – she winced. It tingled in her fingers and stung her chest, *definitely* feeling something, now she concentrated. In the direction of the building. She fixed a glare on the fairy. "You didn't. You couldn't have – you said –"

"I'd get your man out of there," Lightgate said. "Quick as you can."

"You have to stop it!" Pax raised her voice, surging towards the fairy, but Lightgate launched off her perch, out of reach before Pax got close.

She regarded Pax thoughtfully, circling overhead. "If I *could* stop it, why would I?"

"If you could?" Pax answered. "It's *your* plan!"

"Sure but I'm not activating those charges myself. Arnold's boys are – it's the least they could do after failing to hunt the codes. You know what happened? After my FTC contacts said *no*, and Arnold's boys did their lame best to find another source, one of them found a note left for me. My name, two words: *MEE Charges*. Then a bunch of numbers. Anonymous – for all I know it might make the detonator explode."

Pax gritted her teeth, watching the building again. "We discussed it. It's a *bad* plan."

"Oh, you're just afraid of *action*. Don't worry. It'll be fun."

Lightgate was grinning, and Pax saw there was no reasoning with her. The Fae was an unaccountable danger. Pax considered the scooter, back round the corner – the seat compartment, with the glo – it could help – but no, the glo was back in the shopping centre now. Increasingly desperate, she said, "There must be some way you can –"

Lightgate held up a hand for quiet, and for a moment Pax expected another belch, or worse. No, she just didn't want to talk: "We'll chat after this, okay?"

"For Christ's sake!" Pax gaped. "If this happens, there's no –"

"Let it go," Lightgate said, firmly now. "I'm still keen to work with you. Don't run in there trying to help your fellow humans. That would be a waste."

Pax glowered, striving for something, anything to say. She darted across the road.

A wide desk created a barrier to the rest of the building, with two plastic turnstiles to one side. It was manned by a uniformed guard and led to a corridor of elevator doors. She could shout a bomb scare or something, but the guard would stall, questioning her or otherwise not taking it seriously. Her best bet was the fire alarm, get people moving without question. But the closest one was on the other side of the desk, near the lifts.

Pax scanned a hanging board of company names, gold on brown, some with logos. A couple of municipal departments, as she suspected, but companies, too. *Klondike and Feather LLP*, *Burgher Logistics*, even one she recognised, *Warlowe Ltd*, a name you saw on shipping containers bowling towards West Quay. The turnbold plan had been bad enough without Lightgate conveniently failing to mention so many innocent people shared the Ministry's space.

The Ministry's name sat at the bottom of the list, in discreetly small type. *The Ministry of Environmental Energy.* Floor 5/6. Pax opened her mouth to speak to the guard, but the ground spoke for her, a creak below them, like metal being dragged through a tunnel.

The guard smirked at Pax's startled expression. He was young, spotty and skinny, with a nose too big for his face. He said, "Sewage works. Been noisy this morning. I guess they're making sure everything's up to standard after the mess yesterday."

"They?" Pax replied. "What they?"

"Gas company?" he suggested.

It was that easy, wasn't it? The Ministry under their very roof, and you had people assuming some anonymous gas company was doing anonymous work that explained away the weirdness. Pax eyed the fire alarm again. She needed a quick way in. "I'm hoping to surprise my friend, up on the fourth floor, to invite her for lunch?"

The guard raised a questioning eyebrow. "What's her name?"

"Jenny," Pax said, off the bat, playing the ditsy friend. She leant an elbow on the desk, thankful for her awful new clothes. "She tells boats and trucks where to go. Kind of?"

The idea was that he'd suggest a surname, but he didn't bite. "Full name?"

"Jenny Talbot." Common enough to sound real without being generic.

The guard's face said he didn't recognise it. Pax smiled encouragingly.

"Best if I buzz her down," he said, hand going to his phone.

"That'd ruin the surprise!"

"Yeah." He was staring, unsure what to do. He was young and spotty enough to want to please a random young woman, so searched his monitor for an answer that wouldn't put his job at risk.

The ground shook. The monitor rattled and one of the guard's pens rolled off the desk. He twisted to get it, muttering, "They're really at it down there."

"Yeah, and you've got a pretty tall building," Pax stifled a nervous laugh. "I'd like to get up to her floor before the place collapses."

His eyes were hard, not amused, but Pax kept smiling. He took a breath. "You've gotta sign in." He tapped the guestbook and Pax scrambled to write any barely legible shit. He pressed a button and the barrier parted as he tried to make conversation, "It's a – there's a nice place you can go a few blocks down, if you like Mexican –"

"That's *perfect*," Pax beamed, racing past. "Thanks! You've made my day, hers too!"

"Or there's a Nando's!" he called out, more enthusiastic. She pressed the call button as he watched her. Fuck, if she pulled the fire alarm now he'd cancel it before anyone so much as left their chairs.

The lift arrived and she had to enter. She'd go up to 1 and pull the alarm there.

The doors closed, with the guard calling out another helpful flirt, and Pax frowned at the numbers on the panel as she realised she'd hit 5 without thinking. As the lift rose she looked up. Her hand hovered over the panel, ready to press another number, but a sense that there was something up there made her hesitate.

This feeling was getting stranger, her fingers tingling again, chest warming. But it was different this time. She wasn't sensing something below her. It was above, where she was heading, it was *there*. Had Lightgate got something else in the building? Or was it Rufaizu? Perhaps she could sense where he was. Or Casaria? Had she developed a *useful* psychic link?

It burned stronger as she rose higher, coupled with a desire to see what was there, and in the distraction she almost forgot why she'd come. She'd be at the top of the building when Lightgate struck. She'd be stepping into the Ministry's offices, for fuck's sake, what was she thinking –

The lift pinged as it reached the fifth floor and Pax froze.

The doors slowly opened onto a long, empty corridor. No people. Just the burning feeling that there was something waiting for her behind one of these doors. And, equally important, there was the friendly red box of a fire alarm, halfway down the hall.

7

Casaria was mad.

It had always been obvious he was a little unhinged, lacking social skills and operating to an odd personal code. But he was actually *mad*. It was all that Sam could think as he advanced on her. She landed heavily on a chair, rocking it onto two legs, too stunned to resist. But he'd already stopped, muttering to himself, looking away, "You're useless – wretched – never *understood*."

His fists clenched, and his eyes, aflame, rolled back towards her.

She should never have come down here without an escort. She'd been distracted. Bewitched by resolving everything that was going on, forgetting who she was dealing with. Wherever he'd been, he was still Casaria.

He stepped towards her and she curled up into the chair, saying, "Let me help you!"

A flicker of doubt in his face.

"You don't have to do this – " Sam urged.

"The MEE's a mess," Casaria said, voice quavering. "You *are* the MEE."

"So are you!"

"No. My eyes are open. At last. And *you* –"

"Don't," Sam said. "Please. Don't."

He smiled. Sadistic, even as his eyes vibrated with uncertainty. He'd act in spite of his confusion. *Because* of it. He had no idea how to handle his emotions, except this – violence – anger – Sam held up a defensive hand. "You're a good man, Cano – I *understand* –"

Wrong choice. His hand came at her from the side, not quite a punch but hard enough to knock her off the seat. She tried to push herself up onto her hands and knees.

"You don't understand shit," he hissed, by her ear.

"I – I –" Sam blinked into the carpet.

"You were never anything but a –"

He was cut off by the piercing whine of the fire alarm.

Casaria stood. "The hell?"

Sam crawled clear of him as the sound escalated, the unbearably loud chime drilling at the pain in her head.

"Stay here," Casaria snarled, and stormed away. The door slammed behind him.

Have to move. Get out before he comes back.

Sam pulled herself up using the edge of the bed and reached for another support. She found the pole of a drip stand, with its thin metal limbs and a base of wheeled legs. Leaning on it, she wobbled to the door. Casaria was saying something on the other side. Someone was out there. He'd persuade them to leave – everyone would evacuate – leaving her –

The room shook, making Sam falter. Then the screaming started below. Still dazed from his blow, she didn't know what was real – was it her fear bouncing back at her? The world was falling apart – she had to *move*. Sam gathered up the drip and charged. She screamed herself as she burst through the door. Using both hands and all her weight, she rammed the end of the drip into Casaria's head, sending him flying into the opposite door. The wood cracked as he slumped down, lifting his face stupidly towards her. Sam kept screaming, raising the drip over him.

"Stop, you fucking psycho!" a female voice cried into her ear, arms wrapping around her chest and pulling her back. Sam bucked, struggling to get free, but the interruption jolted the madness from her. The drip clattered away.

The other woman wrestled her back against a wall, pushing her weight onto her even after she'd stopped struggling. Sam cried, "He wanted to kill me – wanted to kill me –"

"He wanted your help!" the woman shouted, and Sam recognised the voice. She raised her hands to show Pax she was calm. Pax stared back with madly wide eyes.

"What – you?" Another siren chime refreshed the pain in Sam's head. "You set off the alarm?"

"Fucking right," Pax said. "You need to clear this place out. Yesterday."

Before Sam could ask why, another high-pitched sound joined the alarm. A nasty, wheezing sound, growing in volume with each gasp. Sam had heard it once before, one of the few times she'd been in real trouble in the tunnels of the Sunken City, when Casaria had defended her from a scaled monster. It was his laughter. The base, uncontrolled laughter of a lunatic.

Pax followed her gaze to him. He was propped against the door, legs bent under him, face split in a savagely wide grin as he touched the lattice of cuts Sam's blow had left. Thick blood streamed from his brow.

His laughter kicked up a notch as he tapped the blood, frantic, terrifying.

"Damn," Pax said. "You broke him."

"He's always been broken," Sam said.

Another scream shot up from somewhere in the building, far below, more piercing and distinctly pained than the ones before. Then a crash. Something shattering. A tremendous noise of metal sheared in two. The sounds cut off Casaria's laughter, which reduced to dribbles of sniggers as he started to push himself up. More screams followed. Sam met Pax's eyes again. What had she done?

"It's not me!" Pax guessed her thoughts. "I came to help – so did he." Pax ducked to Casaria's side, getting under one of his arms. "Where's Rufaizu?"

What was happening? Should she fight them off? Sam spotted the drip, lying a few feet away. Almost within reach.

"Don't," Pax said. "Please – everyone in this building's in danger." She lowered her voice to Casaria, positioning him upright like balancing cards. "You good?"

"Every agent in a fifty-mile radius will be here in minutes," Sam said. "You can't –"

"They're already too late," Pax said. "*Please*, give me Rufaizu. We can't leave him here."

"I'll get help –"

"There's no time!" Pax yelled.

There was another crash, many storeys below, and another scream, and Pax stared imploringly, pleadingly, into Sam's eyes. Whatever they'd said about her, Pax had put herself in the path of this catastrophe to help.

"In there." Sam pointed at the door she'd fractured with Casaria's weight. As she approached it, she looked towards the lifts. Casaria was in the way, painted in blood, but he slumped, with Pax, towards the door.

Someone shrieked below, but was cut suddenly short.

The corridor to the lifts suddenly seemed hopelessly long, and the thought of getting out of this building alone desperately frightening. What was happening – half an hour ago everything had been normal – Casaria had walked back in and –

"Can you open it?" Pax shouted. Sam started and her body made the decision for her. She bolted forwards to key in the code to Rufaizu's room.

Pax tried to disengage her brain as she raced to unplug Rufaizu. The machines around the room beeped violently, adding spice to the blaring fire alarm. He was okay, judging from the colour of his skin and the fact that he was able to open his eyes in terror, but his pupils looked like tar pits. His hands lifted and flopped back down uselessly.

"You fuckers drugged him to hell," Pax snarled.

"No," Ward insisted. "I cut it off – he should be clean –"

Pax shot her a look to shut up. Rufaizu had a bandage around his neck and wore a hospital gown, bare at the back, lanky skin and bone on show with no other marks. He tried to sit up, but couldn't carry his own weight, so Pax struggled to help.

"You missed a tube," Casaria said, somewhat recovered but just watching.

"Make yourself fucking useful!" Pax commanded. Casaria moved to the other side of the bed to push Rufaizu her way. She turned to Ward. "Got a wheelchair? Anything?"

"There isn't one here?" Casaria asked, and Pax gave him a savage look.

"Think I missed it behind all the room's emptiness?"

"The other room," Ward said, and rushed away.

Pax and Casaria manoeuvred Rufaizu over the side of the bed, as his head lolled like a rag doll's. His hazel eyes locked on Pax. "Lookit who's here – barfly, pretty barfly –"

Pax huffed irritation. Was this her life now? Tolerating the semi-conscious hindrances of variously incapacitated men? She patted Rufaizu's cheek, saying, "How far gone are you? You in there?"

Rufaizu didn't answer, snapping his head aside like a child refusing peas.

"Here, here!" Ward reappeared, a wheelchair squeaking in front of her, frame mottled with dark rust.

"Couldn't find anything older?"

The floor shook and the lights blinked off. The fire alarm missed a beat but continued screaming as dull white emergency lights flicked on. The brief respite was torn by a massive piece of furniture breaking below, bits slamming into different parts of a room. Was it directly beneath them? One floor down?

"What is it?" Ward asked, terrified.

"I don't know," Pax lied, returning to Rufaizu. She pulled him off the bed as he playfully resisted, too doped up to be worried. "Quit it!" Vaguely aware she was doing all this herself, Pax looked at Casaria, watching her questioningly. Ward looked similarly uncertain.

"What?" Pax shouted. "Think we should stay here?"

"You *know* what it is," Casaria said. "You came in because you know."

"I came up here because you were taking so –"

"Stop bullshitting me!" Casaria shouted, veins popping up under his bloody flesh. Ward backed off fearfully, but Pax just felt fucking annoyed. She stood up straight.

"Turnbold, that's what they called it," Pax told him, bitterly, and Casaria spun away, cursing. "You didn't guess it was serious?"

"Take the boy, go," Casaria instructed. Already halfway out the room.

"Where are you going?"

He pointed up the hall. "*Obviously* there's no one else in this damn building who can deal with something like that. I'm going to get something that can stop it."

He marched out of the room and Pax swore, moving behind Rufaizu and shoving the wheelchair. The wheels caught; the guy was heavier than he looked, moving about, giggling.

"Help me, already!" Pax shouted at Ward.

Spurred into action, Ward joined her and together they shoved the rusty wheelchair into the hall. Pax faltered in the corridor, noticing the sensation tugging at her chest. Her eyes were drawn to a nondescript door at the end of the corridor. It looked small, not even another office entrance – a cupboard – why was this buzzing energy drawing her there? Didn't she have enough to worry about?

A groan from Rufaizu drew her attention back to the chair. She shook herself out of it, leaning heavily on the handles and racing the other way, towards the lifts. Ward scrambled after her. A door was open on the right, ahead, with sounds of equipment being tossed about coming from inside. As she got closer Pax saw shards of wood across the floor, the door busted in. Inside, the room was filled with metal caging. Casaria was somewhere in the middle, searching for a weapon. Pax slowed down and shouted, "The Dispenser, don't forget –"

The lift pinged, drawing her attention back to escaping. She watched the doors open. An older man, square-shouldered, silver-haired, a stern look on his face. At his elbow was a younger suited man, eyes a little too far apart. Both as surprised as her.

"What the hell is going on?" The older man regained his senses first. "Ward?"

"Sir, it's not what it looks like –" Ward started. How would she explain this? She didn't get a chance, as the corridor shook again. They all stumbled, the men cursing as they banged into the walls. Rufaizu laughed.

"Oh, it's coming! Judgement coming up, them that've been bad, it's *coming*!"

"Not a reason to be cheerful," Pax hissed, steadying herself and slamming her weight into the chair. It moved with a piercing squeak, Rufaizu whooping, and the two men staggered out of the way rather than get hit. Speeding between them, Pax couldn't slow down entering the lift, the chair and Rufaizu crashing into the far wall. The doors rolled closed on her leg, sticking out, and rolled open again.

"Sir?" Casaria's voice bellowed beyond it all. "Evacuate! I'll handle this!"

"You're all going to –" the older guy roared.

The floor exploded.

8

In her brief forays into the Sunken City, Sam had been exposed to a number of its creatures. She'd seen a sickle, at a distance, and the shadow of a passing *effundo porcum*. She'd heard glogockles and seen the destructive path left by a migrating tuckle. They all exuded enough horror that she'd never needed to see more. Once she'd negotiated her way into Greek Street, they became names and numbers collated in spreadsheets and bar charts. Recent turnbold numbers were below the optimum level for balance in the Sunken City ecosystem; a good ratio of turnbolds reduced excessive sickle numbers. The problem was too many crusads, spider-like creatures which fed venom into the food chain, deadly to turnbolds. The solution was to increase the coverage of wading moss in the northeast quadrant, stimulating the spread of carnivorous buglooms which would, in turn, prey on crusads.

It was all a game of numbers.

In late February Sam had drawn up a plan to redress this balance.

Seeing it in the flesh, she was thankful that particular plan had been rejected.

The turnbold was a nightmare incarnate: its enormous turtle-like shell slowly rotated above a tangle of thick tentacles, various dark holes in its carapace hinting at the horror of multiple heads within.

Sam backed down the corridor. The hall was thick with debris, lights flickering. Casaria stood nearby, making noises like he was testing his voice or ears. On the other side of the creature, Mathers was on a knee, trying to gather his senses. The agent with him, Devlin, was coughing on dust. Pax punched at a lift button but the doors weren't closing.

The turnbold screeched, a birdlike call that cut to the bone. It came as a series of sounds from different parts of its shell. It rotated out of the mess of the shredded floor, a domed shape the size of a large table. Tentacles rolled up from its base, feeling for purchase. As it pulled itself up, and the dust started to clear, its faces became clearer.

A couple of tentacles reared up and single, jagged claws stretched out of their ends, hooking into the walls. It pulled itself further out of the hole and another head crept out from one of the shell's openings. The face stood on a stalk-like neck, wrapped in leathery green skin. In all other ways, it had the appearance of a human skull, its circular eyes shining like copper as the strobing hall light caught them. No pupils, no irises, but clearly looking Sam's way. Its crooked jaw dropped open and a two-foot lizard tongue flicked out, spraying blood across the floor. It let out another avian cry.

Sam ran.

Another flurry of cries and a sudden burst of action answered her panic.

Concrete and floorboards snapped behind her, the heavy thump saying the turnbold was clear of its opening and advancing. More thumps, the sound of claws tearing through the walls. Someone shouted. A heavy *thwack* as it passed Casaria – had to have hit him, knocked him down. But it hadn't slowed. It was gaining on her.

Sam aimed for the end of the corridor. She couldn't turn, no time to open any of the doors. All she had was a square window to aim for. And what? Jump? It was getting faster – moving faster than her – she wasn't even going to make the window –

The monster's climb must have severed the power lines, because the lift wasn't responding. Pax leant out, looking one way then another. The arrow of a fire exit sign pointed past the monster. There had to be stairs somewhere.

The creature – Lightgate's turnbold, it had to be – tore free of the hole it had created. Like a goddamned turtle-mole. It was following Ward's screams down the hall. The suit by the lift composed himself to stand with a pistol in one hand, but that was it.

"Fucking do something!" Pax yelled, but he only turned to her dumbly.

Casaria hit the wall as the monster thundered past.

Pax leapt out of the lift and tore the pistol from the suit's hand, lifted it and pulled the trigger. It bucked in her hand with a terrific bang and she almost let go. The ceiling erupted halfway down the hall. That snapped the agent out of his trance; he gave her such a look that she held up a defensive hand and offered the gun back. By the time he'd turned, the turnbold was coming back their way. Two skeletal heads poked out of its shell, bouncing on stalk-like necks, bony jaws chattering hungrily together. The agent spread his legs and raised the gun. The older suit pressed himself against the wall as the monster arrived.

The gun went off and some fleshy mass exploded with dark liquid. The monster screeched but didn't slow down. Pax rolled towards the lift as she was hit by a spray of hot blood. The agent smashed into the wall above her and flopped to the floor a metre away. His lower half flapped into the wall on the other side. A tentacle shot over Pax's head, claws ripping through the wall. The lift panel came off with sparks.

Pax made it to her hands and knees, trying to crawl out of the way as the turnbold pulled itself along the corridor, rising on its tentacles, jaws gnashing from multiple heads.

"Casaria!" the older suit yelled, reprimanding on instinct. "Shoot it!"

The mass of tentacles writhed like worms as the shell spun in his direction, jamming against the wall in the tight space. The man's scream was cut off by a wet thunk, reduced to a gargle. Pax saw the guy's lower legs, between the tentacles, raised off the floor, kicking for a second, before they stopped. Blood oozed down the wall behind him. The turnbold lowered itself, the shell obscuring the view but not the sound, as he gargled more desperately, and multiple jaws started chewing.

Pax heard her own loud breath as she tried to crawl away. Her hands were shaking. Rufaizu shouted from the lift, voice echoing in the tinny confines, "Want trouble turny-bold? Think I'm afeared from you?"

He got its attention, the tentacles slapping against the floor again, the shell turning. Pax dived out of the way as it lunged for the lift opening. Its broad shell caught in the metal doorframe and it released a series of frustrated screeches. Its tentacles flapped about as it blindly tried to force its way in. The walls creaked under its immense weight, the lift's frame twisting noisily. Rufaizu laughed. "Best you got? Come at me!"

The sound of snapping jaws bounced out of the lift.

Pax jumped to her feet, and something snapped her way. The shell had openings all the way around it, and another stalk head launched at her. Ducking the bite, she jumped to get past the monster. She slipped on the MEE agent's blood, bringing her down to a knee, just in time to avoid a claw that punched through the wall at head-height. Pax dived out of the way and ran in a crouch, clear of the monster, back to the hole it had risen from. It gnashed and shrieked, and she half-turned to see it was stuck in the lift entrance, heads popping in and out of its shell and tentacles lashing in all directions. The older suit was mangled like roadkill on the floor. Rufaizu drew its attention again: "Ugly sinner, that all you got?"

Utterly mad – she'd pinned her hopes on *him*?

But at least the ferocious attack had woken him up.

Pax stumbled towards Casaria. He was taking deep breaths, leaning against the wall. Impossible to see if he'd been seriously injured or just winded.

"Nu . . . nu . . ." Casaria wheezed, vaguely pointing at a collection of weapons at his feet. A stubby gun that looked like a toilet roll with a handle. A conventional-looking pistol. A couple of small cylinders that had to be grenades.

Pax looked from the weapons up the corridor. A fire exit light stood out over a door at the end of the hall. Sam Ward was there, eyes staring their way. For a moment Pax thought she was dead, pressed horrified against the window. But the woman's head moved, shaking in disbelief.

"Get out, all of you go!" Rufaizu yelled. "I can't hold it much longer!"

Hell, he wasn't a simple lunatic, he was actually trying to distract it.

"Pneumatic charge!" Casaria forced it out, with all his breath, kicking the stubby weapon. Pax snatched it up. Two buttons on the gun, a lever at the side, a basic trigger. She aimed down the corridor at the writhing monstrous mass and pulled the trigger.

Nothing happened, and the tentacles kept snatching at the lift.

Casaria grunted, halfway up the wall and reaching a hand her way. She shoved the weapon at him and he pumped the lever, pressed one of the buttons. It made a hissing noise. But he stopped there, slumping, with barely the energy to breathe.

The lift creaked, the wall splitting around it as the turnbold pressed further inside. Rufaizu couldn't hide the fear in his voice now. "Yeah – ugly – try it – that your best?"

Pax ripped the gun off Casaria and aimed again. She braced herself and fired.

The tube erupted like a bursting air canister, and a projectile shot down the hall with a plume of gas. It cracked through the left edge of the turnbold's shell, multiple shrieks coming from the monster. The thing slumped slightly, many of its tentacles going limp, then its heads drew in with an echo of pained breaths.

"Move your arse, Rufaizu!" Pax screamed as the monster reared up.

"Go, go," Casaria gasped, a hand feebly pushing Pax's shoulder. There was a flurry of movement as Rufaizu scrambled through the tentacles under the turnbold, the creature twitching at its extremities. Casaria gathered his pistol and the grenades off the floor, finally getting his breath back. He gave Pax a harder shove. "It's recovering."

Pax stumbled a few steps, hitting the edge of the hole the turnbold had created. Below, she saw the devastated remains of desks amid blood and lumps of flesh. There was another hole in the floor below. "Fuck. Fuck. Fuck."

"Go!" Casaria croaked, as he clawed at a grenade. With Rufaizu still back there.

"No!" Pax yelled, and he caught her eyes before looking back the turnbold's way. He shook his head, but lowered the grenade, then started moving ahead. Away from the creature, limping as fast as his stunned body would take him.

Casaria waved at the frozen Ward, shouting, "*Go!*"

"Casaria!" Pax ran after him, grabbing his arm as Ward came to life, scanning the doors near her. "There must be something –" Casaria pushed Pax back.

"Only had one shot," he snapped, smacking the tube gun from her hands. "You missed."

Pax stood frozen for a second, looking from the apparently empty gun back towards the turnbold. Its tentacles were becoming more animated, searching the air. One of its heads came out of the shell, eyes dim but widening. As Rufaizu burst out from under its mass, staggering into the open, the eyes brightened. The creature shuddered all over and Rufaizu cursed as he stumbled upright.

Pax raced the short distance back to him as the turnbold screeched again. Another of its heads stuck out, jaws biting at Rufaizu, and he ducked out of the way. The monster wrenched itself to the side, ripping a massive fragment of wall free, lurching halfway clear of the remnants of the lift. Pax grabbed Rufaizu and pushed him the other way. As she turned again, something caught her ankle. It pulled her leg from under her and she met the floor with a knock to the head. She saw one of the tentacles tangled around her leg, dragging her towards an extended head with a wide skeletal maw.

"Get to hell!" Rufaizu yelled, jumping past her, feet first. He caught the turnbold shell beyond the head with both feet. The tentacle came free as the turnbold rolled onto its side with more snaps and screeches, toppling into the lift. Rufaizu landed heavily beside Pax, coughing in shock like he hadn't expected the impact.

Pax jumped up and pulled him with her. "Move, move, move!" He lifted himself, with her help, and they ran arm in arm down the hall. The turnbold writhed in the lift, screeching and clawing and scraping its clawed tentacles against the walls. At the end of the hall, Casaria was waiting, holding a door open.

Ward was already gone.

"This way!" he shouted, uselessly.

The cries of the struggling turnbold were met with a groan from the elevator shaft. Pushing her legs as fast as they'd go, Pax didn't dare look back.

"It's going down!" Rufaizu whooped, twisting in her grip.

Another metal groan. More turnbold screams as it bucked at its confines.

Pax turned to see the elevator break free. With a final splitting of the walls around it and a tremendous crash, the lift fell out of sight, dragging the turnbold down with it. A cloud of dust rose to fill the corridor, silhouetting the flopping shapes of two severed tentacles and a flying head.

Rufaizu was laughing again.

The lift landed far below, and the building shook with an enormous boom. Another cloud of dust burst out of the shaft and there was a second's silence before the avian shrieks resumed. The creature, at the base of the building, sounding angrier than ever.

"This way," Casaria said again. "Out the back."

9

In the Plaza, waiting, ruing Pax for not having a phone, Letty kept scanning through Fae websites, finding articles complementing the first headlines she'd discovered. They confirmed her fears: between the rumours about Pax eating a Fae, and the news reports about the return of the dangerous Apothel Five, the Fae media was being led to believe the humans were fiendishly mad. It would look bad if someone came forward with the Dispenser, claiming some humans actually wanted to help them. Even worse if those humans had been killed by Val.

Arnold had called three times, but Letty didn't answer. They'd be here soon enough, better if they didn't come too prepared.

Letty scanned from her phone down to Rolarn's festering body, forcing herself to look at him. It wasn't right, having to kill another Fae, even a Grade A arsehole. There weren't enough of them, and he was a soldier, one way or another. And she'd done it for the sake of the humans. Weighed their lives against one of her own.

Except it *was* right.

She didn't owe her people loyalty – not when all they did was make things worse.

She needed a better distraction. Who was the guy that'd come visiting? How important was he?

Letty searched for his name. The suited dork's face came up right away, in multiple posed photos. Councilman Edwing, as he'd claimed. A young blood in the FTC government, he hadn't been around when Letty was still there. She checked the headlines relating to him. He'd rapidly risen to Chair of Information, whatever the hell position that was. So Lightgate had the ear of the government. Plotting another coup. Letty bit her lip. Considering Valoria's attitudes to the Dispenser, she wasn't sure if that was a bad thing, but Edwing hadn't been entirely on board, had he? Lightgate's people needed to create a scene that forced him to act. A dead family of humans would do that.

Letty tried the news sites again.

A new headline came up. Well, shit, that had to be another of Lightgate's spinning plates.

The footage was lifted from the human media. Smoke coming out of the Ministry building. Emergency service vehicles blocking the streets. Never mind their plans for the Bartons – they'd gone right for the jugular. Lightgate had activated one of the Fae weapons that had never been put to rest. Early reports said it was a creature. There'd be bodies, with Lightgate involved. No way Pax would've gone in, was there?

She should go – find her. These punks might give hot pursuit of the Bartons, but Pax needed her more –

A noise disturbed Letty's thoughts; men talking on the floor above. One of them called down: "Rolarn, you there?" Arnold.

Letty stood, straightening out the hefty strap of her artificial wing, Rolarn's shotgun ready across her waist. She kept close to the edge of the till, pretty much the only object in this massive room that would provide any cover.

"Rolarn, talk to me, why aren't you answering your phone?" Arnold demanded, angrily, as the dark shapes of him and his men floated into view from above. There had to be six or more of them: the Tupsom Trawlers.

Here to do a job.

"You brought the whole gang?" Letty called out to stop them. They hung in the air near the ceiling opening, all quiet as they understood Rolarn wasn't just being quiet.

"Where's the damn humans?" Arnold asked. "Letty, if you've –"

"If I've what? Interrupted a seriously dumb idea?" Letty said. "How do you think this ends? We *need* those humans to take back the Sunken City."

"Sunken City shit," Arnold sneered. "Where are you, Letty? Get a light on."

"Sunken City shit," Letty echoed, quietly. Was she the only person who gave a damn about their heritage? The only one that wanted a return to something respectable? Of course, this lot hadn't ever known respectable. She called out, "The humans are gone, you should be too."

"You damn idiot!" Arnold snarled. "This is our chance – we're taking our place –"

"Your place is the gutter! What the fuck is there to aspire to, if not the Sunken City?"

"The FTC!" Arnold raised his voice, quick to anger, and his boys joined in with snarls of agreement. "It's time someone with true Fae blood took charge."

"The FTC?" Letty shouted, her own temper rising. "Who wants the FTC? You genital wart, you wanna die trying to dominate a consolation prize?"

The gang went quiet. They'd come here suspecting something, no doubt, but couldn't have expected to have to face *her*. Please, Letty silently begged, give it the fuck up and go home. "You all know who I am. You want trouble, I've got it for you. But the last thing any of us need is more dead Fae."

Silence again.

"We got no beef with you, Letty," Arnold told her. A little cautious. "We just want the humans. Things are moving – promises been made."

"Like what? Kill a human and your three wishes come true?"

"Only one wish. We get people to take up arms against Val. She's been denouncing them, but things are going crazy. They set the turnbold loose – you heard that? The humans show up dead now, at Val's hand –"

"They show up *alive* and Val's in the shit."

"It's not enough. These are humans that took our *tech* – they *killed* our –"

"They didn't kill shit!" Letty shouted. "I'm right here, no one killed me!"

Arnold stalled, logic failing. "They're still human. Still scum. Better off dead."

"These humans can help us, you dense pillock."

"No," Arnold said, mind settling. "This is how it's gonna work – how it's gotta work. Without bodies to pin on Val, it's your word against hers. The Citizen has to die."

"Smoking geese," Letty muttered. It was no use. "You're even thicker than you look. You and the whole damned FTC. You've got the chance to fly away, right now. Take it."

"You know what Lightgate would do to us?" Arnold said.

"Fly fast, then."

"Sorry, Letty." He sounded like he meant it. "We got no choice."

"Then neither do I." Letty took aim with Rolarn's shotgun.

Five flights of stairs (or ten? They doubled up, didn't they?), and Pax was having an unpleasant time breathing. When they burst out of the fire exit into a walled courtyard with a single, narrow exit, she couldn't speak. Sam Ward was blocking the exit, but she didn't look particularly great herself, her frightened skin the colour of porridge.

The sounds inside hadn't stopped, with things continuing to break apart and collapse, people shouting and screaming, the turnbold shrieking. It had slowed down and wasn't getting any closer, though. Maybe still stuck in the lift shaft.

"Step aside," Casaria said, facing Ward with his jacket pushed back over his hands on his hips. A mock cop pose. It looked forced, but Ward took a concerned step back.

"Why?" Ward said. Her pleading eyes found Pax. "How could you?"

Pax said nothing. She didn't have the breath.

"You still don't get it?" Casaria snarled. "There's more going on here than you can begin to comprehend. There's enemies you don't even understand."

It was a fine summary, Pax supposed, especially as she was sure it applied to the man saying it. Good to see his enthusiasm reapplied, either way.

Rufaizu shifted at Pax's shoulder, apparently pumped enough to be standing straight. He said, "Enemies underground, who made them come up, huh?"

"That thing . . ." Ward said.

"This was the fucking Fae!" Casaria pointed into the building. "The Ministry should've seen it coming. Should've purged the lot of them a long –"

"Stop." Pax held up a hand. The courtyard seemed to dance before her eyes, all a bit whiter than it should've been. Oh, to be fit and healthy for times like this. "Wait." They did. This weird situation again, with everyone looking at her like she would speak their troubles away. "*Not* the Fae. Not that simple."

"Have you any idea the damage you've done?" Ward asked, genuinely.

"Yeah," Pax sighed. "But . . ." She took another deep breath, rolled her eyes up, unsure if she was seeing thick white cloud or her vision was failing. "*I* didn't do it. The Fae . . ." She flapped a hand Casaria's way. "This is them – but not all of them." Lightgate had been turned down by the other Fae. It might have been a lone madman that left Lightgate the note with those codes; a conspiracy of two. Without the energy to get all that out, Pax huffed, "Most said *no*."

"You're wasting what little breath you've got," Casaria said. "She's a company man."

"I am *not*!" Ward protested, then repeated it in what she clearly hoped was a more reasonable tone. "I am not. I've been trying to trace where the energy goes."

A siren whined nearby. Emergency vehicles rapidly approaching. Pax couldn't help feeling she needed to get used to these sounds.

"We can't stay here," said Casaria, stating the obvious.

"You can't *leave*," Ward said. "Our people will surround this area." Another birdlike shrill came from the building. "Thankfully."

"Okay." Pax took a step forward. "You can't stop us."

"I won't –"

Casaria moved towards her too, and Ward jumped back into the wall. His fists were clenched, perhaps intending to do more than scare her. She had both hands up, frightened. Pax growled, "She's not the enemy, either, for Christ's sake!"

He looked back at her, confused.

Pax advanced and Rufaizu jumped to her side to help, taking her arm. He, fresh from his hospital bed doping, offering *her* support. She let him. Taking a few more breaths, Pax said to Ward, "Think before you retaliate. There's a bigger picture – the Blue Angel. Not the Fae."

"The grugulochs?" Ward uttered back. In agreement?

Pax paused. "Yeah. That, too."

"What is it?"

"You tell me. You've got the technology."

"Is it the *praelucente* itself?" Ward said, almost hopeful. That would be simple, wouldn't it?

"No," Pax replied. "Whatever's *behind* the *praelucente*. Whatever's moving that energy around. Manipulating everyone. You track that energy, you'll find where that word comes from."

Sam started shaking her head. "It'll take time –"

"Your people are gonna want to hang the Fae," Pax warned, then paused for another breath. She cleared her throat and said, "The Fae won't take it lightly. I don't know . . . the Blue Angel, or your grugulochs, made this happen here. Even if the Fae pulled the trigger, the Angel is to blame."

The sirens were getting closer.

"We need to go."

Ward pushed off from the wall, desperately. "Where? Where are you going?"

Pax walked past her, not looking back, not answering because she didn't know.

10

Letty sheltered behind a metal strut. It was a minor miracle she'd fought her way out of the cover-free shop into the steel rafters of the plaza's loft space. But pretty clear why Lightgate chose Rolarn as a guard over Arnold and his Trawlers. They were amateurs, soft from picking on humans and never tussling with real Fae. She'd left three dead on the shop floor, filling the place with gunfire as she flew for the ceiling. That left another three, by her counting, and they weren't happy following her up here.

"On me, you bastards!" Arnold shouted. "Use your heads!"

Letty leant around the steel support to watch their shapes flitting between the beams. None of them was racing her way. A good chance they hadn't seen where she'd ended up. One movement a few tiers above, another in the opposite direction. Arnold's voice had come from somewhere in between. That put all of them more or less in her line of sight.

She ducked as a bullet sparked off the adjacent beam. The muzzle flash was about two feet back. Had to be Arnold.

"Still time to fly away, Arnold!" Letty shouted.

"You shot my men!" he snarled furiously.

"Like you gave me a choice? No one ever told you I eat street thugs like you for breakfast?"

"Better a street thug than a human-lover!" the one to the left shouted. Pinpointing his position, thank you. A movement to the right indicated the third one, dashing to another beam, trying to flank her.

Letty jammed her pistol in the holster and hefted up the shotgun. Still a couple shots left, there. She kept goading: "I already did for Mix and Fresko. And Rolarn? He must've been worth your whole crew. You got nothing on any of them, Arnold. Fly *away*."

The flanking Fae dashed for another beam and Letty opened fire. A pistol shot would've been impossible, but the guy couldn't fly through a cloud of buckshot. She unloaded both barrels and he spun in the air like a fly in a tornado – one more down. Throwing the gun away and whipping out her pistol, she spun back and fired at the one on the left as he moved to another position. The bullet thunked into the ceiling far behind him, but the message was sent. She heard the goon's heavy breathing. Freaking out. There was a reason he was the only one left, she guessed. Letty threw a comment his way: "Go now or when Arnold dies, you're a free man either way."

The pair of them were quiet, except for the minion's worried breathing.

"Like hell," Arnold snarled, finally. "Let's finish this."

She cursed at the sound of his fluttering wings and ducked to see his approach. He moved fast, springing from one strut to another; she fired and missed by a mile. The next shot glanced him but he took it. Two beams away, a foot between them.

"Now!" Arnold shouted, coming into the open firing. The shots sparked against Letty's cover, making her take shelter, and she turned in the other direction to take on his companion. He didn't materialise, and Arnold started screaming, "Shoot her!"

Nothing.

She spun around to the other side of the beam, into Arnold's confused face. He was coming too quickly to react; she got her free hand on his wrist and twisted his gun away as she turned hers on him. Fired two shots into his wing as his other arm came up to punch her. She fired a third shot into his chest. His own single shot slapped uselessly into the floor. His eyes met Letty's with shock, asking *why*. She returned a grim look. Didn't need to be this way. His wings slowed as blood spread across his chest. She let go and he dropped like a sack of nuts.

Something fluttered behind Letty and she spun. The last Trawler was speeding between the beams towards the ceiling. The only one of them with any damned sense.

"Idiots," Letty muttered, thick with regret. "I don't know."

"Hey," a voice said above.

Letty half-raised her pistol before freezing.

Lightgate was perched one beam up, a shining silver pistol, with a host of gadgets, held in a limp hand, loosely aimed at Letty's head. "Those idiots got us here, at least."

"Where's here, bitchsticks?" Letty growled. "The humans are gone. Your boys are dead. What've you got?"

"My health," Lightgate said. She stood, drunkenly teetering. Letty knew better than to believe it. The barrel of Lightgate's gun didn't stray from her forehead.

"How'd you ever convince the FTC you're not nuts . . ."

Lightgate rolled her arms, gun pivoting to point at Letty like it was tied to her by string. "No mystery. I have great ideas, and I know how to work with people."

"You're shitting me," Letty snarled. "You never could've got close to the humans without me –"

"Yes. Thanks for that. You *are* useful, Letty."

"I'll give you fucking thanks!" Letty tensed but didn't move. Lightgate's lazy-looking eyes were way too ready.

"Letty. We've done good today. Someone's on your side, for once. I took advantage of opportunities you couldn't, that's all."

"Opportunities for *what*?"

"To make a better world, what else?" Lightgate said. "Breaking down old walls, destroying the Ministry, destroying the FTC. Destroying whatever plagues the Sunken City." She'd started laughing, taken by her own words. "Change, Letty. We have opportunities for change. Have fun with it!"

"You're nuts," Letty snarled; even without Lightgate's flippant tone, she would've known the fairy cared about none of that. "You were nuts before, you're only more nuts now, and you used these boys who believed in better, all for what? To stoke violence?"

"Is that a bad thing? No one wanted to lift a finger against the Ministry or Val. I came up with genius ideas – blame the turnbold on Barton, frame Val for human deaths, *all sorts*. The best I got was a coward's note." Lightgate delved a free hand into her jacket, searching pockets. In a brief flurry of irritation, betraying her instability, she pulled a crumpled piece of paper out and tossed it towards Letty. It came nowhere near. Letty watched it fall as Lightgate railed on, "The FTC are too scared to even talk to me face-to-face! You meet Edwing? He's the only one I got more than a phone call from, and he's got all the gumption of a fucking lamp. They've been scared forever. They need this."

"A catastrophic monster attack? The murder of innocents?"

"An attack necessary to take back the Dispenser. To prove Val's been lying. An attack we could blame on the humans, at that – they're known enemies of the Ministry. Except, uh-oh, Val's people kill them? Double-trouble for her!"

"Except *they're gone*. And where's the fucking Dispenser?"

Lightgate shrugged, "Details."

"The Ministry are gonna go apeshit! Val's gonna hunt you down! Aren't you –"

"Looking forward to it?" Lightgate grinned. "You have your love affair with the Sunken City, Letty. My dreams are simpler. And *clearly* more appealing, considering our respective social circles."

Letty stared, aghast. Why *did* anyone follow Lightgate? Edwing had known better, so who had she convinced to do something as daft as set off those turnbold charges? Would any Fae be mad enough to put the FTC at risk like that? Letty's eyes scanned down to that scrunched up ball of paper. No, probably not. "You got a secretive note? Anonymous help?"

Lightgate didn't reply, amused face not seeming to follow.

Letty knew it, deep down, already. Lightgate had brought her own brand of crazy into this and the Blue Angel had seized the opportunity. Active, somehow, in the FTC, wielding the same influence Pax suggested it had over the MEE. "We were getting close – getting both sides talking – trying to figure out the truth of this. The Blue Angel's scared of that, and you've just given it a fucking golden platter of chaos to revive the Fae-human rift. You're insane."

"No," Lightgate said, eyes moving wistfully up, "I am *creative*. We haven't fought for our place in this world in *ten years*, Letty. Don't you miss the conflict? The excitement of battle? Your human friend might step on some toes, but we can do so much more. We damaged the MEE, how are you not impressed?"

"Because *we* didn't do it! You don't even know who set off the charges! That note," she gestured to the paper, "is it written in ink or just scratched into the fucking paper?"

"What?" Lightgate frowned.

"This is what it does!" Letty shouted. "The Blue Angel is playing you!"

"This Blue Angel again," Lightgate sighed. "Aren't you tired of that paranoid talk? Whoever was behind those charges, good for them. If they're playing, I'm *game*. If the Ministry comes, it's open season. The FTC can crumble, if they're not ready – but I'm ready. We've sown seeds. *You* sowed seeds. Let's reap."

"I'm no fucking farmer. You're talking about setting the world on fire."

Lightgate leant in closer, face wicked. "You can't deny it's gonna be pretty."

Letty screwed her eyes shut. With hope finally creeping in, so came the psychos and warmongers and chaos. "Why don't you put me out of my fucking misery?"

"Oh no," Lightgate said. "You're a good soldier. You're going to fight with me."

"Why not imagine my answer?"

"Because I've got a gun on you and you're a survivor. Do we really need to discuss how you're going to survive?"

11

"Are you gonna throw up again?" Casaria asked.

"Fuck off," Pax answered, hands on her knees. "How far have we gone?"

The streets at either end of the alley were busy with pedestrians and fast-moving cars. The mindless bustle of Central, oblivious to the panic a few blocks away.

"We're near the river," Casaria said. "A few streets from Planter Bridge."

"And the Underground?" Pax said.

"On the south bank, sure – but with him? Looking like that?" He nodded to Rufaizu's hospital gown. Pax hardly looked well herself, after the tussle with the turnbold. Her new trousers had a tear down the right calf and her face felt sticky in places she didn't dare touch, worried about smearing the blood of mutilated men. It was nothing compared to the carnage of Casaria's suit, though.

Pax said, "You're the one that looks like an adult abortion."

Casaria scoffed. "These people can't see past a suit. They're locked in their own pointless heads, witness only to their daylight expectations."

Pax stared, unsure whether to be alarmed by his contradictory comments or impressed that he understood the same phenomenon that Letty said kept the Fae hidden.

Another siren wailed as a police car shot past. The pedestrians barely reacted.

Patting her pockets to check for a phone, it took Pax a moment to recall they'd ditched Rimes' phone after Chaucer Crescent. She should've taken Letty's advice to get another one. But they could get to a payphone once they were out of the open.

She gave Rufaizu a look. He pumped his eyebrows playfully, energy redoubling minute by minute. As though he hadn't just escaped government abduction. Admirable, but perhaps indicative of something wrong with him. She said, "Up for a walk?"

"My lady," he said, stepping away from the wall and giving a graceful curtsey. He stumbled on his own feet and had to steady himself. "Yes. Yes I am."

"Okay, the bridge is this way? We'll make like it's no big deal." She led by example, moving into the bustle. Casaria dogged her heels. When he met a businesswoman's eyes, she buried her face in her phone.

"Where are we going?" Casaria said. "The Underground, then *where?*"

"Broadplain," Pax said. "To get the others out of there, if it's not already too late."

"Broadplain," Casaria scoffed. "I told you, never trust those insects, now you've seen the results."

"Result of bad men playing bad games," Rufaizu disagreed.

"Shut up or I'll shut you up," Casaria replied.

"That's what got us here to begin with," Pax said, stopping at a traffic light. "You and your bloody efforts to keep innocent people quiet."

Casaria stopped, slotting into the waiting crowd. One man glanced at Pax's face and sidestepped around a woman and child to stand further away. Pax smiled at the little girl, who stared back, noncommittal.

The lights beeped for them to cross. Rufaizu sprang off the pavement with sudden inspiration. "Barfly! You bust through and showed them who was *boss*."

Pax kept her head low, passing more pedestrians, willing the young man to tone it down.

"I was the one who went in to get you," Casaria said. "And it's me who knows how to face the hell that the Ministry's going to raise after this."

Pax cut through the crowd to a set of steps that intersected riverside office blocks. She said to Casaria, without looking back, "You're sure they've got anything left? Seemed your people just took a blow."

"Hardly," Casaria said. "Mathers? Devon? Those two were dead weight. There's others that'll fill the gaps. London will send people. It'll be weapons-free." He opened his jacket demonstratively. The pistol he'd retrieved was holstered there. Pax slapped the jacket shut again.

They came to the edge of the thick, rolling grey slosh of the River Gader, 200 metres wide at this point. Planter Bridge, with its jagged pillars and worn floral moulding, was accessible by a tall set of steps. Trying to refill her lungs, Pax cursed the architects of Central for taking them down to river level before sending them up onto the bridge. After a five-storey flight from a tortoise-hydra, it was enough to keep them all quiet until they reached the crest of the bridge.

Alongside thinning traffic, Rufaizu skipped to the bridge's edge to look down into the river, and cooed at the cityscape that flanked it, like he'd never seen such grandeur. Pax gave him a warning look, to tell him they needed to keep moving, but what the hell, it was a chance to recharge.

She came to the young man's side and followed his gaze to take in Ordshaw. How long had it been since she'd last seen this view? And during the day? The cityscape was beautiful in its rises and falls, a spectrum of old and new. There was the domed, twin-turreted Hall of Tongues, now home to the mayoral office. The vast gothic peaks of St Margaret's Cathedral. In the distance, it was possible to see the pointed tip of Grant's Obelisk, and near that the familiar stepped riverfront facade of Featherback's Casino. Between those landmarks sat the glass and metal totems of modern business: most notably No. 2 Waterfront, better known as The Spoon, and the Duvcorp building.

"Lot's changed," Rufaizu said, with wonder.

Pax nodded. It was different enough from when she'd first arrived, and she couldn't imagine how it must look compared to his childhood memories; he'd left aged nine, and must have seen some things in between. But at least he'd always known what lay beneath it. For her, she was only just discovering Ordshaw's true layers. Ready to kill them all. She asked him, "Why did you come back?"

Rufaizu's face screwed up. "To kill the minotaur."

His answer was so simple, so honest. The fool. Pax said, "You know it's more than just a monster, right? You know about the Blue Angel? You know what your father knew – that word he wrote in the Ripton Chapel? The grugulochs?"

His face screwed even tighter. "The *what*?"

Pax stalled. Not the revelation she'd hoped for.

A trio of Japanese tourists passed, huddled together with hurried whispers, a wildly conspicuous attempt at subtlety. One of them pointed at Pax and she looked away. A camera clicked behind her.

"What *do* you know?" Pax implored of Rufaizu. "What happened between Apothel and the Fae? Between him and the Blue Angel?" Rufaizu's face clouded in anguish. "What?"

"Don't trust the Ministry," Rufaizu said, reciting it like rote. "Nor the Fae. The Angel, he was our only ally. But don't trust *him*."

"*He – him*? You know who it is?"

"No," Rufaizu said. "No oh no, don't know, don't know."

"He's an imbecile," Casaria summarised.

Rufaizu raised a pointing finger, "Am *not*. I've just never seen him. But I know he made trouble. Got Papa angry, made him betray the Fae. Fairy friends."

"And what happened?" Pax said. "How'd you find the weapon, the book? Why'd Apothel deface the Ripton Chapel?"

"He didn't." Rufaizu frowned. "Never defaced nothing – Papa loved his work. He sent the Fae gun and the book *away* to protect them. Once he knew the gun didn't work – and the Angel told him *wait*. My father died and . . ." Rufaizu spat aside as a curse, almost hitting a dog walker. "I wanted nothing to do with that kind of friend."

Pax tried to piece the frantic account together. Apothel had known the Fae were coming for him, to get their Dispenser back, and the Blue Angel had persuaded him to face them. He'd made provisions to preserve his work, though he couldn't have preserved the chapel – but he hadn't been the one who defaced it –

"The Blue Angel itself?" Pax said, quietly. "It got in there and destroyed whatever hints Apothel left behind, before anyone could see it. Trying to erase his legacy. So why leave the word grugulochs?"

"As a warning," Casaria suggested. "Sign off their work?"

That didn't sound right, but what other reason was there? As a reflex, a joke? Another trick? This was getting Pax nowhere.

A man in a white van shouted "Mentalists!" at them, his laughter punching the sky as he sped off. Casaria snarled, "We ought to keep moving."

Pax nodded. "Let's walk and talk. Rufaizu, how'd you trace what Apothel sent away?"

Rufaizu smiled, trotting at her side, towards the far side of the bridge and the stairs down. "Hard work. The hardest."

Pax watched his expression, listing upwards on the left side like he'd once taken a blow that left permanent damage. "Where've you been all this time?"

"No easy path. Ran just to run, you know, to start. A long way from Ordshaw, making sure those Fae didn't do for me. I looked for Papa's people and found a lot else besides. Secrets of the French Alps. Myths of Gardossa, legends of the Antler King."

"Gar-what-sa?" Pax said, not liking the broadness of any of that.

Rufaizu ignored the question. "Uncle Staryn took me in, eventual. Good as a blood uncle. Papa trusted *him* with the gun, and the book, but he didn't tell me, not for a long time. Didn't know Ordshaw and thought I oughta not know it either. I came of age, though, and I learnt what needed knowing. Learnt why Papa couldn't work the weapon. Had to come back. Had to find Citizen Barton and get the electric weed, to make the gun work. Finish what Papa started."

"And it brought you here," Casaria concluded. "Hobbling across a bridge like an escaped dementia patient. The boy's an imbecile, he's led an imbecile's life –"

"Watch your mouth!" Rufaizu sprang towards him, then back again, hopping like a boxer. "Got me by surprise before, but I scrap – you'd better believe I scrap!"

"Alright, put your dicks away," Pax intervened irritably. "You can punch each other out when I'm through with all this. *What* did you learn that needed learning?"

Rufaizu paused to give her a merry look, like all the answers of the universe were obvious. "That last call from the Angel, that was true as blue. Scratched in the wall when Papa wanted to know how to get the gun going. Told him, real simple, *wait*. Just that. Wait. No other answers – no more help. Not for the first time, I learnt. Everyone out there waiting – ignoring the truth, actively ignoring it. They waited in Gardossa and the city crumbled. What we've got in Ordshaw, it's not the first, might not be the last. The Blue Angel's *moved* and been *around*. He's old and powerful and didn't always have a minotaur or glogockles, but he always had *something*."

She felt like that she already understood this, just hadn't put the thoughts together yet. The thing behind this was more than a person. It had done more than move and manipulate the glo; it had a hand in the monsters themselves. Was it possible the creatures were its creation, somehow produced by it? The minotaur included. "What else did it have, what other things?"

"Hard to say," Rufaizu admitted. "History ain't kind to legend. He had a hand in the demon of Gardossa, I'm sure. And the waywards of the Alps, they were *not* natural – I swear he was there."

"Why?" Pax said. "Why do you think the Angel was involved? How do we *find* it?"

"Ask me?" Rufaizu said. "It's to do with his food. Cut off his food, get him angry, get him making mistakes, showing himself. The honourable Theo Murhaimer, in his saga, claimed the light was revealed, like glo reveals a trail. But whatever he attempted, he didn't succeed. No more than legacy, but it's *enough*, right?"

"Seriously," Casaria snarled. "Utter gibberish." He marched ahead to the stairs down, shoving past people coming up. Pax signalled for Rufaizu to follow, quickly. They caught up as Casaria reached the Underground entrance. At the gates, he pulled back his jacket to show a guard his badge and muttered a few words. The guard buzzed him through, and Casaria waited for Rufaizu and Pax to go ahead. His hand lingered a little too long on Pax's shoulder, guiding her through. Pax was fairly sure he hadn't had that badge before. Nor a holster. The bulging grenades, of course, she'd seen him pocket. He was ready for war, which wasn't necessarily a good thing.

It was another problem she didn't have the capacity to focus on, as she tried to unravel Rufaizu's words. She could see he'd collected hints he didn't fully understand himself, but there were names at least, paths to follow. And her instincts were right; the Blue Angel was a hider. It was possible no one had got close, or lived to talk about it. No one had formed a connection like she had.

Locked in those thoughts, Pax barely noticed them boarding a train, nor it rattling out of the station. The lights flickered and Rufaizu looked out the window at the passing brickwork, creeping up out of his seat. "We shouldn't be down here."

"It's only a few stops," Pax said. She didn't like it either. The air seemed tighter than usual. Down the aisle, a man in a brown coat sagged against a pole, eyelids heavy. Were they being drained right now? Pax took a breath, trying to feel it, and she could all but sense the creatures lurking beyond the walls, ready to claw at her, chase her.

Rufaizu sat back down, but his eyes didn't stop moving.

The lights flickered again. The train slowed. Like when she'd brought Letty underground, when the horde had approached. Pax felt her heart beat faster.

She *could* sense them. Close and far, across the city. Tingling in her fingers, burning in her heart. So many creatures, writhing in the walls. And something else, lit in the blue. The memory flashed up from her dream. *At least thirty*. She put a hand to her head.

"What's wrong?" Casaria asked.

Something sparked outside and she flinched, but she said nothing, trying to focus, to see or feel through the bricks. Imagining the tunnels beyond. Something was stirring in her. Not panic, not fear. She'd felt it in the Ministry building – something she could use.

A voice came on the tannoy, apologising for the delay. A signal problem.

"Pax? Are you okay?"

It was the pull again. As it had been in the Ministry office. As it had been under the chapel, when she knew she wasn't alone. The same in Chaucer Crescent. Not the minotaur's surge, but connected. Was it an indicator, or was she just losing her mind?

"Who is he?" Pax asked, not looking up. "The last one you mentioned, Theo More Hammers? He got close to the Angel?"

"Ah nah," Rufaizu said. "He's a *was*. Left a journal – at least an *account* – of his trials. Long, long ago – before Gardossa. Centuries before, centuries before everything. He spoke of seeing without help."

"Seeing *what*?"

"What we see in the glo. The Bright Veins."

Pax stopped and caught Casaria looking at her. She looked down at herself, half-afraid she'd see it again. Electric tracts, under her skin. Her grubby hands were solid, darker in dirt than her best tan. Definitely not glowing. But she *had* glowed. Casaria questioned it, at last: "What's it mean?"

Pax asked her own questions, "Have you ever touched it? The minotaur? Has anyone?"

"Of course not," Casaria said. "We've lost two or three agents that got too close, might as well jump on the tracks. What did it do to you?"

"You touched it?" Rufaizu's jaw dropped open. "You are *true*. I knew it when I saw her in that bar, I said, she's something special. Look at her now and say it wasn't worth it."

Pax gave him a sideways glance. "I'm not special. It was *nothing* to do with me, I didn't want this – it was pure chance I got involved, and even luckier I didn't die, okay?"

"That's the beauty, right? Blue Angel has his plans, *machinations*, but I'd bet you a tooth he didn't count on you." Rufaizu grinned. "Pure luck is what we *need*."

"Piss off," Pax uttered, but knew he was right. With all the Blue Angel's scheming, the fluke of her randomly bumbling in and connecting to it might tip the tide. Whatever it meant for her mind and body. She took a breath. "It affected me." She looked at Casaria, confessing, "I've been getting a feeling when the minotaur acts. Pains. And more than that. It's hard to explain. I'm sensing something, many things. Sensing when I'm getting closer to them, feeling it . . ." She tapped her chest. "Here."

"I knew it, I told you, I knew it!" Rufaizu said, excitedly. "You're what he never was, what never was in any of them – you can *see* it? You can see the Bright Veins?"

"No, I can't see that," Pax said, "but I did. When I tried that glo."

"We should get you to a hospital," Casaria decided.

"Piss *off*," Pax snarled.

"Listen to yourself! Sensing something? Feeling something? It's messed you up, there could be something seriously wrong with you. *What* are you feeling?"

"The energy, I don't know! Something passing between it all – like, it's in all these things, and moving. I get a feel for how many there are, how close, but I don't know –"

"It's the *Bright*," Rufaizu said, "in the *Veins*. Murhaimer studied it and developed ways to see it – through his own eyes, no glo. Rik Greivous would've danced a jig if he'd known! But Murhaimer did it alone, never again, no explanation *how*."

"This Murhaimer, from ancient history, is the opposite of useful."

"But here you are – connected to the light that passes through all things!"

"You're talking about novisan?" Casaria interrupted. Rufaizu paused questioningly. "The energy in people that the *praelucente* interacts with. It uses that energy, decreasing or increasing levels. You know how complicated it is for us to measure that? How do *you* know about it?"

"Clearly your systems aren't the only ones," Pax said. Her own connection with that energy, the Bright or novisan or whatever it was, had been corrupted when the minotaur caught her. She wasn't mad, she wasn't psychic – she'd become sensitive to a network they were all part of. An energy system that the Blue Angel was part of, too. It was abusing that energy to extremes that made the Angel more visible, too. Her dream flashed on her again. The lightning jumps, the nodes. At least thirty. "I can feel the energy that the minotaur and the Blue Angel have been collecting, or moving, or whatever they're doing. It's spread over the city. That's why it's so fucking confusing. When they use that energy, I feel it."

Casaria stared at her blankly, completely at a loss.

She was feeling the blue screens in use, and the creatures affected by the shifts in novisan or whatever. That's what she had felt in the MEE office; not the turnbold, some other force. She shot Casaria a look. "In your offices, that corridor where we were. What's in the room at the end of the hall?"

Casaria frowned. "What room?"

"At the end of the hall!" Pax insisted. "The innocuous fucking cupboard near the fire exit."

"Nothing," he said. "Some stationery supplies, I think. No one uses it except the secretary, and that's mostly to get faxes."

"Faxes? What the fuck are you talking about, *faxes*?"

"You know, printed messages. Obviously we don't use the fax machine ourselves, that's why it's down there, out of the way. The secretary gets –"

"Jesus Christ," Pax huffed, "you're talking about one of those old phone-email-printer things or whatever? Who the hell *does* use it?"

"London," Casaria clarified. "It receives orders from the Raleigh Commission."

Pax stared for a beat. "That sounds important."

"Well." Casaria twisted awkwardly, like he realised he'd said something stupid. "I suppose, if you care for them. The Raleigh Commission have a commanding say in Ministry matters, when they deign to get involved. One of the idiots on the board won't go online; he only ever sends faxes. Sometimes direct orders, but mostly summaries of nonsense discussions in London."

Pax kept staring. That was *definitely* important. She wasn't sure how, but that was where the Blue Angel had their foot in the MEE. That was what she'd felt. As the train drew into Broadplain, she watched the platform, willing Letty to be ready to help her make sense of it.

12

The smell was horrendous. It seeped up from the fifth floor to pervade every inch of Floor 6. Sam couldn't stop noticing it, a scent she'd associate with toxic waste. Agent Hail assured her it was only the turnbold's pheromones, perfectly harmless. That didn't help.

Hail, returned from the field, attempted to brush off everything with cold professionalism, from the moment he'd found Sam staring at the carnage from street level. He and his partner had taken two barbed zinc harpoons (as they called them) from their car and silenced the turnbold with a series of careful shots, fired from the building entrance towards where the broken creature was stuck in the lift shaft. Then Hail tried to take charge with instructions for Greek Street to be sealed off and a retaliatory strike to be mounted, without any immediate idea of the target. Of course, the Ministry historically only had one true opponent in Ordshaw. Even with a long-established peace, resentment against the Fae ran deep amongst Operations agents. They would blame the fairies as a matter of instinct. As Pax and Casaria had suggested.

But Sam realised Pax had saved her. She'd heard the shout, over the ferocious charge of the turnbold – *"Fucking do something!"* – just before the gunshot. And Pax had insisted this wasn't simple, that they all needed to stop and think before attacking the Fae.

Sam was the ranking officer in the building, again, and she pressed that on Hail as he began issuing orders. He tried to brush it off. "After what you've been through, you should take the day."

"After what I've been through," Sam replied, hearing the words as though someone else was saying them, "I'm ready to *personally* tackle the fallout. And the next time you answer me back, it'll be your badge."

In truth she wasn't sure if the field agents even carried badges any more; she had a feeling that they'd been replaced by laminate warrant cards a few years ago. But, in front of two other agents, she held Hail's gaze, without mentioning her doubts, and he silently backed down.

Sam issued the usual commands to keep the press quiet and keep the emergency services from the building. She quickly decided they'd call it an alligator attack, from the sewer, as too many people had heard and seen things that couldn't be explained without mentioning some kind of animal. They could blame the alligator for the train crash and the movements under the building in New Thornton, while they were at it. The squat in Nothicker, the old library building that got flattened last night, would be more of a problem. Realistically, no natural creature could have caused all that damage, so it would have to be passed off as coincidence.

Such an incident, in Nothicker, probably wouldn't have made the news in other circumstances, and that detail would hopefully stop it from all seeming too convenient, adding credibility.

Alongside the media effort, the remaining staff started rallying back to work, even as the smoke-filled building was still being checked for structural damage. The field agents whispered about the Fae, questioning when they would strike back. They were whispering because Sam had already said no to such plans, but also because the place had an atmosphere like a wake. The lights kept blinking off, sometimes for minutes at a time. Half of the computers weren't working. Everyone trod carefully, wincing at creaks from elsewhere in the building. There was a large crack in the floor near the reception and lift area.

Mathers and Devlin were the only reported casualties from their floor. Ryan from IS was unaccounted for, but Sam suspected he'd headed home in the chaos. Selfish, but understandable. It might have been a lot worse, if Pax and her people hadn't interrupted the attack.

Sam knew the best medicine was to power through. She took a few staff off the job of securing the *praelucente's* location and set them to searching the city for spikes of novisan during the times of the Monday surges. Against complaints, she told them it'd lead to the cause of this attack and they had no recourse to question that. She insisted she'd take care of the Fae herself, and went to Mathers' office. She tried their FTC numbers and got no response. There were no emails coming in, not in her account or Mathers', open on his computer.

That left her looking over the remnants of Mathers' office. He was gone. Dead, before her eyes. Brutally. He'd left books on the shelves, never to be read, and a photo of a dog – who would take care of it now? She shook herself out of it.

Don't think.

Don't think.

The phone rang, and she answered, "Deputy Director Mathers' office, this is Sam Ward, Head of –"

"Yes, quite," Lord Tarrington said. "What the blazes is going on over there?"

The director of the Ministry. Interference she did not need. Sam swallowed, then described the events in as neutral a tone as she could muster. She started with the announcement that Deputy Director Mathers was dead. She moved straight on, ignoring Tarrington's curses, to explain a turnbold had come up through five storeys of the building, until MEE field agents had managed to stop it. For all the damage it had done coming up, it had not reached the real seat of operations on the sixth floor, and they were now focused on the hard, fast pursuit of a potential force behind the attack. Only when she finished did she realise she'd said nothing about Casaria or Pax, and it seemed too late to mention it.

"Right you are, you'll be our Acting Deputy Director, then," Tarrington said. "Congratulations on the media cap – they're lapping it up in London and no one would dare question such an absurd story after a tragedy. An alligator indeed." For the briefest second Sam thought this would go smoothly. But he continued, "That's you done. Pat yourselves on the back, pack up and get out."

"Sir?" Sam frowned. Through the internal office window, she could see the bullpen, heads down, hard at work. "We're on our way to some decisive results already."

"Decisive nothing. You've lost the man in charge and the building – whatever you say – cannot possibly be deemed safe."

"After what we've been through –"

"Everyone must be exhausted, traumatised, not at their best. Shut down the office, with statements that the MEE has suffered a blow, and we'll form a plan from here."

Sam slowly turned to look out of the office's other window, down at the limited view of Central backstreets. How could anyone outside Ordshaw grasp what they were going through, let alone form a plan? "Respectfully, sir, I believe we're in a unique position –"

"You are indeed," Tarrington said. "You've been the target of a terrorist attack, Ward, do you understand that? You're weakened but talking about retaliating, without knowing exactly who staged this little fiasco."

"But we need to –"

"You need to give us a chance to get on the blower with them, see what they *want*."

Sam froze. That was an admission, wasn't it? The assumption of Fae guilt was there in the Raleigh Commission, too, and he was baldly telling her he had access to the FTC. "Sir, if you're suggesting engaging with the Fae, then I think I should personally –"

"Rest assured," Tarrington interrupted politely, "we know how to deal with the important stuff. Now be a good girl and shut down. If – and that's a very tentative *if* – this is not simply a rogue element, your team will need to be rested."

"It's not a rogue element," Sam rushed in. "It's no coincidence that this is happening now – with the erratic surges across town, and these civilians' unusual activities. I believe this is the result of an endemic problem, connected directly to the *praelucente*."

Tarrington digested that. "Where is this coming from?"

"Sir…" Sam hesitated. How to explain it? "I don't like to say before we have –"

"You just *did* say. Explain."

Sam clamped her mouth shut. How could anyone hold a conversation with this man if he never listened to complete sentences? She started slowly, "I've been looking at novisan patterns. And . . . I've had contact with the compromised civilians – limited contact."

"You've had *what*? And they're still out there?"

Sam cleared her throat. "It wasn't by design, sir, I wasn't prepared –"

"Good *God*. I suspect you're right, then, there's no coincidence, Ward. What did you tell them? Anything they could pass on to their Fae contacts?"

Her face felt hot enough to melt the window. "Absolutely not, sir, this is –"

"This is exactly what I am talking about. You're too close to this. The whole Ordshaw office is too close." He wasn't listening, he didn't care. She felt it boiling up inside her, wanting to shake him through the phone. "Send everyone home, seal the building and await further instructions from us. You will –"

"Sir, I will not," Sam said. "Two of our own are dead, including our leader. Our city is under attack, and we have done nothing but hide it. I have a way forward that I intend to follow. I intend to confront the source of the corruption in this city."

Tarrington was quiet. Perhaps waiting to explode. She had to say it, though. It was *her* turn. His voice came back warily. "Ward, I have given you clear instructions. You are experiencing an emotional response to an extreme event. Consider your position. Will you or will you not do as I request?"

Sam gritted her teeth and answered in as clear a staccato as she could. "Considering my position, as the Acting Deputy Director of the Ordshaw MEE, I will act in the way I believe best suits my city. That is what I intend to do." She added, with an air of finality, "*Sir.*"

Tarrington was startled into quiet for a moment. "The rest of the Commission will hear about this, of course."

"I'd be glad if they would give Ordshaw their full attention, sir."

He muttered something that could have been a curt *very well*, then hung up.

Sam breathed a massive breath of relief. She turned and found she had an audience. Landon was back, with Hail at his shoulder.

"How much did you hear?" Sam asked.

"Enough," Landon said. "Assistant Deputy Director. Where do you want us?"

13

Pax left the desolate Debenhams to lean against the railing over the empty shopping centre nook. Rufaizu and Casaria were waiting, the former slouched against the wall and the latter standing stiffly to attention. She wasn't sure of the appropriate way to respond to discovering a group of murder victims when the bodies were so small. It was almost hard to take seriously; these two-inch thugs in miniature pools of blood were once living people. One of them had spoken with her, albeit in an unfriendly manner. Now he had a hole in his chest.

With no sign of Letty, or the Bartons, she assumed (hoped?) that Lightgate's plan for them had backfired. Whatever it was.

"That's that, then?" Casaria said, a little disappointed. He had responded to the scene with particular poise, moving through the shop with his gun out, as though the violence might resurrect itself.

"No, that's not that," Pax said. "What happened? Where did they all go?"

"Fae do that, they do," Rufaizu said. "There a second, gone another."

"With humans in tow?" Pax gave him the eye.

"Got their ways," Rufaizu shrugged.

"He's right, for once," Casaria said. "There have been cases of Fae kidnapping humans. Reported if not proven. They're devious little shits."

Pax raised an eyebrow. She knew well enough about Fae kidnappings, having resolved one mere days ago when they took Grace. "Letty clearly put up a fight; if it was a kidnapping I'm not sure it was successful."

"Either way," Casaria said, impatiently, "we should be going, too. There's nothing for us here."

"You pretend to care for this city and you're not even interested in what happens to an innocent family?"

"Innocent? Barton is a trespasser, a thug, a drunkard, and a Fae sympathiser."

"He's got more beef with them than you!" Pax started, then stopped. It wasn't worth it. "Letty's alive, she's got to be. I need to call her."

"Passed a shop," Rufaizu said. "I can get you something."

He'd stolen her money before, deftly enough. But committing more crime hardly sounded like the best idea, especially not with Casaria scowling. Pax said, "There were pay phones, down by the toilets."

She led the way as they fell in step behind her, and a few minutes later she'd scraped enough change together between them to try the number Letty had given her. It rang through a dozen rings with no answer. She placed the receiver down and turned to Casaria. "Your people can tap phones, track mobiles?"

"We can. Doesn't mean we do."

"Just when you feel like it, huh."

"Anyway, I assume Fae phones are a problem, else we'd have them on a tighter leash."

"They work on our networks, why not?" Pax paused for confirmation, but Casaria's vacant expression suggested he'd be no use. "You got any friends at the Ministry that could do it?"

"You think the office is functioning right now?"

"If it is," Pax said, "have you got any friends there?"

Again, Casaria's blank face said no. Definitely not. He deflected the question. "They'll trace any call you make *to them*, for sure. And they'll be watching for you especially, because Sam Ward will definitely have reported you were there."

"What about Sam Ward herself? We saved her life."

"Pax, give it up," Casaria said. "We have your Blue Angel to hunt, why waste time here?"

"Because people matter!" Pax snapped. "Jesus Christ, why does that need explaining? Letty's put herself on the line for me – she's –"

"A *bug*," Casaria snarled.

"My fucking friend!" Pax jumped at him, a pointing finger shoved into his face. "She's shown more humanity than you!" Her emotion carried her towards Casaria, pushing him back until he hit the graffiti-stained wall. Rufaizu stood up straight, halfway between enthusiastic and frightened. Pax rose onto her toes. "You prick, all the talk I've had to – what? Stop fucking smiling! Why are you fucking smiling? Listen to me – one more time, you call her a bug, an insect, a piece of shit, whatever, I will fucking *hurt you*."

He hadn't stopped smiling. Couldn't stop. Scared, ashamed, maybe, but a little excited too. Damn, that's how he coped, wasn't it? Pax moved away, glaring at him. As he peeled himself from the wall and opened his mouth to speak, she said, "The only word I want to hear from you is sorry."

He considered it. Then chose to say nothing.

"Whatever. Do you have Sam Ward's number?"

Casaria said, in an admonished tone, "Your thugs took my phone. Yesterday."

"Shit. You must have a switchboard –"

"It's okay. I know it."

Pax paused. "Know what?"

Casaria said nothing, letting her catch up. Ward's number? Pax drew out her response, "Okay."

Rufaizu sniggered, and Casaria shot him a look. The young man held up defensive hands. "Not judging, not judging! Sweet, is all –"

"Keep fucking talking," Casaria growled.

"No! Enough!" Pax's eyes locked on his. It was like reprimanding a damned dog. Casaria didn't move, already in his place. Bloody hell, this man. "Give me her number, then."

*

Casaria watched Pax over the shoulder-height plastic partition as she made the call. The pay phones were lined up along a side corridor, opposite the toilets, with the minimum of privacy, but no one was around. Only fugitives and criminals used pay phones and public toilets, after all.

That's what he had become, wasn't it?

Associating with the likes of this street urchin scum. Taking shit from a poker player who'd lose her breath in a ten-metre race. Casaria avoided looking at Rufaizu, to suppress the urge to punch his face off, and fixed his gaze on Pax. She couldn't complain, seeing as she was the leader now, seeing as he needed to follow her. He *had* to watch her, didn't he?

He studied her as she talked. Her soft features were hardened by crusted blood and black smears of dirt. He was tempted to wipe them off himself, seeing as she wasn't bothered to. But it suited her aggressive personality. She was tough. She had come for him, saved him from torture. Insisted he join her. Insisted they talk to Sam Ward, despite that she-devil's flaws. Fought against the turnbold, and fought in the Sunken City for those hapless civilians. Even fought against *him*, risking serious harm for an insect's honour.

If nothing else, he respected her courage. As she had said, she was trying to fight a good fight. The gypsy boy was right. Behind her lack of fitness and lack of style, there was something special in her.

It made sense to partner with her.

He watched her lips, talking into the receiver. They'd almost brushed against him when she'd lost her cool. Casaria didn't suppress a smirk. Why not be positive?

"Is it something you can do?" Pax was saying. "Something you're prepared to do?"

Casaria could hear Sam Ward's voice well enough. The phone made it metallic, cold and distant. An accurate interpretation, which he hoped Pax would soon understand. Sam had answered brusquely, barely responding to the first few comments, no more agreeable than she'd been in the office, or outside when they'd saved her life. "I don't have anyone spare, Ms Kuranes. If you come in –"

"I've got places to be," Pax said. "We can help, better than your lot, I'm sure – all I'm asking is that you check my friends aren't dead."

Ward hesitated. "You realise there's people who think you're responsible for this?"

"Are you one of them?"

Another pause. "No. But –"

"Well, I *am*," Pax said. "I didn't want it or organise it, but I am responsible, aren't I? Because I know what to do about it, and no one else does. Trust me, you trace Letty's phone and I'll take care of your minotaur for you."

"You're wrong," Ward said. Here we go. Casaria gave Pax a knowing smile, but she twisted away. "You're not the only one trying to resolve this."

"I imagine we've got different ideas of what that means."

"My people are looking for the grugulochs right now. They're working – after what we've been through, they're following *my* command."

"Congratulations," Pax replied, flatly. "I guess that makes you head rat?"

"You should've stayed here," Ward said. "Tell me what you've seen, what you know –"

"Yeah, that sounds kind of one-sided," Pax said. "Especially considering part of what I *know* is that you've got fucking cutthroats working for you. To say nothing of the rather worrying level of ignorance in your organisation. The sort that suggests an institutional problem."

Ward hesitated again and Casaria's smile spread. Pax was sharp, fierce. She understood the MEE, even from the little she'd seen of it. The whole organisation was an institutional problem, wasn't it? Particularly the likes of Sam Ward.

Ward said, "I don't disagree that we have areas for improvement, but *you* called me for help. Considering I have the means to trace the source of all this, if you're not willing to talk, I'm not sure what exactly you are offering?"

Pax paused. "You know I can tell you things you don't know. Can you trace this phone for me or not? Find my friend?"

She went quiet and waited, an uncomfortable look on her face. She couldn't want her secret about those electric veins shared with the Ministry. She was ashamed of taking on part of the myriad horde, having touched their world.

Ward took a long time to answer. For her, it didn't get much worse than diverting resources without authorisation. "If you agree to discuss all you've been through with me – at the very least with me personally, even if you don't come in – then I'll run the trace."

Pax immediately set new demands. "Run the trace *and* guarantee the Bartons and myself will be free from your investigations, then we've got a deal. And I want my bloody money back – and someone to stop my landlord from kicking me out."

Ward paused. "I think that can be arranged."

"You think? That doesn't do it for me. Can you make it happen or not? Because –"

"I can make it happen," Sam said, more firmly. "That man you saw ripped apart in our office? He was in charge. Now I am." Her voice got even firmer, making Casaria frown. "*I'm* in charge."

14

In the brief window that Sam had taken to field the phone call and organise Pax's trace, she found the unsupervised field agents had started itching for blood. Every one of these young men (and they were all men) yearned for trouble. It was written on their squared faces, creased with lines of tension and distaste. They gathered around the table in Meeting Room 2, waiting for Dr Galler, their tech specialist, to explain the Fae's Dispenser at the circle's centre, before they could get out and bust heads.

Galler said, "Obviously we haven't had much time, so I wouldn't like to propose exactly how it works – or what might make it more effective than our own tools – but essentially this appears to produce a particularly potent electromagnetic pulse. There's an aspect I can't account for in the conversion of –"

"Perhaps we could stick to how it can be used?" Sam heard herself say. With authority, she'd decided, came coldness.

"Right." Galler regarded her with the same expression everyone had worn the first time she issued them an order. Tackling two questions at once: *do I need to put up with this woman?* and *do I want to risk my job?* "There's essentially two moving parts. After you unscrew the end and put in the fuel, you pull back this lever, and the device goes through a – let's say a charging process. This button discharges it."

"Potentially bringing the tunnel system down on top of you," Hail said.

"Potentially."

"With respect" – Hail looked to Sam – "we've been working on the assumption that the *praelucente* has become unstable because that moron Casaria shot this weapon at it. Right?"

"No." Sam was ready for this one. "That's perfectly possible, but it's equally possible the *praelucente* behaved this way because we threatened it, and what we've seen is a series of revenge attacks. It's possible the turnbold was part of that. The point is, we have no idea what you're going up against, and you need every weapon at your disposal."

This met a murmur of disagreement. They wanted Fae blood, not some new mystery threat. But for once Sam could point them in the right direction: their searches had led to something concrete. During the first Monday surge, when that building had quaked in New Thornton, novisan had spiked, in a massive amount, in one very particular spot.

The energy was moving, as Pax said. It had to be the grugulochs. If that was the force behind this mess they'd stumbled into. It was dangerous, it was using them and it needed confronting.

"Shame we don't have the homeless guy's drawing to help," Agent Farnham commented, sarcastically. It got a few dutiful sniggers.

Sam gave the burly, bearded brute a stern look. "Gentlemen. You know how to do your jobs. If you want to stick with your usual weapons, that's up to you. But this is here, available."

The agents shuffled their feet. Even Landon wasn't volunteering on this.

"Very well," Sam decided for them. "Agent Hail, I want you to take it. Use it or don't, that's your choice. Dr Galler, you've got some fuel for it?"

"Yes."

"Let's discuss how we're going to do this, then." Sam bent over the table and paused with her hand poised to push the Fae device out of the way. She hardly dared touch it, and looked to Hail. He took it gingerly himself. Under the device was a map of the Net, Ordshaw's northernmost borough. The ink was faded from age, but the paper was spotless, testament to how rarely the Ministry ran operations there. When Roper had announced they'd located a focal point for an energy spike, it seemed logical that it would be somewhere so remote, barely populated and scarcely patrolled by the Ministry.

A big cross intersected the corner of two roads in the upper west quadrant.

"What's there?" an agent with a crew cut asked.

"Your ears need cleaning out?" Farnham replied. "We don't *know*, that's the point."

"I meant the building, dumbass. The location."

"*Gentlemen*, when you're ready." Sam kept her voice calm. "It's an old church."

"An actual church this time," Landon added. "Not like Apothel's chapel."

"Thank you. Methodist building, closed down in the '70s, when the minister was charged with indecent activity."

"Paedo," someone muttered, helpfully.

"There's a set of keys coming from the City Council. I want you to secure the perimeter before going in. There shouldn't be any creatures –"

"Never had reports north of Juliacre Boulevard," Hail said. "The tunnels finish a block above the A564." Some of the agents muttered agreement, to demonstrate they knew this already.

"Stay vigilant," Sam said, hoping to sound inspiring. "We don't know what you'll find, but it *is* responsible for all the assaults we've had on this city. This office included."

More grumbles in the audience, and a lot of wary looks, picking her apart. Hail spoke for them: "You think it's another creature, or what?"

"I don't know," Sam admitted. "It might be our perpetrator's apparatus. Whatever they're using to manipulate the *praelucente*." They didn't look convinced. "It's big. The novisan levels are huge, compared to the rest of the city, and they've spiked in line with the *praelucente's* surges. Be *very* –"

"Excuse me, ma'am, sorry!" Tori blustered clumsily in, wearing a nervous smile, flapping a piece of paper in one hand. Sam scowled at her, ready to deliver

a public scolding. The secretary didn't give her a chance. "It's urgent –
correspondence from –" She made a secretive click of her tongue. "You know –"
She cleared her throat. "Orders."

"The Raleigh Commission?" Hail said. Sam turned to him, to say it was none of
his business, that he should back off, and she would –

He had the paper in his hands, and swore under his breath. He slapped it down
on the table, so everyone could read it at the same time as Sam. He even kept a
finger on it so she couldn't take it back. As commander, it was her role to read the
Raleigh Commission's correspondence and –

Her thoughts of command disappeared as she read the first lines.

URGENT: NOTIFIED ORDER OF ENGAGEMENT

FAO: Acting Deputy Director S. Ward.

*Action has been decided and is hereby notarised by the Raleigh Commission, to
be effective immediately –*

She was going to be fucking fired. Minutes away from dispatching her team to
take action. One of the agents pulled back from the table with a grunt, not
especially happy about the news either. At least there was some solidarity here.

*– the Ordshaw Branch of the MEE is to be directed towards the locating and
engaging of the entity entitled Fae Transitional City, enacting Protocol 21. In
respects of –*

Holy what?

Sam's face was slack. Tarrington's instructions for everyone to take a break
suddenly seemed reasonable in the face of what she was seeing. The Commission
had gone away to agree on *this*? Was this a message, because she'd shown
initiative? Lord Asquith's doing, some sort of punishment for them attempting to
contact him directly?

"How's this possible?" Landon said, equally stunned.

"Fucking right is what it is," Farnham said. "It was a direct attack, it was an act
of war – this is what we *should* be doing! Not chasing unknowns with two men
dead!"

"Three men," someone reminded him. "We lost one Sunday."

"This should've happened Friday," Hail said. "The second they fired on
Casaria."

"There's due process to be had," Landon attempted. "Especially if there's rogue
elements at work. Escalation's never a good –"

"No." Hail leant towards him, right into his space, and stabbed a finger into the
Commission's order. "We're being ordered to attack the FTC. Escalation is *exactly*
right. Isn't that correct, Madam Acting Deputy Director?" He turned forcefully to
Sam.

As she looked into the eyes of half a dozen edgy men, her words came out
messily. "I – we – there must be a mistake –"

"It's signed, Ms Ward," Tori said, lingering in the doorway. "Notarised."

"We're good and ready, aren't we?" Hail addressed his fellow agents.
"Different target, same strategy. Seal off the perimeter, advance on the enemy."

"You're talking about a whole city of people," Sam said with alarm.

"Fae." Hail shot her a nasty look. It spread through the room, the majority feeling. "They're not people. They're terrorists, and they did this to us. You can't defend them, the order's right there."

"I'm the Acting Deputy Director, and I say where our priorities lie. This anomaly in the Net could explain *exactly* what put our building in danger."

There was silence. The pack of wolves smelled weakness in their leader. The only soft face in the crowd was Landon's, but even he looked uncertain. Galler and Tori, for their parts, had their eyes on the floor, wanting to be anywhere else but there.

How could she convince them? What had convinced her?

Common sense, surely? It all added up to a force more complex than a simple mindless attack. No one wanted a war, not on the face of their allegiances. Lord Tarrington hadn't given any hint of this on the phone. There was a manipulative force –

"Come on." Hail pushed past Sam, his shoulder barging her into a side-table. She opened her mouth to protest, but he tensed and she flinched, thinking he might hit her. He had the fax, held up demonstratively. "The orders are clear."

He kept staring at Sam, accusingly, as he marched out of the room. The other agents gave her brief looks, concerned or angry, as they filed out after him. Farnham mumbled, "We'll be waiting for your instructions in the field, ma'am." Not serious.

Sam realised she was shaking.

The idiots. The gung-ho idiots. To say nothing of the idiots in London. It made even less sense than Tarrington's phone call.

Finally, only Landon and Tori remained, watching her with concern.

"What do you want to do?" Landon asked.

"What do you mean?" Sam said, a squeak of insecurity. "The Commission's made their decision. It's an awful one, but they've made it."

"Seems to me" – Landon cleared his throat – "that an order was presented, but Agent Hail took it before our acting commander was able to read it. Let alone process it."

Sam frowned. "What can *we* do? I can't send you out there alone."

Landon took his time, not entirely certain, then shrugged. "Yes. You can."

15

It wasn't the first time Letty had been held at gunpoint with the promise of death or imprisonment or some other vile result at the end of a journey. Usually, the idiots could be talked around, or otherwise fought off. But Lightgate wasn't like the guards who had cornered her during Val's coup or the chancers who tried their hand at unsanctioned exile-hunting. She kept her distance, with her finger on the trigger, and appeared to be absolutely flexible about the outcome of her plans.

The best Letty could hope for was to choose when to take a bullet.

They were gliding over the warehouse district already, so it wasn't like she'd be able to pick out somewhere scenic. Maybe over a chimney stack, to give Lightgate a nightmare of a job hauling her body out. But Lightgate wouldn't give a shit about leaving a Fae corpse behind. She hadn't cleared up in Broadplain, after all. She hadn't asked for Letty's phone when it rang, either; merely offered a look to suggest using it was a bad idea. At least its ringing suggested Pax was alive, trying to get hold of her.

Not far from the FTC, as the building itself came into view, Lightgate glided closer to Letty. She had a brown bottle in her hand, and continued to knock back liquor without it seeming to affect her.

"You ever offer it around?" Letty asked.

"People normally say no," Lightgate said, and took another long pull. She slowed down, then threw the bottle Letty's way. It fell halfway between them and Letty hesitated a second before diving after it. When she caught it, Lightgate appeared high above her, limp pistol still trained on her.

Letty hovered still to take a swig, ignoring the smell. It was practically gasoline. She winced it down, then hoarsely said, "I'm used to some strong shit, but that . . ."

"My own mixture," Lightgate said. "I call it Assault and Battery."

A play on battery acid, ground-up ammunition, or worse? Letty didn't ask.

"Now we're chums, you ready to save yourself?"

"Chums," Letty said, taking another sniff of the bottle. It set her nostrils burning. With another Fae, the bottle might have been a weapon. Lightgate would expect that, though. Maybe even invite it. Letty tossed the drink up and Lightgate caught it by the neck, barely appearing to move. In case there was any doubt that she was quick.

"I like you, Letty," she said. "You're too smart to be a hero. Heroes are fools, they get early graves. I've seen too many to count."

"That must've been tough for you," Letty said. She looked ahead, towards the FTC building. The scouts might have picked them up at this distance, might be wondering if they'd come closer. Lightgate followed her gaze with a wistful look.

They'd both been through some shit there, for sure.

"You ever been back?" Lightgate asked.

"Only the outskirts," Letty said. "Nothing closer than the peripheries."

"I got a few ways in. Sympathetic guards, unwatched passages. I used to sit watching them, imagining it. The Fall of the Fae. Their precious buildings burning."

"They've got precious buildings now?"

Lightgate smiled, just a little. "They're dug in like barnacles. Slightly better tech, improved workshops, but the same dark cage. The same pathetic people."

"So why'd you come back?" Letty said. "Why go through any of this?"

Lightgate gave it a second. "I miss the old days, don't you?"

"Not one bit. I want what came *before* the FTC, the days we never even saw. Back when Fae had a stake in this world, instead of a borrowed bit we might lose at any minute. That place has never been worth it."

"We can agree on that." Lightgate saluted with another swig from the bottle. She paused as she lowered it, looking down to the streets. "But would you look at that."

Letty followed her gesture to a flicker of movement through the buildings. A human car, bouncing back sunlight from the windows and mirrors, kicking up dust from the broken road. Lightgate dropped closer to Letty and held out the bottle. Letty looked from the bottle to Lightgate's pistols. One in hand, another holstered within grabbing distance.

Letty took the bottle, had a painful swig, then handed it back.

They watched, side by side, as another car appeared, three blocks over. Unmistakably headed towards the FTC. Lightgate pointed: "And there." A cloud of dust, way off towards the horizon, approaching from the other direction.

"Ah hell," Letty said quietly. Part of her had hoped it wouldn't come to this, that the humans had some sense. Surely they knew it hadn't been a random attack, and they'd stop to ask who was really behind it before doing anything rash?

The two nearest cars stopped at the same time. The dust in the distance settled, too. Lightgate nudged Letty and nodded the other way. Opposite side of the FTC, a fourth plume of dust.

"What do you want to do?" Lightgate asked. "Watch and place some bets first?"

The doors of the nearest car opened. Two men got out. Letty recognised the ginger one, his suit partly hidden behind panels of plasticky body armour. He went to the back of the car and opened the boot. He put on a padded helmet and a chunky backpack, the size and shape of a fridge. His companion came to strap a tube into it.

"What are they using these days, do you suppose?" Lightgate said. "Fire or gas?"

Letty didn't answer. Both were possible.

"Their detectors can't be up to much. Shouldn't they know we're here?"

"They know there's Fae around," Letty said. "At this distance, they can't pinpoint us."

Lightgate took one last long pull on the bottle and belched. She tossed it away, to fall between the buildings, then drew her second pistol. She held it towards Letty.

Letty stared at the gun suspiciously.

"Come on, don't be sour."

Chances were Lightgate would gun her down for trying to take it. Or gun her down the second she got the inkling Letty might use it on her. Might not even be loaded, might have some kind of safety catch.

"I want you to enjoy this," Lightgate said. "How often do you get the opportunity to hurt humans?"

Sam kept her phone in her hand, looking at it anxiously, willing Landon to call and give her something. The field agents blinked on a digital map of the warehouse district, on a mounted wall monitor. Half the Support staff watched alongside her, silently waiting for the dots to move, while the others analysed data from their desks to provide detail.

"Fae guards in the area," one of the analysts announced. "At least half a dozen outside the city walls. Sending it through."

A new set of lights blinked up, yellow this time, closer to the centre.

"Give the word," Hail's voice came through the speakers.

"Hold," Sam said, steadily.

"We're ready," Hail said, clearly irritated.

"I said hold."

A phone rang in Mathers' office. Sam darted between the desks, telling everyone not to move. Please be something. She whipped up the receiver. "Ward."

"You understand that we still possess devastating capabilities."

It wasn't Landon, but a bold female voice Sam instinctively knew, though she'd never heard it before. It had to be the Fae governor, Valoria Magnus.

"Madam Governor," Sam said. "I am —"

"Withdraw your men immediately," the Fae governor commanded loudly, forcing Sam to hold the phone away from her ear.

"I can't," Sam answered, her jaw locked with frustration. "You have to talk to the Raleigh Commission —"

"This is on you!" The woman's voice rose furiously. "*Your* head will roll!"

"It's *not* my —"

"It was the humans that struck you!" The governor was all but shrieking. "The Apothel Five. We have *evidence*, where your people failed — you need to —"

"You know where they are?" Sam interrupted, and Valoria faltered.

"Withdraw your men and I will deliver them to you."

There was enough hesitation for Sam to confirm the governor was bluffing. But Sam already knew the truth of it; Pax hadn't unleashed that turnbold. Her silence told the governor she knew.

Valoria breathed heavily on the other end of the line, making no more threats.

She simply said, "Withdraw your men now and we can still forgive this."

Sam swallowed. Wishing she could do it. She said, "The order came from the Commission themselves. But if you're calling here I guess you already know that."

Valoria snarled and hung up without another word.

It was baffling that whatever peace the Fae leadership had with the Raleigh Commission had been so easily shattered. Heinous as the Greek Street attack was, why were London being so quick to act?

"They're in position," Roper announced, the moment the call ended. Sam gave him a worried look. She could simply refuse to give the order, couldn't she? She *wouldn't* give the order. But it wouldn't matter. They'd take their own initiative eventually; they already had.

"Tell them to hold, for the love of God," Sam said, knowing it would make no difference. As Roper reluctantly relayed the command, she made another call.

The second the pay phone rang, Pax jumped at the receiver, willing it to be good news. *Bring Letty back, tell me everything is okay.* "Where is she?"

"What?" It was Sam Ward alright, but she was thrown. "No, sorry, I don't have that – something's happened. Our people have been diverted. And. And . . ."

Pax was silent for a second. "Diverted where?"

"The FTC. It's Protocol 21. Total extermination."

Pax stared through Casaria next to her, through the world. That amounted to more or less the worst response to the morning's disaster. Countless fairies would die, a whole society erased. "What am I supposed to do about it?"

"You know the Fae," Ward said. "You know what happened this morning, you have to give me something. I don't know why the Commission decided this so quickly, it makes no sense –"

"It's not enough that your people hate the Fae? They'd jump at any excuse."

"The Ministry is procedural, Pax," Ward said. "We do things by the book, according to analysis – usually. I'd potentially found your grugulochs, and –"

"You found it? How? Where?"

"I traced the energy, exactly as you said – but it's too late, our men are about to do something devastating."

"So tell them to stop! If we can confront the Blue Angel we can end this!"

"How?" Ward demanded. "I'm up against my superiors – they don't care and it doesn't add up! You must have some idea of where all this is coming from."

"I don't know!" Pax replied, equally exasperated. She caught Casaria watching her, face sour as ever. He'd invite Fae destruction, like the rest of them. Pax insisted, "There was only one fairy behind this that I know of for sure – Lightgate. She's itching for a fight, maybe nothing more – and the FTC *know* that. She said herself that their council turned her down, they weren't interested in her plan. She got *anonymous* support, from just one source, not a sanction from their whole damn society. That sound like something you want to start a war over? Hell, all she had was a written note . . ." Pax trailed off, remembering the fairy's words. "She had an *anonymous* note. The same sort of manipulative shit this Blue Angel is always doing. Look – you don't have to tell your bosses it's the Blue Angel's doing, just convince them it wasn't the FTC!"

"I *can't* – we have a written order."

"What? Who gives a shit about a written order?"

"You don't understand how this office works – the field agents wanted action, and nothing says decisive bloody leadership better than a Commission order, printed and notarised."

"Which you happened to get as quick as possible?" Pax snorted. "You don't see *that* as a problem?" Ward didn't answer at once, and Pax pictured the insane bureaucratic scenario, office workers deciding things with numbers and printed commands. She paused. The answer was hanging between them; it was in the detail Casaria had already given her, and in the unsettling feeling she'd had in the MEE building. It wasn't just their superiors' speed, it was *how* they gave the order. Pax said, "This printed order, was it faxed?"

"Directly from the Raleigh Commission. From Lord Asquith. It's how –"

"Through the fax machine on that same floor where that monster tried to tear us apart," Pax said. "The room at the end, a little useless stationery cupboard, right? Home to the same fax machine that's been giving you orders for years. Christ, no wonder it's stayed so well hidden."

"What?"

"The Blue Angel," Pax said.

Silence. Casaria was waiting for the conclusion with a frown, and Rufaizu, beyond him, was grinning, anticipating something good. Encouraged by that smile, Pax told herself her instinct was right. The Bright Veins were real, and they told her where the goddamned Blue Angel had its eyes and hands and mouth or whatever it needed to screw the world. She said, "There's a blue screen in your office. Where you've got that fax machine. They can change the appearance of walls, alright? Why not the writing on a piece of paper?"

Ward stayed quiet. Thankfully. It meant she might buy it. She might question everything.

Pax pushed the point. "You've wondered how your organisation could be so incompetent or ignorant of things like the dangers of the minotaur or the behaviour of the Fae. The answer is, they *aren't*. The details that would tip the Blue Angel's hand are hidden – I bet you get numbers through this Commission prick, too? Revised balance sheets about your costs and benefits or whatever?"

"Rarely," Ward answered uncertainly.

"Rarely is good; it knows how to do *just enough* to keep up the ruse. It's *the Angel*." Pax thumped the wall triumphantly. "In your office, under your noses, playing its games."

"But that doesn't make sense –"

"It's not supposed to. It's always had you believing the minotaur's a good thing. That no one should go into the Sunken City. That the Fae are best kept at arm's length. Now it wants you to believe the FTC should be wiped out, because we're asking too many questions, we're *talking*. Someone or something in the FTC can take this thing down, with our help, and it doesn't want us anywhere near joining forces."

"But that turnbold could've killed everyone here –"

"Exactly," Pax said. "No one left to ask questions and a bunch of outsiders coming in to clear up the mess. You got goons on their way from the main office in London? Is that right?"

Ward hummed affirmation, not liking it.

"Dammit, don't you see? It's been manipulating all of you and it didn't even need an inside man, it can just fuck with your correspondence."

Ward was quiet again, giving Pax a second to reflect on that image.

Paper being manipulated, messages coming out of nowhere.

"Jesus Christ, it *was* the Angel. It did what none of the Fae was prepared to do, too. It gave Lightgate that fucking note with the charge codes. Listen to me, this is *all* the Angel; it wants the Ministry torn apart and it wants the FTC torn apart. This is scorched earth."

Ward still hadn't said anything.

"Sam?" Pax said. "You still there?"

"Yeah," Ward answered, voice weak.

"Stop your people attacking the FTC, however you can."

"I will," Sam promised.

"And give me the location of the grugulochs. I don't know if it's another trick or whatever, but I'll know when I'm there, I'm certain. Let me deal with the Blue Angel while you prevent a massacre."

16

The Ministry men were waiting by the front of their car. Ginger had goggles on, now, like these prats might wear to play squash, and he was talking into a headset. His partner had a rifle of some kind. Or the product of two rifles taped together – ridiculously wide and crude.

"Sends out a blast a mile wide, that thing," Lightgate said. "Be behind him when it goes off."

"I don't want to be near any of that shit," Letty said. Were the FTC prepared, in any way? They'd been on alert since the weekend, ready to evacuate, but they would've been reluctant to flee. A thousand people behind those walls, penned in, waiting for death to arrive.

Lightgate held a pistol over her face to stifle a yawn. She shook her head to wake herself up. "Sorry." Reminded of the gun in her hand, she held it out again. "Yeah. Take it."

"You're a goddamned psychopath, Lightgate," Letty told her. "Those bastards could do for our whole society."

"I knew you'd get it eventually."

The ginger was moving forwards, his flame-thrower, or whatever it was, ready. His mate trotted to the edge of the road, taking cover against a building. Letty pushed up with her wing, over the roofs, to get eyes on the next car. Two more pricks in suits, similarly armed. No prizes for guessing what was happening with the other cars. There might be more, even, way out of sight.

They were three blocks out from the FTC. Two blocks from the no man's land where the scouts would open fire. Humans usually got deterred before that, through non-violent means. The roads in one direction were blocked by rubble, in another by a broken-down truck. The rest of them had fields of shattered glass or nails earlier in the approach. These guys were watching their feet, aware of such traps. The ginger's pal with the unlikely rifle called out and the pair stopped. He had something on top of the gun, a blinking panel of lights. He pointed off to the side and Ginger approached it. He took another gadget from his pocket and activated it with a beep. Something puffed from between the bricks of a half-fallen wall.

Well shit, they could deactivate Fae defences.

Sam pulled Mathers' phone as far into the main office as its lead would allow, receiver cradled against her shoulder as she shouted, "Tell them to stand down! Tell them not to engage!"

The phone kept ringing, Tarrington not answering.

The analysts looked at her like she was mad, none of them in any hurry to move. One of them even shook his head, pityingly.

"It's a direct order! No one is to advance!"

Roper took the lead, relaying her words through the radio in an uncertain mumble. He looked sideways at Sam, clearly torn. Hail's voice came back over the speakers.

"We already have our orders. Ready to move."

"The orders have been compromised!" Sam said, louder. "Listen to me, you insubordinate –"

"Ms Ward, I warn you." Tarrington's voice cut her off. "You're in danger of overstepping *many* lines."

"Sir," Sam gasped into the phone. She quickly tried to recover. "Sir, please – there's something I need to ask you – it's crucial in rescinding Protocol 21 –"

"What Protocol is that?"

"The FTC," Sam said, hurriedly. The fool wasn't even aware that they were about to slaughter a civilisation? "We have men in place on the orders of the Raleigh Commission, but I believe there's been a mistake."

Tarrington took a second before replying. "You've questioned my commands already today, Ward, and I can't say I cared for it. Now you're questioning one of my colleagues and, what, expecting my support?"

"Sir, did you actually sign off on Protocol 21?"

Tarrington paused again. "I was sent papers earlier, I suppose, what of it?"

"The order to assault the FTC? To *wipe out* the FTC, you agreed to that?"

"If I did," he answered, "that's not your concern, is it?"

There was uncertainty in his voice; he either didn't want to admit he didn't know what she was talking about, or he'd committed to something he hadn't fully understood. Either way, it was the best response she could have hoped for: confusion. But Sam needed to get him off the defensive. "Sir, I believe a document we've received, issuing the order, may have been tampered with."

"Ha," Tarrington said plainly. "Ms Ward, I told you to take some time off. Your –"

"Please, sir, take this seriously," Sam said, "or a lot of people could die."

Another pause. "Go on, then."

"We received a fax telling us to enact Protocol 21 and assault the FTC. Did you agree to it?"

"I can't keep track of everything I'm sent, and I trust my fellow members of the Commission to act in lieu of assembling the entire board." And that was exactly it, wasn't it? He could pass the buck; if anyone thought to question the details of their orders, it was someone else's problem.

"Ms Ward," Roper called out, voice wavering, "they're advancing."

"Sir," Sam continued, "quickly, please. Have you had any direct contact with the other members of the Commission regarding this order? Have you spoken to them in person, or by phone?"

"No, Ward," Tarrington answered petulantly. "Have you?"

"No, sir, not at all. The order originated from Lord Asquith. *Please* can you speak to him directly and confirm it." Tarrington laughed derisively, making Sam frown. "Sir?"

"Let me get this straight, Ward," Tarrington said, "you want me to talk to Asquith for you?"

"Sir. You are our main point of contact within the Commission."

"But of course."

"Ms Ward," Roper called out again, "you should be monitoring this!"

Sam waved a hand for quiet, as Tarrington continued, "You talk to me because I have my finger on the pulse. No one talks to Lord Asquith, because the man's a veritable recluse. I'll happily ping him a message, but don't expect a quick response. He won't touch modern electronics, you know."

"Sir, we don't have time."

"There's nothing else I can do. I'm hardly going to chase him down in the Chilterns or wherever he's camped out."

Sam paused, realising what he was saying. She spoke very carefully, to make sure he appreciated the gravity of the question. "Lord Tarrington. When was the last time you actually spoke to Lord Asquith in person?"

Tarrington was quiet. Yes. He got it.

She drove the point home. "Sir. You can stop this assault."

"Sharp bunch, aren't they?" Lightgate commented, as the MEE agents defused another trap with an electric pulse.

"You want a fight so bad," Letty snarled, "what are you waiting for?"

The pair of Fae kept pace above Ginger and his mate, as the men reached the end of the road. They checked from side to side, not up and down, and continued. Lightgate said, "Bloody amateurs."

"It's been so long, there's barely a mug left in their cupboard that knows Fae fighting."

"None of them knew it back then, either," Lightgate said. "Our people fled. Our people fought amongst themselves. We *never* get to hurt them. It's delicious."

Letty gave her a sideways glance and Lightgate returned a crooked grin. Then she laughed and shook her head. "The look on your face, Letty. Lighten up. Enjoy this."

The agents crossed the boundary, one foot over the invisible line.

A sniper rifle in the distance flashed soundlessly, like a penny reflecting the sun. The bullet struck Ginger square in the eye, an incredible shot at that distance. He took a step back, head jerking to the side. Then he straightened himself up.

The goggles had taken the bullet.

"Those rifles can put a hole through plate metal," Letty gaped.

"*That*," Lightgate said, "is an interesting development."

Another flash from the distance, and Ginger took it in the chest. It knocked him back, but he kept his balance. He swore, a little wind knocked out of him. That plastic armour was far tougher than it looked. Another shot caught his shoulder as he was straightening up, making him twist the other way and drop the tube of this weapon. He shouted, "Take them out!"

The other guy fired in the direction of the shots, with the crack of a sonic boom, a pulse spreading from his gun like a heat shimmer. Even flying behind them, Letty and Lightgate had to steady themselves against the blast, as it arced through the buildings ahead, shattering the scant remnants of windows and shaking loose brickwork. It hit home as mortar erupted around where the sniper's flashes had come from.

Ginger gathered up his weapon and the men observed the landscape ahead of them.

No more shots.

"Holy shit," Letty said quietly.

"We're ten years behind," Lightgate said. "You see it now? The damage Val's *peace* has done to our people? We should be dominating these scum."

The agents crossed the invisible barrier, walking unhindered towards the FTC building, where the citizens must have been scrambling to flee. There was another crack of sound off to the side, another advancing MEE agent firing his weapon. Then another, and another. Ginger's friend, closest to them, fired again. Letty shuddered in the air, feeling it in her bones.

They were raking the sky, making sure no one was flying up, which is exactly what the Fae would be doing. A thousand or more people scrambling to flee, just to survive. Otherwise they were boxed in to be exterminated like insects, as the humans saw them.

"You want to do something?" Lightgate said. Her pistol was held out again.

The agents' armour wouldn't defend them from a shot up close, not against a gun pressed to their skin. Letty looked at Lightgate's pistol.

"All yours," Lightgate said.

Letty reached for it. Shit, she had to do something.

Ginger pointed and his pal fired another shot. A lone-standing pillar in a bombed-out warehouse cracked and slowly tumbled.

Letty streamlined her arms and legs into a torpedo aimed right at the fuckers. Hurtling through the air, seeking flesh. A gap between the back armour and the helmet, that was hers. A bullet in the bastard's neck.

"Hold up, hold up!" Ginger shouted, suddenly. He put a hand to his headset.

The other guns went quiet.

Letty stopped abruptly, barely a building's width from them. The rifle guy straightened up as Ginger frowned at whatever he was being told. "Fall back. Commission's orders."

"Now?" his friend replied. "This isn't —"

"No, move," Ginger told him firmly. He turned back the way he'd come and Letty flew up, out of his line of sight. The other guy started after him, giving fleeting looks towards the FTC. Ginger was grumbling, both of them pissed at the news.

As Letty floated towards the nearest building, Ginger tried to justify the cancelled attack out loud. "We got a few, hey? At least that's –"

He dropped like someone had cut his strings, offering a startled gargle as his Adam's apple burst out in a small mist of blood-spray. A thin red stream crept down his neck. The tubular weapon clattered to the ground and got in the way of his fall, both his hands limply rising to his throat as he tried to stop the bleeding. He spat up blood as he squeezed his own throat, choking as it filled with blood.

His friend was shocked still, the same as Letty. At the sound of a gunshot, his head snapped back and he hit the floor without so much as a splutter.

Ginger gargled and twitched like a drowning man, then his quivering stopped.

Lightgate floated down between the two bodies, turning in the air to check her work. Her expression was entirely neutral. Letty checked the pistol in her own hand: not even had the chance to check it worked.

"Make your decision now," Lightgate told her. "I'm not having you sneaking behind my back, so you're either gonna help me bury the rest of them or you're joining them now."

"They were falling back."

"Back to a time when they hadn't killed our people?"

There was no arguing. She *wanted* the violence.

They were metres apart, bobbing up and down in the air. A difficult shot with the best conditions, let alone up against this monster.

"Oh." Lightgate steadied in the air, sensing Letty's intentions.

Letty ran her fingers over the pistol handle, tensing. It was only another Fae. She'd faced countless pricks with guns. Just one more. Lightgate raised her free hand in a fist to cover her mouth, a little gag. Burping? Now? A distraction, Letty was sure, to try and draw her out. She knew this bitch was ready as ever.

Lightgate met her eyes, lowering the hand slowly.

Nothing left to say.

Letty whipped up the pistol and fired. The gun leapt from her fingers as she took a blow to the chest, Lightgate's shot coming at the same time, strong as a train driving her back, back into the wall. She hit brick with a crack, the engine of her artificial wing shattering and all her air gone. She dropped and hit the pavement hard, taking the brunt of it on her knee. Once, twice she rolled, then flopped still. She wheezed, trying to breathe, but each breath came shallower. Warmth spreading across her chest.

She rolled her head to the side, searching the sky through the blurry tears of pain. Lightgate's shape was still up there, bobbing a little erratically. Her voice came down, almost annoyed. "Better than most. I'll give you that. *Fuck*." The final curse as she folded over herself. Clutching an injury.

Letty's head dropped back onto the hard floor.

Please let it be fatal, she thought, looking past the buildings to the blue of the sky.

Please let it be fatal.

17

When the Ministry car pulled up, Casaria swore and turned away. "This fuck-up?"

Pax gave him a warning look, but she wasn't impressed either, seeing Landon behind the wheel. He looked even worse than before, with a few added scratches on his rosy face, and he looked about as happy to see them as they were him. He leant over to push the passenger door open, squeezed by the seatbelt he'd neglected to undo.

"Anyone but you," Casaria said.

Pax opened a rear door to invite Rufaizu in, and went round to the other side. She lingered just long enough to make sure Casaria was joining them. He rolled his eyes before getting into the passenger seat. Rufaizu was already playing with an over-large white shirt in the rear seat, exploring his way into it. It must've been one of Landon's spares, but the big driver wasn't stopping him.

"Fasten up, all of you," Landon said, by way of introduction.

"She's scraping the bottom of the barrel, isn't she?" Casaria said. Landon ignored him, pulling the car into traffic.

"There's been a serious development," Landon said. Casaria was about to reply when their driver punched the accelerator and threw everyone back into their seats. As a method of silencing complaints, it worked. Landon said, "I'm not sure this is a good idea any more."

"No surprises there," Casaria said.

"I would've been there by now if I hadn't had to pick you up," Landon reminded him. "And I would've been better off, wouldn't have to think about watching my back."

"What's that supposed to mean?"

"You know." Landon turned away from Casaria to focus on a sharp right turn that made them all tumble. Pax pushed against Rufaizu to straighten herself up. He put his hands up with a smile, showing off the cuffs of his enormous shirt.

"What's this development?" Pax asked Landon.

Landon negotiated another gap in traffic before answering. "The orders came in as Ward was directing me your way, calling off the FTC attack. London got through to the FTC Council directly or something – I don't know – there's calls for a ceasefire from both sides. Except" – Landon looked for Pax in the rear-view mirror – "the situation already got out of hand."

"Out of hand?" Casaria said. "Tell me we've done some damage, at least. How many of ours are out there?"

"Eight," Landon said.

"Eight? Everyone?"

"Everyone but me, you and Vinton. He's on leave."

"Enough to do some serious damage." Casaria looked at Pax, too. "Whatever your feelings, we still ought to wipe that place out, one way or another."

"We already did some damage," Landon said, with aggravated patience. "The Fae agreed to talk, and the Council gave permission for our men to walk away, despite the initial attack, but it seems they weren't all on board with that. We've lost contact with half the team."

"Double-crossing little shits," Casaria hissed. "Forget this Blue Angel, we ought to head there ourselves."

"That's what it'd want," Pax said, shaking her head. No way were they getting in the middle of a shoot-out, not when they were this close. "The Blue Angel doesn't want to be found, what better way to stay hidden than cause more fighting amongst ourselves? Where we're going, *that's* the answer."

Landon gave her another look in the mirror. He didn't want to be at a shoot-out either, did he? He addressed Casaria rather than her. "This all could've been done much neater. You've got a lot to answer for."

"Yeah, neater," Casaria countered. "Neat and ineffective, same as ever."

Landon gave him an unhappy look.

"Cheer up," Casaria said. "We're doing good work now."

His smile was back, Pax noticed. That white, unnatural grin, ready for certain danger. Except she appreciated, now, that it also meant he was scared. And she knew he was right to be.

They'd slipped into silence long before they crossed into the industrial plain of the Net. Rufaizu kept picking at the car door and the buttons of his newfound shirt. From the way they looked at the road and each other, Casaria and Landon were torn between meditative thoughts about their destination and their mutual dislike. Pax left them all to it, focusing on the feeling that was building inside her, the odd pull, the tingling, burning. Was it really her sensing what Rufaizu had called the Bright Veins?

The further north they travelled, the stronger it got. Could she feel the Blue Angel itself? Or its diverted, hoarded energy, at least?

She closed her eyes, trying to feel it more clearly, to picture whatever this odd sensation was. It didn't help. She knew something wasn't quite right, and she knew in what direction. Beyond that, it wasn't clear. But whatever it was, it was getting stronger.

They passed between wide, low-lying commercial buildings, built for storage or the kind of work that required big, empty spaces, like furniture manufacture or industrial laundry. Pax had been up this far once for a game hosted by a man who printed banners for small companies. It had grown uncomfortable when he started threatening anyone who beat him in a hand. That's the sort of place the Net was: an area providing little-wanted or little-understood services, slightly disconnected from reality.

Since they'd left the ring road, they'd barely passed another car. There was no movement in any of the windows. Landon cleared his throat, apparently hoping to break the tension with small talk. "They're converting some of this into apartments. Maybe putting up some new builds. Might be a good investment, before everyone moves here."

"Please," Casaria said. "No one wants to live here."

"I saw it," Landon continued. "I read up on some plans for a development. We went past the site back there."

"You see any building works?"

"Maybe they haven't started yet."

"They never will."

Landon went quiet again. His efforts had failed.

They stopped at the corner of two wide roads, opposite their target building. A free-standing red brick church, with a slanted roof and a large white cross on one wall. It was otherwise unadorned, with no sign announcing sermons and no name, only two massive wooden doors.

Pax felt her pulse racing, maybe from adrenaline, maybe the draw of the Bright Veins. She didn't dare look at her own flesh in case she saw something moving underneath. Unlikely, but why risk it.

"You two should stay in the car until we check it out," Landon said. "I'd appreciate it if you don't take off."

Rufaizu looked to Pax for guidance, and she said, "You wait here. I need to see it."

"Me too," Rufaizu said. "My mission, barfly – I've *been* here for this."

"No," Pax said. With all the authority of a young mum. "Sit this out. If things go wrong, or it's not what we're looking for, I need you to be safe."

Rufaizu held her gaze unhappily, but didn't argue. Pax got out of the car and the sound of the door closing shook the neighbourhood. She started across the road, and Landon called out, "Wait, we've got scanners."

"They won't help," Pax said, sure of it.

"We've no idea what we're going to find in there," Casaria said, briskly following as he drew his pistol. Landon appeared at Pax's other side, giving Casaria a disapproving look, though his hand moved closer to the lump of his own pistol under his jacket.

"I can feel it. I can . . ." As Pax moved towards the building, the sensation grew. The tips of her fingers tingled stronger than ever, and the electric throb pulsed from her heart to every inch of her body. It wasn't like the pained pulses of the surges or the unfocused pulls of being near the blue screens, earlier. It was a dominating warmth, a sense that she was near something big. Stopping at the double doors, she hoped it wouldn't cause a heart attack or a stroke.

"You've got the keys?" Pax said. "Open it already."

Landon looked to Casaria, malice trumped by a need to defer responsibility.

"Pax . . ." Casaria said, sounding oddly nervous.

"You feel it too, don't you? The energy coming from this place."

Neither man answered, but it was clear in their pallid faces.

Pax said, "Let's pull the rug out."

Casaria hesitated a moment longer, then strained to restore his wicked grin. It looked more unconvincing than ever, but he said, "I'll go first." He nodded to Landon, who fumbled a ring of keys from a pocket.

It was getting worse. Like the bass of an immense speaker, the pulse shook Pax in waves. There was something incredible inside, something otherworldly.

"Just a moment," Landon said, testing one key, then another. Casaria tutted impatience. Pax stared at the doors, trying to see through them. The lock clicked. "Got it. Ready?"

Casaria's legs were spread, two hands on his pistol. He nodded.

Landon took out his own gun, less gracefully, and held it at his side as his other hand rested on the door handle. He gave Pax a nod, then turned the handle and stepped back, heaving the door open.

Blue, bright blazing blue. They all raised their hands to protect their eyes from the light, as it flooded out from the far side of the room. At the sound of the creaking door, or the sense of the air rushing in from outside, the light broke and scattered, like massive fireflies dispersing in fear. Shards of blue raced to the corners of the room and faded into the shadows, plunging the room into darkness.

Pax lowered her arm, eyes adjusting to the sudden dark, and tried to make out what was there, way at the back, where the light had been most intense. The feeling inside her faded, the pulse rapidly weakening, diluting, as the force she'd felt moved away. The faintest echo remained.

But their goal was standing near the altar, beyond a scattering of old pews, even as Pax's senses returned to normal. It was staring at them, waiting for them to enter.

Casaria asked the question: "What the hell is that thing?"

18

"Grug . . . u . . . lochs."

It spoke through thick saliva with a gargle. The orb-like eyes with tiny irises traced an unfocused circle, their dullness adding to the impression of a lack of intelligence. Its mouth hung vaguely open, a foot wide and lined by thick, lumpy lips, glistening with dripping liquid. The hideous face, with its porcine nose, sat in a domed head sunk into a gelatinous torso. Its folds of fat were the sluglike texture of the creature in the Ripton chapel. Two arms drooped all the way to the floor, coated in the same grotesquely rolling flesh, almost molten in its excess. The hands, if that's what they were, spread across the floor in bin-lid diameters of tubular fingers. One finger tapped up and down, a hollowed suction cup on its end.

The torso rocked slightly to the side, revealing the rest of the body, a curve of pulsing flesh, marked all over by ancient scars and knotty warts. All flowing into an amorphous base, where the thing appeared to melt into the floor, surrounded by thick slime.

"Grug . . . u . . . lochs!" it repeated, louder, as a toddler might request food. One of its great arms rose and the trio in the door tensed, Casaria training his gun on it. The hand slapped down with a squelch, snapping the wooden flooring. Its fingers twisted and planted themselves between the cracks, and a blue light appeared around them. A blue screen, forming on the floor. It pulsed, and the creature's flesh pulsed with it, something bulging up the arm and into the torso like a snake swallowing prey.

"I think," Pax said, quietly, "I'm going to be sick."

But she felt warmth, that pull, returning. This *was* it. Where the energy was going, where that feeling was leading her.

The creature's head rolled, as though lacking support, from one side to the other. Finally it rested, pivoted on a slanted shoulder, eyes looking their way. Another pulse came up its arm and it exhaled with deep satisfaction. Pax coughed, lifting a hand to her mouth, the smell noxious, even at this distance.

Landon took out his phone, gun still at his side.

"Get ready, for fuck's sake!" Casaria hissed. "Are we culling this shit or not?"

"Wait," Landon mumbled, hurrying to make a call.

In their distraction, Pax stepped between the men, closer to the creature. This was the source of the Blue Angel they'd been hunting? It moved impossibly slowly, sliding its hand to the side. Rounding a pew, she got a better look at its base, where its hard flesh seemed to fuse with the floor. How long had it been here, gestating like this? Feeding by proxy through blue screen emissaries?

The light around its hand faded again, and it deflated slightly, done.

"What *are* you?" Pax uttered.

Its eyes focused on her. Listening. Understanding.

"Grug . . . ulochs," it answered, then gave a series of sharp hisses, like air squeezed through a balloon, its whole body convulsing. "Grugulochs' . . . lair. You . . . people . . ."

"It talks?" Casaria said. He was stunned enough to slightly lower his weapon.

"You're behind all this?" Pax asked, taking another cautious step closer. There was a good twenty metres between them, but something about this thing, hideous and unnatural as it seemed, was oddly unthreatening. "The minotaur – berserker – glo? It's you?"

The hissing chuckle came again, the creature's eyes narrowing with delight. "Grugulochs' . . . city. Belongs . . . to me."

"Crispy. Bloody. Geckos." Pax met Casaria's eyes to share her shock.

Landon shook his head, phone to his ear. "It's me," he said, and in the quiet of the church Ward's voice came through unapologetically loud.

"I know it's you! I need you to get to –"

"We've found it," Landon said. "The . . . thing. It's . . . I don't know what it is . . ."

"It's the grugulochs," Pax told him. "Clearly."

Ward was quiet for a moment. "What . . . but . . . the FTC . . ."

"It just fed," Landon said. "Or looked like it was feeding? Test your theory – is it connected to the *praelucente*?"

"Hold on," Ward replied. She relayed a series of muffled commands. "Just hold on. Jesus Christ. It's there? You're really seeing it? What *is* it?"

Pax took another step closer, trying to move fluidly, calmly, in case she might scare it off. She asked, "You control all this? The Sunken City? The myriad creatures?"

It nodded excitedly, and added, "Gloooo."

"To feed?" Pax frowned.

"Feed . . . good."

"A great fucking parasite," Casaria concluded. In awe, in disgust.

"Yes, two minutes ago," Ward's voice announced. "A minor spike from the *praelucente*, south of Old Ordshaw. Does it mean –"

"You manipulated the Ministry?" Pax asked the creature, loudly. "The Fae? This fight?"

It started shuddering again, pleased with its own actions. "Fight . . . fight . . . kill . . . no one knows. No one knows . . . grugulochs."

Pax turned a look to the others. Not sure what was more alarming: the confirmation of her theories or the fact that the mastermind of all this was some bulbous slug that seemed too dumb to realise it was giving its own game away.

"Did you hear that?" Landon said into his phone.

"I heard it," Sam said, stunned like the rest of them.

Landon looked at his phone for a second, like he wasn't sure what to do next.

"Can you . . ." Pax took another gentle step forwards. She could feel that pull, that energy, but it wasn't as strong as before. It was around her, not focused on that one spot. She checked the walls, the shadows. "Can you explain . . . to us?"

"Explain?" the grugulochs gurgled. Its eyes started rolling again, and a great tongue lapped out of its slot of a mouth, bovine in thickness and texture. "Yesss. Friends?"

"Sure," Pax said. It was the Ripton Chapel blue screen all over again. This thing felt the world through its blue screens and knew people through their words, the way they wrote. It didn't know who she was to look at her. "We're friends. Tell your friends what you've done."

"Tell friends?" Its bulging eyes narrowed uncertainly.

"We can help," Pax nodded. "You're in trouble, aren't you?"

"I don't like this . . ." Casaria said. Pax held a hand up without looking back.

"Minotaur . . ." the grugulochs said. "Feed. Minis . . . try? Find minotaur. But . . . find me. Fairieeees" – it drew out the word, long and high-pitched – "want to hurt. Minis . . . try. Fairieeees. Want to hurt."

"Want to hurt you?" Pax said. "Or you want to hurt them?"

"What difference does it make," Casaria said. "You're right, it's an abomination. All this time, we've been *feeding* this?"

"Feeding, yes!" The monster bounced up and down suddenly, hardly moving from its spot, but sending rumbling shakes that rattled the pews and staggered Pax. The walls creaked as it came to rest. It rolled its head towards Pax, and slowly raised one arm.

"Get back, miss," Landon cautioned, edging into the room. Casaria sidestepped in the other direction, gun rigidly aimed.

"Friend," the grugulochs said, reaching towards her. Pax didn't move, transfixed. It was well out of reach, even with the arm fully extended, its fingers spread. There were suction pads all around its palm. With a great effort and a grunt, it moved, the sluglike base snapping free from the floorboards. Pax jumped back. But for all the volume and power of its movement, it shifted an inch at most. "Friend!"

"Step away from it!" Landon ordered, louder. Casaria joined in.

"Pax, you're too close!"

"Look at it," she said. "It's harmless. An idiot. It does everything through those screens, but in the flesh it's . . . what? Just a filthy mass."

"Filthy . . . mass?" The creature's arm slapped back down into the floor, its face distorting in an expressively pained look. The lower lip quivered. "Friends say . . . filthy mass?"

Oh. Apparently it was a sensitive filthy mass.

Pax took a step back. "Well . . . you have fantastic abilities. You can change things, can't you? The way they look?"

"Change." It fixed its eyes on her again. "Change. Yes."

It leaned onto both arms, arching up like a gorilla. Pax felt the energy coming closer before it appeared; the blue light returned, one square forming around each of the monster's hands. They pulsed again, but this time a bulge came the other way. Out of the torso, rolling down the arms.

"Change . . ." Its voice grew grittier, aggressive. "Friends."

"Step away from it!" Casaria ordered.

Pax didn't need to be told. The blue screens around its hands glowed bright as a flare, and something sparked out of them, spurring her to run. More sparks crackled around them. Around the whole room. Pax staggered to a standstill, Landon ahead of her, and they both looked dumbly up. In the far corners of the room, other blue squares were appearing, lit like sparkling floodlights.

Arcs of electricity lanced into the room.

They cracked like thunder, building in quick succession as the grugulochs roared, bass voice vibrating the entire building, "Filthy mass!"

Casaria fired a single shot but the wall lit up behind him and something struck him from behind, flinging him into a pew and to the floor. Landon turned and ran. Pax couldn't move, feeling the energy, the draw all around her, the creature active, alive in the walls. It was coming from all the different points – alive in every blue screen – dozens of them – *at least thirty* –

"Grugulochs!" The beast thundered its own name as Landon reached the doorway. A fierce whip of electricity snapped out from the doorframe, exploding with a flash that threw him back into the room. His pistol slid past Pax's feet.

The monster roared again and the room grew ever brighter, the sound of lightning bolts piercing Pax's ears, pews snapping in half from the shaking. The energy was building, growing in every screen, and focusing again on the grugulochs behind her. A shard of lightning cracked overhead and Pax ducked, snapped out of her trance.

She twisted to where Landon's pistol lay.

At best she might run and save her own life, for now. But it was going to keep growing in power, going to keep striking, bleeding this city.

She snatched the pistol from the floor and spun back to the beast. It reared up on the great arms rooted into the floor, eyes lit like headlights, brilliant blue flooding out of its gaping maw. A monster full of tremendous power, focusing ferociously on her.

She pulled the trigger.

The lights went out. As the deafening echoes faded away, the monster slumped down, streams of green gunk pouring from the back of its head. Pax blinked and fired again. Again, again, each shot coming easier, hitting the creature's torso like stones thrown at mud.

When the gun clicked empty, the room was silent. Dark. The blue squares were gone.

The grugulochs was dead.

Pax stood stone still, scarcely believing it.

She could feel its energy, still. All around them, in the walls, but receding fast. It was spreading beyond her reach, all but the tiniest feeling left.

There was still something there. The faintest flicker beneath the grugulochs' mountainous corpse. Pax took a step towards it. Then another. She passed Landon, groaning on the floor a short distance away, apparently alive.

"Pax," Casaria croaked wearily, somewhere behind the broken pews.

She ignored them both, approaching the beast. It was an empty husk of life, that was plain to see, but her sense for its energy remained. And the closer she got, the better she understood. The energy was beyond it, now. Not within it.

"Don't," Landon called out, pushing himself onto his hands and knees. "Don't get so close."

Pax frowned, watching the floor and the walls as she felt the energy shifting. The feeling was unclear, unfocused, but she understood it was moving, not fading away. It was still there, that was the crux of it. The monster was dead and the feeling remained, even as it drifted away from her. Its novisan pulsing back into the city through the Bright Veins?

No. It was nothing so innocent as that.

Sam Ward's voice cut through the stillness, shouting from the phone, "Landon? Are you okay? Is everyone okay?"

Silence for a second, as Pax kept staring at the empty vessel of the grugulochs. She said, privately, "I've got you, you fucker."

"Landon?"

"She killed it," Landon announced, finally. "It's over."

19

Pax sat alongside Rufaizu on the bonnet of Landon's car, watching as men in hazmat suits marched into the church. They kept stopping in the doorway as they came and went, throwing unsubtle looks at Pax across the road. She wasn't sure what to feel about any of it. Maybe she should've run, before they arrived, but it was too late now, with two vans here and another ministry car pulling up. She was tired and wanted to go home, that was the only thing she was certain of. And she was happy to sit still, feeling, even for a moment, like she had some breathing space. Her hands wrapped around a disposable coffee cup, a blanket over her shoulders, she told herself she was safe – more useful to the Ministry alive and free than confined or dead.

Sam Ward approached with a forced smile. The sharp businesswoman looked oddly chipper, considering this success was balanced by a simultaneous catastrophe elsewhere. She tugged at the lapels of her suit jacket as she reached them, getting her ensemble in line, then held out a hand. Pax regarded it suspiciously. What the hell. She shook, and from Ward's smile she'd at least made someone's day. Pax caught Casaria watching unhappily from a distance, sat with Landon in the side door of one of the vans. He looked away when she met his eyes.

"The city owes you a great debt," Ward said. "And, I believe, an apology."

Pax knew there were a hundred smart responses on both accounts, but wasn't in the mood. She simply said, "Yeah."

"I'll see that it's not forgotten. The Ministry won't detain you or harm you. We'd like to do a full debrief, with you and the Bartons, that's all."

"I have no idea where they are," Pax said, doubting she'd tell her anyway. She hoped they were okay, but given the results of Lightgate's conquest it was probably an unsafe bet. "But thanks."

"Citizen be fine," Rufaizu murmured, tiredly. The doping and his previous wounds were catching up to him. "Nothing holds Barton down."

"I'm sure," Ward said. "And you *can* trust me. Barton, Dr Rimes – they were left alone before, they will be now. Whatever you think of us, the MEE are reasonable."

Pax gave her a sceptical look, then nodded to Casaria and Landon. "How are they?"

"They'll be fine. With time. It's a miracle you all got out of there unharmed."

Pax hummed. She'd replayed the event over in her mind and agreed. With the force of the attack, and direct strikes on Landon and Casaria, it was remarkable they'd survived. None of the blows had come close to harming her. Almost like it was deliberate. The thought that she'd been *allowed* to live was linked to the feeling that the energy she'd felt hadn't been concentrated on the grugulochs itself. She wasn't quite ready to face her conclusions.

Ward cleared her throat and confided something of her own: "They're all we've got left."

Pax frowned, studying the two imperfect agents. "What happened with the Fae?"

"Hard to say," Ward said. "We've got a ceasefire, but I don't know how long it will last. Lives were lost on both sides and it's unclear if either side's attacks were retaliatory or officially sanctioned. Confusion alone is preventing worse from coming. But . . . eight men." She swallowed. "Eight of ours died out there."

Casaria had said it on the way here. That was everyone. The whole Ordshaw street team wiped out. Which, for their faults, left Ordshaw vulnerable to whatever was left after the grugulochs. Everything under the city. It would also leave the Ministry poised for war, if this ceasefire didn't deliver satisfactory answers.

"We managed to trace your friend's phone, by the way."

Pax's surprise turned to worry as she noticed Ward's uneasy tone. "And?"

"She was there when our people arrived at the FTC. It doesn't look good."

Pax didn't respond. Had they hurt her? "That's all you've got?"

"We couldn't pinpoint the phone, exactly, and didn't find her, but . . ."

"How would you, she's the size of a matchbox," Pax said.

"If she was the one –"

"She's not the fucking one," Pax snapped. "I told you it was Lightgate, all Lightgate. No way Letty would've gone along with whatever happened out there. This" – she waved towards the church – "this is thanks to Letty. It would've been over years ago if people hadn't kept screwing her around. Jesus."

"Gonna be okay," Rufaizu said, quietly, a gentle hand patting Pax's. "She's gonna be okay." His smile was disarming.

Pax told Ward, "Find her and keep her safe. Promise me that."

Ward nodded. "I will, I promise. There's something else, to start. We ran a trace on the phone's usage and got two numbers that tried to call it. One was a payphone in Broadplain. The one you used? The other we traced to a coffee shop in New Thornton. We haven't tried it yet."

Pax stared. Would it link them to more Fae? "Can I have the number?"

Ward glanced at her men milling about the church, concerned they might be watching. She gave a slight, conciliatory nod, with a whisper: "If I can listen."

Pax nodded back, and Ward took out her mobile. She brought up the number and hit dial before handing it to Pax, who held it between them, speaker chiming.

"Reny's Bean Barrel," a young man answered.

"We had a call from this number," Pax said. "Someone –"

"Right you are, I'll get her." The young man raised his voice. "Ma'am, someone returning your call!"

Pax held Ward's gaze as they waited for the caller to take the phone.

"Letty?" Holly Barton's voice came on hopefully. "Is everything okay? We did what we could, but after half an hour on that wretched train it was –"

"Holly," Pax said. "It's me."

Holly skipped a beat, before replying with relief, "Thank *heavens*. You're with Letty? Are you both safe? Should we –"

"Holly," Pax cut in. "I'm with the Ministry."

A slight, icy gasp.

"It's okay. I think . . . Are you all alright? Are any of you hurt?"

"We're fine. Of course. We fled that awful shopping centre but we couldn't stand to be underground too long. Diz wasn't the only one getting antsy about it – we came up for air and have been waiting here – what do you *mean* you're with the Ministry?"

"I found it," Pax said. "The source of this energy. Kind of. They helped me, and they're . . . look, things are winding down. It's going to be okay. But – I'm not with Letty. What happened to her?"

"I thought . . ." Holly slowed down, and her voice said this was bad news. "Have you been back to Broadplain?"

"Uh-huh."

Holly paused again, appreciating this meant Letty hadn't been there. "She said the other one wanted to kill us. She stayed . . . to . . . well . . . where do you think she is?"

Pax didn't answer right away, wary of Sam Ward listening in. "We'll find her, don't worry. I'm going to sort everything out. Stay there for a bit, can you? I'll finish up here and get back to you."

"Are you sure? Shouldn't we keep moving –"

"You're safe," Pax said. Even if the MEE had ill intentions towards the Bartons, they had no manpower left to do anything about it right now. "Wait for my call."

She ended the call and handed the phone back to Ward, whose concerned look suggested it had done some good for her to hear Holly's voice. Now she appreciated they were real, normal people, all of them. Ward said, "We *will* find her. And things are going to change. This has brought the *praelucente* into question. The very figures that demonstrate its benefits might have been manipulated. The Sunken City itself will be reassessed. It's a huge step and you will all be commended for your part in it."

"Listen," Pax sighed, not meeting Ward's eyes for this. It was time, wasn't it? Her voice came out edgy with the truth. "There's something you need to know and you're not gonna like it. But before I tell you anything, I want assurances."

"As I said," Ward replied slowly, "you're safe. I guarantee it."

"I want more than that. Protection and damages for all of us. Him" – she patted Rufaizu – "especially. And that family, they deserve to go back to exactly the life they left four days ago – this was thrust on them, they're nothing to do with it. And you have to make sure I've got a home to go back to. I want my money back and the rest of the money Casaria stole from me."

Ward frowned. "I don't know anything about that."

"So find out," Pax sighed, thinking of all else she'd left behind. Where had she been that night Rufaizu first happened upon her? Her hopes for the next few days had been so much simpler. She said, "I want a ticket, too. Get me a ticket into the World Poker Tour. You can blatantly pull strings and I reckon I've earned that, at the very least."

The confusion on Ward's face doubled, but she didn't question it. "I'll make it happen. But you'll tell me everything, won't you?"

"Yeah." Pax still hesitated. With the Bartons accounted for, and at least some assurances from the MEE, she needed to share her final suspicions, didn't she? Everyone else could walk away, but she couldn't, not with this weighing on her. She pointed at the church and said, "That thing in there, it wasn't what we hoped it would be."

Ward took a moment. "The grugulochs was diverting novisan, wasn't it?"

"You should've seen that idiot monster. You wouldn't believe something that dense could hide itself so well, playing everyone against each other."

"Well," Ward said. She certainly wanted to believe it. "A chameleon doesn't need intelligence to change colour, does it?"

"You *shouldn't* believe it." Pax turned to Rufaizu. "What'd your dad tell you about the grugulochs?"

"Huh?" Rufaizu's face was caught between eagerness at being asked and uncertainty at the question. "Papa never said nothing."

"Never wrote it, either, did he?"

"Not that I saw," Rufaizu said.

"You know why?"

Rufaizu ventured, "Didn't know it?"

Ward's deepening frown looked in danger of leaving permanent creases. She said, "It was in the book. The only word in the chapel –"

"I never saw that word in Apothel's book," Pax said. "And it wasn't Apothel that defaced the chapel, or left that word there. Here's another one: you ever see a creature like we encountered in that chapel? That acid slug."

Ward shook her head.

"No, and if you'd seen what I encountered getting some glo, you wouldn't have recognised that either. I bet you no one" – Pax pointed to the church – "*no one* has seen that creature before."

"Blue Angel keeps hidden," Rufaizu said, "that's what he does best."

"The Blue Angel doesn't exist," Pax said. She let the pair of them stew on that for a moment. "Not in the sense we've been chasing. You're right, though, hiding is definitely what it does best. What better way than this?"

Their eyes all ran back to the church. Two men were carrying some big lump wrapped in black plastic between them, part of the monster for studying.

Pax explained, "I think I sensed it before we got here. It was too easy, us finding the creature like this. I hoped it was that the Angel got cocky, or sloppy. But when I looked that thing in the eye, and I *felt* the energy of that room, there was no denying it. We found that thing because we were supposed to. It wasn't the Blue Angel – but the blue screens were there. And they can do a hell of a lot more than write on walls. More than *transporting* things like glo and creatures, too. These creatures weren't there before, weren't anywhere . . ."

Pax took a breath. Now she'd said it, she knew in her gut it was right. "The blue screens can change the shapes of walls. They defaced that chapel themselves, and changed the writing on the paper in your office, too. Your faxes, Apothel's Miscellany even. They planted the word grugulochs. They sent out the *sound* this thing was making through their screens. They put all this out there to make you think you'd found them. But what we found was another distraction they'd designed. A totem."

"No . . ." Ward said.

"No way!" Rufaizu said, decidedly more enthusiastic. "The hunt's still *on*."

"No, that's not what this is," Ward persisted. "The Fae weapon weakened it and it let out these noises in pain, it –"

"The Fae weapon," Pax said, "hurt the minotaur, but it wasn't drawing energy to recover. These things used that energy more acutely. These random bursts have occurred when these new creatures have appeared. I felt it, trust me."

"How?"

"This thing *got* me, alright?" Pax said. "I'm hooked into their network, whatever – what's important is they were doing something with that energy. They might have been transporting stuff through those blue screens – but I think it's worse than that. I think they created those creatures you'd never seen."

"Created?" Ward almost laughed, but Pax kept a serious face, to impose this tough conclusion on her. It was unreal, but it made sense, considering the ill-formed nature of the slug creature, and that glutinous mass on Chaucer Crescent. Especially when considering the grugulochs itself.

Pax continued, "Who knows what they're capable of, or what they even *are*. But I'm getting an idea, and it's not one mastermind you're dealing with. It's a whole host of these things. I've felt them, moving in the walls, part of the blue screens themselves. They were throwing every trick they had at me because they knew I saw them, suckling at that light monster's teat. They scrambled to give us an answer that would draw attention away from the fact that they were right there, on display. The blue screens themselves."

"And we chased their clues to a totem?" Ward sounded more impressed than upset.

"Towards the truth," Pax said. "You have an advantage right now. The grugulochs is dead – if it takes the blame, they'll think they got away with it. You can find them without them actively trying to throw you off the scent."

Ward looked towards her men. Casaria was saying something to Landon, who was leaning stiffly away, trying to ignore the man's existence. "Clearly, Pax, you're better equipped to deal with this than most of my staff. You'll work with us, won't you?"

"I've done my bit," Pax replied. "I only want Letty back – the rest of this is on you."

"You'd leave this hanging over our city? Where would we start? You at least have some insight –"

"You start," Pax said, exhausted by it even needing to be said, "by *talking* to each other. Open a real dialogue with the Fae, share what you know, and figure out how to obliterate these fuckers *together*."

Ward hesitated. "It's not that simple, and we're on a knife-edge after today. You know them. I don't believe you'll just walk away."

Pax held Ward's gaze, trying to implore her to back off just by looking at her.

Ward stared straight back.

Rufaizu beamed happily, drawing his own conclusion: "Barfly's gonna kick Blue Angel's *arse*."

EPILOGUE

Bright, blinding light.

Dull shapes moving. The taste of plastic, an ache around it. Jaw wide open, wide as it would go. Something in it. All the way down. A long, loud puff of air. A whirring, expanding apparatus.

No other pain than the jaw ache. Head swimming. Body bloated.

"She's coming around." A man's voice. Factual.

"Let me past, come on." Another man. Familiar. A pillar of darkness sliding into the centre of the light. Fuzzy. Vibrating. "Can you hear me? Letty, can you hear me?"

A thinner shape moving from side to side before it. Pendulum motion, testing her vision.

"You expect her to say yes?" The first voice again.

"Letty. You know who I am?" The dolt actually waiting for an answer. "We met earlier today. Very briefly. I've taken a big interest in what you've been up to. I want you to know we didn't agree to any of this."

She tried to grunt, to work the words around the horrendous tube.

"What's she saying?"

She tried louder. Tried to lift her chest to get the words out. Couldn't move.

"Letty. Do you know where you are? A lot's changed since you left, and after – well – now, there's no going back. We need you. We need to build on what you started."

Trying again, louder, but still muffled.

"Can we let her speak? Get that out of her mouth? Letty, we're going to do everything we can to help you. We can do great things together."

One more time. Getting her lips wide of the pipe.

Making it clear, even if it was muffled.

Fuck.

Off.

With the satisfying silence it brought, she sank back into the bed and closed her eyes. Let the machine breathe for her.

THE VIOLENT FAE

AN ORDSHAW NOVEL

PHIL WILLIAMS

PART 1

1

Letty had a simple plan.

When the physician returned to take her vitals, she'd jam the plastic fork in his eye. Well, *near* the eye, close enough for him to hand over the keys and whatever information she needed. The guard, a young one-eyed guy with a half-melted face, would get it, too. She'd recovered enough energy now. Her chest barely hurt, she was breathing freely. All good, considering the last thing she remembered was getting shot in the chest. There was a bruise, but no bullet hole, no scar.

Her captors had healed her, but it didn't excuse them locking her up in a whitewashed room with no windows and an adjustable bed as comfortable as a pivoting plank. She was going to break their jaws and get out. Then she'd tear through Ordshaw following Lightgate's blood trail. That lunatic Fae needed her face smacked into the ground before she hurt anyone else. And to get her back for that gunshot in the chest. And just because she was a lunatic.

With that done, Letty would break into the Ministry of Environmental Energy's offices and take the Dispenser by force – fuck it – and finally lead her people back underground.

She'd do it all, the second she got her hands on that plastic fork.

The lock clicked and Letty clutched the side of the bed, ready to pounce. But the Fae who strolled in behind the one-eyed guard was someone new: a beanpole in a three-piece suit, slim with little round glasses perched on his nose, holding a big plastic disk. He was young, with the aura of a lofty accountant, and spoke in an educated tone: "Letty, good to see you awake." She'd heard that voice while wrestling through drugged-up sleep. And – yeah – she'd met him, in Broadplain, around the time she realised Lightgate was preparing to screw everyone. "You remember me? Edwing. The Chair of Information for the Fae Transitional City. This is my brother, Flynt. I want you to know you're not a prisoner."

So the one-eyed guard was this beanpole's brother. Slim but ripped with muscle under a tight t-shirt and jeans, Flynt stood at Edwing's shoulder, a revolver holstered low at his hip. His dark hair needed combing, and while an elegant black patch covered one eye, he could've done with covering the rest of that burnt half of his face. Words catching in her dry throat, Letty growled, "A locked fucking door is a prison."

Flynt grinned, showing a damned gold tooth. That smile disappointed Edwing. "You can go, Flynt. We're sending the wrong message."

"All the same, *Edwing*," Flynt said, "I might talk her language better than you."

Still, Edwing indicated the door. "I'll shout if I need you."

Flynt took his time leaving and the suit paced further into the room. Past the room's one decorative feature, a mounted flat-screen. "Sorry there's no view, but –"

"I can improve it," Letty said. "Once I ram your head through that TV."

Edwing faced her dead on. Either too arrogant or too ignorant to be afraid. He held up his big plastic disk and turned it around: a concave, elliptical device with three concentric rings on its curved side, the outer two translucent like tube lighting. "Do you know what this is?"

"Robotic human diaphragm?"

"It's a Clear Glider," Edwing said. "Released this spring. Almost silent, mimics a second wing so well you wouldn't notice the substitution. The system of Svenkin propulsion, I'm told, is the closest we're likely to get to an anti-gravity engine."

Letty had no idea what *Svenkin propulsion* was, but got the point: this thing could replace her severed wing. The ability to fly properly would greatly improve her chances of escape. "What do you want for it?"

"Nothing you don't want yourself," Edwing said, resting the Clear Glider on the foot of the bed. "You remember what you went through? You were unconscious for some time."

"Sure. Lightgate shot me when I tried to stop her killing humans. How'd that go?"

"Not well," Edwing replied. "You, however, were lucky. The strap of your artificial wing stopped the bullet. It left you with a cracked rib and concussion from a nasty fall, but nothing a course of medicinal dust couldn't take care of. You'll soon be fighting fit."

"I'm never not fighting fit," Letty said, stirring. "I could be flopping about on bloody stump legs and still be fighting fit. And you know that, with your 'not a prisoner' bullshit."

Edwing didn't blink. "You're tough, Letty, but it's dangerous outside these walls. Half the Fae call you a hero, the other half a liability. Both hold you culpable."

Letty snorted. "And Lightgate?"

"No one admits to having seen her. I'm afraid you have all the attention. Hence, this room."

"Hence, you're a dick." Letty adopted his stuffy tone. "Tell me you know where she is, at least? Tell me I gave *her* more than a fucking bruise."

Edwing shook his head. "Fortunately, Flynt found you before anyone else did, but she was long gone. Well enough to escape, it seems."

"She's never been well in her batshit life."

"Nevertheless, Governor Valoria's Stabilisers are scouring Ordshaw for *you*."

"Let the fuckers come!" Letty spat aside, a globule of saliva hitting the wall. Edwing stared with more curiosity than distaste. Not taking her seriously. They both knew the significance of the Stabiliser threat. Val's elite soldiers, Fae who hunted other Fae.

"We're at a crossroads," Edwing said. "Valoria is still telling everyone that your human friends are a serious threat to our community – that they're on the brink of invading us, even. She plans to cut the FTC off from the humans entirely. Her people are tracking down other Ordshaw Fae exiles to limit potential leaks."

Letty gave him a level look. "So give me that wing and I'll take her down."

"You don't understand. The FTC is locked down. You are *not* a prisoner, but –"

"I understand well enough."

Bracing one hand against the bed, Letty launched up with an outstretched kick to Edwing's chest, a glancing blow but enough to send him stumbling. She swept the Clear Glider off the bed and rolled to the floor, down into a crouch, ready when Flynt rushed in with his gun drawn. He was looking Edwing's way as she charged. She drove her shoulder into his gut and burst past into a short corridor, hatches to other levels in the floor and ceiling, another door at the end of the hall – an exit. Running, she rolled the Clear Glider over in her hands, searching for a way to attach it – the back had a couple of pipe holes. Was this some kind of fucking joke?

Not stopping to figure it out, Letty slammed through the door onto a tight metal platform, a balcony with no railing, four Fae storeys up. She skidded to the edge, catching her balance before falling. There was hard concrete below, a metre or more down. Too far to jump. Breathing into her wounds, she realised fresh pain was already spreading across her torso. She spun and saw rungs beside the balcony, sunk into the wall like staples. The most rudimentary Fae fire escape. Opposite this building was another, about a foot away, made up of stacked metal containers, each the size of a human shoebox, welded together from scrap. Beyond that was empty space, the vast floor of a human warehouse with a wall far away. Hell. It was the edge of the Fae Transitional City itself. The place she'd been driven out of so many years ago. And there was a lot of open ground to cover, on foot, if she was to leave again.

"Letty," Edwing said behind her, urgent, "come back!"

"Piss off." Letty held up the Clear Glider like it would protect her. Flynt was next to Edwing, his pistol down at his side, looking more worried than threatening. These whelps weren't stopping her.

Dropping the useless artificial wing, Letty jumped onto the ladder rungs and started down. She descended a storey before the pain in her chest made her pause.

"Letty!" Edwing hissed, leaning over the balcony, fearfully quiet. "It's not safe!" Flynt was scanning the sky above. Between them and the distant ceiling was a whole lot of nothing.

"Movement," a metallic voice called from somewhere unseen, and a glare appeared, high up. Someone with a searchlight. Letty checked the next balcony, a short distance below. She jumped as the light swung from the opposite block towards her. The voice returned, through a loudhailer: "Peripheral citizens are *not* to move beyond the city limits."

"We got a right to be here!" Flynt called up as Letty darted into a doorway. Just in time; the searchlight scanned the balcony, its source getting closer. Bracing herself against the door, Letty found the handle and rolled inside.

"Scout Chief Flynt?" the metallic voice continued.

Letty scrambled into an unlit corridor, kicking the door closed behind her. A light came on, and Edwing appeared halfway down the hall, pulling shut a ceiling hatch behind him. Trapdoors – the Fae answer to stairs.

"The hell is –" Letty started, but Edwing put an anxious finger on his lips for quiet, floating to the floor. Above them, Flynt was talking to someone, a man.

"They want you, Letty," Edwing whispered, "for the same reason we do. You have friends amongst the humans. Ones outside the Ministry. The difference is, *we* want to nurture that."

He said it almost pleadingly. Talking about Pax, wasn't he? The one human Letty could rely on. Hell, the only *person* she'd been able to rely on. Pax risked her neck to get the Dispenser back from the Ministry's Greek Street office, before everything went to shit. Then what? Stopped the Ministry from decimating the FTC after Lightgate unleashed a monster on them, surely. Pax was the only person remotely capable of convincing the Ministry goons to give the Fae a break. But where would she be now? If not wanted by the human government, then another target for the Fae?

Letty gave the exit another look. She'd need that artificial wing, and more of what this clearly harmless suit was offering. *Perhaps* her escape plan had been rash. She turned back to Edwing.

"You got a phone?"

2

Pax held a pair of queens.

The best cards she'd had in an hour. Half a day into the World Poker Tour, she was barely hanging on. The biggest game in town – maybe the biggest in Europe right now – and a win could cover her bills for five years. Could build a career to replace hustling for pennies. Except tournaments required the sort of luck you couldn't wait for, and she'd barely picked up a decent hand all morning.

The kid in early position mumbled a big raise, turtling inside his grey hood; an internet player who would push with nothing, just what she needed. Except Dutch McRory followed, in middle position. "I'll raise." He barely looked up, as casual as ordering an espresso. He scanned his own stack, the pot in the middle, the young guy's stack, running the calculations. "Six thousand."

He'd tripled the kid's bet and created a pot half the size of Pax's modest stack. A roller-coaster drop: if she wanted in, she had to bet everything. And one of these two would certainly see her. McRory was a legendary poker author and three times World Series bracelet winner. Re-raising in middle position, against an early opener, he *had* something. Almost certainly a pocket pair, aces or kings, ace-king at worst. Or did he just have the gall to move against an overeager youngster? With four people still to act? Unlikely.

The action folded to Pax and she gave her queens another look. The third-best starting hand in Texas Hold'em. Against two guys claiming something big, third-best was dubious. Lose now, with a month's rent spare, and she was back to grinding local clubs. Brushing shoulders with men she now knew to be bloody criminals, who she'd rather never see again. Bees, Jones, Monroe – all men who knew *she* knew they were bloody criminals.

She needed these queens to be good. Go All In, triple up against two weaker pocket pairs or an ace that didn't hit? Or lose and put herself firmly in the gutter? Her instincts said walk away. Survive for later. Or was that just fear? Another way to lose, folding away to nothing . . .

In the background, the central hall of Featherback Casino was loud with spectators and table shuffling. The World Poker Tour's first Ordshaw outing had swelled with the city's recent troubles: poker players were nothing if not thrill-seekers, and the crowd was eager to explore dangerous Ordshaw for mutant alligators, since the news had reported subterranean tremors and sewer monsters attacking offices. The reports were a long way from the reality: those monsters and crumbling buildings were connected to forces no one understood. In case she unwittingly revealed she knew that, Pax had been studiously avoiding TV cameras and loudmouths who hounded her on realising she lived here. She was trying to focus, at least for a minute, on improving her life.

As the minute dragged longer, McRory gave her a gentle look. This man had taught her so much through his books, and they had never spoken. Now he was reading her, this daft woman in loose jeans and a tatty hooded sweatshirt, better suited to loitering on street corners than challenging poker millionaires. And she saw, in his expressionless face, that to go All In with the queens would be desperate.

"I want it too much," Pax said, and slid her cards to the dealer.

Two more folds and it went back to the kid, who immediately announced All In himself. McRory called without excitement and the kid flipped over ace-king like he'd already won. McRory showed aces. Bullets that would've cut Pax down. The dealer drew the community cards: a king on the flop, so the kid would've beaten Pax, too. Instead, he mumbled ungracious defeat and stalked away. McRory offered a sad look, this ruddy white-haired American who'd seen off countless hopefuls. He asked Pax, "Queens? Jacks?"

"Queens," Pax admitted. A rake-thin player in a loose red shirt laughed. It was the table's other celebrity, Yannick "YnkSpotX30". An online millionaire who hadn't met a single person's eye since he sat down, and didn't now.

"Thought you were off with the fairies," Yannick joked in a Scandinavian accent, massive Adam's apple bobbing. Pax blanched at the expression. By pure chance, he'd broached the exact subject she was avoiding thinking about.

Part of her *wanted* to lose, to be away with the fairies. Her Fae friend Letty was out there unaccounted for. Sam Ward from the Ministry of Environmental Energy had failed to make any inroads with the Fae Transitional City; no one knew what the Fae were planning behind their closed doors, nor if they had any idea themselves what had become of Letty. Last located at the scene of a massacre, no doubt caused by Lightgate. No doubt something Letty tried to stop.

What the fuck was Pax doing? Mulling over cards while her friend might be dead –

Yannick continued, "Champion material, she is. Representing for you, girls."

Pax frowned, drawn back into the room. Yannick was addressing his fans, who offered appreciative hoots. The group gathered at the rail comprised spotty, bespectacled guys and glamorous blonds, none much older than twenty. Except one. Catching her eye, Pax half-rose from her seat.

Holly Barton, penned in by younger women, smartly presented with her short bob of hair and ironed blouse, didn't share the mood. She waved with an awkward *not-sure-what-I'm-doing-here* smile. Pax's heart skipped – did Holly bear bad news: another kidnapping, a Fae attack, something worse? She excused herself from the table and pulled Holly aside. "What are you doing here?"

"Joining the zeitgeist, apparently," Holly said, jostling to get free from Yannick's fans. "How long has poker been a spectator sport? I have no idea what everyone's watching – were they impressed that you *lost* a hand?"

Pax almost smirked, but the ill-feeling remained. "Holly, is something up?"

"What? Oh." Holly threw a look back towards the main entrance, the gilded double doors barely visible through the bustle. "Grace wanted to come, but I called and they wouldn't let a teenager in. I told her we'd only be distracting you –"

"Why would Grace want to come?" Pax guided Holly away from the crowds.

"For support, of course," Holly said. "Though Grace shouldn't be walking anyway. Which Diz isn't helping with, jaunting about like his ankle was never broken. Thank you, miracle glowing liquid. And where are *your* family, your friends?"

"The guys I play with would find this game too rich or too public." Thankfully. "But you're not *really* here to cheer me on, are you?" Pax could buy it from Holly's daughter, or the wayward young vagrant Rufaizu, who the Barton family had temporarily taken charge of, but Holly was no cheerleader.

"Well," Holly said, cagily, "you've not answered our calls."

Pax offered a guilty smile; Holly didn't sound entirely serious. In the two days since they'd all escaped the threat of gun-toting fairies, no one could blame Pax for being a little on the quiet side. She had imagined the Bartons, like her, had mostly been sleeping and talking evasively with Ministry agents. Only, where Pax had swindled a ticket to this tournament, they'd had the responsibility of house-training Rufaizu.

"Seeing you here, I'm guessing you're convinced we're safe," Holly continued. "You're not suffering from" – she waved a hand to indicate Pax's body – "you know?"

"Period pains?"

Holly's face shifted incredulously. "What – why would –"

"No." Pax moved closer, lowering her voice. "I've not been suffering from any weird side effects. And we've been out, Sam and me, checking some old locations where Darren saw the blue screens. I didn't feel anything."

Holly's expression was sceptical. The Bartons, like Sam Ward, wanted to believe Ordshaw's Sunken City had given Pax some kind of superpowers. Rufaizu called it the Bright Veins, the universal life energy that Pax had seen glowing under her skin. She *had* felt the force of the blue screens, the two-dimensional creatures responsible for the monsters – responsible for everything – when they manipulated energy. But not since she'd killed the grugulochs, their totem. Her brief trip to underpasses and grim alleys with Sam Ward had confirmed the screens had gone into hiding.

"But the Ministry don't know –" Holly started, conspiratorially.

"They don't know *anything*," Pax said. "Only Sam knows. I'm not giving the Ministry an excuse to dissect me. Being accountable to you guys is scary enough." A cheer rose behind them, distracting Pax. Her chips would be dwindling. Good cards might be passing by. "Holly. What's really bothering you?"

Holly cleared her throat. "Actually, you'll be happy to hear it, I think. We've every intention of lifting some responsibility from your shoulders. Diz and Rufaizu have been getting ideas, about making up for the work they did under the blue screens' trickery. They want a second chance. Down in the tunnels."

"You . . ." Pax trailed off, stunned. And Holly wasn't scathingly brushing the idea aside? She had come for Pax's blessing. "You're not serious?"

"It's not ideal," Holly said, "but we discussed it, at length. And I had a rudimentary chat with Sam. We're all in this now, aren't we? It's our city we're talking about. We can't turn the volume up on the *Bake Off* and pretend it's not happening. My husband coped down there drunk, I expect he can do it sober. With help. You've shown everyone how important a fresh perspective is."

Pax was quiet. Of course, Sam had pestered her about going back underground, so why wouldn't she ask the Bartons, too? "I just wanted to get out alive. Holly –"

"Between you and Sam, we can get some licences to roam or something. I don't see it being a problem. I wanted to see where you stood, though. From here, you look ready to move on."

Pax shook her head. "It's not that, I needed to –"

"That wasn't a judgement. It means it can't be all that bad. Otherwise you'd have felt something, wouldn't you?"

Pax gave her a worried look. Thankful, if she was honest. If the Bartons helped the MEE, she might not have to. If she let these hapless fools risk their lives instead of her . . .

Holly's phone vibrated in a pocket, which she gave an annoyed frown. She frowned deeper as she checked the screen. "Unknown number – could be work. I called in sick."

"Go ahead, I oughta get back, anyway." Pax hurried out a conclusion: "And thanks for coming, Holly – if you think going back down there's a good idea, then, sure. Rather you than me."

Holly nodded and went to answer as Pax turned. The caller spoke so sharply it made her stop: "No time for your shit, Holly, pass me to Pax."

"Excuse me –"

The little, familiar voice gave Pax a light thrill, and when Letty insisted, "Now! Now!" she was ready with her hand out to take the phone.

"You're alive! Where are you?" Pax asked.

"With some fucking nerd. Well, maybe not a *fucking* nerd. We've only got a minute – where are *you*?"

"What? Why only a minute? They said you were at the FTC."

"I still am. Have you seen Lightgate?"

"No – I – I'm in the WPT, but we –"

"Playing *poker*? No, that's good – might convince the Fae you're done. At least as far as the Ministry's concerned. Look, the FTC is on lockdown and I can't leave. They're saying our people are hunting Fae expats to keep things quiet, some serious isolationist shit going on, scared of human corruption."

"What? But the Ministry are trying to reach out to your people – no one's talking."

A pause from Letty. "That's our governor fucking around. But there's Fae who disagree with her. This egghead who I'm with wants to talk –"

"Ten seconds!" another voice said, somewhere behind Letty.

"Fuck." She rushed out the rest. "This egghead thinks we can start talks, but we'll need to figure out how. I'll call back, okay? Keep your head down. Crush that game."

"Letty, if you're –" Pax started, but the call cut off. She found herself breathless with excitement just from hearing the fairy's voice. Alive. But trapped? With Fae everywhere in danger? Didn't matter, she was *alive*.

Holly took the phone back, regarding it like it was soiled. "Why was she calling on *my* phone? How did she get my number?"

"They do that," Pax said, unable to stop smiling. "Guess she wanted to avoid direct contact? Or didn't know I got a new phone – who cares – this is amazing – she's okay. And she has help." Pax checked the room around them. "She knew we were together."

"Indeed," Holly said, looking violated.

"I'm sorry. That was – Christ. I'm doubly happy you came now."

"I'm happy for you, too," Holly murmured, uncertainly. "A little surprising, that's all. The Ministry insisted we were clear of the Fae, they gave us devices to alert us of them. They *said* we were safe."

Pax didn't answer that. The Ministry was anything but infallible. She turned on the spot, taking in the casino anew. Invigorated where before she'd been distracted. Her friend was alive and she would hear from her again soon, *surely*. In the meantime, yeah – she needed to crush this tournament.

3

Sam Ward crept down a spiral stairwell with her Maglite held high, creating little splashes with each step. What liquid collected down here? Did she want to know? At the bottom of the stairs – fifty or a hundred feet below ground? – her torchlight barely penetrated the gloom. No side doors, only a long walk. She resisted the urge to look back. Something might appear if she turned. And her breath was too loud, she hated it.

He'll meet you at the end of the hall. That's what the email said.

London hadn't bothered to mention the hall was a terrifying gauntlet of the imagination. Punishment or a test? Sam Ward, desk jockey – if she's scared down here, how can she manage the Ordshaw Ministry of Environmental Energy?

Sam swallowed. Absolutely she could. In the two days since Deputy Director Mathers' (brutal) death, she'd whipped her staff into a storm of efficiency. You wouldn't know the Ministry's staff numbers had been cut by almost half. Or that their ruling body, the Raleigh Commission, was inert, under investigation for corruption. And Sam had got Pax on board, a woman worth half a dozen, even if they had only taken baby steps towards exploring the Sunken City together.

The light caught the tunnel's end: a riveted door suitable for detaining psychopaths. *The end of the hall* clearly meant *in whatever death-den lay beyond.* The door shrieked open onto a glare of light. It revealed a broad space with brick walls and pillars, with a vaulted ceiling divided by rib-like supports. There was another door in the far wall, and smaller ones to one side. Fluorescent lights buzzed overhead, and at the centre sat a single desk. He was sitting there.

Sam cleared her throat as she approached. He didn't look up, stooped over a mobile phone. "Hello? I'm Sam Ward, Acting Deputy Director."

The phone looked tiny in his hands. The man was built like a golem, square all over and far too big for the desk and chair. He finished typing as Sam considered making a leading statement. *They sent you from London* was ridiculous – as if there was any other possibility.

The man placed the phone aside and sat back. His eyes ran over her, feet to head, his wide mouth open in an expression somewhere between disgust and confusion. His hair was slicked back from an already high hairline, accentuating the size and squareness of his forehead, and his deeply unfashionable wire-frame aviator spectacles added to the overall effect of a human brick. Finally he said, "No."

He kept staring, mouth open – his default expression?

"Excuse me?" Sam said, when it seemed he wasn't going to continue.

"No," he repeated. A low Yorkshire accent. "You are no longer the acting deputy director. I am."

Sam tensed. She'd hoped the choice of location indicated something that needed her attention, not a usurper.

"Wayne Obrington," he said. "Special Agent to them in London. *Your* new chief." He stood and Sam took an involuntary step back. Obrington looked like the worst kind of bouncer; one whose awful glasses invited challengers. Here to obliterate Sam's sensible plans in favour of Management boondoggling. He turned to face the door at the rear. "Come with me."

He marched to the door, opened it and stepped through.

As introductions went, it was an odd one.

Sam hesitantly followed. The dull, off-green glow of old lights revealed another long corridor with an arched ceiling and sweating brickwork. Older and danker than the Sunken City Sam knew.

"It's not the Sunken City," Obrington said, reading her thoughts as he kept walking ahead. "Old post-sorting station, built by a tea shipping company in the 1890s. Been vacant about thirty years. Up to here, anyway." He indicated another door, heavy wood. "*That* is a Sunken City entry point, and it's been making strange noises."

He heaved it open, with effort, and Sam looked around him onto another spiral staircase. They were on the north-west side of the city, while according to the MEE's latest readings the horde of monsters was far south; it should be safe, but the darkness looked decidedly uninviting.

"I was pottering about before you arrived," Obrington said, stepping aside. "Kept hearing a tapping. Thought I'd wait for you to investigate properly." He paused, both of them listening. Nothing. "You armed?"

Sam shook her head. This was *surely* a test, seeing how she performed in the field.

"I've read your reports," Obrington said. "Spreading your limited resources thin, aren't you? Two field agents active at a time, and one of them busy sealing access points?"

"I only *had* –" Sam began to explain, but he didn't let her.

"I get it. A couple days spent closing our least-used doors and we cut future patrols by half, without too much impact on our ability to get underground." There was a sound in the stairwell. Something tapped against the stone. Obrington ignored it. "Except while you do that, places like *this* aren't being guarded."

"We've got sensors," Sam said uncertainly. Support always picked up movement near access points. Had he told them to keep this one quiet, to surprise her?

Something scraped against the stone steps. Then a heavy footfall. Something coming *up* the steps. A pause as whatever it was scented the air. It shrieked, shaking dust from the walls; an avian cry followed by a sudden patter of ascending feet.

"We should –" Sam said, twisting to Obrington, but the stare he gave the shadows stilled her, saying he would not be undermined by some monster. Sam's eyes darted back to the doorway and the charging noise – if it was a test, she was surely safe, shouldn't show fear –

The thing launched out of the darkness with reaching claws, and with a short scream Sam ducked back, hands up. A gunshot made her wince, followed by the loud crash of something big and hard hitting the wall. She looked up again. Melting from the top step into the darkness was the lower body of an animal with thick legs, skin marked by patchy scales, jointed like a horse and finishing in spiky claws. A ravisher: a three-legged, wall-climbing creature with an acidic tongue. The shadows hid its thin-haired head of mandibles and jagged teeth. Obrington prodded it with a shoe, pistol at his side, as its acrid smell invaded Sam's nostrils. She wasn't sure whether to vomit or flee.

Obrington said casually, "You're unarmed, Ward, you oughta have run."

Sam straightened up, heart pounding in her ears. He'd shot it like it was nothing. They should *still* run, lock these doors, call on Support for an explanation and Operations for a clear up. "It shouldn't have been here."

"Likely to be more of them? What is it?"

"Um." Sam struggled for the MEE's exact faux-Latin wording. "*Ultra* – no, *ultro rapientis*. Commonly called a ravisher. They're solitary – only a handful down here." Trivia studied for Ministry exams flooded back to Sam. The ravisher's existence had only been confirmed in 2012. Before then, everyone had believed it to be one of Apothel's inventions. Like the blue screens.

"Good. We'll get someone to clear it up later." Obrington pushed the door closed, jolting the creature's limbs out of the way. He tramped back the way they'd come. Sam stared dumbstruck at the closed door. Heart not quite still. Solitary as the ravisher was, it still belonged near the horde, following the *praelucente*, Ordshaw's great energy parasite, currently on the other side of the city.

"Back in the office, if you please, Ward," Obrington called out, already re-entering the big chamber. That jarred Sam from her concerns.

"*Office*?"

"Complete with plumbing and electricity, all we need."

Sam raced to catch up, throwing one last glance back to the stairwell door and the horror it hid. "Wait. You intend to work down here?"

"Me and everyone else. Exciting, isn't it?"

"But . . ." Sam trailed off. Not only was it far too close to the Sunken City monsters, but there was zero natural light, or air. It couldn't be healthy.

"The word" – Obrington jabbed a blocky thumb upwards, indicating the city – "is we've got rogue Fae and unstable creatures on our hands. This is the safest place in the city. No Fae underground. *Supposedly* no buggers coming this far out of the tunnels." Sam bit her lip. The ravisher had come far enough. But he said, "I've been down here an hour or more and that thing didn't come beyond the door. It *is* secure here. We're circling the waggons, understand?"

Sam said nothing. Pot plants and ergonomic chairs weren't going to make this place comfortable, and she definitely didn't feel secure.

"Sealing off access points is a fine idea," he went on. "Cutting back patrols is *not*. Considering that this grugulochs thing you took down supposedly controlled the *praelucente* –"

"It didn't control it, it *used* the *praelucente*," Sam corrected. "The grugulochs was merely diverting energy from it."

"You make a habit of interrupting people, Ward? No? I'll continue, shall I?"

Sam felt her face flush.

"Considering this thing, now dead, *had an influence* on your monsters, and we had a great beast tear apart your old place of work, the Sunken City warrants clearing out. Yet you're not enacting Protocol 38."

Protocol 38. The plan to purge the Sunken City of its uniquely vile creatures. Particularly the *praelucente* itself. The Ministry had believed it benevolent, so their plan to remove it was entirely theoretical and relied on unproven weapons. Sam had prepared an answer as to why they must wait. Not the truth, which was that she and Pax feared attacking the horde would drive the blue screens into deeper hiding, but something close to it. "I can explain my thinking –"

"Save it for your therapist." Obrington didn't give her a chance. "Hotshot young department head unsettles decades of stability *and* stokes a conflict with the Fae. Doesn't want to make things worse. Sound right?"

"I didn't –"

"You didn't do anything wrong," he said, surprising Sam into silence. He waited for that to sink in, then continued. "But the accepted opinion on Ordshaw is that you leave it well alone. You don't poke it. People itching to poke it, they get moved somewhere that *needs* poking. Mathers should've transferred you two years ago."

"He was effective in his way," Sam replied, only polite now he was dead.

"He was a musty fart with no imagination. But since you *did* start poking, we now need to draw this fiasco to its conclusion. You're scared of following through, which leaves *me* sitting in that chair." Obrington indicated the desk. The chair behind it was a small plastic thing, suitable for a school hall. Did he carry it and the desk down here himself? "You're not an idiot, are you, Ward?"

Sam stalled – trap question? Her hesitation cost her the chance to respond.

"You're gonna be my right hand, because your innovation is bleeding useful. In fact, I'll de facto let you run this show. Give you a chance to prove your mettle. But you're gonna assume I know what's best. Understand?"

Sam replied quickly, "Are you going to –"

"No. See." Obrington drew this out. "I didn't ask for questions, did I? I asked *do you understand*?"

His rocky disposition challenged her to answer carefully. Not voice the nagging thought that poor communication had got them in this mess.

"Yes or no."

"Yes," Sam said, with just a little defiance.

"Yes *what*?" Obrington pressed.

"Yes, *sir*."

"I was going for *yes, I understand*. But that'll do. We'll keep at what you've started, but manoeuvre towards Protocol 38. Once we're better staffed. I'll have more agents here in a few days. Meantime, talk to me about your proposals to use these pesky civilians."

The Bartons, an idea Sam had already relayed to Management. She said, "I'm already working with them. They've been cleared, we can –"

"Some of them have been cleared. Pax Kuranes raises a big question mark."

"We're lucky to have her," Sam rushed out. "Her perspective is refreshing – free from Ministry prejudice."

Obrington's eyes bulged behind those glasses. "You sleeping with her?"

"What?" Sam exclaimed. "No – I'm not *gay* –"

"Try not to sound so offended. We'd *all* do best to avoid prejudice. But nine out of ten potential recruits, it's an agent trying to get in someone's pants."

"That's not true." Sam stopped, flashing on Cano Casaria. The man who'd recruited her certainly made enough awkward passes, culminating in a narrowly avoided violent outburst recently. He'd gone off the rails chasing Pax for the same reason, hadn't he? Obrington's claim might be a little true.

"Pax has connections to the Fae," Obrington said. "Making her suspect. Especially as *you've* not managed to follow up with them since the attacks?"

Sam paused again. This was a bad start. She had been careful about exactly what she'd said to Management about Pax, and her unique senses, aware that her superiors might take rash action against either her or the Sunken City. Obrington's comments were giving her no confidence that she could safely share Pax's full situation with him. Partly to steer the conversation, partly because she had even less confidence that the fairy situation was under control, Sam said, "I hoped London might've heard from the Fae. Management kept such information from me in the past."

Obrington regarded Sam like he'd stepped in crap. "London hasn't heard a thing. This is *your* problem. These fairies took our weapons? All those men dead? And you can bet the Fae aren't sitting idle. Holding off following through there too, aren't we? Haven't you got gasses that could kill a Fae colony?"

"You're not serious? Our priority is diplomacy."

"Purging the Fae would sure make it easier to focus on the Sunken City."

"Absolutely not," Sam said suddenly, and braced herself for a scolding. He glared, waiting. "With respect, the Fae can be talked to. They can *help* us. And enacting Protocol 38 would be reckless considering our current lack of understanding." She gave another look towards the rear door, picturing that errant ravisher. Were there others like it, creatures lurking unchecked?

"We're not performing an academic study," Obrington said. "We're securing this city so I can go home to my tabby in Pelham and *you* can maybe take this chair." He rattled the little plastic thing at the desk. What a reward. "Protocol 38 is the –"

"We've been manipulated," Sam insisted, quickly, before her courage failed her. "We have no idea if our weapons will work on the *praelucente* or just piss it off. But we do know the Fae had a weapon that hurt it, a weapon we ourselves lost, outside their community. We can't move until we properly understand what we're dealing with. If Mathers had listened to me, he might still be alive – if Management listened to me, this city might already be secure."

She stopped to catch her breath, like she'd run a mile. Face impassive, Obrington let out a thoughtful croak. "And you think we can afford to hesitate?"

"Haste is far more dangerous," Sam said, finally sounding confident.

"Well. I'm not gonna be the fool that disdains the woman who dethroned the Raleigh Commission. And I *want* to believe you know what you're doing, so I don't have to *stay* in this bleeding town. So here's this. I'll give you all the rope you need to hang yourself, Ward, but only as much time as it takes to get our pieces in place for 38. Sound fair?"

Sam merely stared for a moment. It almost sounded like a compromise. "As long as it's enough time to revise our novisan scans. Our methods are time-consuming –"

"Ah, the scans," Obrington said. "Here starts a lesson. I can bring in new equipment, and new people, to speed things along, but if I do that, are you gonna accept responsibility for them?"

Ominous and ambiguous. Why shouldn't she? Was it another test? Sam nodded slowly. "That's what I'm here for, isn't it?"

The slightly slanted edge of a smirk on his face warned her it was a mistake. Another part of the test, though, sowing doubts?

"Right you are, Ward. Let's get started."

4

Fresko watched the townhouse opposite, focusing on the wall-mounted air-conditioning unit. The sound of stuff being smashed drifted up from within. It had to be Stabilisers, damaging shit for the sake of it. There wasn't anything in the Fae hideout that'd indicate where Fresko and Mix had gone; the pricks were only sending a message. The pair got the message clear enough from the windowsill opposite, having taken cover after hearing the disturbance.

"Three of them," Mix counted. "We can block the entrance and gun them down."

"You know what happens to people dumb enough to cross Stabilisers?" Fresko said.

"Ain't *they* already crossed us?" Mix grunted. The grizzled veteran looked more grizzled than ever, bruises still visible from the hiding their former chief, Letty, had given him. He'd been itching for another fight ever since, and it was only a matter of time before they got one.

This was their second den the Stabilisers had busted. And from the word on the Fae wire, it wasn't just them. Fae expats all over the city were in for a rough time on account of Letty's mess. If you weren't in the FTC, you didn't belong in Ordshaw, they were saying. Even those that never did a thing to anyone, or those, like Fresko and Mix, that had actively followed Val's orders. After kidnapping a human and trying to cover it up, they were especially high on the Stabiliser shit list.

"Got them!" a voice shouted from above. "Out here!"

Shit – another shape, a dark figure on the gutter of the adjacent roof. One hand to his ear, activating a radio, the other resting a gun against his hip. Mix drew a pistol as Fresko spotted another guy rising from beyond the A/C unit. The shadows inside scrambled for the exit. Fresko pulled Mix back. "Too many, come on!"

The Stabiliser above fired; a sharp crack and the bullet hit brickwork a few inches off. Cursing, Mix twisted to join Fresko in speeding away. Another gunshot zipped past. Fresko called out, "Split up – meet at the bridge!"

Mix peeled away, sticking close to the building fronts, as Fresko dived low, down through a treetop, deftly avoiding branches. A Stabiliser wasn't far behind, radioing sharp reports: "On him – left – through the trees."

Fresko rolled around the trunk, doubling back, and caught a glimpse of his pursuer doing the same. Fast. Human cars passed in the road below. Fresko banked out of cover and flew over a moving van. He turned suddenly, darting alongside the vehicle. The Stabiliser shot overhead. Sensing he'd made a mistake, the guy turned in the air. Fresko pushed himself against the van for support and swung the rifle off his shoulder. He fired and the Stabiliser moved to the side. Missed, but Fresko followed him with the scope while keeping pace with the van, fired another shot as the guy dived behind a bin. Fresko dropped down, under the van's carriage, and watched for a passing car – flew for that one. He caught hold of a metal fixing and hung underneath, bouncing over the road. Checking one way then another. They hadn't seen him, had they?

The car carried him away, turning and continuing up the road. No sign of Fae following. Fresko let himself breathe. There had been a half-dozen of them, at least. Not thugs bullying people out of town, but a bloody death squad.

Another couple of blocks and Fresko ventured out from his cover. He flew up, higher and higher, to get an aerial view of the city. Looked clear. He drifted back towards central Ordshaw, aiming for the river, slow and cautious. Narrowing his eyes, he spotted another Fae converging on his position. Mix had made it. He gave Fresko a brief salute, and Fresko indicated their destination ahead. Midway across the August Bridge he dropped onto a tower, skipping a few steps to regain his balance before checking the sky.

Mix stumbled to an even less graceful stop, a pistol in each hand. "I don't like running."

"You hit?" Fresko asked. His companion's glare said it was insulting to ask.

"We could've taken them," Mix snarled.

"You and what army?" Fresko replied, scoping the central riverbank with his rifle. Plenty of humans, joggers, suits on phones, delivery boys. You couldn't see Fae at this distance, if there were any. "We'll hit Farling next, if they haven't been there, too. Pick up some shit, make for the suburbs till this blows over."

Mix rubbed his nose with a fist and holstered one pistol. "More running? To the *suburbs*? Might as well ditch Ordshaw completely. We want to take charge, Fresko, for fuck's sake. Trade one of those human bitches to Valoria – the poker player – gotta be worth something."

It was a bad idea; the sort that got them mixed up in all this to start with. But the comment drew Fresko's attention to the north bank, where Featherback Casino sat. A crowd was gathered outside, half styled by wealth, the other half with no style at all.

"Oh no." A voice made them both spin. "The Ministry are sure to be watching *her*."

The newcomer stood unfazed by their guns aimed at her chest. She wasn't a Stabiliser, though. The bloodstains on her slender white suit were offset by her bright, toothy smile, the grand mane of side-swept hair, and the gleaming polish of her holstered pistols. Even the sling holding her left arm looked stylish. Lightgate. Not just well-presented, but capable of reaching them unseen, even with all this empty space in every direction.

"Fuck me." Mix exhaled.

She responded with a slow drawl. "You are too old, too fat, and dress like a biker's charity sale. So no, thanks. But I have a better proposal than whatever *you're* thinking."

*

Talking to Pax had a surprisingly calming effect on Letty. So much so that she stopped berating the men gathered in her room long enough to enjoy a hit of medicinal dust while they arranged another call. It was the job of a Fae tech, Newbry, a gangly guy with long, rank hair, a big nose, and a shirt and trousers too loose to look presentable. He had a bulky laptop and smelt bad; probably enjoyed unlit rooms and animated porn. But he was evidently Edwing's resident computer whizz, having pinned down Pax via Holly Barton, and arranged a call the Stabilisers couldn't trace. He said he couldn't repeat it right away, though. Something to do with riding their signal on the back of someone else's, careful timing, concerns about Pax being watched.

Whatever – Letty could wait.

While she did, she planned ahead, most of her ideas centring on how to get a longer conversation with Pax. That seemed to be Edwing's plan, too, never mind what they might actually achieve with it. They both knew if they got to Pax without MEE or FTC interference, things would be easier. That meant directing her to another Fae exile. Letty had precious few friends left, though. Palleday?

It was late when Newbry announced he was moderately confident he could put a call directly through to Pax's phone. He had traced her to her apartment, back after her day in the casino, and connected them with Flynt and Edwing watching. As soon as Pax answered, Letty started, "Big day, champ? The website says you're still in, 84 out of 121."

"Yeah," Pax said. "I'm doing what I can. Hard to feel really safe yet. Are *you*?"

Letty tried to hide a smile. This big idiot, worrying for everyone. "Sure, and I've got some Grade A dust that makes the pain go away. Don't worry, when I get out of here we'll sort out your poker game, get rich on it, buy a mansion, booze until the early hours."

She could practically hear Pax smiling, too. "I'm game. How do we get you out?"

"Well, there's the sticker. Sneaking out is next to impossible, they're saying, which leaves dealing with the lockdown itself. Bringing in fucking Lightgate is option one. Securing the Dispenser would be another starter, force Val to act, once she can't deny the weapon's still out there."

"Wait. You don't know the Dispenser's in there?"

Letty froze. "Come again?"

"The Dispenser, your people have it."

"The fuck they do. Val hasn't said shit about it."

"You were there, outside the FTC, when all those Ministry men got gunned down, weren't you? They had it with them – your people grabbed their weapons before the clear-up crew got there."

"By leopard's ghosts," Letty huffed. "How the hell did you stop the Ministry dropping bombs on us?"

"By opening their eyes," Pax said. "The force behind all this had control of the

Ministry, had been manipulating them for years. Maybe the blue screens got to your people, too?"

"Hold up," Letty said. "You figured that how? You tracked that Blue Angel down?"

Pax took a breath. "Shit. We got time for the long story?"

Letty gave Newbry a look and the technician shook his head. "Better keep it short."

"The blue screens themselves were the problem. They absorb novisan – the energy driving the Sunken City, the same being drained from people – to create things, like the liquid glo, or the monsters. One changed the Ministry's documents, pretending to be a guy called Lord Asquith. Your leader might know him. I'm certain your people can bridge gaps in our understanding here. Your Fae dust, for example."

"You want –" Letty started, but a bang above cut them off. Someone hammering on a hatch higher in the building. She frowned at Flynt, and he in turn looked at Newbry.

The technician tapped at his computer with mounting concern. "There's a trace –"

"Oh you shit," Letty hissed. Another bang came with a muffled shout as Flynt ran into the corridor. "Got to go, Pax. You need Fae help, you won't get it from the FTC."

"Move!" Flynt returned, waving hurriedly.

"– your last warning!" a man's voice bellowed above.

"What's going on, Letty?" Pax asked. "We need to talk –"

"Yeah. Go to Palleday," Letty barked. "Sandwich shop on Dresden Street – our people won't touch him – and watch out for Lightgate!"

She hung up and Newbry closed his computer to run for the door.

"Go, Letty!" Edwing urged. "I'll hold them off!"

Something weighty cracked above, the intruders' voices getting louder as they broke in. Flynt opened a floor-hatch, guiding Newbry down as the hatch above rattled against a lock. "Open up in the name of the FTC!"

Letty climbed through the trapdoor as Edwing shouted, "This property belongs to the Informations Department! We have every right to –"

"Break it!" another man shouted. As the hatch slammed behind Letty, she heard the one above being smashed. Flynt pulled her away as men descended on Edwing.

"You trust Lightgate?" Mix asked, leaning against an upturned tuna tin littered with empty beer bottles. A table they'd used for years, soon to be discarded forever, once they ransacked the Farling den for ammo and drinks. "Swaggers in out of the blue claiming she can rally exiles? A thousand to one she's as crooked as Valoria."

Fresko didn't bother responding. Lightgate had given them instructions to round up whatever friends they had left in Ordshaw for some kind of rebellion, and Mix hadn't kicked up a stink then. Only now that they were alone, getting ready to do as she asked, did he get bold.

"Us getting our mates together while she does *what* exactly?"

"Drinks herself into a stupor," Fresko said. He knew Lightgate liked to delegate; either to get other people in trouble, or to buy time to lose what little mind she had boozing. She could tick off both the boxes with them. Chasing other Fae allies would put them in the Stabilisers' crosshairs, keeping her safe. But you didn't say no to Lightgate. They'd have to bring her someone or she'd gut them.

Tossing bullets into a bag, Mix complained, "When did we lose our dicks? One bitch after another telling us what to do – Letty, Val, Lightgate. Fucking bitches."

Fresko couldn't deny that. Human bitches, too, if you included the poker player. He paused, looking at his old tea-light candle seat, the wax warmed into just the right shape for a Fae rear. They used to be comfortable here. It was Pax who had taken all this from them, wasn't it?

"The fuck you thinking?" Mix demanded, before dragging heavily on his beer. "Always fucking thinking. Never sharing it. Getting some other genius plan?"

"Regretting where we are, is all," Fresko said.

Mix's fist tightened on his bottle like he wanted to smash it. "Yeah. Well, Ordshaw still beats being halfway round the world drinking fermented rice or some shit."

"Better than never drinking again. I got no desire to take a bullet."

Rather than respond, Mix rummaged in his pockets, searching for what was left of his Fae dust. He snorted some greedily, powdering his face in exhales of hungry breath, then rammed the rest into his beer. Maybe it'd calm him down.

"You done?" Fresko asked. "Got any ideas for who we go to now?"

Mix shook his head, focusing on his high.

"We wanna hedge our bets. Go someplace that looks like we're doing Lightgate a favour without putting our necks on the line. Not somewhere the Stabilisers will be watching, or someone that might actually join up with Lightgate."

"One of the dead gangs? Hooky in New Thornton, he moved on six months ago."

"Too obvious," Fresko said. They needed someone more or less hidden. A forgotten Fae. "What about fucking Palleday?"

5

Cano Casaria exuded nonchalance as he entered 14 Greek Street, the Ministry's drab shared office block and his supposed base of operations. Things had been hectic since the various disasters they'd faced, so he didn't fault Management for failing to call him in; they probably assumed an agent of his calibre would return on his own initiative, anyway. But enough time had passed, while things were likely racing ahead, and his supposed injuries were all but gone. Granted, his toe was never coming back, but it wasn't like it *hurt*. He climbed the stairs to the sixth floor, since the shattered remnants of the lift were hidden behind caution tape, and he put on a smile for them all.

There was no one there to meet him.

An old fax machine sat at the centre of the room, like a shrine to offices past, disconnected and partly dismantled. The device Pax claimed the blue screens had used to control the MEE, with faxes supposedly from Lord Asquith. Now, a husk of ancient electronics, dissected and abandoned.

Everything else was gone, as though it had fled from the taint of this shameful object. Not even the reception desk remained. Unattached cables stuck out of the floor, dents dotted the carpet where desks and chairs had sat, and discoloured squares showed where monitors once hung.

Casaria frowned into the unlit gloom. He wandered towards one of the side offices. Through the partition, he saw it was empty too, but went in anyway. In the middle of her office, Casaria considered simply calling Sam Ward. He had failed to force a chance encounter outside her apartment, most likely because she was working all night, and now he had missed her packing up and leaving. But calling reeked of desperation. It was her place to call him. She knew he was an asset.

Casaria inhaled deeply, searching for inspiration.

He could call someone else. Landon, or the Ministry hotline. Merely ask for the new location. But those lower-level minions would delight in thwarting him. He could hear their remarks: *no one told you the new address?* No, thanks.

Hands back in his pockets, he considered another option. He belonged in the field. That's where he'd find his people.

Buzzing from the drama of Letty's call, and the prospect of tracking down this Palleday, Pax had slept poorly. Then she'd woken up too late to go after the Fae before the WPT resumed. She hated putting it off, but she couldn't throw away her tournament. Her chance at creating a life for when this drama blew over. A mansion for her and Letty? She settled into the game with her chips low and a niggling itch to be elsewhere. The lunch break was already closing in when a chance to make a stand came: she hit bottom two pair on the flop, tens and nines – good enough to throw her meagre chips at. Except the opponent ahead, another odorous online player with buck teeth, bet first.

And then she felt them.

For the first time since encountering the grugulochs, Pax was hit by the movements of the screens. She winced and put a hand to her head, pretending she was struggling with the decision to call the bet. But something throbbed under her skin, a pulse of shifting energy, somewhere far away. Beneath the city. Underground, all together – clustered as one. There could be a handful of them, thirty or a hundred.

South of the city.

But – something else – directly north –

The feeling passed and Pax sat back with relief. She needed to tell Ward, the Bartons, anyone. Buck-teeth goaded, "Don't faint on us, yeah?"

Pax tuned him out, searching for the screens. Ignoring arrogant men of all ages was something she'd mastered years ago. She wasn't so used to picking up on disturbances in the world's energy. It had to be something she could use. A sense, an understanding, that could open a gate to the Fae. If she could tap into this, she could do something *useful*.

But they were gone.

"You got top pair," the man guessed. "Not enough to call, not for your tournament."

Blinking to reality, she quickly reconsidered her cards. They were good enough to push in on a bet, if not to call. Sensing the screens made it tempting to just go with the bad move and get away from here, to figure her mad feelings out. Throw away her shot at a big cash injection.

"Do I need to call the clock on her?" her opponent asked, and Pax shoved her chips in, already half out of her seat. Get this done, go find Letty's friend, call Ward, *something*. Murmurs of interest rushed through the crowd. The internet guy looked disgusted as he turned over top pair himself – with an ace kicker. The other players gave agonised groans or impressed gasps at Pax's hand: good, but at risk. The dealer brought out an ace on the turn. The hotshot laughed like he'd planned that sick luck and the audience's heart broke, but Pax was ready to run. A miracle ten came next. Full House. She'd doubled up.

Buck-teeth jumped up, demanding to know how in hell she could make that call – he could've had trips, a better two pair, anything. Pax stared in disbelief. Twice the chance, now, to win big. She shook herself out of it, and let people congratulate her as she left anyway. The extra chips would buy her time. She needed to move.

In the hall, trying to calm herself, she brought up Sam Ward's number. At the very least she could get a handle on what had just happened. But she stopped dead as a man caught her eye. Walked out of one bad feeling right into a monumentally worse one. *Him? Now?*

Stacey Monroe was flanked by two big guys in American football jerseys. With his shaved head, thick woollen suit and heavy gold rings, he belonged in a garage peddling boxes of contraband. Not here, reminding Pax he'd almost made her witness to a homicide four days ago. Monroe's men had captured and tortured Casaria, a government agent, pursuing an interest in Ordshaw's tunnels. She didn't know exactly what Monroe did, but she knew it was nothing good. His head didn't reach the other men's shoulders, but he was dominating their conversation, rough accent audible from a distance. "Trust me, I'll take care of you."

Monroe and his men weren't on the tournament roster, Pax had checked. But there had always been a chance they'd show up. She had a plan: back slowly, discreetly into the shadows. As she took one step back, he saw her and his round face stretched into a lurid grin. Who was she kidding. He might've come deliberately for her. His hands went up to pat his companions. "Here's a local legend you might get a chance to play with."

He sauntered towards her with the men, square-headed Americans of the most cliched variety. Pax stood rooted to the spot.

"The inimitable Pax Kuranes, one of Ordshaw's finest. Sits on all the best games in town. I heard you made fast friends with Dutch McRory, you planning on bringing him to the Baudelaire Club once you're crowned champ here?"

Pax opened her mouth but no words came out. Just as well, because the words were: *last time I saw you was in a torture chamber*.

"Meet Hugh and Brutus," Monroe continued, like she wasn't frozen in awkwardness. "Brothers outta Houston, you believe that? Flew all the way over for this. I'm reckoning they'll make back some of that airfare in the big game. You *will* be there, won't you, love?"

It didn't sound like a threat, but it wasn't a request either. Monroe's eyes said *we've got unfinished business*. And it stank because if he'd ingratiated himself with brutes like this – one even called Brutus, for crying out loud – then whatever game Monroe was peddling would be worth her while. A clear hustle.

"Sure she'll be there," Monroe decided for her, when she still hadn't spoken. "Make a bloody party of it, won't we."

The Americans were confused by her silence, but she pulled just enough sense together to hold out a hand to shake. "Hope to see you there."

Satisfied, the pair let themselves be dismissed by Monroe and wandered off talking at an unapologetic volume. "A chance to play with Dutch McRory? Are you kidding me?"

Monroe watched with amusement, like he'd just given tourists the wrong directions, before turning to Pax. He said, with no indication that it was a compliment, "Well, don't you look a picture. You know I got a monkey riding on you?"

"What?" Pax replied, a weird image springing to mind. But he meant money. A lot of money.

"Ton on you reaching the final table," he elaborated. "The rest to say you'll cash."

She said, weakly, "*Why?*"

"It's nothing." Monroe patted his chest, like she'd touched his heart somehow. "I got faith in you, darling, that's all. Placed the bet with Lorenzo when you were two above the fold, got great odds. Lorenzo out of Ripton, know him? Didn't believe in you like I do."

"You probably should've listened to him."

"Bollocks." Monroe jabbed an authoritative finger towards her, "There's only two of our own left in the field, you know? Yourself and Wonky Gunry, and we both know Gunry used up all his luck standing out of bed this morning. You're going all the way, my girl. Make Ordshaw proud."

"And if I don't?" Pax heard the question before she'd thought it.

"You will," Monroe shrugged. "No question."

Pax gave him a conceding smile. Why not add the prospect of being accountable to a criminal's losing bet to her worries. Desperately wanting to get away, or at least change the subject, she searched the hall for inspiration. At least there was no sign of Bees or Jones, his hired goons. Last seen trying to stab Cano Casaria. She said, "Your men weren't interested in playing?"

"Ah," Monroe said. "Those boys chewed my ear off for a month about sponsoring them. But we know where the smart money's at, don't we? Come by the Baudelaire Club this evening, there's gonna be stacks on the table, substantial buy-in. Bring McRory and I'll stake you. Gratis."

It gave Pax pause. This was all wrong. He should've been angry at her for upsetting his stabby plans. Paranoid about her snitching on him, at least. But he was cheery, offering her a place at a game worth a small fortune. If he wanted to lure the world-class players, they'd be looking at five-figure buy-ins. Four-figure *hands*. "You're serious?"

"As a nun's drawers, you've earned it." Monroe put his hand on his heart again, making Pax frown. "Least I can do. And it's good business, besides."

"Mr Monroe," Pax said, carefully. Again, the words didn't come: *shouldn't we talk about what happened? You vicious bastard.*

"Apologies my dear," he said. "I'm distracting you from the tourney. Don't worry, alright? We're good, Pax. Two locals shooting at the moon, rolling over foreigners come to take advantage of our town. Kind of noble, I reckon."

Pax merely nodded, sure this was a not-so-subtle reference to his business dispute with Jamaican gangs coming into Ordshaw. Monroe, she had learnt, was patriotic in a murderous way.

He finished, like a proud uncle. "That's my girl. You're gonna play some great cards, aren't you? In there, at the Baudelaire. What do you say?"

Fuck, is what Pax thought. Already preparing to face psycho fairies and ethereal screens, now she had to weigh the patronage of a gangster against a good business opportunity. Would he even let her say no? Her eyes picked out a brass-rimmed clock above the reception counter, the second hand ticking away all the time she had for these huge problems.

"Pax." Monroe brought her attention back to him. "You know the sort of figures

I'm talking, right? Your stake in this. Don't that sound good to you?"

She frowned again. Was this something else? His way of buying her silence, or even *apologising*? Hell. She could work with that. "Sure, Mr Monroe. I'll be at your game."

6

Sam marvelled at how the new Ministry chamber had come to life. Though she couldn't quite call it an office yet. Removal men and technicians had swept in overnight, and desks, computers and monitors now lined the underground lair. Tall pot plants *had* added colour, and a ventilation system somehow kept the air moving. Everyone was in early, along with a couple of tough-looking men in dark suits: Obrington's new hires, who were being briefed on something by their resident tech expert, Dr Galler. Sam also had the very promising prospect of taking Darren Barton into the Sunken City today, to expand her surveying – which Obrington showed little interest in observing: "Your people, your problem."

In general, Obrington ignored everything to lean against his desk, thumbing through his phone and making calls. That suited Sam fine; he genuinely didn't look like he intended to stay. She might yet get the chief's chair for herself. The Support team were already turning to her for leadership, things were running smoothly. Mid-morning, there was a flurry of excited activity when the *praelucente* created a surge in novisan. The team checked for fluctuations across the city, to be sure the energy wasn't being transferred, and settled into a congratulatory atmosphere, concluding the surge was localised.

When Sam's phone rang and Pax's name came up, it felt like the cherry on the morning's cake. Besides their rather abortive visit to a handful of reported blue screen locations, during which Pax had been notably quiet, they'd had less contact than Sam hoped. But with time and space, Pax would surely come around to throw herself into the Ministry's work. Sam answered cheerily, "Pax, how's the tournament going?"

"Yeah fine," Pax replied a little shortly, sounding rushed. "About a half-hour ago, maybe more, was there a surge?"

"Yes!" Sam said. Too enthusiastic. She tried to contain the excitement, lowering her voice. "You felt it?" Overcompensated, sounding like a posh gentleman. "I mean – gosh – so it's working?"

"My magic power?" Pax said. "Did you just say *gosh*?"

Sam fumbled her phone to adopt a casual posture, even if Pax couldn't see it. "It was south of the river, between Broadplain and Tupsom, is that where you felt it?"

"I don't know exactly but they were all in one place. And they did something. You caught that? Right in the opposite direction."

"What? No." Sam scanned her colleagues, relaxed at their screens, obliviously continuing their tasks. "Our scan goes citywide now, showing the fluctuation was localised."

"Okay. Except it wasn't."

A moment of dread swept over Sam. She picked out Obrington, breathing through his mouth with an expression like his phone was insulting him. He wouldn't want to hear that their expanded surveys might be flawed. No one would want to hear that. And how could she tell him, short of subjecting Pax to a hefty Ministry investigation? But even without having proved Pax's esoteric abilities, Sam trusted there was *something* in it. She asked, "Where was it? This other . . . thing?"

"I don't know."

"But – are you tracking it now?"

"No. I'm in the middle of something else."

Not the poker; she would've said if it was that. "What sort of something?"

"I'll tell you about it later, best you not get involved yet. Look, all I know is those screens were together with the minotaur when it fed, all of them." The minotaur, her word for the *praelucente*, borrowed from the long-dead civilian, Apothel. "That's a good thing – we can round them up if we can catch it feeding. But they *used* that energy, and that's bad. At best, they've still got a screen roving separately. There's plenty worse options, though."

"But you can't pinpoint it . . ."

"North. I was in the casino, it was north of that, I can't say for sure." Pax gave it a moment's thought. "Relative to the surge? I'd guess roughly the same distance in the opposite direction. Roughly."

"I can work with that." Sam waved at a Support tech. "Pax, I'd like you to come in –"

"Not now. Not today."

"Why? At least tell me what you're doing?"

"Hanging up." And the line went dead.

Sam cursed, but put it aside, with the tech already waiting for orders. She instructed him to recheck the novisan scans to the north, then crossed the office to Obrington. Those scans wouldn't show anything; they needed to get someone out there. Obrington lowered his phone, pushed off from the desk and stared at her to ask the question: *what?*

"Could we spare a couple of agents to investigate an anomaly?" Sam asked, keeping her voice quiet so the rest of the staff wouldn't hear her meek request.

"You tell me," Obrington answered, as loud as she was soft. "We've got Vinton and Bolton sealing doors in Farling, and Marks and Lungen getting ready to hit Nothicker. Or there's your civilians, you want them investigating *anomalies*? Your initiative, your choice."

He made it sound condescending, but it *was* her call. "I think the –"

"Wrong answer."

"But you don't know –"

"Ward," he said, "that creature manipulated your office for a long time. There's gonna be plenty of anomalies. Want to hear one I discovered? Some bright spark had your pulse pistols set to the wrong frequency. Deadly, but *not* the quietest shot. Presumably based on faulty advice from your faxes. Why do you suppose that would be?"

Sam considered it. "To make us less effective culling the creatures?"

Obrington shook his head. "Guess again."

Unable to answer him correctly, Sam merely went quiet. Another Management figure appearing to know everything. If you'd care to share with the rest of us, instead of using information to puff up your own chest, perhaps we could make progress?

"What's that?" He raised an eyebrow and Sam froze.

Did she say that out loud? She shook her head to indicate she hadn't spoken.

"*My* guess," Obrington said, "is it made you *visible*. Your master manipulator was using faxes to communicate, right? It didn't have access to our computers. Didn't necessarily see all that was going on. But it could've picked up on specific signals, like the right energy gun frequencies, to watch your men at work. What do you think?"

That suggested the blue screens sensed energy in a different way to them. Beyond their understanding. About par for the course. Sam said, "Well. We're doing a full review to avoid mistakes like that. But it's not enough."

"No. Good thing I'm here, isn't it? Come with me, there's someone we've got to meet –"

"Can it wait a moment, sir?" Sam blurted out. "This anomaly, it's a *specific* hunch. Related to the recent surge. It's time-sensitive."

Obrington gave her his usual open-mouthed glare, inviting an explanation. She wasn't sure what to say. Without revealing Pax's connection to the screens, and risking more interference, how could she explain why they needed to search an area their equipment showed to be inactive? Her eyes wandered to the office's rear door. That was it. "That ravisher didn't show on our scanners," Sam said. "I'm concerned we might have similar strays, and want to do a sweep to be sure the surge didn't unsettle anything we're not seeing."

"Search the whole city for something we haven't detected?"

"Just an area fitting previous patterns of energy transferral."

Looking entirely unconvinced, Obrington shrugged his big shoulders and said, "Your initiative, Ward. Your choice. You understand, though, that you go chasing enough wild geese and it'll become harder to fill this seat I want to vacate."

"Not if I catch them," Sam said. Which she thought was rather bold and clever. His sneering face suggested it wasn't.

"Do what you have to," Obrington said. "Then join me upstairs. In a matter of minutes." He padded away without room for discussion, and Sam wasted only a moment watching him go. She hurried back to the Support tech, who was already frowning.

"What is it?"

"There's only two access points in that area," the man said. "Not a historically busy zone." He wavered, worriedly. "It's the warehouse district. The closest tunnels to the Fae Transitional City."

"Ah." Not good at all. They couldn't send agents that close to the FTC, not this soon, without communication from the Fae. But that couldn't be a coincidence. Were the screens advancing on the Fae themselves? Somehow planning to use or abuse them? One way or another, they were looking to cause trouble. Sam said, "Message the FTC, saying we're investigating unusual activity in the area. And get hold of Darren Barton, I want him to meet me there."

"But there *isn't* any unusual activity –" the tech protested.

"Just do it!" Sam ordered, drawing a few nearby looks. She didn't meet their eyes, racing after Obrington.

They walked a block away, around the corner to a row of brown office buildings, Sam itching to get away to whatever was happening near the FTC. A man was standing by a car in a parking bay, halfway down the road. Sam trotted to catch up to Obrington, and he said, "I called in a favour. This chap should've been kicked to the curb when he left the Ministry, frankly, but he has some uses."

"Left the Ministry?" Sam echoed. They approached the man too quickly for more.

"Agent Obrington?" He was shabbily suited, wearing a tweed jacket and brown corduroys, and his short mop of curly hair needed cutting. He smiled unhappily as he held out a hand. "Simon Parris."

Obrington shook with a grip that made Parris wince. "This is Sam Ward, *Acting Assistant Director*. Glad you could make it."

Sam held off questioning the title Obrington had previously denied her, as Parris maintained his unsettled smile. She shook his hand too. Clammy. "Anything for the Ministry," Parris said. "This is about the recent troubles, right?"

"It's about you paying your due," Obrington answered bluntly. "What've you got?"

"You know it's risky?" Parris said, his anxiety drawing Sam out of her Sunken City concerns to the fresh worry of what was going on here. "I've said in the past – it's not like we're unwilling to share, but if this gets noticed –"

"Save the patter," Obrington told him. "Ward takes full responsibility, don't you?"

There was that word again. What was he getting her into? She had to play along to see where this was going. "I need to see it first . . ." Whatever *it* was.

Parris nodded obediently and moved to the back of his car, an ugly cube of a Nissan. He opened the boot, looking about in case they were being watched. Obrington's bulk blocked Sam's view of whatever was inside.

"Three of them?"

"All I could get," Parris said. "And I need them back by tomorrow."

"You'll have them back when we're done with them."

Obrington stepped aside so Sam could see. Lying on a rumpled blanket was a set of long, matte black tools vaguely resembling rifles. Each sleek metal barrel split into prongs at the end, like a massive tuning fork, and there was a tablet panel near the back, above the handle and a distinct chrome badge. The logo was immediately recognisable; a D designed to resemble the tip of a speeding train. Or a bullet. Duvcorp. One of the most powerful companies in the world. The owners of Ordshaw's tallest building, comprising a trio of staggered towers that dominated the Central skyline. Duvcorp had made their mark in the American automobile industry before segueing into mainstream electronics and beyond. How had they crossed into MEE territory?

"What's happened?" Parris asked. "The Sunken City –"

"Is something you shouldn't ever mention, isn't it?" Obrington said.

Parris paused, suitably scolded. "Of course. But my bosses will want to know –"

"These things easy to use?" Obrington interrupted again.

Parris gave Sam a look for support, but she was impassive, waiting for this to play out. He answered, "Yes. That button activates, and when the light goes green, that one starts the test. The display" – he tilted one device – "gives you the SURE reading. Expect around a 23 for humans; electromagnetic field manipulations go as high as 50. Atmospheric readings usually even out around 10. Anything below that is strange."

"Fantastic." Obrington turned to Sam: "Think you can handle that?"

"What's happening?" Parris asked. "There were big SURE fluctuations surrounding those quakes last week – we've even got our COO in town asking questions."

"Want to tell your bosses anything," Obrington replied, "say we're testing new equipment and want to check benchmarks. But it'd be better if this co-operation was kept quiet, wouldn't it?"

Parris didn't press the point, starting to wrap the scanners. Obrington bid him a cold farewell, then hefted the weapons up against one shoulder and moved off towards the office. Sam gave one final look to the dishevelled Duvcorp man, now silent, merely waiting for this to be over. She hurried back to Obrington's side and asked in a hushed whisper, "What's going on? How much do they know?"

"*He* knows a lot," Obrington said. "Including that *we* know how to bury people. He's never shared our secrets with Duvcorp, but nor has he shared theirs with us. That company gives us a run for our money in the shady factor."

"And you wanted me to take responsibility to shield yourself?" Sam demanded.

"Obviously," Obrington said as though it wasn't cowardice or betrayal. "You think I'm planning on visiting from London every other weekend to handle the fallout from this? The consequences are on you."

"Jesus." Sam exhaled. "You people can't ever just be straight with me?"

"How's that not straight? You wanted new equipment, fast, I got you some. Return the scanners without drawing attention to ourselves and that's that. *Should* Duvcorp happen to come calling, you'll have a chance to prove you're Management material."

"Without knowing their angle? What do these things even measure?"

"SURE," Obrington said. "Their take on novisan. Special Unexplained Residual Energy, they call it. Special because URE is bleeding awkward to say. They don't know about your Sunken City because, strange as it might sound, Ordshaw's energy levels are curiously *normal* compared to most big cities. But they know a thing or two about novisan in general."

"And the MEE allows this research? Surely they'll –"

"Don't overestimate our influence, Ward," Obrington said. "Our work gets bent by committees and budgets, and the good of society; they are more efficient, better funded and ruthless. We've kept our secrets from them, they've kept some from us, neither of us wants a fight over it."

Sam ran this through her head, thinking of the Ministry's technology. To the best of her knowledge, they had nothing that directly measured novisan, only complicated systems of deduction. The implications were clear. "They could've uncovered things paralleling what we've found in the Sunken City?"

Obrington scoffed, though she couldn't tell whether he was dismissing the idea as silly, or aggravated that it might be true. "Best keep your eye on the goal right now. With these scanners, you'll be properly informed, for once. Perfect your monitoring equipment, test your Protocol 38 weapons, make some bloody progress."

Sam held off from replying. A long way from at ease. But there was something in it. Better equipped, she might make sense of what was going on. Starting with Pax's concerns in the warehouse district.

7

Pax parked her spluttering moped on Dresden Street, thankful that the elusive Dr Rimes had lent it to her, *more use to you than me*. It would've taken an hour to reach Ordshaw's under-served Nothicker on public transport; instead she'd arrived in twenty minutes. She scanned the grimy neighbourhood, walls soiled by the detritus of time, then double-checked the electronic device the Ministry had given her to track Fae. The little black box resembled a metronome, and Sam Ward had insisted it would alert the MEE if any Fae targeted her. She had turned it off, so the Ministry wouldn't blunder in and upset things when she found Palleday. Which they definitely would, given the chance. Ward couldn't have sounded happier to hear from Pax. An echo of Cano Casaria, exposing her to their work with dreams of signing her up. One of us, one of us. Pax's special sense for the blue screens made that all the more uncomfortable: it would be better if she had imagined that latest surge. If it wasn't the blue screens potentially spawning new and more terrible monsters only she could sense.

Putting that cheerful thought out of her mind, Pax approached the shop, *The Sandwitch*. Its barred windows were plastered with faded newspapers, the sign weathered like driftwood. Did local children think the store haunted? No, children living in Nothicker had bigger problems than ghosts. She punched the shop's buzzer, and it produced a fierce buzzsaw sound. The intercom crackled to life. A hoarse, older man's voice said, "You got ten seconds to get clear of my property."

Pax looked up, through the frosted glass of the window, no sign of someone inside.

"You hear me, I said ten seconds! Must've been eight by now."

"Palleday?" Pax said.

The speaker cut out for a moment, then came back. "I'm counting from five. Four."

"You know Letty? She sent me – she's a friend."

"Three."

"We need –"

"Two – one!" He rushed the last numbers and Pax jumped aside. The intercom hissed, something spraying out of it, barely missing Pax. She crouched, a hand over her face, coughing. The gas stung without making contact, burning her eyes, her nostrils.

"There's more, you hang around!"

"You prick!" Pax shouted. "What's – what was that?" She wheezed, spitting burning phlegm on the pavement. Her head spun, ears popped – was it some foul Fae technology, an airborne chemical weapon? Pax staggered against the wall and took deep, gasping breaths.

When the man spoke again, his voice sounded uncertain. "I warned you . . ."

Pax slowed her breathing, the burning slowly starting to pass. She blinked bleary eyes and swallowed to clear her ears. "Jesus fuck, I came to you for help."

"I got no help for a Fae-eating monster." His voice wavered. "Walk away. Please."

"Now that you've . . ." Pax breathed deeper into her recovery. It wasn't mystical, or deadly. "You *pepper-sprayed* me? All I've been through, now I get maced trying to knock on a goddamned door for *help*?"

The man didn't respond. He had to be Palleday, or a friend, knowing the rumour that she'd eaten a fairy. Pax said, "Letty trusted you! She's trapped, and I need you to help me help her." And then *we* can save this whole damned city, can't we?

"Ain't no human helping her," the voice crackled through the speaker. "Ain't no *one*."

"You know where she is? What's going on?"

The speaker crackled off.

Pax took another breath, and the pepper had a minor resurgence at the back of her throat, making her gag. She hit the buzzer again, and shouted, "Give me a glass of water at least, fuck! A tissue!"

"I told you to leave –"

"I'm streaming! Streaked with snot. What's wrong with you? Palleday!" She raised her voice. "Palleday, you bastard, open up!"

He hissed panic through the speaker and the intercom beeped a different pitch at last. The door clicked. "Inside, quick – stop using my name!"

Pax entered onto the stench of wet mould. Clamping a hand over her mouth, she continued past a crusty sandwich counter. With barely any light seeping through the papered window, she squinted through turning dust to the choice of steep stairs or a doorway to an ominously black back room. She called up the stairs, "You here?"

Climbing the creaking steps took her above the smell, and she inhaled an approximation of fresh air. Two closed doors sat ahead, with a small rectangular window to one side, open a crack, casting dim light on the stained red carpet. In the centre of the corridor sat a roll of toilet paper. He must've moved fast to leave it for her.

"Quite a place you've got," Pax muttered, scooping up the roll and tearing off sheets to dab her eyes. She blew her nose loudly.

"I got no water, not for a human," Palleday said from up near the window. Apology in his gravelly voice. He was hidden by the window's glare. "Say your piece, before I do you worse."

"Like feed me a sandwich?" Pax sniffed, pocketing more paper for later. "I'm not the enemy. A lunatic called Lightgate tried to use me to spark war between the Ministry and the FTC. Letty tried to stop her and got trapped in the FTC. She said you were a friend."

Palleday's continued hesitation gave her hope. Pepper-spray or not, he hadn't threatened her life in the usual way of the Fae. He said, "The news pinned it all on Letty. Say she was working with crazy humans. But Letty, she's got a good heart.

Lightgate . . . a pox on whoever brought her back." He spat. "But there's no help here. You know my name, and I guess that's all."

"Yeah," Pax said. "So fill me in. Can I see you?"

"I ain't giving you a chance to snatch me, human."

"It's *Pax*, not *human*. And do I look like the snatching type?" Pax spread her arms wide. "I've got the reflexes of a sloth."

"And the trickery of a fox," Palleday said. "You're such good friends with Letty, tell me why you came here and didn't go to her crew?"

Pax recalled the Fae who had kidnapped Grace and tried to kill them all. "We fell out."

"When you ate young Gambay?"

"No," Pax answered seriously, no idea who that was but fairly certain she hadn't eaten him. "I don't know what ideas they got about me, but they weren't working with Letty in the end. We had the weapon to kill the minotaur, they tried to kill us to get it back. Now it's fuck-knows-where and we're grasping about in the dark. Only I *know* your people can help us finish this."

"Because we're special," Palleday said, defensively. "That sounds like eating talk to me."

"What –"

"Think you'll gain our *powers*. Who knows what ideas you have."

"Your powers? I can be coarse, antisocial and violent without resorting to cannibalism."

"Cannibalism," he said, "is reserved for equals."

"Can we park this? I didn't *eat* anyone and I'm not going to. Bottom line is, Letty sent me to you – you're not in the Fae city, I need a go-between."

"Fat chance," Palleday snorted. "I live out here because I got no love for the FTC, but I got less love for humans. You could do a lot of harm. They just wouldn't let me build no more. They leave me alone, I leave them alone." That brought reflective sadness. "Now. Once, men fought wars over my towers."

"And women knew better?" Pax offered.

He paused. "It's a joke to you, is it?"

"No," Pax said. "I just don't know what you're talking about. What towers, why would they stop you from building?"

"Because it wasn't *right*, not for their kind of living. They said." He made a snuffling sound. Torn between paranoia and wanting to share. "You want to see them?"

"Sure. If they're, say, less than two minutes away?"

"Open that door. The one ahead of you."

Pax looked from the frail door back up to the shadows. She crossed the corridor and opened it. The room beyond was dark, barely lit by one small window obscured by clouded glass. It made the contents unsettling: column after column of organic shapes, each as tall as her, pitted with warped openings, like the mouths of tortured souls.

"Jesus Christ," Pax said. Something moved near her head, making her sidestep.

"Yes." Palleday hovered by the doorway, rubbing his little hands together as he looked upon his work. He was as small as Letty, no more than two inches, but had grand, lacy wings, and a long mane of mucky grey hair, thinning up top. He wore a patchy boiler suit and his long, bony limbs gave him a more insectile appearance than other Fae. The slightly manic look on his face conjured the impression that he hid in the shadows of these massive anthills, waiting for rodents to walk by.

"You built these things?" Pax asked quietly.

"And more, so much more." Palleday hovered a little closer, enraptured by his own achievements. "Wonders of Fae civilisation, forgotten, no longer deserved." With him distracted, Pax realised, she could actually grab him out of the air now. For a laugh. Palleday turned to face her and shot back with surprise. Sensing her intention to prank? "What are you doing?"

"This stuff." Pax ignored the question. "Was this how the Fae cities used to be? The sort Letty told me about, under the city, before the monsters."

Palleday's expression softened. "She spoke about that? What do you know?"

"Not enough."

He made a low, curious noise and flew into the shady room. A moment later, the overhead light blinked on, an old yellow bulb that stretched the openings of the many structures in pained shadows. Palleday resurfaced in the middle of the room. "See it for yourself, human."

Pax placed a hand on the doorframe and said, "I can see well enough from here."

He made a sound of disapproval as he emerged from between the structures, flying with a halting action, his old wings unfit. He perched on a ledge at the top of the nearest tower, eye-level. "One of these fit a family, long ago. A pillar of faith in ourselves. Not *possible* in the new way, they said. Small, mobile, that was all they wanted. Even as – even if –" He floated off the ledge again, pointing a shaking hand across the room. There was something beyond the structures, tucked in a corner; a frame of some sort, pipes and poles with taut wires running between them, arching over the top into a system of pulleys, with wheels at its base. "I gave them options, they wouldn't listen!"

Pax looked from the elaborate machine back to the towers, whose organic, drooping style made them look half-fused to the floor. If he was suggesting he could move these towers with that thing, she could sympathise with the Fae who doubted him.

"I am redundant," he continued, grimly. "A relic. Sculpting alone. A sideshow for a human."

"Letty understood, didn't she?" Pax said. "She wants to restore what you had before."

"She's a dreamer. And you must be, too. Think there's any hope we can live side-by-side? Our own people can't even get along. No. The best, only thing I can do is this."

"Your people had the Sunken City once, it could happen again."

"You seen the things down there?" Palleday scoffed. "The light – the electric arms. Paws, claws, teeth; all coming faster than you can scream. Drove us up here, where *your* people chase us with fire and gas. Again and again, moving. Every time abandoning my creations, watching them crumble to dust."

"I'm sorry," Pax mumbled, aware of the futility of saying it. She couldn't imagine all that had been lost with each forced migration. But it raised another thought. She'd seen it herself, when the Sunken City horde swarmed towards her. The fairies had drawn them her way. She'd felt it, too, riding the tube with Letty. The monsters hunted the Fae. Wanted to feed on them more than anything. "What *is* so special about your people? Why are the creatures drawn to you?"

Palleday gave her a miserable look. "You oughta be able to answer that."

Pax shook her head, but an idea was forming. Even without understanding why, she could imagine how that unique Fae energy might draw the monsters and the screens all together. Then the Ministry could have their purge. If they could get a handle on Fae energy. If they could get the Dispenser back. If she could rescue Letty. A lot of ifs, all requiring the co-operation of more reasonable Fae. Pax said, "Is there anyone in the FTC that actually likes humans?"

"What do you think?" Palleday said. "Even the soft young bloods must be reeling at you, since the return of this Apothel Five and Fae getting" – Pax gave a warning look – "Fae getting *hurt*."

"Someone's with Letty, inside the FTC. Helped her talk to me. Could you get them a message? Find a way we can properly connect?"

"I look like someone with contacts?"

He really didn't, but she said, "Letty thought so. You think of a way, and I'll clear out the Sunken City. You'd have space for your towers. Protection. Maybe people to live in them."

Palleday was quiet. Imagining it. He said, "You know all that's down there."

"Not *all* of it."

"Lot of Fae won't want to return. Most Fae are too young to remember, but I saw things. Troubling things."

"Yeah, me too. But we can explore all that once it's safe to, can't we?"

Palleday's eyes were glazed over in memory.

Pax continued, "I'll be at a card game this evening, at the Baudelaire Club. A good excuse to keep the Ministry from watching. You send someone my way, anyone that can help, I'll be waiting."

Palleday regarded her for a moment. "Don't hold your breath. But I'll see what I can do." After another moment's thought, he added, to remove Pax's smile, "As long as you realise there's plenty more people want you dead than alive, right now."

Once the human was gone, strolling self-satisfied away, Fresko and Mix drifted through the pillars of Palleday's building graveyard. Mix said, "We could've done her here. Like we should've before."

They settled on the ledge next to Palleday as he watched them. A battleaxe of an old Fae, long past his prime. He said, "She seemed genuine."

"Yeah?" Fresko replied. "The human promising impossible things seemed genuine?"

"Says the man under Lightgate's thumb?"

Fresko let him have that; he trusted Lightgate even less than he did the human. But Lightgate was at least a Fae. And much more likely to make them pay for crossing her.

"We can *still* get her," Mix said. "The Ministry aren't watching."

"And they won't be later," Fresko said. "She gave us a time and place. We bring the meeting to Lightgate, it might get her off our back."

"You heard the girl, didn't you?" Palleday said. "Letty's been set up by her that sent you. What you oughta bring Lightgate is a stick up the arse."

Fresko said nothing. If Letty wasn't responsible for the Ministry deaths, more fool her. And if this girl *was* genuine, didn't that just make her another dangerous woman? Why not put her together with Lightgate, see what sparks flew. He caught Palleday reading his face and said, "That human caused us all sorts of shit."

"I'll say it again – you heard her. She's not what you think."

"You want to help her, that it?"

"I see no reason not to reach out to the FTC."

"To fucking Val?" Mix demanded, but the architect was already shaking his head.

"Take me for an idiot? I got people I can talk to, hell. Might even get word to Letty herself."

Mix gave Fresko a look telling him this was his call. Fresko kept staring at the old man; a legend of the Fae world, the sort you left alone. Smarter than most, for sure. Then, it didn't take a genius to know the less you had to do with Lightgate the better. Fresko said, "Alright. We'll hold off. See where this meeting goes and make a decision then."

"Knock yourself out," Mix said. "I'm ready for a fucking drink."

8

When Apothel's Miscellany was couriered to the Bartons by a man in black, Holly had started studying it keenly. The leather-bound tome looked like it belonged in a university library, to be handled with microfibre gloves. She warned Darren off touching it with his greasy fingers, likewise Grace. She especially turned Rufaizu away, though the book technically belonged to him; she had seen him make the dishes dirtier when he washed them.

In the book, partly translated by Pax, Holly discovered fantastic creatures she knew to exist under their feet. Among Apothel's sketches was a plant he called a *seeping sour flower*, resembling a foul thing she'd seen herself. Imagine experiencing such things – widely unknown, radically different – without the looming threat of death. She understood how the place had enchanted her husband. Or ensnared? Regardless, when the call came, Sam Ward giving Darren an okay to access the Sunken City, Holly had to be there.

At the edge of the desolate warehouse district, they found Ward in an empty gravel car park, waiting by a big metal door with an object whose long barrel split into multiple prongs. It vaguely resembled a weed-whacker. Ward regarded Holly with surprise. "Mrs Barton – I'm not sure you should be –"

"It's fine, Grace has Netflix to look after her," Holly said, nodding for her to get on with things. Ward looked uncomfortable, but Darren shook his head to warn her not to argue. She didn't question Rufaizu's presence, either. The bright-eyed vagrant was grinning, washed and groomed and newly clothed, though he'd refused to give up his ever-present tatty turquoise trench coat.

"Well," Ward said, "I appreciate your help. Revising our surveys is a complex task. And this is particularly sensitive, as we're not hugely far off the Fae city. I hoped your presence would make this investigation appear more neutral than if we'd brought our own agents."

"The Fae have little love for me," Darren said, in his typical gruff manner.

"You've never actively attacked them," Ward reminded him.

"Why are we here?" Holly asked. "What've the fairies done?"

"Nothing we're aware of," Ward said. "It's the – something to do with the screens. Our scans don't show anything in this area – the horde hasn't been near here in weeks – but Pax sensed something. We've got a new piece of equipment." She held up the odd device. "An energy scanner. And I brought this." She pulled back her suit jacket, revealing a shoulder holster holding a chunky pistol. "Darren, you might take it, while I –"

His blank look stopped her. "I never needed one before." In his striped polo shirt, with a crutch and one foot in a cast, he certainly didn't look like a gun-toting assassin.

"And hopefully you won't today," Ward said. "But it's an MEE energy weapon –"

"Allow me," Rufaizu offered, reaching towards it, but Ward stepped back. She looked from the young man to Darren, clearly imagining he was the only responsible gun-wielder in the group. He didn't budge, and she let the jacket fall back over it.

"We shouldn't need it. Holly, perhaps you could take notes." Ward took out a phone. "Tap here, and the GPS will record the location." She pressed a button on the big scanner and aimed it into the car park. Various numbers increased on its digital screen before decreasing again, settling on averages. A series of green lights came on, one after another, and the screen lit up: LEVEL 12. NORMAL.

Ward nodded to Holly and she pressed the phone, typed in 12. Ward grinned proudly. "Well done."

Holly shared a despairing look with Darren. Did the woman work with imbeciles?

"Let's go, shall we?" Ward opened the door behind her, revealing steps descending into darkness. Holly's heart suddenly beat faster. They were really doing it. Those things she'd read about, seen before . . .

"Your equipment pick up raptors?" Darren commented, following Ward inside. "They're small."

"Or ripple worms," Rufaizu suggested. "Buckets of them, sometimes, isn't there?"

"Yes, our motion detectors would've spotted those," Ward said.

Holly came warily behind them, unsure what raptors or ripple worms were, and thinking she might do better to spend more time reading about such things than actively seeking them out. Noting her hesitation, Darren let Rufaizu pass him on the steps and said to her, quietly, "You okay? You don't have to do this."

She tightened her hand on Ward's phone. "I hardly think we can trust you to do it alone."

At the base of the stairs, the endless possibilities of the tunnels stretched ahead, lit by sparsely spaced tube lighting. The corridor of concrete walls was interrupted by occasional branching passages and smelt like chalk.

"It's clean," Darren said. "No weeds, no cracks." He ran a hand over the wall. "Used to be no lights down here, we carried three torches each, to be sure. There were plants, too. Creepers. Some of them glowed, for a bit of light."

"We clear the worst of the weeds away, to limit creatures spreading," Ward said, moving ahead with the scanner held up. "Electric weed, as you called it, for instance? Glogockles thrive on it."

Rufaizu whistled. "Been so long, so long. Buda be damned, it's good to be back."

"Why would anyone damn Buddha?" Holly said.

"No! The Buda Labyrinth, what once held Dracula!"

"Of course," Holly said. "Let's bring Dracula into this."

"Ah, it's nothing – for tourists now. Staryn took me, says, here's your tunnels. See there's nothing to see. What do you need Ordshaw for? For the *minotaur*, I told him. That's the fight." He skipped about, beaming idiotically. "I was ready then, I've *been* ready."

Darren slowed to study the base of the wall. Scratch marks surrounded by murky brown patches. Holly asked, "What is it?"

"Trail of a tuckle," Darren said. "They squeeze down the tunnels." He followed the scratches as they passed the first break in the tunnel, a passageway Ward was nearing. "Hold up." Darren took the lead with quick taps of his crutch. He leant around the opening while Ward took an energy reading. "See that?"

Holly joined them. The passage was another identical corridor, this one ending in a T-junction a dozen metres away. A dangling weed hung in the intersection.

"Sickvine," Rufaizu said with wonder.

"Best not go that way," Barton said. "Usually indicates ankle raptors. Little packs of them wait for something to touch the vine."

"But your people said it was clear?" Holly asked Ward.

Ward frowned. "It must be an old vine." She stepped into the tunnel, raised the scanner and took another reading. "Thirty-four. We'll continue the other way."

As she continued, distractedly, Rufaizu resumed his wandering thoughts. "I always had to come back. The other tunnels, other places, they're *lost*. Gardossa and those in the Alps, we never saw it."

Ward gave him a questioning look. She had already listened, with the rest of them, to the young man's stories of old understandings of novisan and the things that preyed on it. A Bohemian city called Gardossa, an Antler King in the French Alps and an ancient hunter named Theo Murhaimer. Though perhaps steeped in nonsense, the stories paralleled Ordshaw's: Murhaimer carved messages in walls, gone by morning. Gardossan legends of an unseen beast. The Antler King's influence spread through caves.

"Have you connected that history to Apothel's book, yet?" Ward asked. The tone of her voice suggested she'd welcome a distraction from whatever was worrying her.

"No, but I'm curious about the Gardossans," Holly offered. "The Sect of Fore, have you heard of them? Not the number four, but *fore*, from the idea of *forward-thinking*. Supposedly they received messages in the catacombs."

"Prophecies!" Rufaizu interjected, and excitedly took over. "They were guided against the *beast* and warned of disaster."

"Apparently not very successfully," Holly added, "as they all died and the city was destroyed."

About to ask something more, Ward stopped suddenly, and they all almost collided. Rufaizu opened his mouth to question it, but Holly hissed for quiet. They all listened. A sound was coming from a distant tunnel. A rush of air.

"Fans?" Holly asked hopefully.

Ward shook her head and continued. The sound was escalating, like a broken gas pipe. Darren growled, "That's a dreadhorn."

"What?"

Darren hobbled quickly towards another gap in the tunnel.

"What's a dreadhorn?" Holly asked.

Darren didn't answer, adjusting his grip to hold the crutch like a spear. The sound was building, blowing up a gale, and a rush of air passed over them. He stumbled to a halt at the tunnel edge, and his grim look spurred Ward into action, dropping her scanner and clawing at her pistol. Rufaizu ran to Darren's side and Holly followed. As she drew alongside him, spying a heavy-breathing critter squatting in the branching corridor, the gusting wind pulled her hair across her face. The silhouette sat in an unlit stretch of tunnel, jagged knees pointed so far out they almost touched the walls. Its head was crested with spikes, as though wearing a homemade mantle, and its torso expanded as it inhaled, the rush of air drawing towards it.

"Get back!" Ward instructed, hopping towards them with her pistol caught in its holster.

The creature's knees bunched awkwardly in as it rotated towards them. The faint light from their tunnel caught the edges of mandibles, and the glint of soulless green eyes. They narrowed, focusing on the group, as its head stretched and chest inflated with the immense inhalation. Holly patted her hair back and steadied herself.

"Cover your ears – its scream will burst them!" Darren shouted, limping forwards.

Ward finally got her gun loose, but Rufaizu ran into the way. "I got it, I got it!"

He sprang through the air as the dreadhorn reared up, its shadow blocking the tunnel. Rufaizu made a shout of attack as he punched at it, and the creature crumpled to the side, cutting off the huge rush of air. It clattered back with crab-like motions as Rufaizu's momentum took him to the floor. It wheezed, mandibles working in and out.

"Yeah, have some!" Rufaizu laughed.

Holly watched aghast as Ward aimed the gun uselessly, blocked by the two men. The dreadhorn was regrouping, backing into the light of the far tunnel, continuing to breathe in and expand. Darren raced past Rufaizu. Visible in bright highlights, the creature's leathery skin stretched over bones as it ballooned with every second. Darren stumbled against the wall and cried out. Rufaizu overtook him again, snatching the crutch.

"In the mouth!" Darren ordered, and Rufaizu jammed the crutch forwards, just as the monster turned to them – caught it right between the mandibles. The dreadhorn deflated with a huge outward gasp, shrinking inwardly. Rufaizu backed off, hands held aloft like he didn't mean to break it. Darren let out his own deep breath of relief and turned slowly back. Ward lowered the gun.

"Done." Rufaizu hopped over the dreadhorn's final death shudder. "Is it done?"

"It's done," Darren said, pushing off the wall.

"How – how dangerous was that?" Holly stuttered. Ward gave her a backwards glance: best not to ask. "What would happen if these things got *out*?"

"That's the point," Darren said, limping back. He eyed Ward accusingly. "Your sensors said there was nothing here?"

Ward bit her lip with clear concern, then passed Darren to approach the monster's body. She leant around the tunnel's end, checking up and down, saying, "This isn't right. Our motion sensors *should* have told us that was here. And the energy levels are much higher than I'd expect –"

"You have no idea what's going on down here," Darren said.

Holly huffed in irritation. "But Pax knew? What's that tell us?"

"For one, we can trust her senses," Ward answered quietly.

"It tells us we still *can't* trust the Ministry," Darren said.

That worried Ward more than everything else. "No – we're fixing this. That's the point! But it's not your place to be here. We should leave."

"Leave?" Rufaizu exclaimed. "You want to *leave*? When it's getting interesting?"

"He's right," Holly said. It was clear enough that between Apothel's book and this government ministry's studies, there were big gaps in any academic understanding of these monsters. The reality was that no one would get a damn thing done without certain intrepid people braving the tunnels themselves. However daunting the place was. "If we leave now, we're no closer to explaining what's wrong. Seeing as your fancy equipment can't be relied on. No, I think it's best we continue."

9

Light spilled into Letty's fresh hovel as the door opened. Fresh was being generous: this box made the white room look big. Just enough space for a dense sponge bed, an old TV and a pile of boxes. Someone's forgotten storage chest. She stood from the sponge as Flynt entered. He'd adopted the same sort of disguise they'd rustled up for her: a dark green plastic poncho, hood up, glasses and a smog-bandanna, like a bookish crossing guard. The disguise didn't hide the concern on his face.

"We're good," Flynt said, pulling down the bandanna. "Edwing convinced Val's people he's been trying to draw outsiders back into the FTC, peacefully."

"But . . ."

Flynt bit his lip, too nervous to say.

Letty regarded him critically. The Scout Chief. Responsible for the Fae's scavengers, youthful, smooth-skinned where he wasn't burnt, and *nervous*. She said, "Hell's biscuits, before the scouts were run by a guy whose voice could've rusted plastic. How'd a whelp like you take over?"

Flynt put a hand on his hip, drawing attention to his pistol bulge beneath the poncho. "Got you back here, didn't I?"

"Got me *stuck* back here."

"With Lightgate still prowling out there."

"Spin on it. What's *happening*?"

He paused, still reluctant. "There's rumours going about. Emergency broadcasts on the big screen. Val's recalling my scouts, saying only Stabilisers are allowed out."

"Because they caught us making a call?"

"Because the Ministry have been spotted nearby. Teaming up with the Apothel Five. Like, ten blocks away."

"Pax?"

Flynt's blank face said he didn't know.

"Fuck this." Letty pushed past him to the door and he reached for her arm; she snatched his hand, twisted him round, lightning-fast, to press his face against the wall. "I ain't sitting around waiting for whispers, not with shit like that happening! You're at least gonna show me what's happening out there."

"Put on the TV –"

"Screw the TV," she hissed in his ear. "I want to *see* it."

She released him, stepping back, and he dropped his arm, more ashamed than annoyed. Defeated, he sullenly nodded and led the way. Out onto the warehouse floor, in the shadows of the towers. Flynt craned upwards, then whispered, "Okay, it's clear."

His wings took him silently across the path, to another building where he twisted back and watched for Letty to follow. He waved a hand and she lifted off, too. The Clear Glider worked. It had taken some painful jabbing and manoeuvring to connect it, but it was worth it. She flew with a graceful spin. Effortless, and a sign her injuries were basically healed. Hell, this would give her the edge once she tracked down Lightgate.

Flynt directed her around a corner, across another empty space to a major thoroughfare. One of the big avenues of the Fae city; nothing at ground level, but walls of homes and businesses looming over them. Having earlier escaped through shadows and alleys, Letty was finally able to see the city proper, and it wasn't pretty. Lit partly by skylights high above, partly from the many-coloured lamps and signs outside Fae dwellings, everything looked so *clean*. The stacked homes, variously coloured structures the size of human shoeboxes, were neatly painted and aligned. The air traffic, with Fae gliding from one opening to another, was eerily well-ordered, gravitating towards the centre and the broadcast Flynt had mentioned.

Floating high above it all was a great screen with drone propellers, broadcasting a news channel for the whole damn city to see. Even from this distance, the image was clear. Footage of that mousy MEE agent alongside Barton, his wife and Apothel's boy. All of them hustling into a tunnel entrance. A headline said: *APOTHEL FIVE WITH MEE ON FTC PERIMETER.*

The image cut to Valoria, the pompous governor. Bulkier than any Fae had a right to be, chains around her neck, hair in loose braids, wearing a velvet dress like a medieval queen. Standing at a podium looking Deathly Serious. Letty's skin crawled with the urge to pummel her glutinous face.

"This is clear provocation from the humans," Valoria announced, her big voice echoing past the buildings. "So soon after their brazen attack, returning to our territory."

"Our territory?" Letty said. "They were going into the Sunken City, how do we know it's anything to do with us?"

"With no word of warning from the Ministry," Valoria continued, "we can only assume the worst. But I have personally been preparing a response to the human hostilities. The Council will meet tomorrow afternoon for a vote to move forward with it."

"Where's Edwing in this?" Letty turned on Flynt.

"Talking to others sympathetic to our cause. There are dissenters, he might be able to delay whatever she's planning, sway this vote –"

"Votes, delays," Letty said. "She's gearing up for a shitshow and you're talking fucking politics? We need to act. Wherever your boy is, we're here now and we know, at least, that she's hiding the fucking Dispenser. You know where?"

Flynt hesitated. "Only place completely secure is the vats."

"Too right, the fucking vats. So we bust down the door and stick it to her where it hurts. You and me, right this minute."

"What?" Flynt squeaked. "There's –"

A shadow passed over them and he ducked against the wall, pulling Letty with him. She shoved him off and leant out. Whoever had flown over was gone. She scoffed, "You ever actually *been* in a fight? How'd you lose the eye, coffee pot explode on you? What are you, twelve?"

He stood taller, trying to show he was a big, grown-up Fae. Hell, him and Edwing both, they were fully mature, but Fae reached maturity quickly, that could've meant anywhere between ten and thirty years old. "I've done things –"

"Screw it, come on." Letty pulled him out into the open. He stumbled after her before regaining his footing. She squinted up, searching for the black armour of Stabilisers, and spotted a couple watching the screen. Letty flew up, sticking to a wall, all the way to a nearby roof. A better vantage point, out of their view but revealing half the city.

Flynt landed alongside her, panicked. "You can't be out here –"

"Look at those mugs." She pointed. "They're all rapt with this fucking broadcast. You need a lesson, Cyclops: everyone here got comfortable, no one expects a beating. Like you. Strike hard and fast, they'll be too surprised to react. Where are the vats?"

"Hell, you can't – come back down, let me call Edwing –"

"Why'd you rescue me at all? You got no idea who I am? How I work?"

Flynt firmed up with a new trace of defiance. "Of course I do. Our old Scout Chief, Bevans, he flew with you, told us all the stories. Syphoned oil from a Warlowe Ltd truck? Ransomed a kid in West Farling? Edwing, he says, *she knows we're meant for better things*. When they said a human *ate* you, I said bullshit. Not Letty. We believe in you, alright. That's why I gotta keep you alive."

Letty took in a breath and let it out. His innocent tirade almost made her feel bad. Almost. "You know me so well, you think I need *your* protection? You know what I see, looking at you? A guy keen on action who's never seen it. Let Edwing do his thinking, he's not *here*. We go in quietly, get proof Val's got the Dispenser, that she's a lying bitch. Give your brother something to talk about."

Flynt hesitated. Long enough to say he was game. "Let me call Newbry."

Letty folded her arms as he made the call with quick, quiet commands. Asking for door codes, camera scrambling, hacker spy shit. While he talked, Letty gave the city another look. There was so much openness. Floor-to-ceiling windows, wide terraces; fragile structures that you couldn't easily move. She squinted at the stacked buildings: the securing clips were still there, these stacks *could* be detached, but this FTC was no longer mobile.

Her roving eyes picked out a familiar word, above a wholly unfamiliar leisure unit. The sign read *Rullion*, the name of the clubhouse the city's best scouts used to frequent. But the building had a pillared facade and a swimming pool visible through the big windows. "What in holy rat rot . . ."

"The Rullion?" Flynt caught her staring, ending his call. "Yeah. Mostly the Council and Stabilisers use it now. But we've got our place, too. The Bloodtooth Bar –"

"Don't, just don't." Letty shut her eyes against the madness. "Are we on or what?"

"Yeah. But we'll need to cut the fence."

"Got my knife." Letty patted her thigh where the sheathed blade lived. "That'll do."

He gave her a sceptical look. "Okay." He flew past her and down, gesturing that she follow him. "Careful – stick to cover."

Letty kept pace with her own concerns. "Why's everyone dressed like mundane humans? Where's the shouting or gunfire or blaring music? This place is fucking *quiet*."

Flynt shrugged, leading her through gaps between homes. He pointed out the bigger landmarks she didn't recognise. "There's the Council Chambers" – ornately carved rotundas, mimicking classical architecture – "and Ducker's Exchange, biggest marketplace in town." A wide-open shopping centre, lined with shelves like a damn human supermarket.

"Oughta correct the first letter," Letty said. At floor level, a couple of slumped, shuddering Fae in rags caught her eye. "What's that? All this opulence, and junkies can't get good human drugs?"

Flynt glanced at the men. "That's dust withdrawal."

Letty followed Flynt until they were one tower removed from the dust vats. Landing on a lookout ledge, Letty considered the dust economy uncomfortably. She'd experienced medicinal grade dust that could heal. Were they also churning out the polar opposite?

The site responsible sat on the edge of the FTC complex, separate from all the other buildings and notably more horizontal; like four overturned bathtubs, connected at various heights by dull pipes, accessible through a foot-wide circular bulkhead in the roof of the farthest one, or via a set of double doors at the base of the nearest. Armed guards loitered around both, and wire fencing encircled the lot like a net. The fencing had one entrance, another foot-wide gate on electric rollers. No one outside Val's inner circle of workers ever got in. As long as the dust kept flowing, everyone was happy with that.

"Over there." Flynt pointed, checking against something on his phone. Newbry had come through quickly. "There's a blind spot. Through that fence, we can get to the walls, then it's the ID checkpoint. See, up there, the guards are turning the corner."

Letty watched the patrolmen drifting out of view, around one of the vat buildings. Both looking over towards the broadcast screen. She darted down to the fence, across the open ground, as Flynt raced to keep up. She drew her knife and slid it through the links; a quick slice and they fell away. Flynt watched in awe at the blade's sharpness, but she gave him a dismissive look. Who'd want a knife that couldn't cut metal?

Letty pulled a gap open for Flynt and they continued to the main gates, where he keyed a code into a number pad. Newbry had pulled his weight there, too. And presumably he'd neutralised the cameras? A surprisingly useful gaggle of nerds, these boys.

Slipping through the door into a small antechamber, Letty spotted a desk behind a glass panel. A single Fae sat watching TV. As Letty's shadow passed over him he looked up, mouth open, and she knocked him to the floor. Jumped on him, spun him around, too quick for him to see her. She hissed at Flynt, on her heels, to find something to tie him with. Together, they bound the guy into his chair with tape, then Letty checked the desk's monitors: familiar outdoor scenes – perimeters like the ones they'd shot across – patrols flying oblivious. Good. Then interior shots. The vats themselves, big cauldrons with pipes running in and out, a couple of walkways over them. Production lines with conveyors, grinders and robot arms processing sludge into dust and pills. One shot of a packaging area. Very few workers, most of the operation automated.

None of it seemed out of the ordinary. What they'd come to find wasn't on camera. Letty checked the screens against a map on the desk, showing the four buildings divided into sectors. The monitors had corresponding labels: Silo 1, Sector B. Packaging North. She said, "What's not being watched?"

Flynt checked. "Packaging West?"

True. No sign of the name on the monitors. Letty snatched the guard's keycard and paused to look at the TV. The broadcast was still going. A sallow-faced Fae in a suit had taken Val's place to talk about the dangers of interacting with humans. Fucker.

Letty ran at a half-crouch from the entrance into one of the silo rooms – a massive chamber, thick with the rumble of machinery and the hum of electricity. It stank like iron and earth. Pipes ran from the base of the enormous vat into the ground. At least a Fae's width thick, riveted shut except at a couple of small viewing panels. Whatever was inside glowed, faintly. It gave Letty a chill.

"What is it?" Flynt asked.

She wasn't sure herself. Pax came to mind. Saying dust sounded like the humans' glo. And here was shit glowing in the pipes. Junkies on new strains of dust getting high somehow. High-grade medicinal dust . . .

Shaking the thoughts clear, Letty dashed down a short corridor to an adjoining building, then skirted a production line to reach the doors to Packaging West, labelled with a big sign. Locked. The guard's keycard produced a red light. Cursing, Letty gave Flynt a look. He shook his head – no solution. In the gap between the double doors, there were at least three bolts holding them together. No way of forcing this one. But with that kind of security, they must be in the right place.

"There," Flynt whispered, pointing at a guy in grey overalls strolling onto a walkway above. Letty shot up between poles and pipes and dropped behind him. As he turned, she got a hand over his mouth and shoved him into the rail. She dug her pistol into his gut.

"Not a sound. You're gonna open the door down there." His eyes were terrified but he shook his head quickly. She dug the pistol deeper. "We can do it quick and easy or slow and painful."

He mumbled a frightened response, eyes desperate, and she released her hand just enough to hear it. "I don't have access! No one gets in from here! Please!

Please. I know you – I've got a kid –"

"To hell with your kid. Who *does* go in?"

"Stabilisers," he said. "And Nimm. But he's not *vats* staff –"

"You got the Dispenser in there?" Letty said, storing that name for later.

"What? I don't know! But – there's a ventilation shaft – not big enough to go through, only to see – but I'm begging you –"

"Move."

Letty shoved him into flight, and the engineer took her to where a metal shaft entered the wall. He opened a panel and she wriggled her head and shoulders into it, keeping one hand clamped on his neck. There was a small grate looking into Packaging West. And there was her goal. The brass and glass casing of the cylinder was unmistakable.

"Satan's mule," Letty said. "That's my fucking Dispenser."

But it wasn't all that was there. A handful of Stabilisers were gathered around a stack of crates with Cyrillic lettering, and behind them sat a pile of earthen waste. A big pile, clumps of mud and tangled roots running through it. Bits of it glowed softly blue. Letty ducked out, glaring at the engineer. "What the fuck are you doing in here?"

He squeezed his eyes shut in fear. She got no chance to quiz him further, as Flynt called a warning: "Got people coming, time to go!"

10

Pax was almost breathless when she made it back to her seat at the casino. Fifteen minutes late; not bad considering she'd been right across town and met with a crotchety fairy. Only a few chips gone. She muttered apologies to the players eyeing her like she must be mad to miss a single second of the game. It was worth it. Palleday had hinted at a way forward, and that was all she needed. Some Fae, somewhere, would help. Now, she could play.

In theory. With one eye on the game, her mind wandered as she bet and folded her way through hands. Palleday's words drifted into her consciousness.

More people want you dead than alive right now.

And a lot of those people thought she was a Fae-eating monster. Trying to consume their powers for herself, he said. A relevant fear, considering something in their energy made the minotaur desperate to consume them. Did they understand it themselves, well enough that they might use it to fight back?

She picked up a king and queen, and everyone folded to her. Three people to go, and she once again had a dwindling stack. To hell with it, she would figure something out later; now she had to get back in the game. She pushed her chips in.

The next player called immediately, to two more folds, and showed a pair of kings.

Oh.

Pax stared with little feeling as the dealer drew the five community cards, whispers of upset as her march towards success was cut brutally down. The kings held up. She was out of the tournament. Her chips were callously swept away. Disbelief for a moment. She nodded to the vague sounds of people's condolences. Pax stood, forcing an uncomfortable smile, and ran a hand through her hair. Oh well. Oh well. It was just an opportunity to get rich. Just a matter of getting her life secure.

"Congratulations," a voice said at her ear, the tournament director, come to lead her away. "You did excellent, Pax."

An announcement penetrated her numbness. "– Kuranes, placed 68. Ordshaw's own, everyone please, give her a hand."

Two tables over, Dutch McRory was standing, joining in the applause. He gave her a kindly nod and she smiled back. Placed 68. In the money. Stacey Monroe would get paid. A camera crew were hustling through the crowd, waving for attention. She hadn't done much, but she was a woman, local. A Story. Bowing her head, Pax turned away. "I've got to go."

Avoiding well-wishers and the disappointed camera crew, Pax hurried into the lobby with the tournament director close behind, chatting about her winnings.

Couldn't face this, needed a distraction. She took out her phone and he backed off, no stranger to the odd behaviour of an eliminated player.

It took a few rings before Ward answered this time. Good for her.

"Pax, how's it going?"

"Yeah," Pax said. "It's gone."

"Huh?"

"Never mind. Where are you?"

"Underground. Scraping the surface of exactly how corrupt our reporting systems might be. You were right, Pax, there *was* something – the true novisan patterns were hidden from us, our calculations misaligned somehow. But we've got new equipment –"

"As long as you're straightening things out."

"That's an overstatement. Pax, we've got creatures a long way from the *praelucente*. Near the FTC, even – it's rare for them to come this way. You were *right*, the blue screens did something."

"The FTC," Pax echoed. She saw a big screen over the main desk, the rankings for the tournament updating. Her name right at the bottom: PLACED 68. What was that worth, a couple of grand? A long way from a house, or retirement, or anything more than scratching about to live. The gains she might've got with a bit more focus – no, stop thinking of it. She had worthy distractions. "What are you saying? There's monsters coming for the Fae?"

"I don't know exactly, yet," Ward said. "And it's only getting stranger. Our new equipment, it comes from a private source. Duvcorp – I had no idea of their research. Christ, I'd really like your read on *that*. When can you come in? Are you still playing?"

Pax dragged a hand over her face, seeing kings and queens and fucking failure. Forget that: monsters were moving towards the Fae. Had the blue screens used their energy to spring an attack? After all these years keeping themselves to themselves? It was a *good thing* she'd gone bust, wasn't it? Not answering Ward's questions, Pax said, "What do you know about Fae energy?"

"What do you mean? They tap into our electric grid, but it's so minimal we –"

"No, their physical energy." The camera crew entered the hall, and Pax hid behind a pillar. "What makes them Fae? How do they impact novisan?"

"Um. I'm not aware of the Fae affecting novisan any differently to how we would expect people to on that scale. We trace them using their heat-signature and sound. Their wings create a pattern unique in nature – that's what guides our shock guns."

"The blue screens kept us apart for a reason," Pax said. "The horde goes mad on their account. These things are controlling, and Fae energy makes them lose control."

"You do have something, don't you? Where were you before?"

Pax paused. *Before*, she had a chance at financial independence. Now, where was she? Twisting in the confusion of monsters.

Dutch McRory came around the pillar and Pax yelped.

"Jesus fuck – sorry, hell –" Pax put a hand over her mouth at the older man's gentle amusement. Great move, cursing heaven before a poker legend. "Mr McRory, I didn't mean to –"

"My bad, I wasn't looking to intrude. I only wanted to say…" Dutch held up a business card. "It'd be good to share some hands again, before I leave town."

Pax looked at the card with alarm, fingers barely daring to touch it. The words come automatically, "Actually. There is a game – this evening."

"Send me the details." He smiled and moved away with a light remark, "Back to work!"

"Pax, was that someone –" Ward started.

"Poker, Sam," Pax replied quietly. Had that really just happened? It seemed less real than the monsters. Was 68 maybe not that bad – she still had a future? Monroe's game would be big. And the Fae . . . there might be Fae there. Yes. She said, "Listen, I've got another game that I need to be rested for. Might lead somewhere good for both of us. We'll discuss everything tomorrow. Deal?"

"What?" Ward asked. "Wait, what is it –"

"I'm out of the tournament," Pax said, to an apologetic sound from Ward. "I need this." Not just for money. Pax stared at McRory's departing back. Connections, security, Fae meetings. This evening would have it all. "It's important. And these aren't the sort of people that'd take kindly to government interference, understand?"

Ward hesitated. "I'd really like you to come in, Pax."

"I will. Tomorrow. Right now you've got to trust me."

"I do, of course I do . . ."

Pax almost cringed at how desperate Ward was for an ally. Pax *wanted* to help, after her own problems were managed. Was there some little way to show that? "You're underground now? Near the FTC?"

"Kind of. We've been moving away, checking the tunnels –"

"Move *further* away. At least until I get a better idea of what's going on. Don't do anything to provoke the Fae, don't go near them."

"The creatures might threaten them, we could *help* –"

"The Fae aren't going to see it as help, Sam. Get out of there. I'll take care of it."

After surveying the Bartons' tidy lawn, Casaria knocked. He turned to watch the house opposite. Casual, hiding his desperation in coming here after he'd found no one from the Ministry at three separate Sunken City entrances, and seen Pax wasn't home. Anyway, there were months' worth of debriefs to be done with this family, so it wasn't unreasonable to drop by.

"Hi, can I –" a teenager's chirpy voice said behind the opening door. "Oh, it's you." Grace, the inexplicably perfect daughter, made cheap ripped jeans and a loose t-shirt look fashionable. Her feet were bandaged and a pair of crutches was propped by the wall.

"Young lady." Casaria showed his teeth in a grin. "Your parents in?"

With no smile of her own, Grace shifted a foot. "You don't know where they are? I thought you might be with them."

Casaria kept the smile. So his instincts were right, and the MEE were in touch with the Bartons and not him. "Of course I know. I thought they were due back, though?"

She looked uncertain, but said, "Do you want to come in? I was making a drink."

It wouldn't do to be found alone in this house with this young lady, but it was all he had. Casaria nodded and she used the crutches to swing down the hall. He followed, finally losing the smile as he watched the strain in her movement.

This is why we do what we do, he told himself. A delicate flower like this needs so much protection. Let them think badly of him for coming here, for all he did in the course of his work. His work was necessary.

"This way." Grace continued to the kitchen. Music played softly from a low-grade speaker. A trashy pop tune, matching the sound system. She added milk to a pan already steaming on the hob, and put a second mug alongside one on the counter. "They said they'd be back by dinner, but I've got some macaroni cheese in the fridge anyway, and enough episodes of *Culture Snap* to last me like a week."

"They haven't been in touch?" Casaria asked. "Not said how they're getting on?"

"Mum messaged an hour ago, actually," Grace said, pouring hot milk into the mugs. "To remind me about my medicine. But they're not telling *me* things. I mean, if I'm really careful Mum might let me look at that" – she pointed at a book – "but I'm supposed to keep out, otherwise. It's okay. Rufe will fill me in. Do you like Rufe?"

Casaria wasn't listening, eyes on the book. The big leather-bound tome of Apothel's Miscellany, the collected thoughts of a madman. Entrusted into these banal civilians' hands. And they were off with the Ministry? Had the world turned upside down?

The girl was suddenly in front of him, smiling, with a mug held out. It gave a rich waft of chocolate. He took the drink stiffly. He hadn't asked for it – likely to give him spots – but her face was insistent. Disarmingly encouraging. He took a sip as she watched, and he offered the slightest nod, which somehow lit her face up with delight. She twirled back to the counter, towards her own drink, using a crutch like a vaulter's pole.

"You probably don't have real chocolate at work," Grace said. "Dad complains about his office; *they* have a choice between sugar water and *shit* wa –" She froze, a hand over her mouth, giving Casaria a secretive, cheeky look. "Sorry, Mr Casaria. I wasn't thinking."

He mumbled a response behind another sip of the drink as Grace took her own. This young beauty, joking with him, knew his name? He certainly shouldn't be here. Did she even understand flirting?

"Do you want to know what I think?" Grace asked. "Rufe's *fun*, but he needs to separate the stories from the reality. His dad might have been the same."

"Is *he* here?" Casaria asked. Surely they hadn't enlisted that bum Rufaizu, too?

"No, he went with them. *I'm* the only one too young. Old enough to get kidnapped by fairies, though."

Was anyone but him not involved in this? "Who did they go with exactly? Where to?"

Grace's eyes focused in realisation. Casaria forced his smile, but wasn't feeling it. Her face didn't shift. Was she going to scream?

"They left you out, too, Mr Casaria?" Grace spoke softly. He gave a dismissive snort, but had no immediate rebuttal. "They keep asking me if I'm okay. Like, do I have bad dreams or something? I told them it was nothing. My dad lived through this stuff over and over, I just had a few bad days. And I was *fine*. This" – she held up a bandaged foot – "wasn't even an *injury*. Too much walking, that's all. I mean, yes, it was scary, but I'm not gonna *stay* scared, am I? I'd rather get over it."

Casaria said nothing for a moment. Was she making a point? He had a bad foot, too. She'd got over her fears, he should too? But he didn't *have* fears. "Is that what they think? I'm not fit for work?"

Grace studied him for a confused moment. "I wasn't . . ." Then her face became very serious and she put her mug down. "Mr Casaria, is this to do with Ms Ward? I think they *are* with her. But listen, there's this guy in my class, Luke Merrick, he spent months talking to everyone *but* Claudia Newman, and when they finally got together, it wasn't even worth it. They split up like three weeks later. You like her but are worried because she's your boss? I'd just get it out there, if I were you."

Casaria's eyes were wide with . . . something. Shock? Anger? The cheek of this brat – the presumption – the same nonsense Pax had spouted. He lowered his drink to admonish her. But hesitated. What if Sam Ward was keeping him at bay out of similarly misguided awkwardness? Perhaps the girl was right.

11

"Stinks to heaven and hell," Letty told Edwing, pacing what little floor space her dark hideout permitted while Flynt watched with his arms folded. "The Dispenser's one thing, but that weed? Your new strains of dust? The glowing shit going into *pipes* – Pax was onto something, wasn't she? There's more behind Val's tricks than keeping us under lock and key. Connections to the Sunken City she's hiding."

"All the more reason to approach this diplomatically," Edwing said. Letty had expected a berating for their little break-in, but he'd come with quiet concern rather than anger. He'd spoken softly to Flynt, worried he might've been hurt. It was all good. They'd gone more or less unseen; the first guard wouldn't identify them, the engineer was too cowardly to raise a storm. And Edwing was looking forward rather than back. "If there's a connection between dust production and those tunnels, bringing it brashly into question could see us connected to the humans as a threat to our society. Raising treasonous suggestions. We can't risk undermining Valoria until we know what the connection is."

"You need to undermine the fuck out of her right away," Letty said. "She'll destroy the Dispenser – the only drastic thing you could do would be *not* storm in and secure it. Drum up a mob and pitchfork your way through!"

Edwing looked to Flynt and the scout said, "I could get a couple dozen guys –"

"All we'd do is expose ourselves," Edwing said. "She could say she was testing it in private, ensuring it was genuine, or safe. She would hide anything truly implicating her before we got in."

"You were there," Letty said to Flynt. "You get the need to act, don't you?"

"I get it," Flynt replied, looking to his brother. "But we've gotta act *smart*, don't we?"

Letty took that in unhappily; an echo of the comments she made to her own boys. They might've simply broken into the FTC and settled here under the radar, if she hadn't always been trying to do things *right*. That's what this kid wanted. She shook her head. "Maybe fast beats smart, right now."

"Short-sighted as ever, Letty," a low voice said, as a man entered. Edwing stayed Flynt's hand going to his pistol, as Letty recognised their guest, from long ago. Smark, pear-shaped and bald with swollen facial features; his loose suit was greasy in patches, perfectly fitting to his yellowing skin and an array of jewellery hanging from his left ear, chosen for size rather than elegance.

"Welcome, Smark," Edwing said. "Letty, this is the Waste Chief, I invited him."

"Chief now?" Letty said. He had been around before she was exiled, a neighbourhood junker back then. With ready access to human amenities, few public industries really mattered to the Fae: dust production and trade, entertainment, health and education were high up there. A few rungs down were the junkers: people responsible for sanitation and, more importantly, for removing all traceable evidence of the Fae. Letty commented, "For someone who's gone up in the world, you look worse than I remember."

"Feeling's mutual," Smark replied.

Behind him came a tall, greying woman with a dark suit and the flitting eyes of the perpetually nervous. Edwing said, "And this is Deidre, councilwoman for housing in the bottom third." An even lower role, really: anyone could manage static living spaces. "Deidre, Letty."

"The troublemaker," Smark surmised. Letty's grin told him to sit on a rusty spike.

"Letty and Flynt entered the vats. They've confirmed Valoria has the Dispenser."

"Entered the vats?" Smark responded incredulously, while Deidre offered hushed surprise: "That's good, no?"

"It's not good," Letty said, "because Val won't use the fucking weapon."

"Is that news?" Smark said. "Why should the Sunken City interest us when we've got humans on our borders?"

"Val obviously cares enough to avoid the place, you pile of bile," Letty snapped, then asked Edwing, "What are these pricks here for? This mug used to spend Saturdays hosing down vomit."

"Letty, please," Edwing intervened, holding up his hands. "We need to approach this from the top, where we can effect wider change. We need the Council – it can't just be my voice. Deidre's district contains our broadcasting equipment, she keeps us concealed while we spread our message, and between Flynt and Smark they have a network of traders. Supply routes, safe passage for our people – none of us can do as much alone as we can do together."

"Our networks have almost zero movement," Smark said, "now that her friends have everyone scared."

"Screw your network," Letty said. "I could put that weapon in the hands of someone that would actually use it, *alone*. We give people a place to go, Val's FTC loses all its clout. And from there we can figure out what else she's hiding."

"Put our weapon in the hands of a human?" Smark countered with disgust.

"One worth a hundred of you," Letty said. "If Pax doesn't already have answers, she'll have people we can talk to. Ways to show humans and Fae can figure this out together. Then Val has to put up or shut up."

"Or history repeats itself," Smark said. "Not the first time Letty had a plan involving a human, is it? Last time they miraculously stole from us."

"*That* human wasn't working with me when he took the weapon," Letty said through gritted teeth. "Because he didn't trust the Fae to use it."

"No, I agree with Letty," Edwing said, carefully. "Building goodwill with the humans, that's where a better future lies, for all Fae. And I have news of my own, in that regard. Now we're all here." From the way he watched Letty, she could tell it was something she wouldn't like; a reason, now, that he wasn't so mad at them breaking into the vats. "I have an opening. I received a hailing from Palleday, the revered –"

"Palleday!" Letty said. "She actually met that dinosaur? Found a way to connect? While we're yakking like arseholes?"

"Pax spoke to him, yes," Edwing admitted, slowly. "She proposed a meeting. But what Smark says is no exaggeration. Valoria has the city scared. We have no idea what the humans were up to in the nearby tunnels, and I very much doubt it was hostile, but the fear has been stoked. The FTC holds its breath. Even the scouts are grounded. The drain tunnels, the crawl webs, are all alarmed. If there was ever any doubt the Stabilisers knew the secret entrances to the FTC, not any more. Yet *I* can go, alone. I've got enough influence, yet, to leave the FTC on legitimate –"

"Like hell you're going without me!" Letty flared up, stepping so close Flynt moved to shield Edwing. The one-eyed Fae looked more worried than threatening, determined to hold her off nevertheless. His courage made her look unstable. She forced herself to act calmly. "She's my human. I need to see her."

"I wish you could," Edwing said, earnestly. "But the borders are sealed. And after a break-in at the vats, it'll surely get worse. But Valoria accepts that some neutral, *important* Fae, like Palleday, may be persuaded to move on without coercion. Under the guise of seeing him, I can go to Pax. While you two," Edwing told Smark and Deidre, "start a public conversation. Raise the questions our people need to hear. How can we truly justify exclusion from the humans?"

Deidre deferred to Smark, and he gave Letty a stony look, not happy even having her in the room. He said, "If it means sticking it to Governor Magnus, I'll do it."

"A true hero," Letty said. "Reluctantly standing up for what's best for everyone."

"Anyone would think you *want* a fight," Smark sneered.

"Yes I fucking do, isn't that why you need me?" Letty turned to Edwing. "And while you're making friends, we're supposed to wait and leave Val with the Dispenser?"

"The Council meets tomorrow afternoon," Edwing said. "Give me until then. I beg your patience – don't rock the boat, and I promise you we'll be ready to act."

Letty wanted to say fuck that. To hell with subtle plans and talking and her being trapped here. But she caught Flynt's eye again. Asking her to stop, to have faith. She huffed. "Tomorrow afternoon. Then, if you don't fuck shit up, I will."

12

One by one, the Bartons climbed out of a manhole in New Thornton, exhausted. Barton was vaguely aware that he should've stopped a few hours ago, when his ankle started aching, but the draw of the Sunken City was hard to ignore. When the women asked, he said he was fine. The place kept him awake. Rufaizu's enthusiasm even brought a smile to his face. The boy hopped about recounting adventures that never really happened, reminding Barton of Apothel, the cheery loon who'd drawn him into this world. It disarmed Holly and Ward, too. Their walk through the tunnels stretched into hours as Ward's worries faded, taking them away from the warehouse district into New Thornton. There were signs of creatures, but not recently. Claw marks left from sickles, scorch marks from helluvian hounds. Just like old times, with the added beeping confusion of the Ministry's scanner informing them things were unstable.

They ran into no more errant beasts, but Ward's analysis, and occasional calls back to her office (*her* phone worked down there), suggested other problems. Her people were reassessing everything they thought they understood of the underground lair. Same as Barton. Hard to believe he'd been so naïve, believing what those blue screens told him . . .

Out on the street, Holly called Grace while they waited for someone from Ward's office to ferry them home. Rufaizu slumped a few paces away. Finally spent. Barton heaved the manhole cover into place as Ward double-checked her readings.

"How messed up is it?" Barton asked.

"Well," Ward said, "the bulk of the horde has evidently stuck together, which is both good and bad. It's not a widespread problem, but it suggests the screens can direct strays to targeted locations. A dreadhorn might've done a lot of damage, unchecked."

"The way we had it," Barton said, "nothing *controlled* those creatures. The screens needed us to report their whereabouts. Needed *you* to do the same. We were their eyes and ears, weren't we?"

"That's the theory. But if we're looking at them manipulating energy, who's to say what control that gave them. Even if they couldn't necessarily track the creatures themselves, perhaps they still had some ability to influence their movements. It might be peripheral, uncontrolled."

"Like a lucky dip. They drop a defence and we see what slips out."

Ward hummed uncomfortably to say it was perfectly possible. "Not to worry; we'll start pinpointing the problem areas very soon."

"The problem is clear enough already," Barton said. "This novisan energy is more complicated than any of us thought. The tunnels themselves could be pooling it or something – if the screens can manipulate where the monsters travel. Makes me wonder if drinking glo hid stuff from us – what are the effects of just being down there?"

"You feel any effects now?" Ward replied. Checking over his body, he wasn't sure. Mostly he felt tired. She continued, "No, if we absorbed any of what's down there, it was too minimal to affect us much. But your glo, our novisan scans, they *were* blinkers. The blue screens didn't want us to understand anything fully."

Barton heard his own instinctive growl. Those bloody screens, with their broken English and cryptic messages. "If I could just get my hands on one . . ." He'd what? Punch a wall? Rufaizu caught his eye with a tired but encouraging look.

"Never met a foe the Citizen couldn't beat," the young man said. "But might not meet them again. Might never see them."

"We'll keep at it," Barton insisted. "We'll find them."

"I'll have more agents in tomorrow," Ward said. "You can take a break."

Barton watched Holly, across the road, with her back to them. Having overcome her initial reservations, she'd want to keep at it, the same as him. "It's fine. We're ready for more."

Holly briskly returned, sighting on Ward like a hawk. "Where's this pick-up?"

"Something wrong?" Barton asked.

"Indeed. Not that I don't appreciate your people's help, but I'd rather Grace *not* be left alone with any of you. Least of all Mr Casaria."

"What?" Ward and Barton voiced alarm together. Ward added, "Is he there now?"

"A fleeting visit, apparently," Holly said, icily. "But not a good start, is it?"

"I'll handle it!" Ward insisted, marching aside to make a call of her own. Barton met Holly's fuming eyes. What were they thinking, leaving Grace alone so soon after what she'd been through?

"Where are you?" Ward barked into the phone, equally incensed. "You've got no damn right, Cano. How dare you?" Her assault stalled with whatever he said. "That's because you're suspended, we're not *hiding* –" She stopped again. Swallowed it. "I'll send you the address. Come in at once. You're on your last warning. Understand?"

She hung up and offered an apologetic, worried look.

"If he touched –" Barton started.

"He wouldn't," Ward said. "I'm sure in his head he was doing something right. I'll take care of it – this shouldn't have happened."

Holly was staring at Barton, imploring him to do more. He didn't know what. He could throttle that smarmy agent. He couldn't shout at Ward, though; she looked as troubled as them. He said, "You . . . you'll handle it. We need to go home to our daughter?" It came out as a question, directed at Holly.

She held her indignation high, but said no more.

*

The Baudelaire Club sat in an upper-floor suite of an old converted bank, south of the River Gader. Its pillars and triangular pediment recalled a grandiose government building, the clubrooms harking back to colonial times, interiors framed in dark, expensive wood interrupted by deep green wallpaper and ornate carpeting. The furniture was big, heavy and sculpted, and every hint of metal was polished to a brass shine. Cigar boxes sat between crystal decanters, and the terrace looked down on a private park.

Pax had been once before, for a game out of her league. Being a token female player was good for opening most doors once, but it took real work to get invited back to the Baudelaire Club. Its members had old money and old values, expecting their women to show flesh, not intelligence. Pax had earned modest winnings on a hefty buy-in, but offended a member who offered her his number to arrange a dress fitting for her next visit. She'd suggested he didn't have the figure for it.

It wasn't something she regretted. But now she'd been invited back, with the many trials the last week had dumped on her, she came in wary of burning more bridges. Her single all-purpose dress wasn't classy enough for the Baudelaire, so she'd opted for a pair of black trousers and the sweater she'd acquired while on the run, striped and inoffensively slim. She'd also tied her hair back in a short ponytail, going for discreet over any attempt to make it look *classy*. She didn't expect to turn heads, but she could avoid turned-up noses. Quite aside from a chance at money and security, it was important, after all, that she stayed long enough to meet any lingering Fae.

A doorman in a burgundy suit led her to the game, past suits sipping cocktails. The poker room held eight men, the locals in their finery, the foreigners notable for their lack of it. The big Americans were near the balcony terrace, as was the pro Yannick (had Monroe approached him after seeing him at Pax's tournament table?). And there by the bar was Monroe, talking to a tall, slim gentleman in a tuxedo. There was something familiar about him. His angular features and narrow, judging eyes exuded power, definitely a few stations above most people. Even his jet-black hair, barely a centimetre long, likely cost a fortune to cut.

Monroe waved Pax over. About to say hello, Pax looked past the two men into the beaming face of the barman. Monroe's big henchman, Howling Jowls Jones, was polishing a glass, dressed in shirtsleeves and braces. A large square block of a man with the chiselled jaw and curly blond locks of a model, offset by a wonky smile and Pax's memories of him stabbing Casaria. Out of character, he said nothing, leaving the introductions to Monroe.

"Pax, our local champion," Monroe said merrily, lightly tapping her arm to break the look of uncomfortable recognition she gave Jones. "You know the most eminent Mr Tycho Duvalier?"

Recognising the name with surprise, Pax took in Monroe's companion again. This game was even bigger than she'd anticipated, and a response slipped out to alienate herself from it: "No, Mr Monroe, playing cards in dark alleys and above Chinese restaurants doesn't often bring me into contact with the 1%."

"You're a pro?" Tycho asked politely, as he held out a hand. His enunciation was so crisp she wouldn't have been able to place the accent if she didn't already know he was American. Pax shook his hand – *ridiculously* smooth skin – and wondered if her peasant fingers just rubbed off thousands of pounds' worth of manicure treatment.

"Yeah, I'm a pro in the loosest sense of the word," Pax said, part of her screaming to stop talking before she ruined everything. Tycho was heir to the monstrous fortune of Duvcorp, richer than a Byzantine emperor. Ward had name-dropped the company earlier, she recalled with a flash of unease. Pax tried to push the feeling away with humour. "I sometimes make enough to buy a takeaway."

"Modest *and* charming," Monroe said. *Charming*, about as glowing as *homely*. He was putting on an act for Tycho, reining in his broad Farling accent. "Pax did Ordshaw proud today, didn't she? Queen of the World Poker Tour. Plenty of pros out of Vegas didn't come close to her."

"They'll write history books about it, the 68th Place Champion," Pax said.

Monroe laughed. "Did better than Dave 'the Cave' Spencer, didn't you?"

"Did I?" Spencer was a two-times WPT champion. Between scheming over how best to stretch out her £4,238 win and her anxieties over the Fae and underground monsters, Pax had paid little attention to who was still in or out.

"And she's bringing us Dutch McRory," Monroe continued. "Legend, ask anyone."

"I know the name," Tycho said, then asked Pax, "He's a friend of yours?"

"About as deep as my friendships go." Pax smiled. True enough.

"Oh for sure," Monroe said. "I'm surprised you didn't come together."

She kept her smile, holding his gaze. Of course, her stake here depended not just on her winning personality but that pro's presence, too. She'd texted McRory the address; seeing the clientele, she wondered if it was even necessary. "I'm sure he'll be here."

Monroe betrayed no aggravation, and said, "Drinks, then, Pax. You're a Scotch girl, aren't you? Jones, whip her up something special."

Something special, Pax saw without looking closely, was a whisky that would've been locked in a safe in most places she drank. It would help ease her nerves. She might even enjoy this. A mediocre prize in a tournament, a seat at the Baudelaire, making herself difficult in front of the world's richest men. A quiet hope of seeing an anonymous Fae. However uneasy she felt, things were on track.

13

Following the club's activity through the floor-to-ceiling windows that looked out onto the terrace, Fresko wished he could see the players' cards. It was obvious who was in charge of each hand – he could pick out the winners from the losers without fail – but it was dull as hell. He shouldn't have let Mix off, even if the man was a drunk liability. Some company would've been nice, waiting in a tree, trying to decide exactly how to handle this situation with Lightgate.

The Baudelaire Club brought back memories. Three years back they'd plotted a raid here. Bigwigs swilled brandies you could trade for cars; even their tiepins were worth a fortune. And they insisted on privacy that kept even the Ministry at bay. Letty's gang had sneaked in, taking trinkets for about a month until it got noticed and was pinned on three long-standing members of the staff. A concierge with decades of spotless service took the main blame. They'd laughed like hell about it, and it still made Fresko smile. But watching the building, waiting for the lummox to step out of the game, he got grim again. Was he gonna chat with the woman who'd torn their gang apart, or what? She was enjoying herself at this big poker table, drinking, chatting with some slick prick, now introducing some old fart who everyone seemed eager to suck off. Her granddad?

"Dutch McRory," a voice said. "He wrote the book on human poker."

Fresko's heart jumped but he didn't flinch, calmly looking up from his rifle scope to find Lightgate had crept up on him. She could've just arrived or could've been there an hour, for the calm way she sat on the branch beside him. How the fuck did she find him?

Keeping his voice neutral, like he'd been expecting her, Fresko said, "The girl doesn't belong in there. Not her class of people *at all*."

"I have decided," Lightgate said, with tired deliberation, "not to underestimate her. Notice anything strange about this place? It's . . ." She trailed off, eyes narrowing, scanning up and down. She sniffed, too. There was a good hundred metres of unlit grass and trees between them and the building. No way this woman could see nor smell anything of note.

"Wanna borrow the rifle?" Fresko suggested.

Lightgate shook her head, and put a hand into her sling. Rather than produce her own scope, she pulled out a hip flask and took a sip. The fumes burnt Fresko's nostrils.

"What is that shit?"

She held it towards him, silently studying the building.

From the way she'd settled into position, he guessed he wasn't in her shit-book. She must've figured he was scouting out an opportunity. There was no way she could know the plan; she hadn't followed them to Palleday's, had she? To appear helpful, Fresko said, "You wanted a chat with her, this could work. Assuming you don't just wanna put one in her from here. Wait till someone steps outside, with the door open, it'll look like an aneurysm."

"You probably don't remember working with me before," Lightgate said, taking another swig. He gave her a disbelieving look. How could anyone forget the ill-advised times they'd flown together? "I remember you guys. You were supposed to be the smart one. I don't want her dead. You moron." She said it so blandly it took a moment for Fresko to take offence. "We'll take our time. See what opportunities arise."

He frowned, dreading whatever plans she might concoct. She definitely hadn't been following them earlier, though, or she'd already know Pax was expecting a meeting.

Pax considered how far she could push Tycho Duvalier. He was a tight player, only getting involved when he had the best hands. And right now, her read said he *thought* he had a good hand, but not the best. A bet before the flop, barely big enough to drive everyone else out. A bigger bet when an ace came with a seven and a three. Then a hesitant call when she raised him.

It was just the two of them going into the turn, when a king came. Perfect. Tycho mulled it over before betting again. A dutiful one, less than a third of the pot. Pax had drunk just enough whisky not to overthink this; she called and let the river come. A nine. No straights or flushes available. Tycho made one last stabbing bet and Pax pushed in big without hesitation. Doubling the pot. He stared at the chips and she knew she had him. Absolutely. It didn't matter that she held Shit All. Or that there was close to three grand sitting there. Almost as much as she'd made after two days grafting in a tournament she'd waited her whole life for.

Well, she couldn't *quite* ignore that. It was a fucklot of money.

But this was her work. Waiting, needling, studying people and picking her moments with craft, unlike the tournament that forced panicking, blundering heroics. This felt *right*.

The room was silent. The only people remotely relaxed were McRory and Yannick, who likely read the hand exactly as Pax did. Monroe greedily salivated by the bar; the bigger the pot, the bigger his rake, as host.

Pax had Tycho's measure after only an hour at the table. Moneyed types usually bullied their way through pots – three grand was nothing to them – but Tycho valued being seen to make the right decisions. His family didn't become billionaires by throwing money away; that was written all over him.

"You put me in a difficult position," Tycho said.

"That's the idea," Pax replied, desperately waiting for him to make the right move. He had to believe she had his ace-queen beat. For sure, those were his cards: good when opening the hand, but not good enough to go mad with. Worried by that king, reminding him of at least one obviously *better* possibility. His thin eyes ran over the cards and chips multiple times. He had to fold, Pax must have ace-king at worst. Possibly a set.

Her eyes rested on the money again.

That three grand might be Pax's only big pot of the night. Yannick and McRory had been taking most of the hands, with her bowing to their more confident styles. This was her moment, and she silently begged Tycho to fold. If he called, she would be close to walking away empty-handed; a big blow to Monroe's generous stake for McRory's arrival.

"You've got something," Tycho concluded. She gave him a sweet smile. More confusing than a blank poker face. But Ward's comment about Duvcorp flashed up and her smile faltered, paranoid for a second – *what's he doing here?* Had he come for her? Was she drawing too much attention to herself?

Silly. He was the COO of a truly enormous company, for crying out loud.

He sighed. "I've enough on my plate already without adding this uncertainty. Well done." Tycho pushed his cards to the dealer.

The other Americans celebrated with loud congratulatory comments. One of them demanded, brashly, "So what'd you have?"

"A gentleman shouldn't ask," Tycho admonished the man politely.

"What I *have*," Pax answered, masking massive relief to drag in the winnings, "is enough money to avoid stealing soap from public toilets this month."

It got a few smiles, icy enough to suggest this wasn't the place. Tycho took it well, though, saying, "We supply sanitary products across Europe, I could get you a deal." It was hard to tell if that was a joke or a genuine offer, given Duvcorp's ubiquitous interests. Then he was standing. "Gentlemen. It's been a pleasure, but my father would disown me to see I was knowingly playing at a disadvantage. That's been made clear. Somewhere in the world, it's daylight, and I have work to do."

He folded his coat over his forearm and waited by the door for Monroe to cash him out. The next hand was dealt and the other players made comments about Pax driving away their most interesting guest. She tried to focus back on the cards. Thankful for the dual reliefs of winning big *and* banishing her sneaking suspicions of Duvcorp.

Then Tycho called over, "Care to walk me out, Ms Kuranes?"

Not good. Either an indecent proposal or Sunken City complications? In both cases, saying the wrong word to a man of his stature might open up doors she'd rather leave closed. God knows she'd done enough of that for one lifetime.

"Won more than you bargained for?" Yannick sniggered.

Struggling not to let the worry show, Pax forced another smile. She excused herself quietly – not quietly, she tripped on the chair – before exiting ahead of Tycho. The hallway was empty, and it swayed as Pax realised she was a little light-headed. The price of her whisky courage, mounting tiredness and high-stakes giddiness.

"I won't keep you," Tycho said, closing the door and lowering his voice to a whisper. "Only, I *can't* simply leave."

Here it was. Come to my hotel, or worse? *We've been watching you.*

"Did I make the right move?" he said.

Pax paused. He'd brought her out here for that? Rather than show crass curiosity in front of everyone? She said, "Ordinarily, I'd say the time to pay for that information has passed."

Tycho's eyes watched hers like a retinal scanner. Deciding whether or not she was inviting a bribe. He chose correctly. "I'm at the mercy of your charity."

"You had ace-queen," Pax told him, and he raised an eyebrow in surprise. Said nothing, waiting for more. She didn't give it to him. That she'd figured out what his cards were should've told him he was beat, one way or another.

"I was right to fold," he admitted. "I should not have been playing."

Correct. Pax smiled to herself. A little more at ease in this territory. Then it just came out. "Can I ask *you* something? Are you in town because Ordshaw's falling apart?"

Tycho's turn to pause. "With the animal attack and the train accident?"

"And the collapsing buildings, yeah. You've got that shiny tower to protect, after all." She heard herself but could not stop. "Why else would you be here?"

"A hundred reasons," Tycho said, amused by her forthrightness. "*Tonight,* I shall be briefing a management team overseeing our plants in China. Likely they need replacing by morning or we're down a few million."

"Must be an expensive garden," Pax said. He stared. "Plants. Like . . ."

"Ah," he said. "No, I meant factories, making computers."

"Got it," Pax said. There'd be no fairy tale wedding to this wealthy prince. "But I'm curious. Why would your city's problems gravitate towards *us*, exactly?"

"Evil lurking under the city targets the government," Pax shrugged, "maybe it'll target other powerful institutions in the area."

The analytic eyes were back. "An interesting perspective."

Yeah, she didn't like piquing that interest. Really should not have spoken. "I'm babbling, aren't I? Look, I'm bursting for a piss, so I'll just –"

"But you're right," Tycho said. "That's the funny thing. My father *was* concerned by Ordshaw's news. Not through any fear for Duvcorp, mind. For more . . . esoteric interests. I'm humouring him, coming here, otherwise he would have sent someone less discreet. But that is an interesting thought. The UK government was *targeted,* wasn't it."

Pax quickly shook her head. Christ, he hadn't given a shit until she opened her stupid mouth. "I've had too much whisky, it's just –"

"Pax." He said her name like they were old friends, moving closer. "Let me confide. My father entertains ghost stories that strain relationships and drain funds. Mostly it's nonsense. Yet, as the whole world knows, he sometimes strikes gold."

Great: exactly the strange sort of turn she wanted to avoid. Still, she had to ask, now they were here. "What sort of gold would involve us, here?"

Tycho's smile revealed too-straight teeth, as he seemed to remember where they were. "That's a game *you* should not be playing. Thank you for this evening. I trust you'll use the winnings responsibly."

And with that, he walked away.

Pax watched him disappear around a corner. He had unwittingly imparted some curious details she wasn't quite able to unpack, while she might've set him on a dangerous path. And she had told one of the world's most powerful men that she was bursting for a piss, to get out of it.

Really. Great.

Fresko watched Lightgate with complete uncertainty. The woman had been sitting staring into the shadows for minutes, seeming to scent the air, ever since some unseen occurrence had drawn her interest. It had happened when Pax left the table, making excuses, following that rich prick out. Lightgate had been suggesting following her when she instead stopped abruptly, entering this weird attentive state. Fresko didn't dare interrupt. If it meant not causing a bloodbath, he could live with sitting still.

Finally, Lightgate held the hip flask out in front of her, arm straight, tracing something in the air. Fresko followed the gesture through the rifle scope. He couldn't see anything. She explained, "We are not alone. *Very* interesting."

There were no humans, clearly, and if she meant Fae, how in hell could she see?

"Tonight, we observe, my dim-witted friend," Lightgate said. "I've got a good feeling about this."

14

Returning to the Ministry's new chambers, Sam was greeted by her young analyst, Ryan, frantic to tell her something. She wanted to brush him off, to draft a report that would slow Obrington's purge down, but Ryan insisted with waves to his desk.

"It's strange. Maybe nothing?" He brought up the Ministry's map of the Sunken City on his computer screen – a three-tier plan of tunnels. It was overlaid by shades of colour, from yellow through to red. "We've been going over *everything*, rebooting the motion sensors, physically going down there. Meantime, I revised our historical markers. This heatmap shows the horde's movements over a five-year period. All the creatures. An even distribution, right?"

"Yes."

"But look here. And here." He pointed from one spot to another. Then tapped the monitor in a dozen more places. "All these spots."

Sam didn't follow. He pointed at a gap between the outer edges of orange colouration. "There's nothing there."

"Exactly," Ryan said. "Nothing in any of these spots. Sixteen of them."

"There's a lot of tunnel space," Sam said. "Some spots are bound to go untouched."

"But *nothing* has been in them. Crusads and bunch spiders, they get all over the place, and look, this one, the horde passed right by this room. Nothing slipped inside?"

Sam's first thought was that the Ministry had been monitoring these tunnels for years; if such a pattern was relevant, someone would have spotted it. But by that logic, they should've spotted the novisan transfers Pax uncovered. The areas were mapped, so the Ministry had been to these locations, but perhaps only once, ever, without movement there. Maybe he had something.

"Prepare a list of co-ordinates," Sam suggested. "Check them against novisan scans and see what's above them."

Just what she needed: a new problem. Thankfully, as she moved to her own desk, Obrington didn't wave her over, too engrossed in his phone to say hello. At least all these additional confusions would build a case for delaying Protocol 38. Sam just needed to get the report written before Casaria arrived, as he would make it next to impossible to complete it with a clear head. It was her own fault, she shouldn't have left him in the wind. Damn, it was a minor miracle the Bartons hadn't gone ballistic.

Casaria swept into the office before Sam had written an introduction to her report. He was clad in a pressed suit and starched shirt, not a hair out of place.

Obrington gave Sam a look, directing the problem her way. She opened her mouth to invite his input, but he was already texting again.

Steeling herself, Sam sat up straight. Casaria limped over, examining the vaulted chamber, his toothpaste grin a little uncertain. He indicated the plastic "guest" chair Sam had on the other side of the desk. "You mind?"

"A little," Sam said. "But go ahead."

"Surprised to see you here." Casaria gestured from her desk, on the outer perimeter of their open-plan workspace, to Obrington's central position. "Shouldn't you be there?"

"Shouldn't *you* have stayed home?" Sam hissed, refusing to let him mock her.

"According to you." Casaria sat down and stretched out his injured leg, wearing his usual arrogant smile. The cut running across his eye was almost healed. His skin, somewhat concealed by foundation, looked its usual tan-tone, with only a few scrapes showing. Besides the limp, there was nothing visibly wrong with his leg; no cast or bandages like Darren or Grace Barton had, though he'd lost a toe. Sam knew he was a mess inside, though, even if his appearance hid it. Casaria had risked his life for Pax and the city, but had shoved Sam, and might've done worse if he hadn't been interrupted.

She raised her chin. "Yes, according to me. Your superior. You want to get fired? What the hell were you thinking, going to the Bartons' home?"

"Relax," he said, cautiously. "I only went because I didn't know where any of *you* were. It's no secret you need staff, how could I sit idle?"

"Casaria, for the shit you've done, you could be *hanged*," Sam said, as firm as she dared without raising her voice. To hell with it, it was time to put him in his place – but his face clouded over with an unfamiliar emotion. Some sort of . . . shame?

He answered quietly, "I waited by your place."

Sam's eyes shot open. He had gone to her bungalow? Her oasis, where the streets were unlit after 10pm because it was *safe?*

"I didn't go in," Casaria continued, some consolation. "I could've, your neighbours aren't exactly vigilant."

Sam was about to question him, but caught herself. How would her neighbours let him in? Then the realisation hit her. They'd shared rides when they patrolled together. Three years ago. He didn't know she'd moved out of her West Farling apartment building. She said, "You should have called."

"*You* didn't. And I don't like doing things over the phone," Casaria confessed. "Not ones that matter." He sat forward, then back, unable to pick a pose. "Pax is okay?"

"You didn't sit outside her apartment, too?" Sam replied. Casaria covered his hurt look with another smile. His demeanour was off, nervous.

"I'm a professional," he said. "Worrying about the people of this city is my job. And I didn't *sleep* with her, before you ask." Said like it should reassure Sam. "Look. I didn't scare the Barton girl. Good *someone* checked in on her, if you ask me."

"How can –"

"I was trying to find *you*," Casaria quickly continued. "I've been thinking – a lot – and it's not good. Before – in Greek Street, when I came for – you know –"

Sam raised an eyebrow. Had the possibility that he might have seriously hurt her stuck in his mind, too?

"I lost a lot of blood," he said. "I'd spent two nights without a bed. I wasn't myself. I didn't want to scare you. I would *never* hurt you."

A derisive snort escaped Sam's nose. She covered her face. "Sorry. Cano. Do you really believe everyone is stupid, or is it just that you keep convincing yourself of your own lies? You're suspended because you can't be trusted. You're unstable and definitely *wanted* to get in Pax's pants." She wasn't proud the last bit came out. But it was true.

Casaria was speechless. Some of the glow was gone from his blue eyes. Yet he would come out with some offensive or dismissive comment. Damned if she would let him.

Sam said, "You see Obrington over there? Your fate's in *his* hands. But I'm pretty sure I can predict what he'll say once I tell him you couldn't lay low."

"Please don't," Casaria said, a shimmer of fear finally on his face. "You're right, okay? Pax spun me out. Talking to her –"

"We're gonna go in circles," Sam huffed, but he hurried on.

"*She* said the same things. Not just her. I've *really* been thinking. In that church, I was there to protect her, but it was me on the floor, her firing the gun. If I wasn't good for that, then what?" He continued with a mad smile, almost laughing. "I don't *know* what I've been doing, and I'm pretty sure she hates me and thinks I'm useless, like you – but I found her, at least, didn't I? She told you about her sensing things, the . . ." Casaria held up his own hands, fingers spread, as if that explained something. "I made mistakes, but it was on her behalf. And I don't want anything more from her – or those civilians – I just want to keep doing a good job. Don't take that from me."

"You want to prove you're professional, wait for us to contact you," Sam said, trying to remain firm. Panic crossed his eyes, like an opportunity was slipping away.

"But you know me," he said. "And this isn't over, is it? You need those tunnels secured, and the Fae –"

"Casaria." Sam held her mouth closed.

He paused and seemed to suddenly sense his own pitiful display. His grin came back, utterly empty, and he stood. "Right. No, I'm sure you're hard at work. Always at it, aren't you?" He straightened his jacket. "I'll go. I didn't mean harm – you know someone should've been checking on that girl anyway." He paused again. Then rushed out a final idea, almost as one word: "Maybe I could get you dinner when you're done here?" Only the briefest pause for Sam to take it in. "You know, to apologise. If I need to? I don't know how upset you are?"

No words came to Sam. Her face was stuck fast, wide-eyed, as she realised this wasn't about his job. Not entirely. This self-pity and apologetic routine, his nerves –

was he psyching himself up to ask her out? Sam feared the slightest movement might make her gag.

Casaria's eyes slowly tracked up to read her stricken face. Then he muttered under his breath. "Of course. Stupid idea." He turned to leave and Obrington finally intervened.

"You two having a good meeting?" he boomed, pacing across the room. Sam gave him a cringing look, not wanting to stretch this out. Had he been waiting to make sure the conversation reached its awkward zenith before joining them?

"I'm going," Casaria said.

"Oh, but we haven't had the pleasure." Obrington made it sound like an order, positioning himself in Casaria's way. Sam hadn't quite recovered enough to know where she wanted this to go. She simply wanted it gone. "Wayne Obrington, your new chief, in case that wasn't obvious. Ward, I take it you're reconsidering sidelining this man? Might be as well – when my next set of steel-dicked agents with fingers on the triggers get here, I've got a mind to –"

They were saved from hearing his plan by a loud beeping, a flashing red light drawing their attention to a Support computer. Ryan raced to check the details, calling out, "Proximity alert – human – maybe a blip."

"You can tell that from the pitch of a beep, can you?" Obrington said, sarcastically, as Casaria gave Sam a knowing look. One that said, *see, this place is falling apart.*

"There's been a couple today while we reset the sensors," Ryan explained, frantically deactivating the alarm. "It's BGb-67, up on the –"

"St Alphege's," Casaria said. "The closest access point's the Victorian sewer, off Meer Street. There's about two blocks between that and BGb-67, no way someone gets that far without setting off another sensor."

The flashing light and the beeping stopped. Sam stood carefully as Ryan's hands went up, denying responsibility.

"Sometimes the myriad creatures trigger the human sensors," he said. "Cloth frogs, maybe."

"This how you usually deal with blips?" Obrington said. "Reason your way out of it with whatever daft idea pops to mind? On a day when we've seen *repeated* evidence of things not being where they're supposed to?" He turned to Sam. "Anyone nearby?"

Sam shook her head, aware that Landon was starting a shift in East Farling and Obrington's new men would be finishing up in Nothicker. "We're closer ourselves, by far."

"How fortuitous," Obrington said. "Guess you recalled him at the right time. Agent Casaria, are you up for some redemptive casual reconnaissance?" His eyes stayed on Sam, weighing her up. "Assuming that's what this is? A rallying of the troops?"

Sam stared back. Definitely not what this was. But she had to get her report written, and this potential confusion certainly needed investigating. Casaria looked hopeful, to the point of restraining himself from speaking. He *did* know his job, despite his faults. And it would keep him away from her. Sam said, "Yes. Let him go. Just for this."

Casaria's grin returned. "I'll be back before you know it."

"No weapons, no heroics," Obrington ordered. "Get eyes on it, that's all. I don't want any extra crap hanging over us tomorrow."

Casaria was already halfway across the room, eager to prove himself, limp conspicuously gone. Obrington turned back to Sam. "I appreciate you being proactive, we might need him for Protocol 38. But you've got a screw loose if you were flirting with that one."

Sam could have screamed, but chose not to. Casaria was out the door. Everyone would be going home soon, tomorrow was a new day. Best, she calmly told herself, to complete this report.

15

Pax leant on the marble counter of the sink unit, staring in the mirror. A little more exhaustion and she'd be wearing panda eyes. She splashed icy water from a gold tap over her face. Her brain warned her it wouldn't *actually* help her stay awake. She groaned, piss off brain. She was having fun, making money in a place where, with these opulent toilets, they literally threw their money down the shitter. The potential danger of Tycho Duvalier had wandered into the night and even if Monroe took back half Pax's earnings it would be a profitable evening.

But wasn't there something else?

"Excuse me, please don't be alarmed," a polite voice said, and Pax turned to search for its source. She was vaguely aware that this was a unisex toilet, but it had definitely been empty. And the timbre of that voice, well-spoken as it was, carried a quiet pitch that she'd been getting used to. She lowered her eyes.

Oh yes. There was something else.

A tiny man stood next to the faucet, hands clasped genially across his waist, lacy wings up over his shoulders. Holding onto the counter, Pax bent to bring her face down to his level, a little too quick in her slightly inebriated state. He took a step back, but just one.

"Sorry," she muttered. "Hey. Are you wearing glasses?"

She gripped the counter tighter to resist the temptation to poke him. He offered an uncertain smile. A businessman of a fairy, he would've fit in at the club.

"Is that a real tie?" Pax squinted. "That knot must be *tiny*."

"Yes." The fairy adjusted the tie. "I understand you proposed a little talk."

"Well, it'll have to be, won't it?" Pax's hand was up near him, then, thumb and index finger held apart in an estimation of his size. "Little, I mean."

The fairy looked from her fingers back up to her face. Hearing her own words confirmed again that the whisky had been a bad idea. Her attempt at an encouraging smile didn't seem to help, so she tried to shake herself out of inebriation, only making him retreat from the flailing hair that came loose from her ponytail. Pax backed off, centring herself, before trying again. "Palleday got a message to you? Wait – where's Letty?"

"Yes – I'm afraid until our political situation changes, she is stuck in the FTC."

"So you've brought me a plan to bust her out?"

"I have a plan to bring *change*. My name is Edwing, I'm a member of the Fae Council. I don't know how much Letty shared with you, but our governor, Valoria, has institutionalised a fear and hatred of humans, promoting *peace* as zero human contact. You said –"

"*Peace*?" Pax said. "She tried to kill me!"

"She's spun many lies. But I believe in the sort of connection you formed with Letty. In an openness that can benefit us all. *I* believe human and Fae can work together." He finished with a proud, upturned head.

"And" – Pax couldn't help it – "you said you're called Ed*wing*?"

He hesitated. "Yes. My parents were patriots."

Pax offered silence to that. Fuck, she really shouldn't have had that whisky. Or spent all day playing poker or delegated anything to Sam Ward – this was the important stuff, *fuck.* "We need to get clear of here for a proper chat. Let me make an exit, we –"

The door creaked on its hinges. Too late.

Without thinking, Pax spun to shield the counter and threw her hand back, closing it over the tiny man. Just in time, as a newcomer strode into the washroom and paused. Jones, hulking in with his shit-eating grin. Acting like she was turning off the tap, Pax moved her hand from the sink to her trouser pocket, Edwing rigid in her loose fist, not struggling. She held him there, keeping her wide eyes on Jones.

"Thought I heard you talking?" he said, brightly.

"What if I was?" Pax answered.

He scanned the room, as if to say: *there's no one else around.* She let her eyes talk, too: *figure it out for yourself.* With no explanation forthcoming, Jones took a big step closer. His lopsided grin, she saw now, was uneven from cuts and bruises, concealed with makeup. He said, "I don't mean to intrude, you know, it's technically not even a ladies', this place. Not sure they *have* a ladies'. I read it wasn't until the '90s that Baudelaire first let a woman through the doors. I swear."

"So who cleared up after them before? Black folk?"

Jones laughed, in a measured way, not his usual whoop. "Stinks, don't it? I said to the boss, he wants to hook us up with this room and swanky company, we oughta take extra for our efforts, right? Bet some of them decanters are worth a boatload."

"Except the *game* is legal," Pax said. She shifted, trying to relax the hand in her pocket without drawing attention to it. Edwing wasn't moving. Hopefully out of caution, not because she'd hurt him.

"Those guys in there," Jones said, "you think they made their fortunes paying taxes? You, schmoozing with Tycho fucking Duvalier? Heir to that corrupt throne? What'd *he* want with you?"

"A goodnight kiss, what do you think?"

"You entertained him? Billionaires on the backs of paupers, Pax, you want to talk criminals, give me strength."

"I don't especially want to talk at all, to be honest," Pax said, meaning *with you.*

"Yeah, you see..." Jones sidled closer, approaching the counter, and Pax took a step back. He was bigger than ever in this space, an impassable obstacle between her and the door. "I thought there might be bad blood between us. The boss, he says don't bother Pax, for the sake of the game and all. But we need to clear the air, don't we, you and me? How am I gonna serve drinks smiling like a prat with you thinking I'm some kind of asshole?"

"Shit, Jones." Pax sidestepped, an eye on the door. "That never bothered you before."

"Ouch!" Jones whooped. "See, I don't want to lose that! You are special, Pax, you're one of *us*."

That rooted her to the spot. She'd imagined threats, mild intimidation or knowing remarks. Not camaraderie. She didn't want that, and was shaking her head to say so. But Jones nodded more vigorously.

"Come on, by now we must be practically family. We work *well* together, don't we? Holy *fuck*, we torture a guy and you get us off the hook?"

Pax felt Edwing shift. "That wasn't me."

"Alright, look." Jones held up big, calloused hands. "I get it. You're cautious and that's good. And the boss, he's super cautious too, so he says, leave Pax be, I do it. This conversation never happened. But I gotta speak, and you know Bees would say the damn same. I'm giving you space, right." Jones moved towards the door. Hands still up. "But I'll give it to you straight, too. Come in, you get compensated good. Real good. You already earned it."

"I don't need space," Pax said. "It's already a no."

"It's already a *go*." Jones winked. "Just a question of you getting paid or not."

Her face twisted in confusion. He wasn't talking about what they'd already been through, but something new. Together with how well-meaning Monroe had been, with his hand-on-his-heart shit, this didn't sit right. "This game *is* legal, isn't it?"

"Hell yes." Jones dropped his hands, suddenly serious. "Fuck, don't even joke on that, we're on a serious earner tonight. And here's me not rocking the boat, right? But be in touch. I feel rotten the way we left things, don't I? You know Bees does, too."

The mention of Bees only made her more uneasy. "Where *is* he?"

Jones stared for a second, then his goofy grin was back and he ran two fingers over his mouth to imitate a zip closing. He continued talking anyway. "You know me, I care about careless talk. Enjoy the evening, Pax. I'm rooting for you."

Pax took a step after him as he made an exit, wanting to know more but remembering the rather more pressing concern of the fairy in her hand. As the door swung shut, something light brushed the back of her hair. Her spare hand was halfway up to swiping at it when she felt a pinprick of pressure at the top of her neck and a harsh male voice snarled, "You let him go right now."

Ah shit, another one. And what, a gun to her head?

Holding up her free hand, Pax slowly drew Edwing out of her pocket, lifting him as gently as she could. "I was trying to protect him."

"A human, protect him?" the man snapped. Young, edgy. "Don't *ever* touch him."

Pax uncurled her hand and Edwing stood out of it. He straightened his jacket and trousers. Then his tie, and finally his glasses. Unhurried, if a little nervous.

"You okay?" his unseen companion asked.

"It's fine, Flynt," Edwing said. "She meant well. Didn't know any better."

He beat his wings, lifting gracefully to float back from Pax. The pressure was relieved from the back of her head, a little breeze hinting the other one had taken off. Pax half-twisted but didn't see him. She said, "Sorry. I *do* know better. You guys can hide like magic, can't you? With that dust of yours –"

"Most humans don't notice us," Edwing agreed. "There *are* exceptions. So thank you for trying. I apologise for my brother's enthusiasm."

"I'm used to it. Last time I touched Letty I got pistol-whipped." She indicated the tiny cut above her eyebrow. "Deservedly so."

"Well. Where were we?"

"Not somewhere good," Pax replied, Jones' words hanging over her. "You've got somewhere else we can meet? I'll go straight there."

Edwing considered their options. "I'd like only a small concession from you today, to take back to my people. You told Letty the Ministry sought peace with us. Valoria Magnus claims otherwise, that there is no safety in trusting them. They've even been spotted near us, unannounced. Can you see a way forward?"

"Absolutely." Pax nodded. "I'm sure they *were* announced, your people must've hidden that. The Ministry are trying to get their act together and them being in your area was nothing to do with you. Talk to them – I can call them now."

"I'm our Chair of Information," Edwing said, "and I cannot guarantee the security of our electronic communications. But if you could arrange a meeting in person, then I can take that to my people, for sure. You have someone that you trust, from the Ministry? We could meet tomorrow – would midday give you enough time to arrange this?"

"It's a date. The Ministry want it, too." Pax paused. It meant another half day of waiting for answers – surely she could get something now? How to quickly explain the blue screens situation? Or that Pax wanted to know everything about the Fae. The whisky helped. "You know what makes your energy special? The Sunken City and you all, the Fae, there's something going on there."

Edwing gave it a moment's quiet thought. "We have much to discuss. Tomorrow. Come to the Tupsom lido."

Fresko watched Lightgate's face as the toilet meeting drew to a close. The white-suited fairy kept drinking from her noxious flask and betrayed no clue as to what she was thinking. There were a couple of bombshells in there: this young suit was undermining Val, and Letty was working with him. With Pax and Edwing going their separate ways, Fresko asked, "Our turn?"

"Next time," Lightgate said. "Wouldn't want to get in the way of this."

"Think that square can make a difference?"

"I told him –" Lightgate choked mid-sentence. She turned away, covering her mouth, and shook her head at her inability to talk. She finished, "I gave him ideas. Ways we might screw with the FTC. With these disruptive humans. We'll see what he comes up with. How close to *revolution* he can take us."

The way she said it, Fresko knew she had a different idea to what Edwing was planning. He was only a disruptive councillor; this woman thirsted for something Edwing had never dreamed of. It was all getting too much; no clear lines in this sand, and Fresko only wished someone would've simply asked him to shoot the human.

16

It took all Letty's nerve to sit doing nothing. They were out there talking to Pax, making plans, and Valoria was scheming, pulling apart the weapon she'd worked so long to find. A city on edge, and people like Lightgate taking advantage on mad whims. But Edwing was right – this was complicated and breaking into the vats had been reckless. On the slightest excuse, Valoria might start randomly executing people.

No, Letty couldn't interfere. But she couldn't stay put.

Pushing aside their warnings, she donned the poncho disguise and slipped out between shadows, off to find Flynt's Bloodtooth Bar. It had a big neon fang flashing on one side, no windows, and inside were grimy, mottled metal walls hung with faded bottle-caps. Heavy metal music played quietly from a jukebox, with scarcely a dozen Fae there, divided between old overweight bruisers and young posers too clean to have ever done anything of worth. A long way from the debauched chambers of FTC revelry Letty used to promise the boys. Euphoric dancing, fistfights at midnight, they used to have that at the Rullion. Now the whole city was stuffy as a fart in a box.

At least the whisky was fine; incredibly smooth. Fae culture wasn't a total bust. She chased that with a mug of mead and slipped into a corner booth, hood up, no one looking her way. She listened in on three old boys grumbling about a lottery of locations permitted for scouting. *If* they reopened the gates. When they lamented not having won the storage facility ticket, the nearest active human building, Letty couldn't hold back. "Are you fucking crying about getting permission to scavenge?"

"What's this?" the one doing most of the talking said. He had long wiry hair and a big old mole on his cheek. "Cocky young blood, thinks she knows better?"

"You might have longer teeth than me," Letty said, "but you ain't got half the experience. We're Fae, we take what we need; you don't get told where not to go."

"We're *Layer* Fae, not Rostov madmen. We work within the guidelines."

"Like fucking cowards," Letty scoffed.

"Who you calling a coward?" The man moved to stand but didn't actually rise.

Letty did, hood falling back. "You, you geriatric wart."

The room got two shades quieter, all eyes on Letty.

"You want to – you want to watch it," the old boy said, hands up off the table, away from the gun at his hip. Showing her with his body he didn't want trouble, even if he said otherwise.

"Yeah?" Letty swept her eyes across the room. "You can all have a go." No one moved. A guy near the bar had a bottle half-raised to his mouth, mid-tilt. "What's happened to this place? You still call it a night out going home without a black eye?”

“Some say it,” a single confident voice replied. Coming from the shade of the entrance. Letty narrowed her eyes at Smark, the bald bastard plodding in with two burly Fae at his shoulders. His minions weren’t dressed in ragged junker getup, but in thick, familiar armour. The bar got impossibly quieter. Letty hadn’t sensed she was being followed. Seeing the pair of Stabilisers explained why.

“You all recognise her?” Smark said, moving into the room. Letty’s hand drifted towards her pistol as the Stabilisers fanned out to the sides. The two men had the utterly impassive expressions of career killers. Smark pointed. “That’s Letty. The troublemaker.” He looked at each Stabiliser for confirmation. Then met the eyes of others in the bar. “Very much alive, and very much still a believer that the Fae can work for something better.”

Unsure if it was her mistake coming here or Edwing’s for trusting this bastard, Letty figured it didn’t matter either way. She told the room, defiantly, “Yeah, it’s me. What are you gonna do about it?”

Men exchanged glances, hands hesitantly hovering over guns. One of the Stabilisers drew something like a cattle prod, a stick that suddenly crackled with electricity.

“How many here think someone like Letty should be cut down?” Smark asked.

No one dared answer as Letty’s eyes bored into the crowd.

“You’re all scouts,” Smark continued. “You’ve seen something of the human world. Or want to. How many of you think we’re where we belong? That our doors should be locked?”

Again, there was silence. His eyes fell on the closest scout, a young guy, staring at the crackling electric baton, unsure how Smark wanted him to answer. Letty wasn’t sure, either.

“I got word from Edwing,” Smark told Letty. “I gather the meeting pleased him. Confident we’ll find human allies.”

“And you?” Letty asked.

Smark indicated the Stabilisers, to let them answer for him. One of them said, loudly, “My uncle died out in the warehouse plains. Because Valoria wasn’t prepared. You gonna stop that happening again?”

Letty met his eyes.

So this was Smark making peace. Coming to protect her? And this whole bar better damned well like it. She said, “Too right I am. Are you gonna drink to it?”

Dutch McRory caught up to Pax as she started down the stairs, hands in pockets along with £2,300 in cash. Monroe, high on the success of his game, said the profit was all hers. Put that together with the four grand from the tournament and she was on her way. Bills covered for half a year, if she was careful. She could buy proper salmon in Sainsbury’s instead of mangled trimmings. When was the last time she had so much at the same time? Three, four years ago? No more waiting until Christmas for socks . . .

"Not tempted to push your advantage?" Dutch asked with his genial smile.

"Not tonight," Pax told him, trying to look equally pleasant. Lying, because she was desperately tempted to try busting these moneyed bastards. But paranoid with Jones lurking and Fae in the air. "Be careful yourself, Mr McRory."

"Dutch, please," he said. "And *careful* is how I made my career. We'll have another game tomorrow, hope to see you there."

"I . . ." Pax stalled. Definitely have other commitments. Don't trust coming near Monroe again, for sure. Don't trust not blowing this money as quick as it came. But would *so* like to recreate the joy of seeing Tycho pay out. Ugh. She said, "I'll see."

"Do. You've got potential. You play in London?"

"Not often."

"Vegas?"

"It's on my list."

"You come out there," McRory said, "you've got my number. Out there, someone like you, your wings'll spread wider."

"Someone like me?" A smile tugged at the corners of Pax's mouth.

McRory nodded without explanation, patting her arm and bidding her farewell. "Take care, Pax. I look forward to seeing you again."

Pax didn't dare say more.

The warmth of the conversation lasted half an hour, until her taxi crept into her neighbourhood of Hanton. She passed a house party with students spilling onto the street, shouting into each other's faces as they waved bottles above their heads. Three blocks from home, the taxi stopped at a red light, the driver cursing. A young man was retching into the drain. Another pair pointed and laughed from a wall.

Without the affluence of a taxi, Pax would be out soaking up such antics. As far from Tycho Duvalier's incongruous accent and Dutch McRory's promises of overseas potential as you got. No responsibilities, like the midweek vomiter there. Fuck it, she told the driver she could walk from here. A voice in her head warned her it was this kind of thing that got her drawn into the Sunken City in the first place. But that voice could spin on it. Pax jumped out and breathed in the night air.

"You looking for the party?" a student called out from the wall.

The house was alive with flashing lights and throbbing bass, so Pax gave the banal question the raised eyebrows.

The young man hopped off the wall. "I got beers in the fridge – Peroni, the good stuff?" He was reasonably lucid for a drunk, only his untamed volume giving him away. A slim, dark-skinned guy with a round face and gentle eyes, talking fast and friendly. "What music are you into?" Citing classic hits, Sinatra, Lee Hazlewood, to prove he was deeper than the pop coming from the party. Then from music to films, as Pax silently searched her own feelings. Watching the building. Her warm well-being quietly faded. Her fingers tingled, not unlike the sensation the blue screens gave her.

Something here, close.

Shit.

Not the screens. Something else. In that building? It wasn't bad, was it? *Good energy?* Was this what novisan felt like when people partied? Bringing out the best in each other? Pax allowed it. It didn't have to make sense. It was enough to feel like she wasn't up against the whole world. Only part of it.

The student's chatter demanded her attention. "What do you think of it? I bet you've seen it, you have to have."

"Huh?" Pax frowned. No idea where his private conversation had taken him.

"*Devilfist Noon.* I must've watched it twelve times now."

The odd title caught Pax's attention. "Devil *what?*"

"Easily Rik Greivous' best. And that's saying something, all he touched was gold."

Those comments jarred Pax. The beat in the house cut out and another tune came on, more muted, to a few groans inside. With that shift, the energy Pax was on the cusp of feeling was gone. Pax stared numbly at the young man. "Come again?"

"Greivous? You're a fan? Oh come on, he was the master."

"The film-maker?" Pax ventured, uneasy at hearing this recently-familiar name. Rik Greivous, Apothel and Barton's friend, had disappeared a long time ago. The name brought the same fears Jones' hints gave her. Something going on she wasn't aware of.

"I could lend you a copy?" her new friend offered.

Pax turned to leave. "I've gotta go."

"Hey no, wait! You didn't see the graffiti wall?" The student pointed back towards the party hopefully, not following. Pax pulled her jacket tighter, to feel for the cash and the little comfort it brought. Her life, back on track, soon –

Another student mocked his friend. "Mate, a woman like that would've eaten you *alive.*"

Pax froze. Echoes of McRory: someone like you. A woman like that. Palleday afraid she was a monster. She felt the blood turning in her veins. Stirred by the energy of the party, the uncertainty over Duvcorp, the complications of whatever Jones was up to, the monsters wandering the city, the blue screens busy – she felt it *in her veins*, and fought down a despairing sound. She was the centre, not the screens, not the minotaur or the Fae. She and her unnatural bloody senses. Unable to flee to Vegas leaving Sam Ward and everyone else holding the ball. Unable to be unassuming, unattached, Pax of the shadows.

She had to own this. Master it, understand it, before shedding it.

She had to *be* something.

But at least she didn't have to do it alone. Continuing home, Pax wrote Ward a message: *Tell your boss we'll meet in the morning.*

The problem with women, Cano Casaria decided, trekking through the St Alphege's sewers with only a torch for company, was that they had *many* problems. Sam Ward, for example, was both arrogant to the point of being above an apology dinner and yet craven enough to roll over for the first boss-figure to come along after she'd usurped control. At once fiercely ambitious and cowardly. Rolling a panel of heavy wooden slats back from a hole in the brickwork, Casaria considered how she revelled in theory but not in action. She probably described imagined dates in her diary rather than ever actually talking to anyone.

Dates – Casaria admonished himself for the word. He ducked into a tunnel, a small unlit cave, taking care to squat low so his shoulders didn't brush the ceiling. That's what she thought he was doing, wasn't it, asking her on a date. That's what Pax would say, laughing. Not even considering that he might honestly be remorseful for his actions.

Fuck the pair of them. And fuck that Barton child for putting such ideas in his head, that he should be clear and straight with any of these women.

Ward should have been thankful for the offer. It would've been punching way above her weight. Or was that it? Was she intimidated? Not from any perceived threat – he had apologised for that, after all – but because she didn't feel worthy? He smirked. When she went home to scribble about it in her diary, would it make her a little excited?

The narrow dugout opened onto a wider tunnel, which Casaria scanned with the torch. No lighting here, either; the passages at the edges of town, stretching north and west into St Alphege's and West Quay, were broadly neglected. Likewise the ones south-west through Nothicker. The *praelucente* and its horde rarely came to these areas, most likely because the energy above wasn't a worthy draw. So, in turn, the Ministry left light bulbs unchanged and power lines untended.

Continuing down a long hallway, Casaria noted a similarity to the Ministry's new office. Older brick tunnels and archways, damp and smelly, fitting to the bloated ogre that had instructed they move. Most likely they had been afraid to give Casaria the new address, knowing he'd disapprove.

He'd have words with them, alright. When his search reminded everyone how much they needed him. Sam Ward would recall he was a good team player. Hell, she was courting Pax herself, she had to appreciate what he'd done for her . . .

BGb-57, Casaria was aware, wasn't much of a place at all. An intersection of a couple of tunnels. He'd reach it soon, see there was nothing, check the batteries on the motion sensor and report back. Quick and simple. Those new agents would probably quake coming down here. Spend all night checking shadows for spiders.

Sam Ward certainly wouldn't venture this far alone. She'd been apprehensive even in his company. He sighed. He'd gone about it wrong, hadn't he, offering himself as supplicant? She needed a guiding hand. He could try again tomorrow. Not ask, but tell her: we'll go to dinner. For my apology. You'll enjoy it.

Women liked that, didn't they? Being told what –

Casaria stopped, torchlight hitting a shape where two tunnels crossed ahead. It was big – not quite person-sized but bulging with muscle. Cracked flesh dark all over, the shade of a *scorpio mites*. A territorial creature that warranted shooting on sight. And Casaria had no gun on him. Only his fists. There were stories that Darren Barton got into fistfights with them, but Casaria had never had the opportunity himself. The Ministry had regulations to prevent that; forms you'd have to fill in. But with the leeway they'd given Barton, they might turn a blind eye for him, too.

He edged closer, turning his rear foot, ready for action. The creature wasn't moving. It was slumped against the wall. There was no glow between its muscles. Casaria traced the torchlight up the wall. A dark splatter.

He approached quickly, then, and checked both directions down the adjoining tunnels. No sign of any other creature. There'd been no reports from Support of any activity here – what did this?

Casaria lit up the creature's grotesque face. Just above its crescent eyes, that was where the wound was. There were a handful of creatures in the horde that might make a hole like that. The needle-nose of the *corno cattus* might – but that speared animals at waist-height. And it wouldn't leave a corpse untouched. The more logical explanation opened a world of darker possibilities.

A gunshot wound.

If a human handgun killed this creature, the Sunken City had been compromised.

PART 2

1

The FTC was stirring.

The secret was out, after the revelry that left Letty, in the morning, with a headache and red knuckles, and her poncho torn on the floor. Fine by her, she had never been one to hide; she felt better in her short shorts, sheath knife and pistol on show. Between that and the marks from last night, the sight of her gave Edwing and Flynt a start. Edwing was halfway to arranging medical aid when she explained she'd only been drinking. Instead, he called up Newbry to see how much exposure she'd had.

The story had reached the Fae media. They took enthusiastic bar patrons' accounts out of context to say Letty had emerged looking for a fight. Defying her exile and their peaceful ways. Smark spoke into cameras saying he didn't know her whereabouts or plans, but that she was welcome in the East Eight blocks. That focused the Stabilisers' search, at least. Meanwhile the news anchors questioned his loyalty to Fae security.

Once Edwing was done taking in Newbry's report, an index finger tapping his chin, he said, "I intended for Smark to approach this subtly. He shouldn't have encouraged you. I have my own message, one that doesn't involve fighting."

"It was a bar brawl," Letty said, sitting on her sponge bed while Flynt watched from the door. "It's in our blood. Isn't it?"

"An outdated concept," Edwing said.

"You're a bloody outdated concept," Letty said wearily. "No one from that bar's ratting me out, Edwing. This morning, some bruised punk with a couple teeth missing woke up thankful he ran into me."

"Meanwhile the patrols are doubling and they'll be aware exactly who broke into the vats," Edwing said. "And any statement I make about the humans will be connected –"

"To *me*?" Letty snapped. "Sorry, your majesty, does my name sully yours, when I deliver such things as a healthy contact with a human?"

Edwing gave her a wary look. "I appreciate it, deeply. I have faith in Pax, and if what she says is true about the Ministry, then there's hope for everyone. But you *have* to go to ground until we get there."

"I'm not running," Letty said. "And I wasn't just boozing. This news is working for us. Smark's got Stabilisers chasing their tails in the wrong part of the city, while *others* are willing to help us out. They can get Val's science prick Nimm's address. A key to his place, even. While you do your thing, I can do mine."

"It has to wait!" Edwing was in danger of showing emotion. "I will make Valoria account for the hiding of the Dispenser, and her false claims about communications with the humans. But targeting her dust facilities and people gives her an opportunity to deflect from those issues. You've done *plenty*, isn't it our turn to do something for you?"

"I don't need anyone to do nothing for me. Never have. Never will." Letty looked away from them, nothing to fix on but stains. Never needed anyone and where did it get her. Hiding while these morons were talking to Pax? The thought gave her pause. She asked, "How was she?"

Flynt answered, "I'm not convinced."

"We didn't meet her at the best time," Edwing explained. "But I trust she is exactly who we need."

"She's safe? Any mention of what the Ministry are doing? Lightgate?"

Edwing shook his head. "From her situation, she seemed at ease."

"I've never been that close to a human," Flynt said. "I can . . ." His nose curled in distaste. ". . . still smell her. Took a lot of restraint not to hurt her." Letty's smile faded. "I don't get it. What makes you so sure she's not like the rest of them? She could've killed him."

"Nonsense," Edwing replied plainly. "She demonstrated quick-thinking."

"What happened?" Letty demanded.

"A man interrupted us," Flynt said, "and she threw Edwing in her pocket. I had to pull a –" He stopped, rather than talk over Letty's laughter.

Pocketing a Fae councillor? The girl didn't give a shit. Wiping a tear from her eye, Letty read Flynt's humourless glower, noting his fear. "Pax is harmless. She's just a bit handsy."

"And you did *not* need to draw a gun on her," Edwing admonished. "Clearly she's given a lot of thought to our people. She asked about our specific energy."

This idea again. "Any insights?"

"I thought it best to leave such discussion for a more formal setting. But I look forward to our next meeting."

"Questions about our *energy* clearly intersects with the Dispenser and Val's glowing crap in the vats. We could be talking to this Nimm chump already. I can be subtle."

Edwing eyed Letty. Surely thinking she was going to do it anyway, wondering how he could prevent a disaster. "I intend to leave Flynt with you. He knows how the city works, how to stay hidden."

"While you head into Ordshaw alone?" Flynt said. "No chance."

"I'm not the one being hunted," Edwing said. "The trouble is here, in the FTC, where you're best able to protect Letty. I'll be fine."

"The hell you will!" Flynt flared. "That human –"

"Will not hurt me," Edwing replied calmly. "I want you two safe and ready, for when I return. Letty, if you can only wait –"

"Like Val will wait?" Letty said. "She'll be covering shit up, smearing her trail, silencing leads. While I wank in a corner?"

"Things will change," Edwing answered calmly, quietly. "Today. I will release a statement, saying I am working with you, and know Pax Kuranes and the MEE intend to vanquish the creatures of the Sunken City. When we address the Council, the FTC will have to act."

Unmoved, Letty replied, "You actually going to use that word, *vanquish*?"

"Yes," Edwing told her seriously. "This *is* a righteous struggle."

She went quiet at the gravity of his conviction. Deny it as she might, she couldn't suppress the hope he exuded. For once, maybe she wasn't alone. Meaning she'd better listen.

2

Pax took in the coffee shop, relieved that they were meeting somewhere welcomingly normal, rather than the tunnel where, according to Sam Ward, the MEE was now based. Apparently that now meant members of the public, or bigwigs out of the government, were greeted in plastic-coated booths over a battered sausage and a milkshake, before the Ministry disappeared back underground like mole people. The waiting staff wore chequered uniforms in the fashion of tea towels, and their customer base comprised paint-splattered labourers whose main criteria for food was maximising calories.

Strangely, Sam Ward and Wayne Obrington fit in perfectly, as though obvious spooks were the other natural inhabitant of a greasy café. Alongside them and the labourers (on a Sunday morning?), Pax alone stood out in her ordinariness, dressed in her least-stained jeans, a green hoodie and her second-best coat. The suits were huddled together on one side of a booth, waiting for her; this bull of a man could've used a bench to himself, and struggled to get around the table to stand and shake her hand. Ward was grinning at Pax, and had probably lost sleep over what they might discuss.

Obrington introduced himself with a smile, gesturing for Pax to take a seat. "You'll eat something?" he suggested, squeezing back into place. Ward gave a quiet hello, with a little wave. Obrington passed the menu over. He already had a large plate overflowing with sausages, eggs and beans. "Forgive my appetite."

Pax gave the menu the quickest glance, aware of the sort of fare available. If they had salmon, it was better that they keep it. A middle-aged waitress joined them, inviting Pax to order with a cocked eye, and Pax asked for a black coffee and eggs on toast. Ward, she noticed, only had a glass of water. Probably ate a salad before starting work, what, eight hours ago?

"I've read the reports," Obrington said, cutting mercilessly into a sausage, "including Ward's weighty new edition. So I'm not gonna insult anyone's intelligence, or time – let's agree the Sunken City doesn't add up and the fairies might be important. That it *might* be prudent to take our time before enacting Protocol 38. And you, for reasons currently beyond me, have some keen insights into that. Correct?"

"It's my natural curiosity," Pax said. "I couldn't do your work with all the questions your lot have left unanswered."

Obrington looked to Ward, inviting her response. She cleared her throat, and Pax picked up an uneasy edge in her voice. "Management tend to believe we can do our jobs without overextending ourselves. Understanding is not an absolute requirement for keeping order."

Pax didn't let her look away, trying to weigh up the conviction in the assessment. Then said, "Management have royally fucked us all for a fair while, haven't they?"

Obrington snorted through a mouthful of food, seeming to approve, and waved his fork for Ward to continue, flicking brown sauce onto the table. Ward waited as the waitress returned with septic-smelling coffee, then said, quietly, "We're starting to uncover the full breadth of the grugulochs' influence. How much we don't know. The truth is, without your . . . curiosity . . . we might never have recognised the fox in our own henhouse."

Pax watched Obrington, as Ward was clearly saying it for his benefit. He shovelled more food into his mouth and worked his bovine way through it, offering no input.

"Okay," Pax said. "I can contribute more, but I want to be careful about how we involve the Ministry. I'd like to borrow Sam, but otherwise have no one else nearby. And I'd like you to press pause on provoking the Sunken City creatures. Definitely don't go near the FTC again."

Obrington stopped eating. "Funny, I thought you came to help, not make demands."

"I *am* helping."

"You're aware the creatures have been moving erratically? Approaching some very compromising positions?"

"Yeah, and I'm concerned that simply killing them might make that worse."

Obrington looked sideways at Ward, and she fumbled for a compromise. "Perhaps if we knew where –"

"I think I can work with the Fae," Pax said. "But not their leaders."

Obrington sat back. "You've experienced their lunacy. They're a bloody nuisance."

"They're more than that," Pax insisted. "The horde go after the Fae with more passion than anything, but the blue – the *grugulochs* never sought them out, not since they were driven above ground. Your leaders were corrupted a long time ago but only took action against the Fae last week. Only now have you seen a creature venture towards them, right? The grugulochs was scared of them."

"They developed weapons dangerous to it." Obrington shrugged. "So have we. Only difference is we had no inclination to use them before."

"The bigger difference is you've no idea if *yours* work, do you? You're finding your existing tools aren't all you thought them to be. Understanding the Fae is the only sure way to get a complete picture here."

"Alright." Obrington put his fork down, like this detail was enough to cost him his appetite. "Say you're right. Say you're not just, for example, buying time to get your little fairy mate back? The one accused of killing our people? Let's say –"

"Oh, piss off," Pax cut in. "She did *not* do that. I'm doing this because you've no idea the damage you might do messing with powers you don't understand."

Ward averted her gaze. Hiding a smile? Unfazed, Obrington said, "Implying you *do* understand. Why would that be?"

"I'm smarter than you? Then, it doesn't take a genius to see co-operation with an otherworldly race with miniature technology might benefit us."

He clicked his tongue in thought, then deferred again to Ward. She said, "I've always promoted a better working relationship with the Fae. I don't see the harm in exercising caution."

"You think it's *cautious* to work with the people that gunned down eight agents?" Obrington said.

"We're looking for the fairy Lightgate," Ward said. "That's –"

"Don't care. You keep this up, I'm stuck lurking in this backwater. Wasn't I clear about that? I don't like to lurk anywhere longer than necessary. Least of all places where you're exciting a dormant force of evil or two that we'd rather *stay* dormant."

"It has been for decades," Pax said. "You can afford a few extra days."

"I also don't like having a civilian presume to tell me my business," Obrington said. "This is really how you do things?" Ward straightened up, not meeting his eyes but steeling herself to defy him. As she took a breath to speak, he continued, "Don't know why I'm even pretending this is my rodeo. Whatever, you take Ward. Get yourselves murdered. Anything else you need, seeing as you got all dressed up to meet us?"

"Yeah." Pax ignored his attempt to wrong-foot her. "I want to know where your Management stand on genuinely offering the Fae something."

"Something like asylum? Some part of these tunnels we'll shortly be clearing out?"

"Something like that."

"It's an option," Obrington said, plainly. "London are open to it, considering the mess our system of miscommunication created. Couple of backbenchers in Parliament might push Fae rights into a carefully hidden reality. Protected under UK law. Without revealing them, of course."

Both Pax and Ward gave him open-mouthed responses. Where had this man come from? Pax said, "You're serious?"

"Theoretically. But it's a big ask, for a very unclear reward, besides general harmony. We're talking about legitimising terrorists. Based on the whim of a pretty young lady with a hunch? I've merely been exploring options. Only seems sensible in case our people *were* gunned down by one rogue agent. But Ward, Ordshaw's your screwy town. You've gotta live with it, I'm just here to put a lid on the bleeding chaos. When that's done, you can make those screwy calls yourselves."

It took Ward another moment to recover, unable to believe her luck. "Of course. I want to do whatever we can to open channels to the Fae –"

"Fine." Obrington waved a finger in the air, calling over the waitress, and eyed Pax again. "But I'm not done with you. Before you two get yourselves killed by insects, you can at least pay lip service to our primary goal. We're tripping over mysteries left and right."

"Like the black spots?" Ward suggested, brightly. Obrington eyed her in a way that said that wasn't necessarily what he had in mind, but that it warranted consideration. She explained to Pax, "We've found pockets of unreported activity, or unreported inactivity, more accurately. Places where energy *isn't* manipulated. But we don't have the manpower to check all this out – the Bartons are ready to help out, and I'll be meeting with them once we're done, but we can't throw them into this without at least some initial exploration ourselves."

"And here we're all sitting not pulling our weight," Obrington said. An idea had started ticking in his mind, a way to lean on Pax and make a nuisance of himself. "We'll take a look ourselves, shall we? Investigate one of Ward's curiosities and give me an idea that you really are in this to help, all in one."

Pax bristled at the sudden demand. Obrington's magnified eyes tested her resolve. His new venture was not optional. And Ward wasn't much better, eagerness trumping concern as she was getting every treat under the tree all at once. Pax in the tunnels *and* a potential meeting with the Fae, what a day.

"Can I eat my eggs, at least?"

Footsteps stirred Casaria. Not from sleeping, he told himself, only rest.

He scrambled up, fumbling at his torch. The switch didn't work; batteries dead after so long waiting. He pocketed it and used his phone. Stopped and listened. Yes, the tap, tap of footsteps, people approaching. At least two; talking in low voices.

Holding his hand over the phone screen to hide the light, Casaria checked the time. Hell, it was morning, no wonder he'd dozed. Should have returned to the office and called for backup or proper surveillance. But those idiots would've sent someone like Landon to scare off intruders by breathing too loud.

Casaria, on the other hand, would catch them red-handed. He'd haul them into the office by the scruffs of their necks. See what Sam Ward thought of him them.

As the footsteps got closer, he made out what was being said, the voices rolling around the tunnel. "– not a bloody gorilla, I keep telling you."

"*Like* a gorilla, I said. That covers a lot."

"It doesn't cover this, see. It's some Big Foot level shit."

Casaria recognised the voice. It had sifted in and out of his mind while he'd been tied to a chair, waiting for injury. One of Pax's uncultured, violent associates. Low and slow and continually churning out ridiculous ideas.

"Things mutate living underground, don't they? It's true what they say about alligators in New York. And pigs under London – monstrous things."

Casaria edged along the wall, hand going back to his torch. Heavy enough to knock a man down; and he'd knocked this particular man down before. But he'd also been knocked down by him. Beaten, a toe severed . . .

"– taken to speculating," the second voice said, a nasal tone, higher-pitched, someone small and disagreeable. "Take a blood sample and prove it's just something escaped from a zoo. You're tired, eyes not adjusted down here."

"I know the difference between sleep-induced psychosis and seeing something unnatural, Vulcher. Would've saved us all time and effort if that were taken as given."

The footsteps tramped past as Casaria tensed. Moving in a parallel tunnel, close but then gone, echoing around a corner. They were looping to the intersection. Casaria pressed himself back into an alcove, a foot or so deep.

They pattered on. Turning, getting louder again.

"You sure this is the right way?" the whiny one, Vulcher, asked.

"I've got a keen sense of direction," the bigger one answered. His voice came through clearer, along with the heavy footsteps, as he drew into the same tunnel as Casaria. Torchlight bobbed past. "Twelve lefts and three rights. Didn't I tell you it was about a twenty-two-minute walk? How long's it been?" Which thug was he? The ashen, ugly one or the infuriatingly blond one? Casaria wasn't sure which face he'd rather rearrange.

"Twelve lefts?" Vulcher echoed. "In that order? *One* wrong turn and –"

"I know what I'm doing," the thug said. They finally passed the alcove, and Casaria froze. The ashen one, with his ugly, stony face and threadbare denim dungarees, filled the tunnel, stooped. A smaller figure followed, a scampering silhouette in the bounced-back torchlight.

The thug mumbled something about trust as they passed, and Casaria braced himself to go after them. A quick step behind the little one, clock him with the torch, a sharp punch to the thug's jaw. That'd do it. Only he'd lose the element of surprise on the small one.

Their footsteps were retreating and Casaria hadn't moved.

He'd race up behind them, a knee to the little one's back, carry the momentum forward and bowl the bigger one down. They'd grapple, but he'd knock the man senseless.

The talking got quieter as it became more distant.

They'd hear him now, hear his approach. He couldn't run after them.

He couldn't.

Casaria realised his heart was beating fast. What in hell. He'd waited all night, and they were getting away. They had got away.

He closed his eyes. What was going on.

3

Pax watched Obrington on his phone through most of the journey underground, tapping away like an addicted teen trying to beat a high score. Hell, maybe that's what he was doing. He led them to an unlit stairway that must've gone down fifty steps at least, and they followed his phone light onto another corridor. Pax was glad he was distracted, because with the tension in this place she had no desire to talk.

Finally, Obrington replaced the phone with a small torch, barely the length of his palm but startlingly bright. A handful of doorways sporadically lined the brick hallway.

"That one?" Obrington asked, and Ward checked against a map on her phone. She looked as anxious as Pax felt, watching the walls like she was looking for something. But this was safe, Pax told herself. The "anomaly" was a place where nothing went. A vacant lot in a system otherwise populated by fiends. And she had the company of the Ministry's finest.

Obrington pushed their chosen door and it didn't move. From the look of it, it had been closed for a very long time. He leant his shoulder into it, using all his weight. It cracked open and Ward flinched, a little cloud of dust puffing back over them. Obrington entered into darkness and summarised: "Huh."

Pax looked in herself, trying to see around him. The cold stillness was oddly noticeable, considering it was already so still and cool in the corridor. Obrington took a step further and Pax followed, feeling the sensation that had made him say *huh*. It was like taking a sharp intake of breath.

His torch lit up a large space. A hole in the rock of the earth, unadorned, without the brick or concrete that lined much of the Sunken City. The chamber was roughly spherical, though jagged around the edges, like someone had extracted a giant round boulder, and the doorway entered onto a ledge about halfway up, over a drop of some ten feet.

Obrington waved the torchlight back and forth. Nothing there but this vast, empty sphere. Ward crept around Pax to see for herself.

"Never seen your Sunken City described as cave-like," Obrington commented. "Tunnels, man-made, that's what they say. Any other parts tap into caves?"

"I don't think so," Ward said.

Pax stayed near the door. The ledge was barely a foot wide, and she wasn't sure she'd be able to climb back out if she fell. But that wasn't her main concern. The place felt weird. There was an emptiness to it. A painful emptiness.

Ward said, "There's no other break in the walls."

"Like whoever was digging down here found an air pocket," Obrington said.

"I don't think . . ." Ward went quiet, as if short of breath. She held a hand up in front of her, into the room, to feel something more.

"Dying to hear your take." Obrington turned to Pax, having waited what must have been an acceptable time for Pax to draw Serious Conclusions. About twenty seconds. Pax wasn't sure what to tell him. Ward's face expected something, too. The dug-out space served no apparent purpose, but she could, deep in her body, sense something wrong with it. It was colder than the surrounding tunnels by degrees, and – it was like looking at a flat lake. Eerily calm, with hidden depth. Capable of great change with the slightest touch. Pax sensed something in its silence, too. Or was it the absence of sound? The expectation that she should hear something?

She let out an uncertain comment, just to say something: "Meditation chamber?"

"For monsters?" Obrington said.

"Why not."

"Right." Obrington moved back out into the hallway. "There's something off with it, I think we can all agree on that."

"Yeah." Pax left quickly, now he'd set precedent, with Ward just behind her. Obrington closed the door and Pax tried to ignore his expectant look, to focus her senses. It was suddenly hard to reimagine the feeling from seconds before. "Did it feel cold to you?"

Shrugging his big shoulders, Obrington took his phone out again. Back to work or whatever addictive app he had. "Not especially. Notice anything else? Let's hear you deliver the same insights that cut down the Raleigh Commission and the grugulochs."

The big texting goon said it deadpan, disinterested. Pax replied, more firmly than necessary, "I felt nothing."

Obrington looked up. "Nothing?"

"Literally," Pax said. "An absence. Emptiness. Didn't you feel it too?"

"Uh-huh." He slapped his beefy free hand into the wall before concentrating back on his phone. "As opposed to out here. You feel something different?"

"We never claimed Pax was *psychic*," Ward intervened with an awkward laugh. Essentially informing Obrington that they were hiding something. He didn't look up again, pausing in his typing to read something. Pax was curious herself, despite his manner. Wondering if she *did* feel something beyond general disquiet.

Carefully, she placed her palm against the moist brickwork, and inhaled, drawing in. Ordinary, lifeless brick. Pax concentrated harder. It wasn't lifeless. There was something there, moving. She could imagine it, like worms in the ground. The same way she felt the blue screens when they were active, only less clear.

"It's different," Pax said. Able to draw that conclusion at least. "That room was different to out here. Lacking something."

"Huh," Obrington said, finally sounding interested. Pax was about to elaborate, if she could, when he explained his surprise. "There's been an alert. I have to go.

We can pick this up later."

"Go?" Ward exclaimed. "We're just –"

"Turns out there *is* someone in the tunnels," Obrington said. "Casaria's called for backup, and we're closest. Did you know he was still down there?"

Ward's stunned look said she didn't.

"Guess he spent the night." Obrington straightened up, getting into action mode. Ward had her own phone out then. "Probably just a bum got in because we're spread so thin – I'll sort it out. Meantime, Ward, this place seemed harmless enough, your civilians might as well throw themselves into the others."

"I've got an alert, too," Ward said, distracted by her phone. "But it's about the horde. Changing direction. Maybe they got unsettled by the intruder?"

"If your equipment tells us anything useful at all," Obrington scoffed. Pax merely eyed the pair of them; only one useful conclusion worth drawing here. She should leave.

"We're really meeting the Fae?" Ward asked, trying to regain her enthusiasm as they paced towards their respective vehicles. Her unassuming but immaculate Honda, Pax's very assuming rusty moped.

"That's the plan," Pax said, checking the time with growing unease. Was this her default feeling now, everything *uneasy*? Or was there something in the tunnels that caused it? Casaria waiting it out. The horde shifting direction, oh, around the same time Pax had been pondering underground. And it was almost midday – where had the morning gone?

"Who is it? Where are we meeting?" Ward asked. "I can drive, no sense us going separately. If I can just get Barton set up first."

"We're kind of against the clock."

"It won't take long," Ward said. "There's another black spot, near here, accessed via a New Thornton entrance. I only need to unlock the door and give Barton a scanner. Maybe point him in the right direction. With Obrington racing towards Protocol 38, the more we can learn about the Sunken City, quicker, the better."

"It's fine," Pax said. "I'll go on ahead, you catch me up."

Ward slowed down. "You're sure? I don't want to turn up late –"

"It's casual," Pax insisted, thinking if anything this might be good. Give her a chance to chat with Edwing before Ward brought her enthusiasm. "Just get to the Tupsom lido when you can."

Ward squinted, committing the location to memory. As they drew up to the two vehicles, her focus further intensified, as if she was trying to think of how to word something just right.

"Take a breath," Pax said, "before you have a heart attack."

"Okay." Ward actually did take a deep, centring breath and released it, like she had had training. "The Fae – this is a big step for us, that's all. I can't thank you enough."

"Don't thank me yet," Pax said. "Like your mouth-breathing boss said, it might end up getting us killed."

Ward shook her head. "That's typical Ministry prejudice." She paused, considering that. "He is a bit difficult. Was there anything you wanted to say? Away from him?"

"No. I would've asked him to his face what the hell he's keeping back from us, but it didn't seem the time," Pax said, strapping on the bike helmet. "But that black spot shit *was* weird. Gives me the same uncomfortable feeling as the Fae."

"Keeping something back, like, about novisan and the tunnels? Barton suggested the system itself might pool energy, which our equipment is starting to confirm. And – we haven't even discussed this business with Duvcorp. If there's unchecked *people* in the tunnels" – Ward gasped in sudden realisation – "what if it's *them*?"

Pax paused, considering Tycho's nonchalance at the Baudelaire Club, the way he'd been, at least initially, dismissive of Ordshaw's problems. Paired with her blundering comments that might have got him interested. "As it happens . . . I ran into someone from Duvcorp last night" – Pax hurried on as Ward's face showed horror – "and I might've got them a bit curious, that's my bad. But he said they were sceptical about Ordshaw's weirdness."

"But – they came after *you*?"

"Pure coincidence," Pax insisted. "This was just talk at a poker table, no way they know anything about me – *I* brought it up. Look, it could be nothing – your boss didn't seem too bothered about this intrusion."

"No," Ward said, taking care not to sound worried. "No . . . homeless people and kids creep in occasionally. Even when we're fully staffed, it happens. But Casaria shouldn't have been calling for backup for homeless people and kids." Ward went quiet. Still trying to convince herself, she said, "Cano was unarmed, probably tired, if he was there all night."

"Yeah? I'm surprised he's back at work at all."

"It's fine," Ward said, though clearly it wasn't. Ah, Casaria, the foil for her happiness. "I can handle him. Half of success in any career is navigating other people's idiosyncrasies. That's *all* it is. And we need all the help we can get." She emphasised that for Pax's benefit.

"I'm doing what I can, aren't I?" Pax replied.

Ward's silence suggested she wanted more. She said, "All of this is in the air. Just when I thought we were resolving our scanning equipment, we get more unchecked activity. And those black spots?" She took a breath. "I'll get the Bartons started, but we could look at a few locations later ourselves, today. Couldn't we?"

"We'll see how this goes," Pax said, cautious of the snowflakes of responsibility that could soon form an avalanche. "Assuming the tunnels haven't been overrun by something else by then. See you at the lido, okay?"

4

Biting back frustration that, of all people, Wayne Obrington had arrived as backup, Casaria led the overweight vulgarian through the St Alphege's sewer. The man sported a superiority complex while wearing an off-the-shelf suit. His tapered head of hair had an awful, slick style that his expensive barber should have advised against. Everything he said seemed to come out snide, even his weighted comment that another agent was on the way to join them, someone to watch the exits. Like Casaria needed help.

Obrington barely fit through the access point, and bore no consideration for quiet as he plodded ahead with his torch. "I'll give you marks for not wading in like a dunderhead, but I wouldn't punish a *little* initiative."

"I'm up for review," Casaria replied, "for showing initiative."

"You know that's not the reason, don't you?"

Casaria had accounted for himself to Sam Ward, he didn't have to repeat it for this oaf. He pointed. "Down there. There was a body."

"The *scorpio* you say was shot."

"It was," Casaria said, struggling to be cordial. Everything the man said sounded like an accusation. "I take it you're armed?"

From a shoulder holster under his jacket, Obrington drew a small revolver, the sort carried by a '70s TV detective on budget cuts. Casaria gave it the look it deserved.

"It's the man that holds it, makes a difference," Obrington told him. "Shall we?"

Casaria continued, leading him past the spot where the body had lain. There was now a blood trail. Obrington hesitated over the mess. Got your attention now? The criminals wouldn't be far; he'd listened as they heaved the thing back through the tunnels, commenting about setting up in a bigger chamber.

"As far as your review's concerned," Obrington said, volume making Casaria cringe, "I don't question your initiative. And I'll defer to Ward for your character. You clearly have a way with the women." Compared to this wart, Casaria supposed he did. "What *I* question is your integrity."

Casaria stopped and Obrington almost bumped into him. "My integrity? I've done everything with honour."

"Except for lying about how you lost your toe," Obrington said. Sounding unhealthily sure of himself. "And your treatment of this Kuranes girl situation. Or, my biggest question, worth everything: how exactly a fellow agent died on your watch."

Casaria didn't flinch, showing the man he had nothing to hide. There was no way he could be held accountable for the massacre outside the Fae city, nor the deaths in Greek Street.

"Gant, wasn't it?"

That stilled him. Landon's partner? The amateur who'd risked getting them both killed? Why ask about that? They'd been alone – and he had no choice –

"Always an awkward thing," Obrington said, "to lose someone in places like this, no cameras, no easy answers, just a stressed man's word over what happened."

Casaria looked from the pistol up to his face, the oaf's eyes questioning. This bastard might be the sort that would do such a thing on purpose. *Accidentally* hurt a fellow agent. Was he threatening him? "Did you come here for these criminals, or to accuse me of something?"

Obrington answered, "You know who these people are, don't you?"

"What? No – I *saw* them –"

The big man put a finger to his lips. "Hey. Let's keep it quiet."

Somewhere in his blank face was the hint of a smile. Enjoying this? Casaria forced himself not to lash out as Obrington continued, walking lighter now. He followed silently.

The blood came in occasional smears, grit on the ground streaked from the weight of the dragged body. It led to a short set of steps that ascended to a doorway filled with the white light of an electric lantern. Obrington slowed down as they crept closer. There was no sound ahead, no talking or movement. Casaria checked back the way they'd come, a long empty hallway, and he started as Obrington's phone lit up. The boss whispered, "Warning Landon to be ready."

Landon? That was their other backup? That fool, *again*?

Obrington pocketed the phone and lumbered on. Up the steps, into a wider room. Casaria crept after him, trying to see over his shoulder. It was another vaulted brick chamber, like a wine cellar. And it appeared empty, besides the big floor lamp and the carcass of the *scorpio mites*. Obrington strode in as Casaria followed. He turned quickly – too late.

The big thug stepped out of the shadow of a pillar, pistol aimed at his head, a block of grey menace with his stubbly chin and dusty clothes. The shorter one, a weaselly man in mechanic's overalls, came from the other direction, a stubby shotgun trained on Obrington.

"Gun on the floor," the big one said. Bees, that was his name, wasn't it?

Obrington held up his hands, turning lazily towards him. Casaria tensed, fists clenched. He should've killed the thugs when he first ran into them outside Pax's apartment; men lingering around with guns, unchecked. And they'd just walked in on them, damn this oaf.

"Gentlemen," Obrington started, unconcerned. "You're aware you're trespassing on government property? And threatening, I might add, Her Majesty's agents."

"We're pretty well aware. As, I expect, you're aware that Her Majesty's agents bleed, and disappear, the same as anyone else."

"Not these ones," Obrington said. "Our men are tracking us. The exits to this tunnel system are covered. I suggest you come quietly."

"Awful sure of yourself, aren't you?" Bees said, moving around the room, keeping his distance. No way Casaria could jump him without taking a shot. But he might turn into it, take the bullet in a shoulder, how much damage could that do? Obrington might be killed, but that was his problem. "Serious business you've got here. With your secrets and your . . . infrastructure. What exactly *is* that thing?"

Obrington gave the monster's body a bored glance. "*Scorpio mites*, looks like. Native to Ordshaw. You the mug that shot it? Lucky it was alone. Typically move in groups, isn't that right, Agent Casaria?"

Casaria's eyes were fixed on Bees. He'd pounce with a hair-trigger, the second that the brute took his eyes off –

"*Casaria*," Obrington said. "Your thoughts on how this one got here alone?"

Casaria snapped out of it, glancing at the monster, while Bees' eyes found him, genuinely curious. The criminal said, "You're telling us there's packs of them?"

"Of course," Obrington replied. Why was he humouring these men? "We tend to cull wandering loners, but we've been understaffed the past few days –"

The shotgun went off. The sound tore through the room as brickwork burst from a far wall, the shorter thug folding over Obrington's hefty shoe in his crotch, a kick out of nowhere. The same time, Obrington crouched, revolver firing at Bees. The criminal ducked aside, barely avoiding a bullet that sparked off the wall. Casaria dropped to the floor as the two men exchanged reckless gunfire. Each shot compounded the deafening echo.

Casaria scrambled for a pillar, and as he rolled around it a bullet struck the brick behind him, the criminal taking a potshot. He leant around the other side, finding Obrington taking cover behind a pillar of his own, as Vulcher wheezed on the floor.

The two men's guns clicked empty at the same shot, both testing their triggers a few times for good measure. With a guttural roar, Bees tore out of cover and pounded towards Obrington. The latter, reloading the revolver, stood just before Bees struck. The revolver flew from his hand as the criminal caught him around the waist and slammed their combined weights into the wall. Vulcher scrambled towards the exit.

Casaria ran after him, and unthinkingly put his weight on his injured foot. Pain screamed through his leg, bringing him down. Damned hell it was supposed to be healed! The little criminal was away, feet pattering down the tunnel. On a knee, Casaria tried to push himself up, Obrington and Bees' sloppy fight sounding in dull thumps and thuds. He lurched forward and supported himself on another pillar.

Bees had Obrington from behind, on the ground, his great arm squeezing the agent's neck, turning his face purple. Casaria sprang towards them but stumbled again – useless fucking foot not carrying him. Obrington gargled, feet kicking, not going to make it. His hand grasped to the side.

The revolver was in the middle of the room. Casaria flung himself towards it and his fingers pushed it further away. The gun skidded towards Obrington as Bees squeezed harder, whispering into his ear, "It's done, mate. It's done."

Brushing the metal of the revolver with his finger, Obrington made a final strained stretch. He caught the weapon and turned it up. It went off and the back of Bees' head splattered over the wall beside them. His grip releasing, Obrington sat up, gasping for air. He shunted off the criminal, aiming the pistol back for good measure.

Casaria half-stood, looking from the thug's body to the doorway, Vulcher long gone. Obrington lowered the gun, rapidly inhaling, and checked his glasses with his spare hand. Impossibly, they'd escaped damage. Without ceremony, he lumbered to his feet and stared at his adversary's body.

Casaria breathed heavily, too, wanting to kick the slow, mouthy bastard who'd taken his toe. Lifeless now, a chunk of head missing. Animal bastard, ingrate, uncul –

Obrington patted him on the arm, hoarsely saying, "You can tell me how you know these prats while we round up that other tyke."

Meeting the Bartons and Rufaizu at a site designated AGb-13, with an access point disguised as a transformer box behind a Tesco Express car park, Sam tried not to rush. Pax would wait, and she owed it to everyone to manage the current situation properly. The trio looked rested, even if Barton's limp seemed to be bothering him more than before. It would be lighter work today, anyway. The entire point was visiting untouched locations, a long way from the horde; it should be safe for them to split up with two Duvcorp scanners.

Sam took them into the tunnel and asked Barton if he knew of the black spots they were investigating, but he said it was news to him. Rufaizu offered, "Empty pockets. Places no one and nothing wants to go. Should be sealed off, the Sect had some ideas about that. No good could come from them."

"This Sect of Fore?" Sam said.

"The MEE of their day, I imagine," Holly said. "Off in mythical Bohemia."

"So you heard of something like this?" Sam pressed Rufaizu. "Untouched rooms?"

Rufaizu gave her a smiling look that suggested he did, but he slowly shook his head.

"He does that," Holly said. "Can your Ministry substantiate any of his claims? This Gardossa city, for instance? I have *so many* questions."

"I've got Support looking through the details," Sam said. She had the same questions, and so far the answer was no. The Ministry had no evidence to support the young man's anecdotes. Beyond the blue screens there was so much more to know. It started down here, with them, collecting data. She couldn't wait to finally meet the Fae, but they needed to see the first black spot together, at least. To be sure it was safe. It would be quick – she'd be just behind Pax.

Her phone buzzed in her pocket. Sam took it out, hoping to see a message from Obrington informing her everything was under control. It was the office. Barton asked, "How does your phone work down here? We always had trouble with electronics."

"Special issue," Sam explained in a whisper, as their secretary, Tori, spoke.

"Ms Ward? I don't like to bother you but this sounded serious –"

"They found the people in the tunnels?"

"Huh?"

"Obrington, Casaria."

"Oh that – I don't know, it's not that. I got a call. Someone from *Duvcorp*. They wanted to speak to you, directly – to put you through to Tycho Duvalier."

Sam was too dumbstruck, thankfully, to say, "*The* Tycho Duvalier?" As if there could be two.

"Ms Ward?"

"You have him on the line?"

"Not right now, I have a number –"

Sam's mouth hung open without words. Duvalier, an international *tycoon*, chasing her for stolen property? Damn Obrington – damn all of this. She covered her phone to address the Bartons, worriedly recalling the scanners in their hands. "Wait here a minute, I've gotta make a call. Tori? Get them back."

5

"At a time when Fae doubts Fae," Edwing said, "I declare *no more*. I have spoken with the exile, Letty. Within our very city. We're told she orchestrated the theft of the Dispenser. The slaughter of many humans. The sharing of Fae secrets. The same Letty who strove for nine years to reclaim the Dispenser – not to clear her name, but to complete the very task we've all forgotten? Her intention in contacting the human Apothel. Her intention in contacting the human Kuranes. She *still* believes. *I* do. Don't you?"

He paused to give space for an answer, minutely correcting his posture. "The Waste Chief Smark came forward in Letty's favour, for he recognises what we must all understand. Letty offers change. Hope for something beyond the Transitional City. Hope so many of us lost long ago. Hope that we *can* get along with the humans. Change is frightening. Risky. But it is necessary. We have seen the true worth of our position here, have we not? The city almost fell last Tuesday."

Edwing paused again, using an adjustment of his glasses to let that sink in. "Governor Valoria Magnus warns us the humans are on our perimeter. She tells us they will not negotiate, that we cannot abide communication with them. She keeps them at bay. As your Chair of Information, I tell you it is not the human Ministry putting these barriers before us. Perhaps they won't negotiate – with her. But Letty and her human connected with them – *their* diplomacy stopped the attack.

"Pax Kuranes, some of you know as a monster. I have spoken with her myself, and I tell you this conscientious human wants peace. She is the bridge we have always lacked. She protected Letty. She protected the Dispenser, and she has not exposed us. Even after *our* people tried to hurt her. She has opened a door which the governor claims does not – cannot – exist.

"This will be painful to hear. You may ask why I trust Pax Kuranes. You have been told that the humans will inevitably betray us. I do not expect to change your beliefs in an instant, but I ask you to give me a chance. I will meet with the Ministry myself to learn exactly what the humans can offer us. What we can offer them. Give me that chance. Give Letty a chance. Give humanity a chance."

He lowered his head, affecting solemn reflection. When he raised his eyes again, his tone shifted, graver. "Many are angry for what happened to our city. Afraid. I do not fault the governor's responses. But one of our own did the damage – one called Lightgate. To my shame, I met with *her*, too. Before it began. And as I go to speak with the humans, it is not their species I fear, but our own. Please – consider our future, as you seek vengeance and security. I appeal to Governor Valoria to address these issues publicly. We all deserve this opportunity for co-operation. The real monsters are those that would prevent it."

The broadcast cut back to a newsroom where the glamorous anchor, behind her TV smile, was thrown by the speech. Squatting on a box watching, Letty commented, "He knows how to switch it on, doesn't he?"

"Yeah." Flynt leant near the door. He hadn't come all the way in, watching the airways outside. "You hear shouts? It's gonna get everyone riled up . . ."

"About time." Letty stood.

"You don't think he should've waited?" Flynt asked. "We could have riots."

"He's the brains, you said. Guess he figured this would make it harder for someone to assassinate him. They do it now, Val's culpable."

Flynt frowned, distracted. "Think I heard someone ask *where is he*."

"He's got his plan." Letty patted his arm, encouragingly. "And we should be figuring out ours. It's time we got Smark and his lads to serve up Nimm."

"We can't –" Flynt started with surprise.

"We'll wait on Edwing, okay?" Letty said. "But we'll be ready. Mark my words, Flynt, you win fights by acting, not by fucking thinking about it."

Fresko found Mix with one arm hanging over a doll's armchair. Dropping onto the matching sofa, Fresko kicked his companion's knee. Mix jumped up, grabbing at the nearest weapon, a second from tossing a bottle into Fresko's face when he saw who it was. Grumbling complaints, Mix sat back, dark rings under his eyes.

"Figured I'd find you here," Fresko said. "Trying to get yourself caught?"

It was actually the third place he'd looked, after their water tower and the summerhouse in a Ripton garden. This den, in the eaves above a betting shop in West Farling, was a favourite, adorned with takings from the rich locals – a likely spot for the Stabilisers to search.

Mix croaked, "No one's looking for us now. You didn't see the reports?"

Fresko narrowed his eyes. Mix stared back blearily, not about to explain. Fresko took out his phone and brought up the latest Fae news. The headlines about Edwing, that prick who'd met with Pax, giving a speech. Fresko had looked him up: the youngest member of the Council. Supported by forward-thinking Fae, known to question Val's decisions. Bunch of do-gooders.

"FTC's gone soft, hasn't it?" Mix sneered. "Peace and love shit."

"Yeah," Fresko said. He could've predicted this. *Did* predict it. Edwing was saying they shouldn't hurt one another. Lightgate wasn't gonna like that. "The human and this guy, they've got a meeting happening in Tupsom. Like, right now. Lightgate's gonna be there."

"To do what? Ice the pair of them?"

It might've been a joke, but Mix was probably right. All this chatter and confusion, now this young one was promoting productive dialogue, open up the FTC. How was that gonna play with Lightgate watching?

"Pass me another bottle," Mix groaned.

"You want a coffee," Fresko told him. "You want a hit of dust and a clear fucking head, because once this meeting goes down things are gonna move fast."

"Things," Mix grumbled back. "Ain't we had enough *things* for a lifetime?"

"You don't want in, that's your problem. But I'm not sitting back waiting for this to wash over us. I'm done living like a fucking degenerate, letting other people dick us around. Sit here and drown in puke – I'm heading to Tupsom."

"What's in Tupsom?"

Fresko strode to the exit, but a jangling of empty bottles and Mix's huffing attempt to stand stalled him. "Wait, wait. Tell me. What's in Tupsom?" He swayed uneasily and his foot caught a bottle, which rolled and almost toppled him. He cursed and kicked another bottle into the wall, putting on a whole show of standing. Finally, he straightened his belt and checked his hip-holster. Empty. He scanned the room.

"I told you," Fresko said. "They're meeting there. Lightgate and all."

Mix snorted. "Fine. Pass me my gun. Might as well see first-hand how we're gonna get fucked this time."

Edwing arrived at the lido early, confident after a few circles of the open-air pool and its visitor centre that he was the first there. There was an old canteen inside, perfect for their chat; benefiting from natural light but hidden from outsiders. He flew through a broken window and settled on a central table, where he straightened out his suit, corrected his tie and practised a polite but welcoming posture. Now it was merely a matter of saying the right thing.

Welcome, Pax, good to see you again. Thanks for joining me.

I'm so happy to work with you.

Too formal?

How're you doing? Having a good morning? Perhaps one of Flynt's expressions would work best: Bet you killed it at the table last night? You're looking fine? No. Complimenting a human's looks could only be considered disingenuous.

Edwing cleared his throat and tried, "Good morning Pax, did you sleep well?"

"I can't speak for *her*" – a female voice spun him around – "but I was too excited to sleep, myself."

Lightgate was standing on the table behind him. One arm in a sling, but otherwise as perfectly presented as the last time Edwing had seen her. Pressed white suit, great mane of hair, and a youthful cheer that he now better understood as madness. He took a step back.

"Edwing, my friend," she said. "You never called."

"I –" Edwing stuttered. "I haven't heard from you, either."

"Me? I left a calling card at the FTC, didn't I? If *shooting people* wasn't a cry for revolution, I don't know what is. And now fancy this" – she moved closer – "finding you cutting out the middle-woman. Chatting with my humans. Promising things to the FTC."

Edwing took another step back, eyes on her guns. One bulging under her jacket, the other holstered low on her thigh. She listed to one side, swaying like she might fall, but she stayed upright. "Lightgate – I *did* come to visit you. I told Rolarn –"

"He's dead." Lightgate was mere inches away now. Edwing glanced over his shoulder. He could make it to the edge of the table. Fly for the rafters? Even if he had a gun, he wouldn't dare fight. Lightgate ran a slow finger under her throat. "Butchered by your friend, Letty. Fae on Fae crime, can you believe that? A bit ironic, I think you started your speech about something like that."

Edwing straightened himself up. No, there was no running. He would face her with dignity. "I'm sure Letty acted with good reason. You understand why I'm here now? We have an opportunity to combat Valoria. Things are going to change."

"Yes." Lightgate smiled slightly. "You make good with young Pax and the Ministry. Valoria either agrees to negotiations or steps down. Everyone talks happily ever after?"

"It *is* possible," Edwing insisted. "A bloodless revolution."

She studied him with a sad face, shifting closer. Almost chest to chest. Her breath stank like petrol. "Peaceful change? Valoria retires to the hills?"

"She won't go quietly," Edwing answered warily, leaning back. "But she will go – Fae won't die for her, not when they understand our alternative."

"Poor, naive Edwing," Lightgate sighed, her alcoholic exhale stinging his eyes. "Don't you realise you're saying *all* the wrong things?"

"Lightgate. You came to me, you know –"

"I came to you with great ideas. And you give me this *peace* nonsense?"

Edwing opened his mouth to respond, but she moved quicker than he could speak. He didn't even see the blade being drawn from her sling, only felt the fierce bite as it slid into his gut, all the energy shooting out of him. As he slumped forward, blood glugging up his throat, filling his mouth, he locked eyes with Lightgate, pleading, and she dug the knife deeper, leaning her weight into him with a lover's embrace.

"Shh, Councillor. This is just step one."

6

The Tupsom lido was a place Pax had been only vaguely aware of. It was not somewhere anyone outside the neighbourhood of Tupsom was likely to have visited, even when it was open. Flanked on one side by a weed-riddled playing field, it sat behind a concrete wall, a single-storey building cracked by age. Its plaster mouldings, arched windows and doors went halfway to an impressive design, but the plant life, smashed windows and rotten door frames made it hard to imagine it as anything more than a relic.

It was also hard to believe the signs claiming the place was monitored by CCTV, under the threatening protection of LuxSecur. Aside from there being no cameras, Pax doubted that a firm trendy enough to drop the *e* from their name had set foot here in years. Across the courtyard lay the empty beer bottles and crisp packets of people who had ignored the warnings.

Rather than wait on Ward, who might have a skeleton key, Pax scouted the wall looking for the easiest way in: the main gate's bars were too tight to squeeze through, and too tall to shimmy up. The wall itself looked scalable, thanks to occasional barred portholes, but it was topped with razor wire. No way the crisp-eaters took such risks. Further study turned up a gap in the side-wall, visible across the derelict playing field, which was encircled by a chain-link fence. The fence's lattice was its own ladder, no razor wire there. She managed the climb almost gracefully.

Pax crossed the overgrown grass and squeezed through the wall where a hole had been kicked through, hardly concealed by a broken pallet. Inside the lido's grounds, she went to the main building and checked through the grimy windows. The outside had got in, as nature partially reclaimed the metal tables and chairs with snaking weeds. Pax skirted the building to the back, where the lido itself sat; a concrete dipping pool, partly filled with dead leaves, sludge and – yes – a soiled pram.

Ignoring that mystery, Pax continued to the rear doors, where a bottom panel had been smashed, creating a gap for a person to crouch through. Which Pax did.

It was cool inside, holes and cracks making it as airy as outside, minus the sunlight. Pax walked between changing rooms, through to the reception area and finally to the overgrown café. A delightfully haunting meeting place; thanks, Edwing.

Pax searched the shadows in the corners, around the tiled ceiling. Tiles were missing above, exposing dark cavities, and in one spot the ceiling had collapsed into the room. Pax called out, "Edwing, you here?" She toed a broken chair leg out of her way, moving into the room. "You guys have an affinity for the dystopic, don't you?"

With no answer, she continued, and spotted a dark shape at the centre of the room. Something standing in the middle of a table, the size of a fairy. But the posture was wrong. Pax frowned, getting closer. It was stiff – and splayed, four limbs out like a cross. Humanoid, at least . . .

"Holy fuck," Pax gasped, bending to take it in. It took a second for her eyes to process the sight, then she turned away, hand to her mouth. "Fuck, fuck, fuck . . ."

She gave it another look – had to force herself, to be sure.

That was Edwing's face alright. His tiny glasses, lying on the table behind him. His little stretched limbs, bound to – what – bent wire? And those were his guts spilt out of his open torso. Pulled apart like an anatomy experiment.

Pax turned on the spot. Every instinct said to run, get the hell away, but logic told her it was already too late. He'd been murdered, *brutally*, and left for her to find. Worse – for her to be found *with*. She checked the shadows again, searching for the culprit, sensing who it was. Fuck, *fuck*. She called out, "What the hell is wrong with you?"

"Me?" Lightgate's familiar voice came from an adjacent table. Pax clenched her fists as the miniature lunatic addressed her candidly: "*You're* the one that did this."

Fresko and Mix stopped at the window, seeing the human's silhouette inside. Wordlessly, they slipped in through a broken pane, to perch on a jutting spur of window frame. From the human's stance, something was wrong.

"The fuck is that?" Mix grunted, quietly.

Fresko swung the rifle up from over his shoulder and checked through the scope. He lowered the gun and gave Mix a disbelieving look. Pax, looking ready to gag, turned away from the table. Mix took the rifle and checked for himself. "Shit on a stick. Did she –"

Fresko snatched the rifle back, targeting the human himself. With the canteen separating them, she'd never see the shot coming. But she was saying something, edgy.

"Put her down!" Mix hissed. "About time, isn't it? That psycho –"

"Shh!" Fresko snapped, following Pax's gaze to the next table. "Lightgate's there."

"Shoot the human before she gets her too!"

"*Wait.*" Yeah, Pax looked ready to crush Lightgate. But the white-suited fairy was unafraid. The opposite. She was smiling, her good arm out to the side.

Nothing about this was right.

Dead bloody councillor, *gutted*. The giant lummox standing over him like she'd done it for kicks? Out of curiosity? No. He'd seen them talking last night. Chatting lovey-dovey bullshit about all getting along. She'd asked after Letty. Fresko had made bad assumptions before, thinking Pax killed Letty, and look where it got them. Mix rocked on the spot with agitation, so Fresko held a hand up for stillness. "Just fucking listen."

"Someone," Lightgate said, her voice rising, "tipped off Valoria's people as to where poor Edwing was meeting with a human. But where are your Ministry friends? I was expecting more of a mess."

"Fucking . . ." The human wasn't able to string a sentence together.

"It's Lightgate," Fresko said. "She killed him. Set her up."

"With Stabilisers on the way," Mix added, looking out of the window. Fresko followed his gaze. The Stabilisers would take them down, along with the human, given the chance.

"Shoot her now," Mix suggested, "we're heroes again, right?"

"You psycho!" Pax snapped. She was trying to find words to break out of her shock. One fist was raised, as if she'd ever be fast enough to touch Lightgate. "How – why –"

"You're upset," Lightgate said, helpfully. With gentle wingbeats, she rose from the table to Pax's head height. "So I'll give you some advice. Run. Val's people are nasty – *I* certainly don't intend to stick around to greet them. But I had to say *hi* before I left. If you survive, we'll talk again."

"Fresko," Mix urged, both of them sensing that Pax was about to make a move. This was their moment to take control. Fresko's rifle drifted; his crosshairs trained on Lightgate's chest.

"She's the one murdered one of ours," he said.

"The human can take the rap *right now*," Mix snarled.

"You know," Lightgate said, through a stifled yawn, ignoring Pax's fierce look, "that clown is more use this way."

Pax lunged and Lightgate moved too fast for Fresko to track. Pax's snatching hand closed on air, the Fae suddenly a few feet above her, silver pistol drawn. "Oh. So close."

Ignoring the gun, Pax jumped at Lightgate, tripping over a chair as she did. Lightgate effortlessly evaded her, floating towards the ceiling. Fresko picked her out again.

"Do her," Mix said, meaning Pax. "We wait until –"

"Enjoy the party!" Lightgate shot into the shadows. Pax twisted on the spot, her only hope to spring wings and fly herself. Lightgate was gone, and that only left the reality of the situation. Her eyes went back to Edwing, the poor brutalised sod. Then something else caught her attention, at another window. Fresko and Mix saw it too. Three dark shapes converged on a break in the glass. A man said, "In there, she's with the councillor!"

"I didn't –" Pax started, protesting her innocence. But seeing the newcomers swarming to get in, she changed her mind. She ran.

"Out!" one of the Stabilisers shouted. "Cut her off!"

They hadn't seen what'd happened, they didn't care. The mission was to stop her.

"We take her, Val's gotta reward that," Mix said, drawing a pistol. Fresko grabbed his arm. He gave him a meaningful look, not sure how to explain it, but hoping to get the message across. There were two sides to this. The right one might not be easy, but they'd been screwed around too much, for too long. He was done playing these games.

"We go after her," Fresko decided, "it's not for fucking Val."

7

Pax crashed through the gap in the rear door, catching her shoulder on the broken panelling and forcing her way through. Not stopping as the wood shattered around her, coat ripping. She stumbled through the dry pool before vaulting the edge and charging the wall. She slid through the hole feet first, hitting the pallet on the other side, and scrambled along the wall edge, low. A voice shouted, "In the field!"

Rising to a half-crouch, Pax sprinted – they'd be here any second. The fence blocked her path, but she'd run through it if she had to.

A shape dropped in front of her, a man smaller than a tiny bird. Shit shit. Pax turned to open ground, no cover, no hope – but better than standing still.

"Stop or I stop you!" the man shouted, almost as loud as a human. Pax ran, and a gunshot popped like a carton bursting. It took a few steps for Pax to stop, fearing the next shot, arms out to her sides. Her chest burnt, just below her ribs – had she taken a bullet? Breathing heavily, she looked down, no sign of blood. Nothing. A fucking stitch, muscles not used to moving this fast, weak bloody lungs. She looked over her shoulder. Her pursuer was approaching quickly, rifle raised. A gun the size of a matchstick, but bigger than the pistols that had lanced her leg and riddled the Bartons' house with holes.

"Got her," said another voice, drawing her attention to the side. A second man hovering not two metres from her head. Armed with a similar gun, dressed in the same black uniform. The first man moved in front of Pax. They wore helmets with visors like fighter pilots. Two inches tall, miniature militant police.

"I don't –" Pax began, but a shout from the lido cut her off.

"It's him – the Chair of Information! What's left of him!"

Pax cringed, looking to the wall, no sign of the shouter. "I can expl –"

"Good a place as any?" the first gunman said. The second scanned the playing field. The only overlooking building was a desolate office block, windows darkly empty. Trees loomed over them in other directions, and the road was a distant, empty dream. She'd fall in the long grass, not be spotted for days. Even then she might be ignored, dismissed as a passed-out junkie. The fairy nodded, and the pair raised their guns. Pax looked down the tiny barrels, and tried one more time. "You've got –"

Something whipped past Pax's ear. The first fairy was struck out of the air. He spun down as the second fairy aimed over her shoulder. Pax flinched at another whizzing bullet and the second fairy was propelled back like a rag doll. He spun into the grass with barely a sound.

Pax didn't move, staring at the empty space that had, seconds earlier, contained her death. Lightgate? That chaotic little shit . . . She turned back towards the lido, and heard the shout of her third pursuer: "Regroup, there's –"

"Have it you bastard!" a new voice shouted. The war cry of a hooligan, followed by a series of roared attacks. Pax stared at the wall, no sign of what was happening, just the huffs of two men brawling with the impacts too quiet to hear. It was over in seconds, before another yell, "Any more? Bring it on!"

She recognised him. Even furiously engaged as he was. One of the men who'd chased her from the Bartons' house. The fairies who'd tried to kill her before. Fuck. Pax took a deep breath and ran for the fence. She crossed the field in seconds and slammed into the chains, vaulting up and over. She ran the second her feet hit the ground, up the road, back towards her moped. Before she got close she saw the wheels – sunk as though melted, punctured beyond repair. *Shit.* She kept going, sprinting towards a bus stop, out across the road without looking, no cars here anyway. No people. The shelter ahead had three walls of Perspex, solid from adverts and torn events posters; she grabbed the edge and used her momentum to swing into the cover of the corner, where she slid to the ground.

Hidden from the outside world, at least partially, Pax shakily took out her phone and raised Ward's number. It pinged, engaged, through to voicemail. Pressing herself better into hiding, Pax hissed at the beep, "I need some fucking help right now. Fae on me." She hung up. She dug into another pocket for the faeometer the MEE had given her and switched it on. It'd send an alert back to their base. As if anyone could get here in time.

When she flipped the switch it beeped. Then again.

Again, and again, getting faster. Faster. Pax stood, eyes wide, as the device panicked: Fae almost on top of her. She looked up the road. Barely a couple of parked cars for cover, and why the hell wasn't Sam Ward here already? The faeometer beeped so rapidly it reached a whine.

"Trying to give yourself away?" yet another male voice said. A higher pitch than the last one. He'd been there, too, on the Bartons' street. Shooting at her.

Pax flipped the faeometer switch, silencing it, as the fairy floated down from above the bus stop. Sharply dressed in trousers and a white shirt, with suspenders and a tie. His wings beat gently, and he held a rifle across his waist that had to be taller than him. Like this tiny man had taken a gun from a toy of a different scale. Was that the weapon that had knocked those two soldiers out of the sky?

"You let her fuck your bike?" the fairy asked sharply, as if it were Pax's fault a fairy slashed her tyres.

She replied with a question of her own, "You're not with Lightgate?"

He looked back down the road, still deciding. His face twitched uncomfortably, and when his eyes rested on Pax he only seemed more troubled. "She's probably watching."

"Got her, Fresko?" the other man asked, the thug, appearing alongside him. He was broader than the others, all denims and leather belts, square head and white hair. Face darkened by something – blood? "What now?"

"We're gonna have a dozen more Stabilisers on the way," the white shirt, Fresko, said. "Twenty minutes at best, out of the FTC, but likely already closer than that. See where Lightgate went?"

The thug laughed with elated bravado from his fight. "If I had, I would've done for her, too!"

Fresko scowled. "Hang around, you'll get your wish."

Great, Pax reflected, at least three separate sets of murderous fairies fighting over her. But these ones had defended her for now, at least. They were Letty's friends once, weren't they? She said, "You guys want to help me, maybe I can get somewhere safer . . . ?"

The pair stared at her like spectators at a car crash.

"Guess she's our responsibility," Fresko said. "But how do you protect a thing like this from *us*?"

"Same trick she pulled before?" the thug grunted. "Toss her down a manhole, back with the fucking critters."

Not the best start. Fleeing into the Sunken City had proved more terrifying than the Fae, last time. Pax leant out from the bus stop again, checking the road. The pair flew higher, keeping their distance.

"There is an entrance," Fresko said. He added harshly, "Lady, you listening?" Pax met his eyes. "About two hundred metres up the road. An underpass with a maintenance hatch, that'll get you in. You'll wanna move quick."

"Yeah," Pax said. "I never *want* to move quick."

The pair exchanged another uncertain look, then the thug said, "You realise you should've fucking died back there?"

"Yeah." Pax moved out of cover. They darted to the sides to avoid her as she looked up the desolate street, in the direction Fresko indicated. "My day's not about to get much better, is it?"

"Ms Ward." Tycho Duvalier's smooth voice finally broke off the incessant chime of a tune that had held Sam waiting. She jumped, anxious to end this call quickly. "I understand that you're in charge of the Ordshaw Ministry of Environmental Energy, correct?"

"Mr Duvalier?" Sam replied pointlessly. Voice too high. "How can I help you?"

"You can start by explaining how you came across our SURE scanners. Imagine my surprise when our inventory showed one of our own was tricked into sharing them with you."

"Tricked?" Sam echoed. Of course, Obrington as much as told Parris to pin it on her. And it was dumb luck they'd noticed at all. Pax's blunder? Sam cleared her throat. It didn't matter. Obrington had insisted she had to own it, and she'd already got in mind what to say. "There was no deceit involved, we requisitioned them for government business of the highest priority."

"I wasn't aware you had such mandates," Tycho replied. "Naturally, we're always willing to help out our friends in the government, but that is *sensitive* equipment and its use indicates rather specific, perhaps unusual interests on your behalf."

Sam was quiet. What else had Obrington said about their research? Likely dealing with things the MEE weren't aware of themselves. Duvalier had to suspect something extreme, and she had to avoid confirming it. She considered their typical excuses. Faulty gas mains, mobile or electrical interference . . . but another option struck her. Complete dismissal. Channelling Obrington's arrogance, making herself *Management material*, she said, "You'll have the scanners back as soon as we're done with them. I can only apologise if it's caused any inconvenience."

"No inconvenience at all. Inconvenient would be getting legal teams involved. Checking the authenticity of that mandate of yours. We're not going *there*, are we?"

Despite the pause, that threat didn't warrant an answer.

"You'll meet me this afternoon," Tycho decided. "I'll come to your office. Shall we say 3pm?"

"Now is not a good —"

"We're talking, Ms Ward, that's all. Two organisations sharing the burden. Let's not make it any more than that, shall we?"

Sam gritted her teeth. Would the world fall apart if she told him to piss off? She didn't choose fast enough.

"Very well," he finished. "I'll have my people call yours. Until three."

And he was gone. Sam closed her eyes. Hell. Forget telling *him* to piss off, she should go back to the office and kick Obrington in the balls. It suddenly felt like a blessing that Mathers had left her out of these sorts of entanglements. But Obrington wasn't *in* the office, he was dealing with his own problem. Which, by the sounds of Tycho's probing, was not of Duvcorp's making. And Sam had other issues, too, missing the Fae meeting. Seeing the time on her phone, she cursed under her breath. She paced back to the tunnel entrance, drawing up a to-do list in her mind.

Set up the Bartons, super fast.

High-tail to Tupsom, solve Fae-human relations.

Speed back to the MEE office, delegate Duvcorp back to Obrington.

Finish the day without any more undue drama.

Simple.

8

The smaller criminal, Vulcher, whimpered like a beaten dog. The sort of coward that creased up at a slap against nearby brickwork. Not that Obrington stopped there, shoving the man into walls, getting in his face. Obrington, Casaria had decided, was unhinged. He'd approached these criminals intending to provoke a conflict, and was now throwing his considerable weight into someone half his size, who was already ready to talk.

When they'd caught up to Vulcher, he was down, hands cuffed behind his back, Landon watching him with a pistol drawn. That piece of human beige explained he'd checked the nearby tunnels, too; found a crate of *powdered narcotics* in a nook. Landon lacked the imagination or experience to say if it were cocaine, heroin or aspirin.

Obrington hauled Vulcher up by his overalls and tossed him across the room. The slight man skittered into the wall, not quick enough to get his hands up to protect himself. He went down, near tears. Landon looked displeased. Had he ever handled a suspect like this?

Casaria had, of course. But only when necessary. Some of them drove you to it. This one hadn't. Obrington was sweating, jacket off, shirtsleeves up, flat mouth letting out occasional wheezes as he relieved the tension left from his brawl with Bees.

That was it, wasn't it? The man could've died. He was processing that. Though Casaria sensed some of this was also for his benefit. He'd told Obrington he only knew the deceased man from Pax's flat, and it hadn't satisfied him.

The oaf thumped over to Vulcher with fists clenched, and finally stopped. "What do you lads think? The boy's ready to talk?"

Landon held his tongue, but Casaria was less shy: "He was ready to talk before we got here."

"That's what you think?" Obrington replied blandly.

"Yes!" Vulcher gasped. "I'll tell you everything – whatever you want! We were hoping to store some things down here, that's all! Just me and Bees, happened upon the place by chance and –"

There was a crack as his head snapped sideways, jaw taking the brunt of Obrington's shoe. Vulcher fell to his knees crying curses through blood. Landon cringed.

"See," Obrington said. "Still needed some tenderising after all." He grabbed Vulcher's chin, drawing his tear-drenched face up. "Who are you working for and how in hell did you disable our sensors?"

"He'll kill me," Vulcher uttered.

That earned a back-handed cuff. Obrington kept hold of him with his other hand and drew him back to his face. "Name."

"M – Monroe," Vulcher spluttered. "Stacey Monroe."

Obrington raised an eyebrow to Casaria, who nodded. Yes, it was familiar.

"And the sensors?" Obrington demanded.

"Anonymous tip," Vulcher said, trying to speak faster, arms up. "I swear – it's what they called *me* along for and I told them I wasn't handling that shit. Obviously government or high-end security, those sensors – no one with any sense would've –"

"So you got blessed by a guardian angel," Obrington said, giving Casaria a look.

"Boss got a note," Vulcher said. "Someone who knew how to get in. Didn't ask for nothing, just gave us instructions – scrambled the signal. I don't know who, it was Monroe's business."

"Anonymous notes." Obrington walked the short distance to Landon, addressing him now. "Lot of disruptive writing going around, huh?"

"When did you get these messages?" Casaria asked.

"Yesterday," Vulcher answered hurriedly. "Morning, I think."

"After your grugulochs died," Obrington said. He put his hands in his pockets and hummed. "Could be a Ministry agent upset at his job, farming out his knowledge?"

Casaria shifted. "I didn't tell them a damn thing."

Obrington turned square to him. "Come again?"

"Yes, these were the bastards that jumped me. Who hurt me. On account of our run-in at Pax's. But I got free, exactly as I reported, and I never said a word to them. I don't even know what the hell they'd want with these tunnels."

Obrington stared silently. Landon, behind him, looked deeply uncomfortable. Obrington said, "You didn't think it might be worth us following up on people who abducted a Ministry agent?"

"We had big enough problems outside Ordshaw's answer to the mafia, yeah," Casaria said. Like hell he was going to apologise. "Management were screwing us on behalf of a *monster*, so I handled these people on my own. There was nothing to follow up."

"Just let them cut off your toe and be done with it?"

"I gave as good as I got."

"He escalated things at the girl's apartment," Landon clarified. "They were there for her things. It's not unreasonable to think it got personal."

"Uh-huh." Obrington gave Vulcher another look, rocking on his heels. "No. You're a liability and a lunatic, Casaria, but I don't think you're a traitor. At least, you're not the first person I'd suspect, not when we've got a girl no one knows from Adam, secretly best mates with gangsters, asking me to keep our people away."

"Pax?" Casaria exclaimed. This lot were Pax's friends, true. She'd talked them down from killing him. But she'd been trying to keep clear of them, hadn't she?

"We'll bring her in," Obrington said. "And get Support to double-check all the sensors in a mile radius. With *luck*, these mugs are responsible for all our complications." He moved past Landon, who stepped aside.

"And him?" Casaria indicated Vulcher. Obrington looked back like he'd forgotten their captive existed.

"How do you usually dispose of them round here? Feed the beasts? Tree-grinder?"

"What?" Vulcher's panic doubled. "You can't –"

"We encourage them to leave town," Landon said warily. Obrington snatched the pistol from his holster and aimed it at the small criminal, whose hands shot up.

"How many more people know?" Obrington demanded loudly, as if talking to someone who couldn't quite hear.

"No one!" Vulcher sobbed. "It was me and him, bringing –"

"You and him's no one, with Mr Stacey Monroe pulling *no one's* strings?"

The criminal reconsidered, squeezing his eyes closed, shaking with fear. "Don't shoot me, please don't shoot me."

Obrington fired, the sound filling the room. The wall cracked over Vulcher's shoulder. "Next one's between your eyes."

"Monroe, yes! Me, Bees – Jones too. Maybe a few other boys in the warehouse, I don't know – it was a big find, but everyone's been busy with the poker game. Monroe didn't want the distraction, not with all that money on the table. So Bees came here alone, seeing how far the tunnels went, and he found that *thing*, but we didn't believe it – I came this morning, to check – Jones would've joined us later –"

"Blow me, what a mess," Obrington huffed. Aiming again towards Vulcher's forehead, he turned a glance back to Casaria, as though asking for approval. Casaria made an effort not to move, to show no trace of feeling at the threat. Landon was less stoic, grunting to say this was wrong. Obrington lowered the gun. "We'll need to make other arrangements; the cancer's already spread too far to disappear with one or two bodies."

Pax reached the underpass out of breath again, after her short dash down a road empy besides occasional old cars. Scanning the sky for anything birdlike coming to shoot her. Mind racing: not just at the disaster of being marked for assassination *again*, but hell, plunging back into the labyrinth? It had shaken off the Fae last time, but she'd barely survived. And the trip down with Ward hadn't made her feel better about it, knowing even the empty rooms were disturbing. Every new thing she encountered in the Sunken City made life worse.

A grim set of steps led to a maintenance panel, exactly as the little shirted man promised, with big screws at each corner, rusted in place. After making sure she was alone, not even the two gunmen for company, Pax reached towards the first screw.

Her phone rang.

Pax prayed for Sam Ward's name – but Unknown Number glowed big and bold. Letty? She answered hopefully, "Yeah?"

"It's me," Casaria said. She winced. Of all the lifelines. "Are you alone?"

"I am," Pax said. "And kind of mixed up in something."

"Whatever it is, this is more important."

"I doubt that."

"Your gangster friends found a way into the Sunken City. Someone *helped* them get past our sensors. The new bastard in charge at the Ministry wants you for it."

"Fuck – hell – whatever. If you can get the bloody Fae off my back, I'll come. Casaria, I'm about to break into the Sunken City myself, otherwise I'm toast."

"What? No – don't go near an entrance. Don't even breathe on it."

His tone made Pax freeze, eyes on the panel. "Three fairies came shooting at me, and more are on the way. So unless you've got some kind of Fae-proof shield you can wire me through the phone –"

"You touch that entrance, the alarms will go off and our people will scramble to you. Aren't you listening, we had a Sunken City breach. The *boss*" – he spat the word – "just killed one of your friends."

Killed her friend? Pax's heart jumped in her throat. Had this hit the Bartons? "Which – what friend? Tell me you're not talking about –"

"Are you listening? I'm calling to *warn* you: he's out to get you."

Pax backed away from the maintenance panel. Her reckless escape plan was shot. Her tenuous alliance with the only people who could protect her was shot. "Who got hurt?"

"One of the thugs – and they're claiming you played a game of poker with his boss, just last night. What am I supposed to say?"

Not the Bartons – something to do with Monroe. And the MEE knew she was with him? "Do they know I met a Fae there, too?"

Casaria paused. "What've you been doing, Pax? Criminals, those vermin –"

"Seriously?" Pax answered with acid. "Considering the nature of this call, you fucking blame me?" She checked the entrance to the subway. No indication if there was a threat far away or just around the corner. "Help me out. Turn off the sensors so I can lie low in these tunnels – at least long enough to give the fairies the slip."

"Sensor interference is exactly what they're after you for. Where are you?"

Far away, was the answer. A taxi would take as long as a bus, out here. What could she do? Wait for Sam Ward, who might already have orders to snag her? Run for the nearest tributary to the River Gader and swim underwater to avoid detection? Could fairies swim? Bloody hell, what kind of idea was that, she could barely swim herself. Pax said, "Is there anywhere else the Fae can't go?"

"Only places we protect." A loud voice spoke in the background of the call: Obrington, returning to Casaria. Casaria covered the mouthpiece and replied, "She's coming in, voluntarily." Obrington responded with something unfriendly, and Casaria placated him with obedient responses before unmuffling the call. "They saw your faeometer alert, Pax. There's already a car on its way."

"No," Pax squeaked.

"Stay put," Casaria said, his tone suggesting she needed to do the opposite. He hung up as Obrington started again.

"Serves you right for trusting those Ministry bastards," the miniature thug in denim said, drawing her attention upwards. He was perched on the tip of a caged light beneath the underpass, something sticking out the side of his mouth. A little waft of smoke came out, distracting Pax for a brief moment of wonder. He was smoking? Fresko was sitting next to him, leaning on the large rifle upright between his legs, watching her carefully.

"I can't go in there," Pax told them, pointing at the maintenance panel.

"Nah," Fresko said. "But you've drawn those Ministry pricks out here. Stabilisers won't mess with them. You'll only have to deal with one side or the other, depending on who gets here first."

"Unless Lightgate's still around," the other one added.

Though her eyes rested on them, Pax could no longer focus. Even if the Fae and MEE shot one another, and Lightgate, they'd only add bodies to the pile without setting her in any way free.

"Of course," Fresko said, "there's always that car we passed."

"Oh sure," the other added. "Old model, no electric key shit there. Shame if someone took it."

Pax glared. "You'd better be able to hotwire a car, because I sure as shit can't."

Sam stood alongside Holly gazing into an empty chamber, soaking up its queer atmosphere. A cube hollowed out of the surrounding stone, so perfectly square as to appear unnatural. The stillness was palpable, at the same time unsettling and impossible to resist. With it came a weird serenity, pushing away fears of Duvcorp and anxiety over Sam's lateness in meeting the Fae. Here, she could be at peace.

Until her ringtone shattered the atmosphere. Both women nearly jumped out of their skins, retreating and slamming the door as though the noise might offend the room.

Sam gave Holly an apologetic look as she answered. Obrington barked, "Finally, Ward. Wherever in bleeding hell you got to, grab that woman, *now*."

"Um, you –"

"Grab Kuranes! We've got a situation, in St Alphege's. Drag her here by her teeth if you have to."

"I'm not *with* her, sir –"

"You're what?" It was almost possible to hear him steaming down the line. "You went off following her cock and bull story and you let her out of your sight?"

"I had to brief our volunteers in –"

"That was an hour ago!" Obrington exploded. "Call her. Tell her we want to talk."

"What's happened, sir?"

"I'm being led to think your judgement's been way off, that's what."

"I don't –"

"Are you anywhere near her, at least?"

"I'm in New Thornton, I could catch up to her in about twenty minutes."

"Bleeding Christ and damnation. Forget it, leave it to the professionals. Come straight here."

"Where –" Sam tried, but he ended the call. She held the phone away from her ear in disbelief. The pendulum had swung back to where the Ministry wanted to capture Pax? Why? And she'd been here *an hour*? She hadn't been on hold to Tycho Duvalier that long – what had they been doing? Was there something hypnotising about these black spots? She caught Holly watching with shock, having heard the call.

"It sounds like that man is *not* on our side," Holly said, cautiously.

"Must be a misunderstanding," Sam said. "I'll clear it up." She brought up Pax's number. Damn, this had to have compromised the Fae meeting. But she could get Pax to come in to the Ministry office and sort things out from there. Thinking out loud, she said, "We should probably all go in together."

"Like hell," Holly said.

"What . . ." Sam ventured, then paused. "We don't know what the situation is, and it's best to co-operate, to avoid confusion."

"In my experience," Holly said, "your organisation's idea of co-operation is a one-way street. I think it's best you go alone. I'll find out what hellish trouble Pax has got herself into myself, thank you."

"Without –"

"Diz!" Holly shouted down the hall. "Get over here, we're leaving!"

Sam tried to think fast. Obrington sounded mad and she had to get moving fast. Not to the lido, it was too late. And she'd seen enough unhinged Ministry retaliation in the last week, she couldn't let that happen again.

Holly took her own phone out as Sam held her gaze. This was a moment, Sam sensed, that was going to define their relationship moving forward. She couldn't very well force them to come with her, definitely not with Darren Barton bearing down on her. And if Pax had any resistance to coming in, she might be more likely to answer the Bartons' call than Sam's. Sam lowered her eyes. "I'm not part of the problem. If she won't hear it from me, you tell Pax that. You can find your own way up?"

9

Letty was hunched over some cards on a wine cork table, failing to learn a game Flynt called cuttle, when the knock came. Three sharp raps, and Letty jumped up, hoping to see Edwing so they could finally get to work. Flynt went to the door with his hand on his pistol, less optimistic.

"It's me," Smark announced.

"About fucking time!" Letty said. "We're ready to bust some heads."

"Oh," Smark answered apprehensively. "You've heard, then?"

Letty and Flynt exchanged a concerned look. Letty waved a hand, let him in, and Flynt stepped aside, peering out for trouble. Smark entered sullenly, and reading their postures decided no, they had not heard. He gestured towards the TV. "It's on the news, story broke as I was on the way over."

As Flynt closed the door, Letty said, "Val's responded?"

Smark gave her an uneasy look. He turned on the television himself. "It's hell. I'm sorry." He addressed Flynt: "So sorry."

The channel was broadcasting a speech from Valoria Magnus, in all her resplendent glory. Talking over a podium again. "– put his trust in beliefs that experience has taught us to doubt. We did our best to find the councilman, but he was determined to go alone. An admirable thinker, and a friend –"

Flynt gave Letty a sideways glance. "What's going on?"

Smark grunted, reluctant to say it. "It's unclear – all we've got is her word."

"The young amongst you," Valoria continued, "may not remember the coup. We've moved beyond those violent days. Edwing, certainly, had moved beyond that. But without a crusade to fight, some still seek trouble. And, of course, the influence of that monstrous human cannot be understated. It's a great loss."

"They showed photos," Smark said. "It wasn't pretty. The Stabilisers claim they tracked him down, to protect him, but what they found – they were too late."

On screen, Valoria continued, "She knew exactly how to isolate him. Playing on his hopes. Now, I appeal for calm and understanding – do not blame our dear colleague for his folly, nor his family, nor friends. One Fae alone is responsible. Her and the humans."

A headline scrolled at the base of the screen. *Chair of Information, Edwing, Murdered By Human*. No. Fuck. That righteous idiot got himself killed? What about Pax?

"Who? How?" Flynt said, horrified. "You said he was safe – Val wouldn't –"

"The truth," Valoria said, "is that Letty has been looking for ways to draw the FTC and humanity into a war for decades, even before she left us."

"I fought for *you*!" Letty shouted. She spun on the other two, Smark edging towards the door. "You know this is bullshit, right? She'll do anything to spite the humans!"

Smark was about to answer, but Flynt's anguished look gave him pause.

"Letty *will* be punished," Valoria continued. "The human will be punished. All that is left is for me to appeal to Edwing's people – those of you that believed in him. Hear me. I am as dedicated to resolving our differences with the humans as he was. I feel his loss as deeply as you. I only ask that you work with us. Help me deliver justice for this tragedy. Smark – our Waste Chief – Flynt, our Chief of Scouts, his *dear* brother – if you are listening, *please* be careful. Letty has fooled many in the past."

Flynt's eye shifted to Letty.

"This," Smark said carefully, "is a time to step back. I don't believe it, but if –"

"Pax would *never* have hurt him," Letty spat. "I know her –"

"She grabbed him," Flynt said. "Tossed him in a pocket like a toy."

"You murder your toys? She grabbed *me*, it doesn't mean a thing."

Smark took another step, into the doorway. "Letty, you see how it looks. What if –"

"Fuck you for suggesting it," Letty flared back.

"Anyone," Valoria continued, "with *any* information about Letty's whereabouts…"

"We need to lay low," Smark said. "If I come forward – say I was mistaken –"

"You bloody idiot! Let her win? She's probably flicking herself silly at her luck; no Edwing, no opposition. I warned him this would get dirty."

"Did you get my brother killed?" Flynt asked, quietly.

Letty froze, looking at him sideways. He didn't move.

"I'm leaving," Smark decided.

"Don't you fucking –" Letty twisted towards him, and Flynt shot into action. He shoved her, hard, both hands on her chest, hitting her bruise with enough force that she stumbled. Then he sprang at her. Letty's body took over: she deflected the attack and ducked to the side. He flew up, gaining the advantage of height as she rolled under him. She took one blow to a forearm before grabbing his wrist. She twisted it around and leapt up at the same time, hooking his arm into the crook of her elbow as she rammed her forehead into his nose. With a crack and a cry, Flynt fell, but Letty held him up by the arm, swinging her other fist in. Her arm was caught and she was twisted into a bearlike grip. Smark's face was terrified and apologetic, one hand on her wrist, the other arm around her waist.

"That's enough!" he shouted, fearfully. "He lost his brother for crying out loud!"

Letty shoved free of him but released Flynt, breathing deep. He collapsed at her feet, sobbing and cursing. Letty told him, regretfully, "You've got balls and no fucking brains. I didn't hurt Edwing, I didn't set him up, and Pax sure as shit didn't either."

Smark said, "You're – I can't stay –"

"Fuck off then," she snapped, "but give me what you promised."

Smark shook his head, forgetting himself entirely. Letty glared until he remembered. With hurried nods, he searched his pockets and took out a security card. He tossed it over with a hushed address: "Penthouse 8. And my guy, he hasn't been involved, but some Stabilisers, they've been up to something. Something else. For – for what it's worth."

With that, he hurried out. Flynt lifted his bloody face to Letty, single eye filled with hate, the eyepatch askew and showing a twisted, scarred hole. He spat blood. "Edwing . . . he . . ."

Letty gave him a sympathetic look. Not the first time a good man got beat, nor died. She held out her hand. He took it, limply, and she pulled him to his feet. Pulled him further, into an embrace, and he let it out. Slumping into her arms. Sobbing into her shoulder. He tried to form words, slowly, painfully. "What – what – what are we going to do?"

Lips set in firm defiance, Letty patted his back and didn't answer. Didn't need to, seeing as it was obvious. He already had the right idea, he'd just chosen the wrong target. *We're going to fucking well fight back.*

10

Pax's nerves were tightening by the second – murder, attempted murder, framing and fleeing were bad enough. Trying to remember how to work a clutch was salt in the wounds. The car moved in starts, something scraping in its pipes every time she changed speed. Christ, did cars have pipes? How the hell did you even describe this mess. All with two fairies giving mad instructions mostly formed of curses. Enjoying it.

"Double shift, for fuck's sake!" the denim one roared from his spot on the mirror.

"Pissing double shift yourself!" Pax shot back, whatever that meant. They jolted onto a long, straight road where Pax could finally relax after what seemed like an eternity of snaking little lanes. She glanced at Fresko, mulling over her phone on the passenger seat. She'd missed a call from Holly Barton, and she didn't dare stop to call back, but the fairy was making little progress doing it for her. Part of her wanted to toss the phone, in case it was being traced, but a bigger part wanted reassurance that the Bartons were safe. Pax said, "There's like three numbers on there, what's taking you so long?"

"I got it, I got it," Fresko grumbled, slapping the touchscreen. It did nothing.

"Turn right, dullard!" the denim one shouted, and Pax hit the brakes. The phone flew into the footwell, fairy with it. When Pax gunned the accelerator again the car shuddered to a stop and went quiet. She stared wide-eyed ahead, thankful that the nearest other car was a long way off.

"Sort it out, Mix, for fuck's sake," Fresko snarled, flying back up to the seat carrying a phone that dwarfed him.

The denim one, Mix, flew down past Pax, complaining, "Amateur."

As he played with the wires to restart the engine, Pax tried to slow her heart.

"You want the clutch totally disengaged when you're moving that stick," Fresko said, almost without malice.

As the engine coughed back to life, Pax said, "How do you guys know this? You've got cars like ours?"

"Ha, hear that, Fresko?" Mix flew back up to the mirror. Unless barking angry commands, he had a hard time addressing her directly. "Thinks we're driving about in toys or some shit?"

"We've got wings, lady," Fresko told her, deliberately obvious. "Just pays to know your big tools."

Slowly moving the car on again, Pax recalled exactly who she was dealing with. This pair of maniacs had kidnapped Grace using a car, hadn't they? She had no idea how, but it didn't surprise her that they were capable of it. "So has one of you bright sparks got a plan?"

They looked to each other, and Mix said, "Seeing as this genius here got us shooting fucking Stabilisers, how about I give it a go? The only place to hide from your Ministry is with the Fae, only place to hide from the Fae is with your Ministry. Failing hiding, you gotta keep moving. Hence the ring road."

Coming up on it now, she could see the sign. Shit, there was going to be a slip road. Pax's knuckles whitened on the wheel as she picked up speed. She twisted quickly, searching every corner of window-space for blind spots. A truck whizzed past and she braked, jolting forward. Then she was there. On a highway stretching into the distance.

It was a straight line, near enough. Other cars shot past her, but she could stay in this lane, without having to steer, without having to change gears. This was good.

"Okay. Okay, we're safe. We can circle the city forever." She gave Mix a look. "You can syphon petrol from moving vehicles, fly in food, and we never have to leave the A564." She could sleep in stolen seconds, a motorway hermit swung around by the centrifugal force of Ordshaw's chaotic heart.

The electric ring of the speakerphone drew her back from that fantasy, Fresko announcing, "Got it."

Holly answered her phone. "At last. I'm not sure if you're aware, Pax, but the Ministry are after you. I can only imagine my family are in danger again."

"No, this is on me," Pax told her quickly. "Tell them it's nothing to do with you."

"*What* doesn't? Where are you?"

"Moving, for now, while I think of something. I've been set up."

"Of course you have," Holly said. "How can we help?"

"Stay out of it," Pax insisted. "I'll sort it out."

"Oh rot! I don't know how people do things where you come from, except clearly *not very well*, but I'm going to –"

"Watch that lorry!" Mix cried out, and Pax swerved with a screech from the car. They banked, but kept going, and she threw a terrified glance at the mirrors to see she was nowhere near hitting the massive vehicle they had passed. The fairy was laughing.

"You little shit," Pax hissed.

"See her face? Dumb fucking humans."

"Not the time," Fresko said, flying up to the rear-view mirror to join him. He sounded amused, despite the warning.

Pax said, "You're *both* shits."

"Who are you with . . ." Holly asked, worriedly. She recognised the voices. How could she not, when these little fiends had driven them into the sewer at gunpoint? "Pax . . ."

"It's complicated," Pax told her. "But I'm safe, okay?" Notwithstanding hurtling along at high speeds in a metal box of death. "Listen, Holly, if the Ministry *do* come at you, ask for Casaria. He's on our side. In his own weird way. As long as you tell him I said so."

"*He* came knocking at our house unannounced."

"He's there now?"

"No – I mean – never mind. What about Sam?"

Pax was quiet. Good bloody question: why wasn't Sam at the lido? "Is she with you?"

"She had a call from her people. She insisted she's on our side, Pax, but she answered their call, didn't she?"

"Uh-huh." That was a dilemma Pax could scarcely unpack. However amiable Sam had been, she was a company girl, wasn't she?

"We're heading home," Holly carried on. "Go there, we'll figure something out."

Pax wanted, deep down, to take up the offer, but couldn't. "I'll get back to you. Take care, Holly."

She ended the call, passing the turning for Hanton, towards New Thornton and, in its vicinity, the warehouse district. The harbour of criminals and fairies. This reckless escape was taking her *closer* to the threats. The Fae might spot her hurtling past on the raised highway, all of them coming after her in a swarm. Shooting at her from the sky. She asked her small companions, "Is there any way to avoid a shoot-first-ask-questions-later policy with your people?"

Mix gave a belly laugh. Fresko scoffed, more disdainful, and answered, "What for? Who's gonna believe the word of a human?"

"*You* know I didn't kill Edwing," Pax said. "Don't you have some kind of judicial system?" She recalled the way Letty had scolded her whenever she questioned Fae society. They had a university, working computers. "How do you hold trials back in the FTC?"

"Simple," Fresko said. "Hang a criminal someplace public, give everyone a chance to make judgements in passing. Good or bad."

"You hang them *before* a trial?"

"In a cage, dumbass," Mix replied. "You think a Fae ever got executed at the end of a rope? We can *fly*."

"It's a trial by the public," Fresko said. "Everyone's welcome to have a go."

"Leading to some kind of judgement?" Pax said.

"Usually a consensus gets reached, sure. Either, *go on let him out then*, or, you know, the other way. Sometimes in hours, days. Sometimes longer."

"Bana swung in his cage for eight years, the wretched shit," Mix recalled. "No one could decide that one. Did he kill his mistress, didn't he?"

"Wasn't so much no one could decide," Fresko said. "No one cared. Bana and the woman weren't well-liked. Usually those closest to the situation make the call. Doesn't work so well when you're dealing with loners."

"It's some kind of due process," Pax said. "A chance to be heard." She slowed down, making the Fae look around. There was an exit coming up, a sign for Brimlane. The warehouse district.

"The fuck are you doing?" Mix said. "Looking for the worst place to lie low?"

"That's the point, isn't it?" Pax said. "I'm supposed to lie low. We're all supposed to be fighting, blaming one another – no one talking. I'm being blamed for people I know getting into the Sunken City and we're all too busy getting chased to ask exactly what happened. Dial Sam Ward for me."

Fresko and Mix exchanged a look, then had a quick, muttered argument, pushing each other to decide who was going to follow orders this time.

"I'd suggest you, white shirt, seeing as you know what you're doing!" Pax took charge. Fresko gave up; with a snort, he flew to the phone.

Pax steered off the ring road and turned into a quieter street. Pulling up behind some parked cars, she held on to the steering wheel to calm herself. Fresko struggled with the touchscreen, looking like he was playing a game of Twister, so Pax reached for it herself. He scrambled out of the way with a hand shooting to the rifle slung across his back. "You fucking try –"

She ignored him, finding he'd somehow brought up a weather app. Rain all day tomorrow. She dialled the number.

"Sam Ward speaking," Ward answered, anxiety masked by her impossibly polite phone-answering instinct.

"Sam, it's me."

"I know – Pax, what's going on? If it's some kind of misunderstanding, you –"

"MEE policy would be to arrange a meeting and make sure I don't talk, I'm sure."

Ward paused. "Certainly not *my* policy." But that implied Pax wasn't wrong.

"That happens, or I run, and we fall into the same pattern," Pax told her plainly. "I didn't do whatever you think I did. I didn't do what the Fae think I did, either. I don't know if it's the same person set me up twice, but I do know *not knowing* is the problem."

"So . . ."

"Where are you?"

"Hanton, heading to St Alphege's. Where Obrington is."

"Casaria says your boss killed someone I know. You weren't there?"

"Absolutely not. But the intruders – is it – maybe you told them about the tunnels by mistake?"

"I haven't talked to –" Pax paused. She hadn't stopped to think about it. Monroe, Bees, Jones. They knew the tunnels existed. They'd dropped the subject when she convinced them it wasn't safe underground. Or because they didn't need her to get in? Jones and Monroe had given her those cryptic comments, suggesting she had helped them out – somehow given them access? Pax slammed a hand into the steering wheel. "Bastards! This is Lightgate again – she saw me with them, she knew they knew me."

"Good," Ward said. "We can do something about that."

"No, not good, because Monroe thinks I helped him. Your people go to him, they'll believe the same. Shit. We need to get there first – figure out how she got to him, *show* it wasn't me. Sam. Do you trust me?"

There was hesitation, but it was short. "I do."

"Can I trust you?"

"Definitely."

"Buy me some time. Send your people *anywhere* but after me."

"I can't, Pax, I have to meet –"

"I'm going to the warehouse district. I'd appreciate it if you'd join me. Only you. So at least someone'll know if it goes tits up."

Ward was quiet for a moment. "I'll come." Another pause. "But Pax. The Fae? I heard your message . . ."

"One catastrophe at a time, Sam. Please."

Barton clambered up the stairs back into daylight at a pace that was wearing his ankle back to breaking point. By his side hovered Rufaizu, ready to catch him at any moment, face full of concern. He swatted him away, leaning against a wall instead, squinting into the sunlight to see Holly finishing on the phone.

"Anything?" Barton asked.

"I spoke to Pax," Holly said. "Then I got an address. The MEE switchboard told me where I could return Sam's scanners. So we can at least go *there* and do what we can. Assuming Pax survives the fairies, anyway. I heard them, Diz, on the phone with her – the ones that kidnapped Grace – and –"

Barton heard the crack of the wall before he felt the pain in his knuckles, as he realised he'd punched brickwork. His chest heaved, shoulders rolling, those bloody Fae – he should've killed them before –

Holly's face told him to stop. "Can you engage your brain instead of your testicles?"

Barton shook bits of chipped wall off his hand, cowed.

Rufaizu said, "Where is the bar fly? Can we fly to her?"

"I don't know," Holly said. "But whatever she thinks, I doubt we're safe from this."

"I'm not running," Barton said firmly. "They've been fucking with this city for far too long – the blue screens, the Ministry. I'll go to their office and make them see sense."

From the way Holly stared at his clenched fist, his wife remained unimpressed, but she didn't scold him this time. No better ideas of her own.

"You go," Barton continued. "Take Rufaizu back to Grace. I'll –"

Holly folded her arms. "I think you'll find I can handle these people better than you."

11

When Sam caught up to Obrington, she found the Ministry had created a crime scene out of a white van. Yellow police tape and bollards sectioned off the road, courtesy of one uniformed officer and a patrol car, and beyond that stood Obrington and Casaria, slightly apart from the vehicle, which was being searched by Landon and their tech-head, Dr Galler. Sam ducked under the tape and approached Obrington as he said, "Ah Ward, so *good* of you to join us."

"Apologies, sir, the traffic was –"

"Don't care." Obrington gestured towards the van. "What do you know about this? Exactly how pervasive a system of lies have we got here in Ordshaw?"

"Lies?" Sam looked from the van to Casaria, who slouched like a grounded teenager. "I haven't had a chance to –"

"Drug dealers in the Sunken City," Obrington announced, "who conveniently got access right around the time their good friend Pax tells us to back off, distracting us with stories of the Fae. Arranging things at conveniently unmonitored card games."

Sam's mouth was open, unbelieving. "Drug dealers?"

"It's the same van," Landon said, approaching from behind. Sam gave him the slightest smile of a hello, good to see his familiar face, but his expression warned her worse was to come. "These people were outside Casaria's, remember?"

The issue they'd never fully resolved, his abduction, which he'd claimed was unrelated to the men at Pax's apartment.

"Like I said," Casaria said, "I never got a good look. It could've been them. All I know is they wanted to leave me for dead in a rival gang's territory."

"Yet somehow over the course of this home invasion and abduction," Obrington said, "we get them happening upon a Sunken City entrance, and the means to deactivate our sensors. The same gentlemen who *happened* to burglarise Pax Kuranes' flat?"

"That's how it seems." Casaria wasn't even trying to sound convincing.

"You're effectively Management now, Ward." Obrington let his gaze rest on her. "What do you do in this situation?"

Sam paused, trying to appear in thoughtful control, rather than internally panicking. Casaria had proven himself unreliable, but Pax? Could she have orchestrated anything like this? Why would either of them help criminals?

"I'll make it easier on you," Obrington said. "Start with Mr Casaria. Who you seemed ready to forgive. Suspension, investigation, let him off?"

The *mister* was an insult that made Casaria twitch. Sam gave him an assaying look. Blame him and they'd limit the growing complications of this situation. It would get Pax off the hook, at least. But words came out at odds with that grave chain of thought: "I'd keep him closer, sir. If he's trustworthy, he's an asset; if he's not, he needs monitoring."

"An asset?" Obrington sounded surprised.

"Unless proven guilty, he's one of us," Sam said. "Trained, capable."

Mouth open again, her superior looked down his nose at her, not what he wanted to hear. "Respectfully, I'd say his trustworthiness is well in doubt. I wouldn't permit him to fart in the wind without a full account of his dealings this past week. But we shouldn't let him out of our sight, certainly." Before Sam could respond, he added, "Now where's Kuranes?"

"I honestly don't see her involvement in this," Sam said defensively. "Is it not possible these men, who intruded on her apartment, might have discovered this place without her knowing it?"

Obrington fired back at once, "*Are* you a dyke, Ms Ward?"

Sam tensed in shock. "That's the second time, sir, and I –"

"You seem awfully rosy thinking about Kuranes." Obrington turned to confide this to Landon. "Had them together this morning, can't say I didn't notice a few sparks. Thought I was imagining it, but here, this is a funny old place to be, with a fugitive –"

"You're out of line," Sam interrupted.

Obrington looked amused. "Touched a nerve?"

"Once was ignorant. Twice, it's insulting. To me, to her and to your office." Seeing Obrington's stirring anger, Sam puffed herself up rather than back down, chest high, shoulders back. "How are we supposed to trust your judgement when you say things like that? Do you think it's acceptable just because I'm a woman? Or that I *must* be driven by sex? That'd make it half the population you don't understand."

Obrington's open-mouthed grimace of disbelief was back, and Casaria had rediscovered his own grin. Landon made a noise of discomfort. If words failed Obrington long enough, Sam wondered, would he simply smack her face? His bear paws would flatten her. His goggling eyes vibrated, looking her up and down, until he settled on his best response. "Mathers really kept you in a box, didn't he?"

Sam glowered straight back, tight-lipped. No way she was going to let him dismiss this so blithely. "I respect Pax Kuranes. I believe the Ministry owes her a debt. Whatever you think you have against her, I suggest questioning it."

Obrington narrowed his eyes. "Why?"

"Because she's got a connection to the monsters that we don't, you fat fuck," Casaria blurted out, and it was Sam's turn to stand shocked. Obrington didn't turn to him at once, which was good because Casaria was grinning like he had no idea how else to wear his face. He hadn't meant to say it; Sam's outburst had drawn it out.

With perfect timing, Dr Galler appeared, lightly saying, "Yup, definitely Fae shots."

Obrington's broiling rage subsided in an instant. "What the bleeding hell does *that* mean?"

"The van. You said check for everything – there's bullets in the door. One in the wing mirror. Looks like your average scratch but that's what this baby's for." Galler proudly held up what looked like a microscope from a children's playset.

"You're telling me these mugs had a shootout with the Fae?" Obrington scowled.

"Well, their van did."

Obrington rounded on Casaria. "And you wouldn't know anything about that?"

The answer was clear on Casaria's face. Fully unprepared. He knew exactly who the criminals were and how they'd come to be shot at by fairies. Sam gave him a weak look. For all she'd said, Pax and Casaria *had* kept a lot back. Were her instincts wrong?

"Care to revise your assessment?" Obrington asked her, considering the same.

Sam shook her head but said nothing.

Obrington's pocket buzzed and he drew out his phone. He frowned at the Caller ID and held up the index finger of his free hand. "Getting more interesting by the second." He answered. "Governor Valoria, I assume? Now is not –" The Fae governor interrupted, talking deeply but not loud enough for everyone to hear. Obrington's brow folded. "Huh. That so." He listened as the Fae railed on, then said, "You understand we're willing to co-operate." More listening. "It's come to our attention, too." He looked unhappy at the next comments. "That might be best for all of us. Good day."

Putting his phone away, Obrington looked at Sam. He adjusted his jacket, and said calmly, "Seems I owe you an apology, Ward."

Definitely a trap.

"I was wrong about one thing. Ms Kuranes wasn't spinning a yarn about her Fae connections. And it has got her in all sorts of fresh trouble. They're connecting her to some kind of political assassination. And you weren't with her at the time?"

Sam's doubts mounted. They'd planned to go to Tupsom together – but Pax had been keen to go on ahead, hadn't she? Hell, why *were* there Fae bullets in this van? And these people knew how to get into the Sunken City – was it possible –

"Know what we do with her now?" Obrington said, self-satisfied. "Besides marvelling at how big a cocking mess she's producing."

The best Sam could do was stare back.

"No?" Obrington said. "The Fae want us to hand her over, or otherwise *handle* her. They're not above capital punishment, yes? Frankly, I'm not in Ordshaw to tango with gangsters and this kind of bloody politics. Remove Kuranes from the equation and it seems to me we've got a much clearer shot at the end goal, don't we?"

Sam shook her head, but still no words came.

"Sounds settled to me. You two" – Obringinton indicated Casaria and Sam – "need a few lessons taught hard, but I can see you've been caught up beyond your station. Here's a shot at redemption. Help make all this go away, *including* Kuranes, and you get to keep your jobs, and your freedom, how's that? But we'll leave hunting her to the boys, shall we, to make sure a proper job's done, Meantime, how about all of us find this bloody Stacey Monroe, whoever he is, and see what he has to say about your star civilian. Casaria, you're with me" – Obrington clicked his fingers at Landon – "and you'll kindly follow on with Ms Ward. Get us a home address. Assuming none of you have any problem with that?"

12

Letty barged through a sleek entrance hall into an open-plan living area. Nimm was at a kitchen counter, startled from chopping vegetables, a gleaming knife in his hand. Pistol drawn, Letty sprang over the sofa then the counter with a quick wingbeat and the hum of the Clear Glider. She knocked the knife away and pushed Nimm into a stainless steel fridge, then jammed the barrel of her gun under his nose before checking the room.

A black leather three-piece suite, polished tile kitchen, resembling the worst, coldest human styles. Right down to a shrieking hussy in an open silk robe, scrambling out of an armchair trying to cover herself up. Flynt pushed her back down, waving his gun shakily. "Not a sound, not one fucking movement."

He looked at Letty, scarred face unsettling with its dried blood and the raw, trembling emotion in his eye. He was straining to hold back. But he was in control. Just. Letty bore into Nimm. "We're gonna have a chat and you're gonna want it to go well, because my mate's looking to work through some emotions."

There was no question Nimm had power: despite the big nose, skin patterned by liver spots, and hair coming out of his ears, he owned a pad like this, waited on by this pretty escort. Letty dragged him around the kitchen counter and kicked him onto the sofa. He scrambled back, hands up.

"There's no need," he squeaked, "the compound is gone!"

Letty paused. "Compound? Of what?"

Nimm's face mirrored her confusion. "You're not here about the septjad?"

"What fucking septjad?"

Nimm looked from one intruder to the other, worry mounting as he reassessed the situation. His eyes rested on Flynt, with a gasp. "No – they're preparing it now, in response – you don't think I had something to do with Edwing . . ."

Flynt's face hardened. "There a reason we should?"

"Shit." Letty stepped between them. This was supposed to be the safer, subtler option, going for the guy knee-deep in the *why* without losing their cool chasing murderers. To Nimm, she said, "We're not here for your fucking *compound* and we don't think you killed anyone. You're gonna take us to the Dispenser, your other fucking sins can wait."

"What do you mean? There's no –"

"'There's no question I'll do exactly as you ask, Letty, it's wonderful?'" Letty's fist was raised, making Nimm push himself deep into the sofa.

"But why? The Dispenser is secure –"

"Not as long as Val's got a hand in it, it's not! Tell me you're not trying to sabotage the thing? Make like it never worked?"

"Of course not, why *would* we?" He genuinely didn't follow.

Letty explained, slowly, "Because Val doesn't want us to retake the Sunken City." It only softened Nimm's features, the threat diminishing as he grasped the nature of the misunderstanding.

"But disabling the Dispenser has nothing to do with that."

Letty cocked her head to one side. He was almost smiling as he saw she didn't have the first clue what Val and her people were up to, even regarding the Dispenser. She met Flynt's eye again, and could see the same concern caught him. He needed clear, cold retaliation – what the hell was this?

"Explain," Letty said, holstering her pistol.

"You're Letty, aren't you? I –" Nimm cut off his attempt to get friendly as she unsheathed her big old hunting knife.

"Explain *well*," she advised.

He swallowed. "Valoria sought to conceal the Dispenser, yes, but only to avoid public concern. There's no need to risk disabling it, it could be easily recreated, and" – he hurried on, past Letty's startled reaction – "anyway no Fae would use it, or *could* use it, safely. The energy it sends out – surely you understand, the interplay with dust production, with electric weed as a fuel – it could kill us."

"What the fuck are you talking about? What's electric weed got to do with dust?"

"They're the same genus," Nimm said, surprised at her not knowing. "There's similar energy stored in dust fungus. Different strains, but similar enough to make the weapon's discharge dangerous. It could create a chain reaction – essentially drawing on that same energy in *us*."

"You . . ." Letty focused on the edge of the knife, trying to keep calm. "You already understand it. You understood it before?"

The scientist twisted in the seat, appealing to Flynt for reason. "Yes, well. The issue with the Dispenser was never that we couldn't rebuild it. We can neutralise Sunken City energy in controlled conditions, with the right materials. The *unknown* is what comes next."

Letty dragged a hand over her face. Of fucking course. She shouldn't be surprised, after Val's betrayal, with all this about the Fae settling into their transitional culture. They weren't ever waiting on her for salvation, the one person that could find the Dispenser. It was *always* replaceable and they let her believe otherwise. For nine years. Nine fucking years. She threw her knife with a snarl – half the blade sank into a wall, the impact making Nimm jump out of his seat. She said, "You fucking . . ."

Flynt moved past her, quickly. In front of Nimm.

"How many people know about this?" he demanded. "How many people know we already had the means to fight the creatures down there?"

"Plenty!" Nimm blurted out, frightened eyes on Letty. "It's not a well-kept secret. Half the workers in the vats must have an idea of it – knowing where dust comes from –"

"What the fuck's that mean," Letty snapped, "where dust comes from?"

"We cultivate a – a particular type of energy." Nimm's voice wavered. "The similarities in the Sunken City creatures are obvious. Likewise, how we might neutralise it –"

"So what's your damn *unknown*?" Letty said.

Nimm stared gravely. "Many tools were tested, before Valoria took power. The Dispenser was merely the last of them. They worked, of course they worked, but the berserker never *stayed* neutralised."

"Didn't . . ." Letty trailed off. They'd actually tested it – attacked the berserker before, that amorphous minotaur, the Ministry's protected *praelucente*. The heart of it all. They had *hurt* it? "This is bullshit. Why not keep trying until it was gone?"

"Because it's next to impossible for Fae to get close unharmed! All for the possibility of removing a force of energy that's likely to *come back*?"

"But the humans can –"

"Work with humans? For what? We have the resources to expand our dust production here, what more does the Sunken City offer, worth that risk?"

"A home!" Letty shouted. "It's our fucking home! It *belongs* to us!"

Nimm looked at her like she was mad. "But you can't honestly believe it? Those tunnels weren't made for the Fae – I would say quite the opposite."

Letty glared hard, unsure exactly where to direct her anger. Valoria, the lying snake. This whole society, implicitly following her abandonment of the place Letty always aimed to return them to. How many scores of people were simply ignoring that option? She turned to the pretty escort in the armchair, sat in terrified silence, and said, "You know about this?"

The woman shook her head quickly, lost in fear.

"Reckon there's ordinary Fae that would like to know? Might kick up a fuss?"

The woman nodded desperately, agreeing with whatever Letty might say. Flynt came in, speaking low: "Of course they would. Else it wouldn't be secret. Else they wouldn't have killed my brother."

Nimm swallowed uncomfortably. "That is *not* my area. Your brother – Valoria would *not* have dared. She didn't think it necessary. And the things that have been said about *you*" – he gave Letty a look – "it is politics. All she wants is *security*."

Letty frowned. None of it was anything to do with him, from his perspective. "You thought we were here for something else. What's this compound?"

Nimm went quiet again.

"Speak," Letty said, leaning closer to him again, "or I'll cut your fingers off."

He croaked, "The Stabilisers are distributing the septjad compound across Ordshaw, as an insurance, to be ready for when the Council meet this afternoon. With the humans moving in the tunnels nearby, and now Edwing's death, it's our answer – but only as a *threat* – I thought you came to make it a reality."

"I asked what the fuck it is."

"Uh. A poison, water soluble, virtually untraceable. Cultured in Russia. Perfectly harmless in its current state, but placed in a water supply it becomes deadly. A way to disable high-profile humans."

Letty glowered. A poison from fucking Russia. A chemical weapon. The boxes that had been in the room with the Dispenser, all covered in Cyrillic. A gift from the Rostov Fae? Their closest neighbouring Fae community were a collective of unscrupulous psychos who experimented in vile, vicious technology. Perfect examples of what happened when Fae gave up on being civilised. Which was actually most Fae, most places. If anyone knew effective ways to kill humans, Rostov would. While Letty was itching to get back a weapon that was apparently never special, Val's people were preparing something that clearly was. "Val's going to threaten Ordshaw? Poison the humans?"

"She's planning…" Nimm averted his eyes, scared to repeat the governor's spin. "It's merely for the purposes of *negotiation*."

"Fuck's sake. Where the hell do we find it?"

"Why?" Nimm asked. "After what they did to Edwing, surely you want –"

"The humans didn't do that!" Letty told him viciously. "If anything, Val planned this shit herself. How the fuck do we stop it?"

"You're too late," Nimm said. "By now, it's already in position across the city."

Near Monroe's derelict lair, waiting on word from Sam Ward, Pax leant against the stolen car and reflected on her terrible choices. The car in itself was bad; the second time she'd committed grand theft auto in a week. Now she was wanted for murder, too, alongside suspicions for associating with dangerous criminals. Before this, the worst crimes she'd committed involved recreational drugs and drinking underage.

"About a half-mile walk to the FTC from here," Fresko mused from the car roof.

"Trying to make me feel better?" Pax said. He shrugged, not bothered how she felt. Mix was even less interested, standing further away, puffing on another Fae cigar.

"Never knew these guys were here, that's all," Fresko said. "Big city, isn't it?"

"Yeah," Pax said. "But then a pint of beer would be big for you."

"Listen." Fresko took a breath. Something on his mind. "Before you go get yourself killed, I gotta say. Things got out of hand before. Mistakes were made. Things happened. Okay?"

It *almost* sounded like an apology. Pax said, "One of you shot me in the leg."

Fresko looked her up and down. "You're walking, aren't you?"

"Yeah." What was the use. They'd saved her now. "I guess I'm glad you had a change of heart."

"For today," Mix told her. "Or until someone makes us a better offer."

As Pax regarded him warily, Fresko said, "Ignore him. It obviously wasn't Letty, or you, that screwed us. They weren't ever letting us back in the FTC."

Pax folded her arms over her chest, watching the road. "Yeah, we're all victims. Look, you'd better clear off. Seeing as you don't play nice with the Ministry."

"Uh-huh," Fresko said. "But if they don't kill you outright, come find us. I'm interested in what happens next."

"Find you where?"

"Palleday's. Couldn't say your Ministry won't track you, but the Stabilisers should steer clear, considering him neutral, near as I know."

The casual suggestion said they knew she'd already been there. How long had they been following her? When the Ministry was supposed to have her back . . .

Fresko shouldered his rifle and signalled to Mix it was time to go. The pair lifted off. Pax watched them flying with birdlike grace, becoming dark shapes against the cloud. How many times had people seen such sights, assuming delicate birds or big insects, when it was in fact a sweary little man with an attitude? There was something to be said for how far she'd come, and all she'd learnt, no matter where she'd ended up.

Checking the road again, she had another thought. How often did people survive learning these truths? And as if on cue, something throbbed in her. Her fingers tingled, something happening, movement, somewhere far off. The minotaur was feeding again. Drawing energy. It barely felt surprising now, tapping into whatever they were up to. She closed her eyes and focused.

Out east, moving north. The horde was getting closer. The screens were still together. Surrounding their minotaur and drawing energy like limpets. But they were reaching out, probing with tiny transfers. Interacting with their tunnel networks, or their monsters? It was too faint to tell, and faded as fast as it came.

Pax opened her eyes to the road again. Much calmer this time than before. Had she somehow triggered that feeling herself? A little casual probing. Ward would be here soon, and they could figure that out together. Once they overcame the Monroe mess. One step at a time. Provided Ward wasn't coming to shoot her.

13

"You said she had a connection to the monsters. What'd you mean by that?"

Casaria avoided looking at Obrington as they drove to the address Ward's Support team had found for them. If he concentrated on the oaf's face for more than a few seconds he was going to punch him. "I don't know."

"You don't know?" Obrington echoed. "Slipped your memory between hurling insults liable to get you hurt?"

The prick. Casaria saved his life, didn't he? That two-bit thug would've choked him, and where was the thanks? Somewhere behind vague threats of losing his job or violence. Like this overweight buffoon could match him in a brawl. Casaria would break his knees.

"I wasn't thinking." It was true, he hadn't meant to say it. Obviously he wasn't going to share Pax's secret, not if Pax and Sam Ward had kept it hidden. "I meant these criminals. She understands them."

Obrington hummed a sceptical noise.

On the radio, they were discussing the city's news. Someone commented, "It's Ordshaw, Steve – they don't exactly have the same building standards there, do they? Don't they say, those that can, do; those that can't move to Ordshaw."

Seeing Casaria's glower, Obrington said, "Funny because it's true, no?"

"Funny," Casaria replied with venom, "is the thought that people don't even realise how special this city is. You've no idea how important it is, what we do."

Obrington gave him a cock-eyed look. "You think what you do is important, but undermine it by being an insubordinate ass? How about that."

Casaria didn't deign to respond.

They were entering the outskirts of West Farling, and the affluent neighbourhood reminded him it wasn't monsters they were regulating, here, but people. Casaria thought of Pax and that unassuming teenager, Grace. Obrington had shot a man in the face, in the tunnels. He might've killed the small one, too, if there weren't so many loose ends. What Casaria did *was* important, because he kept the Sunken City in order without ruining the lives above. He didn't beat up defenceless people, or resort so quickly to murder.

He decided he did have a response, after all: "It's become clear we need to question Management's decisions if we're to do our work properly."

"Is that so," Obrington replied. "There's assuming you know how to do your job properly. Where'd we get to, before, when we were interrupted? Think I was asking, *how exactly was it that the only agent to die in the Sunken City in six years did so on Casaria's watch?*"

He clearly had an axe to grind over Gant's death. "If you're looking to crucify me, I'm sure you'll find an excuse. Your type usually do."

"You're not shy, are you. Whatever *my type* is, Casaria, you've plainly got a lot to account for. You didn't get on with the young lad, did you?"

"Did he file a report?"

"After he got killed?" Obrington made Casaria face him. The big man was staring, ignoring the road for longer than was safe. Casaria broke eye contact first. "You *believe* you're a good agent, don't you?"

They were passing ever-bigger houses, some of Ordshaw's grander mansions. Typical of a man like Monroe, living amongst the elite. It'd be good blowing off some steam here. Casaria said, "I put myself on the line, every day, to keep this city safe. I do that well, on my own, because I understand those tunnels and those monsters. I only have problems" – he directed this at Obrington – "when other people bring them to me."

For a moment, he couldn't tell if the wide-mouthed goon was going to keep pushing. Obrington focused on the road, and said curiously, "You'd lay down your life for this city, would you?"

"Any day of the week," Casaria said. Hadn't he already proved that, saving Pax and the civilians? Ready to take their secrets to the grave, toe severed while tied to a dentist's chair? A knife in his gut? A shield for Pax when she faced the grugulochs?

Obrington was quiet. Hopefully thinking the same.

A short distance down a hill, they pulled up next to a red-brick mansion, square and tasteless, the grass and bushes of its large open driveway trimmed so neatly it could've all been artificial. "This is it, isn't it?"

The car rocked as Obrington heaved his weight out the door. Casaria exited the other side, pulling his jacket closed over his gun. He studied the road, quiet. Obrington looked unimpressed. "Where's the others got to, then?"

"Sam Ward is very strict on the rules of the road," Casaria suggested, checking the car in Monroe's driveway. A gleaming black Porsche, most likely belonging to a trophy wife half built of plastic.

Obrington had his phone out, dialling. No answer after a long wait. He grunted and tried another number, with no answer there, either. With the third call, he said, "Tori, anything from Ward or Landon?"

"I thought they were with you, sir?" the receptionist chimed back.

"Evidently not."

"So you're not calling about the Bartons?"

Obrington mouthed a disapproving curse to Casaria. "Why would I?"

"They arrived a few minutes ago – insisting that –"

"Arrived in our office?" Obrington said.

"Yes. I thought –"

"For crying out loud, who's running that place?"

There was a muffled disagreement on the other end of the line, and Tori urgently came back. "Sorry, sir, would you mind speaking to her?"

"To who? This is a bleeding –"

"Mr Obrington." Holly Barton announced her presence sharply. "I'll have you know that there are problems under Ordshaw that you are clearly too short-sighted to understand. You know that Ms Ward enlisted our help for a good reason, don't you? Thanks in no small part to Pax's involvement."

Obrington paused at her brusqueness. "Mrs Barton. I'm not sure *you* fully understand the situation with Kuranes."

"*Whatever* it is, it's a damned sight better situation than you were in a week ago," Holly said. "Have you even asked *why* Pax might keep things from you? Perhaps because your blundering management have already screwed this city so successfully for so long? Touch a hair on that woman's head and you'll have a city to answer to."

From the set of Obrington's shoulders, he was not happy about being undermined yet again. Casaria twisted away, to give himself space to smile. "Mrs Barton," Obrington said. "It's not a question of what Kuranes has kept from us, so much as what she's *done*. Though perhaps you'd like to share exactly what you think I should be upset about?"

"Is Sam with you now? Frankly, it's time she explained it to you herself."

Obrington looked at Casaria, then Monroe's mansion, and finally the car, his mouth open in thought. He was piecing together the deception. Pax's connection to the monster, everyone lying to him. Sam Ward not here now. He drew a slow conclusion, and said, simply, "Huh."

Sam was not aware of making a conscience choice to subvert the chain of command, but the moment Obrington's car had turned out of view she advised Landon that they would not be going to Monroe's family home. Landon watched Sam with many questions in his eyes, unhappy about changing course for the warehouse district without telling their colleagues. He asked only, "We planning on arresting her or helping her?"

Sam said she wasn't sure, and he segued into comments about his new Ministry-issued car, to change the subject. A Mercedes. He was pleased about its MPG, engine size and various electronics. Aware that Sam didn't care, but trying to demonstrate two things: he appreciated that Sam had once shown an interest in upgrading his car, and he appreciated that she didn't want to talk about their current situation.

In truth, she was terrified that meeting Pax would mean coming head to head with the very criminal Obrington expected to confront in West Farling. But she was even more frightened about the very shaky ground regarding Pax. She shifted in the passenger seat. Her instincts, her gut, said trust the woman. It was too crazy and dangerous for her to have orchestrated such a mess, with herself at the centre. But doubt crept in from all angles. Casaria's kidnapping and the way he had been swayed further against the Ministry. These illicit meetings with the Fae . . . what *had* Pax been getting up to? What were they walking into now? Pax wanted her alone, might she be planning something heinous?

What was Sam even doing out here, she belonged in the office – telling others where to go, analysing data. Even if Pax was to be trusted, they had field agents to follow up on it.

"You're not carrying a gun," Landon said, his mind in a similar place.

She gave him a wan smile. Of course she wasn't carrying a gun. Having an energy weapon in the Sunken City hardly helped. It had been years since she last used the Ministry's firing range.

"There's a spare in the glove compartment. You've had basic training?"

Sam let her eyes answer the question. Yes, she could shoot. No, she didn't want to.

"I'll take the lead," Landon said. "It's just in case."

14

Letty expected to find Edwing's war room empty. Newbry should've jumped ship the same as Smark, but Flynt insisted it was the place to go. If they were to have any hope of thwarting Val's citywide disaster, they needed help. He barely said anything else, retreating into his misery once the destination was established, with no discussion over exactly what use an abandoned comms station would be. The basement dwelling wasn't abandoned, though. Newbry was there, sitting amid a heap of wires and computer monitors, and he wasn't alone: in the little remaining space were Deidre and one of the Stabilisers from the Bloodtooth Bar.

"The fuck are you all doing here?" Letty asked, surprise coming out hostile. "The man's gone, shouldn't you be, too?"

"It's because –" Deidre started anxiously, higher than she intended. She tried again: "It's *because* we've lost Edwing that we're here. Flynt . . . I can't imagine." She half-raised a hand in consolation, but didn't come closer. Flynt nodded quiet appreciation.

Letty asked, "Do we know how it happened? How it *really* happened?"

The Stabiliser offered his input. "Near as I can tell they've reported the truth – our people weren't the first on the scene. They're hiding the fact we lost men, too, though."

"What?" Letty said. "How?"

"Only heard rumours," he replied. "Stabilisers got an anonymous tip to be there, but the first ones on the scene got taken down – three of ours. I don't see a human pulling that off, unless it was the Ministry, but why would Valoria hide that?"

She wouldn't, but she might downplay Fae involvement to keep the focus on Pax. Letty worked through that. Pax had other Fae friends? Who would intervene to help her? She asked Flynt, "Your people?"

Flynt shook his head. His scouts had been locked down with everyone else. No, it was stranger than that. If they set this up, the Stabilisers should've been prepared for trouble. If there was another Fae involved . . . Suddenly it hit Letty. "Fuck, it's her again, isn't it?"

Deidre asked, "Who?"

"Lightgate," Letty said. "Why the hell wouldn't it be? I knew I shouldn't have waited on Edwing's war of words and this shit – and you lot" – she pointed at the Stabiliser – "don't have the first clue about stopping her, do they?"

"Lightgate?" he replied. "We couldn't find –"

"I'm telling you it's her. She saw him vying for peace and that's the worst thing in the world to a psycho like her. Val didn't need to kill him, she could've connived around it, but Lightgate revels in this kind of brutality, *fuck*. Give me your armour. I'll get out, go –"

"No," Flynt cut in.

"What? You listening to me, your brother –"

"Can *wait*." He closed his eye at the pain of having to say this. "Whether Valoria pulled that trigger or not, she's taking advantage of it. She meets the Council in under an hour. We have to stop her using this to do even more harm."

"How's that?" Letty said. "Storm the Council, put one in her head? The FTC doesn't matter."

"No," Flynt repeated, determinedly, "with the vote she'll be pushing retaliation, segregation. It's more important than ever we stand up for what Edwing believed in. Lightgate wants us to fight; we need to be voices of reason."

"Edwing wanted human support," Deidre said. "Without that we have nothing."

"We know what she's doing," Flynt said. "Planning to force her demands through by threatening the humans."

The Stabiliser said, "They've been moving something, Val's closest men."

"We know," Letty huffed. "It's a poison."

"I can tell Valoria *no*," Flynt said. "Make the Council see sense." Emotion bubbled into his voice. Desperate to do this. "It's what Edwing would've done. Stayed the course."

"I . . ." Deidre struggled. "What would we say? I don't know –"

"*I'll* do it," Flynt said. "I got a right, don't I? As a community leader – as his brother. I'll say what he would've. It's not right, Val's way forward."

Deidre joined the rest of the room in looking to Letty for a decision.

"What? Why ask me? You think you can actually make a difference?"

"I can argue for peace," Flynt said. "For calm, measured justice."

"And we can record it," Newbry said. "I'm set up. Even if the Council votes in Val's favour, we can expose the details to the FTC."

Letty tried to picture it. A Council meeting where they managed to make a lot of angry Fae question Val's corruption. Throw in the message about her disregarding the Sunken City and the Dispenser, they might have something. At least delay what she had going on. Flynt wasn't the orator his brother had been, but it was better than busting heads. Letty asked, "You're up to this?"

He nodded, with the determination of a kid about to jump in water for the first time.

"Alright. But it's not enough. This one's right" – Letty indicated Deidre – "we *need* that human element. Can you get me another outside line?"

Newbry turned to a second computer. "Already on it."

At the ring of her phone, Pax felt a pang of stupid guilt. She still hadn't tossed it, inviting trouble. A tracking device in her pocket. Come get me, lock me up, shoot my knees off, whatever. And now another Unknown Number. She answered, "Yeah?"

"You sound down. Been wrongfully accused of murder or some shit?"

"Letty!" Pax jumped to attention. "Thank fuck! How –"

"You're in the shit," Letty cut in. "We are, too, for what it's worth. An hour or so and Valoria's gonna make contact like this completely impossible. So we gotta talk quick. First, some good news: our weapons *can* get rid of the berserker – your fucking minotaur."

"Great. Can they take out Lightgate, too?"

"Shut up and listen – this thing's still a clusterfuck and we need your help. Specifically, *you*, because you're always finding answers to questions no one's asking. I'm hoping for an answer to stop our people kicking the world in the balls. Point one, the Dispenser wasn't never some unique, mystical weapon. Like you fucking thought, our energy's all connected, and my people already *know* that. They baulked at it because the buck doesn't stop at the berserker. The Dispenser *worked*, but the berserker came back."

"Came back . . ."

"That's their excuse for giving up and going with whatever the hell Val wants. Our Council's meeting in an hour and Val wants to draw a line we won't come back from. She'll threaten your people with some fucking poison. But if you can give us a solution – if we can resolve the Sunken City, put serious faith in humanity – then we avoid disaster."

Pax said nothing. Not panicking, or creasing up at the responsibility. Calm, strangely, like it made sense. For once, she wanted to be needed. "I'll do it. I'll be there."

"At the meeting? No, that's –"

"I mean I'll figure something out. If I'm not dead by then."

"Get your Ministry mates to earn their keep, they can hold off a few Fae."

An engine grew louder as a shining black car pulled into the road. The sleek heartless vehicle of government spooks, not Sam Ward's Honda. Tracking the phone call?

"Yeah, about that," Pax said quietly.

"What *about that*? Pax –"

"Let's both of us just try and stay alive. Speak soon, okay?"

She hung up as the car got nearer. Through the windscreen, she saw Ward, giving her a wave, but she wasn't alone. Behind the wheel was the older, overweight agent she'd crossed a few times now. Landon. Pax didn't run. It was what it was.

They pulled up and got out, Landon checking the sky, Ward holding back, watching Pax. Dreading the answer, Pax asked, "What's he doing here?"

"Whatever I tell him to," Ward said, with forced confidence. Having satisfied himself with their surroundings, Landon turned to her for instructions. There was a dark look on her face. "Obrington wants your blood. And the FTC got in touch."

"Saying I killed someone and you should hand me over, I guess?" Pax said. "Did they suggest I single-handedly took out the Fae hunting me, too?"

"I don't know." Ward hesitated. "The others are on their way to Monroe's house, thinking we're behind them. It's just us here."

"They'll trace us before long," Landon added. Prompting a decision. Pax gave him an uneasy look; thinning dark hair dusted with grey, badly dressed and an overall picture of lazy tiredness. She could see why it was this one, in particular, Ward was able to control.

Ward held Pax's gaze, looking like she wanted to ask something, anything, that would make everything clear and easy. Rather than speak, Pax spread her hands openly. She had invited them there, trusted them this far; it was on them now. Ward took a deep breath and shook her head, going with a feeling that her logic was raging against. She said, "We might not have much time. What are we going to do?"

"Alright." Pax fought down a relieved smile, and raced quickly on. "Monroe and his boys, they *think* I'm their mate. They'll give me the time of day – I want to talk to them. Figure out how Lightgate got to them, maybe see a way I can prove it wasn't me. At least to satisfy you. But these are career criminals. If things get ugly . . ."

"We'll have your back," Ward said.

"I've got the impression," Landon said, "these men don't much respect the authorities."

That raised another question. Pax asked, "What happened in the tunnels?"

Landon checked with Ward. She nodded and he said, "They were looking to move contraband under the city. Prepared to kill over it, it seemed."

"And they had help," Ward elaborated, "disabling our alarms. Their interference probably caused our more widespread problems, letting some of the creatures through our sensors. It was pure luck they missed one."

"Lightgate could've got that info," Pax said. Pinning this on the fairy would mean the blue screens weren't conspiring as actively as they feared. To convince herself, she continued, "She has connections. She saw me with these guys, knew we were . . ."

Friends? Bees and Jones had almost killed Casaria, after she'd shared years of banter at the poker table with them. Bees, with his rambling trivia, as close to a friend as Pax had. She asked, "The men down there? Big guys?"

"One big one small," Landon said. "The grey-haired one was at your apartment. He got shot."

"He . . ." Pax averted her gaze. Shot meant dead. Just like that. Bees. She didn't know what to say. This whole damned affair. That little maniac fairy. Well, if Lightgate was here, they would trace a path back to her. Create a gap between the lies and deceits to see a way through. She said. "Come with me, but stay out of sight."

15

In the dim mid-afternoon, Stacey Monroe's dentistry office was lit from the inside, with at least one light on in the opposite warehouse, where his men did their work. Pax had taken grotty alleyways to the back of the small building, rather than risk the direct route, but she might be noticed walking between the buildings anyway. Fine, just as long as there was no sign of Ward and Landon.

She knocked at Monroe's door and waited. There were voices inside, the low chatter of two men. No response to her knock, so she tried the bell. It didn't ring. Pax opened the door, unlocked, and crept in. Through the reception hall, listening for conversation.

"Not what I agreed to, was it?" Monroe said, chewing someone out. "2009 was a good year. The best. Snobs in glass towers write poems about it. 2007 was a year you could wipe your arse with. Understand? I ask for a Jag I don't want to see bloody Peugeot on the bonnet, do I?"

The scolded person mumbled a response.

"You got something to say, say it, but it better be fucking good."

"Sorry, boss. Won't happen again – I promise." A man used to servitude.

"Can't happen again, can it? There's no one else offering eight fucking crates of 2009 Pomerol. The question is how you're gonna make up the difference."

"Two journeys in October," a woman's voice answered, decisively.

"Love, when I'm talking to you, you'll bloody know it."

"Two journeys in October," she repeated, "double your take, that'll cover the loss. If you take the truck off us, we can't earn you a thing."

"The truck? Take the fucking truck? Think your truck's worth that much?"

Christ, enough. Pax couldn't let Monroe get murderous punishing smugglers, not before she'd even begun. She knocked on the doorframe and cleared her throat. "Mr Monroe, you got a minute?"

Monroe froze mid-threat. Opposite him was a tall trucker, slim with facial features all out of proportion; big lips, long ears, bushy eyebrows. At his side was a short woman, wide and stern. Both had peaked denim baseball caps and desperate eyes. Monroe hid his surprise to address the pair: "Saved by the bell, Lucky. Get the fuck out of here and await my call."

The pair looked at him like it was a trick.

"Now!" he barked, and they scrambled to the door. Pax stepped out of the way. "And you'd fucking better run two trips, October. Back on the road by tomorrow!"

"This evening, boss, I swear!" the tall guy promised, not slowing down. The woman gave Pax a passing nod. When the door slammed, Monroe's face flicked like a switch to warm and welcoming.

"I'm blessed, got you making visits now, have we?" Whatever trouble he had with the truckers, he clearly hadn't heard about Bees in the Sunken City. They were alone now, no sound of anyone nearby. He indicated the kitchenette. "Cuppa?"

"Best not," Pax said.

"If it's the game this evening, you could've just called," he said, approaching the counter anyway. "This is no place for a lady. Got your own stake, we're happy to have you."

The game. It felt like she'd left that world a decade ago, even as the WPT was still in swing today. She wondered who was winning. "I'm not here about the game. It's our . . . other business."

Monroe stopped. He put his thumb to his chin, in thought. Really pressed it in, like this was some special technique he had for problem-solving. "Something more you gotta offer me, or something you want for yourself? Be very careful with the latter, I've given you a *lot*, sweetheart."

Pax bit her lip. "It's neither. It's something I heard. Bees was in the tunnels. The ones I warned you to steer clear of. I'm guessing that's why he wasn't at the game last night."

"You heard all that." Monroe's voice was strained. Not liking this. Friendly and reasonable as all hell when it'd work for him, less so faced with a problem. "And, what, you thought these rumours were worth something more than your current compensation?"

Pax shook her head. "I'm only asking. About the how of it. I mean – how you –"

"How, how," Monroe said. "We got a bloody Indian in here?" He opened a drawer. Please don't pull a knife, please don't pull a knife. He took out a folded piece of paper, walked to the middle of the room and placed it on the coffee table between them. "How we fared with the advice we were given?"

It was futile to answer not knowing what was on the paper. Hedging her bets, Pax said, "After my warnings, I hoped you might consult with me before . . . you know."

"Between that and this," he said, flicking his hand at the paper, "you're sending me very mixed messages, darling. Haven't I done right by you?"

So the note had supposedly come from her. Tightly wound already, he was unlikely to appreciate the idea that someone had tricked him. She gestured. "Can I just check that?"

"I asked you a fucking question."

"There might be more –" she tried, hoping to explain.

"Ah, there we go." Monroe gave her a faint, fuck-you kind of smile. He took a little phone from his jacket, a two-decade-old plastic lump, and he pressed two buttons. Holding it to his ear, he said, "It's been a long morning, love. We were all up late." Someone answered. "Jones, get down here." As Jones replied, Monroe suddenly yelled, "I don't give a shit about your nails, get your lazy fucking arrogant arse down here this second!"

He hung up and placed the phone calmly back in a pocket, using his free hand to pat a bit of sweat from his brow, face red. Pax was frozen stiff. Damn Lucky and his trucker girlfriend, they'd sowed the seeds of a very angry little man. He didn't even know what Pax wanted and he was furious. He said, "Sorry. I've got staff obviously can't take care of their own business today, haven't I? Now. You want to tell me how it is you see I *haven't* done right by you already?"

Pax held his gaze, not particularly wanting to tell him anything. The wrong word could make him explode. But that paper was her clue towards the real culprit. "You have done right by me, Mr Monroe. I'd only like to double-check the note you received."

"Oh, you're leading me up the garden path now," Monroe said. "Thinks she's fucking" – he drilled an index finger into his temple – "*smart*. Let's have out with it, shall we? Tell me what it is you're after to give me an idea of how big a moron you are."

Pax shook her head, taking a step back. He grabbed the piece of paper and thrust it her way, barely reaching her with its weightless flight. "Go on and tell me, love, what it is you can add, and what it's worth, above what I already done for you?"

The paper flopped open. Pax couldn't make out what it said at this distance, but she recognised the handwriting. There were numbers, a couple of paragraphs of instructions. All in *her* writing. "Fuck . . ."

The door burst open behind her and Pax jumped. Howling Jowls Jones filled the exit, his usual cheery face fixed with concern, hair swept sideways from the run. "What's the beef –" he started, before spotting Pax. "Boss?"

"Pax is back, as you can see," Monroe said.

"As I can see," Jones answered carefully, picking up on the room's tense mood.

"Says Bees has been down those tunnels of hers. Wants to consider a few details about how it is we came to know about that business. Seems sore about it."

Jones kept quiet.

"I think it's about time," Monroe said, "that you took her for a ride. Far enough to, I don't know, have a conversation about manners, coming to my place of work, talking about what people owe one another. You know?"

"I didn't come looking for a handout!" Pax stepped towards him before she realised she'd moved. "I came because I *didn't* write that note – and whoever did got Bees killed!"

The temperature dropped by degrees. Jones shifted, looking from Pax to Monroe and back again, hands opening and closing like he didn't know what to do with them. Monroe didn't blink. He said, "Second thoughts, she oughta take a seat."

"I'm not taking a seat," Pax said, eyes running back to the note. If the Ministry proper were on their way, that was exactly the incriminating evidence she'd feared. Worse than she feared: with *her* handwriting, perfectly recreated, it pointed to the blue screens. How could she convince Obrington of *that*? "I just want to take –"

Monroe snapped ferociously, "Come in here talking about Bees killed and then you're talking about fucking taking? Jones. Help her out."

"Wait, you're –"

"Not another fucking word, you're doing my head in. *Jones*."

Jones' face was a regretful, horrible grimace. Pax stepped back, into the wall. There was the barest slither of space between Jones and the door – the outside world, freedom. Shit, there was a torture chamber somewhere here. She ran, hard and low, driving her shoulder towards Jones' crotch. He moved deftly, a big hand slapping her off balance. The other lifted her deftly off the ground, making her spin as she kicked and cried out.

"Let her go," came a voice from the door.

Pax kept kicking as Jones went still, his grip like steel. She connected her heel with his gut and he wheezed, hands releasing. She darted out of his range, and found he hadn't moved. The massive man steadied himself with a recovery breath, staring past her, with Monroe motionless beyond him, equally still. Landon was standing in the doorway, Ward watching over his shoulder. His legs were spread, arms up, both hands clamped on a pistol.

"Don't know what your game is, my man," Monroe said, voice thickly aggressive, "but you are trespassing."

"Mr Stacey Monroe, we can get onto who's breaking whose rules," Landon said, "right after you both step away from this young lady."

"Bollocks," Monroe answered. "You're not going to shoot a couple of upstanding citizens in their own place of work."

"I'd prefer you didn't make me."

"Fucking desk jockey, isn't he?" Jones said. "Security guards playing at being spooks, I swear."

"I told you about the Ministry!" Pax said hurriedly. "There's still a –"

She jumped as Monroe's phone rang. He lifted it as Landon warned, "Don't move!"

"Relax," Monroe said. "Unlike some people, I believe in good manners. Someone calls, you answer." Unchecked by Landon, he pressed a button, "Monroe." A pause. "Yeah, we do have company in fact. Glad you bloody noticed. What the fuck you think I want you to do?" He hung up. Eyes fixed fiercely on Landon.

With failing conviction, Landon instructed, "I'm going to ask you to both back off. Through there, come on with you –"

"You think we're alone here, you daft bastard?"

Landon said nothing, giving a sideways glance to Pax. Yeah. This was escalating.

"You got a tool?" Monroe said, eyes still on Landon.

"Yeah, I got a tool," Jones replied, one arm moving slowly towards his waistline.

"I said don't move!" Landon raised his voice.

"That you did, mate." Jones put on his wide, white grin. It looked psychotic now. "But there's something I *got* to show you –"

Landon fired.

16

Outside, Pax took cover behind a low wall, hands on her ears as gunfire punctured the sky. Each explosive sound made her flinch. It was a miracle she'd made it out, she wasn't even sure how it happened; in her short darting sprint she must have dodged one or two bullets.

Now there were at least three criminals shooting, and with Ward having produced a pistol there were two shooting back. Pax had no idea exactly where any of them were, save some enterprising lunatic who kept popping up in the upstairs windows of the warehouse, spitting bullets into the street. Landon had rushed inside as Monroe fled, roaring orders. Ward had sprinted to skirt the big building, looking for another way in. And here was Pax, crouched, under fire, jumping at every sound.

The gunmen shouted the nonsensical shrieks of men fuelled by adrenaline. Howling Jowls Jones, back in the dentist's office, bleated, "My leg! My fucking leg! You fucking fuck!"

Pax searched for a way out. Across the road, there was a dumpster, good cover before getting into an alleyway, out of sight. But it was a ten-metre dash, at least. Up the road, there was a pick-up truck, another ten-metre dash. It had already sunk on a rear wheel that had been shot out. Taken bullets without anyone near it.

Then there was back the way she'd come. The dentist's office, with that bit of paper lying somewhere on the floor. With luck maybe Jones would drag himself over it and soak it in blood.

A bullet hit the road near Pax, chipping tarmac with a spark. Beyond that – a manhole cover. She'd never open it in time.

"You're fucking dead!" someone screamed from a high window, followed by another volley of gunfire that scattered around Pax's wall. Holy hell, that was directed at her – why did that frenetic bastard want to kill her?

"Get me a fucking medic!" Jones yelled, close to hysterics.

Pax fought her nerves, the instinct to stay put, not move, not make a sound. She shouted, from her gut, "Jones! Tell them to stop and I'll help!"

"Shove it!" Jones replied at full volume. "Right up your fucking arse!"

Rude.

He kept going, stringing out insults until they degenerated into blubbering, and finally an odd stream of consciousness. ". . . Cottage on Whistler, fucking A . . . never had it . . . small, handy size!"

The maniac inside opened fire again, half a dozen shots tearing through the side of the pick-up truck, shattering a window. He was no more in control than Jones, lashing out madly. Had Monroe simply armed a couple of madmen with instructions to raise hell if anyone started trouble around here?

Pax watched the sky. Where were Fresko and Mix? They'd saved her from one shootout, why not now? Letty would've made short work of this mess . . .

Far on the other side of the warehouse, another gun fired. Lighter, one of the pistols? Small rifle fire (presumably) answered it. Another pistol shot, from off to the right – that sounded like two people advancing on one? A pincer movement, both Landon and Ward still alive? Christ, hopefully.

The madman aiming at Pax had taken a break, and Jones had gone quiet, leaving the road in silence as the wispy mist of gunsmoke rolled over it. Keeping her head down, Pax reassessed her escape routes, left and right. A man dashed across the road, the heavy woollen suit of Monroe. He had the ungainly run of someone who'd heard how to do it from a mate down the pub. But he was getting away, trotting between another pair of buildings.

Bloody hell.

He was getting away to what? Call more boys to finish them off? Send men to watch her home? She had enough unknowns hanging over her.

More gunfire erupted, way off, and a strangled shout said the madman had moved, opening fire at the other side of the building. She was clear. Maybe. Just her and Monroe out here, now. Hell. She had to see where he was going, at least.

Rising to a crouching run, Pax raced after him. She cringed as she went, arms cocked high at her sides as if she might deflect bullets, expecting a shot at any second. But she made it across the road, around the corner, with no one shooting. Another pistol sounded in the distance. Pax picked up speed, breathing hard, and saw the flap of Monroe's jacket disappearing into an alley. She ran after him, and slowed at the alley entrance. He'd slowed too, up ahead. His laboured breath came with curses, phone up at his ear. "Insolent fucks. Reggie? Reggie, I'm gonna cut your balls off when you hear this. I got a job for you."

Pax pushed down her concerns. Any job he wanted to organise at this minute could piss off. She charged down the alley after him, bracing herself, and he turned at the sound of her approach. She jumped, taking no chances, and hit him with all her body. He fell like he weighed nothing, landing heavily on his back to cushion her. Pax bounced, air knocked out of her, but held on, hands on his arms. He tried to buck, snarling and snapping, spit spraying her face, so she dropped her weight onto him, a knee either side of his gut, pinning him down.

"Get off me you fat bitch, I'll cut your throat out!" he snarled, but she held fast, riding him like a bronco. In any other position he might've had the strength to throw her off, but he couldn't lift her weight off his belly, not with her squeezing his arms in – in his thrashing, he snapped himself back into the ground and hit his head. The fight went out of him with a grunt, and he was suddenly limp. His head lolled to the side, a trickle of blood on the concrete behind it. Pax sat back slightly.

Fuck, she'd broken him.

He groaned again, blinking in dazed pain. Hurriedly, while he was stunned, Pax repositioned, hiking her knees over his arms, freeing her hands. She grabbed his jaw and turned his face towards her, his eyes rolling back in his head.

"You done?" Pax asked, breathlessly.

"You fat bitch," he wheezed back.

"Yeah, you're done."

He hawked up phlegm, but before he could spit she pushed his head away and the spit sprayed up over his own nose. He spluttered on it with increasingly severe curses.

"Some gentleman," she said, breathing deep. Running down this alley, she'd sealed a particularly shitty fate for herself. He had friends who would burn down her house or cut off her fingers. But right now she was sitting on him and this was a victory. She patted his face, vaguely aware of the sound of a car braking nearby. "Come on . . . apologise and I'll let you up. You can walk away, no hard feelings." She even smiled. The Ministry wouldn't let him walk away, would they? "What was your plan here? Disappear government agents? Police must be on the way."

"Out here?" Monroe snorted. It was a point. She'd seen his men at work with torture, wandering around in bloodstained overalls. Now, firing rifles across the road. The area was abandoned. Maybe even because of the Ministry, steering the population clear of the Fae.

"Just you and me, then," Pax said. "But you know what? I've killed bigger monsters than you, this past week."

His weary eyes said he didn't believe it.

"Yeah." The gunfire, the panic, or something else, stirred the memories in her, all this shit she'd endured. "Want to count? Hairless creature with pincers and jaws like" – she gnashed her teeth – "which I took its head and *rammed* it till it popped. Like nothing. And the great – this big bastard tentacled turtle thing with skull heads – I helped drop it down a lift shaft. Then the grugulochs, the simple-minded bloody grugulochs – I put a *bullet*" – Monroe gave it another go, bucking under her, and she shifted her weight, shoving him firmer into the ground – "I put a bullet in its fucking head! You hear me? I'm not scared of you – I'm not scared – and I'm not letting *your cock up* get me killed."

Regaining some of his breath, he snarled, "You're crazy."

Seeing the look in his eyes, she could believe it herself. Beyond frustration and anger: he was genuinely frightened by her. And how else did she get here, if she wasn't mad? Pax said, almost to herself, "I need to be, don't I?"

"You oughta thank her," a man's voice said, and she shot a look to the side. The entrance to the alley was filled by the imposing form of Wayne Obrington. "Now she's gone and caught you, we don't get to say you died trying to escape."

Pax sat motionless. The big man had a pistol out, down at his side. There was no getting past him and she'd used up all her energy for running. She said, "Can we talk?"

Obrington stared at her impassively for what seemed like an age, then reached a conclusion. "You're gonna do a lot more than that. Monster whisperer."

PART 3

1

The FTC Council met in a chamber bigger than most Fae homes, with a massive table encircled by tiered rings of desks. Flags hung from near the ceiling; an FTC coat of arms, the wing badges of the Stabilisers, the colours of old families. It could've fit a hundred Fae, but there were only eleven stuffy suits gathered around that central table, and a half-dozen less-presentable people scattered through the peripheral desks, with Stabilisers at the perimeter. A big projector screen took up one wall, presenting a list of proposed laws. Number One said *Unauthorised Contact is a Capital Crime*.

Valoria had given them a dry intro with references to Edwing's tragic death. Her condolences went out to Flynt, who was doing all he could to keep still at an outer desk. "He had so much to offer us, and shall be remembered. The measures we propose today honour his spirit."

She ran through various forms of rhetoric to explain how great it would be for the Fae, and the FTC. A new era, combining solidarity and security, backed by firm, decisive measures arranged by her people, which need never burden the public. Regrettable events had led them to this point, but the outcome would be historic.

And so it went, softening up a Council that were already hers.

Did she just enjoy hearing her own voice?

Newbry's camera showed the room from up high, a cleverly placed bit of kit. Letty squinted at the screen to read the projection of laws that demonstrated Val's end goal: from punishing contact with humans down to ID and visa laws, regulating Fae movement across Ordshaw. It was probably laced with clauses ensuring Val never lost her title and the FTC never relocated, to boot.

"It's not subtle," Letty said, more to herself than Newbry. "Talking and talking without actually saying anything, all the while hanging this bullshit behind her that basically says we're locking our doors. Can't Flynt just say *look at what the hell you're doing* and be done with it? They got no sense at all, how crazy this sounds?"

"And it'll be with this Council's blessing," concluded Val, "that we address the Ministry of Environmental Energy. I am honoured that you entrust the delivery of this message, and the necessary means to secure it, to myself and the Stabilisers."

The councillors obligingly shuffled papers, all having access to more written down that hadn't been said. Deidre and Smark were there, unhappily reading what was in front of them. Flynt craned forward; no one had printed a copy for him.

"It's a drop in the bucket," Valoria said, looking his way, "but justice for Councilman Edwing is at the very top of my considerations. Followed by an impartial investigation into Tuesday's attack and the Ministry's more immediate movements."

One of her sycophants took the chair for a minute, praising her efforts, saying these terms would benefit the Fae for generations to come. A thin, older Fae Newbry named as Mullon. Not someone Letty recognised, except maybe from the broadcasts, meaning he'd been a nobody before these days where talking was enough to make people important. Finally, he gushed, their children could sleep easy. Letty watched Deidre for a reaction, the councilwoman frowning as she read. She looked like she wanted to speak, but didn't.

Smark, for his part, was statue-still, playing the penitent now.

"As we know," Valoria told the room, "the Ministry plainly have plans of their own, and the sooner we establish new boundaries the better. If I can put it to a show of hands –"

"You're not going to discuss it?" Flynt said. Councillors twisted to face him.

Valoria put on a patient smile, which Letty could've kicked off her face. "We welcome your views, Flynt."

"Seems," Flynt continued, voice high and anxious, "something we should discuss. You've got the means to secure this –" He gestured weakly towards the demands. "But we don't need to discuss how else we might do it?" What?

"Of all people," Valoria said, "I thought you'd approve of this show of strength. For Edwing."

"You can't say it's for him," Flynt said, going for defiant but coming off petulant. He looked ready to stand, unsure if he should. "It's not right – you've got – what about moving?"

The Council wore pitying expressions. He was fumbling.

"This isn't peace," Flynt offered. Every extra word made him seem more uncertain. All the ammunition he had, the fact that Val was provoking humanity with the worst weapons, keeping the Dispenser from her people, that the notion of *hiding* was mad – he wasn't saying a thing. And Deidre kept her head down, too shy to help. Flynt said, "Edwing, he didn't want – wouldn't want *threats*."

"And we all appreciated Edwing's eloquent dissent," Mullon responded, "but this is a matter for the Council, young man, and perhaps not the place for your concerns."

"Young man?" Flynt replied angrily. "What's my age got to do with it?"

"Apologies," Mullon continued, bordering on sarcastic. "It is rather your grief."

"You puffed-up old bean –"

Newbry cringed, and Letty felt the same. This wasn't what they'd discussed, and she really shouldn't have been surprised.

"Can we stay on track?" another crusty councilman said, this one wearing a waistcoat and a toupee like a soiled mop. "Madam Governor, I think I speak on behalf of all the members of the room, when I say we trust your wisdom."

"You don't speak for me," Flynt said. "I see this better than you – it's a cage we're talking about! Not peace, imprisoning us – and using poison to do it –"

"Perhaps," a woman councillor said through her nose, "the Scout Chief should take leave –"

"Balls!" Flynt stood. "You're flying on an ugly wing! Edwing believed in that human! She was gonna help us, she still *can*, but you're not even discussing it."

"That human that killed him?" Mullon boomed suddenly, taking personal offence. "Regardless of your troubles, Flynt, I will not hear such talk in this room!"

"Who says she did it? Some of you must think differently? Smark –"

The Waste Chief kept his eyes down, refusing to get involved.

"We all *know* the humans to be a threat," Mullon said.

"The governor's proposal is sound." Back to Toupee. "With secure borders, we can focus on internal development. We can –"

"Words," Flynt said, "it's bloody words to avoid the point."

"Yes, please," Mullon said, all sympathy gone, "let the young man explain why we shouldn't be talking using words!"

Nods and sniggering followed. In the furore, Deidre tried to help, with easily missed quietness. "Surely there is a case for delaying to investigate?"

This was what the FTC government had become? The language they were using, their trim suits – a perfect mimicry of the humans' vile Parliament. And Valoria at the centre of it, watching smugly, letting them squabble, knowing it made fuck all difference except to ultimately stroke her ego. She *owned* this. As the volume escalated, she finally slammed a fat palm into her lectern, for quiet.

"Your caution is appreciated, Flynt," Valoria said. "Doubly so as we can see your brother's passion lives on, here in this room. It is a passion the FTC sorely needs. But it's time to take action. Can I see raised hands for the Ayes?"

Ten hands shot up, Smark's quicker than most. Deidre eyed the room with concern. She looked like she was going to raise her hand too, just to fit in. But she kept it down, with effort. Val said, "A clear majority, then. If the Council will take a recess, I will make the call."

"No – you can't!" Flynt tried again, standing, panicking. The two closest guards were moving towards him. "Threaten the humans with poison and we destroy any chance we have!"

Most of the councillors regarded him with annoyance, now, but Val's face shifted in a more calculating way. Understanding the specific nature of Flynt's concerns. She said, "It's best we proceed without further interruptions."

The Stabilisers grabbed his arms as Flynt shoved back. They took his pistol and marched him towards the doors, his shouted complaints going unheard. Valoria looked to her right-hand man, Hearlon, and he followed the others. Letty swore under her breath as Val made a final announcement: "Today, our position is secured."

There was nothing in this they could share with the FTC public that would sway anyone. The phone was quiet, no last-minute save from Pax. No way to delay the threats Valoria was about to make or the laws she was ready to ratify. And worse, her people were taking Flynt.

"What a cockspasm of a mess," Letty said. "Can you jam her calls? Mustard gas the room or something?" Newbry's blank face said she was on her own. She straightened out her gun belt. "Fine. Back to Plan A."

2

With the Ministry crawling over the scene, Pax sat wearily on a low wall, waiting for the axe to fall. She was getting used to this sullen feeling that came after a period of intense life-threatening madness. She just wanted to peel back the tarmac and crawl under it to sleep. Instead, she contented herself watching the MEE at work, avoiding thoughts of the trouble she was in by wondering, distantly, about Letty's plight. How was Pax going to help her from a windowless prison? Or a coffin.

Having apparently tracked their phones, there were three black cars in the road now, along with two ambulances and a police car. Landon had returned from his shootout to give uniformed officers and paramedics bland instructions about cordoning off the area and tending to the wounded. His suit jacket was torn at the shoulder where he'd been grazed by a bullet, and he had a profusely bleeding head wound that needed dressing, but Pax heard him dismiss the ferocious drama: "They'd probably never fired a gun before, any of them."

The backup MEE agents were hard-looking men with hunters' glares. Pax wanted nothing to do with them, though she wished they'd been around earlier. Casaria was there, but he shot her only the briefest look before dashing inside. A body bag and two occupied gurneys were rolled to the ambulances before Pax caught sight of Sam Ward. She drifted out like a ghost, dusty, sweat-wrecked hair in strands across her face. After a few words with Obrington, who was grilling Monroe with one of the police officers, Ward wandered across the road to join Pax on the wall. She said nothing, eyes still focused on whatever she'd seen in there. Pax asked, softly, "Good gunfight?"

Ward's thin, humourless smile said it was far too soon. Dark rings had formed under her eyes and she hadn't quite stopped shaking.

They sat together in silence as Obrington chewed Monroe out, gesturing their way as he threatened the crime boss over any future problems. Pax doubted the Ministry could protect her from gangsters. Then, she needed protection from the MEE, too. The police were finally gifted Monroe, and drove him away cuffed with a Ministry car for an escort. He regarded Pax viciously through the window as they passed. She tried to ignore it, while Obrington approached, blocking out daylight.

"One dead, another two in critical condition," Obrington summarised, catching Ward's concerned attention. Was it her or Landon who'd scored the fatal shot? "Three dead if you count the guy who throttled me earlier. And here you two are, like a couple of schoolgirls caught pinching pennies from the tuck shop."

Pax processed that slower than she usually would. It was an oddly flippant remark considering the gravity of the situation. She said, "Is this where you take me behind a dumpster and shoot me? Tell my parents it was a random mugging. They'll claim they saw it coming."

Obrington didn't answer straight away. He looked around, as though he needed to double-check exactly where they'd got to. The first ambulance was leaving, and one of his agents was carrying an armful of guns towards his car. "This has spread beyond something a few disappearances would contain. Now it'd be more trouble than it's worth."

"Seriously?" Pax said, giving Ward a glance. "Not *oh no, the Ministry would never do a thing like that*?"

"We do what's best for the majority," Obrington answered simply. "Mostly that doesn't involve being deeply evil bastards, but not always. Especially *difficult* people can require special consideration. In your case . . ." His eyes lingered on Pax, the sentence unfinished like he wasn't sure himself. "The chap who actually *saw* something down there will need extra attention. Otherwise, it's a case of some gun-running lowlifes being locked away for shooting at government agents. They had serious gall; the gentleman thought he had friends in high places. Fortunately, it doesn't come higher than us. But even so. Ward. How is it we find ourselves in this situation?"

Ward gave him a look that said she was considering that question from afar. Pax said, "She didn't know about them. I thought I could talk them down and I convinced Sam to help. To avoid bloodshed."

"Because you wanted to get hold of this before we did?" Obrington took the handwritten note from his jacket pocket.

Inwardly wincing, Pax played it honest. "Yeah. I didn't think you'd understand."

"*We* didn't," Ward came in, a tired fact. "How could we tell who to trust, after what happened with the Raleigh Commission?"

Obrington's face was as readable as a rock. "Third time today I've been told people are willingly keeping things from Management. What is it, exactly, you're all so delicately hiding? Not this criminal enterprise."

Ward wasn't ready to elaborate.

He addressed Pax. "Plainly, with half of Ordshaw fawning over you, you are more in control than me. Agent Casaria got his career tied in knots over you. An intensely irritating housewife gave me an earful on your account. This woman here, with aspirations to head a government department, is covering for you. Why?"

"It's not something I asked for," Pax said.

"I didn't ask for your opinion on it, did I? I figure you're smarter than this. Both of you. I figure there's a reason my gut says don't believe *this*" – he indicated the piece of paper – "is what it appears to be. Likewise, I don't like believing the Fae saying you're a murderer. Is my gut right, or is it last night's curry playing up?"

Pax frowned. It wasn't what she expected from him, and her dislike for the man made her reluctant to simply co-operate. But he was giving her a lifeline. She said,

"I was set up, when I went to meet the Fae. And I was set up with these guys. Different people behind it, but the same reason. Neither of them want me building bridges."

"And the one we're talking about here," Obrington said, "would that be the sort of person that could pose, say, as a member of the Raleigh Commission?"

"I think so."

"Back from beyond the grugulochs' grave. So if this manipulative force is not really gone, what have you got against us culling the *praelucente*? Is it not, as you claimed, what our enemy uses to draw strength?"

"We don't know what they are, so it's reckless to attack the one thing we know has value to them." Pax let it out with what she realised was relief. Coming clean felt safer when she knew the guy might listen. "These things seem to exist in surfaces, and they warp how things appear, and they can create lifeforms. Beyond that, all we know is they've gone to a lot of trouble to hide their existence. We go on the attack, they hunker deeper down."

The ideas rotated behind Obrington's eyes. "You're talking about the blue screens themselves. A conclusion we reach because?"

"I've felt them," Pax said. "After I touched the minotaur, I picked up a sense for it. When I killed the grugulochs, I knew they were still there. They've abandoned the places Apothel used to meet them, but I *keep* feeling them." It jogged her memory with a moment's clarity. "You had another surge. In the last hour or so. I felt that."

As Ward gave Pax a concerned look, Obrington took out his phone and called to check, eyes on her all the while. The report from the office came back quickly: yes, there was a surge.

"Somewhere in the east," Pax said. "Moving this way?"

Obrington relayed that and got clarification. Whoever was on the line suggested they were hurrying to check if there'd been any wider effects. Obrington put his phone away, staring hard.

"It wasn't just paranoia that we kept this quiet," Ward said in a hushed tone. "I was concerned for Pax. That you'd want her trapped and tested. Or that *they* would target her."

Obrington's eyes widened, deliberately looking towards bullet holes in the nearby truck, across to smashed windows. Landon was talking to one of the new agents, wiping an absent hand over his bloodied face. "That's what this was, huh. Whatever bastard's got its claws in your town, it wanted us to declaw *you*."

Pax's gaze rested on the handwriting on the note in his hand, a perfect imitation of her own. He was right. The blue screens weren't randomly stirring chaos like Lightgate; this was designed to get rid of her, specifically.

"Why?" Ward asked of the world, slumping forward, elbows on her knees and head in her hands. Pax was unsure if she should pat her shoulder, offer a hug, something?

Obrington asked, "What more do you know? They exist on *surfaces*?"

He was taking all this remarkably calmly. Pax nodded. "They communicated through touch, scratches in walls or whatever. When I encountered one, it couldn't tell who I was by sight. But they're linked to each other like a hive mind, I'm sure. They're organised, somehow, able to communicate through some other means."

"As are *you*, evidently," Obrington said. "Making you a little bit psychic."

Pax gave him a warning look, preferring that not to be true, but it was disarming how seriously he made the suggestion. "You guys know something about this? I'm guessing there's more you've got hidden from the rest of us."

"That might be, but I don't know jack about your blue screens and this grugulochs business. Might've been useful to know when I got to Ordshaw that this wasn't yet a clean-up operation. What were you hoping to do next?"

"Study their patterns," Ward softly rejoined. "They expose themselves through novisan. When they feed, when they make things, when they transfer the energy."

"But they're sticking close to the *praelucente*," Pax said. "Maybe so we mistake their novisan fluctuations for its. They'll find new ways to stay hidden, if they're forced out from under its shadow. They infiltrated our government, hid their own existence –"

"I got the picture," Obrington said. "And you wanted to study this on your lonesome until you could be sure they're not listening. Except you can't ever be sure of that because you don't know what they are. And here we are, with them targeting precisely the person thinking she's got one up on them."

"You believe us, though?" Ward said, hopefully.

"Does it make a difference? Beyond believing neither of you would be idiot enough to join these low-rent gangsters, the details aren't important. You're telling me there's something still out there, suckling at your *praelucente's* teat. They're of the same energy, they'll burn just the same when we fry it."

"We'll send out a party invite, then?" Pax said. "*Come to an all-you-can-eat* and lock the doors? We don't even know how they communicate."

Obrington gave her an unsettling look through his magnifying lenses. "You know why Management sent me up here? Me, specifically. Not a bookkeeper like Mathers. I see a thing needs doing and I find a way to do it. I don't prat about overanalysing it."

"It's an otherworldly creature no one understands! How much analysis is too much?"

"Ward's words," Obrington said. "Understanding is *not* an absolute requirement." Hell, he'd accepted their reality, but it was making no difference. "We can still take a pop at damaging these things. Your problem, in a nutshell, is how do we make sure they're in the right place when we pull the trigger?" Pax began to say they couldn't, so he added, "These things targeted you specifically, Kuranes. You."

His glare told her to really consider that. The screens had plotted to attack the Ministry and the Fae using the turnbold situation. And they helped the Fae kill Apothel, years ago. But true enough, this wasn't them taking advantage of an existing situation, today. They knew things about her and her associates. Meaning . . . Pax said, "They sense me in some way, the same as I sense them. Even after this trick with the grugulochs, they know I'm a threat . . ."

There *was* something in that mantra, that understanding was not a requirement. However the blue screens thought, with rationale or reason, the horde swarmed feverishly when it scented energy – might their targeting of her be the same? And if they had a gentle attraction to her, their attraction to the Fae was uncontrollable. She said, "Certain energies inspire them to act stronger than others. With Fae energy, we *can* get them in one place."

"The girl's a genius," Obrington said, flatly. "So we tie a fairy down as bait."

"What?" said Ward, startled. "The Fae are *people*."

"More important than the entire population of this town?" Obrington replied. "Want to wait until next time these things screw us over?"

"We've already provoked the Fae," Ward said. "There's no way we can ask this."

"Wait," Pax said. The image of Edwing came back to her. That poor, small man, torn savagely open. "I have an option."

"Pax –"

"If I can find Lightgate. We *need* to stop her, anyway. She's as bad as those bloody screens. If I can get her, we can trap the creatures that way." She looked away from them, hearing her own voice. That was where she'd got to. Using a living person as bait for monsters? A maniac responsible for a lot of deaths. Yeah.

"Lightgate," Obrington echoed. "The Fae our people were scouring the city for? Shall we add a few needles in haystacks to our shopping lists, too?"

Pax shook her head. "No. She's crazy but she's . . ." What had Obrington said? Pax had the whole of Ordshaw fawning over her. Lightgate included. "She sees something in me she likes. I can get close to her." And then get killed?

"Alright," Obrington said. "We'll head back to the office, make a –"

"I can't," Pax said, and explained it to Ward rather than him. "She'd have to believe I'm not with you. Between now and me getting in one of those cars, that's the only time I could make a break for it. They might be watching. *She* might be watching."

Obrington pulled back his jacket, revealing a small bulge in his inside pocket which he tapped. "This would tell us, within a hundred metres. Not just Fae presence; if they were running any equipment. There's no –"

"Thanks but your scanners can piss off," Pax told him. "This is how I've got to do it. I get away from you; out on my own, she might believe I'm desperate, looking for other angles. Help from the likes of her."

"Even if she does . . ." Ward said, but let the question go unasked. How was Pax going to ensnare the city's most dangerous fairy? It didn't matter. She had to. Ward's face shifted. Searchingly, trying to understand Pax's bravery. "You'd do that?"

Pax almost laughed. "I have a choice? It's up to you guys now."

She looked to Obrington. He asked, "Got a weapon on you, Ward?"

"I'm unarmed. Now."

"Right. You'll be on your own, Kuranes. See this gun I'm watching so loosely?

Be a shame if you took it. And these car keys. Might be something I'm too big and slow to prevent. But you know what happens, this proves to be anything other than what you're saying?"

"I know," Pax said.

"I'm gonna take out some cuffs. To take you in. Understand?"

He had accepted her proposal, setting a scene for escape. Leaving the only complaint at the back of Pax's own head. It was the best way forward, the only clear path. If you ignored the definite risk of her own violent death.

After taking a breath, Pax grabbed his gun.

3

Sam was not quite able to focus. The spark of action with Pax running for the car, Obrington shouting at his men not to shoot – they needed her alive – scarcely enlivened her. Obrington pursued Pax himself, with his most vigilant agent, in what was bound to be a carefully unsuccessful car chase, while another agent escorted Sam back in.

She tried to strategise, but the face of a young Chinese man kept springing to her mind, lifeless eyes staring at the warehouse ceiling. Shot through the chest. At least, she thought he was Chinese, he might've been Japanese, what did she know. Not even that. Only that he was dead because he'd picked up a gun he wasn't trained to use. Or rather, because he wouldn't put it down again. Why was he dead. Not even connected to the Sunken City.

When Sam finally suppressed that image, she imagined a future not much better. Pax murdered by a fairy, or worse. The blue screens could build a monster to tear her apart. While Sam did what? Managed an office. Overanalysed, as Obrington said.

All heads turned to her as she entered the Ministry office. In Greek Street, late afternoon had been about the time they all started zoning out. Down here, the time of day was less obvious. The receptionist asked what was happening and Sam replied automatically, "Get me reports from everyone, and whatever we've got on Protocol 38."

"And your meeting?" Tori whispered it like a secret. "They weren't happy –"

"Meeting?" Sam frowned.

"I directed them to the café you used this morning, I hope that's okay. We're not setting up meetings here, are we?"

It dawned on Sam like the breaking of a wave. Tycho Duvalier. Oh. Hell. It was almost 4pm. An hour after they'd arranged to meet. "Is he still waiting?"

"I got a call ten minutes ago saying so. Seems they just arrived."

Well, at least there was that; Tycho probably turned up deliberately late. Top-floor office power-plays were the last thing she needed. But after that gunfight, she didn't have the energy to be worried, regardless of Obrington's warnings about Duvcorp. "Tell him I'll be there in five."

Before Sam could leave, Holly Barton raced to her side, ahead of her hobbling husband and Rufaizu, having apparently been waiting her turn. "Mrs Ward, where's Pax? I've got a lawyer in the family, and we'll contact Pax's people – her disappearance will *not* go unnoticed."

"What?" Sam blinked, trying to follow. The civilians' presence was almost surreal down here. "Pax hasn't disappeared. She's fine."

"She's not here now, you're –"

"Honestly, Holly," Sam said. "We let her go."

Holly was ready to keep complaining, but something made her stop. Reading Sam's face, she changed tack. "Are you okay? What happened?" Her hand was up, towards Sam's collar; there was a bloodstain. At Holly's shoulder, Barton's expression was equally concerned. He didn't say anything, but his stare begged for answers.

"Not my blood," Sam mumbled. "They gave us no choice."

"If Pax –"

"Holly, what are you doing here? You should go home."

"Where is she?" another voice hissed, Casaria appearing from behind, slinking into the office with Landon in tow. The latter gave Sam an apologetic look. They must've raced back after Sam. "What *was* that, give her thirty seconds then you come shooting?"

"What?" Sam said. "We let her *go*."

"We?" Casaria snorted. "In cahoots with that fucking oaf?"

"*Yes*," Sam said. Everyone was watching, she was aware. Even those pretending to work. Casaria looked ready to hit something. It must've stung him, missing the shootout, and now being excluded from Pax's flight. Sam explained, "Pax has gone to find Lightgate. The fairy that killed our people. She's going to bring her in."

"You're out of your mind!" Casaria said. "How is Pax supposed to take –"

"She's going to bring her in," Sam growled. Not louder than before, but sterner, going by the startled look on Casaria's face. The rest of the office was absolutely still. "Then we're going to use Lightgate to lure all the worst creatures of the Sunken City together. *Then* we purge them." She turned on the spot everyone staring, finally focusing her – time to take charge. "Revise the terms of Protocol 38. Test our weapons against the new scanners and produce an action plan ready for this evening. I want the current locations of the myriad creatures, optimal choke points to place field agents. I want *everyone* on hand." She turned back to the Bartons. "If you're staying, Holly, I've got reports you can study. Darren, you can liaise with Support, share what you know about combating the horde." Holly looked like she might protest. Sam didn't give her a chance, clapping for movement. "That's it, people, let's go!"

Staff raced in different directions, a rush of comments passing between them. The older analyst, Roper, guided Barton away while Sam diverted Holly, saying, "Your daughter, is she safe?"

"She's not going to open the door to strangers," Holly replied, with a significant look Casaria's way. "What's Protocol 38?"

"It's where we nuke the Sunken City," Casaria said, bitterly.

"It's nothing without the Fae element," Sam said.

Casaria was about to continue, but Landon intervened. "Didn't get a chance to say so back there: you performed admirably under pressure, ma'am."

Sam squinted at him. Was *ma'am* good or bad? Just a distraction, to block Casaria?

"The city owes you a debt," Landon continued, definitely for the others' benefit. "Scumbags like that might've done some real damage."

Sam hesitated. *Thanks* was the easy option. *All I did was shoot an Asiatic man,* was more honest. Did it make her racist? Three white guys got away alive. This wasn't the time. Everyone was rallying around *her*. She looked from Landon to Casaria, one kindly supportive and the other dangerously aggrieved. She made another snap decision, pointing at Casaria. "Something else I need to take care of. You're with me for a second."

Not sure exactly what she was going to say, Sam entered the café with her head high. Like she wasn't ready to collapse with stress. Her determined energy had kept Casaria tensely quiet for their short walk, with only scant instructions: "We enter together, but you take a seat by the door. Say nothing. Do nothing."

"What –" Casaria started.

"Say nothing, do nothing." Zero room for discussion.

Tycho Duvalier had a booth to himself, sitting patiently upright. The waitress behind the counter was shamelessly staring, somewhere between awe and disbelief that this sharply dressed, familiar face was in *her* diner. A group of builders paid him no heed, but another man in a suit, two booths back from Tycho, stood out. Wearing dark glasses, hunched over a menu but patently observing the surroundings. Yes, Casaria's conspicuously shady appearance made a good choice for backup.

Standing, Tycho wore a welcoming smile, but gave Casaria exactly the sort of wary look Sam had hoped for. He began in a genial tone: "I'm not used to being kept waiting, so I hope you're planning to take us to your *actual* office –"

"Here is fine," Sam cut in. "We won't be long." She hadn't thought this through, and didn't intend to. She had a feeling to latch onto, stirred by surviving a shootout, observing Obrington, watching Pax put herself on the line – Sam let it flow. "You are not being shown our office or our work. We had information that you'd developed scanning equipment that we needed. We'll use it until our benchmarks are reliably satisfied, then we'll return it. We won't be studying the equipment itself, and you will not question our activities. Consider it a tax for doing business in our city."

Tycho's smile was gone. "There were proper channels to go through for –"

"No, see," Sam said, invoking Obrington to sound tougher than she felt. "This is a matter of national security. I'm *telling* you, not asking. The only question you should have is if there's anything more you can do."

The man's face was professionally blank; taller than her, more powerful by a thousand degrees, he studied her carefully. Her skin was sheened with sweat, suit marred by dirt, still smelling lightly of gunsmoke. His eyes lingered on her bloodstained collar, but he didn't ask. Finally, he said, "It's not so much the co-operation that concerns me, as the subterfuge. I discovered this situation on a chance hunch, and I remain in the dark as to exactly how *you* came to know what we were working on."

"Let it concern you," Sam told him, "but think carefully before crossing the Ministry. There's no authority higher than us." She didn't indicate Casaria, but Tycho's eyes went there. Who had the more dangerous goon, here?

"If I wanted that kind of trouble," Tycho murmured, "I would have brought lawyers. I wish simply to see where our interests align."

Sam reached into her jacket, not buying the friendly act. Obrington wanted to distance himself from Duvcorp for good reason. She took out a business card. "Prove that with a meeting in *your* offices. Explain your research to me and I'll consider what I can share with you. How's that?"

Tycho looked at the card. Sam's thumb had left a black smear. She needed a shower. But he took it, the billionaire tycoon pocketing her soiled business card. He said, "It's a dangerous game, believing yourselves untouchable."

Out of nowhere, Sam said, "Less than an hour ago, I shot a man dead." She wasn't sure if it was meant to sound threatening, unafraid, or what. Just had to say it. To own that, acknowledging the weight of things getting out of hand. His sly eyes betrayed no surprise. She continued, "Don't test me. It'll be as before; we won't step on your toes, you won't step on ours. I guarantee we won't do any more than use your scanners to take readings. And then, if you truly want to talk, that will depend on *your* openness. Want to start by explaining what Duvcorp has been measuring?"

Tycho's face gave away nothing. He avoided the question, reaching a businesslike decision. "I'll have them send papers. Properly inventorying the scanners' use. Invoiced at a rate we consider fair. With appropriate NDAs and other legal documentation."

He had bowed to her. In his way; there was no doubt that invoice would be steep. But that was Management's problem. Sam gave him a respectful (thankful?) handshake, and turned to leave before she lost her bottle. She marched outside and up the street. Walking strong, aware she was still visible through the café window. Casaria hurried after her and came close to say, "What was that – what's –"

"Not now."

Right around the corner, onto another street, into cover, and there Sam slumped, energy puffing out of her. She continued quietly back to the office, ignoring Casaria's questioning stare. Christ, she'd just stood up to Tycho Duvalier. Did that make her tougher than Obrington? She allowed herself a faint trace of pride, that maybe she could make inroads into Duvcorp relations where Management had presumably failed.

She was up to this. She was in her element.

Except why had Management failed? What were Duvcorp doing, that Tycho would let them use their scanners to avoid the slightest discussion of their own projects? Hell.

When she re-entered the office, Obrington was back, standing dead centre. Her face lifted, ready to tell him what she'd done, but his grim expression warned her off.

"Got another bleeding call from those little Fae menaces." Obrington's voice bounced off the walls. "Making a whole *heap* of demands. Rights, borders, the full gamut."

Sam frowned. "They want to open a dialogue? Isn't that a good –"

"It wasn't a request. They've got a weapon that they, I quote, *are not afraid to use*. Care to tell me what in bleeding hell septjad is, Ward?"

She stared blankly. Not a word she was in any way familiar with.

"You want to do something about it?" Obrington asked.

From one confrontation right into another. And Fae relations, her burgeoning obsession, threatened to dominate her again. But she shook her head, somehow still riding her authoritative high. "Sir, we're preparing to enact Protocol 38, and I'm confident if Pax succeeds then the Fae situation will become a lot less complicated. I'd respectfully ask that you keep them at bay while I prepare the team. I've just pacified Duvcorp myself."

Obrington almost looked impressed. "Did you now? Then I guess I can hold off the little buggers."

Sam had to fight to keep the satisfaction from showing on her face. This was good. This was how you moved on after murdering someone.

Having missed the drama with the criminals, Casaria had hoped to do at least *something* in Ward's shady meeting, but he was just there for show. While *she* put herself forward as the big dog. What an act. It should've been him protecting the city, then and before. Not nervous Ward and plodding bloody Landon. The criminals were gone. The chance for *justice* was gone, with Monroe on his way to jail, and that blond one maybe bleeding out. And back here, with Pax out on her own, Casaria was wasted. They wanted him to demonstrate weapons to the new agents. Dr Galler's job. Casaria watched Ward instructing Holly Barton, instead. Giving another civilian more attention than her own staff.

Darren Barton limped over, two steaming paper cups in hand, making Casaria square off uneasily. What did this lout want? He held out a cup and Casaria regarded it like proffered vomit.

"Too good for filter?" Barton said.

"Generally, yes," Casaria replied. What was it with this family and hot drinks? Barton kept it out, so he took it. It did smell inviting, even if it likely tasted piss-awful.

"We haven't properly spoken, you and me," Barton said.

"I wonder why."

"Another time, I would've given you a concussion for paying a visit to my daughter," Barton stated, idly.

"And I could've erased you from history for all the irresponsible crap you pulled."

"Sure. I owe you one, though. For helping Grace. And Pax."

Casaria was silent. Unsure how best to respond to gratitude from a man he could not respect. He looked at the coffee and realised what this was. A peace offering. He tried again. "I had no intention of calling on your daughter unannounced. I was looking for Sam Ward."

"I know," Barton said. And left it there. No words of advice about chasing the woman, or that she didn't want to talk to him. Barton took a sip of his own drink, breathed in satisfaction, and gestured to Ward and Holly. "I kept the tunnels from her for years. Figured she'd leave me if she knew. Now look at her, more involved than me."

Casaria nodded. He knew that feeling. "I trained Ward. Introduced her to all this. But she was always too good for me." He stopped dead, not knowing where that had come from. He left it too long to correct himself.

"Guess we both had high opinions of ourselves. It's what happens when us foot soldiers think too much. Word of advice?" Barton said. Here it was. "Stock some beer down here."

With that, he limped off back the way he'd come. Casaria wondered if the man even heard what he said. Ward left Holly, heading for the kitchen area, and Casaria sucked it up to follow. He caught up as she reached the coffee machine and he cleared his throat to announce his presence.

"Jesus, don't creep up on me."

"I didn't," Casaria told her, sharply, and got a sharp look back. Quickly moved on. "Are you hurt? From the shooting."

A pause, like she had to consider it, and Casaria's heart skipped. Had one of them –

"No."

"I would've taken them all down," he told her. "In the café, too. In a heartbeat."

"Maybe a good thing it was on me, then," Ward said grimly.

"I mean I wouldn't have let you go through that. It wasn't right. Obrington had –"

"He's doing okay," Ward interrupted. Casaria clamped his mouth shut. Unable to say anything right. She saw his frustration and softened. "What happened, happened. We survived. And for what it's worth, you were right, Cano. Pax *is* an asset to the Ministry."

Casaria went quiet. Did Sam Ward actually just admit he was *right* about something? He resisted deriding her for it. "I should be out there. Tell me where she went, she needs protection. These new bastards from London don't know the city, do they?"

"No."

Casaria smiled. "So you'll tell me where she's gone?"

"No, I mean you can't go after her. And you're not the first to offer."

Ugh. Fuck the others, what could they offer? He'd –

"Cano, stop, okay," Ward said, and he tried to unravel that. He hadn't been speaking, had he? "Can you just try not to think too much? In that café, just now, that was perfect. Follow instructions, don't second-guess, just assume we're doing the right thing, and none of it's personal."

Casaria stared at her, unsure where this was coming from – twice in as many minutes, told not to think. But he sensed it was important to her. Say no, and she'd remember it. Have what she deserved, perhaps, for all the spite she'd shown him. He didn't, though. He nodded. "Whatever you need."

She gave him the faintest smile before turning back to her coffee. Something moved in his throat. Not risking another word, he turned towards the weapons area.

4

The Fae Council building was a whitewashed monument to opulence. A tapering ringed tower decorated by pillars and arches in a neoclassical style. It stood taller than any building in the FTC, topped by a terrace with a low-walled rock garden, lording it over the city. Ambient spotlights highlighted it, soldiers hovered nearby. They didn't matter: Letty had a way in. She streamlined to approach as quickly as she could, down towards the base and a small ledge. A guard stood by a maintenance door, idly watching the sky.

As Letty got closer, he jumped to attention. She came fast, hitting him as he started to raise his gun. The guy went down and his gun slid off the ledge. He scrambled onto his knees as Letty bared her teeth. The soft-faced fool's eyes ballooned in recognition. "Shit –"

Letty rose to pounce, drawing her pistol, but the guard lifted his hands in surrender. A little whiff of something – hell – he'd pissed himself.

"Get up," Letty instructed. "Open the fucking door."

The man sprang to his feet. "Yes – of course –"

What had happened to this place, were they all this lame?

She dragged him inside, finding a row of hatch-tunnel entrances, labelled for different floors. "Where's the meeting?"

"Level eight," the guard told her. "Concourse."

"Good. Now, I need to punch your lights out, or you gonna keep quiet?"

"I won't say anything, I swear –"

"Yeah, whatever." Letty holstered her pistol. It wouldn't matter either way, they'd know where she was soon enough. She could spare a little sympathy for this loser.

Flynt fought his escort every step from the Council chamber, through the circular corridor and up the hatch. He bucked in their grips, snarled at Hearlon, their leader, and shouted about the mistake they were all making. Val was making her move – *had* made it, while he was being taken away. It was too late. The Stabilisers thrust Flynt into an empty room and locked the door. He clawed at the door, the walls, the ceiling, but there was no way out. The bastards had taken his weapons, and it was only a question of if they shot him right here or moved him somewhere more discreet.

Hearlon returned alone, light silhouetting him from behind. Flynt jumped to his feet and backed into the far wall, fists up. "You try me, man –"

"Shut up," Hearlon said. He was larger than most Fae, with a concrete face, head too big for his body. His black armour added extra bulk. The pistol at his hip was nearly the size of his thigh, and his hand hovered over it.

"That's it, is it?" Flynt said. "Edwing out in the wilderness – me right here in the Council building? Think the FTC won't notice –"

"It wasn't us did your brother," Hearlon said, coldly. "But he had it coming. Arrogant little shit. Guess it runs in the family."

Flynt glared back. "You honestly don't care that Val's imprisoning us?"

"*Protecting* us," Hearlon answered simply. "Like always." He drew the pistol.

"You're gonna bury this city," Flynt said, voice wavering.

"Nah. Only you."

Letty's words came to him, *strike hard and fast*, when they weren't expecting it – but there was no element of surprise here. Hearlon raised the gun and called over his shoulder, to the hall, a long way from convincing, "Ah, no, he's going for my –"

A bang shook them from below.

Hearlon looked down as though he could see through the floor. Another bang followed, distinctly a gunshot, and Hearlon's distraction was complete. "What in hell –"

Letty's words exploded in Flynt's mind – *win by acting, not fucking thinking* – and he sprang forward. Hearlon twisted and the gun went off, but Flynt was already past it. He drove a knee into the big guy's crotch, the same time he slammed his forehead into his face and got a hand on the gun. As Flynt pulled away, Hearlon stumbled into the wall, growling like a bear. But Flynt had the pistol. Right in his face. A corner of Hearlon's mouth rose in distaste and he started to speak. Flynt cut in, "I'll shoot, I swear I'll do it."

There was shouting below.

Hearlon didn't move, face bloody. Not his own blood; Flynt blinked a trickle out of his own eye, wounds reopened from his scuffle with Letty. He flicked it away and said, "Open the door. You son of a bitch."

"I want a talk, that's all!" Letty yelled over the shoulder of a Stabiliser a head taller than she, her pistol digging into his temple. The closest man when she had smashed her way in. As the other guards went for weapons, she fired a warning shot into the ceiling. Anyone who hadn't already leapt for cover did so. "You all keep calm, don't do anything stupid!"

"Letty." Valoria took charge, standing from behind the podium where she'd ducked. Her dignity returned with defiance. "You can't possibly expect this to work."

"Where's Flynt?" Letty shouted. She sidestepped along the wall with her hostage as a shield, getting closer to Val. "Get him back here!"

"He was disrupting the meeting," Valoria answered snidely.

"Did I fucking ask? You want to test me?" Letty flicked the gun from her hostage to the governor, and Valoria's arms went rigid at her sides. She was shitting one, even if she knew how to hide it. "You bring him back, and you – all of you! – sit the fuck back down!"

"Letty –"

"Now!" Letty's voice shook the room.

The guards all had their eyes on her, looking for a way through, as she shifted around, keeping her hostage between them. Fuming on the inside, Valoria held up a hand and spoke with acid. "Everyone keep calm. We are a civilised people, are we not?"

"We'll see, won't we?" Letty bit back.

Valoria slowly pressed a button on her collar, activating a radio. "Bring the boy back in here. In case you didn't hear, we have company."

"Good," Letty said. "Now. You lads – bunch closer together, over there. Where I can see you. Everyone else, in your seats. You're gonna listen to me, seeing as you're all incapable of talking sense. Now!"

The councillors hurried to sit back down, hands up, curling and hunching fearfully. Valoria stayed rooted to her spot. Letty said, "We're gonna have a reckoning, you pestilent grub. Tell these people exactly what you've done."

"There are no secrets here," Valoria answered. "The Council backed the actions we've enacted. For the good of the whole FTC. Whatever you hoped to find, it's not here."

"Uh-huh," Letty said. "They know all about the septjad poison, do they? How you'd risk threatening a chemical weapon rather than fucking *negotiate*? And all about the Dispenser? How you killed Apothel for it, but the weapon was never found? Not then, not now? How about the one about the fact that it never *needed* to be found? That we've got engineers that could've made a new one. Tell me, Val, how none of those are secrets *here*."

Valoria glared in furious silence.

The door creaked open and Stabilisers filled the gap. The governor ordered without hesitation, "Hearlon, join us. Let's see how tough she is with a friend on the line."

Letty watched the door, but the trio of guards who entered were unarmed. The two in front had their hands up. The trailing one was Hearlon, ahead of Flynt rather than the other way round. Flynt gave Letty a triumphant smile. Even better was the look on Valoria's face, crushed.

"Time to talk, Val," Letty said. "Time you fucking answered."

5

By the time Pax reached *The Sandwitch*, the sense that she was doing something remarkably stupid was deeply entrenched. It combined with a rumbling in her stomach, as the coming dusk reminded her she hadn't eaten since breakfast. Hopefully passing Palleday's rotten shop floor would stifle her appetite. When he let her in, the scent of mouldy bread did make her stomach churn. Then it rumbled more. Great.

"In here," Palleday called from the room of towers, where the crappy light was on. Pax strolled in, thinking how best to broach the subject of hunting their most hated felon. She found Palleday standing on a ledge with Fresko and Mix sat next to him, legs dangling over the edge, drinking from miniature bottles.

Fresko said, "You survived, then?"

"Apparently. Is that beer?" Pax leant closer. Did the Fae have glass manufacturing plants? What kind of tiny branding did they have?

"Not so close, *please*," Palleday insisted, holding up a hand, cringing.

"Sorry." Pax backed off. She was right by his buildings now, able to see into the nooks of their cave-like hollows. Empty.

"Yes, well, shouldn't expect a human to realise how big they are. How imposing they might be." Palleday distanced himself from the other two, folding his arms. The pair of mercenaries ignored him.

"Want one?" Fresko said, pushing himself up to approach what she saw was a tiny cooler. As he removed a beer, Mix snapped, "The fuck you gonna waste one on her for? Might as well throw it away."

"It's reckless," Palleday agreed. "Sharing that."

Fresko, apparently driven more by drinking etiquette than logic, opened the bottle with a tiny hiss before holding it up to Pax. She was torn: it was definitely a waste, and it would only irritate the other two, but she definitely wanted to try it. After a bad day and a worse week, hadn't she earned a little merit? Taking great care, she took the bottle in thumb and forefinger and poured the contents onto the tip of her tongue. It was hard to judge the taste from what amounted to a drop, but she told herself it was good. Very good.

"Bloody pointless," Mix huffed.

She dwelt on it for a moment, trying to savour it, and as she did she felt something. A refocusing of her eyes, a tingling around her fingers. The very barest trace of what the blue screens' energy manipulation stirred in her. She frowned, focusing back on the fairies, all three of them watching her.

"What's in it?" Pax replied. "This isn't like our beer . . ."

"It *is* your beer," Fresko said. "We rebottle what you lummoxes make. With twists."

"Twists, like . . ." Pax's voice got deeper. The liquid was taking a familiar but unsettling effect. She sensed her glow without looking down. The electric blue under her skin, the one the blue screens' liquid revealed. And the glow around the Fae; each of them a slightly different colour. Fresko was red, Palleday orange, Mix a steely grey. And the building behind them, it pulsed like it was subtly, slowly, breathing. "What did you put in it?"

Fresko answered slower than she could comprehend, lips barely moving. Pax scanned each Fae in turn as they looked at her with expressions shifting, at glacial speed, towards concern. Palleday's arms started to uncurl, Mix was lowering his beer, Fresko's head tilting to one side.

Pax leant in closer. Time had slowed down; she backed off again, raised an uncertain hand, dropped it, all in the time it took them to widen their eyes.

Then it was like someone hit play again, and all three of the Fae leapt backwards, shouting in surprise; Palleday fell over, crawling away, Mix scooted back, grabbing at a pistol, while Fresko jumped half a foot in the air and hovered there.

"The fuck was that!" Mix roared.

"She – bloody hell!" Palleday gasped.

Fresko kept quiet, staring.

With them watching her like she might explode, Pax remained frozen. "What just happened?"

"You moved like a twitching fucking bird," Fresko said, settling back onto the ledge.

"Bird's not that fast," Mix snarled, getting to his feet, slapping off dirt. "Never seen nothing move like that. Specially not some human."

Whatever it was had passed as quickly as it came. Pax's hearing, vision, and movements were all normal again, no more glow, no unsettling feeling. "What's in that beer?"

The fairies exchanged worried looks. To them, it must've been the opposite of what she'd experienced; in the space of time it took them to breathe in and out she'd gone through all those movements, spoken. Warped time?

"It's standard crank brew," Mix said. "Only a fucking beer." Pax let her eyes express the idiocy of what he was saying. He asked Fresko, "Think it's the dust?"

"Of course it's the dust," Palleday said. He, too, turned on Fresko. "What the hell are you thinking? Born yesterday, giving a human that?"

"There was Fae dust in there?" Pax asked.

"Alright, my bad," Fresko grumbled. "Forgive me for being fucking companionable. Figured you'd already crossed that bridge with Letty, seeing as you're such great mates."

Pax *had* discussed human consumption of Fae dust with Letty, and the conclusion, she recalled, was that it had never been done. That they were aware of. And it wasn't the same as glo, but it was similar. She blinked, trying to clear her mind. There was no more glo, but maybe . . .

"You with us?" Fresko asked. "Gonna tell us where your head's at, human?"

She refocused. "Yes. Yeah. That . . . we'll come back to that."

"Want more, you gotta earn it," Mix said. "It's time you told us what *you* are gonna do for *us*."

"Didn't I make that clear? An end to the monsters – the Sunken City, better relations between our people –"

"Letty gave us the same promises, and where'd that end up? Her fucking fist in my face? You don't have the Dispenser, don't have the Sunken City, or any leverage with the bloody Fae Council, don't even have the Ministry on side. What the fuck do you have?"

"Right now," Pax admitted, "I've got you guys. But I can get those other things, with your help. I need Lightgate."

The three Fae were stunned still for a second, then Mix burst into laughter. Fresko shook his head in similarly amused disbelief, but Palleday wore a look of abject horror.

"Hear me out. As long as she's out there, I figure pretty much everyone is at risk," Pax explained. "And I need a Fae I can take up against the minotaur. What you call the berserker."

"You're mad," Fresko told her, frankly. "Got us shooting at the Ministry and civilians. Got the Dispenser in all the wrong hands, got Letty spun out. Now you want to fuck with Lightgate? You're a fucking blight, you are."

"A blight with a plan. We're on the same side, aren't we?"

"Jury's out," Fresko said.

"This isn't just for me. We can help clear Letty, make things right between our people. If I can get hold of Lightgate –"

"You'll do what, tie her up?" Fresko said. "Someone like Lightgate, it's frontier justice or nothing, a fight to the death. You think no one's tried before? Val's Stabilisers gave up long before Lightgate skipped town. She's a nutcase."

"You're all nutcases," Pax pointed out.

"Not like her," Mix said. "Besides which, you got no chance of finding her. *She* comes to *you*, and you better believe that'll be on her terms. Nope. Double nope." He opened the cooler and took out another beer. "Big fucking mistake sticking up for this one, Fresko. Best thing we could've done is left her to take the fall, like Lightgate wanted. Big fucking mistake."

"Let Letty take the fall," Fresko replied with aggravation, "then this lummox? We end up taking the fall too, eventually. You saw those fucking FTC reports about us. You wanna be called Rogue Fae all your life?"

"If it means living longer," Mix said.

"Guys," Pax said, "this is on me. You don't put your necks on the line. Reach out to her, arrange a meeting, put me in a room with her. Convince her I'm on your side, that's all I want. I'll handle the rest."

"How? Jump down another sewer hole?" Mix said.

"I'll think of something."

"Without help, you'll die," Palleday weighed in. He gave the others a disapproving look. "Letty always deserved better than you two ingrates; look what happens when she finally finds someone useful. You're no-good cowards, you know that?"

"We're survivors," Fresko said, coldly. "Nothing more. You want to duel with Lightgate, you go ahead."

"Maybe I bloody will," the architect snapped. "Seems someone has to, before she tears the whole city down. Now, did you thick-skulled morons, or did you not, just see what I saw when this behemoth took a sip of our beer?"

They hesitated. Mix mumbled, "Saw her waste a good brew."

"I've got dust," Palleday said. "Plenty enough for a human to huff. And Lightgate's been banging on doors around town, I'm due a visit. You give her the message I wanna talk and she'll come, won't she? The human can nab her as she waltzes in."

Though appreciating the vote of confidence (other than being labelled a behemoth), Pax didn't jump at the idea herself. Huffing Fae dust sounded like an unreliable plan.

Mix swung his bottle around. "We set Lightgate up like that, you know what happens? She rapes *her* face with a knife, then *yours*, then *yours.*" He pointed at them each in turn. "Then she skins yours truly alive."

"Go hide under a rock, then, like you're good at," Palleday answered, looking at Fresko instead. "Only takes one of you to give her the nod."

"Anyone gets through to her via any of us," Mix said, angering, "it's on *all* of us. You know what happened at the fucking Grit Plateau? That wasn't just a couple of bumbling goons, she killed like forty elite soldiers. On both sides, because they *pissed her off.*"

"Hold up," Pax said. "She wanted to see me, didn't she? She wanted to meet with Palleday, too? You'd be doing as she asked."

"Until you fuck up," Mix said, "and the trap becomes obvious."

"Then we make sure I don't fuck up, don't we?" Pax said. So she was accepting the really bad idea. "If that beer was something to go on . . . I just need to take a *lot* of your dust."

6

Letty grouped her hostages around the right side of the main table, she and Flynt covering them from up the sloped floor opposite. The guards' guns were piled on a table, and the corridor outside was empty. Letty perched on a desk, pistol loosely aimed at the crowd. It was time to face the music and she had no fucking idea what came next. Flynt's face mirrored what she felt. His adrenaline was shifting back to doubt.

Valoria, at the front of the crowd, got them started. "You know there's no way out, Letty. Whatever you do, my Stabilisers will hunt you to the ends of the earth."

"We'll see," Letty said. "Might be they're not so loyal when they understand how screwy you are."

"You have the faith of the deranged," Val said, blandly. "There is nothing you can say that will shake the foundations we've built. The FTC has thrived without your sort here. Haven't you seen it? Edwing" – she addressed Flynt – "he understood. This behaviour might have worked ten years ago, but not today."

"Ten years ago," Letty echoed. "The coup – that was bloody work, wasn't it? You had no problem with the rule of the gun back then."

"As a means to an end. I do not deny the origins of this peace, but –"

"*But*," Letty hissed, "it was more than a Fae uprising. Ten years ago, you didn't just take control – the humans stopped chasing us. The FTC got cemented. You made human friends – who royally fucked you last week. Don't talk about that, do we? There goes Letty, screwing us by talking to humans, while everyone keeps quiet about Val's contacts."

Valoria shimmered with restrained hate. Hit a nerve. It wasn't going to surprise anyone, but it was still shameful. "None would begrudge my efforts to deliver peace. We had a whole decade –"

"*Had*, Val," Letty said, loudly. "Fucking *had* peace, until someone else called it quits. What kind of peace was it? No one even knows. How can we say what went wrong, make sure it doesn't happen again, when you kept it to yourself."

"What went wrong," Valoria snorted, "was that you gave the humans –"

"Stop. Stop talking. It's all you do. Talk and talk in circles so no one's right but you. Let's focus on what *I* know, shall we? Your contact in the Ministry? Some corrupt fucker, Lord Asquith?"

The governor said nothing.

"He was a goddamned *plant*. You want to know why the Ministry attacked us? The same reason *we* attacked them. Because *you*" – Letty pointed sharply – "made fucking pacts with the devils underground. The second we got a clue to their real nature – 'we' being me and a human – then your mates, the *monsters* in the

Sunken City, they panicked. What they were doing was scorched fucking earth. And what you're doing now is no better. Threatening the humans, locking our doors, burying your head in the sand."

"What I'm doing," Valoria rumbled, "is securing what's best for our people."

"With a poison out of Rostov? Where'd you get that idea? You prats all know about this?" Letty's eyes ran over the crowd. Many refused to meet her gaze, some returned it stubbornly.

"You are delusional," Valoria said, "if you think these good people will be swayed by your insolence. They recognise the need for decisive action." She stood, pulling her overcoat closer around her shoulders. "Letty focuses on the means, instead of the end. Yes, we have a poison, delivered by the Rostov Fae. A carefully poised, highly targeted threat, which we hope not to use. But such a threat requires a willingness to use it. A steel resolve, which human-sympathisers, such as Letty, would undermine. I shoulder that burden so you don't have to."

"Oh you noble sack of blubber," Letty said. "Does your neck ache from carrying gold chains on your people's behalf?"

"Indeed, show your true colours, Letty," Valoria warned. "I expect no civilised discourse from you. You believe yourself a victim, forcibly cast out, lied to. What have you ever done to earn a place here?"

Letty stared fire across the room.

Val sighed, heavily, like this was beneath her. "Flynt, it saddens me to see you keep her company. She set you up, can you not see that? The human Pax Kuranes, now working with the Ministry, is everything we stand against."

"She talked the Ministry round!" Letty replied hotly. "Unlike you, who took handouts until they decided to stop giving them."

"Quite," Valoria continued calmly. "I have, indeed, been betrayed by the humans. Regrettably, on the back of your disastrous involvement. But our new measures guarantee such a thing will not happen again. We will never again rely on human trust. They will ratify our demands. We will be recognised, and securely separated."

"You can't threaten your way into that kind of peace."

"Says the one holding our government at gunpoint!" Valoria laughed with haughty bass. It inspired some of her supporters to snickers. "Dear Letty, your head was always in the clouds. You criticise my methods while bringing violence to this very chamber. You talk of sowing ill-will when it was *you* who murdered human agents?"

"That was Lightgate!" Letty jumped off the table.

"At least I own my mistakes, while you lay the blame at the feet of ghosts."

"Half your fucking Council's heard from her! They won't admit it because it was your head she was after!"

Valoria gave her Council an amused look, not taking it seriously. Her sycophants shook their heads. "Convenient –"

"She's telling the truth," Flynt said, plucking up the nerve to speak. "I've seen her, too. Edwing confessed to meeting her, didn't he? I was there when he turned her down."

Valoria's face turned steely. "And you didn't report it."

"They discussed human support," Flynt said. "Edwing knew you'd disapprove."

Deidre, at the back, cleared her throat to speak above a rush of murmurs. "I had the same offer. I also feared punishment for even entertaining human interaction."

"Deidre?" Valoria turned a heavy stare to her.

"Aye she wasn't the only one." Smark found some spine, at last. "Fust and Nailer received messages from Lightgate, too." The two councilmen both vigorously shook their heads. "And no one would be foolish enough to *pretend* to be Lightgate, would they?" He held Valoria's stare, acknowledging that it was exactly what she was accusing Letty of.

Valoria huffed. "It's no matter. The Stabilisers have tracked half the exiles in Ordshaw; they'll find her too. *If* she's out there. And it hardly exonerates Letty if she associated with the Scourge."

"You accept Lightgate's out there," Letty snarled, "maybe you'd accept someone else might've been vile enough to murder Edwing, not a human I consider a friend."

"A friend?" Valoria answered through tight lips. "Heaven forbid it should be what it appears to be. The inevitability of history repeating itself."

"Meaning Apothel? A man whose crime, let's face it, was wanting to *use* the Dispenser? Killed so you can keep us from the Sunken City?"

"You choose to believe –"

"It's the fucking truth!" Letty shouted, making her audience jump. She walked through the room, pistol arm up, stiff. "You're keeping the Dispenser from us, you always have! I *know* it works – your people could've made a new one any time they wanted. I've been in your fucking vats."

Valoria had a tremor in her wings. Council members muttered concern, even some of Valoria's closest supporters. "To not pursue such a venture was –"

"For the sake of the FTC?" Letty said. "Or just for *your* sake? So nothing ever changes. You'd give up everything for this seat." Letty gestured to the podium, the throne-like chair behind it. "You'd risk completely alienating the humans for it."

"To defend the FTC?" Valoria said. "Absolutely! How dare you –"

"How dare *you* keep the Sunken City from us!" Letty yelled, now only a few paces away. The gun shook in her hand. "You let me search for that weapon for nine years! Nine fucking years grubbing about under human feet, believing I could make up for everything! You never wanted it back and Apothel was fucking well *right* to steal it! That was the only hope we ever had of using it!"

Her audience gasped in shock.

"You simpering moles! You seriously think this bitch wants what's best?"

"You have no idea!" Valoria said, hands balling into fists. "We have a civilisation to consider, the survival of a culture, our infrastructure! An untested weapon, monsters underground, humans that have betrayed us – why should we *choose* that!"

"The weapon *was* tested," Letty answered, slowing down. "Why hide it?"

Valoria paused. "Then, as now, I bore the burden of a question too difficult to share."

Letty glowered. The woman was clinging to her righteousness like it was a life preserver. She wanted to punch it out of her eyes. "Well, it's time to open it to everyone. We have a weapon that can threaten the monsters. It's time we went for the heart –"

"What *heart*?" Valoria demanded. "The berserker is not the problem, you ignorant fool! How could anyone truly believe it was that simple, with the humans bending over backwards to protect the monstrosities below? The humans can keep the Sunken City. We do not need it. The FTC survives alone, as it should be."

Letty lowered her gun. It was a confession; Valoria knew of and ceded to whatever force operated behind the berserker. She had given up the Sunken City without apology. Still, the councillors weren't stirring. They looked like they would have preferred never to have heard all this. Easier to leave it to the governor.

"Are you satisfied?" Valoria said, reading the reluctance from the room. "Do you understand the futility of all this? The *necessity* of what I have done?"

"No," Letty said, straining to keep equally calm. "I'm a long way from satisfied. You're going to recall your Stabilisers, rein in that fucking septjad. Tell the Ministry it was a mistake and we'll make up for it. We'll work with them on securing the Sunken City."

"I won't, Letty," Valoria said. "I have only done what is best."

Letty tried again, angrily, "Make the call. Tell your men to stand down."

"No."

"Make the fucking call!" Chairs scraped and short shrieks met Letty's movement, her gun suddenly against Val's head. The bulbous Fae glared with trembling indignation as Letty hissed, "Do it, or I'll do you."

Despite her fear, Valoria said, "You will not. Not if there's an ounce of truth in your belief in Fae society."

Braced there, wanting to do it, wishing it was as simple as pulling a trigger, Letty looked to Flynt. He had that same expression she'd seen on him a dozen times now: worried she might go too far. With an angry growl, Letty dropped her arm and addressed the Council. "None of you got a damn thing to say? Edwing the only one of you with any balls?"

Smark ventured, "This *has* moved very fast."

"Should our future be made to wait?" Valoria replied, emboldened. "Whatever you say, Letty, the FTC needs my leadership. They *want* it. I am willing to pay the cost of peace."

Letty's fingers rapped against her pistol handle. Smark and Deidre's backing wasn't going to make a difference. This was Val's domain. But there was a whole city of people that might disagree. Surely, would disagree. To reach them would mean signalling what was happening here. Val's soldiers would be all over them.

There was no running now, anyway.

"Flynt." Valoria tried again to appeal to the scout. "Surely you see this is *for* your brother. You are angry, and grieving, anyone would –"

"Piss on it, Val," Letty cut in, meeting Flynt's eye herself. "Edwing wouldn't ever have wanted it your way and Flynt knows it. This chamber might not be willing to stand up to you, but there's thousands outside that might." Letty waved to where the camera was hidden, somewhere up above. "Put it out there, Newbry! Now!"

7

"Height of goddamned sacrilege, this is," Palleday complained, despite his hand in the plan. If it was so offensive to him to rest a (human) bottle of beer here, perhaps he shouldn't have built these towers with conveniently spaced ledges, including the one around chest height that Pax was using.

Trying to keep her hand steady as she carefully tipped a little tub of fine white powder into the neck, Pax said, "These sculptures would be great in pubs, you know. Lot of surface area for storing drinks without taking up a ton of space."

Watching with Fresko from the next ledge up, the architect made a noise that said she was making it worse. Mix, sat by them, focused on his own beer.

"But I bet they looked more stunning in use," Pax tried again. "Teeming with Fae."

"Oh, like a dream," Palleday assured her.

"With about as much substance," Mix contributed. "Ain't no one seen Palleday's towers in use for decades. Even longer since we had a city of them. If you believe there ever was one."

"Course there was, you disrespectful punk," Palleday said. "How you gonna understand, you ever even sniffed those tunnels?"

"Only you," Fresko said, "are old enough to remember *that*."

"What'd it look like?" Pax prompted, the chatter helping distract her from spilling their precious powder. So far only a few grains outside the bottle; Mix winced at every one.

"The population bringing these beauties to life was one thing," Palleday reflected, "but the plants made it. If you'd seen the way they lit the place. Ah – the *colours* –"

"Like, glowing plants?" Pax frowned. "From the weird underground weeds?"

"The Magnus family harvested them," Palleday explained, "for medicinal uses and the like. This was before dust was so ubiquitous. They took a real blow when we were driven above ground. But Valoria's people weathered it better than most." His bitterness returned. "Found new interests, didn't they. Kicked the old ways to the dirt."

"We're working on that," Pax assured him. She stepped back from the fizzing beer, thoughtful. "You must've known the Sunken City well, back then. You ever come across caves that nothing went in? Older chambers, shaped like –"

Palleday scoffed. "What're you messing with Chasm Shrines for?"

"Chasm . . .? Okay, so that's a firm *yes*. Tell me what you know."

"What's to know? Rooms where things never worked proper? Difficult to fly, even. Religious types used them for meditation, superstitious Fae steered well clear. Rumour was some Fae held out in the Shrines, when the monsters came, but you couldn't get out again, could you? One entrance, one exit. Bloody open graveyards."

Did that negative energy keep the blue screens at bay, too? Something for later.

"You done already?" Mix interrupted Pax's chain of thought.

She indicated the beer. "You think that's enough?"

"Would've done about two dozen of our stubbies," Fresko commented.

"Should work about twenty times longer than what you gave me before, then," Pax decided. Then paused. "If I down the whole bottle."

"Yeah, better put more in," Mix said.

"Unless the effects are exponential," Fresko suggested.

"That amount could kill a Fae," Palleday said.

Pax stared at the cocktail. Equally likely to be too weak to give her time to complete their plan and too strong to survive. "This is really idiotic."

"And exactly why *are* you doing it?" a female voice asked from above, and Pax jumped back. Unannounced, there she was, the brightly-suited menace of a fairy, posing at the peak of a tower, just above Pax's head height. Lightgate's face was impassive as she watched, the opposite of the others' fearful concern. Mix uttered, "Ah, fuck."

"How long have you been following me?" Pax asked, scolding herself for thinking she'd ever been safe from the fairy. Besides senseless murder and holding her liquor, Lightgate's chief talent was sneaking up on people.

"You think I have time for that?" Lightgate sighed. She tilted her head, demonstratively, to show a smear. Blood, or a charred patch? "Fresh from Salt Wharf, where a spirited young lady was being harassed by Val's people. She went to join the others. Third one today. Makes fifteen, twenty total? I'm not sure."

"Twenty what?" Pax said. "You're rallying an army?" The suggestion had been there before, with Lightgate's continual disappearances. Rounding up the outcast Fae. "Where?"

"They're out working. But I got the ball moving and thought, hey, the old man's missing out." She pointed her index finger and thumb in a pistol at Palleday and winked.

"We were about to invite you," Fresko said, tense.

"I'm sure you were," Lightgate said. "What else would you be conspiring about?"

"Well. We might've hesitated after seeing what you did to that councilman."

"Ah, you were there?" Lightgate beamed. "That's how you got away, Pax? I should've stuck around, but I never quite trust that lunatic Valoria's swarm."

"You're calling *her* a lunatic?" Mix said. "Saints alive."

Lightgate laughed. "Yeah, well, she outdid me. Have you heard she took deliveries from the Rostov Fae?" She directed the question to Pax, who said nothing. "Poisons. Spread across Ordshaw. Though I wouldn't trust her to follow through."

"What are you doing here?" Palleday rumbled. "You could've guessed I want nothing to do with you."

Lightgate looked at him like he was talking a foreign language. "You've got two deadly klutzes and this volcanic mess of a human with you. You clearly need help."

"They're here because this place is neutral. Everyone knows that."

"Oh, no one's neutral," Lightgate said. "As to what I'm *doing* here, now, I'm discovering what on earth you guys are up to?"

"Trying to survive," Pax said. "At least long enough to see whatever insane plan you're going to throw up next."

"Mixing Fae dust in beer? You know what that does to a person?"

"You do?" Pax replied with concern.

"I've tried it. Twice. Not that they knew it. One went into this kind of" – Lightgate raised a hand, covering a wide yawn, like she was boring herself – "seizure. Shaking all over, eyes moving a mile a minute, then nothing. Second one, it was the opposite. Slowed. Right. Down." She spoke in an extra drawn-out drawl. "Like wading . . . through . . . mud. Sort of fell asleep and never woke up."

Pax stared wide-eyed. Of course Lightgate had experimented with this Fae taboo, spiking humans, and of course she had killed two people doing it. With wildly different results.

"It's not a good idea, Pax," Lightgate continued flippantly. "Feeling particularly adventurous today?"

"Yeah," Pax answered, fighting down her own uncertainty. The startled looks on the other Fae's faces said they were thinking the same thing. Had they just mixed her a death elixir? "Certain toxic people keep making my life more difficult. The more extreme relaxation the better, frankly. Don't think it's worth the risk?"

Lightgate glided down from her perch with a few wing-flaps, onto the lip of Pax's beer bottle. She looked into the liquid to assess its contents. Pax waited, watching her. There was no telling how much dust Lightgate had given her victims; it might've been a huge amount. And Pax had tried it once . . . If she could get a good swig of that bottle, she could make a grab for the fairy. That's all it would take. Right?

If the beer worked the same way as before, and didn't outright kill her.

If Lightgate wasn't too quick anyway.

"How are your Ministry friends?" Lightgate said, stepping around the bottle rim idly, amusing herself with her own steps.

Pax took her time. Did the fairy know about Monroe and her feigned escape from the MEE? Would she even care? "Hopefully they're working on stopping your governor from getting everyone killed, right now. But I thought it best to leave them to it, seeing as no one entirely trusts me."

Lightgate raised an eyebrow. "Aren't you their golden child?"

"Not quite," Pax said. The fairy hadn't kept abreast of the day's events at all. "They got suspicious of my associations this afternoon. After someone tipped off my less-desirable contacts with a way into the Sunken City."

The fairy's eyes lit up. "Why didn't I think of that?"

"Because you're second fiddle to the bigger threat in this town," Pax said. "You remember, the one I said latched onto your turnbold plan? *Used* you."

"Used me to get what I wanted," Lightgate replied. "Tragic."

"What's your endgame, Lightgate?" Pax demanded. "Where are we, now? Three attempts to spark a war? All you've done is helped the bastards below."

Lightgate shrugged with a lazy smile. "Fun's fun, isn't it? I got Val shaking things up, for a start. That's where Fae thrive, in the *shaking* of things."

"Not all Fae. Edwing wanted peace. The FTC want peace. Valoria even wants peace, in her way."

"Those aren't *Fae*. They've lost their way. Know where I was two months ago?"

"Timbuktu?" Pax shot back. "Atlantis? Surprise me."

"Varanasi." Lightgate waited for a response. Pax eyeballed her, *so?* The fairy gestured towards their host. "Tell her about Varanasi, Palleday. Bet you've got some stories."

"What's to tell?" Palleday grunted. "Another lowly Fae city. Practically every Fae colony outside Ordshaw's barbaric, them included."

"They play a game, it roughly translates to the Moon Cull. Every full moon, there's a prize to the Fae that pulls off the most public sacrifice. Without putting the Varanfae at risk. One of them cut the throat of Varanasi's mayor. Or whatever their equivalent is. Probably made the news here?" No one responded. "Anyway, *most* places, Fae still know what it means to be Fae. What's important."

"That sounds like the exact fucking opposite of what's important," Pax responded irritably. "You're saying the Ordshaw Fae are the only ones remotely close to being civilised, so you absolutely *had* to stop them?"

Lightgate sighed and turned on the bottle again, stepping over the gap, stepping back again. "For *my* turn, I took out a kid. Son of a tech millionaire, died in an unfortunate hiking accident. But they never found the body. Kind of . . . missed the point of the game?" Lightgate looked to Pax for sympathy. Pax was sure she just wanted to highlight her own cruel depths. Such a small thing, capable of such terror.

"I'm happy to see you," Lightgate moved on brightly, lifting up off the bottle and hovering before Pax. "All of you. You were discussing what to do about me, weren't you? Will we, won't we, where will we go . . . I've got good news. You don't have to *do* anything. I've got enough people to blow a hole in Valoria's world without you. Of course, I would consider it a personal favour if you *would* consider joining me. All of you."

"Bollocks," Mix said, loudly. "I've heard enough. We're screwed, they're screwed, what the fuck ever. You win, Lightgate. You're a bloody star and I'm sure by the time the week's out you'll have ruined everything for everyone, big fucking deal. Can we drink already?" He raised his own beer bottle, and gave Pax a look. "If you're gonna burn the city down, I at least wanna see this human lose her shit on dust, first."

Lightgate grinned. She floated higher up, giving Pax space, and took her hip flask from a jacket pocket. As she undid the cap, she said, "You're really game, Pax? I think we can do big things. If you survive."

"Now you've painted me as a deranged killer?" Pax asked, pointing loosely at her beer bottle, asking permission. Lightgate tipped the flask towards it, go ahead.

"True Fae respect deranged killers," Lightgate said, as Pax lifted the bottle. This was the moment of truth, then. Liquid hope. Or disaster. "You think I'm mad – imagine, Edwing thought we might talk our way to happiness." Lightgate laughed. Pax felt the others' eyes on her, tensely waiting.

Pax took a breath and said, "Fuck it."

She threw back the beer bottle, gulping it down. The dust made it taste of earthy mushroom, and she gagged but kept going. She scarcely heard Mix's impressed cursing. She put the bottle back down and breathed deeply, checking her body – not dead yet.

"I like this girl," Lightgate told the others. "She doesn't do things by haaalllllf –"

Her words stretched out, long, low, and as Pax looked up from the tower to Lightgate hanging in the air, the dust had an instant effect. The towers shimmered a ruddy brown; the three Fae on the ledge lit up, and Lightgate glowed brighter than all of them. A great, scarlet flare.

The fairy's wings beat in a smooth motion; the only object fast enough to counter Pax's slowed-down time. Lightgate's mouth pursed, impossibly slowly, and Pax narrowed her eyes. Yes. It was working – she was focused, she had time. And she was glowing, too. Pax raised her hands, gently, in wonder at the colour bursting from them. Bright enough to show through her sleeves. It wasn't the same as glo: there was the blue, but not only in her veins. It was all over her. Blurry, dazzling.

Something to explore later, Pax told herself, with an aside that she was calmer than she should be. With the world slowed down, she found serenity. She half-smiled at Lightgate. Zen Pax. Ready to seize the day with perfect clarity. Ready to seize the Fae. She laughed, a sound that bounced back as dull booms. The opposite of huffing helium, oh –

Pax shook herself out of it. She was giddy. Focus, *focus*, she picked out Lightgate again, and the Fae was slightly further back. Her face now fixed with concentration. Shit; she was moving away. Pax raised a hand, but it came slower than her thoughts, dragging through the air. Each passing moment, Lightgate flew further back, crazily slow but dangerously high. Her good arm drifted towards her hip-holster. Pax's hand lifted, marginally faster than the fairy. She stretched her fingers, pushing, hard, towards the Fae. She glanced at the others: Mix's mouth opening in a shout, Palleday and Fresko watching fearfully. She had to do it, for all of them.

Pax's arm was fully outstretched above her head when she closed her fingers. Snatching them shut. Time shifted gears again, catching up with accelerated speed, and Pax stumbled amid shouts from the trio of Fae at her side. Clarity was replaced by a painful, thrumming throb that made her vision blur, as her shoulder smacked into one of Palleday's columns. She lost her footing as the tower cracked.

The walls shattered around her like a breaking vase, and she fell heavily onto her back. A rain of building shards crashed onto her as she looked up, willing her eyes to focus, bracing herself against the floor to stop the whole world rolling.

Way above, near the shadows of the ceiling, Lightgate floated free, a white silhouette in the dark. She called down, "Have a nice trip?"

8

Sam watched one of Obrington's hatchet-faced agents heft something large and dangerous-looking against his hip. Something near its centre hissed and gave the agent the smile of a child with a magnifying glass on a sunny day. Casaria jumped up and adjusted the man's gun strap with some judging comment.

Unlike when the Operations team had geared up to take on the Fae, Sam was eager to see these preparations. She had half a dozen men taking up arms and a dozen more hunkered over computers, all to help Pax. To help *the city*. And Obrington was arguing with the London office, trying to establish back channels to the Fae. He genuinely seemed to be preparing her to take over, which might leave Ordshaw in *her* care at last. As long as her agents didn't march into another slaughter.

"Reservations?" Obrington asked as he joined her in surveying the office. She shook her head, but he wasn't interested anyway, continuing, "I've got a few okays from London, things I might offer the buggers. Creating a no-go zone around the FTC actually works well for us. It'd help if they'd talk to us, though."

"We definitely can't give them Pax."

"Cross that bridge when we reach it. Talk to me about the purge."

Sam did so, grateful for a sounding board. Protocol 38 was, as she might've expected, a half-baked idea. The more they recalibrated their weapons according to what they were learning from the Duvcorp scanners, the less effective they appeared. The main gun they assumed would neutralise the *praelucente* was a glorified taser, which Dr Galler freely admitted had only a 60% chance of damaging it. Pushed, he also admitted that percentage was a guess. From the little time he'd had studying the Fae weapon, he was confident the Dispenser was a much better option.

The other complication was that Protocol 38's strategy assumed they would track the *praelucente* and its horde, advancing on it from the rear, whereas the new plan assumed it would be coming to them, lured by Fae bait. Support were plotting the best tunnels to defend, to channel the horde down a particular route. Darren Barton was advising them on predicting monster movement by sight, while Holly, comparing her own findings to the papers Sam had given her, had concluded there was no evidence, anecdotal or otherwise, that the black spots were harmful. The horde's aversion to these areas might make them ideal pockets for defending their bait until they could strike a finishing blow.

"And you've assigned the man responsible for that?" Obrington asked, once Sam was done explaining. He said it lightly, like the suggestion was harmless, while looking across the room to Barton. "Would be bloody good to use one of them, save us risking a better-trained, more trustworthy asset."

"Sir?" Sam replied with shock. "We're here to *protect* the people of –"

"*Would be*, I said," Obrington told her. "Obviously we can't rely on a civilian for something that important. It was a rhetorical question, Ward, we both know the answer."

Sam paused. Her first thought was: does the captain go down with the ship? She'd already proved herself against those criminals and Duvalier, now she might have to shoulder the ultimate responsibility – but, no. That philosophy would put *his* role in question. The obvious choice, in risking losing someone, was the man they didn't quite know what to do with. Too competent to discard, too unstable to embrace.

"Casaria shouldn't even be here," Sam said, quietly, watching him explain some detail of a pistol to another agent. "He lost a toe."

"He could've lost a lot more and you know it."

"But we don't know what will happen, with the weapons discharged, with the *praelucente* hurt –"

"Someone's got to do it. Perfect combination of skilled enough to do it and not too skilled to replace, should something go wrong." Obrington paused. "Not that it will, Ward. Keep that in mind. We might pull it off. And either way, he gets to be a hero. You gonna tell me he'd want anything less?"

Sam frowned. Given the choice, Casaria would surely volunteer. He'd been fearless going up against the grugulochs and in rescuing Pax before. But it was still a cold, dark responsibility. "Let me consider it."

"With what other options in mind?" Obrington said. She said nothing. "Heavy weighs the crown, Ward. But you'll do fine. Just make it sound like he's doing a good thing."

He lumbered away. Apparently the Fae weren't the only ones capable of dropping bombshells without negotiation. Sam wondered again if this would actually last, or if this illusion of control had been to force her to take on this responsibility. Once the smoke cleared, even if Obrington left, might someone else like him step back into the fold for the easy days?

Across the office, Casaria caught her watching him, and offered a light, gentle smile. She gave him a noncommittal wave back. What other options *did* she have?

Above the centre of the FTC, the news screen replayed choice clips from Letty's summit, Letty and Val's voices booming over the buildings: "We'll work with them on securing the Sunken City." "The humans can keep the Sunken City." Traders, manufacturers and skilled professionals hovered out into the airways between buildings, gathering to exchange concerns, slowly gravitating towards the Council tower. While the citizens hung in growing swarms, Stabilisers collected in the sky, near and far. The building was surrounded; there was no slipping away, no hiding, so why not embrace it.

Letty shoved Valoria, pistol at the small of her back, out onto the grandiose roof terrace. Flynt held back, watching the rest of the Council and the guards. The idea that Valoria could shield Letty, vast as she was, was ridiculous. Fae watched from all angles. No point even pretending she had cover now. Letty lowered her gun and strode away from Valoria, readying herself for the worst. Valoria's eyes were aflame as she waited for the salvo of unprovoked gunshots Letty half-expected.

"Tell these people exactly why you're keeping the Dispenser from us!" Letty's voice demanded from the giant screen in the sky. Newbry had done a good job rushing together the footage.

Valoria watched Hearlon and the other Stabilisers following Flynt out, armed again. None of them dared make the first move, though all looked ready to gun the rebels down. Val addressed Flynt loudly enough to reach the very back of the crowd.

"Your friends are being hunted, right now. Spreading lies, manipulating our communications channels, bringing such equipment into the Council chambers – you cannot get away with this."

Flynt stared coldly back and said nothing. Letty loved him for it. Valoria reddened, forced to continue. "Your brother was an insolent fool!" She turned to the Stabilisers. "What are you waiting for, arrest them!"

Hearlon's crew were hesitating for the same reason as the Stabilisers in the sky. The same reason Flynt had the gall to follow them out here. The whole damn city had questions, a thousand people or more around them, now. Letty squinted at the floating soldiers. She made out one of Smark's friends, and he was saying something to another. Indicating they see how this played out. The hesitation was infectious.

Their openness, being out here, made all the difference. This wasn't a fight, it was an unfinished conversation. Letty approached the edge of the building. Comments rose up:

"It's her!"

"What's going on?"

"What now?" Valoria shouted. "You have driven the city to confusion, congratulations – what *now*?"

"Why don't we ask them?" Letty shouted back, likewise making sure the crowd could hear. "If they're all happy for you to use fear and poison to seal off this city for good, you can fucking put one right here." She tapped a finger to her temple and turned to the citizens. "Or would you rather work with the humans to take back the Sunken City? Something we'll never do by suggesting we *kill* them."

Valoria set her jaw stubbornly. "Yes, I threatened the humans! I wished to avoid making our entire society complicit in it, and I wished – yes – to keep the Sunken City *out* of it. This is our home now. This is where we belong."

It didn't hit everyone the same way, or at the same time, but disagreement swept through the gathering crowd. Valoria had always known better than to make this a public discourse. Letty watched the governor as they soaked up the rising responses.

"There's a chance of getting the Sunken City back?"

"What *have* they negotiated?"

"Didn't Letty threaten the humans?"

"They butchered our councilman!"

"Did they fuck!" Letty railed at that comment. "I can *talk* with the humans! Get to the bottom of all of this! Follow *her*, and all you'll ever have is what she gives you!"

"Oh yes, talk with the humans." Valoria had a ready response. "Shall we befriend the female human who killed Edwing? Letty's new Apothel."

"Apothel was a maniac!" a woman cried out from within the hovering swarm. A score of angry comments, boos and demands followed.

The big screen went black for a moment, drawing everyone's attention up. It blinked and came back with the Fae media's usual logos. Valoria's people had regained control of the network, showing footage of where they were now. The crowds in the FTC centre, headlines scrolling: *TERRORISTS STRIKE COUNCIL.*

"I'm a terrorist?" Letty shouted. "According to people spreading chemical warfare through Ordshaw! You believe in making everyone safe, withdraw your fucking threats!"

"I will not –"

"We can talk to the humans!" Flynt shouted with an excited edge. "Edwing showed us that! I met Pax with him, she wouldn't hurt him!"

"We *have* to question this." Smark added his voice, stepping out from amongst the Stabilisers and other Council members. "If there are chemical weapons –"

"Waste Chief Smark, know your place," Valoria said viciously.

"My place is not knowing why in hell you're sullying our chances to spread our wings! We need *public* accountability, to give the humans a chance. At long last."

It silenced her, and he turned on the other Council members, all eyeing the growing public swarm with great caution. Mullon said, "Perhaps, Governor Magnus, it might be prudent to slow down."

"This . . . " Valoria's voice shook with anger. "This is precisely why I took the lead. We cannot establish autonomy with half measures."

"Nor if we drive the humans to destruction!" Smark replied. "We barely survived last time." Shouts of agreement and complaint swept through the crowd.

"We took their weapons – we better understand them now –"

"Stand down your men, Valoria," Mullon suggested, quietly. "We need a recess."

Valoria's gaze could have melted iron, but she was not fool enough to resist the entire city's demands. Letty said nothing, letting the momentum of the FTC carry her. Shaking her head bitterly at Letty, Valoria raised a hand to her lapel, activating her radio, and the gathered audience quietened hurriedly. She spoke softly, but the rabble were so intent on hearing that her voice still carried. "Fang, this is Valoria. I have orders."

Letty looked to Flynt with swelling pride. This was working. The bastard governor was backing down, the people seeing sense –

"Fang, answer me," Valoria snapped, and the stiff silence was broken by mutterings of uncertainty. "Fang, now is no time for tardiness!"

She went quiet. No response was coming.

"Madam Governor . . ." Mullon ventured.

"There is a problem," Valoria said. She tried one last time, adjusting the radio. "Fang? Hooper? *Anyone* from Team 14?"

Still silence.

Valoria narrowed her eyes. She was as confused as everyone else, but Letty noted a calculating look as the governor saw an opportunity. Not knowing what was coming, Letty stepped towards her, about to shout *stop*, anything, but Valoria yelled, "This is a distraction! Letty's people have struck, they mean to take control of the very weapons she claims to fear!"

"What the fuck are –"

"Stabiliser Team 14 is compromised, Letty's people have them! Seize her, seize them all!" Valoria roared, taking quick steps away from Letty. The soldiers moved quickly – they didn't need to know what was going on, in the face of such firm orders. Rifles were raised, two men were suddenly on Flynt, Smark too, and guns were aimed at one or two dissenting soldiers in the sky. Letty, with her pistol half-raised, had three men around her, rifles pointed at her head. People shouted and panicked – Letty's complaints were lost in it – Valoria alone seemed to have a handle on the situation. "The rebels would spark a war under a white flag! Make true the threat against the humans! Send them to the cages!"

Letty bared her teeth but didn't take another step, more guns on her than she could count. In the mounting chaos, all reason was lost. She tossed her gun aside.

9

The world came back into focus as columns of Fae architecture loomed above like tree trunks, the ceiling a distant, grimy smear. Pax's head throbbed like she'd been hit with a bat. When she moved, a blanket of ceramic chips shifted over her with a clatter. She craned her neck to get a better idea of her situation. Fragments of a Fae tower covered her torso and legs. Worse than that, a tiny woman was standing on her chest with a silver pistol in her hand.

"I *really* like you," Lightgate told her, amiably. "I guess humans *can* take dust."

The gun pivoted idly as Lightgate swayed on the spot. Seeing the fairy rise and fall with her chest, Pax slowed her breathing, barely daring to move. It was fair to say this had gone badly wrong, and any sudden movement now might inspire an execution.

"Betraying *me* isn't really what I'd hoped for," Lightgate continued, "but the willingness to do so, I value that. Most Fae wouldn't stand up to me, so for a human to have a go . . ." Lightgate whistled with satisfaction. "Don't try it again, though."

"Seeing that it worked out so well the first time," Pax said.

Lightgate smiled. "You're too late, anyway. Whatever you thought you could do, there's war coming. For your courage, I'm still willing to deal. I could use you, yet."

"No, thanks."

"Pax. I'm a patient person, but I will take offence eventually."

"You framed me for murder."

"And you made some friends out of it!" Lightgate exclaimed, like she'd done Pax a favour. She gestured upwards to the towers where the others must've been lurking. They took it as a cue. A red dot appeared on her chest.

"I wouldn't call us friends," Fresko called from up high, "but yeah. We'd prefer you left her be."

"You'd prefer?" Lightgate replied with what sounded like genuine confusion.

"We've got you covered," Mix added, making her snap her head to the other direction. He was lower down, much closer, speaking from inside a tower. "Don't care how fast you are, we've got you fucking covered."

"You should care," Lightgate said. "You'll shoot her tits off. Not a good result considering how soft you've all gone for the humans. By the spirits, I should've come back to Ordshaw a long time ago. Where's the *spine* in this place?"

"Standing up to you, right fucking now!" Mix said.

"And don't overestimate," Fresko added, more calmly, "how much we care about this bitch's tits."

Pax kept as still as she possibly could, eyes flitting from Lightgate to the sides, where she couldn't pick out either of her apparent protectors. She'd gone from the champion of resolution to the scenery of a potential gunfight, and from the way Lightgate's posture was tightening, there was no question it was going to get ugly.

"Well, Pax," Lightgate said. "Any advice for your irresponsible saviours?"

"Honestly," Pax said, bracing herself, speaking clearly so Letty's men would understand, "I'm hoping they'll hit you between the eyes."

Lightgate gave her a withering look. "That's not very nice."

Fresko fired first, a crack of a shot that Pax felt rush past. Mix fired a split second later, two weapons at almost the same time. Pax flinched, throwing her body up and creating a rain of shattered debris, which Lightgate spiralled through. The fairy bent back in the air with the grace of a gymnast, pirouetting past the bullets. Arm outstretched, she fired back. Pax rolled, as quick as she could, shoulder rising past where Lightgate had hovered, and the Fae whizzed by her head. Another shot whooshed over Pax's hair, barely missing. Christ – they really didn't care about hitting her.

Pax darted forward at a crouch, picking out the scant space between the towers, head low, hands up. The firing continued, quick and loud, cracks rising from all angles; Mix roared as he flew from one side of the room to another, small flashes of light appearing where he went.

"I thought Letty might've trained you better," Lightgate goaded from the forest of pillars. "Come on boys, don't be shy."

To answer her, the other Fae guns barked back. Again, again.

Pax crabbed from side to side, trying to find a way out. The gunfire and her own panicked breathing almost blocked out another approaching noise; whirring and creaking. Heavy machinery coming to life, getting closer. She turned to it as Lightgate shot back into view. The miniature woman darted before her eyes, tossing an empty magazine from her gun and reloading by hammering her pistol into her gun belt. She slowed to face Pax: a mistake.

The towers exploded around them, cracking and shattering, falling in walls of ceramic. Pax cried out, hands over her head, and tried to dive clear but only fell deeper into the chaotic crumble, the weight of a dozen pots bringing her down. In the collapse, she saw flashes of white as Lightgate tried to dodge debris, but there were too many chunks to avoid and she disappeared beneath the mess, alongside Pax. A tower came down on Pax's side like a log, slamming her into the floor. Another crashed down in front of her, missing her forehead by an inch and shattering on impact.

When everything was still, Pax checked her body. Buried by Fae ruins, partially trapped, but alive. Definitely Not Dead. She twisted, knocking chunks of building off her, and coughed on the dust. Through the scattered remains she picked out a patch of white. Not moving.

Pax stretched under the weight of the tower that pinned her. She tossed chunks of building away, revealing Lightgate sprawled at the bottom. Her white suit was ripped and stained by terracotta dust and her hair was a disaster. Wings bent. But she moved, a hand reaching to the side, towards something tiny, a speck in the rubble. Her flask, bent savagely out of shape, torn and wet with a tiny puddle of spilt liquid. Lightgate took it, and titled it, one way and another, the flask empty. The fairy suddenly pushed herself up onto her elbows. Eyes picking out Pax, wings rapidly lifting her up, she bared her teeth in a snarl. Not so fast, having taken a heavy blow. Pax grabbed forward, but Lightgate evaded her closing fingers. She spun in the air and changed direction, down towards the floor. Pax saw the glinting metal of a gun, and forced her way desperately out from under the debris. Lightgate swept down to the pistol, plucking it up from the mess, and rolled, turning back as Pax's hand came down again. The gun went off with a crack and pain cut into Pax's palm as she slammed her hand through broken shards of tower.

She froze, then, wincing not just from her stabbed hand but with the realisation of what she'd done.

For a moment the room was completely still, Lightgate gone, under her hand.

"You got her?" Palleday called down, and Pax pulled her gaze up to him. His pulley device stood over her, with the fairy operating it at the top, like the pilot of a crane. It rocked on its wheels, hooks and chains swaying as they hung from the high arms; rams he'd used to smash through his works of art to bring Lightgate down.

"Yeah," Pax said, voice hoarse with the dust caught in her mouth. She spat aside, to speak more clearly. "I got her." She slowly lifted her hand from the floor, and cringed as Lightgate peeled off it, broken and sticky with blood. Pax sat back on her haunches with a resigned sigh, holding up her bloodstained hand and observing the body. There was little white left on the maniac Fae's suit. Her booted feet were twisted at odd angles to her body and her face, thankfully, was hidden by a mess of tangled hair.

"Better have," Fresko said, swooping down onto the machine next to Palleday. Something was wrong with his posture. "Because she fucking well got us."

Mix was dead before they got him clear of the carnage of Palleday's ghost town. Pax laid him gingerly down by the edge of the room, and Palleday landed next to him, supporting Fresko under an arm. It was hard to see where Mix had taken the bullet – he might have taken many – but his eyes were open and glassy, his face fixed in an angry death grimace. Pax knelt over them as Fresko slumped at his friend's side. The sniper was clutching his gut, shirt soaked red.

"Hold up, I've got stuff that'll help," Palleday said, and flew out of the room. Fresko made a pained, wheezing noise as he bent over Mix, then muttered what sounded like a string of curses, scolding his friend for dying.

"I'm so sorry," Pax said quietly.

"She dead?" Fresko asked, looking up. Pax held up her closed hand, Lightgate's legs hanging out of it. Shit, she didn't want to look at what she'd done. She placed Lightgate down a respectable distance from the others.

"I didn't mean to," Pax said.

"You should've," Fresko replied angrily. His voice was choked with emotion: maybe the agony of his wound, maybe grief. He tried to stand, but his legs wouldn't carry him and he slumped back down. "Fucking . . . coming to our town . . ."

"We needed her," Pax said. Would it still work? Would a dead Fae lure the creatures of the Sunken City, the same as a live one?

"Needed her like cancer," Fresko spat, but with his words came a splatter of blood, and he slipped onto his back, legs twitching. He tried to continue in broken syllables, fading.

"Fresko!" Pax bent over him, raising her free hand. To do what? Poke him?

Palleday landed next to him, an armful of bandages and plastic-wrapped supplies, and muttered in irritation as he went to work, trying to tie the wound. "Don't be a baby, come on now. What's a gunshot, what's it to you?"

Fresko answered with some wicked whispered curse.

"I'm so sorry," Pax repeated. "I should've – or shouldn't have –"

"You did fine," Palleday huffed without looking up. "Don't flatter yourself thinking this was all over you." His voice got lower, masked in fast breaths as he worked to keep Fresko alive. "If there's anything can be done, I'll do it. You want to go. Make this worth it."

"Uh . . ." Pax looked at Lightgate's body. Not wanting to touch it again. "I don't know that I can. This was – I mean – I wanted her *alive*."

Palleday paused to look up. "Well, the FTC should give you a bloody medal for finishing her, no fooling."

That was true. It might buy some favour, at last. And Letty – she needed help. How long had it been since that desperate phone call? Hell, hell. The Fae had the Dispenser, they had her friend, they had *poisons* hanging over the city, and what did Pax have? A dead criminal. "Can you get a message to them? The FTC leadership?"

"What?" The old Fae scowled. "You're serious? I didn't mean –"

"Please."

"Craziest darned human I ever encountered." He shook his head, then took his phone out. "Maybe Edwing's people still –" He froze, something on his phone chilling him.

"What is it?"

"Not good. Not good at all." He turned the phone towards her, as if there were any way she could make it out. He said, simply, "It's Letty."

10

Only after going through the arsenal thoroughly was Casaria truly satisfied that they stood a chance. His input clearly was needed. The revised plans that Support were feeding them, with choke points for fast-moving, dangerous creatures, suggested this was going to be messy. A battle bound for death or glory. And half the men hadn't handled MEE energy guns before. A rough guy out of London, Agent Marks, even commented, "It's usually *people* we need to stop." Obrington's hires appeared up for a fight, at least, but that wasn't enough. Good thing they had Casaria to instruct them.

No sign of Pax to see his results, but she'd be here. And Ward had offered more than a few encouraging looks. When she approached at last, a little shy, Casaria could see she wanted to make up. She said, "You're ready?"

"As we can be," Casaria said. "These guys are green, but they'll do."

Ward glanced across at the other agents nearby, ugly guys with scars and cold eyes. She looked unsure, so Casaria offered an encouraging smile.

"Can I have a word alone?" She indicated a side door. Casaria jumped up, quicker than he intended, and slowed himself down. Ward took him to the new medical bay. A brick chamber with a cot and some supplies, far from sanitary. Ward started, "We've had our differences, Cano, and you know my doubts well enough. This past week in particular. But I want to say we value you here. A lot. You're one of the most effective field agents we have in Ordshaw."

Casaria found he couldn't look at her, fearing he might smile. Didn't want to make it more awkward, knowing this must be difficult. He mumbled nonsense she'd hear as thanks, probably.

"You know our plan is to lure the *praelucente* to a trap. To strike it once we're sure it's all there. If there's . . . you know."

"The screens," Casaria said. "I know."

"Then you'll know someone has to – well – spring the trap. It's not a decision I take lightly."

It took him a moment to appreciate her point, and even then it was only because she was staring at him so earnestly. So worried. He frowned. Was she letting him down? Saying *she* would fire the killing blow? Or one of these vicious newcomers? He said, "Moving up in the ranks doesn't mean you're the best for everything, Sammy. This is mine to do, it's what I'm *good* at."

Ward was motionless, taken by surprise. He pushed the advantage.

"Obviously," he sneered, "it's *your* decision. But it'd be a big mistake to let anyone else do it. Most of all you."

"That wasn't my –" Ward started, but whatever feeble excuse she was going to make, Obrington cut it off with a shouted command.

"In here, Ward! Where the bloody hell is she?"

She gave Casaria a look, not wanting to leave this unfinished, but raced out into the office. He followed as Obrington said, "Kuranes is stirring trouble again."

Everyone was listening. The Bartons were up, Darren ready to hit something, Holly rigid with concern. Rufaizu bounced nervously on his feet.

"Where is she? What happened?" Ward demanded.

"Got an alert," Obrington answered, "saying she's taking herself right to the FTC. No word from her. Sound like our plan to you?"

"She'll have her reasons!" Ward protested, taking out her own phone. She cursed, no doubt missed a call on this. "I need to talk to her."

"Think we haven't tried? And I'm *still* not getting through to the FTC."

Casaria was already halfway across the office, nearing the exit.

"Where the hell are you going?" Obrington demanded.

"Where do you think?" Casaria replied hotly, and saw the warning on Ward's face. After he'd finally started making a good impression. He collected himself and tried again. "Permission to bring her back, sir. Before she gets herself killed."

"Denied," Obrington said. "She's practically there already, and *your* place is here." He looked to Ward. "You're aware of the responsibility resting on your shoulders, Casaria?"

Casaria met Ward's eyes instead of his. Her face was crestfallen. What? She hadn't intended to pull the trigger on the *praelucente* herself. The woman was reluctant to ask him to do it. She didn't think he was up to it? Or . . . she thought it was too dangerous? She did care, she –

"Sir, there's something else," a plump analyst called from across the room, face in a computer. The man started to panic. "Uh. Sir! I'm getting alerts –"

Amid the office's flurry of concerned movement, Casaria himself was at the analyst's computer in a flash, at Ward's side. Shoulder brushing her shoulder.

"The creatures are moving." The analyst pointed at a map. "Spreading out – going in – this isn't good – that's a glogockle moving into Westlane Station –"

"Bleeding hell," Obrington said. "Something's tipped them off. We need to get down there *now*."

"They're not just scrambling," Casaria observed, eyes wide at what he was seeing. "That one's leaving the Sunken City."

The Trial Cages hung from a crane arm that protruded from one of the FTC's taller central towers, over a wide gap between buildings, fifteen storeys high or more. Six square lattices of rusty metal, each dangling from a chain with nothing but a drop beneath them. Letty, escorted by three Stabilisers, sent frequent looks to Flynt to draw strength from his quiet resolve. The bastards had taken her pistol and knife, and another soldier approached from the other direction with a couple of steel wing clips: pin two wings together so a Fae can't fly. But all they had to do was remove Letty's Clear Glider.

A great swathe of the population followed them between the buildings, a lot of bustle between them, dozens of soldiers brandishing guns one way and another, some shouting for justice against Letty, others that she should be set free – no one completely understanding what was going on.

Shoved into a cage, Flynt shouted, "It wasn't us, dammit! They're lying –"

"Hang fast, Flynt," Letty called out. A Stabiliser pushed her towards her own cage, and she spun to him but held off at the sight of a crackling baton.

"Your wing." Hearlon pointed at the hump on Letty's back. "Get in, toss it out."

"They'll stand trial, under all our watch!" Valoria boomed from high up, with a smattering of councilmen around her. Smark was there, flanked by a soldier. "Until we have confirmation that the septjad is secure – and of our men's safety!"

Glaring at Hearlon, Letty drifted back into the cage. She landed on the bars and growled, "I'm gonna tear your ribs out, you little bitch."

"Speak up, Letty," Valoria said. "Your trial's begun – let everyone hear your threats."

"Spin on it," Letty spat back.

The governor regarded her with a triumphant smile, twisting towards the onlookers. Over her shoulder, the edge of the big screen was just visible between the buildings. The anchor's voice drifted over with snippets about the disappearance of the Stabiliser elite, and fears that Letty and "her people" had plotted a citywide uprising.

"Is this not proof?" Valoria demanded, caught up in her own raving. "The threat of the exiles! The inability to hold civilised negotiations, with them *hijacking* our weapons! But the criminal Letty is caged! Her plot foiled!"

"You brought the septjad here, you delusional –" Letty shouted.

There was a crack of lightning as a Stabiliser hit his electric baton against the cage. The bars lit up with bright sparks and Letty was jolted into the air before landing, juddering all over, barely able to swear.

"Terrorist scum!" the soldier shouted, to a volley of agreement.

"Confess, Letty," Valoria said. "You invaded the Council at this sensitive time. You commanded your exile friends to assault our finest soldiers. You intended only to –"

"Look!" someone gasped.

People were turning away. Something was happening. Letty pushed herself up, regaining her breath. Her guards turned away, following the general sway. Up towards the big screen. It had changed from the news channel again, to a shot outside the warehouse. Newbry must have regained the network. An image of a desolate street, an empty landscape of ruin. A sole figure walked down the middle.

"The fuck . . ."

A human at the perimeter. A human getting closer.

Not just any human.

The camera angle changed, closer.

"Pax . . ."

Letty gave Flynt a look; from his angle he probably couldn't see the screen, but his face was hopeful. Letty wasn't so sure. Pax had to be out of her mind, coming here.

Valoria regained her composure quicker than anyone. "Part of her plan, no doubt – but the human does not know we have thwarted Letty's coup. Activate the defences –"

"She's on our side!" Letty roared. "Would any human risk coming otherwise?"

A ripple of questions ran through the crowd, many pointing to the screen – text rolled across the bottom, like with the news stories. Impossible to see from here. Valoria began another order, but Smark cut her off. "We need to see what she wants."

"She's one human," Deidre agreed, "who must understand the danger of coming here. We should hear her out."

"Should we?" Valoria rumbled. "Are we not all aware of the threat that giving humans the *slightest* opportunity offers? Need I –"

"What's she holding?" the councillor in a toupee asked. Watching the footage rather than listening. "What's that *say*?"

"'Kuranes requests an audience'," someone closer to the screen read. "Via Palleday. The architect?"

"Palleday –" Valoria started derisively, but the cameras picked out the jar in Pax's hands. Half-finished questions swept through the crowd.

"Is that –"

"How did she –"

"Why would –"

"Are we to consider," Valoria started, unevenly, "that a human who could capture a Fae is someone to *listen* to? She may be carrying a weapon – a –"

"A peace offering?" Letty snapped. "You can fucking *see* what she's carrying. Proof of what I've been saying."

"She's close to the defences," a Stabiliser warned.

Before Val could say another word, Mullon shouted, "Deactivate them, for heaven's sake, she's caught *Lightgate*!"

11

In the orange light of dusk, Pax was walking down an avenue of derelict warehouses, towards the one she believed to contain the Fae Transitional City, when she finally answered a call. She'd ignored half a dozen from Ward, Casaria, and another number she assumed to be the MEE, on Letty's warning that the FTC were watching. If she wanted to get close, she needed to assure the fairies she wasn't an enemy. She ignored calls from Holly too, for good measure. But now that she saw the building, an imposing brick structure with black-iron-framed windows, she baulked at doing this alone. It was a call from Holly she picked up, but Ward spoke.

"Thank God, Pax – stop, please stop. What are you doing?"

"Helping a friend," Pax said. "Seeing as I've screwed everyone else." Ahead, the huge metal doors looked rusted shut, not opened in decades, and the street in front had the dusty, debris-littered sweep of a post-apocalyptic plain.

"The Sunken City's stirring," Ward said. "The creatures, they're breaking their patterns, moving away from the centre – with our sensor resets, we can see exactly where they're moving – something spooked them and you *shouldn't* be there."

"I can't help that, can I?" Pax said, not wanting to hear more. "But I can do something here."

"You'll get hurt – there are traps – no one's gone that close to the Fae in years!"

Pax tried to breathe calmly. One step at a time. "They know I'm coming."

Another step, and nothing exploded or harpooned her.

"Pax, we're moving into the tunnels – this is happening – did you find Lightgate?"

"Yeah," Pax said. "She's dead."

A brief pause from Ward. "Do you have a body? Bring it here – we've got our own negotiations going on with the Fae. They could kill you and we need you *here*."

"Yeah." Another step, and it looked safe to continue. They probably wanted her to walk right on in. It'd be neater to kill her indoors. "They must've seen me by now." She held the jar aloft, turning it from side to side, trying not to look at the bloody corpse inside.

"The first agents are already going in," Ward continued urgently. "You don't understand, the creatures might *surface*."

Pax stopped. That was bad. Their fears coming true, of what the screens might be capable of under threat. But why now? She frowned, studying her feelings. There was something. Far away, subtle, but movement, nonetheless. The screens sending signals. Were they still in the Ministry offices? Reading the computers?

Aware of their plans? But they'd had half the day, why now . . .

"Fuck – they know I'm here," she whispered. They had felt her. The same way she felt them. If they didn't know exactly where she was, they knew she'd had a spike of her own energy, she'd tried Fae dust – they knew she was interacting with the Fae. Quickly, she told Ward, "I have to be here. It's *why* they're panicking."

Ward was quiet, not liking it.

"They're scared, Sam," Pax told her. "That's a good thing."

"But . . ."

"I'll call you when I'm done."

With a quiet voice, Ward conceded, "If you – *when* you get out, I'll have a car waiting."

"Thanks." Pax forced a smile and hung up. Never mind that she had Obrington's car back there, the promise of company was nice. She looked up at the door, tall and wide enough for two lorries to roll through. She expected Fae guards, warning shots, anything. There was no movement. In both directions, the road stretched away along the front of the warehouse, a fortress of a building, utterly abandoned. All this real estate, left to ruin . . .

Pax knocked on the metal door. The rap twanged up and down the adjoining streets. She hit it again, the sound strangely satisfying, then called out, "Hello? Anyone home?"

She paced to the side of the doors. The nearest windows, though huge, were a good ten feet off the ground, no way she was climbing in. "You know who I am? I've got a peace offering."

With no response, she continued searching for another way in. After the buildup, from what Letty had told her of the FTC, and what the MEE reported, she'd expected a minefield, snipers, barbed wire, *something*. This was just a dead building at the end of a dead street.

"Human," a small voice called out. She looked up the wall to a gap in the window. On the ledge stood a fairy in black armour, like the ones she'd run into at the lido. He had a rifle aimed down at her, and spoke with deep uncertainty. "You . . . stop."

Pax showed her free palm, indicating she was no threat.

The guard shifted position uncomfortably, clearly uneasy under the gaze of a human; he must've drawn a short straw for this.

"You know who Lightgate is?" Pax asked.

He made an unhappy noise, then said, "State your business."

"I'm selling jam, what do you think?" Pax said. "I want to talk to someone in charge."

The guard ducked back, conferring quietly. He pushed his cohort, neither of them wanting to get any closer. When his companion didn't budge, he reluctantly flew off the ledge. "I'm to search you. Do not move."

"You're . . ." Pax started, but gave in. Better let it play out.

The guard swept down to her, and stalled about two feet away. He hovered, looking her up and down fearfully. He muttered again, "Do not move." Then came closer. Pax followed him with her eyes as he flew around her. Up, down, between her legs, over her head. Finally, he hovered back in front of her face, an uncertain expression on his own. They shared a mutual understanding that it was an ineffective search.

He looked back to the window, swallowed his uncertainty and called out, "I can't see any weapons." No one replied. He gestured to the side with his gun. "Down there."

Pax looked along the wall, to a shaded area. There was a hatch, a drop-box for deliveries. She walked up to it, a two-foot square panel. The guard was gone. She pulled on the handle and the hatch opened with a heavy, rusty creak, pivoting down. The chute inside was barely wider than her, and dropped into darkness.

"Fucking seriously?" Pax muttered to herself.

She tucked the jar into her coat pocket and climbed into the hatch. It took a bit of manoeuvring, the panel rocking back as she tried to get her second leg in, and once in position she slipped on the chute, down, quickly, into the shadow. Pax yelped as she rolled out, and the jar flew free of her pocket, clunking on the floor. She grimaced, expecting a crack, for Lightgate to burst free, alive again. But it merely rolled clear of her, the fairy inside flopping about. Pax snatched it up and scrambled to her feet. She dusted off her knees and stood up straight, looking across the expanse of the warehouse. The chute had deposited her at the edge of a huge open space, big as a football field, enclosed by four bare brick walls, high metal beams crossing a dark ceiling broken up by grimy skylights.

At the centre, lit with a cascade of tiny electric lights, with a good twenty metres of space around it, sat the Fae Transitional City. The towers stood taller than Palleday's sculptures, glowing blocks of metal and glass, a modern city in miniature, with neon-lit bar signs, iron balconies, torn adverts plastering walls, pipes in complex networks snaking one way and another. There were dozens of towers, in all sizes and colours, stretching as far back as the city was wide.

And rising from the gaps between the buildings were the residents, a thousand fluttering winged people, all looking Pax's way. She stared in awe and slowly raised her free hand. With a small, insufficient wave, she said, "I'm Pax. Please don't kill me."

12

With no one coming closer, Pax took a step forward herself. The entire population of Ordshaw's fairy community were hanging there, countless eyes analysing her. They could speak loud enough to be heard by humans; there must be a hell of a din in here when they all got talking. Wrong time to wonder. She took another step forward and handfuls of Fae moved for the edges of buildings, ducking behind cover. The more stubborn ones, the vast majority, held their ground – their *air*. Pax spoke in what she hoped was a calm voice, "You see who I've got here? I know you know her."

"We know *you*," an aggressive male snapped, and a dozen or more agreed.

"I . . ." Pax stopped. It was an audience like she'd never imagined, like being on a stage at a great concert hall. And they hated her, didn't they? What was she thinking? Her skin tingled with the attention. What could she say that wouldn't get her killed?

The stirrings of a commotion drew her focus to one of the taller towers at the perimeter, where hovering fairies parted with noises of disapproval. A bulky fairy emerged from the crowd, her fine regal clothing out of time and place. She flew weightlessly, despite her round, bee-like proportions, and behind her came a trail of black-armoured soldier fairies, armed with batons and rifles. The governor and her retinue. She commanded, boldly, "Into the light, woman."

Pax did as she was told, approaching the outer glow of the Fae city. Drawing nearer, she saw the floating fairies were as varied as a cross-section of society anywhere in the world, from labouring overalls to suits, through to casual jeans and shirts, flat-caps – one in what looked like medical scrubs. Fat and slim, round and jagged, long flowing hair, unfortunate bald spots, moustaches, everything. Their skin colours, too, were as cosmopolitan as Ordshaw's more ethnic neighbourhoods: the darkest-skinned Fae were almost black, the lightest definitely anaemic. The only uniform thing was their ages: almost all young adults; no children, very few over forty or so. Did they not age?

And this vast crowd showed equal wonder for Pax. Questioning, curious looks, and fearful, disgusted stares. Of them all, their leader looked least impressed.

"Pax Kuranes," Valoria snorted. "Devourer of fairies. Murderer of men."

"Sixty-eighth best poker player in the world," Pax added for herself.

The responses were too quiet to hear, but were likely shocked remarks: *did you hear her speak?!* The memory of her first meeting with Lightgate came to mind, an unimpressed comment: *why is she talking about cards?* Cautiously, Pax held the jar a little higher. "I've brought Lightgate."

It chilled the crowd into silence, and Pax doubted her strategy. What if they didn't hate Lightgate as much as she'd been led to believe? Then she was just a human with a bloody Fae body in a jar. "Palleday messaged ahead. To let you know I was coming?"

That helped, murmurs of recognition for Palleday's name. But he hadn't done much to pave the way. Pax came another step closer, now barely two metres from the edge of the city, and the wall of fairies darted back an inch in fear, focused on the jar. It was Lightgate, more than her, that they were scared of.

"Stop," Valoria commanded. "Place the jar on the floor." To her guards, she added, "Keep her in your sights at all times."

"Got her," her closest bodyguard replied, for the purposes of the crowd. He had a rifle aimed at Pax's face. The handful of men around him aimed variously at her and at the jar in her hands.

"She's dead," Pax said, slowly crouching to put the jar down. She kept her hands on it, as though the body might yet break free and kill them all. "It was an accident, kind of. She tried to kill me. And everyone else." Pax stood back from the jar, carefully, as two soldiers swooped down to inspect it. "You know she was planning an uprising?"

A further flurry of concerned noises, but Valoria said, "And you kept her company."

"You call stopping a maniac keeping company?" Pax replied. The indignity of being addressed by an unreasonable woman trumped the anxiety of being watched. "More than *you* managed to do, wasn't it?"

Valoria replied curtly, "And we should be pleased, not concerned, to see one of our most notorious criminals dead at the hands of a human?"

"With Fae help," Pax said. "One of your own gave his life for it, another's clinging to his. And we trashed half a dozen of Palleday's best towers to trap her. I'm not some Fae-hunter extraordinaire, if that's what you're getting at."

Again, Palleday's name impressed a few people, a detail Valoria was quick to move on from. "Then what are you? You, aligned with Letty, a criminal no different to the one you have brought us."

"Yeah? Did Letty scourge any gritty plateaus?"

That impressed the crowd, too; another point for knowing something of their culture. Over their surprised comments, Valoria said, "Letty killed *humans* —"

"The ones Lightgate shot, you mean?" Pax lifted a foot to prod the jar, making the two nearby soldiers fly nervously back.

"And she's rallied exiles," Valoria went on, undeterred. "Disrupted our —"

"Again," Pax interrupted, "Lightgate's right here. Is there anything you're laying on Letty that wasn't *her* doing?"

Valoria went quiet. Despite her demeanour of intense distrust, the crowd was siding with Pax:

"Just like Letty said!"

"The Scourge *was* behind this!"

They were finally questioning the reality that their council had presented.

Pax rocked the jar under her shoe, demonstratively, and said, "She thought you should all be fighting. Against us, against each other. Letty tried to stop her before. I'm hoping, now, I actually *did* stop whatever army she's been mustering. I don't know where they are, but they'll disband without her, won't they?"

Valoria's closest guard leant in to confer with her. She flapped him away irritably, a *you think I don't know that!* dismissal.

Pax continued, "Edwing, God rest him – Lightgate killed him because he believed in peace. And obviously she didn't want you to trust me or Letty, hence how it all looks. But I just want to see Ordshaw safe. For all of us. Thanks to the Fae that talked to me, we've got some idea of the real source of all our problems."

"Whatever you bring," Valoria said, "Letty has shown her true colours today." For the crowd's sake, she added, "Forcing her way into the Council. Holding us at gunpoint."

Pax turned to the closest fairies, gathered around head height. A woman in a pantsuit, not dissimilar to a Ministry worker; a man in a checked shirt, with a beard. "You know all she wanted was to take back your home? She got desperate. Where is she?"

"Awaiting trial," checked shirt responded. "For . . . them things you said Lightgate did."

"For everything!" Valoria corrected. "For the –"

"Great, so I can help clear the air. Is she in your cages? Take me to her." Pax stood taller than she felt. With so many people watching, there were a lot of guns out there, but they needed to see her confidence. "If we co-operate, talk to one another, I know we can reach an understanding. Not just here, with my government, too." She gave Valoria a look, to make her point clear. "You want that, don't you?"

Valoria's face was a picture of malice.

"Would you rather bring Letty out here? I can wait."

"Once sealed," Valoria's gruff bodyguard answered, "the cages may not be opened until judgement is passed."

"That sounds dogmatic as shit," Pax told him.

"It is the way of our people," Valoria snarled. "You know nothing, and are –"

"Willing to learn," Pax said. "If you're finally willing to talk."

Valoria didn't respond at once, bubbling with resistance. But it was clear the crowd wanted answers. She said, "Very well. We will try these criminals together. To the cages."

Pax gave her a sweet smile. "You got one big enough for me?"

The fire alarm was screaming as Casaria leapt down the steps of Westlane Station, the arse end of the K&S Underground. Probably wouldn't have been anyone here anyway. But it had been cleared out, giving him a clear run at the monster lumbering in. Landon huffed along behind him, calling for Casaria to slow down. Fuck him. Casaria skidded around a corner and along the final tunnel, breaking out onto the platform.

There it was. The stocky humanoid beast, lines glowing between the panels of its carapace, pincer limb twitching over its shoulder. Right there on the platform, where on another day there might be twenty people waiting for a train into town. Its clawed feet crunched against the tile floor.

Casaria fired, catching its stomach and dropping the creature to a knee. It reared a horrific face towards him, glowing eyes screwing narrower in fury, and it coiled to charge. He fired again, one shot, between the eyes, flinging it back to the tiles.

Landon came panting to his side, pistol ready. As Casaria steadied himself, checking the rest of the platform and the shadows beyond, the overweight agent frowned at the body. "On the platform? If there'd been people –"

"Get on your bloody radio already," Casaria said. "Where's the next one?"

"Westlane's secure," the Support tech announced, to the relief of the office. "And Agents Vinton and Bolton have arrived at Lyle Park."

"Tell them to move faster," Obrington said, readjusting a gun holster. He was the last agent not already out in the field. Not including Sam. She had training, she should be down there. Reading her look, he told her, "You're staying put. Someone's got to co-ordinate this shitshow."

The readings were clear. Though still vaguely encircling a central point where the *praelucente* was, the creatures were spread across as much as a mile's radius now. It was questionable that their small group of Operations agents could contain it. Arming the civilians and support technicians would be futile and reckless, but with every passing minute their targets moved further apart. Casaria and Landon were under Ripton, another team outside Central, one more moving down from Ten Gardens; no one covering Nothicker or Farling, yet. The *praelucente* itself had reached the outskirts of New Thornton.

As Obrington prepared to join the fray, Sam helped him into something like a bulletproof vest, which likely defended against more than bullets. He gave her sharp instructions: "You've got charges set up in some of these tunnels; if it looks to be going south, blow them. And it might be barmy to send any of the rest of you down there, but better we swing bad punches than none at all."

He indicated the civilians as he said that, and stalked off towards their rear door. So it wasn't just her thinking it. Barton and Rufaizu were watching, one grimly ready and the other itching to join the fight. Holly, behind them, looked horrified. Sam hurried to them, to offer reassurances. Barton spoke first: "This is everything I expected from your Ministry. Heavy-handed goons fumbling over distractions, while the screens go to ground. The years they spent hidden, you think they haven't got out already?"

Sam gave him a stern look. She wasn't sure it was fair to call her agents heavy-handed, nor the monsters distractions. It would be hell for Ordshaw if just one of those creatures broke free, and so far they'd prevented that. She said, "We're doing all we can. And if they could disappear that easily, would they need a distraction?"

"It'll take days before you cull even part of the horde," Barton replied. "A good portion of them will have reproduced by then, you know? Assuming the screens don't generate more themselves. In that time –"

"In that time, Pax will come back," Sam said, firmly. "And we'll be ready." Except there was no one in the office not fully occupied. She fixed on Holly. "I hate to ask, but –"

"I'll go wherever I'm needed," Holly said, giving her husband a look that said yes, he would join her. Rufaizu sprang up, too, ready for action.

"I need someone at the FTC," Sam told them. "Not within their perimeter, but close enough that if Pax gets out, if she can get the Dispenser, then . . ." She hesitated, looking across the room to the table of guns. Half-empty now, and none of it proven to hurt the *praelucente*. "We're spread thin. We need all the help we can get."

"I'll take care of her," Barton said.

"We all will," Holly corrected.

13

Pax tried to focus on the positives, such as witnessing a marvel of a society that no other human had set eyes on, rather than the creeping sense of disquiet at being the centre of attention for an entire city. *Bloody Gulliver, I am.* An explorer, admiring a miniature apartment, chrome-framed windows, modern furniture a fraction of the expected size. Tiny steps on metal fire escapes. Tiny posters advertising . . . toothpaste? Faces of Fae celebrities? And delicate little pipes and lights; even the amenities a marvel. The thousands of faces following her weren't creepy, they were . . . well, not cute, but *interesting*. Surely?

The guards led her around the side of the city, instructing her to follow slowly, no sudden movements, and she trod carefully, the Fae population floating with the single-mindedness of a school of fish. She rounded the corner of the city to see it stretching back with the variety of any metropolis. A glowing vertical sign read *CINEXPRESS*. A tiny cinema? An architectural feat even stranger stood to the left, separate from the main city and enclosed in fencing so fine it looked like a net. Four buildings the size and shape of upturned bathtubs. No prizes for guessing that was where the Fae magic happened. Pax's fingers tingled as she focused on the buildings. Was there a blue screen in there? That would be a satisfying reveal – toss back a building and announce, "Ah ha!"

She edged along the city, glancing at the vats, trying to unravel exactly what she felt. A disquiet, blurring her senses the same way the dust itself had.

"Pax!" Letty's voice drew her attention away, and she almost hit one of the Fae towers as she turned. Shouts of anger met her, a dozen Fae flying near her head, guns out. Pax threw up her hands, taking a step back, and got more shouts. Her shoe had almost hit the vats' fencing. Letty yelled from between the buildings, deep in the maze of towers, "You great bloody loon! Out of your mind coming here!"

Despite the insults, Letty sounded absolutely delighted, and as Pax peered through the crowd to see her suspended cage, her heart lifted too. "I couldn't leave you hanging."

"You've got answers, right?" Letty shouted. "You gaggle of pricks, she's gonna change everything!"

As the Fae between them parted, creating a channel, Pax carefully repositioned herself, getting as close as she could without touching anything. More wary now than ever that *everyone* was watching her. "Thanks, Letty, no pressure . . ."

"So what is it? The Ministry figured out these monsters? Agreed to clear out the tunnels and let us down there? How are we going to fuck that Blue Angel?"

The crowd was quiet, with confused exchanges being shushed by those eager to know how, indeed, Pax was going to change their world. Valoria settled on a rooftop close to Pax's head, with her entourage of suited Fae and soldiers. Beyond them, back over the centre of the city, a pair of Fae carried Lightgate's jar. They placed it on another rooftop, near the cages, and quickly retreated.

"I had a solution," Pax said, deliberating, "but it's a little complicated." Suddenly, the suggestion that she use one of these people as bait for a monster seemed dangerous. "It involved keeping Lightgate alive, so . . ."

"We're not here to brainstorm your plans," Valoria said. "You are being given the opportunity to defend your actions. Shall we start with the most recent? Why did you kill Edwing, one of our dearest and *kindest* statesmen?"

Pax gave her a vicious look. "Why *would* I? Edwing and I were meeting to discuss how *you* wouldn't let anyone talk with us humans."

Valoria scoffed, "You plot to destroy us –"

"Never," Pax said. "The Ministry didn't, either. There was corruption within their management. The blue screens of the Sunken City, the ones that created the monsters, were responsible. Now we know, the Ministry want to settle things peacefully. But again, *you* won't talk to them."

"Because the word of a human –"

"They could've killed you, in return for the attack on Greek Street," Pax said. "You took their weapons, you know what they could've done. But they withdrew. *I* persuaded them we might need each other. Only to have you insist we have nothing more to do with each other."

Silence followed. The majority of eyes were on Valoria instead of Pax.

"All this is," Valoria said, "is confirmation of how unstable and unreliable the Ministry is. We are right to demand boundaries."

"Boundaries, sure." Pax glanced at the dust vats, concentrating on the feeling for what was in there. She wondered what she'd see, through the eyes of glo, or dust, looking into this city. Lightgate had lit up like a star; would this whole city sparkle? Would the blue of a screen show somewhere? No. She would sense that presence, for sure. That wasn't it; this governor's resistance wasn't as simple as following the screen's lies. And it was something more than vying to cement her power here. Pax thought out loud, "Obviously staying hidden from humans, and away from the Sunken City is important to you."

"Quite," Valoria agreed, like she'd scored a point.

"But it's not like we couldn't find ways to agree on it. You're avoiding us for another reason. Are you that scared of the minotaur's horde? Knowing how they go after your energy? Because I get the idea they're scared of *you.*"

"Trivial questions we discarded long ago," Valoria sneered. "Our society is established, here, and that is not in question. You stand accused of murder, of the highest –"

"No – stop," Pax cut in. "I brought you Lightgate. I've told you she's responsible. If you want everyone to believe I'm your enemy then you *have* to justify why. I want the screens gone – you have the means to defeat them. You want me to be your enemy – because if you avoid humans, you avoid the Sunken City – why?"

Valoria's fuming silence confirmed Pax was on the right track. Some of the governor's suits had drifted a little away from her. The countless onlookers were raptly watching, not sure what to believe. The governor said, "We do not have to justify ourselves to *humans*."

"Okay, but can you justify yourself to them?" Pax jerked a thumb to their audience. "Do they all know your real reasons for avoiding this discussion? Your dust manufacture is done behind closed doors; how many people actually understand your connection to the Sunken City?"

"Our dust is –"

"I know," Pax said. "Specialised, unique, your own recipe. Also closely connected, somehow, to whatever the minotaur – excuse me, what you call the *berserker* – feeds off. The energy that its masters manipulate."

"Nonsense!" Valoria erupted. "More diversions, while our septjad is unaccounted for! The monster before us is –"

"Not sure exactly what you're talking about," Pax said. "You lost control of your weapon? If that was Lightgate's ploy, then whoever she forced into helping her is unlikely to keep going with her dead. And I heard you were trying to suppress Fae across the city, so dealing with rebel Fae sure sounds like a mess *you* created."

Valoria was speechless, at last, whatever paranoia she'd been sowing undermined.

Pax continued, "It's you that's looking for a diversion. Soon as I talk about your dust?" She twisted, looming over the vats, arms out to her side, trying to take in that feeling. It wasn't much, but she got it. A little piece of the Sunken City in there, for sure. Whatever energy pervaded those tunnels was here, too. Hadn't Palleday said Valoria's family, the Magnus clan, had adapted outside the tunnels?

"That's it!" Pax turned back to the governor, eyes wide.

"Hearlon," Valoria said, "this has gone far enough. Prepare the System of True –"

"The Fae thrived in the Sunken City," Pax said, quickly. "Or at least they could have. It wasn't just the freedom of Ordshaw it offered, it was something in the tunnels, too. You farmed weird crap down there, and the blue screens were drawn to some similar opportunity. They ousted you – but if you returned, if we got rid of them, you'd have options again. You wouldn't need . . . this." She pointed at the vats.

The Fae uneasily shifted on roofs and tilted in the air. Glaring wickedly, Valoria said, "Enough!"

Pax moved closer, ignoring the fairies scattering around her. "Letty's crime wasn't talking to me or wanting a space you could all call your own – it was raising the question of the Sunken City at all. Down there, you couldn't limit dust, could you?"

"What –"

"Whatever's in there" – Pax raised her voice, pointing at the vats – "is the reason you don't want to work with humans. You're not scared of conflict; you just don't want to reclaim the Sunken City because that would expose what you use to control everyone. What is it? The means for Fae to grow their *own* dust?"

"Utterly ludicrous!" Valoria gave a bellowing laugh to prove it. "In the generations that the Fae lived underground, you think such a truth would've eluded everyone?"

"Yeah," Pax said. "Between the bickering, and the running, and the fighting for survival. And a coup that cost the lives of those that held onto that truth. You built this city on the blood of people that wanted something better."

Pax rested a hand against the wall of a Fae tower as she drew as close to eye-level with Valoria as the city would let her. The governor stared defiantly back, big torso heaving with angry breaths. She said, "Each word you say draws you closer to sealing your fate, human. Tie your own noose."

"If it's not true then what have you got to lose? Give me the Dispenser and we'll clear out the Sunken City. You can go back –"

"We're not giving butchering humans the slightest advantage! *Enough* – execution is too kind –"

"Stop," a bald, rotund Fae with many earrings said from close to her. He regarded the governor with suspicious eyes, and he wasn't the only one. Many of her companions were distancing themselves, even some of the soldiers. The civilians watched uneasily. "These claims require due consideration."

"This human wishes to divide us," Valoria hissed. "Her words are poison – it's time our Stabilisers did their job." She raised her voice to the barrelling tone of one passing judgement. "Pax Kuranes, the human, stands accused of devouring a Fae. Further, of conspiring with the Ministry to harm our people. Of murdering Councilman Edwing, and plotting our destruction by scheming to subvert the septjad!" Many shouts of disagreement rose in protest, but Valoria continued, "Further, she admits to the murder of Lightgate!"

As the voices of discontent rose, with Letty joining in, Valoria built towards a final instruction with her soldiers readying guns. It didn't matter if all these Fae saw reason; even with a clear majority, it'd only take one of Valoria's zealous supporters to shoot Pax. Her eyes flitted back to the vats. If they could feel what she felt, if they understood –

"Escort her to the wall!" Valoria commanded. "She will be –"

Pax took a step back and drove her shoe through the roof of the closest vat. The fencing tangled around her leg, scratching where it caught above her ankle, but offered little resistance. The roof and curved walls cracked like an egg, with an eruption of dust and debris. Cringing, hoping there was no one inside, Pax drew her foot slowly back out and wafted the air clear to reveal one of the vats. It was open-topped, the substance inside slowly revolving. Glowing, faintly, a murky green-blue. A miniature conveyor channelled something mossy into the mix.

A moment of confused shock passed before Valoria screamed, "Shoot her!"

"No! She'd crush the rest of it!" another Fae roared, spreading rapid dissent as Pax crouched and grabbed moss from the wrecked building. A figure darted between shards of the crumbling building – there *was* someone in there – apparently unharmed. Half a dozen soldiers fluttered into Pax's face, guns up, as she stood, amid the yelled arguments of the Fae councillors calling for her to be shot or spared – a contest joined by the crowd. Civilians were drawing guns, and Letty yelled at Pax to get down. One soldier shouted above the others, "Hold your fire! I'm ordering you, hold your fire!"

"There's heaps of this shit in the Sunken City!" Pax said, her raised voice shaking the towers and causing Fae to stumble. She held the glowing moss up, and as the Fae grew still she realised it was affecting her. Her vision was changing, energy pulsing into her through contact alone. The Fae glowed. She put it on the roof in front of the Fae Council, taking deep breaths and blinking away the effects. Trying to ignore that sensation, she said to Valoria, "This grows down there, doesn't it? You already know that?"

The room was deathly quiet.

Valoria glared at the moss, exposed for everyone to see. The pale horror on her face confirmed Pax's hunch. Her councillors and soldiers alike looked from the moss to her, no one quite sure what to do. Valoria's bodyguard, a pistol held firmly in two hands, took a defensive step in front of her. Across the city, Letty rattled her hanging cage and shouted, "I fucking love you, Pax! Give her a fucking medal!"

Pax fought the urge to smile, or even look Letty's way, standing firm, serious, waiting for the reality to settle in. It was on Valoria now, and the governor knew it. The large Fae didn't look up from the moss. She swallowed and said, "Everything I have done has been to protect our community. What would we have, if our systems broke down. What chaos, if everyone had access –"

"Just say it's not true," a thin, sallow-faced councilman demanded. "The Fae fungus was cultured in France. There are no means to harvest it here, in Ordshaw."

From the way Valoria winced, it was clear his disapproval carried a particular sting, and even clearer that she wasn't going to deny it. "I kept peace –"

"When it suited you!" Letty shouted. "Aiding the monsters you should've resisted!"

Valoria went quiet again. Other Fae were finding their voices, muttering disbelief.

"It's a lot," Pax said, trying to speak softly. "It's complicated, but – I have a way forward. Your Dispenser was designed to destroy what you call the berserker. I want to use it –"

"It won't work," Valoria said, sounding more defeated by the second. "It'll come back. The Sunken City was never worth –"

"Upsetting your seat of power for?" Pax cut in. "Yeah, I got that. Only, I think *I* can stop it coming back. The berserker's not the boss down there, it's the blue screens. And if I can draw them together, your weapon might wipe them out. Then we can talk about recognising your people, officially. Restoring your home."

"We have our place . . ." Valoria said.

"This is too much to process now," the sallow-faced Fae decided. "You will leave –"

"We're all out of time," Pax said. "The Sunken City is unstable. It needs to be now. Seriously. What have you got to lose?"

"Our technology –"

"For heaven's sake, get on with it," the bald councillor commanded. "Let the humans fight the fight we should've fought ourselves." To Pax, he said, "You truly have the means to stop these monsters?"

Pax paused. Of course, there was still *that* problem. The maniac Fae that deserved the fate of the horde bearing down on her was dead. She needed Fae energy to drive the entire horde to one target. An invalid Fae, not long for this world? A criminal up for capital punishment? There might be brave-hearted volunteers, even. Letty, shaking her cage, ready for release. She would do it, for sure. If she only knew.

But how could Pax ask that of any of them?

And then she understood, looking at that lightly glowing moss on the roof, that there was another option. She wouldn't just draw the creatures together, she could also confirm they were there to strike. Could confirm whether or not the weapon worked. Pax had felt it, time and again, the pulse of the screens. The glow in her veins. The feeling when her mind buzzed on dust, the tingle when she picked up that moss.

She gave the suited Fae a weak smile. "I *will* have the means. With your help."

14

Outside the Fae warehouse, Pax rolled the Dispenser over in her hands. About the size of a big water bottle, all glass and brass, and as esoteric now as it had been when she'd first set eyes on it in Rufaizu's slum apartment. She said, "Hard to believe I had this in my cupboard all that time. For all the trouble it's caused."

"Probably the least hard thing to believe about you," Letty replied, sitting on her shoulder, eyeing the road ahead as they left the FTC behind. There was a car waiting, lights on, people inside. "I cannot believe you just did that."

"You and me both," Pax said.

"Put Val in her place. Stomped on a building. I thought you might go full Godzilla for a minute. Not that you didn't do enough damage. Unbalanced our whole fucking society."

Pax smiled uncomfortably.

The car doors opened, revealing the familiar bulk of Darren Barton and Holly's angular shoulders. Waving her over, Holly called out, "Thank heavens, you're alive!"

"I got it!" Pax held up the Dispenser.

"Then you might want to hurry up!" Barton said.

Taking a breath, Pax picked up her pace, trotting towards them. Another Fae flew down, announcing, "Wait!"

She recognised the voice: Edwing's protector. He kept a careful distance as he hovered near Pax, holding a plastic canister about the size of a D battery. Letty stood, saying, "Pax, meet Flynt. The only person in that whole city I could count on. Had my back. And I broke his nose."

"It's not broke," Flynt replied with a nervous smile. "And don't forget Newbry." He flew closer, holding out the canister. "This should be enough, right?"

As the Bartons approached, and Flynt backed off, Pax gently took the canister and peeled back the lid. Full of white powder.

"If that's all for you," Letty said, "it could be lethal, Pax."

"Yeah," Pax said. It was a king's ransom in Fae dust, and reportedly higher grade than what she'd got from Palleday. Hopefully that'd make it more effective, rather than more likely to kill her. She explained for the Bartons, "If my theory's right, this'll draw those creatures. And help me stop them."

"Draw them where?" Barton frowned. "To *you*?"

"I'll explain on the way," Pax said. She looked over to Flynt. "You coming?" The tiny man looked moderately terrified, so she held out a hand to him. "I can give you a ride."

"We can't go down there . . ." Flynt said.

"Not all the danger's below ground," Letty said. "You want some adventure, don't you?" Flynt took a bracing breath and nodded. He didn't go near Pax's hand, but flew closer.

Moving towards the car, Barton said, "They're already securing a position. One of those dark spots. They'll have at least a few tunnels cordoned off by the time we catch up. You really think it'll work?"

"Hey," Pax said, "I've just overturned the Fae seat of power. I did the same for the Ministry, so I'm quietly confident I can achieve a hat-trick?"

It was a five-minute drive to the closest Sunken City entrance. Holly kept sneaking glances at Pax and the fairies in the mirrors as she drove, trying and failing to ask questions, too many to know where to begin. Rufaizu, in the back, with Barton, was less restrained. "Great to see you again, Letty, little Letty, told you we'd do big things!"

"Less of the little, you bloody idiot," Letty said, not without affection.

"I'll take the weapon," Barton said, developing his own strategy. "I might not be able to run fast, but I take a lot of knocking over. Once you've got that dust in position, or however you want to do it, I'll be ready."

"I've got a better idea," Pax said. "How about you guard the least likely tunnel for the monsters to use? I'm not going through all this only to have Holly bite my head off for letting you die."

"It was my fight long before it was yours. Before it was any of yours." Barton leant forward in his seat, a hand on Holly's shoulder. "You know I'm the best person for this. Our whole city's at risk. For Grace, I can do it."

Conflicted, Holly refused to answer.

"It's not up for discussion." Pax saved her the trouble. "Near as I'm aware, you never developed a sixth sense for what these things are, or tested how fucked up you get on Fae dust, or had the universe basically shouting at you from all directions that this is, like, your shitty fate."

It was said partly in jest but definitely not taken that way. They all realised, as one, the gravity of her own strategy. Letty glared from the dashboard and said, "You planning on facing this thing alone or something?"

"Doing what I have to," Pax said.

"I thought the Fae –" Barton started. She quickly interrupted.

"The energy that draws the creatures, it's connected to this dust, and it's something the screens sense in me. They want me dead, they've made that clear. I'm pretty sure when I'm down there, tanked up on this shit, they won't see me much different to the Fae. They won't be able to resist, whether they like it or not."

"You barely survived being touched by the minotaur the first time," Holly reminded her. "We didn't come this far to –"

"Yeah," Pax sighed. "Yeah, we did."

"What's this *pretty sure* bullshit?" Letty asked, quietly. "You're talking about pissing them off to the highest degree. You want bait, fuck it, I'm right here – anyone gets to screw them, it should be me."

Pax shook her head. "Like Holly said, I survived the minotaur before. And a human needs to set off this weapon. I can do both jobs."

"Pax, you're out of your mind if you think I'd let you do that alone," Letty told her.

"And you're out of your mind if –" Pax began, but the fairy raised an angry fist.

"We need to be sure to get all those things together. I'm not banking on you being *pretty sure* they'll come for you. They'll definitely come for me."

Pax was quiet. Exactly what she'd hoped to avoid. But she knew how stubborn Letty could be. She conceded, carefully, "Let me get in position, first. Then come down after me?"

There might still be a way, if she was quick with the dust. She could keep Letty out of this. The steely look on Letty's face said it would be difficult.

They pulled into a parking bay for a low-rise complex, near a row of garages. Obrington was waiting, jacket and shirt crumpled, slick hair out of place, flecks of dark liquid across his face. With the barest squint at the Fae on Pax's shoulder, he waved a big hand to invite them all over and opened the end garage. "Hope you've got something good for us, Kuranes. Called me away from an important meeting."

Humouring him with a weary smile, Pax held up the Dispenser. He nodded, satisfied, and stepped back to reveal a trapdoor inside the garage. They all entered and he pulled the door shut behind them. "We've got men converging on here from all directions. It's messy but we'll have you secure." He handed Pax a radio, opened the trapdoor onto a set of descending stairs, and asked, "Who's first?" When no one moved, he said, "Kidding, of course. Follow me. Not you lot." He waved a hand generally, unclear who he meant. He took a few steps down before turning back. "Come on, Kuranes. The rest of you watch this space while we handle the beasts below. Ward's on her way, with medics."

"I'm coming too," Barton said.

"And me –" Rufaizu chimed, but Holly caught his elbow, shaking her head.

Obrington looked to Pax, deferring to her the same way he did to Ward. Christ, Pax wanted them all to come, just to surround her and keep the rest of the world at bay. But it'd be madness. She said, "You've all already done enough – Darren –"

"I'm coming." As impossible as Letty. And no sign that Holly was going to stop him. Pax accepted it and Obrington gave them all a broad smile.

"Right you are," he said. He drew a second pistol from the back of his belt, chunky like a nail-gun, and offered it to Barton. "Take this. Little recoil and barely needs to be aimed in the right direction." Without further explanation, he continued into the tunnel.

Pax raised her eyebrows to Letty as a cue, expecting the fairy to insist on coming right away. But Letty jumped off Pax's shoulder and flew to land on Holly's instead. "Holler when you're ready."

Pax nodded. Sure. As if. Barton embraced Holly with a whisper of love, before they continued after Obrington.

"I should –" Rufaizu whispered, but again Holly held him back.

"You should live a full life," she told him, plainly.

He cheered them on instead. "Kill a few for me, Citizen!"

Back in the Sunken City, they entered the older variety of tunnels; wet brickwork, greening at the edges, dimly lit. Arched doorways branched off every hundred metres or so. Obrington led a winding route, constantly referring to his phone.

Their advance was interrupted by the patter of feet ahead, and the breathless arrival of an unfamiliar agent. Also splattered with blood, his tie almost undone. He saluted Obrington like a soldier, not out of habit but from being caught up in a situation he didn't fully understand. "We're clear to the black spot; Agent Vinton's up the east tunnel."

He rattled off a series of other names, agents coming as quick as they could. Casaria was a way off yet, with Landon, engaged with a tuckle. It might be five minutes or fifteen minutes before they got here. Not good enough, Obrington said; the longer they waited, the more chance a monster might break loose. Report given, the agent mumbled something encouraging to Pax then broke away to cover another passage. The trio moved forward to a hefty metal door. Obrington opened it, took a look in then stepped back.

"Bleeding weird, but it's all yours. Give me a minute to take up position myself."

Pax let him go, staring into the abyss of the empty chamber. This one was formed of four walls sloping towards each other, meeting in a sharp point, designed to house a toppled pyramid. Pax mouthed, "Why . . ."

But the why didn't matter. It was a refuge, that was all. Somewhere the monsters didn't go, making it as good a place as any for them to make a stand. If it could help her get the minotaur alone, that was all she needed. Stepping inside, she was hit by the same emptiness that had struck her in the chamber they'd visited that morning. Hell, was it only that morning, when she'd woken up secure in her poker winnings, determined to help put her city to rights, unaware she'd be a human sacrifice by nightfall. It felt like a lifetime ago.

Barton followed and voiced a shudder. The slope was shallow enough that they could go in a few paces before it started to become uncomfortable, so they stopped before the centre of the room.

"I can still take it, at least pull the trigger…" Barton held out a hand to Pax, but she only handed him the radio Obrington gave her. He frowned, seeing she had no intention of calling Letty, but he said nothing. She drew the Dispenser closer to her. Fully fuelled with moss, cranks turned and ready. She adjusted her grip, finding the button that would set it off. Resting it against her hip, she popped open the canister of dust with her other hand.

"Get out of here," Pax told Barton. "Stay safe. I'll scream if I need you." Pax forced a smile. Fairly sure she'd be screaming anyway.

As he dutifully left the room, she tossed a heap of dust into her mouth.

15

Sam hauled the garage door up and ducked into the light of the tight space. Holly and Rufaizu stood either side of the gaping trapdoor, startled to see her. She said, "You should wait in the car – I'll keep an –"

She froze, seeing the tiny woman sat on Holly's shoulder. One wing, a pistol hanging over a knee.

"Yeah, we've got it covered," the fairy said, like it was nothing. Letty, wasn't it? Sam had heard her voice before, on the phone. She couldn't close her mouth for surprise. They were here, just like that. Sitting on a civilian's shoulder – armed – "I do autographs for a tenner."

"I – just –" Sam tried to shake herself out of the surprise. This wasn't the time. She dragged her eyes away from the fairy and drew a pistol. "I'll take watch here, you can all go."

"You ever fired that thing before?" Letty said.

"I think between being here and in the car," Holly offered, more reasonably, "it's not going to make a difference where we wait. So we'll wait together, shall we?"

"All pray on the bar fly," Rufaizu said, determinedly.

Taking in their companionable looks, Sam lowered her gun, hoping she wouldn't have to shoot again today. It was more likely a fleeing human would come up these stairs than a monster, surely? A distant, horrible moan rolled out on cue, the sound of immense pipes heaving, but belonging to something far less ordinary. Beyond that, something chattered rapidly, like a bird's sinister laughter. Mercifully a long way off. A bang followed, a short, sharp gunshot. The tunnels carried sound well.

"They're converging," someone said through Sam's radio. Letty snapped around with alarm.

"What the fuck's that mean? No one –"

Sam's radio crackled again: another agent. "I've got sickles."

The thrums of energy weapons followed. From another far-off location, the same agent's voice bounced up the hall. "Two down. Two. I'm seeing movement!"

The escalating sounds of discharging weapons blocked out his further shouts, as Holly whispered quietly, "God save them . . ."

"Oh hell no, Pax, you bitch!" Letty jumped off Holly's shoulder, readying her gun. Another Fae rose from the shadows, making Sam's eyes widen further. Letty instructed, "Guard these fools, Flynt. I'll be back soon."

"You don't –" the second Fae protested, but Letty shot down into the tunnel like a bullet. As if responding to her approach, a series of pained groans echoed up the hall.

"I can go, should go too," Rufaizu insisted, but Holly's disciplined look told him *no*.

Sam stared blankly at the stairs. Should she go herself? There were countless threats, a horde that they'd always made it their business to avoid.

"Get some!" Letty's voice rose from the tunnel with the barest crack of miniature gunfire. Flynt flew by Sam's face, making her jump, as a screeching trill came up. The fairy steadied himself in front of the tunnel, silently waiting, not so eager to be here himself. She had to do the same: they were the last line of defence, here.

The horde moved quickly.

Only minutes after the radios had announced that Pax was in the tunnel system, another message reported, "It's working."

Casaria was running, ruing the fact he had entered so far across town. He hadn't expected Pax down here. Didn't even know if Ward had intended for *her* to draw the beasts all along – surely not, she'd come to *him*. Raging, he fired into the face of a screeching creature as it launched at him from the shadows. Not even stopping to check it was dead, not caring what it was. A terror goose?

It didn't matter. He'd carve a hole in the horde all the way back to Pax, to the centre of the chaos. He'd find Pax and protect her, as he had before. Pluck her from the clutches of the *praelucente*. Protect the city, as he –

More fiends came with the clicks of bone on brick. Tapping hurriedly down the halls, racing towards him. Casaria skidded to a halt and spread his legs, aiming ahead. The clicks got louder, moving fast, and were joined by a great groan far behind them. Come on you bastards, come to me.

With a fierce clicking cry, a bunch spider scuttled into view. Behind it, a dozen more.

Barton stood with his back to the wall, watching the corridor past the doorway to Pax's chamber, unable to keep his hand still as he clutched the Ministry gun. A weighty, impersonal device. He'd never shot anything before. He hoped he wouldn't have to now. Better that Pax's plan not work; that the horde not come, and they give this up. He could track the minotaur the way he used to, quietly, with minimal conflict.

When the sounds started he knew that wasn't going to happen. They were advancing with the wretched shrieks and scratching claws of unholy beasts. Ones that would kill Holly and Grace, given the chance.

The Ministry men were firing, far off. One man was shouting, somewhere. The creatures roared closer before going quiet as they were cut down.

They were definitely aiming for Pax, with a speed and fury Barton had never encountered before, funnelled between gaps in the Ministry's defences. The men firing on the monsters would be making way for the light of the approaching minotaur. Let that one pass, as they culled everything else.

The clucking of a glogockle sounded in an adjacent tunnel.

His old friends, it had to be one of them.

But an electric discharge silenced that. Then came the rapid patter of something else, scraping on the floor. Barton aimed down the corridor and called to Pax, "Get ready!"

A sickle raced into view, a slick-skinned centaur with pincer arms stretching ahead of its gnashing zip-jawed mouth. Barton roared a challenge and pulled the trigger. The gun emitted a dazzling ball of blue light that startled him into throwing his arm, the projectile hitting the ceiling with a snap. He blinked to refocus. The sickle was halfway to him, about to pass Pax's door. He fired again and the second shot burst over its shoulder. The sickle kept going, ignoring Pax's chamber. Barton threw the gun down and hopped from one foot to another. The other being his bad ankle, which flamed with pain and made him trip.

Just in time – the sickle leapt the last few metres and its great pincers narrowly missed his head, slashing his shoulder. He rolled under it, down onto his rear, its bulk taking up most of the tunnel above. He threw his fists and knees up as the sickle fought its own momentum to twist back at him, mouth snapping. He caught it with a good strike to its gut, but barely slowed the thing down. It slashed at him, a blade-like limb slicing his face, and he cried out. Pax shouted, "Darren!"

"Stay there!" he yelled, blocking the monster with his forearm. It was heavier, stronger than him, and its jagged teeth bit close to his nose. He yelled at it and with a last effort drove his forehead into its jaws. It shook off the blow, regrouping, and screeched into his face. But the screech was abruptly cut off as the lower part of its jaw shattered, struck from the side. As it turned it was struck again, in the centre of its head, with a little snap of gunfire.

Barton winced as the creature collapsed beside him. Letty sped down the hall, firing two more shots into it for good measure, shouting, "Pax you motherfucker, you –"

A great cascade of noise made her turn back. Barton struggled to push himself up as a sea of shadows followed the fairy into the tunnel; at floor level, three-feet armoured bugs, giant roaches. Above them, a flock of leathery-winged, skeletal-faced birds. Flying to Pax's doorway, Letty shot at the mass expertly, dropping a handful of birds, but her bullets chimed off the roaches' shells. One scuttled up a wall near her, feelers probing ahead.

Barton grabbed it before the thing could reach the fairy, twisting it away from the wall and pounding it with his fist, the shell cracking. Letty fluttered by his head, reloading, and fired again into the approaching swarm. A screech drew Barton's attention back the other way; some other horror coming from the opposite direction. The tunnel was alive with movement, everything the Ministry hadn't held back descending on them – and as he shouted, punching, kicking, surrounded by clawing limbs, something serpentine slipped past, into Pax's chamber.

"Missed one!" he yelled, and Letty zipped past him, firing away.

Twisting to try and keep track, Barton was caught from somewhere below and dragged down, smacking a knee into the floor. Something tore at his upper arm, pushing him further down, and more roaches scuttled in – overwhelming him. He roared again, thrusting back at them with all he had –

A brilliant blue light burst through, and the shadowy mass of advancing creatures subsided with the speed of retreating spiders. Roaches rounded the far corner as ethereal tendrils of electric blue snaked into the hallway, the first hints of the Sunken City's vilest monster. It came in tentacles of light, exactly as Pax described, and Barton stared with wonder. Without the goggles glo had given him, he saw it now, in all its blinding glory. Definitely not a minotaur.

Time had not stood still for Pax, not like before; not once she realised that with the intense power of the dust high, she could *control* this feeling. Once she latched onto that, after the initial stretched-out sounds of advancing creatures and devastating weapons, she sped it up, the screeches and scratches reaching helium pitches. Then slowed it down to something like normal. She could feel the activity better than ever: every creature moving, even the people. The vocal agent, nervous and firing his weapon too soon. Obrington, businesslike, just doing a job. Landon, dispatching one creature after another with dogged determination – be good to get home again. Good to get home. Then Casaria, his aura unmistakable, tightening like a spring, wrapped in something that blurred excitement with deep, unspeakable fear. And Barton. Pure. More afraid of failing than dying.

Her feelings stretched to Sam Ward at the top of the stairs. Hopeful, quietly dreaming of success. Keeping a silent tally of possible deaths. Worried for her. Everyone worried for her. Them watching, waiting, and the others fighting, overwhelmed by the pressing monsters, all of one thought. *She's counting on me.*

Then Letty. A furious little ball of lightning rapidly approaching.

Hell, she should've stayed out of here. But she was in the thick of the fight, gunning down creatures fearlessly, and Pax sensed, with relief, that the horde wasn't going after her. They felt Pax, as she felt them; the dust worked, she was their target.

It was coming closer by the second, her nemesis. The beast, minotaur, berserker, *praelucente*. She felt its true heart – and knew it to be none of those things. There was nothing conscious in it at all, it wasn't a malevolent force, it was pure hunger. An unthinking, unfeeling parasite that would drain the world if it wasn't trapped here. If it didn't have the limitations the Sunken City held over it.

And with it came the screens.

All the screens, she felt each of them as individuals, racing through the city as fast as the beast itself, gliding over surfaces. Drawn impossibly along, some against their will, unable to resist her promise: combining the Fae dust and whatever part of the Bright Veins' magic ran through her, Pax was a magnet to them. And as they flooded towards her, she started to understand them. Their fears, their wants, their burning, arrogant scorn for humanity. Pax crouched, hands on the floor, feeling the whole system of the Sunken City, like the tunnels were a part of her. She started to get it. Even this room – this black spot, dark in her mind, fit a necessary part of the whole. She couldn't put it in words, but it made sense, she *felt* it.

Various energies competed for dominance, some with truly ancient roots. The screens, connected to the walls, locked it in place, preying, simply preying. The screens behaved according to their nature – aggressive, devious. They formed patterns of unthinking deception, manipulation that came as naturally to them as the design of a hive came to a bee. Even now, unhinged by their surge, ideas formed: *blame the Young One for theft – release the criminals from prison – poison her family –*

Then came the sickle, charging down the hall. Past her doorway.

Barton shouted. The fight going badly.

Pax couldn't move to help, caught as she was in the grip of the entire energy of the Sunken City. She cried out, but was fused to the spot, her own stubborn mission holding her as much as the conflicting sea of life energies.

Worse followed the sickle, a flood of creatures rolling over each other to fill the tunnel and claim her. Shapes passed the doorway in rapid, ferocious flurries, Letty out there now, firing without remorse, Barton doing all he could to keep from drowning. And then one shape slid in, a jagged-spined snake of a creature, red eyes fixing on her. It shuddered on the threshold, pained to enter, but pressed on, revealing a mouth of crooked, spiky teeth. Behind it, another monster crept around the entrance, a dozen limbs venturing in.

Pax stared, transfixed, unable to move as the world's energy held her.

The snake's head popped like a tomato and it dropped lifeless. A second later the other monster was thrown back into the tunnel, shot off the doorframe. Letty hung in the air between them, a ball of light in Pax's warped vision. The fairy gave her an angry look, but Pax smiled back as time stood still.

Then something changed. Letty darted over and landed on Pax's head. She could feel her crouched, reloading, as the shapes outside hurriedly retreated.

A gentle glow suffused the doorway, a beautiful wash of blue. Gradually the minotaur stretched into view, intensifying to its full blinding self as it slid inwards, bright as a star. Pax slowed time again, one arm covering her eyes and the other closing over Letty, like her fist might protect the fairy. She knew the beast, what it wanted, what it would take. And they came with it, the blue screens swarming in, surrounding her. It hurt them, entering this chamber, but they couldn't resist. They called to the minotaur and its limbs stretched into them, anchoring into a score of locations around Pax with terrific lightning cracks. They didn't think in language but she understood: *her, her, of the human of the Fae, suck her dry.* Fear and hatred mixed with hunger. A tentacle quested towards Pax at tremendous speed, and she let it come, as she took the Dispenser in her hands.

Her senses slowed it right down. Almost to stillness.

Letty shouted something, low, too slow and muffled against Pax's hand to be heard.

Were they all here? Pax couldn't tell, their power boxing her in. Dozens, at least, had joined the feast. It had to be enough. She could wait no longer. With a defiant cry, the minotaur's grasp inches from her, Pax pulled the trigger and the Dispenser exploded forward. She felt that energy, too. Understood the raw power of the weapon, and exactly what it would do.

Cancel them out with a fearsome short-circuit.

The screens pulsed in realisation as the charge hit the minotaur's foremost limb and rolled through it. None of them was fast enough to detach from its suckling position, as the room was filled with devastating white light. Time accelerated again, faster than before, playing catch-up, and the terrific energy that burst through the room hit Pax full force as she screamed.

Abandoning an approaching host of scuttling creatures, Casaria ran towards the sound. The walls shook around him, dust tumbling from the ceiling and cracks spreading like it might all come down. He ran, and ran, vaulting a hound that crossed his path. Around a corner, striking out as he passed a veering sickle, the thing moving in the opposite direction, afraid. Finally he skidded into a hallway filled with a deadly scent. It bit at his eyes, a wall of smell he had to fight his way through, the tunnels quaking about him. Barton on the floor, bleeding, wheezing. Casaria ran past to reach Pax in darkness.

Pax, lying on her back, one arm out to the side with the discarded Fae weapon. The other on her stomach, fingers twitching – not with life, but being pushed, a fairy trapped within fighting her way out. Letty squirmed her way free of Pax's hand to look up at Casaria. She snarled, "Stop gawking and save her while I finish the rest of those fuckers."

16

The ground quaked, rattling Sam off her perch on a step. It shook for a full minute as Sam and Holly moved away from the stairs, garage door rattling. As the world rumbled gradually to a standstill, the sounds of the Sunken City were quietened. The remaining shrieks and groans came with a questing quality.

Then a horrific smell burst out from the tunnel, making Sam gag and cover her face. Somewhere between rotting meat and burnt hair. She coughed on the fumes. A monster screeched with murderous rage.

Flynt shuddered as though he could shake off the smell, and said, "That's it. That's got to be it."

The radio crackled. Obrington: "Did you do it, Pax?"

The answer came from Casaria. "It's gone – Pax –"

"I – I need to go," Flynt said, drawing a miniature pistol. Despite his frightened tone, he flew into the tunnels. Sam watched as Rufaizu ran after the fairy, whooping like a jester, "With you, I'm with you!"

A moment later, the sound of a firecracker cut short a horrible groan.

Somewhere further away, Letty's voice screamed insults.

Holly met Sam's eyes with quiet, frightened wonder. "What now?"

Sam had no answer.

One by one, as the sounds died away, the agents exited via the tunnel, and the garage became increasingly tight. Three of the new agents left with little to say for themselves, consummate professionals even as they were plastered with burn marks and blood. One came out shaking, wide eyes filled with fear as he collapsed against the rear wall. Landon arrived and went to comfort him, after checking Sam was okay. The agent who'd been making all the noise came next, erratically recounting all they'd been through. "Should've seen them – worst I've seen – just kept coming –"

Obrington calmed him down with a few brotherly pats on the back, his presence carrying an air of steadiness. He leant against a wall himself, though, and exhaled tremendous relief. His left hand was covered in blood, dripping at a terrible rate. When Sam approached him he dismissed her. "The girl comes first."

Casaria and Barton carried Pax up, each under an arm.

Her skin was dark, marred all over by something like ash, her clothes singed. Her head rolled forwards, no support from her neck, her feet dragging along the floor. Sam and Holly leapt towards her together, taking her from the men, lowering her.

"She's breathing," Barton assured. "It's okay, she's breathing."

Nothing about her looked okay.

Sam crouched to check her face, lifted her head from behind, tried to open an eye. It rolled in the socket, away from her, then back.

"We got a medic?" Casaria demanded. "Where's our fucking medic?"

"Outside," Obrington said, listing towards the garage door. He grumbled, betraying anxiety, as he opened the door. "The fuck did she do? I thought she had this covered."

"Fuck you, why wasn't someone with her?" Casaria frantically answered. "You all went down – didn't even consult me, left her with a fucking civilian!"

Obrington's eyes warned him off, but he said nothing.

"Easy," Barton said, a hand on Casaria's arm. Telling him it was done, over. Obrington waved to an ambulance outside and two paramedics hurried forwards.

Casaria watched, quiet for a moment, tears on his cheeks. As they passed him, his eyes were drawn to Sam. He hissed, "You let her do this. Her? I could've handled it, you *knew* –"

"This was *her* plan," Obrington said, as the paramedics crouched. "Kuranes chose this. But everyone – you did a fantastic job."

Sam stared, not so sure how fantastic any job could be that left a young woman in a state like that. The paramedics were fast at work, checking her vitals, getting her in the right position, reporting to one another.

"Should've been me," Casaria said, almost in a whimper, circling them. Sam regarded him uncertainly, no idea what to do, what to say, until she caught the eye of one of Obrington's grim agents over Casaria's shoulder. She nodded to him, *do something*, and the man obliged.

Marks nudged Casaria, and he flinched from the touch but calmed when he regarded the scarred man with some kind of recognition. The agent whispered something Sam didn't catch, but the gist was clear. We've done our bit, time to let them do theirs. The fellow agent's assurance somehow settled Casaria, as he looked beyond Marks to the rest of them, blackened with blood and burns, a host of people who'd given their all.

"You did great," Sam whispered her own summary. "You all did."

Barton tightened his grip around Holly as they watched Pax.

"She's alive," the lead paramedic said. Big bushy ginger beard, Scottish accent – Sam recognised him. But his face was not reassuring. "Got a strong pulse, responsive. Superficial burns."

"But . . ." Sam prompted.

"But, you tell me." He pulled up Pax's top, around her midriff. Lines snaked over her gut with the clawlike spread of varicose veins. Gently glowing, under the skin. A string of curses went through the garage as the medic said, "I don't know what that is – what to do about it –" Even as he spoke, the glowing faded. The light dimmed as though being absorbed back into her body. An illusion that was never there. "What the hell happened to her?"

"We won," Pax rasped, with effort.

Everyone surged towards her as one, to embrace her, thank her, touch her, anything, but Obrington forced them all back with a quick, sharp command: "Give her space, for pity's sake! Pax. You're still with us. You sure it's done?"

Pax considered it, barely opening her eyes, then nodded.

"How do you feel?" Sam asked.

"Probably worse than I look," she answered wearily. She drooped back into the ground. "I'd like to go home."

Casaria tried to approach again, but Marks stayed him with a hand. Not now.

"I've done for them," Letty shouted, speeding breathless up the tunnel. "You'd better have fucking done for her."

The crowd parted around her as she flew into its centre, face and clothes awash with blood. She ignored the startled medics and agents to hover down to Pax, chest heaving, shaking with violent energy. "Fuck – they did a number on you."

Pax raised a creaking hand, offering a thumbs-up, and said quietly, "I'm fine."

Letty stared, a furious moment. Then her gory face stretched to a smile. "Fine, she says. Someone take a photo. Call the press. Pax: gets fried, pretends she's okay with it."

Pax turned her hand and raised her middle finger instead.

EPILOGUE

From the notes of Holly Barton:

In the two months since Rufaizu first walked into Pax's life, everything had changed, and yet Ordshaw remained mostly the same. With a final set of tremors to complement the series that had already shaken the city, the MEE, under Sam Ward's guidance, came clean. Under the guise of a proxy gas company. They explained that an old, disused system of tunnels and pipelines had been breached during routine explorations. Once blame had been duly assigned, the big story became the City Council's talks to sell a small section of the tunnel system to a nightclub owner, to enliven Ordshaw's South Bank and bolster the city's coffers. With those promises, people lost interest in exactly where these tunnels came from, generally assuming they formed part of an abandoned third metro line.

Sam Ward managed a meticulous cleansing of the tunnel system, ensuring all the vicious phenomena were removed. The task was smaller than anyone imagined, thanks to the help of bands of roaming Fae and the unexpected widespread decline in the health of the creatures underground, once the *praelucente* (minotaur / berserker) was gone.

And it was, assuredly, gone. The Ministry's scans showed no further "novisan" surges. With that settled, Acting Deputy Director Obrington passed his position back to Sam. Deservedly so, he said, though he hoped to see her in London one day, where she could be put "to real use". She was happy to stay in Ordshaw for the time being, now the Fae were talking to her, and it appeared that the city was due some exciting changes. She became the Ministry's youngest ever (and *only* female) regional director.

Communication with the Fae remained limited, but even the slightest trickles were milestones. They entered into quiet negotiations about which parts of the Sunken City the Ministry were willing to trade off, and made agreements as to the Fae's behaviour in society at large. Generally, the status quo of *we leave each other alone* was properly ratified through MEE Management and Parliament. Things moved slowly due to the Fae having their own issues to resolve: it was understood that a new voting system was established to bring in a more democratic leadership. The MEE's Raleigh Commission, meanwhile, was decommissioned, and the director, Lord Tarrington, established a new governing body with better vetting. The first point of order was to decide a title and structure for this group, which was to be workshopped by the following spring.

That suited Sam Ward and Ordshaw just fine. She was left with general command of the Ordshaw Ministry, which was more than occupied with unravelling the complex background of the Sunken City. She kept the Barton family involved in this, as they had all proved themselves to be potential Ministry material – even the daughter might be considered once she came of age (should her mother allow it). Darren was happy to convalesce for a time, returning to his ordinary life, but Holly proved less passive. She valiantly took charge of documenting and analysing Apothel's book in her spare time, and became a frequent visitor to both the Ministry office and botanist Dr Mandy Rimes' renovated telegraph station. Between these visits and extensive research, with guidance from the eternally grateful Ministry, Holly began drafting accounts of events that would prove both entertaining and educational. She insisted that, given time, her husband would be happy to offer his full input, too. He was just being bull-headed as usual.

Rufaizu also accepted a Ministry offer, once it was made clear no one wanted to kill him. He came to their offices to receive general tuition and guidance in applying for a job, but despite Holly's best efforts to civilise the boy, his old habits resurfaced after things quietened down. One evening, he didn't return to the Bartons' house, and a rumour emerged that he had stolen from someone in West Quay. A letter arrived quashing everyone's worst fears, written in his familiar scrawl; he thanked the Bartons for their hospitality and informed them that he had "found ghouls behind Iceland". It was postmarked from York.

Agent Landon, the man Ward credited with the most world-weary knowledge amongst her staff, and an infrequent contributor to Holly's tireless accounts, claimed the Ministry had no interests in Iceland. However, he did reveal a general knowledge of more widespread activities that Sam Ward suspected existed beyond Ordshaw. He couldn't say exactly what was going on around the world, only *where* it was happening. Many international hotspots, including known Fae locations, have drawn MEE attention, but to our knowledge a bigger, clearer picture is yet to be drawn.

Against such concerns, Sam Ward began her own investigations (with specialist support from Holly, experienced in such matters after years toiling in offices) into the Ministry's wider interests. A chief question was how the big corporations were encroaching on their work. Ward had had only the smallest glimpse of Duvcorp's capabilities, but it was enough to worry her, and Obrington's parting advice was that she steer well clear of them in future. So, she made attempts to touch base with the company, but they pleaded ignorance regarding all concerns she raised and insisted that she had never had a meeting with their COO. When she raised this with Management, they echoed the attitudes she'd previously encountered surrounding the Fae and the Sunken City. It was above her pay grade. Ward vented frustrations about this to Cano Casaria, and he suggested they break into the Duvcorp offices and see for themselves what was going on.

Casaria had many such suggestions, which for the most part were, as Ward had come to understand, his way of saying he was up for whatever tasks might be thrown at him. Eager to prove himself, he had the enthusiasm of a loyal dog. Yes, he was still awkward, and mostly antisocial, and no, Ward had not encouraged his clear infatuation with her; but something in him had changed, leaving him somehow more desperate to please. Perhaps he regretted that his more unruly behaviour had cost him a chance to actually be a hero. Or perhaps he simply, finally, understood his place in the grand scheme of things. On one occasion, Ward told him he'd done good work and he was later heard crying quietly in the toilets. Much as Ward wanted to better understand what he was going through, she didn't want it quite enough to get closer to him. It would come with time, she imagined.

Or it wouldn't.

There were bigger, more important enigmas for her to unravel.

Chief amongst them was how to handle our dear Pax.

Pax huffed as she dropped onto the bench, finally. Sweat ran down her back and her face had to be red as a beet. It didn't help to hear Letty laughing at her discomfort. "You bloody walk it, instead of flying, see how you feel."

"I could walk it a thousand times over, the time it takes you," Letty answered, landing on Pax's knee. She pointed at Sam Ward. "You've got a long way to go before reaching this robot's standards."

Ward smiled guiltily back, standing off to the side, pretending to admire the view.

The view *was* impressive: Black Crest offered an incredible vista of the Drumdon Hills and Ordshaw combined. The climb was a hundred times worse than Pax's little hill in Weirway Park, which she now appreciated barely constituted exercise. She would never motivate herself to come here alone. But in this company, she was exposed to a new perspective: sweeping greens and oranges and a city as contained at this distance as the FTC had been up close. Still, out of breath and irritated that the others weren't, Pax preferred not to admit it was worth it. "I could see this on the internet."

"It's not the same," Ward replied. She always bit at such comments, and Letty always shared a knowing smirk with Pax when she did. Obvious enough for the Ministry lady to notice, otherwise where would be the fun? Ward caught them smiling and said, "Well you're getting much better, anyway. We only stopped once this time."

"When I get all the way up in one," Pax said, "do we get to never do it again?"

"Grow a pair," Letty said. "Hark at Ordshaw's champion, eats fireballs for breakfast but runs scared at gentle inclines."

Pax went to poke her and Letty hopped out of the way, staying close enough to punch playfully back at her finger. The fairy floated up in front of her face.

"In all honesty," Ward said, "I hope you'll stick at it. You're doing so well. You know how much potential you have?"

Pax eyed her warily. Another veiled suggestion that she delve back into the life that had left her twice burnt to a crisp. Made her a murderer of monsters and fairies and a deposer of corrupt regimes. Given her some kind of psychic gift, now dormant, and a modest drip of disability pay that was close to dry. As if being able to climb a hill would make her more likely to survive any easier in future.

"I'm thinking about it," Pax said. And it was true. She was considering that she definitely did not want a boss, nor to wear a suit to work, nor to write reports for anyone or do any work for people who would knowingly withhold information from her. Nor did she want to stick to work hours, or be expected to be somewhere at certain times, or talk in a certain way or anything like that. But the problem was, she also found it hard to sit at the card table, day in and day out, without her mind wandering. Like, maybe making a living wasn't enough. And Ward assured her of compensations: leeway with certain workplace demands, and a steady pay she could shove in Dad's face. But much more than that. Answers. More excitement than hitting a Royal Flush. People cheering her name, desperate for her to save them?

Part of that made her cringe, but then it also gave some queer warm feeling.

She'd saved this city from something no one understood. She'd visited a city of Fae. Where did you go from that?

Letty's visits to her apartment frequently reminded her of that conundrum. Letty had responsibilities of her own, what with the Fae expanding underground, with new towers going up and new enterprises emerging. That kept her from having too much time to spend goading Pax, but it also peppered their drinking sessions with weighted comments like, *Making a difference feels orgasmic, doesn't it?*

"What you want to do," Letty told Ward, "is not to keep asking what she wants. It's to just give it to her. She doesn't know what the fuck she wants."

"I know what I don't want," Pax countered.

"Bullshit, you don't even know that."

Ward looked thoughtful, warming to Letty's idea. "Well. There's a few cases that might interest you, Pax. I know you've got questions."

"That's why we're out here." Pax flapped a hand to dismiss the surrounding beauty of nature. "I always get you to spill fresh gossip to tide my curiosity over."

"But that only works when *I* have the answers. I need *you* to figure out some for us. *If* you'd grace us."

"Hey," Letty said. "I think we're exposing the snark in this square."

"Thanks." Ward took it as a compliment. "Pax, the blue screens are gone, as far as we know, but we still have explaining to do. We don't know that they were confined to Ordshaw. We haven't explained the apparitions that Apothel and Barton reported, things we've never seen or understood. The drummer horse and the invisible proclaimer?"

"What happened to Rik Greivous?" Pax brought up a bugbear, lightly.

"Exactly!" Ward said. "And we don't know how you came to sense novisan, or what really affects that. Your reactions to Fae dust . . ."

"Those experiments are on our to-do list, trust me," Letty said, and Pax smiled. She did not intend to try dust again any time soon. Eventually, maybe . . .

Ward turned to take more inspiration from the view. "And Duvcorp's experiments really trouble me. Their technology intersects closely with ours, and we're on their radar as much as they're on ours, now. And they're not the only ones. Mogami Industries, Warlowe, Raystaten – they all have projects we're not privy to, and Management insists I leave them alone."

"I'm not going to war with multinationals," Pax said. "That's *much* scarier than what we've been through."

"You wouldn't be alone," Ward said. "And it brings its own rewards, I'm sure. An international agent just yesterday requested permission to visit Ordshaw regarding Mogami. He's been to Detroit, Tokyo, Berlin, and now he sees an angle to pursue here."

"Sounds like he's bullshitting you to get a round-the-world ticket," Pax said. Ward didn't look amused, so she added, "That's my thinking at work, Sam. You want me on board, you'd better believe I'll hold your jet-setting international agents to account."

"I would like that," Ward insisted, seriously. "And if you'd put joking aside I think you'd see you want it, too."

"But if we put joking aside," Pax groaned loudly, "what have we got left?"

Ward went quiet. Letty gave Pax a mock sad look. The fairy drifted down onto Pax's shoulder and whispered, "You're a cruel, hard person, Pax. How much longer are you gonna keep her waiting?"

Pax stared at the back of Ward's head. Letty knew it as well as her, of course. She couldn't walk away. Had no intention of walking away. She said, "Until I can run a bit faster and further, at least. If we're gonna take on the world, it's not going to be with me bent double vomiting."

Letty gave her an assaying look. "You poor, deluded fool. It's going to be so much worse than that."

A NOTE FROM THE AUTHOR

Thanks for sticking with me through *The Sunken City Trilogy*, and I hope you've enjoyed the ride. As you might have guessed, there's more to come – and you can return to the world of Ordshaw right away with the next book in the series, *The City Screams*. The series is already rapidly expanding, with *The Ikiri Duology* (criminal jazz musicians, psychic children and more!) and *Dyer Street Punk Witches* (does what it says on the tin) to follow.

I love to hear from my readers and do my best to keep everyone informed on my progress; you can find me on the various platforms below. For special offers, and to be the first to hear about Ordshaw and other news, join my mailing list via my website.

And fresh from completing the trilogy, please take a moment to review the books online (even short reviews can make a big difference). A few positive words from fans like you helps massively to spread the word!

www.phil-williams.co.uk

You can connect with me through:
Facebook: **www.facebook.com/philwilliamsauthor**
Twitter: **www.twitter.com/fantasticphil**
Email: **phil@phil-williams.co.uk**

ABOUT THE AUTHOR

Phil Williams is the author of the Ordshaw, Estalia and Faergrowe series. Living in Sussex, UK, with his wife, he also writes educational books and spends a great deal of time walking his impossibly fluffy dog, Herbert.

Acknowledgements

The Sunken City Trilogy is the culmination of a project that started many years before I'd conceived of Ordshaw. And I must lead by thanking my incredible wife Marta for her support throughout this lengthy process. Her belief in me made it all possible. My editor Carrie O'Grady is also deserving of the highest thanks, as she's helped me make sense of this labyrinthine story. It would have made a fraction of the sense without her input.

Now, back to the start: some of the first seeds of these books were sown when I visited New York, back in 2005 (maybe?) – so the first thanks are due to my brother Fran and my brother-from-another-mother Chris, whose companionship helped shine a light on the minotaur lurking under that city. The story germinated as a screenplay, *Penguins and Seahorses*, and thanks are also due to everyone who got involved in that project (even those who wanted the story completely changed). The film never happened, sapping a lot of my time and energy, but this series is richer for the journey.

Thanks next to my other brothers, Alex and Nick, who are always amongst my first readers, and Kat and Lou Fish who I'd count amongst my first fans. My advance readers throughout these books also deserve great praise for their timely encouragement: Brian Busby, Eric Crawford, Lea Pert, Stephen Fielding, Ami Agner, Jan Drake, Yvonne Evans, and Adawia Asad.

Massive thanks also to the reviewers who have encouraged me through their warm reception: Maddelana from *Space and Sorcery*, Steph from *Bookshine and Readbows* and Hayley Hart of *Paper Plane Reviews*. And extra special thanks to Lynn Williams from *Lynn's Books* who first gave *Under Ordshaw* a chance under the SPFBO contest. All these blogs are well worth checking out, give them your patronage! And of course on top of that, thanks to Mark Lawrence for hosting such a contest in the first place.

In the course of writing the Sunken City trilogy I've also developed an excellent network of supportive authors who've helped me along the way, and big thanks to Phil Parker, Jon Auerbach, Dave Woolliscroft, Carol Park, Josh Erikson, Travis Riddle, Kayleigh Nichol, Devin Madson and Steven McKinnon.

Thanks also to the rest of my family for their support, especially my sister Christen and my father Peter, and most of all my wonderful mother Pauline. She never got to explore Ordshaw, but she knew better than most the magic in everyday life.

ALSO BY PHIL WILLIAMS

ORDSHAW SERIES
THE CITY SCREAMS

THE IKIRI DUOLOGY:
KEPT FROM CAGES
GIVEN TO DARKNESS

DYER STREET PUNK WITCHES

ORDSHAW SHORTS
THE ORDSHAW VIGNETTES VOL. 1
THE DOGS OF DREAMS
THE WRONG WAY

ESTALIA SERIES
WIXON'S DAY
BALFAIR'S CONFINEMENT
AFTAN WHISPERS

www.ingramcontent.com/pod-product-compliance
Lightning Source LLC
Chambersburg PA
CBHW060934190726
48286CB00005B/1277